The Choreographer

"It takes a lot of strength to step into perfection."
- Roshinaie Johnson.

This book is dedicated to my grandmother, Shirley Johnson.
She has taught me so much. She has always been my number
one motivator. All that I've become is because of her.
Rest in peace.
November 26th, 1944 – May 1st, 2007.
I love her so much.

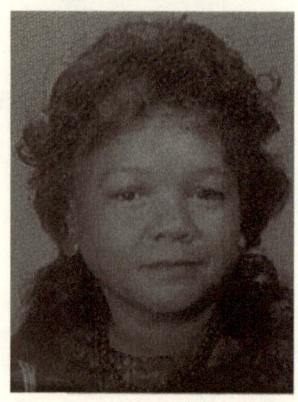

The Choreographer.

By: Roshinaie Johnson.

The phones ringing. It's my mom. She wants to know more about the assault that happened to me. I text her about four days ago and she finally has time to give me a call. She says *mmm hmmm* when I say hello, and I already know she wants me to just tell her what happened. She sounds like she's relaxed, wants me to know that she's not worried, and is happy that I'm okay.

I sit at the table in my dining room and get straight to telling my mom the story.

I tell her I was leaving a motel and was headed to a friend's house. I had my blanket, a pillow, my purse, and my backpack with me for the night out.

On my way walk to my friend Robert's house, I almost forgot he asked me to pick up some tissue for his place because he had ran out. I went to the nearest store. I wasn't feeling good, so my head was down most of the walk. When I got in the store parking lot, I looked up and there were some big kids standing in front of the store. Some were blocking the entrance. These kids looked between the ages of twelve and sixteen. There was about fifteen of them. All of them were taller than me. Some were obese.

My names Shona Jackson, and I'm thirty-five, and have a healthy and beautiful body. I love my beautiful brown skin. All anyone has to do is pronounce the *Ro* in front of *Shona* and they can say my full name correctly: *Roshona*.

When those kids at the store saw me, I knew they were bothered already because they could not compete with my looks. They probably thought I was only five years older than them.

I looked in the store and could clearly see that no one was in it. I had a feeling that it could be a bad idea to go in the store. It was like a gust of wind or a spirit told me to turn around because these kids were trouble. The same spirit told me that these kids could be a part of a gang. However, for some reason, that serious and hard thought left quickly. It's like I had it in me to do the right thing and leave, but my mind couldn't develop the correct actions. I went against what my mind knew was wrong. The thought was in me, but I couldn't hold onto it, or get it to cause me to react off of it.

Instead, the thought of these kids being trouble kept rubbing my head and allowing me to do the opposite of what I should have, which was leave. So, it was in me to leave, but my conscious naturally made my body act and continue to try and go into the store. So, the right thing pinched my thoughts, and I still did the wrong thing. However, I did want to do the right thing, but I had no control of myself to leave. My body naturally went against what was right, and I was conscious of that the entire time.

My mom hasn't said anything yet. I just keep telling her what happened.

As I got close to the store door, no one wanted to make room for me to get in.

"This is a set. This is a set," one of the real skinny girls said. It's like the girl was warning me to leave. I felt like that's what she was doing to get me to turn around. I felt like she was trying to help me in a sense. It's like I knew she meant I was in gang territory, but my body naturally went against the fear of knowing what gangs are capable of.

My conscious was allowing me to take the real skinny girl serious, and at the same time my facials displayed worry and concern for myself, but I still kept moving forward. I didn't know what was wrong with me. What I knew was I could still actively walk into danger with everything about me displaying and feeling the complete opposite way. It's like how could I be completely aware, afraid one hundred percent, and still walk as if it's naturally in me to be stupid?

It's like I was a stupid type of human being. The right emotions mixed with doing the wrong things were labelling me. I was in a moment of truth. I knew exactly who I was, and I was going against my own better judgement. So, with my mind made up that I was doing the wrong thing and should leave, I naturally was entering a situation that could get me killed.

2

It's like my mind was practiced on. That the right thing for me to do would be to enter danger with all the right thoughts of protecting myself in my head, and I would die that way.

When I reached the store door, I tried to squeeze through the kids, but that was not working. Especially not with my blanket and pillow in my arms. While I was close to the kids, I viewed them as if they were hanging out like they were at school or something. They just happened to be at this store on this particular late night.

It was about eight at night. The real skinny girl finally moved to her right and made room for me to get in the store.

"This is a set," the same real skinny girl continuously said. I got in the store and no one was in it except for the two workers. "You touching me?" the same girl rudely asked.

"No, I'm not touching you," I said annoyed.

I went searching for the tissue. Only a couple minutes had passed before another girl and a boy came up behind me. I grabbed my tissue and turned around.

"What happened?" this other girl asked.

"She asked me was I touching her," I said annoyed. "I said no, I'm not touching you."

It's completely left my mind that these kids are trouble makers, a part of some gang. I'm just in the store hoping to grab the tissue and some candy and leave. When I look at the second girl that said something to me, I can see that the girls in the crew wear their makeup a certain way around their eyes. There was a thick line of black eyeliner around their eyes.

I wound up calling the cops. I forgot how the conversation started.

"Ma'am, do you need an ambulance?" Officer Blake, the lady on the phone asked.

"No," I said.

I can't remember most of the conversation.

While I was going through this situation, I also didn't have any words to remember to give me an upliftment from anyone that I knew. Especially not Nadia. Not from Nathanya either. Nathanya is my sister. I was completely empty.

I turned my head away from the girl and boy in my face while on the phone, and the boy threw a liquid at my face. It was in a small candy container. I wiped my cheek to see and smell what the substance was.

"They're throwing alcohol," I said to Officer Blake.

"That was not alcohol," the girl said shocked.

I was hysterical though. It naturally came out of me to say alcohol. It's like that was programmed in me to say the most exaggerated response.

As I'm repeating this to my mom, I'm starting to really wonder what was wrong with me. I can't react normally sometimes to my thoughts, and I'm saying outrageous things, like alcohol instead of spit.

I feel like I'm telling a story of me in a comedic movie. One of those movies where people take other serious films and remake them into comedies.

"Where are the store workers?" Officer Blake asked.

"They're at the counter," I said. "I tried to give one the phone, but he didn't want it."

"Where are you?" Officer Blake asked.

"I'm on Manchester and Figerine," I said.

"How many kids are there? Ten? Fifteen?" Officer Blake asked.

"Yes. There's about fifteen," I said.

I really didn't count the kids at the time. I just guessed because I was hysterical. I had never been in a situation like this. These questions were easy, yet very hard for me to answer. I feel like because I was in danger, every answer should have come out of me quickly and honestly without any hesitation.

After all, I was the one not going to get in any trouble.

I somehow ended up outside. I was standing with the kids while I was on the phone with Officer Blake.

As I visualize this event, I feel like something is wrong with me. I was on the phone with a cop and standing with the people I was snitching on. I looked like I completely thought I belonged right where I was, and it was okay for me to be right next to those kids.

4

I may have been trying to make sure I was giving the right streets to the officer, but I still should have stayed away from those kids. I should have asked the store workers for the street names, but it wasn't a thought.

"You snitching?" the real skinny girl that kept saying *this is a set* asked.

I ignored her.

Next thing I knew, I got punched on the right side of my jaw. I couldn't believe it. I still didn't move away from the kids. I turned to my right and saw that it was the boy that came in the store who punched me.

I didn't do anything back because I knew they were children, and I was unsure of how much trouble I could get into. I also knew there was a good chance that I would get jumped if I touched the boy.

It disgusted me that these kids would always have the fact that they are kids in their defense.

"One of them just punched me in my jaw," I said to Officer Blake panicked.

"Take her phone. Take her phone," the real skinny girl said.

Someone pushed my phone out of my hands. It landed in a puddle of water next to a car. I still didn't want to fight any of those kids. I just went and got my phone.

Officer Blake was disconnected, so I had to call her back.

Meanwhile, the two store workers didn't want to get involved in the activity going on right outside of their clear glass walls.

The kids left and went different directions.

I held my phone out and started recording the kids.

"She's recording," the real skinny girl said.

I ended up getting seven of them on camera. I recorded walking backwards as the boy that hit me kept coming closer to me. He had on a white sweater with his khaki pants.

The boy walked towards me with a huge feel of power in him. He was acting like he owned the parking lot. He made eye contact with one of the obese girls and then looked at me again walking faster.

5

I was surprised the boy didn't try to attack me for my phone before turning around to leave. Another one of the obese girls almost fell trying to get around the car as if she didn't need more space to do so. She was trying to approach me. She must've forgot how much more space she would need to fully get around the car. Her face looked hideous.

I apologized to Officer Blake for losing connection and told her what happened with my phone.

"I'll send an officer out," Officer Blake said.

I was not feeling good at all. I remember when I was staying on Florane Street and called the cops on a man who assaulted me, and they literally took two hours to show up. I told them I would be standing outside of the weed shop. When they did show up, they drove by and didn't stop. They were looking for someone to be standing right outside of the weed shop, and no one was when all that time went by. I was standing in an apartment area, but I still saw them slow down to see if anyone would flag them down. I saw them, but they didn't give me time to get in their sight.

My mom is still just on the line listening. By the way, her name is Nadia.

After the kids left from the store, one of the store workers came outside and leaned on the wall. I forgot what I asked him. All he said was, "You see me every day." He was basically saying that I should know he's a cool person.

I went back in the store and got the tissue and a few pieces of cheap candy.

"Can I get this for free being that I was assaulted in front of your store?" I asked the other store worker.

"It's two dollars," the other store worker said.

In disbelief I asked again, "This is not free being that I was attacked in front of your store?"

The other store worker didn't say anything, so I just gave him the money.

I walked around the store. The whole time I was not even thinking about when the cops would show up. All I could do was hope it didn't take two hours again. I had somewhere to be, and those bastard ass kids interrupted my night.

Cars started to pull up to the store once the kids were gone. People were going in and out quickly.

"Aye, why you didn't hit that boy back that punched you?" some man that was entering the store asked me.

"You already know I'm gone start capping," another man who was leaving the store said to his friend.

People were pulling up and dropping people off to run in the store and run out. I started to think these people were a part of those kids' crew. Only these were adults with licenses. I thought they had the kids doing the dirty work for the night.

While I was waiting on the cops, I noticed the store had surveillance cameras up. There were nine different views of camera angles in the store. Even though the cops hadn't arrived yet, I felt confident that they would find the kids because of all the surveillance. My spirit lifted.

I kept walking up and down the aisles, and in and out of the store waiting on the cops. I was thinking about Robert waiting on me to arrive to his house. I didn't want to call him though. I just wanted the cops to show up.

When the two male cops arrived, I was fine. When they actually got out of the car, and I had to tell the story, I could barely speak.

I basically told the cops how the kids were blocking the entrance, and the real skinny girl kept saying *this is a set*. I told them how someone pushed my phone out of my hand and I lost connection. I said how the kids threw liquid at me, and I was punched in the face.

"Can I file a report?" I asked the officers. One gave me a card. "What's the next step after this?" I asked. "Do I call someone? Something needs to be done about this."

"An officer will get in contact with you regarding the case," the officer doing all the interrogating said.

"I told the woman on the phone that I didn't need an ambulance, but I'm starting to feel a little pain," I said to the officers. "I don't know if you can see anything," I said to the officer interrogating me.

I touched my jaw where I was punched.

The officer interrogating me used his flashlight to examine my jaw, and he said it looked fine.

"I can feel it swelling. I'll most likely go to the clinic tomorrow to have it checked out," I said.

I showed the officers the footage I captured on my phone.

"Is that him with the white sweater?" the officer interrogating me asked.

I said yes.

"Which way are you going?" the officer interrogating me asked. "We just want to make sure no one follows you."

I told the officer I was going to a friend's house and pointed down the street I was going to walk down. I thanked the officers before they left and went on my way. I was thankful my phone wasn't ruined, and I was able to call the cops back because the store workers surely didn't want to get involved in the activity outside of their store.

I was so angry. I was holding a blanket and pillow. Those kids didn't know if I was homeless or not. They just attack innocent people. The reason I was walking was because Robert didn't live far, and I wanted to enjoy a nice walk.

I'm still telling my mom the story.

I'm letting her know how I couldn't believe those kids didn't have anything better to do with their time.

"They fight innocent people. There's nothing there," I said.

I can hear my mom breathing. It's not something I usually pay attention to, but for some reason her breathing is more noticeable through the phone. It's a lot heavier. She's exhaling deeply. She still doesn't have anything to say, so I keep speaking my mind. At least she's willing to listen.

I tell my mom how I went to the clinic across the street from my house and had them take a look at my jaw to make sure nothing was broken.

My mom says, "Mmm."

I just talked to Nadia for over thirty minutes about being assaulted, and that's all she has to say.

It gets silent for a few seconds.

"Jania!" my mom powerfully says. "She said that you harmed your younger step brother Allen and his cousin Emmanuel when y'all was coming up. She said they said you harmed them in a lot of ways."

When Nadia says harmed, it just kills me. I've heard Nadia talk to other people spreading bullshit about people harming people. She could be talking about fighting, running them over with a car, putting their head in a toilet, throwing a brick at their head, pouring hot water on them, pushing them down the stairs, trying to push someone to suicide, killing. Just any criminal activity. This woman is ugly in so many ways.

I space off. My grandma pops up at the table in my dining room. "She's trying to say things that can cause you a heart attack," my grandma says, referring to Nadia. I snap back into reality.

"Jania," I disgustedly say responding to Nadia. "Jania's just mad because every time someone looks at her, they can't remember what they were thinking. She's lying about that."

"She said they *told* her that," Nadia says.

My mom listens to me rant about Jania for over thirty minutes just like I did the assault I just told her about.

Jania's appearance is very disturbing. There's no room for her to be making up lies. Nadia doesn't have anything to say. She just keeps listening to me talk negatively about Jania. I haven't heard from Jania in over twenty-four years, and this is what Nadia wants to say.

Nadia is such a fucking liar, that I think Jania never said that.

I space off and see my grandmother again. We're at my dining room table still.

"It was after nine at night," I say to my grandmother.

"That's how she wanted you to go to sleep," my grandma says.

I look at her.

"Tell her that's why I did it," my grandma says.

9

I hear glass break and shake my head. I snap out of my thoughts. Damn it. I hate thinking about the assault and Nadia's response. It's causing me to miss all the action in Hollow's Cave. Damn. The glass from that candle is fucking with me.

I never knew what my grandma meant when she said *tell her that's why I did it.* To this date, I'm still trying to figure that out. My grandmother is dead, but I heard her voice for the first time since she passed away around the time I told Nadia about my assault.

I think somethings wrong with me. I feel like I can really hear my grandmother.

I was just remembering telling Nadia about my assault and her *I don't care if you die* response, then the next thing I knew, some kind of way I heard my grandma's voice.

I think I'm going through some type of illness because I can't really deal with my grandmother being gone.

I'm at what is called Hollow's Cave by Greeks. Hollow's Cave is a place where Greeks have step offs, battles, and other activities that we don't want strangers attending. Sometimes we bring pledges here for sets. Only select people can come to our secretive events at Hollow's Cave, and sometimes it's just us.

Me and my Sorors of Alpha Eta Nu, A.H.N., are watching Phi Phi Alpha train their pledges on just how tough of skin they are going to need to wear the letters of the fraternity.

I'm sitting next to my line sister Deliana in the nose bleed of Hollow's Cave. We're both staring hard at the events going on with Phi Phi Alpha and their pledges. We look real serious and don't have a care in our bodies for anything illegal that's going on.

My line consists of six other girls: Deliana, Caya, Casha, Telana, Shemina, and Asayla. We're all beautiful brown-skinned women. Me and Deliana are the only ones sitting down. Our Sorors are engaging in all the action with Phi Phi Alpha members. We care none for how weak and sorry the pledges look. We need to see live action on innocent souls. We're all grown as hell and been through too much shit in life.

One of the pledges that is walking blindfolded bumped into a table that has a glass of liquor on it. Brenden, one of Phi Phi Alpha's alumni, just watched him walk right to it. Brenden is the oldest person here. He's thirty-seven.

"Don't cry got damn it!" Brenden shouts. "Ain't no weak ass niggas allowed around Phi Phi Alpha fraternity under any circumstances.

The pledge that made the candle break is about to fall to the floor. Brenden and his frat brother Zack notice that the boy is about to throw up. They unblindfold him and walk him to a trash can in the center of the cave.

There's a potential pledge for next year named Eric, who is here to clean up any mess that is made. He has frequently had to take the trash out tonight. These boys keep puking.

In my opinion, Eric is dumb as hell for telling people he wanted to pledge Phi Phi Alpha before the year he is allowed to. Of course, the members would pre-pledge his ass. They could use a dummy to run errands for them and do whatever else they say. In the members eyes, Eric and anyone else that is being pre-pledged, want to secure a spot in the fraternity. They are basically sucking up so that if too many people want to join, they have a better chance of getting in.

Phi Phi Alpha has a maximum of twenty-one members that can join each year. Sometimes they have very little interests and sometimes they get a number greater than their cap.

Eric should have kept his damn mouth shut, but I know some people don't know anything about pre-pledging.

Eric stands off to the side, and me and a few of my Sorors approach him. He's a nice-looking young brown-skinned boy.

"How is being pre-pledged?" I ask Eric.

"It's easy," Eric says.

"Oh really," I say. "Heard you went a day and a half with no sleep doing things for Phi Phi Alpha. That's easy, huh?"

Eric looks shocked.

"Don't worry," Caya says. "We won't tell anyone that you said that it's easy. It's enough going on in here tonight."

"Besides, we like you," Telana says.

"Yea. You work hard," Caya says.

Eric looks less shocked. He's smiling now.

"You think you are ready for all of this?" I ask Eric.

"I'm ready," Eric says.

Eric changes trash bags in the center bin and another one.

I know it sounds crazy that there is a trash bin in the center of the cave, but the members of Phi Phi Alpha have a very strict lesson going on.

One of the pledges who is breathing heavy asks, "Why is there a trash in the middle for everyone to see while we're going through this?"

"We're going to show you all how disgusting you are," Carter a member of Phi Phi Alpha says. "Y'all keep throwing up anyways."

The pledges are sniffing things blindfolded, and being asked what they think the substances are. So far, they've sniffed stinking socks, cat litter, dog food, white out, nail polish remover, and gasoline. All of which have terrible smells. Some worse than others. None of the Greeks give a damn though. These pledges better do what the hell they are told. They not just about to join this fraternity in an easy way. They won't die from sniffing any of the shit anyways.

The members of Phi Phi Alpha all look serious as hell while they dictate their pledges, but they are having a lot of fun.

"Boy, I'm happy it's not me sniffing all this bullshit," Austin, a member of the frat says. Austin is my boyfriend. He is fine as all hell. He's light-skinned with naturally curly hair, but he always straightens it. People think he's mixed, but he's fully black.

I've been dating Austin since my senior year of high school. We've been together for seventeen years. I wouldn't trade him for the world. He loves me, and I love him. We make each other laugh. We both are arrogant as all hell when it comes to how we look, and that turns us both on. We always look at each other intimately.

12

Me and Austin are both thirty-five, but we don't have any children. We never say it, but we both know that we fulfill each other's lives. We don't need any mini-mes of us running around.

No one bothers Austin and me when they ask if we ever plan on having a baby either. My baby and I just make jokes out of their inquiries, or give smart remarks like, "If we wanted kids, we would've had them. If you don't see them by now, we never wanted them."

All of the members on Austin's line are: Brenden, Zack, Carter, Tevin, Travis, and Devon. Their line is seven people strong. The boys hang out a lot, but they rarely talk about their experience when they were joining the fraternity. Austin's line is helping the prophytes of Cupperton University bring in their line.

I know on television and in movies it's like the people that crossed the year before do all the work with the new line coming in, but not in this part of New Orleans, Louisiana. Everyone from Cupperton University basically wants every new line to suffer just as much as we did. Cupperton needs professionals. When I say professionals, I mean people that have crossed and have had plenty of time to think of new ways to torment the new pledges.

One of the pledges is sniffing the socks.

"Pledge, what are you sniffing?" Carter asks.

"Funky socks," the pledge says.

"That is incorrect," Carter lies. "Ten push-ups." The pledge does the push-ups blindfolded. Once he finishes, Carter takes the blindfolds off and lets him see the funky socks.

"But I got it right!" the pledge shouts.

"So!" Carter shouts. "I knew you would yell after, so I lied to you." Carter's full of it. Him and his line are saying and doing anything to make the pledges mad. Carter makes the boy sniff more things, then escorts him to the trash in the center, so he can throw up.

Austin has two pledges walk towards the broken glass that has yet to be cleaned up.

"My brothers, we have a situation," Austin says funnily. "I don't know about y'all, but I'm devastated that my liquor has run away from the glass."

Zack gives Austin a high five.

"Make them lick it off the ground," Zack says.

"They can lick it off the ground, and buy us some more," Tevin says.

"I don't know about y'all, but I don't feel like picking this glass up," Austin says. "Let's just walk around the area, and see if we can think of a way to clean it up."

What the fuck? Austin is leading the pledges blindfolded in a circle around the broken glass.

"Damn, them niggas about to fuck they feet up," Deliana says. She puts her arm around me and laughs.

One of the pledges loses his balance and falls on the glass. He's bleeding on his arm. The cuts aren't deep though. The frat brothers are all in shock. They help the pledge up, and sit him in a chair. They take the blindfolds off the other pledges and have them stand in a line along the wall.

Shemina rushes to the pledge that fell with towels, alcohol rub, and bandages. The boy is crying and cursing.

"I'm sorry I fell," the boy says. "It won't happen again. Give me another chance. I need to make this line."

"Pledges, when someone is injured during a set, what is said when asked what happened?" Brenden asks.

"We never mention anything we do with our brothers while going through our process," the pledges all say. "We trust that our Big Brothers know best."

The bandaged boy stands off to the side while the other pledges continue to sniff things, guess what they are, and walk to the center if they need to throw up. Once the frat brothers are tired of watching the pledges sniff and puke, they have the pledges circle around the trash bin in the center of the cave.

"Y'all need to hurry up and get that shit out of here," Casha says about the trash. "It's starting to fuck with us, and we are ladies of Alpha Eta Nu."

The pledges are blindfolded circled around the trash.

14

"Pledges, what is it that you smell?" Brenden asks.

None of the pledges have an answer. Austin bends one of them over the trash so he can puke. Then the pledge says, "It's everything that has come out of our system. It's our throw up."

"And how does your smart ass know that?" Brenden asks.

"I didn't move far after you let me clear my system," the pledge says.

"Guess he told you," Zack says to Brenden.

"Get smart again and your ass will get in this trash bin," Brenden says.

"I wasn't trying to get smart," the pledge says.

The pledges remain circled around the trash and Telana brings the fraternity members shots on a tray. My sorority and Phi Phi Alpha are drinking, smoking, and laughing at the pledges.

I have to say that I am the only person here that doesn't smoke. I've just had too many bad experiences, and I have nothing to blame them on but marijuana and cigarettes. I'm done with that mess.

Me and Deliana go down and join the other Greeks.

"Take the blindfolds off," Austin instructs the pledges. They're now staring at their trash of puke.

"Look. One of they asses is about to fall over," Travis says. "Them boys look pathetic as hell."

Some of my Sorors are kissing Phi Phi Alpha members, and they don't date them. Everyone is getting drunk and enjoying a good time. My Greek friends are being flirtatious and making plans to see each other later.

Me and Austin are kissing. He grabs my ass and says he loves me. Some of my Greek friends hear him, and that makes me so happy. Austin doesn't care where we are at. He will express his love for me in front of anyone.

After a few minutes of enjoying some personal time, my crew and I remember the pledges are still here. We walk over to them. I'm walking in front of Austin with his arms around me. Some of my Sorors are hugged up tight with some of the frat members as well. They continue kissing and flirting while we walk over to the pledges.

"You guys need to realize that this trash symbolizes everyone who is not a member of our fraternity," Brenden says. "We are fine men who have defeated all the odds against us. We have careers, and we have unbelievable great lives. We are brothers for life. No one can break our bond."

Brenden has the pledges take the trash to the dumpster outside. When they return, they have the trash bin with them.

"Now who's dumb ass idea was it to bring the trash bin back, instead of putting it in the dumpster too?" Austin asks. "Throw that shit out!"

Carter and Travis are laughing at Austin. "They going to be here all night," Travis says.

When the pledges return, Brenden gives them all a rope. He has them put it around their necks and lets them wonder what is next. The fraternity men put chairs in a circle and have the pledges stand on them with the ropes around their necks.

"The last time we did this, we were in my garage," Brenden says. "Damn near all of you were crying before you put the ropes around your necks."

Me and my girls are shocked. We are drinking and laughing while Brenden tells this hazing story that we haven't heard about this new line. Everyone except me is passing blunts around.

Phi Phi Alpha members are walking around their pledges. They are slapping them, moving their chairs so they can lose balance, and calling them *ignorant* and *stupid*. The pledges are shaking and some are tearing up.

"I remember when I had each of you hung from the ceiling. Why the hell were you all scared when I let you stand on the chairs?" Brenden continues. "You have plenty of room to breathe. The only way you would've died is if you slipped off the chair."

"Certainly, you wouldn't lose your balance because of fear after all we have done for you," Devin says.

"All we want is for everyone to remember that night in the garage," Brenden says. "We are making real men out of you. We are going to knock every fear in you out, before you get to wear these letters."

One of the pledges passes out because he can't stand the memory of them having to be hung as if they were real slaves. My girls and I help him regain consciousness. Water over the face usually does it.

"Stop crying," Austin says to one of the pledges. "All you're doing is holding the rope around your neck. It's not like you're really hanging."

My girls and I are laughing. My boyfriend is just as comical as his frat brothers.

"These damn pledges are fucking annoying," I whisper to my girls. "They are weak as fuck to me."

"Girl, who you telling?" Asayla says. "They too damn emotional."

"They supposedly grown ass men at that," Shemina says taking a shot out the bottle.

"One of you almost fell trying to get on the damn chair," Zack says.

"One of your clumsy asses fell backwards and cut your arm with the knife that was on the table," Austin says. "Someone didn't have a knife to cut their steak with that night."

I'm shaking my damn head and laughing with my hand over my mouth. This is supposed to be serious, but none of us Greeks are taking it that way. This liquor is getting to me, and Austin is here. I'm enjoying myself. My man is doing his thing, and I am a member of Alpha Eta Nu. My girls are here too, and they are tipsy and some drunk. I will show no signs of sympathy. I never do.

"Pledge Meantime, show the scar," Brenden says.

Pledge Meantime keeps the rope around his neck and rolls his sleeve up. Damn. The scar runs down his left arm. It's long as hell. This boy needs his ass beat for being so clumsy.

"Pledge Meantime, when asked how you got the scar, what did you say?" Zack asks.

"I said I was at home minding my business," Pledge Meantime says. "I said there was a knife laying on the floor in my room, and I fell."

"Everyone knows that everything we do together is not to be heard of by anyone else," Brenden says. "Whatever scars you may get, whether they will go away or not, are never to be blamed on men of Phi Phi Alpha."

"That's a friendly reminder," Austin says.

"You've seen the news," Brenden says. "Some of the people who have snitched on frats have wound up dead."

"Don't let it be you," Zack says.

"Shut up," Brenden says to Zack. "I know our pledges are trustworthy. We won't have that problem. As your Big Brothers, we won't let anything happen to you, but keep your mouth shut."

"Besides, we have women that need to know the ropes," Tevin says. "They can't be hearing about no snitching ass pledges."

The girls and I laugh sarcastically while the frat members jump up and down laughing, hit each other's hands, slap each other on the back, and drink. We didn't think that shit was funny.

Austin has the boys recite one of their oaths.

"I promise to be loyal and faithful to my brothers," the pledges say as one. "I will never harm my brother. I will only defend him. I trust my brother. He will be there for me, and I will always be there for him. I am privileged to have my brother and be in this fraternity with him."

My girls and I clap for the boys and nod our heads.

"Impressive," Casha says.

"That was dope y'all," Telana says. "I mean it. Y'all stay strong, and make it through this shit. I felt that."

Austin looks at me and winks. I smile at him.

"I liked that a lot," I shyly say blushing.

"Y'all have to excuse her," Casha says. "Her man makes her get like this sometimes."

18

The pledges give Austin the ropes, and they put their chairs up against the wall. They bend over and grip the chairs for balance. Phi Phi Alpha members have wooden paddles. Zack hits each of the boys once and allows them to sit on the chairs. The frat boys are making the boys recite information about Phi Phi Alpha Fraternity. While they do that, my girls and I go to our own spot in Hollow's Cave and say what we came up with to talk to the pledges about.

"I think we should get on them about ditching school in the past and showing up late for class," Caya says.

"I think we should get on they asses if they plan on joining a gang later in life, or if they have already, or are thinking about putting they hands on a woman," I say.

"Girl please," Asayla says. "You know sororities and fraternities are a gang in their own way." Some of the girls agree with her.

I don't know what Asayla is talking about. I never looked at sororities and fraternities as gangs. We do all types of fucked up hazing acts, but we don't harm people for fun, or because we don't have anything to do. I want to say something to make Asayla correct her fucked up statement. I was really assaulted by some bullshit ass kids that were in a gang. Alpha Eta Nu and any other sorority and fraternity is not a gang.

"I think getting on them about the gang life and putting they hands on women is a good idea," Caya says.

The girls all agree. My topic wins. We all take shots out of bottles and watch the pledges recite their information. Some of them are stumbling. When I say stumbling, I mean that they are mixing up words. Everything is supposed to be said verbatim. Some of the pledges are getting hit on they asses more.

The girls and I go back to the frat and their pledges. They give us the floor.

"So, how many of you have ever thought about putting your hands on a woman, or joining a gang?" I ask.

The pledges all say no or shake their heads no.

"Come on," Caya says sitting on a chair. "You all know you've thought about hitting some smart-mouthed bitch who wouldn't shut up and played the *a man should never hit a woman* card."

"So, no one is going to be honest and say they've at least had the thought?" I ask.

None of the pledges say anything.

"My lady asked y'all a question," Austin says.

The pledges all shake their heads no.

"I don't hear y'all," Austin says.

All of the pledges say they have never had thoughts about hitting women. They all say they've never put their hands on a woman either.

"Everyone hold your hands out," Caya says. She takes off her belt and hits the pledges on their hands. Then she has them turn around and hits them on their asses.

I have the pledges turn around and face the wall. I push each and every last one of them. I'm mad as hell about my assault. I'm drunk as hell and don't give a fuck about none of these pledges at this point.

"Don't ever think about punching a woman," I say. "Especially if you're the only man with a bunch of bitch ass females."

Austin and Brenden push the boys after I do.

"I know y'all didn't think my baby was gone be the last one to push y'all weak asses," Austin says. "I'm the damn man." It pisses Austin off that he has to say that. His crazy ass grabs a piece of wood and hits the boys on they asses again.

I'm getting real angry and mad. I want to punch one of the pledges on the mouth or give him a black eye, but I'm not the type to take a chance on making someone lose teeth. Let alone take a chance on someone being a snitch. I'll never be that damn stupid. People have been caught hazing before, and I'm not the type to think it can't be me one day.

Once I get done pushing all of the boys against the wall, not giving a damn whether I fuck around and make them hit their heads, Caya pulls me to the side.

"Girl, you okay?" Caya asks. "You seem to be getting a little too serious. I think you have had too many drinks."

"I'm fine," I say.

"Then why are you about to start crying? You're getting teary eyed," Caya says.

I haven't told my Sorors or Austin about my assault. I'm too embarrassed. I don't want to admit that a big ass boy put his hands on me.

"I'm alright," I say. "Just give me a minute."

"Girl your man is walking over here," Caya says standing me straight up.

"What y'all over here talking about?" Austin asks.

"Just how I had more drinks than I should have," I say.

"Oh word?" Austin says like he knows I'm lying. "So you more faded than everyone that's smoking and drinking?" Austin doesn't believe my excuse.

I stopped smoking a long ass time ago. Once I felt like someone was pulling and yanking at my body, I knew I was letting them damn drugs go. I'm still having side effects, but at least I know I'm on my way to a full recovery. Fuck smoking, and I mean that.

I hate looking at these niggas smoke, but whatever. It is what it is. I have learned my damn lesson though.

Austin, in his drunk and high ass mind, goes over to his pledges and has them stand with one leg in the air. He hits them with the belt on their legs, then tosses them the ropes.

"Make sure you never make a woman get emotional about being hit by a man," Austin says.

Damn. I just got these damn boys in deeper water. Oh fucking well. They need to be properly taught why they should never hit a woman.

The pledges are in pure pain. Brenden gives them time to drink water and relax after Austin is done hitting them with the belts.

One of the pledges prophytes named Ossin is overweight.

"How the hell did this damn fat ass boy make the line?" Austin lowly asks. He has his arms around me and is keeping me warm.

It's time for the pledges to be fed before they go home. Ossin and his line brothers set up tables and put lots of pizzas on them.

"I know y'all tired of smelling bullshit," Ossin says. "But it's time to chow down now. Now I know y'all probably can eat between three to four slices of pizza, but today y'all will eat ten pizzas."

"Don't act like y'all never threw no food away when y'all was young, instead of saving it for later," Tevin says. "It's people homeless and hungry. Look at this as y'all punishment."

"Overeating is how you will be paid back for throwing away food when you were young, and not giving a damn that there's people out there that would eat it off the ground," Ossin says.

I find this comical.

Ossin and his line brothers put slices of pizza on all of the pledges' plates.

"Where you going babe?" I ask Austin. He took his arms from around me.

"To get the timer," Austin says.

Austin sets the timer for three minutes.

"Austin that's crazy," I say.

"That's how much time y'all asses got to eat all those pizzas," Brenden says. "Three damn minutes."

"Don't fucking smack either," Austin says.

My boyfriend has manners for days. He doesn't play about people having good table manners when they are eating with him. He likes to enjoy his food. Some of his frat brothers say he acts like a bitch because he's aggravated easily when someone has bad habits when they eat.

"Go!" Ossin says. The pledges begin eating their pizzas. They are chewing hella fucking fast. They should feel good right now because I know they are hungry. We been in Hollow's Cave for over six hours messing with they asses. They have been moving around constantly. Even if they ate right before they came, I know they done burned all that damn food off.

After the fourth slice of pizza, some of the boys begin to slow down chewing.

"I said don't fucking smack," Austin says.

"I know y'all know that damn three minutes is up, right?" Ossin asks.

I'm so damn glad I already crossed. When asked a question, it doesn't matter if a pledge responds or not. It's up to the prophytes on whether they will get upset someone opened their mouths, or just relax.

None of the pledges respond to Ossin.

"I asked y'all a question?" Ossin shouts.

I know the pledges hate this shit. If someone would've answered, Ossin could've still gotten mad.

"Yes Big Brother," the pledges say as one.

"How y'all know if the timer didn't go off?" Ossin asks. He cut the timer off. He wants to fuck with these boys real bad.

Ossin's overweight ass needs to sit down. He's trying to make these boys gain weight, so they can get just as big as him. I hate to admit that I know some people are just fucking not all there. I've caught Ossin staring at a few people today that are thin. He was looking real bitter. I knew he just wanted to punch the wall. Austin saw him too. My man joked that Ossin's eyes would pop out of his head before the weight ran away from him.

I know Ossin is taking out his frustration about his weight on his line. I can't say he is stupid for that. If someone is not all there and needs people to take their frustration out on, fraternities and sororities are the way to go. The pledging process is the perfect opportunity to release anger on innocent people.

None of the boys answered Ossin's question.

"I know his fat ass can't stand looking at them eat all that damn pizza knowing they not gone get as big as him," Carter says.

"I swear y'all got jokes for days," Caya says laughing.

23

We're all still drinking. I'm the only person not smoking. I don't mind inhaling the second-hand smoke though. It smells good. I know I'm not supposed to do that either, but I don't care. I miss how good smoking used to make me feel.

Austin is smoking with his arms around my neck. I'm loving it. His bad ass never asks me why I tolerate him smoking if I hate it so much. He also knows I'm not stupid to the effects that second-hand smoke can bring about; he still doesn't ask me why I inhale it though. He just loves his girlfriend, and that's all I care about.

Some of the pledges are throwing up pizza.

"We said don't waste no food," Ossin says. "That's only a few damn pizzas," he sarcastically says.

Phi Phi Alpha members are surrounding the table. They haven't eaten any of the pizzas. I'm waiting to hear Ossin acknowledge that.

"It's not our fault you can't eat good no more," one of the pledges named Charlie says.

Hell no. I can't believe this damn boy. I know he's burned the hell out because they've been here all damn night, but he should have held that comment in. Ossin is mad as hell, and I know he's embarrassed. He's the only damn person here that's overweight.

Ossin and his line brothers put the ropes around the pledges' necks again. All of the pledges start fighting Charlie. None of the frat boys try to stop the fight immediately.

"Let's see if his smart ass can get up," Ossin says. "You in shape. If you had some more weight Charlie, you could get some of them boys off of you."

These damn pledges are punching the hell out of Charlie and stomping on his ass. Charlie's crying, yelling, and throwing up.

My girls and I can only take so much of all this damn fighting and throwing up.

"That's enough y'all," Caya says. "They gone kill his ass."

Once Charlie starts bleeding, Ossin makes the other pledges sit down and finish eating their pizzas. He walks Charlie to

24

another table and gives him cotton balls and alcohol rub. Ossin sits down and talks to Charlie.

Everyone else is watching the boys continue to eat.

"Damn," Brenden says. "I didn't know a damn rope could make y'all that damn mad." The frat boys are all laughing. "Don't worry about Charlie," Brenden continues. "We all have bled before. He'll make it."

"I'm high as hell," Deliana says.

"In other words, she's hungry just like the rest of us are," Shemina says.

The frat boys are walking in circles around the pledges now. I know these young niggas don't think these grown ass men are going to let go of the fact that they are high and hungry while they are eating. These damn members of Phi Phi Alpha are on another level with these pledges tonight. Something must have happened. I don't know what though. I know I'm angry as hell because I had thoughts about my damn momma.

The truth is, it doesn't matter though. These damn fraternity men could be mad about anything. It could be from yesterday, a couple years ago, or when they were in grade school. These pledges are basically torture toys for the night.

It really just hit me that these boys got high and drunk and watched the pledges eat. I know they mad as hell.

The pledges finally get told that they can stop eating.

"Look around boys," Brenden says. "Do y'all see anything else in here for us to eat?"

"No Big Brother," the pledges say.

"So why didn't y'all save us some damn pizza?" Brenden asks. "Y'all can see we high and drunk as fuck."

Brenden is on his bullshit again. He's saying dumb shit to fuck with these boys.

"Don't answer that," Travis says. "My man is just trippin' right now. Go stand in the back while the boys and I talk."

"Hell no. Be still," Brenden says. "Everyone get on your knees and put your hands behind your heads."

"Who's been arrested before?" Travis asks.

25

As Greeks, we intimidate our pledges and make them tell us whatever we want. It sucks for people that want to join that we don't like. We make sure to get all in their business, just so we can throw it in their faces and spread it to whoever we want. It's not wise to join a Greek organization with members that hate you.

One of the pledges named Tariq admits that he got caught stealing. Another pledge named Hectin, admits he got caught eating in a store.

Brenden wants to know how long the boys had to stay in a cell, and how they handled being arrested. He wants to know the officers' names and anyone else the boys had to talk to. He wants to know what they ate while they were locked up. He wants to know if they made any new friends while locked up. He also wants to know how much paperwork the boys had to fill out.

Neither Tariq nor Hectin remember half of those answers.

"Damn man," Carter says to Brenden. "I know your ass done got locked up before. All them damn questions nigga?"

Some of the Phi Phi Alpha members are laughing at Brenden. Me and my girls start sighing and looking uneasy. We keep drinking and they smoke as well. One thing the pledges don't want to happen is for the frat brothers to laugh at each other.

Brenden is not one to like his frat brothers laughing at him, and he certainly doesn't want the pledges to have any good feelings arouse because they're mad they're being hazed.

"Shut the fuck up!" Brenden yells.

The girls and I take a shot. We are drunk as fuck.

I'm kissing Austin. We are ready to leave, but he needs to finish dealing with these pledges.

Brenden makes the pledges get on the floor and lift their legs up. They can barely lift them. They've been on their feet almost all night. Brenden has them put one leg down, then has them switch. He has the pledges count while they hold their legs up. The girls and I can't help but laugh when the pledges count and sometimes don't make it past three seconds before their legs drop.

"I have to record some of this," Telana says. "Don't worry boys. Me and my girls will only watch this when it's just us together. I can't let all this funny stuff go to waste."

Telana isn't the only one of us recording. I am, and so is Casha. Me and Casha exchange phones and look at each other's videos. It's the same footage, but we are so damn drunk that it doesn't matter. She's high too.

I can't say enough that I miss getting high. I know damn well that I can't go back to smoking though. The symptoms I have from it are not worth going back to. I'm so damn mad. I really wish I could hit the blunt. I wish the symptoms I'm having were from something else. I miss how that damn marijuana would make me feel.

One thing I have to keep in mind is that some of these damn Greeks are experiencing the fucked-up symptoms that made me stop, but still won't quit. I have to keep my head on straight and just know that my body is my body, and it said if I didn't quit, I would die soon.

"Have a seat," Brenden tells the pledges. "Bring the water," he says to Eric.

"Damn. We fucked up," Caya laughs. "I didn't even notice they ate all that damn food without anything to fucking drink."

Brenden has the pledges tilt their heads back and pours water down their throats. They all damn near choke on the water. Some of them throw up water and food.

"Eric is really being put to work," Telana says. Asayla and Shemina are laughing at the damn boy.

"Come on cutie. You can do it," Asayla says to Eric.

Eric is serious as hell. He makes sure to clean up every mess perfectly. He does not want to get on these frats bad side. Anything wrong he does, these damn men will not forget. That's why it sucks to be pre-pledged. Eric better not do anything that pisses the frat members off, or they will hold a grudge. It's really no point in even being pre-pledged. The only thing that will be remembered is what the potential does wrong.

Brenden has the pledges line up side by side and link up. Their arms are intertwined.

27

"Squat!" Brenden yells.

The pledges get in the squat position. Brenden makes them hold it. He's really on his Big Brother status. The girls and I can only look on in disbelief. We know Brenden's making them hold it until one of them falls, or tries to stand up. I'm so glad I already got my letters.

Hectin is the first person to fall to the ground. He makes everyone else fall because their arms are intertwined.

"Boy, what!" Brenden screams adjusting his shirt and pulling his pants up. His brothers are laughing and slapping hands. I can't believe how drunk everyone is. I'm the only person that's not high too. Some of us can barely stand up straight we're so buzzed.

It's obvious Brenden's trying to show out for his brothers that were just clowning him. Greeks will do stuff to each other so that the pledges have to go through worse.

"Come stand in front of everyone Hectin," Brenden demands.

Hectin looks scared as hell walking to the front.

"Link back up!" Brenden demands the rest of the pledges. They interlock arms again. "Mug!" Brenden tells Hectin.

Mug means make a mean and ugly face. The pledges usually have to hold it for a long time. We're all Greeks that have been through this, so we know how much holding our face in a messed up position can hurt.

The pledges are doing good taking their brother serious. Sometimes pledges have their moments when they laugh at their brother for making such a hideous face, but not this line that Hectin is on.

My girls and I are laughing. We can't help it. Hectin's face is hideous, but we can't help but take in how he went from a regular hurting face, to a hideous mean mug so fast. He's in pain too from all the hell he's been through today. All this liquor and drugs has me and my girls fucked up mentally. We are here to enjoy a good show, and that's exactly what we are going to do. The pledges feelings don't matter not a damn to us.

Hectin's line brothers seem to feel the pain their brother is going through. Charlie doesn't even seem to care that he was jumped anymore.

Brenden has Hectin get back in line with his brothers and link up. Brenden has the boys turn their heads left and right. He wants to make sure they are in unison. He makes them look up and down. He even says something that's in the cave, such as the jackets that are lying on the seating area, and sees if the boys will all look the same direction to spot them. Those that don't look the proper direction get hit on the forehead.

"Alright man," Travis says. "That's enough. Let they asses stand off to the side for a minute."

In other words, Travis is saying give the boys a decent amount of time to digest some of that damn food.

All the members of Phi Phi Alpha surround me and my girls. There's beer in the mix now. Some of the frat and my line sisters are chugging it. We're even mixing it with alcohol for the hell of it. We are getting pissy drunk tonight. None of us are in the mood to be trying to initiate members.

It's not easy bringing in a line. I know it sounds like it is fun and easy, but it's really not. First off, we have to take time out of our schedules to do it. Then the time has to fit for us all to meet. My girls and I don't have to be here tonight, but the frats as well as us, have to try new things for the pledges to get the full experience. Sometimes that means bringing in another sorority or fraternity.

Secondly, we have to come up with things for the pledges to do. As Greeks, we know eventually some people will tell another line what they went through. None of us wants to suffer the embarrassment of copying what we went through as pledges. We want our status to remain high. We never want the thought of anyone not taking us serious, or laughing at us later.

It takes a lot for letters to be taken from a Greek member. One way to get taken out of a Greek organization, is to be caught hazing. There's definitely a certain level of respect for Greeks because each year we haze, and each year we remain with our letters.

So not only do we have to find time to meet up with everyone, come up with things for the pledges to do, and risk getting our letters taken for hazing, we have to make sure the pledges learn their information.

The entire Greek process is just crazy indeed, but none of us ever question how things popped off with our organizations. If this is how Greek organizations have been run since the day they were founded, then this is what it is. We love our sisterhoods and brotherhoods. Whatever the process is for them to continue, is what we will do.

Let me not forget to add that we have to spend money out of our pockets to feed these damn pledges. We have to put gas in our cars. We don't hesitate to think about the miles that are added to our vehicles as well. We are very stingy and selfish when it comes to what we have to do to bring in a line. We wish this damn pledging process was free, but that's not the case. We have to do a lot for these damn pledges that we don't want to do.

Oh, and as Greeks, we make sure to take out all of our frustration on these damn pledges. We don't care what it's for. There's money that we work hard for that is going to people that have not even crossed yet. They get a few hits and nasty comments for that alone. Everyone in these Greek organizations is grown and would really love to save our finances for things we want for ourselves.

"These pledges need they asses beat some more," Austin says.

"They messed up on some of the information, and they can't even say it as one like they need to," Carter says. "Look at how pathetic they look right now. Their brains have not even been tested like they should."

The pledges look run down, but I know they are happy they get a few minutes to breathe and get some of their energy back. I think some of them are acting more tired than they are, in hopes that the frat will feel sorry for them. Little do they know, we've been through too much as Greeks. We don't care how tired or frustrated they look, even if it is genuine. We have no sympathy for them.

Some of the pledges start talking to each other.

"Aye, who the hell said y'all could talk?" Brenden rudely asks.

The pledges quickly stop talking.

"Stand straight up," Travis says. "Don't be fucking bending over. Put your arms to your sides."

"That's what y'all asses get," Caya says. "Quit all that fucking talking."

"Y'all heard the lady," Devin says. He's caked up with her.

"All y'all had to do was be quiet and no one would've even paid y'all any attention," Caya says. "Y'all could've moved however y'all wanted."

Caya's drunk as hell. She would still be talking if Devin didn't start kissing her.

"Don't spill that on me," I say to Casha. She's had way too much liquor. She's feeling real good.

"Turn on some music," Brenden says.

Eric turns on the radio. Casha is the first one to start grinding. Her ass is all over Brenden. She can barely stand up straight. She's holding the bottle and getting down.

I'm dancing with Austin. He's whispering in my ear.

"You are the prettiest girl here tonight," Austin says. "I'm glad you wanted me." I'm grinding all over him. I'm dipping down to the ground and shaking my ass back up all over my man.

"I'm glad you wanted me," I say turning around and kissing him.

"I see you Shona," Shemina says. She's damn near about to fall to the floor; she's so damn drunk.

"You can hold your liquor better than half they asses too," Austin says. "Oh, I forgot. You don't smoke no more. You not as fucked up as we are."

Damn that weed smells good. I really want to hit the blunt, but I'll be damned if I deal with any of these side effects again. I have to fight temptation. I low key want to start crying, but I'll be damned if I get weak in front of my line, my man and his crew. I will not embarrass my man. I don't want to bring any attention that he does not want. It's tough to watch everyone enjoy something that I once did.

Telana, Shemina, and Asayla start strolling. I join in with them. We are in the middle of all the Greeks doing our thing. We do the basic Greek train movement with our hands in fists and our arms pumping forward and backward. We do small steps so the circle doesn't need to expand. We move to the right and clap two times, then we move to the left and clap two times. Our heads are swinging both directions as well.

"Sssskkkiiioooo!" Telana shouts.

"Sssskkkiiioooo!" Shemina, Asayla and I shout after her.

Sssskkkiiioooo is Alpha Eta Nu's Greek call. We also shout it when we want to know if anyone else in our organization is in the building. Anyone that shouts our call that is not a part of Alpha Eta Nu, can get they ass whooped.

Don't get me wrong, we can't fight anyone. It's against our Greek morals. However, if we are at a party, or anywhere that we know we won't get caught, we will knock the hell out of somebody. We worked too hard to get our damn letters. We don't appreciate that shit.

Sssskkkiiioooo is something our founders put together for our members only. Greek organizations have been around long enough for people that are grown to know not to play around with our calls.

If we are out and about and someone shouts our call out, we approach each other and get to know one another. We are sisters automatically. We pledged the same sorority. No matter what state or country, if someone pledged Alpha Eta Nu, we are sisters.

The expectance regarding the calls is the same with any sorority or fraternity. If people call out the call and they are not in the organization, they are a waste of time. It's like they are playing around, which some people do. They think the calls are funny to hear and repeat them to make a mockery out of our organizations. That gets under our skin. If we can remember that while bringing in a line, we'll take it out on them. We play no games about getting all our monies worth that we spend on these damn pledges.

When we start the stroll line over, Caya, Deliana, and Casha join in.

My girls and I are having a good time. We are smiling, laughing, and flirting with the boys. We know how to make them not take their eyes off of us, even when they are high.

"Pledges, sit on the ground," Brenden demands them.

The young boys look more relaxed. They surely look thankful for all the time they don't have to hear us tell them what to do. I know what the hell that feels like. When I was pledging, I couldn't wait for the damn prophytes to get busy doing something else, and leave me and my line sisters alone.

"Pledge Hectin, why are you yawning?" Travis asks.

My girls and I have stopped strolling. They start smoking with the frat. I'm jealous as all hell watching them get high. I keep drinking though.

"These damn boys are going to get it," Asayla laughs.

"I know right," Shemina says. "They keep getting caught doing stupid stuff."

"When I was pledging, I was too damn scared to change facial expressions sometimes," I say.

"I'm with you Shona," Shemina says. "These damn boys must not have enough fear in them," she says looking at some of the frat boys. She's being messy trying to make them haze the boys more.

I'm just like her. I'm bitter behind all the things I had to do when we were pledging too. I want to make the members of Phi Phi Alpha do the most to these damn boys.

"Remember how we used to do our prophyte's hair?" I ask my girls.

"Girl hand me another bottle," Caya says.

"Somebody pass me a blunt," Telana says.

"Hell yea I remember doing they damn hair," Caya says. "Them bitches had me fucked up."

It's naturally in us to hate our prophytes. We don't want shit to do with them. The people that beat our asses to even get in

33

the sorority can kiss our ass. They have us fucked up. I don't know about anyone else's lines, but as far as me and my girl's line, we could care less to associate with them bitches that brought us in. Even the girls my line brought in don't want to talk to us. We hate the fucking pledging process. It's pure torture.

The correct way for things to be done is for each individual to learn the history of the organization and pass the tests. Really, they are not even supposed to have to take a test. It's common sense that no one should be hazed. When the hazing is taken out, there's only information to be learned. The test is bullshit though.

My line and I know how to do hair, and we had to do our prophytes' hair after they hazed us sometimes. We hated hooking them up. Every time we did our prophytes' hair, they looked better than they ever did before. My line just had natural talent for doing hair.

"Girls, remember they would tell us how they were going to see they man when we finished hooking them up?" Caya asks.

"Remember how when we would do their hair at they houses and they would order the food and get they houses ready for they man?" Telana asks.

Me and Shemina are laughing. It's that hurtful laughter. We made it through all the hell we had to endure and got our letters.

"You know good and well we would not help them bitches out with anything today after all that hell," Shemina says. "I can't believe we kept our sanity after all the hell them bitches put us through."

My line had to run in the rain one day. None of the neighbors gave a damn. They probably weren't even up because it was the middle of the night. My girls and I used newspapers as umbrellas. Our prophytes would drive next to us and yell, "Hurry the hell up! We're tired! I hope y'all get the message!"

My line and I weren't sure what the hell the prophytes meant by any of the things they were yelling at us. We were too focused on all the damn mud piles we kept almost slipping and falling in. We didn't even care that our prophytes were yelling at us. We were more concerned about getting sick, falling, and busting our heads. We had to run around our prophyte Timaina's neighborhood for an hour. None of us could run for an hour straight, and Timaina and her line made sure to keep up with how many times we stopped.

When we returned to Timaina's house, her and her line sisters would recite to us every time we stopped running. My line and I were shocked because we thought they were correct about every time they said we stopped. They told us when we fell, when we threw up, when we coughed, and many more things that we knew we did.

That same night, Timaina made us shower, then asked us what we needed. Some of us needed food, some of us needed sleep, and some of us just needed to sit down. We were all dead tired. If we did anything else, we may have passed the hell out. The girls and I were young, but we hated how we were desperate for any nice gestures the prophytes would give us. We hated how we were made so weak that we didn't care what good was said to us. We were desperate for the prophytes to say anything good to us.

"Girl I don't' care to see any of them mutha fuckas again," Telana says referring to our Big Sisters.

"Me either," I say.

"Eric, come stand in front of the pledges," Brenden demands. Brenden is drunk and high. He's wrapping another blunt. Travis lights it for him. "Eric get in the squat position," Brenden continues.

The pledges look shocked. My girls and I look surprised. The pledges are shocked because they can't believe Brenden has called on Eric. They don't know if it was planned or not. Me and my girls are surprised because we know them damn pledges deserve so much hell that Eric should be damn near invisible.

This damn boy Eric is scared out of his mind. However, he didn't even get in the squat position yet.

Brenden is walking over to Eric.

"Did I stutter?" Brenden asks.

"No Big Brother Brenden!" Eric yells.

The frat boys, my girls and I are laughing at Eric. Clearly the damn boy is scared.

Eric gets in the squat position in front of the pledges. These boys are young, but they are not naïve to the fact that Eric knows damn well they don't care to see him being hazed ahead of his damn time. Eric knows the pledges will take any new event and anyone who they think will get them more time to relax.

The music is still playing. Brenden has his brothers line up and they stroll around the cave.

Brenden leaves Eric in the squat position. When his legs give out, he falls to the ground. Brenden and his line stop strolling.

"Eric," Brenden says.

"Yes Big Brother," Eric says on the ground.

"First off, get your ass up," Brenden demands.

Eric gets up and wipes his behind off.

"He didn't tell you to wipe your ass," Travis says looking angry as hell.

"Sorry Big Brother," Eric says. He's not crying. He feels like because he's not even technically a pledge yet, that he can't get in any real trouble. He has a lot to learn about people that have become Greeks.

"Sorry Big Brother," Brenden says mocking Eric. The Phi Phi Alpha members start laughing and slapping hands. They are just enjoying picking on all these damn young boys who can't do anything about it. The pledges either do what the hell they are told, or get thrown out. For some of them, that would mean messing up a family legacy, and for the rest of them, that would mean not fulfilling all of their college dreams.

"Eric, why the hell did you fall?" Brenden continues. "You caused our whole damn stroll line to have to stop."

"I'm sorry Big Brother," Eric says.

"First off, I'm not your Big Brother," Brenden says. "You just the damn clean up boy, by your damn self."

"Sorry Brenden," Eric says.

36

The frat boys are slapping hands and smoking. They are laughing at this poor boy. My girls and I are doing the same thing. It doesn't matter how Eric answers anything. He knows damn well we know he doesn't know how to go about responding to us.

"There's a fresh box of pizza over there," Brenden says. He stares at Eric. "What the fuck are you supposed to say?"

Eric looks at the pledges who are taking all this time to regain their energy.

"They can't help you," Brenden continues.

"Yes Brenden," Eric says.

Brenden slaps hands with Travis. He's laughing with his boys and acting like the jock that he is.

"That nigga stupid," Tevin says.

Again, this is us Greeks acting like the jackasses that we can. Any answer given, we can decide if we want it to be right or wrong. We can acknowledge that it's right, and still act an ass as if this damn boy Eric answered it wrong. This is just us on our bullshit.

"Bring the pizza over here nigga," Brenden says.

Zack is the closest to the pizza, so he brings it to Eric.

"Sit your ass down and eat it," Brenden continues.

Eric sits on the ground and eats the pizza. The pledges look relieved to get more time to not hear our voices. They act like we don't know they feel that way. Everyone here has pledged before besides them and Eric. We know what it's like to need any and every moment that we don't have to hear our prophytes talk to us. We know what it's like to not want to hear any dictation when we are tired as all hell. Most importantly, we know what it's like to hear the words, *it's time to go.*

Eric begins eating the pizza and the pledges hearts start to calm down. I know from experience. However, it doesn't take long for Travis to have the pledges get a partner. He's about to make them do trust exercises. He has the boys stand in front of their partner. They have to fall backwards and trust that their partner will catch them, and not let them fall to the floor.

After the trust exercise, Brenden blindfolds the boys and has them crawl on the floor.

"Go the other way," Caya says to one of the boys that's about to hit the wall. She didn't say his name, so he crawls and hits his head on the wall, and it starts bleeding. The frat men start yelling and my girls and I quickly learn this pledges name is Arnold.

"Damn it!" Brenden yells. "Everyone take off your blindfolds!"

"I swear it's like these niggas trying to get our letters taken," Travis says.

"I swear we're not!" Eric yells.

Phi Phi Alpha members make this nigga Eric do the crawl exercise too. It doesn't take long for Brenden to get angry with him.

"Man get your ass out of here!" Brenden yells. "Don't ever bring your ass back!"

Me and Shemina put alcohol and cotton balls on Arnold's forehead.

"Man, what the hell were you thinking?!" Brenden yells. "Don't you know we could get in fucking trouble for you fucking up!?"

Brenden is too damn high and drunk. It's time to call it a fucking night.

"Y'all, we need to wrap this up," Telana says. "Phi Phi Alpha is done for the night." She means they are too drunk and high.

"But they still need to perform," I say.

"Aye, yall ready to do y'all show so we can get out of here?" Telana asks Travis.

Travis says yes and has his line get in two rows in front of the pledges.

Eric has already left the cave.

"Phi Phi Alphaaaa!" Travis yells.

Travis and his line break into some fast and intense choreography. They lift their elbows up and have their arms go across their chests while their heads turn the same way. They lift their knees and hit them in unison. They move to the right a few steps, then to the left a few steps, and clap in front. They do a few moves in a circle and bend down to the ground in unison. They end their routine with their call *PhiiiiiHiiii.* Brenden's line plays no games letting the pledges know who is in charge.

"Grab your things and get the hell on," Brenden says to the pledges.

My girls and I make sure everyone is bandaged that needs to be, before they start to exit.

"It's sad that Eric didn't last," Shemina says to me.

"I know right," I say. "Damn. Poor boy."

"Oh well," Caya says. "They'll get another boy dumb enough that wants to be pre-pledged."

"I hear you girl," I say. "There's no room for weakness around these parts."

Some of the frat boys are walking in circles.

"What's wrong?" Caya asks.

"Something's not right," Travis says.

"Wait, bring y'all asses back here!" Brenden demands the pledges.

"What's the problem?" I ask.

"They need to clean up this fucking place before they go," Brenden says. "Eric is finished. He won't be bringing his ass back anymore."

The pledges have to pick up any trash that's lying around. That includes: beer bottles, liquor bottles, blunt wrap packages, and the remains of cigarettes and blunts. It includes: pizza boxes, water bottles, bandages that fell off, and candy wraps.

"Y'all are moving too damn slow," Tevin says. "Hurry the hell up, so we can go. I'm hungry as hell."

Charlie spots a blunt that wasn't properly put out. His dumb ass really is smoking it. It's not much, but he still can get his ass beat. I can't believe this damn boy really thinks no one will notice that he is smoking.

"He must've forgotten already what he's been through," I say.

"No. He so damn out of it from all the hell he's been through, that he's not in his right damn mind," Shemina says.

Brenden goes over to Charlie and sprays him with the hose.

"I'm just putting out the damn blunt," Charlie says.

Charlie falls over because he's being so drenched with water. Brenden is getting this boy soak and wet. Charlie is choking on water.

"Stop man," Charlie says. "Please stop."

"What the hell is wrong with you?" Brenden asks. "Are you trying to embarrass me in front of my crew? What do I look like stopping after only a few seconds of punishing you?"

"My nigga, after everything that's happened tonight, you got the nerve to fucking pick up a blunt that wasn't put out, and smoke it?" Travis asks.

"Keep soaking his ass in that water," Tevin says.

Charlie is moving all over the place trying to avoid the water. He's crying while the Phi Phi Alpha members continuously call him disgusting words. They call the damn boy a bitch multiple times. Brenden says Charlie is worse than woman pledging.

"Nigga, don't be talking about us," Caya says. "We didn't have no weak ass girl start smoking. We never knew no disrespect like that bringing in a line."

"Fuck you," Brenden says to her.

"Nigga, fuck you," Shemina says defending Caya.

"Fuck you and your momma," Telana says defending Caya too.

"Aye, watch how you talk to the ladies," Tevin jokes. "Easy girls. He's just drunk and high."

"So are we," Caya says. "This is y'all sorry ass pledge that's out of line. Handle his ass, and don't disrespect us."

"I'll disrespect whoever the hell I want to," Brenden says.

"Well fuck you again nigga," Caya says.

The rest of the pledges continue picking up trash.

"At least the rest of them niggas know to keep following they damn orders," Caya continues.

My girls and I step to the side while Brenden and the rest of Phi Phi Alpha handle Charlie.

"Girl don't trip," I say to Caya. "You know them niggas are not there mentally at all."

"We'll get they asses," Caya says. "I want to key one of they damn cars."

"No. Not tonight," Shemina says. "We are going out after this."

"So," Caya rudely says. "We keying their cars, not slitting tires."

"Calm down," Telana says. "Don't let them make us argue. Damn y'all. Now I really want to fuck with them."

"Them niggas know not to disrespect us period," Caya says. She's mad as hell. "I don't give a damn that they feel disrespected. Nobody talks bad about our sorority."

"We need to get they asses," I say. I know Austin is in Phi Phi Alpha, but that doesn't matter. Whatever my girls and I do, his ass won't know. We are a sisterhood, and all frats know to give us the same respect they want.

"He's not that drunk," Asayla says.

"Think fast y'all," Telana says. "What can we do? I'm not gone feel right if we don't fuck with them. Not one of them got that nigga Brenden in line."

My Sorors and I look over at Brenden and his boys going off on Charlie.

This damn boy Charlie done got us arguing with each other. Brenden is not taking that lightly. He's making sure Charlie shows remorse for being disobedient. Charlie keeps falling and hitting his head on stuff. Sometimes he does it on purpose because he knows Brenden wants to keep showing his boys that he's not no bitch, and isn't going to let a pledge disrespect his frat.

"Why did y'all let Eric go?" Charlie cries. "He wasn't even a pledge."

"Nigga, we gone let your ass go in a minute," Brenden says.

"Don't fucking question us about what we do," Tevin says. "No weak ass niggas are staying. If you fuck up, you better be able to deal with the punishment. We men. We real niggas. It ain't shit we can't come up with to fix y'all asses."

"But he didn't do nothing!" Charlie cries. "Y'all were picking on him."

"Is that your brother or something?" Brenden asks. "Or is he your man?"

"He was cool peoples!" Charlie yells.

"Lower your mutha fucking voice," Brenden says. "I mean, shut the fuck up!"

Charlie is real angry now. He is saying any and everything out of frustration. He thinks Brenden is trying to kill him. He's still choking on water. He's even shivering.

"Shut the fuck up nigga," Travis says sparking another blunt.

"The water is too cold!" Charlie cries.

"If you don't shut the hell up, you gone lick it off the damn ground," Travis says.

"Think y'all," Shemina says.

I'm drinking out the bottle with Caya. The blunt is being passed around our circle too. We are watching Charlie squat and stand up. He's lifting his legs, and putting them down when instructed. He's even doing leg lifts. All the while, water is still being sprayed with the hose, and poured on him.

It's a windy night. This boy is going to be sick.

"I know you brought a change of clothes, right?" Travis asks Charlie.

"No Big Brother," Charlie cries. "I didn't think I would need them."

The girls and I are laughing. We know Charlie is not in his right mind. Charlie knows good and well he's supposed to always bring an extra set of clothes with him when coming to a set. The pledges parents are always told that they work out and do many trust exercises that cause them to need a change of clothes. We have lies for days to cover our asses with this hazing.

Phi Phi Alpha is laughing. They know Charlie is not in his right mind, but they have no way to one hundred percent know, so they go with their gut feeling that he is trying to make a mockery of them.

Brenden hits Charlie on his face.

"Wake the fuck up," Brenden says.

"I mean, I do have more clothes," Charlie says.

42

"Don't pass out damn it," Brenden says.

The girls and I are getting excited. We're ready to do some mischief to these frat boys. We need to make up our minds before the frat calls it quits for the night. My girls and I keep looking in each other's eyes trying to see who will finalize what we will do. We can't keep still. The boys keep looking at us.

"What y'all getting excited about?" Austin asks.

"None of your damn business," I joke.

Austin smiles at me, then kicks Charlie in his stomach. Charlies throwing up. Austin's not taking a chance on me really joking. He knows his boy just pissed us the hell off. I know all this damn smiling and laughing we're doing doesn't overshadow what the hell Brenden just said to us. Austin should have kicked Brenden.

"We're laughing at your damn pledges over there looking scared as all hell cleaning up," Caya says.

"Y'all better be good," Brenden says. "I'm drunk and high. Cut me some slack."

My Sorors and myself can't think of anything to do to these damn boys. We are the only ones here with them aside from the pledges. That just gave me an idea.

"Whatever we do, we can say one of the pledges did it," I say.

"That sounds bomb girl," Caya says. "But we monitor the pledges every step of the way, so how is that going to work? You're too drunk girl."

"Let's just fuck up one of their cars, and say it was already done," I suggest. "They'll think some people came by, fucked they shit up, and left."

"Who wants to do the honors?" Caya asks. "I'm definitely going to Brenden's car."

"What y'all whispering about?!" Tevin shouts.

"None of your damn business," Shemina says.

Me, Caya, Deliana, and Casha go out to the cars. As soon as we step outside the cave, Deliana shouts that someone has keyed Brenden, Zack and Tevin's cars. At the same time, me, Caya and Casha are hurrying and keying the cars.

43

Deliana tells us Zack, Carter, and Tevin are coming to check.

"Get those damn smiles off y'all faces," Deliana tells me, Caya and Casha. We are laughing and having a good time like a bunch of angry men aren't heading our direction.

"Fuck!" Zack screams. "Why didn't y'all pick another spot?"

"Nigga, how the fuck were we supposed to know this shit would happen?" Carter asks.

"Chill out," Tevin says. "Let's deal with these niggas, and figure this shit out later."

"Yea. Maybe they got some damn money," Zack says.

"Damn. I just needed to get my damn purse, and we saw this," Caya lies. "I'm glad them niggas didn't get my car."

"Aren't you just the damn lady?" Zack says. "Our fucking cars get fucked up, and you're over here feeling good because yours didn't. Some damn sorority."

"Nigga shut up. Maybe if y'all weren't so damn rude to people, this wouldn't have happened," Caya says. "Y'all clown all types of folks. You don't even know where to start looking."

I pull Caya close to me. I think she's hit the blunt too many times. It sounds like she's about to accidently admit that we just keyed these cars.

"It's his damn fucked up remarks that got us to do the shit," I whisper to Casha.

"They just don't quit," Casha says.

Zack, Carter and Tevin are in deep thought while their brothers are inside with the pledges.

I go back in the cave and see all the pledges lined up getting sprayed with the hose. The frat boys are screaming loud. The pledges are all broken completely. They can barely stand straight up. Brenden is getting on them for losing their posture when the cold water hits them.

"Does anyone else want to smoke tonight?" Brenden asks the pledges. They all say no, then jump Charlie. Another damn fight. I can't believe this.

"Aye Brenden?" Zack says. Brenden turns the hose off and looks at his brother. "We got to get out of here man," Zack says. "We got to get to the bar. Fuck them niggas."

"Who the hell keyed my damn car?" Brenden asks.

"Nigga I don't know," Zack says. "We'll figure out how to deal with this shit later."

That usually means that the frat boys will take their anger out on somebody random that they don't like. Sometimes they'll find someone they don't even know and give them hell. These frat boys don't let anything go. If something happens to them and they can't find out who did it, they feel obligated to get revenge in any way on any person.

"Grab they clothes man," Brenden says. He already knew Charlie had his clothes, but didn't give a damn. He wanted to see how Charlie would respond while he was frustrated.

The pledges switch clothes and the frat boys drive them home.

My girls and I get on the road. I'm driving and so is Caya and Asayla. Telana and Shemina are in the car with me. We're all drunk as hell and should not be behind the wheel. What can I say? We are accustomed to what this Greek life has done to us. None of us have on seatbelts, and I've ran a few red lights. Our windows are down. We are doing our call. The radio is turned all the way up.

The Greek life is a fast life. We party all the time. When we are hazing people, we party. When we meet new Sorors, we party. We always feel the need to have a good time when we are together.

So far, with all the laws that we have broken while driving, we haven't been caught. Some people have to get in trouble to learn a lesson, and that's the Greeks from Cupperton University. We know the truth, and we still can't get ourselves to get a designated driver.

I call Austin and ask him what he wants to eat.

"These boys keep throwing up," Austin says. "We gone be further behind y'all than we thought."

"What's all that damn screaming?" I ask.

"We in a vacant parking lot," Austin says. "You know them niggas mad as hell they cars got keyed. They got these boys linked up saying information."

"They linked up, reciting information, and throwing up?" I ask. Telana and Shemina are looking puzzled like me.

"Uh unh," Telana says. "They lying."

"We figured out who fucked up our cars," Austin says. "It was Eric."

Me, Telana and Shemina are in complete shock. If the boys think it was Eric, so will we. We don't give a fuck. Brenden was not about to clown our sorority.

"I'm high as hell," Brenden says. "Have that damn food ready." Clearly Austin has me on speaker. "Aye, I think people spotting us. We done for the night," Brenden continues.

"We gone clean these boys up and be on our way to y'all," Austin says. "I love you."

"I love you too baby," I say.

"Damn. Them niggas is on one," Shemina says.

My girls and I go inside Sharmane's Bar and order hot wings and fries for ourselves and the boys. We don't wait on the boys to eat. I'm drunk, and they are drunk and high. We are hungry as fuck. This food has never tasted so good.

When the boys arrive, their food is already waiting for them like Brenden asked. Now why the hell is Brenden arguing with the waiter asking for fresh food? The argument is completely stupid. Of course his food was ordered before he got here and wouldn't be as fresh as it could've been had he ordered it when he arrived. I have to tell my case to the waiter because I don't want him to think I'm stupid.

Me and Caya look at each other. We are glad as hell we fucked up they cars.

The members of Phi Phi Alpha and my Sorors are all grubbing. We order drinks and cheers to a successful night. We do our calls and converse about everything but what actually happened tonight.

"We gone need to order some more food," Tevin says. The boys are really stuffing their faces.

I miss how much I enjoyed eating after smoking a blunt. Food tasted so much better after I was high than it does after I'm drunk. I can still remember how good it felt to smoke and eat.

46

I'm jealous of the other Greeks. I'm glad they still get to enjoy the feeling though.

Austin whispers in my ear and me and him follow behind a waiter who brings us to a booth.

I sit in front of my man and ask why he wanted to be separated from the group.

"I wanted to stare into your eyes and get you alone for a while," Austin says. "You stuck with me through this crazy ass night, and I wanted to make sure I told you how much I appreciate you."

"I appreciate you for being such a good man to me," I say. I'm still mad he didn't knock the hell out of Brenden for dissing my sorority, but I'm not gone say nothing. The girls and I did what we had to so that we wouldn't be so bothered by Phi Phi Alpha later.

"What you want to do after this?" Austin asks.

"I can look into your eyes and tell what you want to do," I say. "You want to go to my house or yours?"

An argument at the bar takes me and Austin's attention. Brenden is arguing with the waiter because he ordered twelve wings and counted eleven. He's high and drunk, so I know he made a mistake while he was counting. Either way it goes, he's too damn loud.

"He still mad about his fucking car," Zack says. He's explaining to the waiter why his brother is acting like an asshole.

Brenden keeps walking closer to the waiter. Austin gets up and moves Brenden away from the waiter, who is going to get the manager.

"You've had too much to drink," Austin tells Brenden.

"Nigga I'm mad about my car still too," Zack says with his mouth full of chicken. Shemina is wiping around his lips. Everyone in our circle who is not dating someone, treats whoever they want that's single however they want.

Zack is really on one. I've been trying hard not to laugh at this damn boy tonight. The way he talks and his personality are very humorous at times.

Brenden says he is fine, and Austin lets him go. Brenden goes outside and leans on his car. The waiter and the manager go out there and tell him to pay for his food. Brenden punches the waiter in the face. He ends up getting arrested.

A man accidently bumps into Zack at the bar, and Zack ends up fighting the man. Zack is punching and pushing him. His line brothers join in. They get the man on the floor and start kicking and stomping on him.

When the cops question Phi Phi Alpha about what happened, they all say the man was violent towards Zack, but the cameras show otherwise. All the members of Phi Phi Alpha end up getting arrested.

My girls and I are in complete shock. We pay for our food and get to-go-boxes. We go to my house and finish eating.

"Girls, I never want that to happen to us," Caya says.

Days like these, the girls and I get real close and make sure we advise each other the correct way. We don't want any of us to get arrested behind some dumb stuff.

I sit on the couch with some of my Sorors and the rest of them sit on the floor. We want to be together tonight.

"I can't stand when niggas act crazy like that," Caya says.

"I can't stand that one of them was my nigga," I say.

"It's like damn, y'all with a sorority. We just got done smoking and drinking," Shemina says. "Why the hell can't y'all just relax and enjoy the rest of the night?"

"You got something to drink?" Telana asks me.

I grab a wine bottle and the girls and I pass it around.

"Let's just be thankful we not dumb enough to join in on no action like that," Casha says.

"I felt like they just got done doing enough to them damn pledges," I say.

"I know," Caya says. "They just don't get enough."

"I even forgot they had them boys tonight," Casha says. "They act like they didn't take out any frustration on them."

"We were at a nice bar," Caya says. "I go to that bar a lot."

"Me too," I laugh. "I can't have them making the staff think I know a bunch of crazy niggas."

"They gone think that now," Caya says. "They all got arrested. Not one. Not two, but all of them got taken in."

"I hope they know that's not easy for us to be looking at," Shemina says. "We don't just see a lot of people getting arrested, and we know each and every one of them, all of the time."

I put on a movie for us to watch. I get some shorts and big t-shirts for the girls to get comfortable in.

I get some blankets and pillows. The girls end up falling asleep and staying at my house for the night.

3

The lights dim in the auditorium of Ann High School as their step team walks on stage and takes their places in the school theater.

Dressed in black slacks, white fitted shirts, bright red jackets, and with curly wigs on, the girls take their positions. Dressed in red suits, white button up shirts, and black ties, the boys form a row in front of them. The DJ starts the music, and the crowd gets loud instantly when they hear the fast-paced beat.

As soon as the bass drops, Ann High bursts into their choreography. They clap above and under their legs. They face the sides and move backwards with crisp claps. The boys start to do movements while the girls freeze. They're moving around and every stomp is together while moving their arms up and down just like professionals. The girls energetically join in.

The song goes off with a boom effect and the team ends in a four-row formation. Heads facing down. Everyone stiff as a board. The girls with their hands on their hips, and the boys with their hands in fist by their sides.

Everyone has lots of attitude and energy staring out at the crowd which is loving every second of the performance that is just getting started. Parents are shouting their kids' names and students are hype watching their friends perform.

One of the male steppers walks to the front and shouts, "Ann! High! Steppers!" Two stomps and everyone puts their right hand on their forehead. "Break it down!" the same boy shouts. With tons of energy, Ann High bursts into complex combinations. Not missing a beat, all the stomps and claps are together. Everyone's heads are turning sharp in the direction their arms point, and they sound like it's one person on the stage like stepping is supposed to, even though there's twelve people on it. The formations continuously change from circles, to crosses, to rows of three, to rows of four.

Ann High Steppers are the real deal.

Midway through the routine, a song plays and the squad keeps the same beat with their hands and feet. The beat goes off for a couple seconds and Ann High keeps stepping; the song comes back on and they still keep the beat. Even though the music went off, it's like it never did because Ann High's steppers use their bodies as instruments to make it seem like the beat is still going. It takes the crowd a minute to realize the actual music track went off and the step team kept the beat alive without the beat and lyrics. This drives the crowd wild. Everyone is on their feet either clapping, shouting, jumping up and down, yelling their friend or child's name, or smiling.

This is unlike anything the city of New Orleans has ever seen. There's no high schools here that can compete with Ann High. Everyone on the team is gifted, sharp, precise, energetic, and smooth. There's not one odd ball because everyone works hard at rehearsals, as well as puts countless hours into perfecting their choreography outside of it.

Everyone's so hype in here that Ann High has to shout their chants louder to outdo the crowd's loud noise. The teams' working so hard that they're sweating now. I know their energy mixed with the lights shining on them is making them hot.

To close the show, Ann High strolls off the stage to music. They're in one line energetically and enthusiastically dancing and moving forward to leave out of the theater while their friends and family shout: *Get it girl! Go head! Y'all better work! That's my son up there!*

Ann High knows they have delivered one of the best step shows their school has ever witnessed. They know without a doubt that they have proved they are the best high school step team at their first ever Ann High Step Spectacular.

Everyone in the audience shouts and gazes on in amazement as the steppers make their way out the door.

Everyone except me.

I'm gazing on with jealousy, disgust, and anger.

I wanted the team to do terrible, not have something to smile about in my face at school. I look over at the advisors on the side of the stage with their jolly smiles on their faces observing their team and the audience. I hate them with a passion. They were the people that took advantage of having the upper hand. It is because of them I'm not strolling off the stage right now. I'm supposed to be in front of the stroll line leading the team out of the door.

The advisors are turning my direction. Before they look me in the eyes, I quickly look away. I know they want to witness my agony. I'm not giving them the satisfaction. I sharply turn my head and look away, but now I have eye contact with someone else I despise, one of the members on the team, Jasmine Pent, who is all smiles as she strolls off and witnesses my anger. She knows damn well if I was on the team I would be in her front spot position in the stroll line right now, and she would be behind me.

Jasmine's not better than me at stepping. When I was on the team, I was the best and everyone knew it. I was always front and center unless we had a step that required positions to be switched. No one could match my fierce attitudes, facials, energy, enthusiasm, let alone my natural ability. No one could touch me or came close to my talent. Stepping is in my blood. I was born with the talent. My mom always told me I was kicking her too much when she was pregnant, and I used to tell her I was in her belly making up routines.

Some people think I am cocky and arrogant. I think I'm just pure confident. There's a difference in being cocky and arrogant from confident. There's a difference that the two advisors that are hugging each other tight and laughing, while the crowd goes wild, didn't see and that's why I'm sitting in this audience looking bitter instead of outside with the team that's probably jumping up and down and congratulating one another on a job well done.

The fire alarm is pulled and I quickly pick my head off the desk. I'm chillin' with one of my old teachers from Cupperton University, Professor Tobin. I've been coming to see him a lot in the last few months. I fell asleep during the lecture. I remember Ann's Step Spectacular was only a few months before I started college. The memories are still fresh in my mind, which is why I constantly drift off and think about that horrific day I was sitting in the audience when I should've been on stage showing out and letting everyone see, that hadn't before, what someone with a natural stepping gift can do on the stage.

"Class is dismissed until next week," Professor Tobin says in the middle of his lecture at the sound of the alarm. Everyone grabs their books and rushes out the building with the other students on Cupperton's campus. The alarm has my ears ringing. I couldn't get out of that building fast enough.

As soon as I step out, one of my best friends Ciera rushes over to me. I feel relieved. Walking on this huge campus is a drag, but with someone to walk with, it isn't as painful. Ciera was supposed to sit in the class with me, but she was too lazy to get up on time. She didn't even get to let Professor Tobin see her face because the alarm was pulled.

"Girl, I can't take it anymore," I say.

I can't hold it in anymore.

I need to vent.

"Wasup?" Ciera asks.

"What the hell happened to our campus?" I ask as I look

around disgusted at the lack of activity.

"Girl you know that's just today," Ciera says. "My cousin goes here. She said they been having too many fights and security has been getting on people's nerves asking questions."

Some students are studying on the bench, others are walking to class, and some people are at the vending machines. No one seems to be enjoying the day. Everyone looks bored and lifeless. This is not usual at Cupperton.

I love Cupperton University so much. One of the best things about the school is I met and have such a great friend in Ciera who comforts me and says, "Girl who are you telling? Things will look up soon today."

Any time I come to Cupperton, something always pops off. I'm not used to coming up here and everyone seems to be uninterested in being on the campus.

I absolutely love Ciera because I can talk to her about anything. We've known each other since we were in college, we're really close, and I feel like we are sisters. We met in the hour-long financial aid line the weekend before school began. She was standing behind me when I asked the boy in front of me if he knew how to get to President Deon's office because I wanted to meet this successful black man that is the head of my university. The boy in line turned his head around, looked at me rudely, and shrugged his shoulders. I turned my relaxed face into a disgusted one and rolled my eyes at him.

I was mad it was only my second day on the campus, and I already had to encounter someone with a nasty attitude towards me that I didn't even know.

After I got myself together and calmed down, Ciera told me where President Deon's office was. She told me she could walk me over there, so I waited for her outside when I was done with the financial aid people and she took me.

On our walk, I vented about the mean boy from the financial aid line. I kept talking about his ugly haircut and that ugly looking face he made.

Ciera laughed the whole walk to President Deon's office.

President Deon looked so happy to see two black women show up to his door. Cupperton's campus has a lot of different ethnicities; however, there is a significant high amount of black people here than any other race. We definitely outnumber everyone severely. Ciera started to leave me, but President Deon asked her to stay and talk with us. I told him I just wanted to shake hands with the man in charge and he said, "It warms my heart to know he's appreciated." I already knew where he would take the conversation. He told us to have a seat and went on and on about blacks not taking their education seriously. "I hope the both of you make it out of here with a degree," he said. "Don't drop out of school like most of our people do. If funds become an issue, then get a job, mow lawns, babysit, do what you can do to obtain what people don't expect our people to."

Ciera and I smiled the entire time President Deon was talking. When we left his office, I found out she felt the same way I did about the visit. We just wanted to go in, say hi, shake hands, and say how happy we were to be attending Cupperton. We both told each other *bye* when we got out of the building President Deon's office was in because we both assumed we would be heading off campus to go home. We started walking the same direction and laughed.

"Is your car this way?" Ciera asked me.

"No," I said. "I live in the dorms."

"Me too," Ciera said.

On our walk to our designated dorm buildings, me and Ciera started learning small stuff about each other. We both were born and raised in New Orleans. I'm focused on being a TV writer and she's focused on being a TV personality like those people that give interviews on the red carpet. We were both freshmen, and we both had no intention of walking away from Cupperton without a degree.

Ciera was cool and good to talk to, so I gave her my number and told her to call me whenever she was bored.

I love her so much. She genuinely wants the best for me and helped me with anything I needed. Anytime I wanted to get out of my dorm because my roommates were too loud, arguing, or I simply just wanted to be in a new atmosphere, she let me come over and sleep on her couch. Anytime I needed someone to read over my assignments to make sure my work flowed smoothly, she did it with no problem. Anytime I needed to borrow a few dollars, she gave it to me, and anytime I didn't feel like going to buy food or make anything to eat, she invited me over.

Ciera is the type of person I have always longed to have in my life. She's a good friend just like my sorority sisters are. Everyone I knew at my middle and high school were fake and phony. I always heard them talking bad about other people in our crew saying they can't dress, or get on their nerves always bickering about an ex, so I knew when I wasn't around, they did the same to me. I would be a fool to think otherwise.

I never understood why people show their true colors to others when it comes to how they treat their friends, and don't expect anyone to think they are being fake to them as well. I knew once I got my diploma and exited my high school walls for the last time, I wouldn't associate with any of them again. Ciera is a good friend I have who is not in my sorority. Almost everyone else I know is an associate.

"Remember when we went to visit Greg Johnson

University?" I ask Ciera.

Greg Johnson (G.J.) is a Film and Media school. I love to go there sometimes just to meet people. I might meet someone that could land me my dream job.

I'm visualizing G.J. University's band playing on the sidewalk, the band's dancers having rehearsal, the football players playing catch, and cheerleaders laughing over lunch. The students socialized and talked about the party they went to the previous night, and even the staff had smiles on their faces walking around the campus. People had on t-shirts and hoodies with their school's name and colors on them. No one was in a hurry to get in their cars, and when classes were out people sat on benches, ate, read a book, talked to friends, or had a study group at one of the tables. Everyone seemed so proud of their university, and like they didn't want to leave it, even though they would return the next morning for class.

Ciera and I were visiting the campus because we were bored sitting on our school benches one day, and we wanted to compare our surroundings with another college's. We both didn't want to leave G.J. University. As soon as we approached the campus, we heard the band playing and saw cheerleaders drinking in the parking lot. People were handing out flyers for parties, and the school even had vendors that were selling burgers. G.J. was full of life and the way some people depict college to be in the movies. It was the way Ciera and I both thought all colleges would be. G.J. University is just like the movies we see on the big screens.

G.J. University is just like any other school because sometimes the students just go to class and go home unless they participate in some of the school activities. Some of which are: basketball, tennis, track, and volleyball. I've only attended a basketball game, and it was a joke because the players kept double dribbling, air balling free throws, and carrying the ball. The basketball team here sucks completely. The good part about the basketball team is they still have a huge audience. G.J. students have a lot of school pride and always support their teams. Some of the sports have really good teams at G.J. University such as: swimming, baseball, and football. That's only to name a few.

I'm one of those people that wonders why high school is free and has everything possible to offer and why students are actually paying for college and some don't have the activities they would like to participate in.

I love coming back to Cupperton. People socialize a lot on the promenade or at many tables that are sitting outside of some of the buildings.

Cupperton is huge and beautiful. The scenery is gorgeous with the plants and bushes aligning some of the buildings. There's nice exterior designs on the buildings. Campus housing is so beautiful. The dorms are very spacious. I love how big the living rooms are in them. The kitchen has a nice amount of space in it too, so that roommates don't keep bumping into one another.

There's so many beautiful sites to see at Cupperton. It's a real tourist attraction. I love the days when the campus theme is comprised of black and gold colors.

Cupperton's campus is like a city to me because it's so big. I love to brag to people about the college I graduated from.

I stop on me and Ciera's walk to our cars, to continue my rant.

"Look around Ciera," I say. "The students just got out of class. Why does it seem like no one is here? It's usually packed as hell out here between classes. This has got to be one of the most uneventful days I've visited this campus."

I'm mad as hell I chose today, out of all days, to come up here.

Ciera and I are slowly walking to our cars. People are rushing past us we're walking so slow, but we don't care. We aren't in any hurry to get to my house.

Ciera tries to comfort me for being down about picking an unusual day to come visit my old university.

"You will be alright," Ciera says. "You just need something else to keep you busy."

Ciera knows I am someone that has so much potential, but I need to have someone motivating me to keep going. I'm not good at encouraging myself to do something, unless I absolutely love doing a particular thing, or there's something I must get accomplished.

"The step team you created is going great though, right?" Ciera asks.

I look at her as if she is my worst enemy. I say everything without saying anything.

I started a step team at Cupperton to have something to do in my spare time. I started this step team this year. I'm the coach, just like I was at Ann High School.

I hate to think back on the process I had to endure just to begin this step team, and have it considered a club, so that the students could get school recognition. I had to have a sheet filled out of officers which included a president, vice president, treasurer, and two secretaries. Of course, I am the president of the club and I just had four of my members sign their names as any officer. We don't need any titles for the team to run properly, but its protocol to have officers. The only thing that being considered an actual club benefits us in is being able to reserve the gym for rehearsals and perform at school events such as basketball games and pep rallies.

Well, now that I actually said those things, I can see that it was definitely necessary to fill out that paperwork. The gym for rehearsals definitely comes in handy.

Aside from having officers, I had to type up the history of stepping in which I drug out the fact that back in the day slaves were not allowed to speak so they used their bodies to communicate.

I had to tell what was expected of my members, when and where rehearsals would be held, the maximum number of people I could have on the team, what our uniforms would look like, and who our advisor would be.

I had to roam up and down the dance hallways looking for a school advisor to whom I would give the following speech: *Hello, my name is Shona Jackson, and I am trying to begin a step team here on campus so students can have another extracurricular activity. All I need for my proposal to go through is an advisor to be a part of the program. Would you be interested?*

After about eight *no's* from different people, a Ms. Ileen finally said yes. I started this team this year on Cupperton's campus, so I didn't have a relationship with any staff to make my life easier finding an advisor. On every team I've ever coached, it required an advisor which is something I never understood because I am the one making up all the choreography. All the advisor is to me is a babysitter.

After putting my blood, sweat and tears into getting the program started, all I needed was to find some members who were interested. The ones I got were the complete opposite of what I wanted: always late, full of excuses, and take advantage of knowing I do not have enough people to remove anyone.

I always feel like my members take advantage of me primarily because they know I don't want to lose the team. It seems like people know me so well from step shows with Alpha Eta Nu when I was in college, and they tell new attendees at Cupperton about me.

My step crew has no idea about all the hard work I had to put into getting this team started, and I don't think they care. As long as they're a part of something and can go back and tell their mommy and daddy that they're spending their extra time in college wisely, then they're good.

I can't win. I go from one issue to another when it comes to being a coach. I wish I was like Ciera and was content just going to work during the week and going out on some weekends. However, I'm someone that can't spend time doing the same routine, which is spend time with Alpha Eta Nu, come home, take a nap, go to work, and come home again. I just can't be hooked on the same thing. I like to be involved with at least one thing I created on my own to make my life a fun one.

I wasn't interested in joining a team. I wanted to coach one. If I want to perform with the team I started at Cupperton, I can at any time. Most likely I will perform with my crew a few times because I'm getting older, and eventually my body will tell me to slow down with all the stomping.

Cupperton had a lot of clubs I could've joined while I was in school, but I wasn't interested in any of them. Most were subject clubs like Math and Science Club, and others were ethnicity clubs. I didn't want to be involved in any of that boring mess. It would have been better to take an extra class so I could graduate faster.

While I was attending Cupperton, I started a step team. I wanted to do something that was fun, had a good team, and wouldn't require me to leave campus every weekend to participate in the event, so I created what I was born to do: a step team. I gave it a rest when I graduated though. Now I'm back coaching it. There wasn't a team all those years I was on hiatus.

I'm just so happy I have participants. I create the practice and performance schedule, as well as have control over who can be a member and the routine. Having control over who can join and the choreography guarantees that I will have a good team because I don't allow anyone to participate without any talent. If someone can't stay on beat, they have to go. I'm good at teaching people the art of step though. Me having control also guarantees that our shows will be great because I don't just put together any mediocre steps. I go all in and create the most complicated steps and unique beats. I have yet to be a part of a team that didn't do well when I was coaching because I've always had great steppers and great routines.

Although Cupperton is full of activities to offer, there's still a lot of students who are inactive. They're too lazy to do anything that requires leg work, except walking to class.

I didn't cut anyone from my step team because I only have thirteen members. If I ever perform, there would be fourteen of us. I figured some people would quit, so I played it safe and allowed everyone to join. I've learned that a lot of people like to watch the art of step, but they don't want to participate in it.

Now all of my college members are not excellent steppers who know how to mix attitude, energy, enthusiasm, and hard work into one, but everyone is at least good enough to where they can at least mix two of the four things I mentioned together.

"I wish I had more members," I say.

Ciera doesn't cosign with me. I look over, and she's not there. I turn around and she's about five feet behind me staring at something on the campus.

I walk over to her.

"Look," Ciera says.

There's a bunch of high school students in different uniforms standing outside of Cupperton's basketball gym.

"Wonder what they got going on over there," Ciera says.

Girls and boys between what looks like the ages of thirteen and eighteen are practicing different types of routines. One group is dressed in light blue and silver cheerleading uniforms, doing twirls, and transitioning into splits. Another group has on red, black, and white sweat outfits and are break dancing. I can't help but notice the coach looking proud and cocky at her girls as they nail the moves. Me and Ciera continue to look around at the dozens of teams that flood our gym area. Some are krumping, others are doing ballet moves, and some are even doing stiff military moves.

"You want to go check it out?" Ciera asks.

I say yes; it's the most action I've seen on this campus. This is how Cupperton usually is, it's just usually by the college students, and not high school kids.

"At least there's another reason why the students from the school are inactive today," I say.

These teenagers are excited, anxious, and ready for whatever performance they're about to do.

As Ciera and I get closer to the gym, we see the line leading to the entrance. It's comprised of mainly parents. Although it is stretching all the way down the sidewalk and into the parking lot, it's moving pretty quickly. It doesn't stop moving. Thank goodness.

"How much does it cost to get in?" I ask a lady checking in teams at a table in front of the gym door.

"Admission is free," the nice lady says.

Ciera and I walk to the back of the long line. Even if the event wasn't free, I would've still paid to get in because just watching these kids rehearse outside has me excited. They're so hype and ready. Some are jumping up and down, and others are helping their teammates review their routines. I can't wait to watch the performances.

As we get closer to the front, Ciera makes conversation with the woman in front of us to get more information on what's going on.

"This is a drill team competition that's held three times a year here," the woman says. "It doesn't get much better than this. These kids work hard for months to put these routines together."

"How long is the show?" Ciera asks the woman.

"There's three segments that last three hours each. Sometimes they go over," the woman says. "Select high schools from all over New Orleans come out for this show."

"So are you from around this area?" Ciera asks the woman.

"I live in Baton Rouge," the woman says. "And thank goodness this competition is held at Cupperton. Some of these people came further than I did."

"I'm one of them," the lady in front of the woman we're talking to turns around and says.

"So it's a drill competition, and everyone is doing all types of dances," I say. "So is everyone doing what their school specializes in and competing for the same trophy, or is it broken up?"

"It's broken up," the woman in front of me and Ciera says. "Hip hop competes against hip hop. Military competes against military, and so forth. Even though everyone's competing against their particular genre, the show is mixed up. So the pom squad might go first, then a hip hop group might go, then a props group might go. And I actually enjoy it that way. Mixing it up keeps me alert. I get tired of watching the same types of dances over and over."

I wonder why it's called a Drill Competition if there's all types of dance styles welcome. Might as well be called an All-Around Dance Competition.

I'm so excited and can't wait to take a seat in the gym. The line is still moving, but it's so long that me and Ciera are still a good distance from making it to the gym doors.

I can't believe Cupperton is actually getting turnt' up by some high school kids. They are showing a lot of school spirit and have a lot of happiness being with their team. I can feel the competitiveness in the students as well as the coaches who are making sure every movement is together.

4

Ciera and I are almost to the door to get in the drill competition.
I can hear people cheering. The closer we get, the more anxious
I get to get in. I can't wait to see all the teams from all over
Louisiana showcase their talents. When I was stepping in high
school, we only competed against step teams. I've never went
to a competition where dance, pom squads, hip hop teams,
props, and military routines were mixed together.

Cupperton didn't have this activity when I was attending the
school.

A kid squeezes out the door to the gym as I'm trying to walk
in, and I have to step outside to let his hyper self out.

In the lobby, there's a nacho and popcorn stand to my left,
and there's toddlers running down the hallway tossing a small
ball back and forth.

Ciera and I follow behind everyone into the gym. We can't
believe our eyes when we take a small step in. The gym is
packed and we can't find anywhere to sit. The line outside is
super long, but we thought we would find seating easily.
Cupperton's basketball team and other athletics always have
packed audiences. When Ciera and I were in school, we always
got to the games early.

Everyone at this drill competition is having fun and is full of
excitement. Shouting parents, screaming kids, and loud
announcers bring excitement to the atmosphere. Me and Ciera
laugh at how these high-schoolers really think they can turn up
like Cupperton's students.

This gym looks like one big party. All the high school students
have on their uniforms, everyone here is happy and loud, and
the little kids are having fun with each other. This is like a family
reunion.

It's so packed in here that Ciera and I can't even find

anywhere to sit at first glance. People are walking past us searching for spots, but we're not moving until our eyes spot somewhere to sit. What's the point in walking around when we don't know where we're going to sit yet? It's too crowded and congested in here to just be wandering around.

"You two need to keep moving," one of the staff members says to me and Ciera.

I'm not paying him any mind, and neither is Ciera. We're still standing in the same spot. She's still looking for seating, and I'm still completely shocked gazing around at all the people in the stands. Some are holding up signs with their team's names on them, some with the performers' names on them, and others sit anxiously waiting for the show to resume. There's two teams waiting on the opposite side of the gym. I take it they're waiting for the announcer to tell them to take their places.

After a few more seconds of not moving, Ciera spots a small vacancy at the top of the bleachers close to the aisle, and we head up. There's a very thin space separating Ciera from the person next to her, and me from Ciera. Half of my body is in the aisle. There's no room to even stretch my arms out if I want.

I'm looking at all the competing teams sit on the opposite side of the gym shouting their calls and doing small dance moves on the bleachers. Each team tries to prove they have more spirit than the other by out-doing the shouts and putting a little more attitude into their dances that they're standing up doing in front of their seats. What I'm seeing now is exactly what I see in the movies on college campuses, except the movies are with actual college students and not a bunch of teenagers.

I am completely wowed. Why are these teenagers trying to have more spirit and fun than Cupperton's students? Not one high school in Louisiana should try to outdo the life that

67

Cupperton has. Even when the students here aren't hosting an event, they show the hell out. I know me and Ciera sure did when we were attending. These kids need to sit they asses down and just watch their school perform. They really think they are doing something.

"They are very comedic," I say.

"Pure embarrassing," Ciera says. "They need to take their seats."

"We not getting that damn old," I say. "We still get turnt' up, and we get better every year."

"Good evening Ms. Shona," Ciera says holding her hand like it's a microphone and pretending to be a news reporter talking with a professional tone. "How does it feel to be at this spectacular dance competition where high school kids try to have school spirit greater than college students?"

"It's a bit embarrassing," I say matching her professional tone. "I mean, to have teenagers come on my campus and believe they can actually outdo the students is completely shocking."

"This is beyond words for me," Ciera says. "I've been surveying Cupperton for quite some time now, and I haven't seen anything like what I'm seeing now. This is high school students with a little too much confidence. I guess it's the thought and effort that counts."

"Girl, at least they have a lot of support," I say. "I can't wait to see what they're about."

Me and Ciera both laugh and slap hands.

"Ladies and gentlemen, put your hands together for Claritin High School," the announcer says.

Claritin High professionally walks stiff onto the court in two straight lines, their heads facing forward and moving sharply as they turn to their left to face the audience. The crowd is loud

68

and excited, and the music hasn't even started yet.

With their purple and black cheerleading uniforms on and pom poms, Claritin High holds their position at different levels until their coach cues the music. The first row begins on their knees, the second row stands with their hands by their sides, and the third row begins with their hands on their hips.

The music comes on and the girls energetically begin a dance composition. Lots of arm movements and formation changes put astonishment on everyone's faces including, the judges that are nodding their heads and smiling at the team full of girls. The girls form a single horizontal line across the court and do high kicks in the air. They even have parts where everyone is doing three different combinations. Everything they do is in unison. I can tell they're well trained and rehearsed. They smile most of the routine and give attitude at certain parts when the song changes tempo.

Ciera and I are completely amazed. The teens are very talented, and we can see that they really enjoy dancing just as much as me and Ciera are loving to watch them.

My girl and I watch several teams deliver complex routines.

All of the teams we've watched have delivered spectacular routines.

The last group is taking center court to close off this three-hour section of the competition.

"Give it up for Peyton High," the announcer says.

Peyton High performs a hip hop routine. They're bodies are moving so fast to stay at the same pace as the instruments in the music. They're faces are fierce and there doesn't seem to be an ounce of nervousness in them.

Ciera squeezes her way down the stairs and gets two programs from a staff member who has a bundle of them.

"Thanks," I say as Ciera gives me one.

Over thirty high schools are registered for day one of the event, and thirty more will participate on day two tomorrow. There's nothing indicating which teams are hip hop, military, and so forth in the program like I hoped.

Ciera and I want to get up and walk outside to stretch our legs, but we know our seats won't be here when we get back.

Peyton High waves to the audience as they exit the court to their standing ovation.

The announcer tells everyone to stand to their feet as the coaches of all the teams take the court and perform a routine they put together while the judges deliberate.

The coaches excitedly run on the court and the kids go crazy as their instructors' dance to a compilation of hip hop songs.

Ciera nods her head and freestyles to the beats.

"We at this drill competition and it is tight, Cupperton is the turn up spot alright," Ciera freestyles.

I look at her crazily. She is a terrible freestyler, but I love that she is not scared to try anything. Sometimes her rhymes make me laugh. Still in amazement at the atmosphere, I continue to look around the gym. I have to admit I miss having this much fun when I was younger. I should be out there dancing with the instructors, not sitting in the audience.

I'm too talented to not be out there dancing, and I feel like I'm wasting my life away when I see people doing what I can do a million times better than them. I'm getting jealous and upset. The students should be cheering for me out there. I know they've never seen someone with my poise, attitude, fierceness, and talent, perform before. They couldn't have, unless they saw me perform with my step team in high school or with Alpha Eta Nu.

Thankfully this competition was free because if the parents paid, I'd really be upset that they didn't get to witness one of the best dancers, who is me of course.

Looking at these coaches dance and change formations without being out there is really killing me. They're good, but not as good as they could be if I was out there, or at least had a say in what they're exhibiting. If I created their choreography and formations, they would be so much better. If I created the choreography for one of the high school teams, then the crowd would still be in a trance completely shocked at how good the performance was. They wouldn't be able to focus on anything else.

Finally getting over what I'm lacking, I recognize that most of the coaches appear to be between the ages of eighteen and forty.

"I should be out there," I say.

"You should get a business card," Ciera suggests.

After the coaches finish their routine, get a standing ovation from their students, and the trophies are presented, Ciera and I walk over to the announcer's table.

"Hey, if I'm interested in becoming a coach for this program, who do I speak with?" I ask the announcer.

The announcer reaches into his pocket and pulls out a business card.

"Ask for Stephen Banks," the announcer says. "If you can't get through to him, send him an email."

I say thanks and put the card in my purse.

It takes a minute for me and Ciera to get out of the gym. Parents are congratulating their kids and people are talking about other activities their kids participate in while walking slow.

I hate listening to parents try to make it seem like their child is better than someone else's because of all that he or she is involved in. I couldn't get away from these annoying parents fast enough.

When we get out the gym doors, kids are running around and members of teams are taking pictures with people from other teams. This is such a lovely sight to see. This is how my life was back in high school when I was on the step team. Me and my crew always had a great time after winning all of our first-place trophies, talking to other teams that always let us know how good we were at stepping, taking pictures, and getting standing ovations from the crowds. We felt like we were celebrities because that's how we were treated. Once a little five-year-old girl asked me for my autograph and a picture.

My high school step team was the bomb, and it was thanks in huge part to me because I came up with all the choreography and formations. I put in all the extra time to ensure people that were behind for either not making it to practice or simply not catching on fast enough could get on everyone else's level, except mine which is unmatchable. I always made sure my team was better than any team I'd seen perform on television.

I should be the one taking pictures with my students right now outside of the gym. I really hope this Stephen person I'm supposed to contact comes through and gives me a shot at coaching another team. I know once he sees one of my shows or even a single rehearsal, he'll want me to stick around as long as I can. I just need him to give me an opportunity and the door to be opened unto me so I can show him and all those spectators that came out from all over Louisiana what one of the best choreographers can bring to the table.

"That show was nice," Ciera says. We're walking to our cars.

"I know," I say.

"Not once did I get tired during the three hours I was sitting in the same spot," Ciera says.

She's right about that. Usually after an hour of watching

72

something, I'm ready to go if I'm in a congested area that I can't move in. I'm someone that gets annoyed sometimes sitting in movie theaters.

"I feel so good," I say. "And it only took some high school students to come here for me to feel this way."

"I feel you on that," Ciera says. "Girl, I'm thinking about going back to my high school to visit."

"Okay," I smile. "That's the best thing I've heard all day."

My high school definitely has more spirit than these schools that were here. My friends and I used to sit in the senior commons, eat chips, and talk about what we were going to do over the weekend. We'd chill outside on the track and watch the boys run. We'd even stay afterwards in class with our last period teacher just to relax for a little bit until the teacher left.

While I was at Cupperton, I would rehearse with the step team I started and chill at my dorm with Alpha Eta Nu members. I was depressed a lot trying to keep up with my schoolwork while pledging. I know I was at Cupperton strictly to get an education, but sometimes I wished it was different. I had too many friends and there was too much I could be doing.

My freshman year I would sit outside to watch and enjoy things that were going on like sororities and fraternities having a random step off, nice looking football players play catch, and the band playing good music. I couldn't wait to join Alpha Eta Nu and teach them step routines. I knew they would know what I came up with was better than anything they probably ever did. What can I say? I just have a lot of confidence when it comes to my craft.

"I never want to lose that fire I had when I was in school," I say. "Now as adults, we have bills and other things stressing us out. I can't let the stress of adapting to life define me."

"I feel you girl," Ciera says. "I miss looking at them fine

73

football players."

"I know I'm coming to this competition again," I say. "That lady said every three months right?"

"Something like that," Ciera says. "Make sure you contact the person that's on that business card. You need to be out there with those coaches and taking one of their teams. The whole time I was watching them I was like *Shona need to be out there.*"

Me and Ciera depart to our cars.

I'm sitting in my car remembering the five different dorm blocks Cupperton has: A., B., C., D., and E. Each block has over twenty-four apartments, some of which house four people and others house eight people. I lived in block E, which is the furthest from the classrooms in a four-bedroom four-person apartment. Ciera lived in E as well in a four bedroom, but each student had a roommate, so eight people including herself resided in her dorm building.

I made sure to ask for a room to myself when applying for housing to ensure that I could come home after class to peace. Having a roommate would've meant I'd pay less for my room, but it also would've meant I'd be taking a chance at living miserably throughout my college experience.

Having a roommate is a risk in so many ways. People have to worry about them talking too loud, waking them up in the middle of the night, leaving food on the floor and attracting bugs, not keeping their side of the room clean, having company in their space, and most importantly, their things being stolen. I didn't have time for any of that.

I'd rather pay the extra money and come home to a spot that was guaranteed to be peaceful. Most of the time I change clothes in my room instead of going to the bathroom, and I wouldn't have been able to do that if I had another girl in there.

Bored and nonchalant about life, I walk in my house, go straight to my room without picking up the phone, turn on the TV, and throw my belongings on the floor. In this room I just have a bed with sheets, a trash bin next to the door, a desk with a few notebooks on it, a flat screen TV, and all my clothes in my closet. I live in a two-story house, and I live alone.

I remember in college I had housemates. I hated them and never spoke to them, unless I had to. We had too many issues. I didn't move out because I loved the fact that I didn't have to walk far to get to campus. I also couldn't afford to live off campus, even if I wanted to. I was living off of the little money I had left over from my refund check.

I take off my shoes and turn on the television. I go through my purse, and Stephen's business card falls out. I immediately get my laptop and email the director of the dance team competition: *Hello. Does your program fund for step choreographers, and if so, is there any openings? I've been a step choreographer for over five years and have a lot of experience with high school kids because I started coaching my alma mater alone when I was only a freshman. Thanks Shona Jackson.*

I've never typed that fast in my life. I need another job, and what better one to have than something that comes naturally to me? Coaching step wouldn't even be work to me. It would just be another team I had besides the one at Cupperton. It's crazy that when I was in high school, I didn't get paid to coach the team even though without me they wouldn't have had a coach those years. However, the advisors that just showed up and babysat everyone, got paid a good four thousand dollars to play chaperone. That money should have went in my pocket, but I wasn't bitter behind not getting paid because I loved and still love to step that much.

I did think that the advisors shouldn't have gotten paid though for doing nothing. But since they were paid, I felt like they should've paid for our school uniforms with the money they were given, instead of making all the members come out of our pockets, but like I said, I didn't care. Ann High, like every other high school, requires a staff member at the school to be the head of every program.

I really hope Stephen gives me this job.

I always wanted a job that is hands on, and not one where I would be sitting at a desk staring at the computer all day. I am not the type to stay alert staring at the same thing for hours, and definitely not sitting at a desk. I always wanted a job that is something I enjoy doing like most normal people do.

Being a choreographer of high school students would be so good for me while I'm also coaching college students. I know I wouldn't be able to take on a job that required me to do a lot of thinking on top of work at the warehouse. I'd either get fired for falling asleep at work, or not showing up at all. I have bills to pay, so those are not options.

One thing I learned when I was in college was that the professors could care less if I came to class or not, passed an exam or not, or failed their class. They're either going to get my money for one semester or they're going to get paid twice by me taking the class over. They didn't care about school causing me to need years to pay off the loans that I needed. I sure as hell didn't want to take out any extra ones.

It's the same thing at my job. The managers don't care if I get fired, can't pay my bills, and end up in a living situation that I don't want.

I'm so tired after a long day with Professor Tobin and staying three hours for that drill competition. After only reading a page and a half of one of my books titled *How to Become a Successful*

Scriptwriter, my head falls on my desk and I drift off.

I'm remembering the time when my mother Nadia angrily and bitterly said, "I helped you get kicked off the team," when I was a senior in high school. I was sitting on my bed when she decided to reveal to me that she played a part in me getting kicked off the team that I founded by myself.

Angry and wanting to hurt my mother, I tried to get up and leave the house so I didn't have to hear anything else she would say, but she blocked me from exiting and pushed me back on the bed. She stared at me for a good thirty seconds without moving, and looked at me like she wished I would collapse and die. I was staring into her eyes just like she was staring into mine, like I could care less if someone shot her dead. I think Nadia was having a bad night thinking about my father.

From what I was told from relatives, my father left Nadia the second he found out she was pregnant with me. He began ignoring Nadia's phone calls and having his family say that he wasn't home when she would stop by. She later learned that he had moved to another state. All Nadia saw from my father after my arrival, was a child support check.

My father was Nadia's first love. She had several complications during her pregnancy due to stressing over his absence, but I still made it. However, as I got older, she would treat me worse as the years went on. She was constantly spreading lies about me to my friends saying I talked back and didn't do things like chores to help her out, and my friends would always tell me.

Nadia would push me around at times when I walked by her just to make me mad. She also made me stay home a lot. Sometimes my friends would have sleepovers or birthday parties, and she wouldn't let me go. On top of not letting me go, she would call my friends parents and make up a story to why she wouldn't let me. The worst lie she told was she caught me having sex with an adult man when I was just sixteen. She purposely walked past my room door so I could hear her.

Nadia denying me much of a social life caused me to be a bitter adolescent. She ruined my senior year. I knew she blamed me for the love of her life leaving, but I didn't know she would stoop so low as to get me removed from the one thing that I participated in, and made my high school years exciting. Of all the things she's done to me, I didn't see that coming.

I'm still very hurt to this date that my own mother contributed to my removal on the step team. I wanted to ask her what she said or did, or why she would do such a thing, but I knew she would say her classic lines, "I'm an adult. I can do what I want. I don't need to explain nothing to you," with the nastiest look and attitude.

I never looked at Nadia the same ever since she told me she helped get me kicked off the team. Sometimes I hated to look at her, and other times I wanted to push her down the stairs. I never let my anger get the best of me because I knew just like I didn't mind putting Nadia behind bars, she didn't mind putting me there. I also knew people would find out, and I didn't want to be the girl known as the person who got her mother locked up.

Let me say that Nadia wasn't always angry towards me. She didn't start doing little irritating things until I turned thirteen. I don't know what it was about that age, but that's when she started to put her hands on me, and make up lies. When I was younger than thirteen, she would take me out to eat every Friday, allow me to stay at my friends' houses, and stay up with me late on school nights to watch movies. She even helped me with my homework. As soon as I started preparing for high school, she did a complete three sixty, and started acting mean.

I don't know why she waited all the way until my senior year to try and have me removed from my team. Maybe she was planning it all along, or maybe she was waiting on the advisors to start disliking me to make her move.

Either way it goes, there's nothing I can do about it now because what's done is done. I can't get back my senior year and even if I could, I would still be dealing with the same mess because I'd still have the same mother and advisors. The only way things would be different, is if I got adopted and found new advisors that believed what they thought was arrogance was confidence.

Although, Nadia and I didn't have the best relationship, I always kept in mind that she could have been worse. She could be one of those parents that beats the hell out of her child until he or she bleeds, or puts poison in their food because she is so angry.

I didn't let my removal senior year take away my love for stepping, and I know Nadia hates that. I'm the founder of the team here at Cupperton, and I will step for as long as my body allows me to. No one will take away my love for what I was born to do, and have been doing ever since I was in my mother's stomach.

My mother and I can't stand each other so much that we talk a maximum of once every six months, and it's usually only about what we're doing at the current moment. I think it's her way of just seeing if her daughter is alive. Despite how less often we talk, I still hesitate answering the phone when *Nadia* pops up because I have to question whether she's going to ruin my day. I never call her, she always calls me. I could care less about a woman that got pregnant by a no-good man and blames the innocent child, so she mistreats her.

I don't know where my dad is today, and I don't care. Even if he didn't like my mom and only wanted her for a night of sex, he should've still taken responsibility for his child and had partial custody of me.

My room door slams because of the wind. I open my eyes and dry my face. My book is soaked with tears from a nap thinking about my mother. Her admitting to me she helped get me removed, and me not having any closure on how, is one of the worst memories I have to deal with.

I close my book. I always hated reading and because I do, I always drift off thinking about something else.

When I was in college, I always wished someone would sum up my homework assignments for me, and I could just listen to them drill the information in my head. Reading makes me sleepy. Don't get me wrong, I did love my Film major, but I have always been more of a visual learner. I learned quicker and retained the information a lot faster when my professors did examples on the board of the subject matter, or gave hands on activities to do.

I glance over at my laptop and notice I have a red one on my inbox.

Stephen has emailed back: *Are you available to meet tomorrow morning?*

I'm smiling so hard and am so happy that I can't remember why I was crying. This email alone tells me I have an interview, and the only way I won't get the job is if I don't handle it well, or don't meet the requirements that I know I will meet if they're based off of experience.

I type: *I sure am.*

I go in the bathroom to wipe my misty eyes. I'm now full of hope, anxiousness, and excitement. Getting this coaching job would be one of the best things I got put onto because of Cupperton University. Another would be something like meeting Ciera.

I quickly go back in my room to look at my computer and see I have another new message from Stephen: *Great. Let's meet at 10am on the fifth floor of the Unified Student's Building downtown.*

I type: *Sounds good.*

I'm all smiles while I put on my pajamas, brush my teeth, and wash my face. I have an interview, and I'm almost one hundred percent positive I'll get the job. If Stephen needs me to do a demonstration, that won't be a problem because I have a lot of steps drilled in my head. I remember all of the ones I created in high school, as well as the ones I teach my team now. I'm ready for whatever he throws my way, including to do a history on stepping. There's nothing he can say or ask me to do that I won't quickly be able to answer. All I need to do is make sure I get up early and arrive on time to my interview.

I snap out of my happiness temporarily when I remember the day I was in college and my housemate that lived in the room next to me, Melinda, came out from using the bathroom, and her hands touched me before she washed them. I felt like she touched my arm on purpose. We didn't look at each other or speak that day in the bathroom. I wanted to hurt her.

I didn't converse with any of my housemates, but occasionally I was forced to speak to Melinda, the one I couldn't stand the most. Melinda was the housemate from hell. She ate everyone's food, but never admitted to it, and she used everyone's toiletries and denied it. She spent so much money on fast food and new clothes, no one understood why she didn't buy what she needed.

On top of that, Melinda was dirty and loud. I've never been either of those things. I'm just loud when I'm participating with my Greek family or step team at Cupperton.

81

It upset me that when people visited my dorm, they might think I was responsible for the leftover food and trash in the kitchen and living room, but it was really Melinda.

For some reason, Melinda would always take an awfully long time washing her hands. There were two sinks in the bathroom, so we never had to share one when we were in there together. I wanted to slap this girl watching her dry her hands off on my dry towel that usually hung on the shower rod. Every time she did, I looked at her with anger and she didn't care. I tried to refrain from speaking to her, but sometimes I couldn't let her actions go. Especially when she'd do it in my face. Melinda was one of those people that would make people show her their frustration. She enjoyed that. Something was wrong with her.

"Can you please not use my towel again?" I asked her in a nice tone the several times she did.

I tried to keep things calm. I didn't want my dorm life to be chaotic. I sure didn't want to lose my housing fighting with a bitch who seemed to not care about anything.

"Oh, sorry," Melinda would say. "I didn't know it was yours."

I wanted to tie a towel around her neck and hang her for saying that bold faced lie. Me and her are the only ones that shared our bathroom because the other two girls shared a bathroom that was in front of their rooms. Melinda knew good and well that the only things in our bathroom were either hers or mine. If it wasn't hers, then it belonged to me, and she would really try to convince me with that sweet tone that she had, that she had no clue of that.

I didn't even understand why Melinda would want to put her hands on a towel that dried off my entire body. She knew I always hoped she would leave the bathroom after washing her hands, but she would stay longer and play in her hair looking in the mirror. She would brush the same piece over and over.

I would quickly brush my teeth, toss some mouthwash in my mouth, spit it out, and go back in my room when Melinda was in the bathroom with me.

Anyways, before going to bed, I do an old step routine I created while I was attending Ann High School. The hand claps and feet movements are so fast, complex, and one movement after another, that there's no time to take a good deep breath. If people were watching me, they wouldn't even know I was breathing.

That's how I like my routines: fast, hard, and complicated. If someone can learn what I'm doing just by watching it once or twice, then it's not hard enough.

I'm happy while I'm doing my intense choreography, nailing each and every move I still have drilled in my brain without messing up, until images of the members of Ann High who were on the team when I wasn't were doing the routine I'm doing right now at the school pep rally come to mind.

Remembering the audience go crazy watching Ann High perform is making me upset. I get angry and stop stepping as I remember myself walking by the performance and seeing one of the advisors, Mr. Mason McGruder, of the program smiling at me.

Mr. McGruder grinned at me harder and harder the longer he saw me watching the show looking upset because he had the pleasure of knowing he was the reason I was at the door and not on the court. He was ecstatic watching me wish I was out there. That was his way of letting me know he was the king and I was the peasant.

Mr. McGruder was very boastful looking because he knew everything he said ultimately went at all times because he was one of the advisors, which means he had influence over who could and could not remain on the team. There's nothing I could have done about it.

I'm now frustrated and doing my choreography looking angry and putting even more effort into it as I'm envisioning myself competing in the present with the people in the past from Ann High. I'm outdoing them at that pep rally in our school gym. They can't keep up with me. I'm working so much harder than them that I'm sweating. Jasmine can't keep up with me. My adrenaline is pumping as I do my complex routine with the images of Jasmine front and center at the pep rally doing them at the same time as me. She can't keep up with me. I was better than her then, and I know I'm still better than her now. I was probably outdoing her when I was in my mom's stomach.

I'm getting angrier the more I think about Jasmine doing my choreography like it was something she created on her own. She was front and center at the pep rally. That was my spot.

I was supposed to be performing. I'm getting even angrier. I'm doing the choreography faster than Ann High was, but the only bad thing is when I speed up presently, so do they in my mind. My head is spinning, and I feel like the room is shaking. I feel like I'm in tornado.

My blood is heating up. Now Jasmine's doing things in my head that she didn't even do at the pep rally. My whole mind is focused on her, and she's laughing hysterically like she knows I'm in my room right now miserable thinking about the day of the pep rally. She's laughing louder and louder.

I stop stepping and put my hands on my head and yell, "Stop!"

I feel like a crazy person that needs a strait jacket. I don't think I should do any of my steps from high school anymore because I always think back on the times I saw the team doing my steps without me. I hate thinking about the happy look on Mr. McGruder's face every time he got the privilege of seeing me watch miserably.

My head hurts, and to make matters worse, I keep having memories of Melinda. I remember she would sometimes bang on the wall that made our room's border.

"Be quiet in there please!" Melinda would yell when I would step in my room.

I take a pill and pour myself some ice water in my house. When I was in college, I couldn't even enjoy a nice glass of water in my dorm because there would be gnats flying in the kitchen because the same piece of bread that was sitting on the counter the day prior would still be there the next day, in the exact same spot. I never wanted to throw it away, but had no choice. Some days I would open the door to the long cabinet the trash bin was in and it would have flies in there too because the trash would be flooded with all types of leftover pasta, rice, bread, spaghetti sauce, and other foods.

I used to get mad sometimes and just let the trash pile up to see how long it would sit in the cabinet before someone took it out, and it usually took a few days. Being that four days would pass sometimes and no one would touch it, I used to think that we would get rats or maggots. I thought my dorm would be infested with all types of bugs and rodents.

Sometimes I just angrily took out the trash.

One day, on my way back to my building after dumping trash in the dumpster, I heard someone doing a sorority call. Whoever the girl was stretched out her sound. When she stopped, someone shouted the same call back to her, but a lot shorter in length.

The sound was coming from behind me. There was two women walking towards each other. They gave each other a hug. I was observing them from head to toe. They had on Greek letters. I was trying to see which organization they were a part of, but I couldn't make out the symbols with the girls standing so close together, and in the dark.

The two women were stationary as I walked to a bench to sit down. I hoped they didn't move until I got a good look at their Greek letters.

I told myself that the moment I'd been waiting for had finally arrived. I always told myself I would pledge. I'll be honest and say I never considered pledging to help out the community even though I wouldn't mind. I never even considered pledging just to be able to put it on my resume so I could get hired faster or for networking like so many other people do when they realize the benefits of Greek organizations.

I just wanted to join so I could be a part of the step shows and have a sisterhood.

I knew the Greek world had never came across a stepper like me. I knew I could enhance any sorority I became a member of and have the interest rate go up just because people want to step and stroll with us.

I've been interested in joining Alpha Eta Nu just because their step teams are better than any other sororities I've viewed online, and I want to work with the best lines. They're colors are pink and blue.

The two Alpha Eta Nu members who I saw out of the corner of my eyes were laughing and talking about something in the same exact spot.

I knew Cupperton had Greeks, but never decided to eavesdrop on them until that night. They come out at night a lot. Usually, they are attending a campus party. Sometimes they're the ones throwing the party. They host a lot of events giving things away to show people they care about the community.

When I was in college, I saw so many new faces of people in

Alpha Eta Nu letters, that I was sometimes not sure if they attended Cupperton or not.

I was frustrated. I needed to see the girls letters a little better. I didn't want to approach the wrong organization.

The girls began walking my way. As they got closer, there the letters I'd been longing to see were. The letters *A*, *H*, and *N* had never looked so pretty going downward on a jacket. They were the people I'd been hoping to come across.

I needed to gain the courage to approach them. A lot of Greeks pull out their cocky and uppity demeanor when they're approached by interests, and they come off as rude and stuck up, even though that's not how some of them are on a regular basis. They just do it to intimidate people that want to be on their line, to let them know that they mean business when they start the pledging process, and it won't be easy.

I was so nervous and scared to approach the Greeks in fear that they may not like me, that they were already a few steps passed me and I hadn't moved. After they took a few more steps, I finally gained enough strength and bravery to get up and walk fast to catch up to them.

"Excuse me," I nervously and sweetly said.

The two women turned around and looked at me from head to toe. They didn't look pleased that I stopped them, but then again it was late, and they didn't know me. I didn't even know how to go about expressing myself, but I needed to say whatever came to mind because I didn't know if I'd ever come across any more Alpha Eta Nu members again.

I wished I was prepared and did research on how to express interest to Greeks.

"I wanted to say I love your organization and the things you guys do for the community," I said. "I really want to be a part of the sorority, so I can join the sisterhood and take part in the events with women I'll consider my family."

The girls looked at me from head to toe again, and they looked hardcore and a bit disgusted.

"What's your name and what year are you?" one of the girls asked me folding her arms across her chest. Her hair was in a ponytail.

How stupid could I be not to introduce myself properly before going into what I want from them.

Living with Nadia could blank my mind out at some of the worst times. She never wanted me to excel in anything. It hit me that I knew a lot about pledging, but couldn't utilize the knowledge at the moment. Something was wrong with me. Nadia's spirit was bothering me.

"Shona," I said. "And I'm a freshman."

The girls both started laughing.

"I'm sorry. I should've said that first," I said.

"First off, freshmen can't pledge on this campus," the same girl with the ponytail said. "You need to at least be a sophomore."

I honestly thought any college student could join a sorority or fraternity at any grade level.

"And Shona, do you have a last name?" the girl with the ponytail asked.

"Shona Jackson."

"I just asked for the last name," the girl with the ponytail said. "Can you hear?"

"Yes," I answered.

I couldn't get smart with the girls because they had something I wanted, and that's the letters so I can step with their crew. I knew they would have nasty attitudes: I just wasn't sure how nasty.

"So Shona," the other girl said. Her hair was flat-ironed.

Both women were staring intensely in my eyes.

"You want to join our sorority to serve the community," the girl with the flat-iron said. "Is that right?"

I nodded my head.

"Hello?" the girl who had the flat-iron yelled.

"Yes," I said.

"You sure you don't want to pledge Alpha Eta Nu just to put the title on your job application or be a part of our Greek events?" the flat-ironed girl asked.

I was confused as to what events she was talking about being that I had yet to go to one at the time. I usually just minded my business on Cupperton's campus. I was always so busy with other things that I never approached any Greeks or went to any of their events at the time.

"I sincerely want to join to be a part of a family that helps the community," I lied.

"*I sincerely want to join to be a part of a family that helps the community,*" the girl with the ponytail mocked to her Soror that laughed with her.

I assumed the girls never saw me step with my crew because I'm sure they would've assumed what is true, which is I only wanted to join their organization to get the letters so I can step.

They didn't know that I could make their routines and members better than what they were.

"What's our names Ms. Shona?" the girl with the flat-iron asked.

I looked confused. I had no clue what their names were. I'd never heard anyone say them before.

"I'm sorry," I said. "I don't know."

The girl with the ponytail walked away and said, "Can you believe the people that try to join our line?" looking up at the sky. She continued saying, "She had the audacity to speak about

Alpha Eta Nu to us, and doesn't even know our names."

"It's pretty ridiculous that you want to join a sorority with women on this campus and don't even know the alumni's names," the flat-ironed girl said.

"Teasha can you believe she wants to join our line, but doesn't know our names?" the ponytail girl said to her Soror. "Listen Shona, my name is Queela A. K. A. Zero Tolerance."

Queela walked away and came back again while Teasha laughed. I had really made the wrong person upset. Queela was acting like I was the stupidest person she'd ever met.

"You know why they call her Zero Tolerance?" Teasha asked me.

I stared at her waiting for the answer. How would I know if no one's ever told me? I wanted to say that, but I had to keep my calm, relaxed and at her mercy face, no matter what they said until I got my letters. After I pledged, I could say anything I wanted to them, including what I wanted to say at that moment, even though it would be old news.

"Hello!?" Teasha said really loud.

"No I don't know Teasha," I said.

I repeated her name because I was trying to drill it in my head, so I could say hi when I saw them again so they could become familiar with my face.

"Because she doesn't have a tolerance level for anything," Teasha said. "She doesn't accept stupidity, and definitely not people that don't do research, and also make it clear that they haven't been to any seminars held on this campus. If you'd have came to one, you would know our names because we attend all the meetings to support our Sorors."

"The nerve of you to come up to us and you don't even know our names," Queela said. "I bet you don't even have a clue about any of the programs my Sorors hold here, or what they're about do you?"

"No," I shook my head and shamefully said.

I'd never seen anything about Greek organizations posted on the campus, but then again I never looked. I never took interest in reading any bulletin boards or postings on the poles on campus because I didn't have a reason to. I wanted to become a Greek, but something twisted was going on in my head while I was pursuing my degree. Something only a mother could do to me. I just can't put my hands on what it was.

When I visited Greg Johnson's campus, I saw plenty of people walking around wearing their Greek letters, and that's what I expected from any campus I went to that had Greek organizations.

"Of course she don't know Act A Fool," Queela said to Teasha, whose line name is clearly *Act A Fool*.

I knew if I pledged with these girls, they would be strict and mean and I had reasons to fear what they would do to the line I'm on because of the line names they were given.

I knew in the movies pledges were beat with paddles, had to run a lot of errands for their Big Sisters or Big Brothers, were woke up late at night just to get yelled at, sometimes got slapped, had to do intense workouts, and sometimes forced to do their superiors homework.

Teasha and Queela were definitely giving me the vibe of crazy Big Sisters that would do all the things I just mentioned.

"If you want to be an Alpha Eta Nu member, you have to support us at our events, as well as functions we hold at our homes or our fellow Sorors dorms," Teasha said. "You think we wanted to attend a movie night in one of our Sorors that's a juniors dorms, when we have jobs and boyfriends? No, but that doesn't matter. We are sisters and we always stop by to see each other no matter if it is just sticking our head in the door

91

and saying hi. Shona, you need to get up on game. If you can't support us before you're in, why should we believe you will when you get your letters?"

I felt beneath the dirt at that moment. These girls were not playing around with me. They were telling me everything bluntly and with such a nasty attitude. I didn't even know what to say because they were both right about me not attending seminars or knowing their names. Those were little things that would cause them to remember me every time they saw me. I was looking like a sad puppy at that moment. I felt like I'd already blown my chance at joining Alpha Eta Nu.

"Listen," Queela said, "We saw you looking at us, and already knew you took interest in our organization. You're just like all the other interests that don't know how to approach us. You need to really do some research on Greek life. This was not the time for you to express interest to us, when you don't know our names and can't name a single program that Alpha Eta Nu has put on."

Queela had me feeling like an ant.

"And a word of advice, don't approach us in your pajamas again," Queela said.

The girls walked off and I headed back to my dorm feeling little and low as ever. I was upset that I'd already messed up. It was no wonder they looked disgusted when I approached them and said I wanted to join their organization after looking at me from head to toe.

The first impression is a lasting impression, and the first thing I knew they observed about me when I walked up to them was what I had on before I opened my mouth. They probably wanted to decline me when I went out for the sorority. I didn't care though. They allowed me to join. They couldn't deny my natural talent of stepping either. Every time I performed with

Alpha Eta Nu, we made other teams want to shred to pieces when we beat them at step competitions and out-strolled them at Greek fests.

Even though Teasha and Queela made me feel like an ant and idiot that tonight, I could make them feel the same way at step rehearsals, and I made sure to do so. It wasn't often they performed with my line, but when they did, I made sure they felt small. I outshined them and everyone else on the line.

5

I remember that same night after talking to Teasha and Queela, I went back in my dorm, and had to put another trash bag in the trash bin and there was already fast-food bags in the bottom of it. I angrily dumped the trash in the bag I had, then put the bag in.

I went in my room and slammed the door out of frustration.

"Stop slamming the doors!" Melinda yelled.

I paid her no mind because I was so mad. Because of the garbage, and because of the stupid mistake I made of going up to the Alpha Eta Nu girls without being properly clothed in business attire, or at least jeans and a shirt. I knew they were probably laughing on their walk wherever they were going about the stupid freshman that approached them in pajamas and didn't even know freshmen couldn't pledge at Cupperton, which really confirmed to them that I didn't do any research on the organization or attend any of their seminars.

I didn't like the stuck-up attitudes Teasha and Queela had. I didn't care if it was an act just for interests and pledges. I didn't want or need to put up with any attitudes fake or not. I definitely didn't want to deal with being hit and pushed by anybody just to get some letters. I definitely didn't want to be attending or putting on seminars all throughout the week. I didn't want to do research on extra things.

Schoolwork was enough for me.

I knew joining a sorority came with a lot of other sacrifices that I didn't want to make. I was not fond of those stupid line names anyways. *Zero Tolerance* and *Act A Fool*? Who would want to be referred to as those dumb names? I sure didn't. All I wanted to do was step at the time and be a part of a sisterhood. I didn't mind serving the community, but I could do that on my own if I wanted.

I didn't need Alpha Eta Nu for anything. They needed me to make their step shows and strolls better. I knew I could make their organization look better. It wouldn't do anything for me except put me on a bigger platform to showcase my talent to the world. I knew if I continued to step throughout college, the right person would see me and give me a choreography job that would pay me well.

I already got this interview with Stephen tomorrow and who knows, he may put me in contact with some other people that take my career to the next level.

But with all that being said about Teasha and Queela, I almost changed my mind. I almost didn't join a sorority just to step and showoff my talent to more people. I felt like my audience would expand in due time.

I started to just think and remember that I'm a choreographer, and I'm great at what I do. I don't need to be a part of a sorority to make that statement more evident to the world. I had my team that I started and I was content with it.

Hopefully I will have another team in the works by tomorrow with Stephen.

I almost was like fuck Teasha, Queela, the rest of Alpha Eta Nu, and any other Greek organizations. One day they would be begging me to join their lines and I would happily tell them no. Of course I ended up joining the sorority though.

Although I didn't do any research on Greeks, common sense told me that I could be kicked out of the organization just like any other activity or group if I made a mistake like get expelled from school for fighting, or too many letters being written by fellow Sorors to the president over the entire sorority.

I didn't want to be under anyone's control, but changed my mind and ended up pledging.

I already had to deal with Mr. McGruder and Mrs. McGruder

in high school kicking me off the team I started, so I could only imagine how quick I could get removed from Alpha Eta Nu if the members started to mistake my confidence for arrogance and cockiness before I was accepted in.

I started to think what if I teach Alpha Eta Nu a lot of routines and one day they decide to let me go? Then I would have to deal with another group getting a standing ovation from an audience using the steps I created. I'd be watching with anger and bitterness from the crowd wanting and knowing that I should've been front and center on the stage.

I didn't need any more memories of people doing my steps while I was in my room practicing my routines at Cupperton.

I hated when Jasmine popped in my head doing steps I created with no shame or care for me not being on the team any longer. She should have came up with her own original material for the pep rally. I don't care if it was a week after my removal and she didn't have time to come up with something simple, or time to copy moves from other teams on the internet.

It wasn't right for Mr. and Mrs. McGruder to allow the team to use my steps without me participating.

I couldn't stand Jasmine for going on the court and standing in my spot like she owned my moves. The stupid girl didn't even know I was watching the pep rally because I was standing by a door that had the entire team's backs towards me. I wished she could feel how evil I was staring at her.

I just wish Mr. McGruder couldn't see how evil I was looking at Jasmine because he was happy I was disgusted standing at the door. I'll never forget his grin. He tried to keep his cheeks low because of the audience, but he failed tremendously. It was natural for his face to start shining when he saw me looking upset because he's evil.

Certain actions and reactions of people that hurt me never leave my mind, and that situation with Mr. McGruder was one of them.

How can someone be so wicked? I always thought that Mr. McGruder was one of those sick individuals that no one ever sympathized for when he was young, so whenever he had the opportunity to make someone feel angry, he did, and enjoyed doing it. He is definitely one of the ugliest people I've ever seen appearance wise. I bet he was like those kids in the movies that always got picked on in school and forced to hurt himself by other students.

Upset, I get in bed and lie down early. I stare out my opened window. There's nothing but silence, and a nice breeze in the atmosphere. Just like I've always loved it. I can't fall asleep because of my negative thoughts about Mr. and Mrs. McGruder, Jasmine, Teasha, and Queela. Any time I experience bad things or reminisce on them, I have a hard time going to sleep because my mind's not at ease.

The cool breeze and still of the night don't put me to sleep until one in the morning.

6

The next day I get up early because I'm so anxious for my interview to start, and plus the later I go to bed the earlier I wake up. I never understood that about myself. If I fall asleep at nine at night, I'll wake up around ten in the morning, but if I fall asleep at one in the morning, I'll wake up at six in the morning like I did today.

I go in the kitchen because I want to make some breakfast. I make eggs and bacon. I don't feel like making too much. I sit at my table and really take in the opportunity I'm being given today. It's an honor to even be considered for a choreography job doing something I love.

I feel so grateful. I feel like a real woman that's accomplished something major, even though I haven't gotten the job yet.

I go to the store and get some chips and a bottled water on my way to my meeting with Mr. Stephen.

While I'm in the store, a little boy is in front of me playing with two toy buses. I remember when I was visiting California not too long ago and I would take the bus everywhere. I used to sit all the way in the back because there's no eating or drinking allowed on the bus, but no one follows those rules. I used to see old men drinking beer out of bottles. No one would follow the rules of not eating or drinking period on the bus.

Even though I know I will do great at my interview, I'm still nervous when I walk in Mr. Stephen's office, which is located on the fifth floor of a large building. I'm amazed at how big and spacious it is. Nice pictures of landscapes on the walls, as well as pictures of some of the dance teams and other after school programs holding up trophies.

Mr. Stephen's sitting at his desk reading a sheet of paper.

"Hello," I say. "Are you Mr. Stephen?" I still ask.

My heart starts beating when I realize I didn't knock on the door. It was wide opened, so I just naturally walked in like I would anywhere else. I hope Mr. Stephen doesn't get upset.

Mr. Stephen turns around with a smile.

"Yes," Mr. Stephen says. "Have a seat Roshona. Can I call you Shona?"

"Of course," I say.

Thank goodness there's no indication that he's mad I just walked into his nice-looking professional office.

"Am I saying your name right?" Mr. Stephen asks.

"Close," I lie.

He said my name just like it's spelled like everyone else does when they read it, *Ro-Show-Na.*

"Call me *Shawna*," I say and take a seat right in front of him.

"Nice to meet you," Mr. Stephen says. "I will cut straight to the chase."

I have no problem with this because I am hoping to hear that I've got the job quickly.

"I have been looking for a step choreographer to put in my program for quite some time now," Mr. Stephen says. "That's why I responded to you as quickly as I did."

"Okay. I'm so honored you got back to me," I say.

"So why don't you tell me a little about your background in stepping," Mr. Stephen says.

I am a bit on edge. Mr. Stephen's corporate demeanor and professional tone is something I've never had to encounter. I didn't work in high school, and don't remember being taught interview etiquette. I'm not even sure if the blue jeans and black shirt that I have on is appropriate. I wasn't sure if Mr. Stephen would want a demonstration, so I chose these clothes.

I'm nervous also because this is my first job interview alone, and I'm sitting across from a man that stares deeply into my eyes. At the warehouse, everyone sat in one big room and was told we got the job.

"I have been stepping for about twenty-three years," I say.

Mr. Stephen has a straight face on. I need to say something more valuable to get the job.

"Don't mind me," Mr. Stephen says. "It's early."

I inhale, exhale and continue.

"I started a step team my freshman year in high school where I coached ninth through eleventh grade, and the team is still going to this date," I say.

This is the first time I've ever had to verbally say that I coached three years in high school and not four, and it makes me sick to my stomach. Not because I have to say it to Mr. Stephen because he doesn't know why I coached only three years, but because it makes me start thinking about Jasmine. She's laughing in my head again. She knows I'm embarrassed internally, and I hate rolling those words off of my lips in that order.

"So, you have a lot of experience with high school kids?" Mr. Stephen asks.

"Yes," I say. "I've always coached on my own, and every move I've done is original. I create my own choreography. My high school team has always won first place at competitions, and I have a lot of trophies wrapped in newspaper and put in boxes."

Mr. Stephen starts laughing.

"You have that many huh?" Mr. Stephen asks.

"Yes," I say.

I store them in the basement because I didn't want to look at them anymore when I graduated high school and college. I was over all those years of my life.

"Stepping is something that comes natural to me," I say. "No one taught me how to do it. I currently coach my school

Cupperton University's team, which is how I found out about your program. I saw the coaches from the drill competition do a routine together, and they looked either the same age as me, or a little older. My friend suggested I get a business card, and I'm so happy I did. I really hope this works out, and I get a chance to be a part of your program."

"Sounds great," Mr. Stephen says. "Well Shona let me tell you about Luminous LA. We are a non-profit organization that prides ourselves in giving high school students more activities to join that aren't embedded into their school activities. This year will mark our twenty-fifth anniversary. Our mission for Luminous LA is to keep students off the streets and from partaking in the wrong activities such as sex, drugs, drinking, stealing, and so forth. Now no one is perfect, and neither is our program. We aren't saying that students that participate in Luminous LA's events never get involved in the wrong things, but we are confident and happy that we help reduce the chances of students getting involved in negative activities. Last year one of our students was arrested for stealing from a store, and we've had other issues with our students. So, believe me when I say we have a very humble staff, and we know our program won't affect everyone for the better, but we are happy like I said, that we are making an impact in students' lives. Ninety-five percent of the students that have participated in Luminous LA have graduated and went on to college."

That's a lot of damn students who were successful after participating in Mr. Stephen's program.

Mr. Stephen's gets up and picks up a photo from his shelf of a pom squad holding their first-place trophy.

I'm loving everything Mr. Stephen is telling me. I agree with everything he's said thus far. I love the reasons why the program was started. Especially the one about keeping students active, and their minds from wanting to do the wrong things.

"These two girls right here," Mr. Stephen says pointing to two really pretty brunettes smiling holding up their trophy. "They attend college now, and in a year, they'll have their bachelor's degree."

Mr. Stephen sits back down and stands the picture on his desk. I commend people like Mr. Stephen that take their time out to affect young people in a positive way when there's so many people that don't believe there's any hope in the future. Mr. Stephen is one of those people who give others something to be hopeful for. As people, we never know what can make someone change their life around for the better.

Stepping or any of the other Luminous LA programs may cause some of the students to want to be choreographers one day. Luminous LA is a great program. I start to wonder why it never came by Ann High School, then my slow self remembers Mr. Stephen said he only offers programs to specific schools in certain cities. Ann High didn't make the list.

Even if Ann High didn't have a step team already, I wouldn't recommend it to anyone myself. There were two shootings there six years ago, and fights break out a lot. The only way I would recommend that school to somebody is if I didn't like them and wanted to take a chance on them losing their lives. The only reason Mr. Stephen should send someone there is if he wants them to quit the job.

"Now, you would be the first step instructor to work for Luminous LA, but we have many different art forms that are presented to our students such as hip hop, actual arts and crafts, performing arts and theater, piano classes, drum classes, and many more," Mr. Stephen continues. "I am excited to finally sit down and talk to a step instructor. I'm a huge fan of the craft. I have asked members of fraternities and sororities to take on the task, but every individual had some type of excuse to why they couldn't do it, such as schoolwork, not enough time, or some people just flat out said they don't want to work with high school students because it's tough to get them to listen. Some people said they don't want to end up hurting disobedient young people who think they are grown. Now these are things that people assume and aren't true. We have had good reviews with all one hundred and fifty-six sites."

Maybe at his sites people don't take advantage of the coach looking so nice and young, but I'm dealing with this problem at Cupperton right now; however, I didn't when I was at Ann High. At Ann High I was the same age or around the same age as everyone I was coaching, and they always listened and followed the rules. All of the participants respected the queen stepper giving them instructions and always came on time.

Mr. Stephen keeps talking about the sites getting good reviews. I think he is working hard to ensure that I stay if I get the job, which I will because I want the money, and as long as I'm being paid, I can put up with a few attitudes.

If I wasn't being paid, I'd leave and ignore any email or call he gave me.

"I do have another meeting, so I'm going to speed and wrap this up," Mr. Stephen says. "The staff at the site you will be working at will show the students a video of stepping in advance because most of them will probably have no clue what it is."

I hold in my smirk because I know for a fact now that I've gotten the job.

"There will be an arts assistant with you in the room at all times for liability reasons," Mr. Stephen says. "You will only be able to practice with the students for thirty days over the course of three months. After those three months, you will be moved to another high school."

So I have thirty days to instill in my students a routine and have it perfected. I hope I get a talented group. When I was teaching Ann High, I had at least twenty days a month to get my team where I needed them because we practiced at our regular practice hours and outside of school at times, so we were always great. I wouldn't accept anything less than the best.

I really hope I get some students that have at least rhythm and stamina. If not, I'll just have to whip their ninth through twelfth grade behinds into stepping shape. We'll go through different core movements every day. I didn't have to at Ann because mostly everyone had rhythm, but if I get a bunch of uncoordinated people, I know just how to get them performance ready.

"My goal is to put you at as many schools as possible to spread and teach students about the art of stepping," Mr. Stephen says. He pauses for a moment before saying, "I have one last question for you. Do you have a car?"

"Yes," I say.

How the hell else would I get around? I guess riding with other people or taxis, but that's just not me.

"That's great," Mr. Stephen says. "You should never be late."

"I won't," I respond.

"Well Shona, the good thing about this program is we are willing to work with our instructors and place them at schools that are close to their homes," Mr. Stephen says. "Do you have any questions you want to ask me?"

"No," I say. "I'm just excited for my students to perform at the drill competition you put on at the college I graduated from."

I don't like how Mr. Stephen's joy just left his face. I already know he's about to tell me something I don't want to hear.

"Unfortunately Shona," Mr. Stephen's says.

I hate when sentences start with *unfortunately*. It confirms that I'm about to hear something my ears will want to reject.

"Your team would be the only step team," Mr. Stephen continues. "They can showcase, but they cannot compete."

So pretty much we're exhibition. That's boring. I'm about to work my behind off with my students, and they can't even win a trophy for their effort. I don't like it, but I'm being paid and more people will be exposed to a great choreographer.

"Usually, our students at Luminous LA only showcase for their parents at their schools, but I'm willing to allow your team to perform at the drill competition instead, if you're okay with just showcasing," Mr. Stephen's says.

"I am," I say.

I'd rather my students perform in front of thousands than tens. Even though we won't win a trophy, everyone will know that we would've won first place if we'd have competed, and I'll take that.

Mr. Stephen gives me a schedule, tells me what's expected of my arts assistant, tells me about some of his most successful shows, and shakes my hand by the door.

Before I walk out, I say, "Thanks so much Mr. Stephen. I appreciate the opportunity to work with Luminous LA."

"I look forward to seeing what you can do with our students," Mr. Stephen says.

As soon as I get outside of his building, I rush to my car.

I get in my car and remember a day when I had to rush to class at Cupperton. I was leaving a friend's apartment and had to hurry to my dorm, grab my books, and head to class.

I was super late.

My instructor, Ms. Clemens, was lecturing about different camera shots when I took my seat next to Ciera. I felt Ms.

Clemens' eyes on my back like a burning flame the entire way to my seat.

"Who can tell me the difference between a wide shot and a long shot?" Ms. Clemens asked.

Two students raised their hands.

Everyone seemed to be intrigued in the lesson except me and Ciera who were chatting about her getting a job around the corner from Cupperton, at a grocery store. I was so excited for her because she wanted to pay off some of her loans while she was in school.

Ciera's knocking on my door right now. She's excited to hear about my new gig. We go in my living room and chat with a glass of wine.

"So when do you start?" Ciera asks.

"Next week," I say.

"You got a routine together already?" Ciera asks.

"I got some ideas in my head," I respond. "It's not like I have to teach all of it in one day."

"You nervous?" Ciera asks.

Ciera's asking me questions rapidly like we are in a hurry or something.

I remember we were in class when she told me about her job. We still had an hour left. We were talking as low as we possibly could. Some students were looking back at us angrily, annoyed and disgusted. I wasn't mad about it either because I would be angry too if I was trying to learn and couldn't hear every single word coming out of the teacher's mouth. However, Ciera wanted to share her good news about her job with me as soon as she saw me. She couldn't wait. She didn't want her excitement to die down. She wanted to tell me while her adrenaline was high.

"Nervous about what?" I ask. "I coached my high school team

for three years since I was a freshman."

"How come you didn't coach all four?" Ciera questions.

My heart beat speeds up and I'm no longer in the mood to talk about my new job. Jasmine is in my head, and Mr. McGruder's happiness at the pep rally is too.

I sadly walk to my room and sit at my desk. Ciera follows me. With an obvious look of not wanting to answer Ciera, I look down at my desk and distastefully say, "I don't want to talk about it."

I'm so bitter about not being granted my senior year as a coach to make my high school years good, while I was dealing with my bitter mother, that I've never told my best friend about my removal.

Despite Ciera telling me she was angry when she got cut from the cheerleading team each year she went out for it because her skill level wasn't up to par as far as flexibility, certain flips she was required to already know how to do, as well as the coach having favorites from previous years, on top of the required talents, I still couldn't bring myself to open my sealed lips about my termination because it's so painful for me to talk about.

"It hurts," I say.

I was going to finish my sentence by adding *it's one of the worst memories of my life,* but I didn't want to because I knew I would go on a huge rant elaborating about it.

When Ciera and I were in class talking about her new job at the grocery store, I noticed that Ms. Clemens was no longer lecturing. I looked at her and she was staring back at me and Ciera looking frustrated.

"Shona and Ciera, would you two like to share with the rest of us what you are talking about?" Ms. Clemens asked irritated.

Ciera and I sat shocked as we listened to Ms. Clemens put us on blast.

"Shona you just came in the class less than five minutes ago and already you're being disruptive," Ms. Clemens said.

"Right," a female student mumbled under her breath.

The entire class was looking back at me and Ciera with pure annoyance.

"We are paying to be here. Go to the playground and talk," the same girl said disgusted.

I wish it was possible to have obtained my bachelor's degree by just taking the classes I needed to get the occupation I wanted. I wanted to be an entertainment writer. I also wanted to be a well-paid choreographer that didn't have to do an extra job, but in the meantime, until I did make a lot of money stepping, I pursued scriptwriting in school. I always knew I wouldn't take dance classes for step because I wasn't wasting any money on something I knew how to do naturally.

I still can't find a good writing job, so I do projects on my own and submit them places. I haven't had any luck making any money yet, but at least I'm trying.

I never had any intentions of being behind a camera and shooting movies or television shows. I wanted to write the shows and have people shoot them, so the truth is I didn't need Ms. Clemens' class, and it was a waste of a loan for me and Ciera who wants to be in front of the camera interviewing people and not behind it. However, I did understand that some of the students did want to be cameramen and women, so I respected that and kept my mouth shut unless talking about the subject matter from that day on, after Ciera told me about her job.

Ms. Clemens was so upset at Ciera and me that she started to write on the board, but stopped and said, "No, why don't you two come to the front and write the definitions down to these words."

Establishing shot, aerial shot, deep focus, long shot, pan, and *high angle shot* were written on the board.

Ciera and I walked to the front, picked up the chalk, and stared at the words on the board.

"We haven't learned any of these camera shots yet," I shyly said.

Ms. Clemens turned in circles and pulled at her hair as she tried to hold in her anger. I hated how dramatic she acted when she was upset.

With a strict tone, Ms. Clemens said, "Yes, we did. You would know that if you weren't in the back talking. Even though you haven't been here long, I did manage to say all of these definitions during the time you've been in here."

I put down the chalk and Ciera did the same. I hate when people keep reiterating something that's already been said. I knew I came late and so did everyone in the room that saw me walk in. Ms. Clemens didn't have to keep repeating it. I didn't know any of the words she'd written, and she needed to get over it. The most I could do was make up a definition, but I knew that would add fuel to the fire and make her angrier.

"You are paying for your education, so why not utilize it?" Ms. Clemens said. "Everyone needs to write down the definitions to all the words in Chapter Three and turn them in by the next class. Good day."

All the students grabbed their things and exited the class. Some looked at me and Ciera like they wanted to punch us, and others were happy they didn't have to stay in class. Truth be told, a lot of us just showed up for class because attendance was ten percent of our grade. After the first two days, we were automatically enrolled permanently in the class, so the staff couldn't drop us if we came late or didn't show up after them.

This was the first time Ms. Clemens had ever released us early, so I knew she was mad. That, or she was just waiting on an opportunity to release us so she could get out of the class for the day herself. She probably had a sugar daddy somewhere she wanted to get to.

Ms. Clemens is a beautiful Caucasian woman. She looks like the models on TV with her long legs, pretty brown hair, and slim waist. I've seen her leave campus with a different man a few times and every one drove either a Ferrari, BMW, Benz, or Hummer.

7

I'm sitting outside the basketball gym where I'm holding practice with the team I started here at Cupperton in two hours. I'm sitting on the bench because I'm early and don't want to go in the gym just yet. A few people walk by and say hello to me.

A couple days ago there was a bunch of high school kids that swarmed this area; now that they're gone, Cupperton's students are back to normal. I don't think they liked them high school kids being here at all. Now that they're gone, everyone's socializing and enjoying their college experience again.

The men walking by smile at me, but I don't take any interest in them. I smile back at them to be nice, but once they look away from me, I roll my eyes.

I slouch back on the bench and look up at the sky which is a prettier sight than watching people socialize. I smile as planes fly by. I see myself on one of them headed to another country to do a step workshop. The trip is completely paid for by a sponsor. My hotel, food, transportation, and a stipend are given to me by people that are impressed with my natural talent. Someday I'll be on that plane going to spread the art of step and paid well for it.

Mr. Stephen's paying me fifty dollars an hour to work for Luminous LA, so I can't imagine how much a big-time artist or TV producer would pay me to come up with a routine. Probably a few thousand.

I fall asleep on the bench thinking about coaching different races all over the world. Hundreds of people at a time. I see myself on a stage in front of a big arena with my image projected on screens so everyone can see me in the back. My billboard will be hanging outside of famous buildings. People will see my image up high when they're driving on the freeways. I'll be the first person to be a worldwide stepping sensation.

I fantasize about the life I hope awaits me someday long and hard until water starts dropping on my face. It takes me a few seconds to fully wake up because I was in a deep sleep. The sun is no longer out and it's drizzling so I almost forgot where I was at. I fully come to and look at my phone. I've been sleep for over an hour and a half.

I slowly get up and the rain starts pouring down. I run inside the gym building and lean against the wall. I'm wet, but I'm not soaked.

I go in the bathroom and wipe my face and arms off with paper towels, which doesn't satisfy me because I still feel wet and nasty from being outside on the bench.

"Hey, can you bring me some clothes and an umbrella?" I ask Ciera.

Ciera meets me in the bathroom with some jeans, a shirt and socks. We both can fit each other's clothes. We practically have the same figure. Small waists and nice hips.

"Very funny," I say noticing she's laughing at me.

"What you was out there doing?" Ciera asks. "I thought you came in here early?"

"I was outside on the bench and I fell asleep," I say. "I wonder what people were thinking when they walked past me knocked out on the bench, since none of them thought to wake me up?" I say. "I know they couldn't have thought I casually take naps outside of the gym with a bunch of strangers walking past ever so often. The rain woke me up."

Ciera's shaking her head now.

"You better be careful with that," Ciera says. "You know its crazy people around here."

"I know girl," I say. "Thanks."

"No problem," Ciera says. "You know I got you."

Ciera puts my wet clothes in a bag and takes them with her. I love her so much. I can rely on her for anything.

On my way in the gym, I see that the rain has stopped. I hate this Louisiana weather sometimes.

I can't believe my eyes when I walk in the gym where I hold most of my step rehearsals for Cupperton's step team. I drop my bag on the floor and angrily look around. Only six out of thirteen members have arrived on time for rehearsal.

The six members that are here look at me then look away, as if to say they don't care about me being upset that once again, everyone is not here on time.

I was in the bathroom for at least fifteen minutes getting myself together, and it doesn't take long for them to walk from the dorms to here. It didn't even take Ciera long to drive here. All the members except one live in the dorms.

I pick my damp bag off the floor and put it on the bleachers.

I put my calm face on like every coach has to even when they're upset having to be professional and carry on with their craft.

I meet the six members on the court and immediately begin practice.

"Alright," I say. "Let's take it slowly from where we left off last week. Five, six, seven, eight."

The team breaks up the movements from the step. The stomps and claps are slow so that we can make sure everyone is moving the way they are supposed to be. We keep the beat, just at a slower pace. This combination we're reviewing is very simple. It's just a few basic movements put together. It has claps above and under the legs, as well as movements to the left and right with our arms like blades.

As the routine keeps going, I have to hold my composure as I watch Abbey Rodrigues and Charity Tims continuously stomp and clap off beat, as well as combine stomps and claps in areas they are not supposed to be combined.

Abbey and Charity aren't the most rhythmic people, which I don't mind because they'll get better; however, it's obvious that the only time they practice is when there is rehearsal.

My complex choreography requires practice outside of the two hours every Tuesday and Thursday. I offer to help people with my spare time, but no one wants to go the extra mile with stepping except me. No one on this team loves it as much as I do, so they're okay with being mediocre and not the best at the art. So because everyone doesn't want to put the extra time into perfecting the steps, I have to pick on every little thing they do wrong at rehearsals individually, and slow down practice for everyone, so they know exactly what they're messing up on that's making everyone sound awful as a whole.

Whereas, if they would allow me to work with them one on one outside of practice hours, I could continue teaching new steps and personally tell them every detail that's wrong at a different time, instead of singling them out at practice which causes them to have attitudes sometimes.

I have to perform with the team sometimes so that I can carry the sound of the beat with everyone else that has it.

I can't let anyone's annoyed looks and sighs get to me because we need to sound like a group. Even though I know I will kill the choreography effortlessly because I did make it up and stepping is a natural talent I have, no one in the audience is going to hear me alone. They're going to hear everyone as a group. No one is going to say *oh Shona is tearing that choreography up* because no one will know our routine. They won't know who's keeping the right beat and doing the movements right. We're either all going to sound good or terrible as a whole.

"Abbey and Charity, you two need to separate the stomps

and claps," I say. I slowly demonstrate the portion of the step they mess up on. I do the moves one direction, then I do them another direction. "Nowhere in this particular step do you clap and stomp at the same time," I continue.

I observe Abbey looking at me out of her peripheral vision up and down with a disgusted look, but pay her no mind. I turn around.

"Five, six, seven, eight," I say.

I do the routine with them.

In the middle of it, Shanell Lewis and Regina Martin walk in. They slowly put their things down and join the rest of the team. They take their positions in the front row next to me. I absolutely hate how they walked in here like they're showing up for a picnic and not a rehearsal. Others won't care if they don't get a plate at a picnic, but I care if I have to go over choreography again. Shanell and Regina should have thrown their things down and ran to the court to show their remorse for showing up late, but they don't care that they are late.

Shanell and Regina are best friends that think the team needs them, they don't need the team. I only put up with them because I don't want the team to get any smaller, and they are two of my best members. They catch on fast and have more rhythm than a lot of the members. Shanell and Regina catch the beat and join in on the step.

The steps already sound better than what they did without Shanell and Regina because they help me drown out the people that don't have the beat down pact. I decide to start the routine over just to hear how much better and louder it will sound from the top with two of my front liners.

"Let's take it from the top," I say. This time I watch. "We Are!" I shout.

"Legit!" everyone lowly says as they start the routine with a crisp stomp that sounds as one.

Everyone starts off together: heads following hands wherever they go, claps together, feet stomping as if one person is in the room. I'm loving it.

After a minute into the routine, Shanell and Regina begin to mess up on different parts. Shanell turns her head right and stomps with her left foot while everyone else is looking left and stomping with their right foot. Regina is clapping where there is supposed to be a stomp.

This wrecks my nerves because the reason my two best members are off is because they came late to the last rehearsal and didn't learn it. By the time they arrived, I had already broken the step down completely and everyone else already learned it. I was so frustrated that I didn't go back and reteach it.

For one, it's not fair to everyone that did show up on time to have to watch me reteach something they already know because two people finally decided to show up. Second, I don't like to keep reteaching. Definitely not for anyone here that likes to come and go as they please. I like to move forward, not backwards.

I never ask Shanell, Regina, or anyone else why they're late because I know they will either give me a stupid excuse, or catch an attitude saying it's not my business. I already have to deal with them showing up late and catching attitudes when I correct them on steps they mess up on; I don't want to deal with attitudes because they don't want to admit to me that they were too lazy to get up on time, didn't want to practice the full two hours, stayed up late partying so they couldn't get up, didn't feel like practicing a particular day so they didn't come, or simply had other plans.

I know as a coach I have a right to know why my members

are tardy or not coming, but sometimes, to keep the little peace I can with this team, I just keep my questions to myself.

I try not to make it obvious that I'm upset that Shanell and Regina are messing up by keeping my face relaxed and my tone calm. As my old advisor Mrs. McGruder would say, "An attitude is transmittable." I still can't stand that ugly witch Mrs. McGruder for kicking me off the team.

As practice continues, more members show up. They take their time like Regina and Shanell to drop their things before heading on the court. I position my team in different spots a lot today. Towards the end, the rest of the members arrive.

Practice only lasts an hour and a half before I call everyone to a huddle at the bleachers. When I'm fed up, I usually shut it down early. It makes me angry that no one here cares about the time I put into creating this team, the steps, reserving the gym, and helping their stepping ability improve. These are the most ungrateful and uncaring people I've ever met in my life.

Agitated and irked, I get straight to the point.

"We have been booked for the boys' basketball game in a couple weeks," I say. "I want us to squeeze in as many practices as we can, even if we have to practice in someone's dorm."

I've only performed one other time with this team and that was at an elementary school. I didn't want to start with a big audience because most of my team had never performed a day in their lives when we started, so I knew some would have stage fright and they weren't ready to perform in front of crowds that know stepping is supposed to sound sharp and together without anyone being off beat. I was surprised the performance actually went well despite everyone scattering into practice all the time. Everyone showed out and stayed together. If I didn't know better, I'd think they met up without me and rehearsed.

Whatever the case, I'm just hoping that they shock me again

at the basketball game and deliver the routine perfectly, despite the late arrivals and absences increasing tremendously over the last few weeks.

"Any questions?" I ask.

Regina quickly asks, "What time is the game?"

"I will email all the details to everyone," I say.

I'm not about to verbally say the specifics because I made the mistake of doing that last time and everyone still ended up calling me to ask again because they didn't write it down and forgot.

"Anymore?" I ask.

"I don't have any extra time these next few weeks to meet any time outside of practice hours," Shanell says.

I'm looking at her with a blank face because for one, that doesn't sound like a question, and two, she was off beat today so she really needs to meet up with someone other than her buddy Regina who was off as well, and correct her mistakes.

"Can you try to get us a performance at other campuses?" Abbey asks.

"Yea," Charity says. "I want to meet some new people and get off this campus."

"I'll see what I can do," I lie.

I'm not putting any time into getting us performances on different campuses until everyone here starts to respect me. All I want them to do is show up on time so we can all learn together, and not be worried that the performance is going to sound terrible. I'm taking a huge risk putting us on that court with lots of people watching us, knowing people haven't been showing up consistently and have been coming late all the time. I'm going off of a little hope that we may do alright, considering how they did well at the elementary school. I know everyone is anxious for another performance, so before people quit because we're not going anywhere, I booked this game.

When I was coaching in high school, I never let the McGruder's send us out and we weren't ready, but now I'm faced with a different situation. I fear that my passion of coaching this team will dismantle because ensuring that everyone is together and has the routine down perfectly with only two practices a week could take several months. I feel like these members will know they are the reason things take longer, but won't care. They may quit if they feel things aren't right, even if it's their fault.

"Anymore?" I ask.

Everyone looks at each other. No one says anything.

"Alright," I say. "Have a good day."

I didn't want to say that last part. They definitely just ruined my day.

I mope the entire walk to my car. I started the day happy about receiving a position with Luminous LA, then went to the team that I'm coaching for free and am a part of and they killed my joyous spirit. Despite having thirteen members not including myself, I could never be friends with anyone on that team because I'm always bitter with how they show up late or just don't show up at all.

When I started this team, I just knew I would develop thirteen people I would associate with on a daily basis, but I learned fast that being associates with people on this team, let alone friendships, wouldn't work out because I'd be too bitter looking into their eyes knowing they don't appreciate the time I put into ensuring they have an activity to be a part of.

I slowly unlock the door to my house not wanting to be cramped up in it for the rest of the day. A horn honks. I look back and see Ciera sitting in her car parked on the side of the street.

Not surprised to see her, I still ask, "What are you doing here?"

"Came by to relax," Ciera says. "I'm bored. Did I tell you I was thinking about going back to school? I think I want to get my masters." She has different books in her hand about television and film.

Ciera's flipping through the pages of her book. I put my things on the table and sit next to her.

"Do you have to sit so close?" Ciera asks. "I need all the space in the world to read through this hectic ass book. It's bad enough my brain is already crammed."

"Well, if you want more space, this is my territory, so move," I say nonchalantly.

I'm never in the mood after dealing with my team at this school. Ciera moves to the couch adjacent to me huffing and puffing, and continues to skip through pages of her <u>Camera Shots</u> book. I look through it with her.

Knowing my attitude is foul right now and that Ciera knows why, I straighten my attitude up and ask, "Are you going to write the definitions to these words?"

"You thinking about Ms. Clemens?" Ciera asks. Ms. Clemens seemed to pick on us a lot making us write definitions all the time. "I should do that right now since I got the book opened huh?" Ciera asks.

Ciera takes out a sheet of paper and hands me one too.

"Can you write them for me? Your handwriting is better like Ms. Clemens always said," Ciera says.

"Remember how we used to alternate with the homework assignments?" I laugh.

I used to hate writing definitions. Ciera and I used to take turns writing the definitions twice. Once for ourselves, than each other. It would help us study. It sounds stupid, but it

120

helped us stay calm after being asked so often to write them because Ms. Clemens was a bitch.

Ciera is copying definitions for *establishing shot, aerial shot, deep focus, long shot, pan, and high angle shot* out of her books, then tosses the books on the living room table.

"So are you thinking about going back to school, or are you already enrolled?" I ask curious to why she's writing definitions.

"I'm thinking about it," Ciera says. "I'm just refreshing on things I forgot just incase I decide to go enroll at a random moment one day.

Ciera leans back and closes her eyes for a minute. I notice she has a book on writing and I start to read the scriptwriting section. I'm intrigued reading the formats and looking over scripts for movies that I've seen, but I still wish everything was just thrown in my brain and I was a robot so I didn't have to read it.

I hate reading. It's like a medicine that makes me drowsy.

Ciera opens her eyes and stares blankly at me because I am smiling while reading the information in her book.

"I'm already tired of reading this shit," Ciera says. "I can't open another book. I have to take it a day at a time. I don't want to take out any more loans as it is. If I'm going to do this, I need a head start on my studies, and I want to get my monies worth."

"I bet you are tired," I say. "I'm tired just watching you study. Just take it day by day like you said. Study a little a day."

I still have a scriptwriting book from when I was in college. I remember I used to read the same page three times to retain everything, and I would get so worn out from copying definitions.

I used to wish there was something I liked to do that required me to actually get up and move for my major. I didn't want to be a dance major because I didn't want to learn ballet, jazz, and all that other stuff. I just wanted to step, and Cupperton didn't even offer that class.

Watching Ciera yawn and slouch back on the couch is taking a toll on me. Now I'm getting sleepy.

I toss my old scriptwriting book on the table on top of my Camera Shots book.

I turn on the television and browse through the channels. Ciera opens up her laptop.

"Nothing's on TV," I say and turn it off. "What are you looking at?"

Ciera's smiling and so am I now that the TV volume is no longer drowning out the sound of her computer. She's on *Video to Video Vault (VVV)* watching a video of me stepping when I was younger. I know because I recognize my voice. I've been recording my step routines along with tutorials since I was real young with a basic camera. I even have videos stepping to songs.

There's a lot of people online that upload themselves doing my routines and I love it.

There's this one kid named Alibi Orisadele that has done many of my steps and posted the videos. I have over three hundred videos posted. Orisadele comments a lot on my videos and asks me to upload more. He tells me how much he appreciates what I do.

There's young girls in school that use my steps for their teams, and I absolutely love it.

Even though my videos don't get that many views now, I know someday I'll be well-known everywhere. Everyone will refer to me as *Shona Jackson, The Choreographer*.

"You're really entertained by my younger days as a stepper huh?" I ask Ciera who's nodding her head listening to the beats I

122

make.

"Yea girl, you tight," Ciera declares.

"Thanks," I say.

I love to hear people tell me I am good at what I do.

"Almost time to start that new job," Ciera says excited for me.

"Yes," I happily say. "Thanks for getting me to get that business card." I never wanted to work anywhere I wouldn't like. "Guess it's true what they say: *ask and you shall receive,*" I excitedly say.

Ciera goes to a video of one of the teams we saw at the end of the dance team competition when we got the business card.

"I'm just excited to see your team win that competition," Ciera says. "I mean come on, you saw those teams. They were good, but their coaches are not as good as you. Your choreography is a lot harder, faster, and exciting to watch. I already know with your talent and coaching skills your team will win first place."

My excitement has left my body once again. I'm now looking sad.

"Unfortunately, since my team will be the only step team, they can't compete in the competition; they'll just be exhibition," I say walking over and sitting next to Ciera.

"You should try and enter them in The Big Bang Step Off," Ciera suggests.

"What's that?" I ask.

Ciera grabs the flyer out of her backpack.

"It's a step competition for high school students," Ciera says. "Found this flyer on the ground this morning."

She hands the flyer to me and I cautiously look it over from top to bottom. The nice layout and red, black, and white design around the masked steppers looks great.

I read over the same information Ciera just told me with my own eyes.

I need to start taking my black behind to the bulletin boards and poles outside places I go to, including Cupperton when I'm coaching, so I know what events are going on. Most likely this flyer fell from one of them.

"It's in four months," I say. "Can you go to this website?"

I give Ciera the flyer so she can copy the address in the search bar.

Ciera scrolls through *The Big Bang Step Off* website. It's nicely designed with a bunch of stepper silhouettes. This year will mark the first year this competition is held.

Ciera continues to slowly scroll down on the website. I browse through the list of coaches aligned on the left side. I think I may have seen a first and last name that I'm sure many people don't have, that I've seen before.

My blood is heating up.

"Scroll back up," I say to Ciera. "Stop."

I was right.

Jasmine Pent's photo that says *Ann High School* next to it is right in my face. I can't believe she's taking Ann High to the competition.

I know she better make up her own steps and not take mine or any she stole from sororities and fraternities. I can't believe she thinks she's good enough to enter in a competition like this one. I bet if she saw my name across the screen she wouldn't have.

I'm furious the McGruders' would call Jasmine back to coach Ann High and not consider getting in contact with me, knowing I am the reason for all those first-place trophies sitting in her office when I was and when I was not coaching, because when I was removed the team still used my steps. And if it wasn't my

124

steps, they were someone else's. Either way, they weren't Jasmine's, who Mrs. McGruder is falsely advertising as a coach.

Jasmine is not a coach. She's a thief.

"Let me see your computer real quick," I say to Ciera.

I email Mr. Stephen: *Hello Mr. Stephen. Are you familiar with The Big Bang Step Off? If not, here is a link to it. I was wondering if I could register Mission High to be a part of it? Have a nice day.*

Mission High is the first school I'll be working with as a Luminous LA employee.

I close my eyes, inhale and exhale. Then I give Ciera her computer back.

"How crazy would it be if you competed against your old high school?" Ciera asks excitedly.

I feel good on the inside to know that Ciera sees this as an opportunity for me to prove I am the best; however, I am still in competitive mode as I watch her scroll down and look at the rest of the teams that are competing.

"I hope that dude says yes, then everyone can judge for themselves who the real choreographer is," Ciera says.

I can't really focus on anything she is saying. I'm just staring at the website hoping and excited that this competition may jump off.

"Go back to my email please," I demand.

"Here," Ciera says and hands me the laptop.

I click on my inbox happy to see that Mr. Stephen has already responded. He's really good at getting back to me promptly. His email says: *I think that would be a great idea. I will be in contact with you about adding a few more practices after the drill competition.*

I go back to The Big Bang website, scroll up to Jasmine's photo again and smile as I look with happiness.

I wish I could see Jasmine's face when she sees my name and face smiling on this website. I'm going to submit a photo of me my junior year when I was out with Ann High's step team and crop all the members out except me to make Jasmine, Mr. and Mrs. McGruder even more upset.

The submission deadline is in two days, so I make sure to submit Mission High the next morning.

Luminous LA is such a prestigious program and Mr. Stephen is so well respected that I don't have to have a submission video. The producers of the show trust that whoever Mr. Stephen backs up is definitely worth having in their show.

Mr. Stephen sent me another email after saying it was okay to enter the competition that says: *Don't let me down.*

I respond saying: *Believe me, I won't. You can count on me.*

8

I can't wait to meet my new team at Mission High School. I
don't care if the students don't have any talent, I'm going to
whip them into shape. I don't care if I have to blackmail them
with dinner at my house, we will rehearse until they are perfect.
This is no longer just about drilling the beauty, art, and
discipline of stepping in their minds and bodies, this program
just became more than just spreading my craft, showcasing my
talent, earning a check, and getting more people to know who I
am.

This is personal.

This is about more than my team winning a first-place trophy.
It's about showing Jasmine and Mr. and Mrs. McGruder that I
am the best once and for all. There's nothing they can do or
anyone they can hire that will outshine me. They will never get
the satisfaction of thinking that they killed the stepper inside of
me.

I've been waiting for the day that I can laugh and smile in
their faces, especially that Mr. McGruder. The McGruders' are
going to regret kicking me off of my team and they're going to
hate that I will have a team that will make them wish they never
entered into the competition. They're going to respect me, my
talent, and never be able to go another year coaching Ann
High's step team without thinking about me.

I'm the choreographer, and there's no one like me.

I'm headed to my first day of work. I practice step
movements in my car and I listen to music. I'm lightly stomping
and clapping so my legs are still fresh when I get to work. I'm so
happy that I'm waving to all types of people that have their
windows down and speaking to them. I'm being super friendly.

I can't help but notice some of the children on a bus that's
going by smiling at me as they watch me step. A little boy claps

his hands to try and copy me and the bus driver keeps looking through his rearview mirror to figure out where the noise is coming from.

I'm doing small movements to minimize some of the attention although the children are so cute to watch.

I sit back and enjoy looking out at the beautiful scenery. After a little more driving, I reach my destination and walk towards Mission High School.

While I'm walking down the sidewalk, a woman taps me on the shoulder from behind and says, "Hey."

I say nothing, stop walking so I'm not rude, and just look at her through my shades.

"You know this the most black people I've ever seen on this street," the woman says. I say nothing. "Me, you, and this dude I just passed," the woman says. I say nothing. The strange lady continues on her walk.

I'm early for my first day of work, so I'm scoping out Mission's small theater. As I walk up and down the rows to kill time, I have nothing to gaze at really. The theater is comprised of the necessary components: seats and a stage. Nothing is fancy about it.

Cupperton has a much nicer theater than this. I'm not going to lie when I say I've been to a few high schools that have had better looking theaters than my old college. Cupperton's theater is suited so that professional plays can be performed there. The stage is a lot bigger. I went in there once to watch a step show from people that came all the way from California. They were good, but they're nowhere near better than me. Even though they get paid to step all over the world, I wouldn't join their crew because from what I researched, they all come up with their routines.

I like to work solo and don't want anyone mistaking what I

create for someone else's work. I don't need help creating choreography.

School lets out and ten girls and three boys come in the theater with a lady.

They all take a seat except the lady who comes to introduce herself to me. "Hi Shona, I am Ms. Ross. I will be the arts assistant in the room with you."

Ms. Ross shakes my hand. I can't believe what I just heard. Ms. Ross is the arts assistant that is supposed to stay in the room with me and the students at all times, so that means the people that followed her in here are my students.

I look around at my new team. This will be the first step team I have ever coached with no black people.

Ms. Ross is looking at me like *when am I going to greet her back.*

I snap out of my shocked state and say, "Hi, nice to meet you."

"Well, we are ready to start when you are," Ms. Ross says and takes a seat in the audience.

I walk to the center of everyone and say, "Hello everyone. My name is Shona Jackson, but you all can call me Shona, Ms. Shona, Ms. Jackson, whatever is the easiest for you to say. I'm a lot older than you all, but I don't mind if you just call me Shona. Call me whatever makes you feel comfortable. I will be your step coach for the next few months."

Luminous LA would typically fund me for three months, but because of the step competition, they're going to give me an extra one.

I don't know how I should feel about everyone sitting in the audience with no expression on their faces, including Ms. Ross who looks like she was in a raffle to be a chaperone for this class and doesn't want to be in here. I carelessly continue because no matter how anyone's feeling, they will be the best high school team in Louisiana, and they will help me make my statement to Jasmine and Mr. and Mrs. McGruder.

"I will be teaching you all a routine that will be performed at the Dance Team Competition at Cupperton, and you can look at that as practice for The Big Bang Step Off that I have entered you all in," I say.

"We're going to be performing at The Big Bang Step Off?" one of the girls ask.

I look her up and down. Her demeanor says it all. Legs crossed, slight attitude as she speaks, and chewing gum. It doesn't take me long to label her as problem child number one.

"That is what she just said," another girl says.

Ms. Ross finally intervenes and tells them to be quiet.

"Yes, you all will be performing at The Big Bang Step Off," I say. "We only have thirty practices together, which will be two hours each to prepare for the dance competition, which by the way, we are not competing in, we are just showcasing. However, I am confident that with my direction, you guys will win The Big Bang Step Off in which you will be competing. If everyone is on time, and practices at home as well, I know that this team will be very successful. We will practice a few days a week. Each practice will start with stretching and go into learning the routine."

Little Miss Attitude, the first girl who spoke, has another question. "Will we be using any music?" she asks.

"Don't say another word Alexis," Ms. Ross says.

With a forced smile, I explain, "Well the beauty of stepping is that you use your hands and feet to make rhythms and beats. We will be using music, but very little. Now before we begin, I want everyone to introduce themselves, then I will do a demonstration of what I will be teaching today, then we will begin. Let's start from the far left on the second row, then go right to left on the bottom row."

Alexis stands up.

"My name is Alexis Thomas. I am a freshman. I am on the Culinary Arts team, head captain of the cheerleading team during football season, I also play basketball, and am the future valedictorian."

Alexis is absolutely beautiful. She is a pretty Caucasian girl with long blonde hair. She looks cute with her side ponytail. However, after hearing her speak for a few seconds, it's easy to know she is full of herself. Not to mention, she's already let me know that she has an attitude problem.

One of the girls on the first row interrupts and says, "All she said to do was introduce yourself."

This girl read my mind. I was expecting Alexis to stop after she said her name.

"Alright. Let's keep it going," I say.

Alexis sits back down.

"My name is Alina Marks," Alina says really low when she stands.

I can barely hear her. Judging by the looks on everyones faces, they didn't hear her at all. I ask her to repeat herself.

"Alina Marks."

Alina barely says it higher. Although she has no pitch in her voice, she is a beautiful Hispanic girl. Her blue tights and black top, along with her two pigtails, really show off her nice figure and pretty face.

"Speak up! She can't hear you!" another member from the first row says rudely. I can tell this one might be troublemaker number two in the clan.

"She said her name is Alina Marks," Alexis says.

Alina sits back down. The girl next to her stands up.

131

"My name is Delia Perry," she says. I begin to say thank you, but Delia is not finished speaking. "I am very excited to be a part of this team," Delia continues. "I want to thank you for taking your time out to come here and teach. I know you could've been anywhere else in the world right now."

Delia sits back down and flips her flat-ironed blonde hair behind her ears. She seems very nice; however, judging by everyones annoyed expressions, she is not the one to take anywhere.

"Thank you," I say to Delia. "For the sake of getting a little practice in, everyone just state your name. You do not have to stand up."

This role call is taking too long.

The rest of the students state their names.

Desiree Armstrong, Keasha Armstrong, Michael White, Jose Terry, Jason Soto, Aisha Todd, Sheela Gonzalez, Kiara Tips, Casey Miles, and Mya Long are all in attendance.

I could tell this Sheela girl had an attitude before she even stated her name. Her head was resting in the palm of her hand, she had an angry expression on her face, and not to mention she kept rolling her eyes at Ms. Ross, and uttering a few words under her breath in a different language. Judging by her attitude, I know she didn't say anything nice. Probably not even appropriate.

"Alright now, everyone can come on stage, we can stretch and get to learning some steps," I eagerly say.

Ms. Ross stays seated. She's supposed to practice with the students to help them stay encouraged, but I guess she's not going to. Although it's in her contract to do so, I do not care. Mainly because I don't need her. She's just another chaperone in the room besides myself. She really serves no purpose like all the advisors I've dealt with.

Ms. Illeen doesn't even attend any of Cupperton's practices. Her names just on a sheet of paper that makes it seem like she's active in the organization.

"Let's get two horizontal lines," I say to Mission's team. I lead them through a few stretches standing and sitting. "Alright, let's get to work," I say.

I'm so excited to get going with this team and teach them steps. Jasmine and the McGruders' have no idea what they're up against. They'll expect my team to be good, but they won't expect me to have a diverse team that doesn't consist of any blacks.

Ann High is a predominantly black school, and all of the members on the step team have always been black there. Everyone expects black teams to show out on stage because stepping originated from blacks, but no one will expect a team full of whites, Chinese, and Hispanics to hop on stage and upstage everyone in the competition.

What I observed about Mission High when I was walking in, is it's a melting pot. No one will know what they're going to bring to the table. People try to front like they don't instantly think of what race a certain school will be comprised of when they walk through the door of a step competition, but they do.

Anyone that's visited Mission High will assume that the few black people that roam through it will make up the step team, but that's not the case for Mission High and I'm loving it. I can't wait for this team to perform and show people I am capable of whipping anyone into step shape, no matter what race they are.

I have everyone getting arms distance apart. The first annual Big Bang Step Off has no clue what they're in for. This competition will be one for the record books. No one will expect for my team to walk away with that trophy.

I can't wait for them to get on the stage and hit the first beat.

I want the audience in shock as soon as my team walks on the stage, and I want their breath to be taken away with how good my team will be. I want Mission to do so well that nothing but smoke is left on that stage when they leave, and no one wants to perform after them if they don't go last.

It's up to me to have my students ready, and I'm going to do just that.

"Watch first," I say.

I do a complex fast paced step, just so the students can see that I'm the real deal. The first impression is a lasting impression, so what would I look like doing a simple and slow step when these kids have never seen me step before? An idiot.

When I finish the step, everyone looks like they've just seen a ghost.

"We're going to learn all that?" Desiree asks. "Yea right."

"You'll know that step and plenty more," I say. "In fact, by the time I'm done with you, you might be able to teach me something."

Now I'm thinking about how I am unsure of everyone's stepping ability; I try to think of a simpler combination than the one I was practicing in my car.

Needing to spare myself some time I say, "Take a minute to do whatever stretch you need to that I did not do."

I'm making sure I'm doing the simpler step I made up correctly. When teaching a step, I have to teach it right the first time, otherwise people will get thrown off if I say: *I'm sorry, it actually starts on the right foot and not the left, and the clap is above the head, not behind your back.* Plus, I would have to teach it over again.

Everyone is looking at me strangely because I'm nodding my head like an actual song is playing while I'm making sure I have the step in my head ready to teach.

I smile at them and continue nodding my head while I'm making sure I'm doing the step properly.

While everyone is stretching, Ms. Ross is in the audience, and I'm doing the same step repeatedly, Alexis talks to the twins Desiree and Keasha.

"Are y'all cheering tonight?" Alexis asks them.

"Yes," Desiree answers. "At least that's what we're going to tell our mom."

Keasha laughs.

Desiree and Keasha are very close. Neither twin will ever talk bad about the other. I know, because before the door shut behind them when they came in, I heard Keasha defending Desiree to some boy that said she needed to pay attention in class, and was the uglier of the two, which is a lie because the girls look identical.

Keasha told the boy that if his mom truly cared about the future, she would have done the world a huge favor and took the pill.

I thought that was a harsh comeback, but I was proud to hear her defend her twin. If someone lets one person disrespect their family, then more people will.

The Hispanic boy then got on both girls for being born in Mexico, but not knowing any Spanish.

"Quiet down please," I say to the twins and Alexis. "I am going to show five basic movements to get your bodies used to basic combinations. This is one."

I stomp my right foot, then clap above and under my left leg.

"I want you guys to try," I say. "Stomp with your right foot; clap above and under your left leg."

Everyone tries, but no one is able to do it correctly. It's not a good sign that no one here can do a basic step combination, but I'm not panicking. This team will need, by far, the most help out

135

of anyone I've ever coached, and I'm willing to put in the work to do it. All I need is a little patience.

I have to remember my goal with Mission is to make them the best high school steppers in Louisiana. I'm thinking too small when I say that. They need to be the best high school steppers in the world, so people all over will blow up my phone to work with their students. Mission definitely needs to win that competition.

I break the basic movements down further for everyone.

"Alright, stomp with your right foot," I say.

Everyone stomps with their right foot. Then I have them clap. Then I have them pick up their left leg and clap under it.

"Now let's do all of it together," I say.

Everyone does it except Sheela, who rudely says, "We got it!"

I already want to hurt this girl. Everyone does the movement correctly the second time.

"Great," I say. "Now for combination two."

I stomp with my right foot, then my left. Everyone follows along and does it perfectly.

For combination three, I stomp with my right foot, put my left arm in front of my chest with the palm of my hand facing down, extend my right arm all the way to the right with the palm of my hand facing down, and turn my head to the right all at once.

Jason does it perfectly.

Everyone else except Alexis attempts to do the position.

I turn some of the members palms that are facing the ceiling face down, and demonstrate the movements again before paying Alexis any attention.

"Do you plan on trying head cheerleader?" I ask sarcastically.

Alexis looks aggravated and says nothing.

"Stepping's not as easy as cheerleading for you, is it?" I ask.

I need to calm down. I don't want anyone coming up with something dumb to quit.

Plus, Alexis is so flawless that I really want her to remain on the team. Not only will she be a great stepper when I'm done with her, but she'll really have the girls on other teams hating her because she's talented and beautiful. I need her to stick around, so I'm going to watch my tone.

I feel like my frustration from Cupperton's practice is coming out of me. Alexis is doing what some of them do at practice, which is be lazy.

Alexis does the position irritated. At least she does it right and is not like Shanell and Regina who slack off at times because they think they can catch up and learn any combination I do, and they prove themselves wrong each and every time.

I do combination three again. Everyone attempts and mostly everyone does it right.

Some people look a little discouraged, so I give a little pep talk.

"I want everyone to know I understand it's the first day, and I don't expect anyone to have it perfect," I say. "It takes time to get used to. Has anyone here ever even seen stepping before?"

No one says anything and some people start to look around.

"Alright," I say. "So don't get discouraged. I guarantee by the end of this program, most of you will be stepping better than me."

I demonstrate the movements for combination three again.

"We have to be stiff," I say. "Your arms shouldn't be weak. If I put a brick on them, they shouldn't move."

I do combination four, which is the opposite of three. I stomp with my left foot, put my right arm in front of my chest with the palm of my hand facing down, my left arm is all the way extended to the left with the palm of my hand facing down, and

137

my head is facing the left.

"I still don't have the moves for one and three," Mya says looking drowsy.

"As the days go on, you will get better at them and you'll remember them more," I say. "I will state again, I don't expect you to have it perfect today."

I demonstrate the moves for combination four again. I have everyone try them. Some of the kids stumble.

I repeat it a few times and can see that the boys are at least trying and most of the girls are.

It's only Alexis and Sheela who have a lack of effort. It's obvious Alexis can't get over the fact that she is finally not a natural at something, and Sheela seems to have a lot on her mind. Sheela's face is so stern and angry looking like mine was when Nadia told me she helped get me kicked off of Ann High's step team my senior year.

For combination five, I throw my arms up parallel and look toward the ceiling.

Everyone does position five perfectly. I hope that gave them some confidence.

I tell everyone to pay attention.

"I'm going to demonstrate the first step I'm going to teach," I say.

I demonstrate a step that includes movements one through five.

Everyone stares at me in disbelief.

"Don't panic," I say. "I'm about to break it down. Spread back out for me."

I hold it together while day one is not going smooth for me at all. My attitude is right, it's just some of the students are not feeling practice today.

I have to continuously tell Sheela to stop sitting on the stage and practice. The twins talk about their personal lives more than they practice. Everyone else either gets frustrated that they cannot pick up the choreography, or stand around and think about other things. Everyone else, except my boys who are trying their best to get the choreography down pact.

"Alright everyone, listen up," I say.

I'm getting frustrated with this lack of respect due to the fact that I know these students chose to be in here.

"Why did you guys sign up for the class if you weren't going to give it your all?" I ask. "You weren't forced to be in here, right?"

"You guys need to give Ms. Jackson the respect she needs!" Ms. Ross shouts. "You guys did sign up to be in here! It was your choice! Now if it's too hard for you, tough! There's no quitting! You're not going to be in here socializing Desiree and Keasha, having a bad attitude Sheela, and being lazy Alexis! Give Ms. Jackson the respect she deserves!"

I now love my arts assistant.

"Look, I don't know everyone's reason for joining, but I do hope you guys stick it out and put in the work to be a great team," I say. "I know it's not easy at first, but it will be soon enough."

I go around and help everyone individually. I spend a lot of time with Alexis, who still puts in very little effort to perfect the moves. She's barely even trying.

"What's up with you Alexis?" I ask her.

"Nothing," Alexis says. "Look I have it."

Alexis does the step and has the beat wrong in a couple places.

"I know you have the potential to be great at stepping if you put your all into it," I say. "I'm only here for a few months. Let's make the best of it. Besides, if you do this, you can have

139

something else to add to your resume."

I go through the step slowly with Alexis while everyone else is working in groups. Sometimes students need a little bit more encouragement than others, or want to be babied a little. I don't mind for the sake of the competition. If Alexis needs me to act like her mother from time to time to give me a good effort, then whatever.

The more time I spend with each person individually, the more they get better and pick up the rhythm and tempo of the routine.

After our two hours together, everyone has the movements down. All I have to do at the next rehearsal is work on them keeping the beat and making it clear to everyone that we need to sound like one person. I'll have to start off with two people doing the step at once, then add people on to figure out where the problem resides.

I'm not too annoyed at how today went because my team at Cupperton gives me more of a headache than Mission's team. At least everyone here arrived on time.

"Hey, Ms. Ross can I talk to you for a minute?" I ask her while the students leave out the theater.

Ms. Ross sits down next to me in the audience.

"Did everyone here join this class willingly, or were some of them forced?" I ask.

I know sometimes parents will make their kids take part in activities just to keep them off the streets. I don't care if I have any of them, I just want some closure on why it's the first day and most of the students already seem unenthused.

"I only know what you know which is the students chose to participate," Ms. Ross says. "The only observations I will give you is that Alexis' parents enforce in her that she needs to be active and outshine her cousins. I overheard a conversation her

140

mother was having with her. They push her to do any activity that her schedule won't conflict with. The twins and the boys you have just like to try new things. Sheela has always had an attitude problem. No one knows what's wrong with her. I've asked her if she wanted to talk numerous times, and she looks at me crazy and walks away. Everyone else is a mystery just like her, but they did all sign their names in the blank space to join the class."

"Thanks Ms. Ross," I say. "I appreciate that."

"Don't let them get to you," Ms. Ross says. "I've been working here at Mission for ten years now, and I've seen the same pattern with some of the students that join activities that they've never tried before. They start off a little discouraged, but slowly come around and enjoy it more than anything else. You'll be fine."

"I know," I say. "I just really want them to do well and show everyone that step is not just a black thing. I want them to do well at the dance competition and definitely The Big Bang Step Off."

"I'm really excited about that step competition," Ms. Ross says. "I'm glad you entered them into it."

"I am too," I say. "I can't wait."

When Ms. Ross leaves, I stay seated in the empty theater and get my mind right. I'm not happy about how today went, but I am being paid to deal with this team. And I do have an opportunity to make Jasmine never want to coach again, and the McGruders' have to see me in all my happiness when Mission completely outshines their team. The only problem is, I'm going to need more than these two hours each rehearsal to get my team into shape. Some of the members are going to need extra help. They need one on one practice.

What I usually do is move on with the choreography when six

141

people can carry the routine because for others it may take a few days to get used to, but I don't see this team catching on in days without the proper one on one help.

I'll have to become friends with my members and learn if I can trust that they won't snitch to Mr. Stephen or Ms. Ross that we met up outside of my work hours. How I'm going to get this team to want to be my friend is a mystery right now. I'll figure something out though.

When I walk outside of Mission High, there's students all over having conversations, sitting on cars, dribbling basketballs, and showing school spirit in their basketball and cheerleading uniforms. I feel like I'm walking on a college campus.

I lifelessly walk to my room when I get home. I'm drained.

9

"Stay in line until instructed otherwise," Caya says to the new line of girls from Cupperton University. My Sorors and I are at Caya's house along with the new line which has twenty-three girls on it. We're meeting this lines prophytes at Hollow's Cave.

Everyone's getting in their cars. We have all the new pledges meet us at Hollow's Cave. My Sorors and I are already tipsy. My girls are high too. Our last shot before getting in the cars was to us not going insane from taking time out of our night to be with the new girls.

It's late as hell. It's past nine at night.

My girls and I are watching the new girls stand in a straight line in the driveway on the side of Caya's car. We all have our phones on speaker and windows are down so we can all hear each other.

"How much longer y'all want to make them stand here?" Caya asks. "We got all damn night."

"I'm ready to whoop some ass," Shemina says.

"Let them stand like that until they ready to fall over," I say.

'Yea Caya," Telana says filing her nails. "You getting soft or what? This is what we always do."

Caya opens her door and yells, "Don't move your fuckin' legs! Y'all ain't even been standing there that long!"

"Let's hit the blunt a few more times," Telana says.

"Ugh. I'm not even ready to leave yet," Caya says. "I just want to hit the blunt, eat, and chill with my damn girls. I hate when this shit interferes with my damn usual routine. My normal hype at night is too fly to be doing this pledging over again. I don't care if we on the other side this time or not."

"Let's go back to the backyard and chill a little longer," Shemina says.

Before the pledges got here, we were getting drunk in the house and my girls were getting high too. We were dancing and taking our minds off of the events we have coming up tonight. We were gaining energy and trying to find happiness and excitement in all this time we're about to spend with the pledges. We were laughing at the things we plan to do to them.

Caya has the girls follow us to the backyard. They have to keep standing in a straight line with their hands to their sides and their heads tilted back.

Me and my Sorors sit on the wooden tables and get back to chilling and having a good time. Caya turns on some music and we start dancing with each other. We grind on each other and look like we are dating. That's just how we do. We're close sisters and enjoy each other's company.

I'm dancing with Telana. I'm dropping low and popping my ass on her. She's looking me up and down as if she was my nigga, Austin. She compliments my dance skills and twirls me in circles.

"Where your man at?" Casha asks.

"He not her man tonight," Telana laughs. "She my girl."

"Well, I don't know how your girl can not hit this blunt," Caya says. "This weed is doing a number on relaxing me with these damn girls here."

I'm so damn weak behind not smoking.

"I want to toast to Caya letting us use her house tonight," Casha says. "I also want to give her mad props for no one who is a true friend of hers being able to come to her place without giving any thanks." She's talking about the pledges.

One of the pledges is whispering to the rest of them.

My Sorors and I are looking at them in shock. Some of us are laughing. They are going to be under our instruction tonight.

"Thank you Big Sister Caya," the pledges say together.

My Sorors and I look at each other and don't pay the response any attention.

These damn bugs keep biting the hell out of us. We keep hitting our damn legs and spraying Off on ourselves. We're not even paying attention to the pledges.

Caya brings out a tray of already made sandwiches and a vegetable platter. She disgustedly tells the pledges to face the fence so they can't watch us enjoy our food.

"I can't wait to get rid of these damn girls," Caya says.

144

I really miss being high and eating.

My girls and I lose track of time.

"Pledges, go get in your cars," Caya demands. My Sorors and I stay in the backyard a little longer.

While we're getting in our cars, we notice the damn pledges having conversations. We don't play that. We don't want them saying anything because no comfort needs to be given. When they're on our time, the time that we have to squeeze into our schedules, they are not supposed to talk unless instructed to do so. They know that.

My Sorors and I are ready as hell on our way to Hollow's Cave. The pledges are driving their own cars. We don't have enough room for twenty-three girls.

On the drive, Shemina calls me asking if I saw what she did with her forty dollars. She says she had two twenties and they were in her purse. She doesn't think she took them out, but still wanted to know if someone saw her do anything with them, like drop them. I let her know I didn't see her with any money.

"Call everyone else and ask, then call me back," I say.

When Shemina calls back, she says no one has seen her with the money. "That only leaves the pledges," Shemina says.

When we get to Hollow's Cave, the pledges start getting out of their cars before we do.

"Get back in y'all damn cars!" Caya yells. "Y'all fucking hard headed!"

My girls and I all go by Shemina. She's getting teary eyed because she can't find her money. Telana pulls out forty dollars from her purse and tries to give it to Shemina, but she doesn't want it. We all know that sometimes it doesn't matter who we're with. When we are missing something, everyone around is a suspect.

"Don't trip," Caya says. "Let's get these pledges inside."

"Let's do it," Telana says.

Caya pulls the shortest pledge who is in the front into the cave with everyone else following behind her. The pledges are in a horizontal line in front of us with their hands in fist across their chests. Caya is making sure they know their left from their right by making them turn their heads. She makes them bend down, turn around, and look up a few times.

"Pledges," Caya says.

"Yes Big Sister Caya who we absolutely love with all of our hearts," the pledges say together.

"We're missing forty dollars and we want to know who took it," Caya says. None of the pledges say anything. "It seems like they don't have it," Caya continues. "I don't believe that. If my sister says she is missing something, someone here took it. It definitely wasn't me or my line. That would leave you all."

"Let's talk to them individually," Telana says. "Maybe someone here has killed someone before and we don't know. They probably are fearful for some reason."

"Why the hell would they be more fearful of each other than us?" Caya asks.

"Please Caya," Shemina says. "I want my money back. I want to know who the damn thief is while we're together too."

My girls and I end up questioning all of the pledges individually. Some of the girls get questioned three to four times by different members of my sorority. We are getting on they asses. However, no one snitches on anyone.

Shemina is furious. She wants to know who went in her purse.

"Wait. Strip down to y'all damn panties and bras," Shemina demands. "My money didn't just run out of my damn purse."

My mouth drops and I stare at the pledges. Making them strip was not on the agenda for tonight. I hear Caya and Asayla whispering to each other. They are mad at all the time Shemina has us wasting on her carelessness. Especially since Telana offered to give her money.

The pledges are down to their panties and bras. Shemina goes over to them and starts checking their pants pockets. Caya and Asayla are whispering again. They are wondering if Shemina is really about to check twenty-three peoples' pants. They're looking at her in disbelief. Shemina is shedding tears which is definitely not a good sign. We never shed tears in front of pledges.

146

After checking three pair of pants, Shemina looks at her line sisters. We all know she wants us to help her, but we can't believe she is actually doing this. She should have had the girls empty their pants pockets themselves. Surprisingly, Shemina doesn't ask us to help her. She just continues to go through the pledges' clothes in search of her money.

When Shemina reaches the tenth pledge, she finds forty dollars in her pants. She slaps the girl and pushes her to the ground. Her names Trayna. Trayna quickly gets up, slaps and pushes Shemina back. My Sorors and I run over to Trayna and start jumping her. We punch her repeatedly and push her around in a circle. We get her to the ground and start kicking her.

Trayna's line sisters do not even think to help her. They know we can cause them not to become members if we talk to their prophytes. Some of these girls are trying to carry on family traditions. They don't want to upset us at all.

Trayna is bleeding a little on her face, but we have everything we need to patch her up. We have her sit down on the floor and gain her strength back. Shemina puts the forty dollars in her purse.

"So, no one knew she took my money?" Shemina asks the pledges. "Speak! Someone say something?"

"Y'all sure as hell didn't say nothing when we were questioning y'all one by one," Asayla says.

"That's her money. She put her check in the bank and left out forty," a pledge named Canila says.

"Canila, are you calling me a liar?" Shemina asks. She's on her bullshit. She just wants her money back. She can say whatever she wants.

"No. I'm just saying I know that money is money Trayna earned," Canila says.

Shemina pushes Canila and says, "Don't get smart."

Caya laughs and says, "Check it out. Let Shemina have that money and we won't tell your prophytes anything about Shemina's money coming up missing."

147

"Y'all know they gone be pissed," Asayla says. "We don't come around much, and y'all done made us angry. Y'all prophytes like us."

"Not to mention y'all got to deal with them throughout your pledging journey for quite a bit more time," I say. I just want this mess to go away. Shemina found forty dollars and doesn't want to take a chance on us leaving and being idiots. We would rather be wrong and take the money, than take a chance on the pledges ridiculing us about Trayna stealing the money. Canila could be lying about the check.

"Put y'all clothes back on," Shemina says. "Y'all prophytes will be here soon."

"Speaking of their prophytes, where the hell are they?" Caya asks.

"We're here," Tashina, one of the prophytes says. "What happened to Trayna?"

This new line of pledges has ten prophytes. My line and I are laughing at them. They are sober as fuck. It finally hits us that we've been so focused on Shemina and her money, that we haven't been getting drunk. My girls haven't even been getting high.

Caya looks mad as hell. "I need to go to my car and get my stash," Caya says.

"Trayna is fine," Shemina says. "She was leading the stroll line and tripped over her own feet. How the hell did she do that? Y'all don't know how to coach her?"

Shemina is mad as hell still. I can tell she wants to fuck Trayna up more. She keeps looking at her evilly.

"Trayna get your ass up," Tashina says. "Why the hell are you crying?"

Trayna shakes her head no. She doesn't want to admit anything.

"We beat her ass for stealing my money," Shemina says. "What the fuck is wrong with y'all bringing this bitch in on this line?" she asks.

"I thought you cashed your check today?" Amy, another one of their prophytes asks Trayna.

"I did," Trayna says with a little smirk. She thinks her prophytes are about to defend her. She wants to know how we will respond to being wrong about whooping her ass.

"That's probably really her money," Amy laughs.

"It's probably not," Tashina says. "You know how it goes when we don't got no way of knowing the truth."

Amy and Tashina talk regular to Shemina. They aren't mad at all.

"It's the exact amount that I'm missing," Shemina says.

"If it's yours, it's yours," Tashina says to Trayna. "But it doesn't look like you're going to get it back. You shouldn't have had it on you in the first place. So what did we miss?" Tashina asks my line.

"Y'all didn't miss nothing," I say. "We're just getting started."

"We're just getting this party started. They have to recite their information," Caya says.

My line and I are dictating this gathering. We're supposed to for the majority of it. We're special guests. This lines prophytes asked us to come and be in charge the majority of the time. They also want the pledges to experience a different classes' way of bringing in a line. My line is a lot older than these eighteen- to twenty-year-old pledges and prophytes that we're here with.

Trayna says she is capable of joining her line. My Sorors and I know she doesn't want to be the reason they have to do everything again. By now she knows we can play whatever cards we want. Any decision we make can be spontaneous, and one we've never made before. If we're in a good mood or a bad mood, we can still cause the pledges hell. Nothing matters when people are pledging.

"Alpha Eta Nu was founded on the campus of Julliard University in 1913," the pledges say. "It was founded by sixteen beautiful and voluptuous women who strived to achieve excellence. They wanted to achieve many career goals in life and help others at the same time. Their goal was to indite as many members as they could to help make a difference in this world."

Some of the pledges are struggling. They are supposed to sound as if one person is speaking, and they didn't. My girls and I planned to have the history done before the prophytes got here so they could just witness how we haze pledges, but Shemina messed that up.

I know I'm not the only one mad at Shemina. Caya has looked disgustedly at Shemina a few times.

Caya has three pledges recite the history individually, then she has a few more of them recite it together. To be honest, it doesn't matter if they say it right or not, they will still be fucked with because we don't want them to forget it like we know they will. My crew is all over thirty and we don't remember some of the damn information. We're going to make the pledges recite it so much that they will remember it forever.

I'm laughing and so is Caya and Asayla. We don't remember half of this information the pledges are saying. For one, they have to know the first, middle, and last name of all the founders. My line and I have forgotten all of these damn people. We remember some of the names, but not the first, middle, and last of any of the founders. We sure as hell can't recite them in alphabetical order. That doesn't stop us from making the pledges recite the founders' names until we can get some of them back in our memories.

I know there's been times when I've been out and about, and met older Sorors from other schools at the store or somewhere else, and I wished I could have a conversation with them about our organization. Instead, I just say hi and what school I crossed in. Then I find a way to get back to whatever I was doing because I know I don't remember damn near all the history.

My line and I are trying to figure out what we want to do to punish these girls for not being able to say their history together. Some of them didn't even say some of the names. It's like they didn't study. They give themselves away that they don't know their information. My girls and I really don't remember all them damn founders.

"We should have whooped they asses while they was stripped down to they panties and bras," Caya says. "They can't possibly think that being ignorant about our history is worth forty dollars."

"It's worth they whole damn lives," Asyala says.

My girls don't mean that shit. We just getting on the pledges nerves because we can. Their prophytes get to see how we get down and play around with people that can't do anything whether we are wrong or right.

Tashina asks to hit Caya's blunt. I'm watching the prophytes and my line pass the blunt around. I keep drinking out the bottle.

"Girl I work at Ryan's Bar and Seafood Spot," Amy says. "I have all the ingredients in my car to make you a nice fancy drink. Don't worry. I got ice too. Come with me to my car."

I go with Amy to her car and she makes me a Blastball Margarita. She hooks this damn drink the fuck up. It has Tequila and Patron in it. She's about to go back in Hollow's Cave, but I say, "Wait girl. Chill with me for a minute in the car. You want to get in mine or stay in yours?"

"Let's get in your car," Amy says.

I can hear Caya and Shemina yelling at the pledges. The pledges are getting hit with wooden paddles that they made themselves. Trayna doesn't get hit that much because she's already fucked up from being jumped. The rest of the pledges asses are turning red though. My Sorors are screaming all of these things.

Amy gets in my car. We sit in the backseat. She's rolling a blunt too.

"You don't mind right?" Amy asks. "I see you don't smoke."

"No I don't mind. You see my girls smoke in front of me. I actually love the smell of it still," I say. "I know I shouldn't. If I quit, I quit, but I still cheat and take the scent in whenever I can."

Amy starts laughing. She's a young college student, but I can tell she's thirty at heart. She's not nervous at all smoking or drinking around me. She seems like a real party girl. She doesn't choke or cough when she hears the pledges screaming while being hit with wood. They're still trying to recite their information as one.

"Why'd you quit?" Amy asks me.

"I just thought I needed to. It didn't hurt to spend less money either," I say. I don't want to offend anyone when I say the side effects were whooping my ass. They still are, but I don't want to detail them or risk Amy telling my line sisters. They still enjoy it, and I'm not one to get in no damn debate about no damn drugs.

People that love to smoke get offended and mad real easy when they hear about the truth when it comes to drugs. Some of them are already experiencing side effects and don't want to quit. They sure as hell don't want anyone hounding them on stopping.

"So how you like bringing in a line?" I ask.

"Girl to be honest, I could've done without this," Amy says. "I mean, don't get me wrong, it's cool knowing I can tell people I did my damn thing bringing in some new Sorors, but got damn, this takes up a lot of my time and my damn money." I start laughing. "That's why I don't care about the damn girl getting her money taken by Shemina," Amy says. "Hell, my damn money is disappearing itself dealing with this pledging process. I'm tired of feeding them damn girls and wasting my gas."

Amy has me cracking up.

Tashina comes and gets in my car. She has a drink with me and Amy. She's tired of watching the pledges get hit. She says they still keep messing up on the history and now they're acting like they have pronunciation issues. Tashina starts mocking some of the pledges and imitating how they are sounding and acting.

I'm laughing because of how nonchalant Greek life makes people. Of course after being hit with wood, the pledges gone start struggling.

"They are crying rivers," Tashina says. "Let me get some." I pass her my cup.

I always hope that something happens so the night can end early. Don't get me wrong, I do want the pledges to be hazed just as much as I was, but sometimes I just want to turn around and punch somebody because I'm still mad at all the time I spent bringing a line in. My girls and I don't have to show up and help, but we wanted to because we knew the new prophytes and pledges would talk about us and keep our names swirling around Cupperton University.

"You want to hit this?" Amy asks Tashina.

"You know I do," Tashina says. "Where the lighter?" Amy passes her a lighter.

I'm in a car with two college kids getting they smoke on. I miss these days. My car windows are down, but I'm still enjoying the smell of the weed.

"They about to be reciting information for a while," Tashina says. "Let's go to the gas station and get some snacks."

We're not supposed to leave, but we are. Hopefully no one comes looking for us. On the drive, I tell the girls how members of Phi Phi Alpha got arrested when we went out to eat.

"I'm not surprised at all," Amy says. "Them frat boys be on one. I dated a few boys in fraternities that I knew before they pledged. I know they go through hella more shit than we do because the person they become after is nothing like the person I knew before."

"That's what we hope for our pledges in the end though," I say. "We want them to be stronger individuals and have no fear when it comes to handling things that life throws at them. This world is not made for the weak."

"I mean damn though," Amy says. "All the nice qualities I once knew my boys had all went out the door. I mean don't get me wrong. In public they'll put on a front, but behind closed doors they have real anger built up and real frustration. It's like they can't get over any of the things they went through."

"You have to excuse her," Tashina says. "She's real bitter because some of the people she's dated put they hands on her."

"They never did before they joined they damn fraternity," Amy says. "Two of the boys I dated that pledged, ended up hitting me while they were pledging and after they crossed."

I pull up to a gas station and fill my tank. Tashina and Amy go get some snacks. I notice them start talking to two men that are standing outside of the store drinking beer. I hope they know them because Tashina has her ass resting on one of their thighs, and Amy is letting the other one kiss all over her.

There's a liquor store across the street. Tashina and Amy go with the two men over there and don't tell me a damn thing. Never again will I be taking these young girls with me anywhere. I'm not even in the mood to ruin their fun though. I just want this night to be over with. I had too much fun at Caya's house for me to be ending the night with a bunch of damn pledges and they prophytes.

I get a parking spot and lean on my car. I see some people talking to each other in different cars discussing the club they're about to go to. Based off how the conversation moves around, they're six cars deep going out tonight. They're on the road and some of them are switching cars. The light turns green and people that aren't a part of their party start honking at them. That doesn't make the girls walking in their heels move any faster. They curse at the people honking at them and continue to take their time. One of the girls bends over and has a conversation through the car window.

People keep honking at them, but that doesn't stop another girl from getting out the car. To my surprise, the six cars leave and this girl is not in one of them. She's still walking. I guess this girl isn't going to the club. She's out to make money.

I'm shaking my damn head.

Tashina and Amy have my nerves bad now. They're still over at the liquor store standing outside and talking. I hope them niggas bought them something to drink. I drive across the street and park. It doesn't hit me until after a few minutes of sitting in my car, that Tashina and Amy probably wanted me to do that the whole time. I know these two damn girls not trying to make me out to be no dumb ass which is how I'm starting to feel.

I hope they are not expecting me to act like a big sister and get out and meet these two fools. For one, these men have no respect. They keep touching and kissing Tashina and Amy all in

154

public. I am supposed to be correcting their behavior; however, I don't feel like it tonight. Plus, I hate when Sorors know better than to do something, but do it anyway because they know I have to do something about it. Then I feel like Tashina and Amy are really some stupid ass hoes who make people correct their behavior, but won't stop any damn ways. I don't want to waste any energy on these two fools.

My mind gets lazy and takes me to a bad place.

I'm thinking about what I told Nadia. The assault is a nightmare I have often. Actually, Nadia is more of a nightmare. My grandma always wakes me up though. My grandma passed away the year I graduated. Every now and then I feel like she's still alive and comes to sit and talk to me.

"That's what real love can do," my grandmother says popping up in my car. She quickly disappears. I keep having flashes of her making me feel like she's still alive.

My mind floats to another day.

It was a day when I was walking unsure in my room and hopped into a visual of me clothed in white.

I was saying, "Well I'm beautiful. I'm pretty and cute. Anybody would date me. It's not my fault I look good. Even with my hair not done, I still look good. Other girls are jealous of me. There's people that wish they were me. Nothing bad rushes to my head when I think of my looks. I am uniquely and beautifully made. My hair is the perfect length. I am the perfect height. I never wanted to be someone else. I've overcame so many things with all the haters in my life. I'm a lovely girl." I said all of this in my head.

After I finished saying that, somehow I got out of that girl clothed in white.

Then I remembered what Nadia said to me after I told her about those big kids that assaulted me. She told me about Jania saying I hurt those boys, and she told me right before bed.

Then I hopped out of that thought and was curious to who kept helping me get out of these blackouts that were strong enough to make me walk off a bridge.

Then I was stormed with the words, "Tell her that's why I did it." It was my grandma.

I was very curious to who could be so strong and get me out of the trances I was having. I went from complimenting myself, to remembering Nadia's hate words, to wondering how I kept being pushed to keep loving myself, to hearing my grandma's voice.

I recognized that the girl who kept complimenting herself reached a state in her life where she needed family love. She was going to think she didn't have any. She was walking blinded. However, my grandma told me she loved me all along.

My grandma popped up in my room. "Was she about to kill herself?" I asked. "Was she really about to exit this world after reciting such good thoughts about herself?"

I hadn't heard my grandma's voice since I was in high school. Nadia actually let me talk to my grandma on the phone. It was shocking because Nadia was mean as hell to me in high school.

The day Nadia allowed me to speak to my grandma, my grandma spoke to me in a way that had me thinking she had something else she wanted to tell me, but never did.

My grandma always said she had some tricks up her sleeve. She had to for Nadia to have given me the phone. I talked to her the summer before my senior year in high school. I was very unsure of something when my grandma hung up with me. I barely could understand what she wanted to say. She wasn't pronouncing everything correctly, and her speech was chopped up. Somehow, I knew she was speaking to me exactly how she wanted to. She knew something was wrong with Nadia.

I remember sitting on the couch when I hung up with my grandma. I can remember the phone was located right next to the computer in the living room. My mouth was opened and I looked quizzical. I looked the same way Nadia had me looking without any love from her.

The difference was my grandma did love me and speak to me with love. She wanted me to see that anything Nadia did, she could fix it. A lot of my grandma's words were broken a part. I started to blame it on her being so old. Now that I'm older, I know she knew I would do that.

Looking back on that summer, I was afraid. My grandma knew Nadia was the type to listen on the phone when I was on it. I made sure to really keep with me how my grandma shook me after speaking with me that summer. I took that with me my senior year of high school.

I'm really in my feelings.

I'm seeing visuals of my grandma. "Sit up straight," my grandma says. "Hold your head up high." I keep spacing off thinking of her in different ways.

Nadia wanted to show me that anything good I was thinking was trash. That's how I should die. If that was successful, then she'd have felt like she was right all along in me not existing.

The difference between how Nadia hates and how I hate is, Nadia sees an individual and has a need to torture the individual by any means or studies necessary to get them to die. Me, once I wake up to the bullshit, I don't see an individual. I see nothing. Nothing that can move and talk. What it says will never matter. It has a function and that's for any actions it does to be as clear as the wind and as nonexistent as the last thought it had or movement it did.

"Good girl," I hear my grandma say.

I was supposed to die in a rant of me saying nothing but good things about myself with no love present from family. Well no love that I was aware of. Then a love so sharp cut through that and kept me alive. Who the hell hit me in my grown woman mind like that, I thought.

"I loved you all along," my grandma says.

I snap back to reality when I hear a woman sounding disgusted and shocked.

"Is this your man?" a woman walking up to the store asks Amy.

"No. He my fling for the night," Amy says. Her and Tashina start laughing. "I'm just joking," Amy continues. "He's real cool."

"Okay because I thought I saw him kissing on another girl the last time I was here," the woman walking up to the store says. "I wanted to make sure I wasn't trippin'."

"I don't give a damn who it was," Amy says. "This man bought me drinks."

"Don't get smart," the woman opens the store door and says.

"You can continue on in the store," Tashina says.

"You wouldn't want to make those cops across the street work tonight would you?" Amy asks the woman who's continuing on in the store.

"Whether you over here or on your corner, they'll get you eventually," the woman says. The store door closes behind her.

Amy sounds like a cheap hoe. I've never known anyone like her. Some people go to college and just don't know how to act. I bet Amy's reputation is fucked up at Cupperton. She never knows who lives around this damn store. She's in a sorority so a lot of people gone know her that she doesn't even know exist.

I'm sitting in my car drinking. I don't feel like going back to the cave. Them pledges gone be reciting information for a good minute. I'm not in no rush. I don't even care who the hell gets mad that I left and didn't say nothing. Tashina goes in the store and comes out with small toy water guns. She gives one to Amy and they shoot the two men. They're having a good old time outside of this liquor store. I'm starting to think these two girls don't give a damn about me sitting in this damn car.

Austin's calling me. "How's the cult meeting?" he laughs.

"Ha, ha, ha," I sarcastically say. "You know damn well I'd rather be with you. It'd be better if you were here."

"True. I'm at home. I'm not doing nothing. You want me to stop by?" Austin asks.

"I'm not even there," I say. "I took two of the girls to the store. I didn't even care to tell no one we was leaving."

"You thinking about your grandma again?" Austin asks.

I space off.

I start thinking about when my grandma called me my senior year again. She spoke in way to say she was patient, and that she understood that I kept losing my speech at times in school.

She knew Nadia had my mind in a confused state, which now I know was her practicing, trying to get me to commit suicide.

"It wasn't practice," my grandma says. "She had the strategy down pact. But she never knew me." I see my grandma sitting in front of me at my dining room table.

The drugs keep taking my damn thoughts and running with them. I can't wait for these symptoms to go away. I regret using marijuana so much.

"You are to never touch that stuff again," my grandma says. "Does it make sense for young folks to copy who they consider are original gangsters, and do drugs with the effects you know they have?" my grandma asks. "Do you think we really wanted to continue smoking when we started having them symptoms? There's a lot of evil going on around here and mind manipulation Shona. There are some real bitter people out here."

With the drugs taking my memory and instant thoughts, I sometimes start wondering where the love is in my life. I have to literally recite the entire story about the girl dressed in white, to Nadia's hateful words, to my grandmother's words repeatedly to feel and find the love.

I always start with telling myself I talked to Nadia for at least thirty minutes about the assault and she brought up Jania saying I harmed my step brother and his cousin. Then I have to say I hopped into a coma with myself with no love in it, and the girl kept saying good things about herself. Then I have to say I hopped out of her not knowing who kept releasing me and remembered what Nadia said after the assault conversation.

Then I listen to my grandmother say, "Tell her that's why I did it. A mother's love is serious," my grandma says. "Nadia is crazy. But she'll never know how crazy I am."

"Babe, you there?" Austin asks. I snap back into reality.

I pick my phone off the floor. I'm glad I didn't crack the damn screen.

"You know I have," I say.

"What?" Austin asks.

"I mean yes I'm here," I say. "And you know I have been thinking about my grandma."

"Just tell your girls that and they should understand," Austin says. "It's not the first time you done acted out of the usual because you can't deal with her being gone."

"I know, but they deal with relatives that's passed too. I can't keep using that excuse," I say.

"Well I'm bored as hell," Austin says. "Come see me when y'all done."

"No. Talk to me for a second," I say. "Tashina and Amy are no fucking fun for me at all. They underage asses bet not get carded tonight. They don't have any self-worth when it comes to men. Ugh. They are just disgusting."

"I can hook them up with some of my frat brothers. They'll mess with any damn body," Austin laughs.

"That's not funny," I say. "I'm gone let you go though. I need to get back to the cave."

We've been gone a while. I tell Tashina and Amy that we need to leave. When they get in the car, I'm as fake as I want to be. I don't show any signs of being annoyed. I let them think I have no problem with how they acted tonight. I know some young people like to be around older people that don't care what they do, but in this damn sorority we're supposed to act like ladies. They know I know that and could get in trouble for watching them act like hoes, but I don't care.

We get back to the cave and the first thing I hear is, "Alpha Eta Nu was founded on the campus of Julliard Univesity in 1913," come from the pledges' mouths. My mouth drops to the floor. Me, Tashina, and Amy walk out the cave and reenter. If we're still hearing the information, these pledges must really be fucking up.

Caya and Asayla look at me and laugh.

"We just fucking with y'all," Caya says. "We didn't know where the hell you went, so we thought we'd scare you and make it seem like we didn't get nowhere."

"You sure as hell scared us," Telana says. "We like to know where our girl is. You know that."

160

"Especially when you run off with two youngsters that we could give a fuck about," Asayla whispers in my ear.

"Well did they at least figure out what they were fucking up on with the information?" I ask.

"Hell no," Caya says.

These damn girls are going to have to pass tests to be in this sorority. It doesn't matter how many sets they come to, if they can't get a B or higher on their Alpha Eta Nu tests, none of this hazing matters. No one will ever believe they went through the process.

Caya says they moved on to more things the pledges were supposed to learn. These pledges are on one. They were instructed to learn everyone's first, middle, and last name on their line in alphabetical order with the last names. Caya has them say the names and they say them in any order.

Telana has the girls line up shortest to tallest and lean backwards. They need to hold this position until they necks fall off. Not knowing their line sisters' names is a huge fucking problem, even if it is twenty-three of them. Two of the pledges in the middle that are linked together start to struggle and fall over. The whole line collapses to the floor.

"Uh unh," I say. "Why the hell are y'all taking so long to get up?"

My Sorors and I look at this lines' prophytes with disgust. We're not sure why these girls don't know their information and think it's okay to take their time getting up on a broken line.

"Hurry the hell up!" Tashina yells.

My line sisters' let Tashina and her crew take over for a few minutes. They take three silver chairs out of Amy's trunk and place them in the center of the cave with water balloons on them. The first three chosen pledges stand in front of the chairs.

"How'd you guys punish them when I was gone?" I ask Telana.

"We made them hold their mouths open and put peppers on them," Telana says. "Then we blindfolded them and held flames behind them while they walked around the cave."

"At the sound of my whistle, sit down quickly," Tashina tells the three pledges in front of the chairs.

When the whistle blows, two of the girls sit down and get they asses soaked, and one of them doesn't. She says she's too scared because she never knows what to expect.

One of the other prophytes named Kilana pushes the remaining pledge down. Kilana makes the pledges stand up and hits their asses with a belt. She unblindfolds the three girls and has them dry the chairs and place more water balloons on them.

"Go to Soror Amy and recite your information again," Tashina says to the three girls that got soaked. All of the pledges go through the same process: sit on water balloons, get they asses hit, then have to recite the information again to Amy.

I'm mad as hell about Tashina and Amy going to the liquor store and waiting for me to drive over to them. I'm not sure how to take that shit, but I'm not about to leave feeling like they think I will do what they want, and I'm definitely not about to be feeling stupid.

"Tashina and Amy are two damn hoes," I tell Casha. Casha's one of the messy girls on our line that likes to clown dumb ass girls. She also doesn't play no games when she thinks one of her line sisters are bothered about something and doesn't really want to talk about it.

"What's up? What they do?" Casha asks me.

"Girl come talk to me for a second," I say.

Casha and I go stand off to the side in the cave. I tell her about how Tashina and Amy were all up on some men that they didn't even know. Then I tell her how they just walked they asses off with they new company and started getting more drunk with them as if I wasn't even there.

"No them two bitches didn't," Casha says loud enough for everyone to hear. Some of the pledges and prophytes look over at us.

"Talk lower," I say not really caring that everyone heard her.

"No, because I don't appreciate them acting ignorant with you there," Casha says. "They might not be well known, but we sure as hell do our got damn thing around this city and people know us."

"I thought I saw some Sorors and wanted to do the call, but I was scared they would know I was with the two college girls that don't know how to act," I lie.

I just don't care at all to start tension between my line and these young ass prophytes. They have me severely fucked up making them damn men think their presence is stronger than mine when we are out. They didn't even introduce me to them.

Casha sparks her blunt.

"I say we make these damn pledges do some things in public," Casha says. "Since they prophytes don't know how to act, let's make the pledges pay for it and ridicule Tashina and Amy's asses in the process."

"What you got in mind?" I ask.

"I'll think of something," Casha says. "Let's get through this first. Grab those towels so they asses can dry off. Now we got to wait for they asses to change clothes."

The pledges don't get to change clothes before holding the squat position along the wall and reciting the history of the organization. Tashina makes them do it wet.

"It's only your asses that's wet," Amy says.

The pledges keep messing up on the information. They had to memorize it in a particular order too, and some of them forgot that. They're mixing up dates and places. It just keeps getting worse. However, we knew it would. If they didn't know it the first time, there's no way without the sorority history packet that they would figure it out. We've heard them say it wrong plenty of times to know they won't have it right by the end of the night. Their prophytes aren't helping them out at all either. It might be because me and my girls are here and they want to seem real tough.

Kilana lets the girls change clothes, then has them sit on the ground.

"Ladies we cannot let you slack off," Kilana says. "Next year you might be doing the same thing we are. Make no mistake about it, you girls are not Greeks yet, and this opportunity can be taken from you at any moment."

Kilana has two of the pledges stand back-to-back. She makes them keep bending down and standing straight up. Whoever falls has to do push-ups. Whoever remains standing has to take on the challenge with the next pledge.

Casha is looking at me with a smirk on her face. I'm starting to regret telling her about Tashina and Amy. Now I sort of feel like a loser in the eyes of my line sister. I know Casha is cool though. She never cares what any of her sorority sisters says. If we need her to do some dirt, she'll do it.

My girls are laughing at the pledges that bend down and can't get back up. Not one person here is giving a damn about the weight difference amongst these girls. I hope none of they asses bust they damn head on this hard ass cave ground.

Casha, Caya, and Telana are smoking. I'm getting memories about when I used to smoke. The dreams I would have were so much better when I was high. Now I have to get rid of these symptoms and try to remember what my dreams were like before I started smoking.

Fuck it. I'm about to take my anger from not being able to smoke out on these girls. I'm so embarrassed and feel like a loser. I know the pledges are wondering why I'm the only one not hitting the blunt.

After the pledges do their back-to-back exercise, I take the floor.

"Okay pledges. Let's make a horizontal line, and I want everyone to stretch their hands out in front of them," I say. "Make it fast." The girls quickly line up side by side. "Shortest to tallest!" I demand.

"Tashina, what the hell is wrong with this line?" Casha asks. "Why the hell don't they automatically line up shortest to tallest?"

"They must've woke up on the wrong side of the bed," Tashina says.

Amy and Kilana laugh a little then look at me and my Sorors and stop.

"I don't see nothing funny," Casha says.

I have the pledges do a ripple effect of squatting and standing with their arms out in front.

"I'm testing your peripheral vision," I say. "Y'all been fucking up all night. Maybe there is something really wrong with y'all."

I'm circling around the girls reciting the Greek alphabet. My Sorors and Tashina's line join in with me after my third time saying it. I swear if one of these pledges falls or loses balance, I'm going to lose my mind. There's twenty-three of them, so there's no way that anyone should get tired when they are doing a ripple effect.

We must've sang the Greek alphabet ten times before I say, "Nu, Omicron, Pi, and Rho," and space off. I'm still circling the girls. I'm just not singing or paying attention to anyone.

"At least it will be on they minds that I called the cops," I remember myself saying to Nadia. "Instead of them going home with nothing bothering their fucked-up minds about how they accomplished some bullshit of harming an innocent person. I know they'll remember the cops were called."

Nadia knew I was recovering from drugs too. I should have never told her ugly ass that. I was already angry because there were times I kept losing my thoughts because I was recovering from using drugs. I couldn't get my thoughts out in order sometimes. Other times I couldn't remember what the next event that took place was. I usually am stabilized when I'm engaged in a conversation.

I snap out of it and pay attention to the pledges.

The girls are still singing the Greek alphabet when I come back to myself.

"And Omega too," Casha says in my ear. I squat down and put my head in my hands. "You alright?" Casha asks me.

"I'm fine," I say irritated. I hate when I lose my conscious because of the hate Nadia gave me. If only she would've been a good mother, I would have better thoughts and wouldn't space off so much. She's fucked up my brain. I need to get myself together.

165

I'm mad as hell. I've only told the pledges to do one thing, and my mind has already gone to a bad place.

"Alright," Casha says moving backwards with her hands up. "I just want to make sure my girl don't need me to whoop somebody ass."

"That's your sister," Caya says not liking my tone. "Get it together Shona. We all got shit going on."

I have the pledges make two rows and interlock arms. I recite some of the Greek alphabet and pick someone randomly to say the word that is next. Every time someone messes up, they have to close their eyes and take three steps backwards. If they hesitate while stepping backwards, they get blindfolded and hit with wood. They also have to keep the blindfold on until we move onto another exercise.

I know some of the pledges smoke, so I ask Telana and Caya who have their blunts, to come closer to the pledges. I give Caya's blunt to Scalina.

"Go ahead and take a puff," I say.

Scalina does as she is told. I let two more pledges take a puff and have the girls sit on the ground.

"I'm not as mean as you think," I continue. "We have been here a while, but no one is ready to leave. Anyone know why?"

"We don't know the information like we should," Scalina says.

"And you don't know you need permission to talk," Caya says disgusted.

I have all the girls lay on their backs on the ground. They're doing leg lifts.

"I don't think they had enough peppers," Amy says. "All this damn speaking out of turn."

Caya is pouring water over some of the pledges faces.

"This is for all that whispering at my house," Caya says.

"If that is you choking, please sit the hell up," I say.

I'm kicking some of the girls' legs.

Tashina and Amy are placing the paddles the pledges made on a table. These paddles are decorated nicely and my line and I can tell the pledges put a lot of time into them. The paddles have the prophytes names on them and their line names. The paddles have glitter, ribbons, strings, colored cotton balls, and stickers on them.

Some of my Sorors go to the table and keep saying how much they admire the work the pledges can do. Some of their prophytes look jealous.

"I need all of the pledges attention really quick," Tashina says. I have them sit up on the ground.

Tashina puts all of the paddles in the trash with a smile on her face.

"This girl is a fucking bitch," Telana says. "She knows she didn't have to do that shit."

"You seem to be developing sympathy for these girls," I say.

"I think I'm getting so tired, that recognizing how much money went into them damn paddles caught me by surprise," Telana says. "We should have made paddles with our line names on them."

"It's never too late," I say.

My line name is *The One*. Caya's line name is *Unique*. Deliana's line name is *Straight Up*. Casha's line name is *Turned Up*. Telana's line name is *Terror Traits*. Shemina's line name is *Baby Girl*. Asayla's line name is *Red Rojo*.

My prophytes said they named me The One because they loved my stepping ability. They said they never met someone so talented as me when it came to stepping. I was their *go to* girl whenever they needed a routine. They said anytime someone would talk to them about stepping, they would always think of me.

"Look Shona. Some of them are crying," Telana says to me.

"No need to cry ladies," Tashina says. "You can always make another one on your own time."

I whisper to Casha and ask if she has something in mind yet to do to the girls in public. She says yes. Casha tells our line sisters what the plan is while I still watch over the pledges.

I have the girls crawl and follow me to the door. Then I allow them to stand before they get outside. Some of the pledges are saying the Greek alphabet on their way out.

"Big Sister Shona you have a beautiful voice," Scalina says.

"Speak when spoken to," Tashina says.

I say thank you to Scalina because I can't stand Tashina at the moment.

When we get on the road, Casha calls all of the pledges and has them meet us at Caya's house. She's not informing their prophytes because there's no need to. We know the pledges will tell them what happens tonight anyway. I don't need to see Tashina and Amy mad. Just knowing they are is enough for me.

We're at Caya's house just to meet up and make sure we're all together, as well as make sure their prophytes are long gone. I let everyone know about Tashina and Amy's behavior.

"Girl some fucking college kids don't have no fucking sense," Caya says. "I'm glad we didn't have to bring in none of them damn girls. They fucking slow as fuck. Why the hell would they be bringing in a line and acting like that?"

"They know people talk," Shemina says.

"All they gone do is take they frustration out on they pledges if they wind up finding out about it," I say. "They do need they ignorant asses beat more though."

"They couldn't recite anything completely tonight," Deliana says.

Casha pulls next to Scalina and tells her to go to the liquor store I was at and start an argument with one of her line sisters about two girls that were flirting with two men they didn't know. She tells Scalina to make sure she acknowledges that the two men were touching all on the girls. She also tells Scalina to make sure she says how two ladies should act when they are around strangers.

"I want everyone to end up getting in on this argument," Casha says. "Talk to three or four of your sisters at a time. You always remain outside dictating the lesson. Don't let me down."

The pledges pull off.

My girls and I know the girls will do it because they are fearful of us, but we still want hard evidence and that's witnessing it. They think we are always watching them.

Now me and my line sisters are trying to figure out who is going to spy on the girls. We're talking to each other from our cars and calling the ones we can't hear. It doesn't take all of us to go.

In the midst of our phone conversations, Shemina says, "Shit. I found my fucking money."

"What? Where was it?" I ask.

"In my damn glove compartment. I was looking in it to make sure I put my registration back in it, and my money fell out," Shemina says.

I'm mad as hell. All that damn time we wasted on them pledges trying to help this damn girl, and she forgot she put it in her damn glove compartment. She's the damn reason we leaving later than we fucking wanted to.

"I'll go check on the girls," Asayla says. "By the time we come to a conclusion, we won't know for sure if they did what the hell we said."

Asayla pulls off.

"So are you going to return Trayna's money?" Caya asks Shemina while she sparks her blunt.

"I don't think I should," Shemina says. "Them niggas didn't remember half the shit they needed to. They have packets with all the information on them. They didn't have to go search for anything. You know all the things prophytes and alumni have to do for them damn pledges. Them niggas can't even show up prepared to recite the information. They are ungrateful bitches. That's only one damn pledge who's short forty dollars. She will be okay. One of her damn sisters will probably spare her the damn money anyways. They don't fucking respect they damn prophytes enough to come prepared. If discipline doesn't teach them nothing, maybe knowing we'll take they damn money will."

I think the pledges are wrong for not knowing they information, but I do think Shemina should give the girl her money back. That's one thing we never did to our line of pledges was rob them. They're in college, and that mess is high as hell as it is. We don't know what any of their living situations

169

are, and we sure as hell don't know why she was even carrying forty dollars on her. Their prophytes know if any of the girls have difficult living situations, but me and my girls don't.

"If she really needed that money for whatever reasons, one of their prophytes would have said something," Caya says. "Girl don't worry about giving that girl that damn money."

"I'm headed home," Casha says. The rest of the girls go home too.

When I get home, I get straight in the shower. Living alone is boring as hell. I need some company. I'm still not happy about going to the store with Tashina and Amy. Had I had known they would act like sluts, I would've never left the cave. I sure as hell wouldn't have made my girls uneasy about me leaving without saying anything.

Asayla calls me laughing. "Girl I cannot get tired of this story," Asayla says. "Scalina is quite the fucking actress. She really is giving a great performance talking about acting like women."

"None of the store workers are bothering them?" I ask.

"Girl no. It's good we only had a few of them get out their cars at once," Asayla says. "And you know how it is around here. As long as no one is shooting, nobody gone bother us."

"What is Scalina saying?" I ask.

"At first she was going on and on about how no one should just let strangers touch all over them and how people need to have respect for their bodies," Asayla says. "I started dying laughing when she said she knew members of Alpha Eta Nu would never do that. If only she knew her damn leaders were the ones acting like whores."

"How long you been watching them?" I ask.

"When I got here, they were just getting out of their cars," Asayla says. "I didn't miss nothing."

"Hold up," I say. "Didn't we let them leave way ahead of you?"

"Hell yea," Asayla says. "Them damn girls didn't give a fuck. After all the hell we put them through tonight, they still act all nonchalant."

170

"Girl, Scalina not making up any names for her story is she?" I ask.

"Girl, she not using any names," Asayla says. "Some people walking in the store are blown away by her good performance and are asking her who she's talking about, and say they will beat the hell out of them."

"I can't believe Tashina and Amy," I say. "People were walking by with their kids. I mean people on the road waiting at the lights could see they asses. I don't know how the hell they don't care that people could see them."

"They was probably raised by some fucked up people," Asayla says.

"People could have recorded them. We wouldn't know," I say.

"Girl I'm drinking. I'm still here watching this live movie. I need to go get me some more blunt wraps," Asayla says. "I don't want them to see me though."

"Girl go get you some wraps," I say. "The only way I would say don't go in the store is if you were Tashina and Amy because the store workers would recognize you."

"Okay hold on," Asayla says. "I'm gone go in real quick."

I'm feeling like being messy right now. I want them bitches to know it was Tashina and Amy for a fact. I know if they tell their prophytes the story, their prophytes will just act like it wasn't them acting like whores. I want them to know I was pissed off about their behavior. I definitely want them to know that we took our frustration out on their pledges and told them their prophytes were acting like sluts and whores.

I'm trying to figure out how to go about the situation. I could have Asayla tell them while she's in their faces. I think I would rather be with Casha when I give them the news.

"Girl I'm back," Asayla says. "Why are the pledges getting some men to buy them a drink? Oh shit."

"What?" I ask.

"Why the hell are they talking about us?" Asayla says.

"Girl didn't you just walk by them?" I ask. "What do you mean they talking about us?" I know these pledges aren't that

171

disrespectful and nonchalant to a point where they just saw Asayla and are now disrespecting our line.

"I didn't go in the store," Asayla says. "When I saw they interrupted their performance by talking to some men, I sat back in the car. I couldn't even bring myself to speak. I want to know what all they about to say."

"Let me know what you see," I say.

"They smoking and drinking," Asayla says. "They saying we ain't shit. Just bitter black bitches who need to get a life."

"Oh really," I say.

"Girl I'm done," Asayla says. "I'm going home. These pledges ain't shit."

"Go get your wraps," I say.

"Oh yea. Let me do that," Asayla says.

I hear some of the pledges speak to Asayla when she walks by.

"Don't look all shocked now," Asayla rudely says. "Don't even trip. Y'all might not even see my line again."

"Girl I feel you on that," I say. "Something is not right with these pledges and they damn prophytes. Some of them seem a little strange."

"We're just playing around," Trayna says.

"I'm rolling my blunt," Asayla says when she gets in her car. She sounds angry as all hell. I know that weed will calm her down.

"I say we don't waste our damn time no more on them niggas," I say.

I'm mad as hell. The pledges are definitely on our nerves, but we are not supposed to be hazing them in the first place, so it's not like we can do anything when they don't obey us. We just have to wait until the next time that we see them at set. We sure as hell threaten them enough so that they will be scared to snitch, but the reality is they can do it at any moment. If for some reason we see them again at another set, we'll just take our frustration out then. Our whole line doesn't even have to attend the set. If two or three of our members visit the new lines' set, then we can just tell them some things we want to be

172

done. Either way, we can get our revenge for dealing with bullshit ass pledges whenever we want.

I hang up with Asayla and call Casha. I already forgot what I just told Asayla. I want to go see what them damn pledges are doing on my own. I just want Casha to be with me instead of Asayla. My mood is all over the place. I'm thinking about my grandma and I'm missing how weed would make me feel.

"I'm on my way," Casha says. She's coming to my house and we're going to drive to the liquor store. I tell her everything that Asayla said.

"Speaking of her, she's calling me right now," Casha says. "I'm gone let her know you told me everything."

I ask Casha what she was doing at home, and she says nothing but enjoying sitting by her fireplace. Tonight was a waste of time for her. She wants to think of something else to make the pledges do.

I tell her we should just make them act out the same skit again. I want to see it. I don't care if it does ruin how they feel being drunk and high.

"Call them and tell them we're going to watch them," Casha says.

I let the pledges know. They lie and say they aren't there anymore. I pull up and they still are.

I call them and tell them to look at my car. All the pledges look shocked when they see me and Casha. Me and my girl smirk at them and laugh. We slap hands and Casha smokes and drinks while I only drink.

"We want the same performance from the beginning," I say.

Scalina orchestrates the girls on what to do. It's like she not even drunk and high no more. She seems to have her right mind back. That's what fear of alumni from my chapter can do.

The girls are starting off with just a few of them talking about two girls that act like sluts and whores and let men do whatever they want to them.

"Why would anyone want men thinking that women are easy and vulnerable?" Scalina is asking her line sisters. "How could those two girls get any sleep knowing they let perverts go home thinking they are real men by devaluing a woman?"

The pledges are agreeing with Scalina and trying to calm her down. Some are arguing with her saying that this isn't the place to be giving a lecture. This is their way of letting the store workers know that they are trying to calm down Scalina and they don't have to come see what the problem is.

Asayla was definitely telling the truth about these girls giving a stellar performance.

The pledges are flirting with each other and feeling on each other acting like they think me and Casha want them to act. Some of them are telling the seductive ones why they should straighten up and act like women.

"At least we know each other," Trayna says.

"So what," Scalina says. "We in public."

Me and Casha are laughing. Scalina is getting teary eyed talking about women that devalue themselves. Only now, her ass is drunk and high as hell in public, so she seems like she's making a mockery of her own damn self. She can handle her liquor really well though.

There's some other people in cars watching Scalina and the pledges performance. Some are eating, some are high, some are drunk, and some are sitting with their kids. I know when I don't know the people in front of the liquor store that are drunk and high, I just hope they don't start no fights or start shooting.

"I wish I would've went with you to the store with Tashina and Amy," Casha says.

"Girl you didn't want to see that shit," I say.

"Yes I did," Casha says. "Watching these girls would've been a lot more fun if I had seen the original material."

"I feel like Tashina and Amy think I am a joke because I didn't stop them from acting a fool," I say.

"Girl it is not your fault them damn girls don't know how to act," Casha says. "But if you want, let's get on the pledges case about being dumb asses. You know when they get older they'll wish they still knew girls who knew how to check them when they were young and foolish."

174

I'm looking like I don't know what I want to do. Casha is a real bitch though. She's my down ass girl. Casha looks at me and says, "Girl let's show these girls that we real women that got our shit together."

Me and Casha get out the car and slap a few of the pledges. We ask them what the hell is wrong with them?

"We didn't actually think y'all would bring y'all asses out here and do it," I say.

"Y'all know better than to be in public and acting stupid," Casha says. "We could all get in trouble."

"Look, y'all drunk and high as hell," I say. "Y'all not supposed to do all the shit we say. Sometimes we want to know if y'all got sense. How the hell you gone be talking about bitches acting like tramps in public, and here y'all are touching on each other and flirting?"

Casha slaps Scalina.

"You gone have to do better," Casha says. "I feel like some of them damn bitches are jealous of you. That's why they always getting on your case." She's talking to Scalina.

"We all been in y'all shoes," I say. "Y'all are way better than this."

"Let this be a lesson to y'all," Casha says.

"We supposed to be sisters one day," I say. "We just trying to wreck y'all minds a little so that when y'all get older y'all won't be out here stupid to what the real world can do to you. Mutha fuckas don't care where you end up."

"Get in y'all cars so we can go," Casha says.

"And hurry the hell up!" I yell.

"I'm mad as hell they lied to us about not being here. What's going on at the sorority houses tonight? Are any of them poppin'?" Casha asks me.

"Let me hit up my girl that goes to Pepton Nickel University," I say. "She cool. She graduating this year too."

"Wasup Shona!" Chaysa says.

"Hey baby girl. I love and miss you," I say.

I met Chaysa at the mall. We were both buying some decorations for our house around Christmas time. I was drunk at the store, so I asked her what color pattern I should get for my Christmas lights. I had all white and a mixed color pattern box in my hand. Chaysa said that I should just get both. She said she could never make up her mind when buying Christmas lights herself.

I never met anyone that was just like me when it came to buying things for Christmas. Everyone I talk to about purchasing things around Christmas is stingy as hell when it comes to they money, and always can make up their mind on purchasing specific things. They never need to purchase two of one thing because they can't figure out which color they like. They can't get past all the money they spend on buying Christmas gifts.

"I love you too," Chaysa says.

"Girl you having a party or what?" I ask. "I'm so happy to hear your voice."

"It's just me, my sisters, and some of Phi Phi Alpha," Chaysa says. Alpha Eta Nu is always with Phi Phi Alpha fraternity because they are considered our brother fraternity.

"Listen, we been dealing with some of our pledges from Cupperton tonight and they just been acting an ass," I say. "Can we come through?"

"Girl hell yea," Chaysa says. "Let's get they asses straight."

"They drunk and high as hell too," I say.

"That's alright," Chaysa says. "We have extra clothes and unopened packages of panties and bras here for the girls to stay the night. Make sure they hit up whoever they need to and make up something good so they can stay the night at the sorority house."

Me, Chaysa, and Casha are laughing. Using the sorority as an excuse for the girls to stay out all night always works.

I call Trayna and let her know to have their line meet us at the sorority house at Pepton. I hear excitement in the background. They must think they about to have fun.

Often times when someone brings up a frat house or sorority house, people think that a party is going down, but that's not the case tonight. I don't tell the pledges that. I'm going to let

176

them think they are about to have a good time, despite how fucking dumb they've been acting tonight.

Casha and I pull up to the sorority house at Pepton Nickel University. Some of the frat boys are outside playing beer pong.

The frat boys have alcohol in some of the cups, and a mixture of beer and alcohol in some cups. They are having a good time with their brothers. This is how it's supposed to be instead of how Tashina and Amy were tonight. Brotherhoods and sisterhoods get drunk and have fun on their own time. That way if anyone gets too damn drunk, they don't have to worry about doing anything crazy in front of any strangers.

Some of the boys are chasing each other around the sorority house. They are having a good time at Alpha Eta Nu's house. I can tell my sorority sisters are good hosts. All of the men are happy. They are either playing games, enjoying each other's conversations, flirting with some of the girls, or enjoying spaghetti and meatballs and nachos.

"I'm so happy they cooked," Casha says. "I been drinking and smoking all night. I'm hungry as hell."

"I'm hungry as hell too," I say.

"Damn. I wish we had our damn letters on," Casha says. "Now we gone look like strangers to these damn boys."

"Sssskkkiiioooo!" I shout. Now all the boys know we are members of Alpha Eta Nu.

Chaysa comes out eating nachos. I get out the car and give my girl a hug.

"You look fabulous Chaysa," I say. She has on her letters. Anytime one of our members has on their letters, they look good. That's just how proud we are of our sorority. Chaysa gives me her nachos. She always shares her food with me. I'm not hesitant at all to take them.

I give Chaysa a hug and she gives Casha one. We feel like family. I feel real good now that I'm eating too. I give Casha some nachos.

"We have plenty of food," Chaysa says. "You know we always make extra when niggas gone be in attendance."

We go in the sorority house. I look out the screen door to the backyard and see some of the boys stepping with canes. They're jumping in the air, hitting the canes between their brothers' legs, and doing a shimmy dance. Their movements are real precise.

10

The sorority house is really on tonight. I have to admit I haven't been to one in a long time.

Phi Phi Alpha starts strolling.

One of the members shout, "PhiiiiiHiiii!" and his brothers do the call back. It's loud as hell out here.

Chaysa comes to get me when the pledges arrive. Me and Casha go to the front yard and have the pledges drive around until they find parking.

"Don't take all night," Casha says.

Some of the pledges keep circling around the block. Me and my girls laugh at them. We know what it's like for there to be literally no parking and to keep driving around hoping someone leaves.

Some of the Phi Phi Alpha members introduce themselves to us. Casha is very under the influence. She is flirting with them. I'm really good at remembering I have a man. I ask the frat boys if they know Austin.

"That's my boy," one of the frat boys here named Tedran says. "I met him at a party not too long ago. The women love Austin." This boy is high. It's no telling how long he's been smoking his marijuana. I want him to tell me more about his encounter with Austin.

Chaysa and Casha pick up my vibe. They know how we do as women. We act stupid until we can get all the information we want out of people. Sometimes we won't even reveal what the hell needs to be said. In this case, that would be Austin being my man.

"So Tedran, did any girls leave with Austin after y'all gathering?" Chaysa asks.

Tedran chokes on his drink. Damn, he's quick as hell with being suspicious. I'm hoping the weed is his worst nightmare tonight and turns him into a snitch. "I didn't see him leave," Tedran says. "For all I know he was someone else. You know I be high."

"Fuck it. I don't care. I'm saying it anyways," I hear Chaysa whisper to Casha. "Um, Tedran, do you know that Austin is my girl's boyfriend?" Chaysa asks. I really didn't want her to say anything.

"Oh yea," Tedran says. "I remember him mentioning he was dating someone. If it wasn't him, it was someone else. Austin is cool peoples."

The pledges take so long finding parking that Chaysa pulls out foldable chairs and we sit down.

"Uh unh," Chaysa says. "This is her fourth time passing in front of my house. You need to get your girls. We don't got all night to be playing with them."

"I got this," I say. I have Delisha get in the backseat while I drive her car looking for parking. I take my cup of liquor with me. Luckily, I see some of the pledges walking to the sorority house. I see someone leaving on the next street and take their spot.

Delisha looks nervous as hell walking with me. She almost trips a few times on her own damn feet. She looks like we're on the set of a horror movie or something. This liquor has me feeling real easy. I'm having a good time watching this horrified ass girl. People driving by us probably think something is wrong with me laughing while this girl looks scared out of her mind.

When we get to the sorority house, I ask Chaysa if there's anything she could use help with. She says she has laundry that could be done. I have the pledges hand wash all of the dirty clothes that are in the house. They have everything they need: soap powder, water, buckets, and most importantly, their hands to handwash everything. They can clearly see that the washer and dryer are in the same room as them, but the pledges don't dare ask if they work.

Me and the girls leave the pledges downstairs in the laundry room and shut the door. We stomp up a few stairs and walk down quietly to hear what they are talking about.

"I wish it wasn't like this," Scalina says. "I wish we could all enjoy being with our big sisters and earn our letters by doing things we all like to do. I never knew it would be this bad."

"Yea. It seems like all the prophytes and other members want to do is make us mad," one of the other pledges named Jamia says.

"Why don't they ever want to see us happy?" Delisha asks.

"They have tried to make us happy before," Jamia says.

"Girl giving us invitations to be pledges does not count," Delisha says.

Me, Casha, and Chaysa burst into laughter. I know the girls heard us.

"This sorority house is nice though," Delisha continues.

Now we know they heard us.

"Yea, but look what we have to do in it," Jamia says.

"Shut up," Trayna says. She knows me and my girls can barge in at any time.

I honestly don't care what they are talking about. As long as I hear water movement, I won't interrupt their conversation.

Tedran comes downstairs and tosses the girls some dirty boxers.

"Ill. Did these just come off of someone?" Trayna asks.

"Just wash them," I say.

Me, the girls, and Tedran go back upstairs and everyone is playing beer pong or strolling. It's a beautiful night, so I want to go outside. As usual, I get jealous watching people smoke. I go by a crowd that is just drinking. They are talking about good times they've had when they were pledging and weren't with their prophytes.

I know when I was pledging, me and my line met up on numerous occasions to have fun, but most importantly vent and talk about the people bringing us in. Although we all knew we hated our prophytes, we still needed to hear it verbally from each other. We still needed our nights where we talked bad about them and made them so little in our minds that we had more strength when we went back to sets.

It gets loud inside, so I go to the door. I see Casha dancing on the dance floor. She is the center of attention. She's walking it out, moving her hips side to side, and shaking her ass. She's not nervous at all, which is what I love. She motions for me to join her. She takes my arm and turns me in circles. We dip to the ground together. The men love watching two girls dance close to each other. Me and Casha know that. She starts whispering in my ear to give them more of a show. She whispers things to boost my ego. She tells me I'm sexy and if me and Austin ever break up, I can always get another man. I don't mind. I love Austin, but I don't mind hearing things that let me know I'm such a fucking beautiful lady.

I'm looking for Chaysa while I'm dancing. I spot her leaving the kitchen with some nachos. She dances her way to the beer pong table. We make eye contact and she shouts, "Sssskkkiiioooo!" All the members of Alpha Eta Nu shout the call back.

After dancing, me, Casha and a few other members of the sorority cheer on Chaysa playing beer pong. She's the only girl playing. She gets a ball in a cup on her second chance.

I just don't know how people can keep touching the same ball, throw it in cups, then drink whichever one it goes in. Too many germs for me, but just like any old idiot, I participate too so I don't look like the outcast in the group.

Chaysa takes a sip of her cup and her face shrivels up. It's clearly alcohol instead of beer.

"Y'all gone have me fucked up," Chaysa says. "I'm already drunk."

"This is Greek beer pong," Patrick, one of the Phi Phi Alpha members says. "Everything's a mystery. You don't know what's in the cup you get."

"Where have I heard that before?" Tedran asks.

"Nigga, I made it up," Patrick says.

"I could've sworn I heard that before," Tedran says.

"Nigga, shut the fuck up," Patrick says.

"You heard it last night when you were explaining to that girl that she should take the cup on the left with the liquor instead of the cup on the right with the beer, so that you could get in her panties," a Phi Phi Alpha member named Derrick says.

"Nigga, I ain't never had a hard time getting no woman," Tedran says.

"Yes you did," Derrick says. "Your momma taught you everything you know."

Tedran pushes Derrick and the two men are quickly separated by the other men. They keep trying to get closer together, but more than one person is holding each of them back. The two boys continue to exchange insults.

"You just mad my momma had a fine ass son and yours had a fucking scuff," Tedran says.

"Scuff my ass nigga!" Derrick shouts. "Return your momma that skirt you got on under there."

Tedran pulls his pants down and says, "Where you see a damn skirt at?"

The fraternity boys are getting real serious and frustrated. I'm not feeling this change of events at all.

"Let's go check on the girls," Chaysa says.

We casually walk down the stairs, then I tell Casha and Chaysa to walk silently so we can hear what the girls are saying.

"Girl it's too late. They heard us by now," Casha says.

"Shhh," I say.

We get close to the door and the pledges are trying to figure out where they should hang the clothes.

"I told you they heard us coming," Casha says.

Casha tells the pledges where to scatter the wet clothes in the laundry room. She gives them hangers and has them hang some from pipes, on the door, and anywhere else something is poking out of the wall that can hold hangers. Then she has them lay some of the clothes on flat surfaces.

I have the girls line up.

"Great job ladies," Chaysa says. "I want to say how much it is a pleasure to have pledges in the sorority house," she says sarcastically. Me and Casha are laughing and slap hands. We really hope the girls don't think they deserve to be on this property. They should feel privileged just to be here.

"We know y'all prophytes never brought y'all to a sorority house," I say. "Y'all should feel honored." I'm drunk as hell looking at these pledges. All that damn complaining they was doing when they first got down here, they need they asses beat.

They are definitely going to pay for all that shit at the liquor store that they did, and Tashina and Amy did. I can't let it go.

Chaysa looks at me and motions if she can instruct the pledges on what to do. I nod my head and motion for her to go ahead. This is my girl. Even though she's more than ten years younger than me, she's my girl. She's real mature, she's caring, and she's just fun to be around.

"Follow me pledges," Chaysa says swinging her head from side to side. She has the pledges line up on the stairs. She gets to the top and looks down at them. "When you get up here, you are to say something that you don't like about another pledge," Chaysa continues. "I will instruct you all on when to talk."

"Give them a second to think," Casha says. "We been with them all night. We know they slow as hell. They was slow when we first saw them."

Me, Casha, and Chaysa stand at the top of the stairs and discuss if we want to continue our long night after the party at the house. We're unsure because we never know how much of a show the pledges will give us. They may test us to see if we will give them more to do being that it's so late. They may do things on purpose to make us mad. We never know what the pledges will do being that we run them ragged damn near every time we see them. The only time they have time to breathe a lot is when they meet up to take the tests.

Chaysa has the pledges follow her into the living room where everyone is eating. They stand in front of each other. Chaysa has Trayna and Jamia go first. The rest of the pledges stand behind them. Chaysa cues Jamia to begin.

"Trayna thinks she's all that and needs to stop being so arrogant that she's on the line," Jamia says.

I'm drunk as hell and can't believe Jamia just said that.

"What?!" Trayna shouts. "You the one that's talking about all the niggas that's gone want you once you get your letters."

"You started doing your hair more and dressing nicer once you made the line," Jamia says. "Before you were just a raggedy, dusty bum."

"No I wasn't," Trayna says. She's getting teary eyed. "I was always at the top of my game. You just don't got nothing to say, so you making up dumb shit."

"Watch your mouth," Chaysa says. "You, as a pledge, better recognize where you are standing."

Chaysa has Delisha and Scalina go next.

"You need to wash your hair more than twice a month," Delisha says to Scalina.

"My hair is always clean," Scalina says. "You're the one walking so damn close behind me all the time because you wish you were me."

"Girl please," Delisha says. "Not even your little sisters want to be you."

Me, Casha, and Chaysa cheers to that. That was a good insult. They're smoking weed and cigarettes. We have nachos too. We are enjoying the show.

"You know you wish you were my blood sister," Scalina says. "You wish you could see me as much as they do."

"Girl please," Delisha says. "You are not all that. I've seen way prettier girls than you."

"Then stop being so close behind me all the time," Scalina says. "At least you know I'm prettier than you."

"I never said that," Delisha says. "You're so full of yourself."

"I'm more confident than you," Scalina says. "I'm a natural. You need more work. The big sisters can pick up on weakness. You need to get better, and maybe our sets won't be as tough."

We give the girls clothes and have them go change.

"Saying bad stuff not gone help us! Y'all know that!" Trayna cries on her way to the bedroom.

Trayna needs to get the hell on. She's embarrassing us in front of company.

"We don't make the rules, we just follow them," I say.

"It's just going to make us hate each other," Jamia cries.

"So who the hell do you think you talking to?" I ask. I hate when people think I'm ignorant to this pledging process. I've been through it. I know the results. Chaysa asked them to do

185

this, not me. "You're the dumb asses that keep returning to the events," I continue.

I never understood why Greeks haze their pledges. There's nothing good that can come from that. I have common sense. I know hazing people only fucks up their mentality. It's what I have to do though. I wanted to pledge. I did everything I had to do to make it. I wanted to be a part of an organization. I loved watching Greeks hold events, stroll, step, dance, and most importantly, I loved the sisterhood. My sister Nathanya sure as hell wasn't shit.

I didn't know how bad it really was to pledge until I actually made the line. One of the worst things I hated about pledging was the fact that my sleep was broken a lot to meet up with my line. When my line brought in a group, we didn't break their sleep much. The girls that brought my line in didn't mind breaking ours all the time though.

I remember one day when I was on line and me and my sisters were woke up in the middle of the night. We had to cook for our prophytes in Caya's dorm. We go to a habitually black university. People that suspect we are pledging don't even say anything. This particular night that I was so pissed off, we had to make a late-night breakfast for the prophytes. It had pancakes, waffles, syrup, bacon, sausage, eggs, and grits. It even had steak.

I was pissed the hell off because my prophytes made it a priority to look in all of our fridges to see what we had. We were living on campus, so the only way there would be a problem is if we snitched. But anyways, my girls and I made the prophytes their plates and had to watch them eat. We didn't get to taste any of it.

Our prophyte Tisha made us recite the founders first, middle, and last names. Alpha Eta Nu has fifteen founders. I only remember Laya Miles Timber, Yesana Arlin Tan, Michelle Kye Dimps, and Portia Ashley Lin. They were my favorite founders because their quotes were the main ones that relaxed my heart when the big sisters were around. Anytime the big sisters were around, I always experienced fear, just like all pledges. My girls and I never knew when we would be hazed.

Laya Miles Timber said: *No one can take away anything I've started. No one can ever fill my shoes. I'll always be a trickster that no one can figure out. I will never harm my sister, and I know my sister will never harm me.*

Yesana Arlin Tan was probably my favorite of them all. She said: *No pledge will ever be harmed. No pledge will have to do anything that she does not feel comfortable doing. Alpha Eta Nu is about love. Alpha Eta Nu is about sisterhood.*

I loved when my line had to recite Yesana's quotes because I hoped they would make the big sisters go easier on us. I hoped the quotes would warm their hearts, but they didn't. We would still be hazed. My prophytes knew all about getting relaxed when reciting comforting history. They were not going to give us the satisfaction of going easy on us.

Michelle Kye Dimps said: *Alpha Eta Nu is the best sorority. The women that join our sisterhood are ambitious. They are caring and helpful. Women in Alpha Eta Nu are strong women that strive to excel in anything they want to pursue in life.*

Portia Ashley Lin said: *Alpha Eta Nu is a great sorority to join. We turn our pledges into even greater women than they were before. We encourage them and teach them to go after whatever they want in life. We teach them to never let anything hold them back from accomplishing what they want.*

My line and I had to learn at least two things that each founder said verbatim and recite them. It was the middle of the night, so we had to say everything low. We were upset that we couldn't eat anything when we had made enough for ourselves and the big sisters. The big sisters said they were going to save some for the next day.

My girls and I stumbled on a few things with the history. It hurt because we knew everything verbatim, but we were so tired and hungry that we kept messing up. We really wanted to be fresh when we recited the history to make the big sisters proud that we had studied hard, but we were unlucky. We had to say everything on a day that we were tired.

My prophyte Teralin didn't like eating such a good meal and listening to quotes about the founders. We were in Caya's dorm, so we couldn't do a step show and wake up everyone. Teralin ended up making us hold different step positions. We held our arms in several directions. We put one hand in front of our chest and held the other extended out. We did that the reverse direction as well. We would stretch our arms all the way up. We had to squat. We had to hold one leg up at a time.

After holding so many positions, my prophytes were still bored. They ended up watching television in Caya's dorm room. They made me and my sisters stay in the living room area. We ended up falling asleep in there. When we woke up, it was the morning and all the prophytes were gone. We were pissed the hell off that there was really no food left.

Our founders made it seem like we were joining an organization that would be generous enough to let us wake up to food. Being that we made the food, we thought there was no excuse for us to wake up to a kitchen that needed all the dishes washed in them. My line and I helped Caya clean her kitchen, then we all got whatever we could find in our fridges to cook.

We were so hungry and wanting to eat good like the prophytes did, that we made anything we could find and combined it. We had steak, fried chicken, macaroni, shrimp alfredo, and steamed broccoli. My line sisters and I threw down. We ate in Caya's living room and talked hella bad about our prophytes. We talked about everything from their sorry ass sounding voices, to their sorry ass side conversations about the men they were talking to. All they did was say how the men they talked to were fine as hell.

Some of my sisters hated the prophytes so much that they would mess around with people they knew our prophytes were messing with. We had more fun than they did watching television.

But anyways, me, Chaysa, Casha, and the rest of Alpha Eta Nu in attendance at the sorority house, walk the frat boys outside to their cars. They play music, dance, and smoke in the middle of the street. I'm the only one just drinking as usual.

There's no one driving on this street we're on, so some of the frat is strolling in the middle of it. I'm enjoying watching them have a good time and not having a care in the world. I'm getting scared that someone will call the police because it's real late and the boys are doing their call super loud. They are high as hell.

Some of Phi Phi Alpha members are on cars doing their stroll in place. They're putting their right leg out and back in. Then they are turning their heads right, and clapping above and under their legs. They are spinning and clapping above and under their legs as well. They jump and hit both legs in the air.

Some of the members of Phi Phi Alpha are performing like they are at a competition. The others are real smooth and relaxed enjoying their high. They are half doing the choreography.

Some of Alpha Eta Nu members form a stroll line. Of course, my girl Chaysa is doing her thing. Me and Casha don't know this choreography, so we just can't join in.

After Chaysa and her girls finish, me and Casha start our line of just two people. We have our cups in our hands, so we aren't doing the moves full out. We are clapping to our left and right. We are pumping our arms forward and backwards with our hands in fists. Other times our hands are opened while we pump back and forth moving forward. We step to the right two times, then to the left two times. We do a dip and spin around. Then we pump our arms to the front again and move forward.

"I see y'all Casha and Shona!" Chaysa yells. It is too loud out here. Everyone needs to calm down.

Me, Chaysa, and Casha go check on the pledges. We give the girls sleeping bags and blankets and have them sleep in the living room.

"We'll be right back," Chaysa says. "We doing our thing outside."

"Real Greek life going on out there," I say.

"We'll be back," Chaysa says.

Me and the girls go back outside and join our Sorors. We continue to dance and have a good time. Tedran and Patrick are flirting with a few Sorors. This isn't like it was with my line and Phi Phi Alpha at Hollow's Cave. We were more intimate with our frat brothers there.

I see Tedran sitting in his car and go talk to him. The breeze feels real good. I love enjoying company at night.

"You want to hit this?" Tedran asks.

"I don't smoke no more," I say. I at least want to sound cool letting him know I smoked before. "I just drink now," I continue.

"Why'd you stop?" Tedran asks.

I hate this question. The truth offends people. "I just needed a change," I say.

Tedran gets out the car and starts dancing. He's doing a little shimmy too. I love when frats do the shimmy. They rub their hands together, spread their legs, and get low to the ground with a hip shake. It's so damn sexy.

I copy Tedran and do the shimmy too. I'm smiling and giving him props on how good he is at it. He's doing it all around his car. Patrick joins him. I love these Phi Phi Alpha boys. They know they look good dancing.

"So how long y'all plan on staying out here?" I ask.

"Until someone makes us leave," Tedran says. "Man, I wish that was the case. I hate leaving scenes like this."

"Me too," I say. "I feel too damn good."

"You look good too," Tedran says. "Damn. Why you don't got nothing to eat?" Tedran asks Patrick.

"I was just thinking about that," Patrick says. "We should have made a plate to take with us."

"Don't trip," I say. "Let's just go make y'all some plates."

I tell Chaysa me and the boys are going to make them a plate. She comes with us because she wants another bite herself. The weed gave her the munchies just like the boys.

Some of the pledges are still awake.

"Damn. Where they car keys at?" Tedran asks.

Me and Chaysa look at each other. It never crossed our minds to drive around the pledges' cars.

"Hold up," I say. I wake up the pledges and make them go in the backyard and line up. They are slow as hell getting up.

190

Chaysa and Casha start hitting pots with silverware. I have all the Greeks go to the backyard. I really need the pledges to show me any steps that they have learned. Me and the other Greeks circle around them.

"Cupperton!" Trayna shouts and the pledges all stomp with their right foot. Trayna sets their first step. She hits her thighs and moves her arms across her chest. Her arms are real sharp. I notice that her thumbs are tucked in, and she doesn't lose her form. She claps above and under her legs in a circle. She bows her head down when she stomps, and hits her thighs at the same time. She hits her right thigh with her left hand, then stomps and hits her left thigh with her right hand.

After Trayna does the step once, the pledges join in with her and do the same step. They're not in unison. They don't sound like one person. They sound like twenty-three damn people, which is just pure, fucking awful. They should never perform anywhere. I am completely embarrassed.

"They have me messed up yawning while doing the routine," Chaysa says.

"I want everyone to know that none of their prophytes that taught them this little piece are here," I say.

"Damn. They need a lot of work," Patrick says. "You should have let they asses stay sleep."

"We're trying," Canila says.

"They getting too damn comfortable with us," Mianala, one of Chaysa's line sisters says.

I hit Canila on her arm. "I'm not your prophytes, damn it," I say with attitude. "Don't give me no shit."

"I don't know why it's so hard to just do what we say, and keep your damn mouth shut," Casha says. "Just saying that made me want to hurt one of y'all." Casha pulls her fist back and acts like she's going to punch a few of the pledges.

Scalina starts to set another step, but I stop her. The frat boys agree with my decision.

"That performance was too fucked up to do another one," Tedran says.

The pledges performance was weak as hell.

191

"One thing I don't want is for the frat boys to think that because we're women, that we can't outstep them," I say to Casha.

Casha gets in Patrick's face and does a step. Her face is full of expression when she gets inches between her and Patrick. She goes full out exploding into choreography that I taught her. She's clapping high and low. She's hitting the ground and stomping in a circle with her claps. She does a lot of moves in circular motion. She's snapping her neck left and right, and bending low with her arms extending to the sides.

Some of the pledges are smiling and the other ones are in complete shock at what they just witnessed.

Patrick gives Tedran his drink.

"Yo, handle that," Tedran says.

Patrick tilts his neck left and right then begins his intense choreography. He does his fraternity call and gets right into stomping. He stomps and hits his chest, moves his arms in blade positions, and hits the ground. He makes sure he spins in a circle like Casha did. He does a step looking at his boys with his back towards Casha. His boys are loud as hell watching their frat brother.

Me and Chaysa can tell the frat boys aren't taking us serious because we are women. They are acting like their boy isn't even giving a full effort battling a woman. They are saying things like *I remember you did this routine against my mom when she was clowning you* and *didn't we freestyle that beat?* Me and Chaysa don't care. We laugh and slap hands. We know they gone act like men regardless. She's high and I'm drunk anyways. We love to see how men act that are a part of fraternities. We, as sorority members, live for the moments we get to see how frats behave around sorority women.

The pledges are looking at me and cheering me on to go next. They know I have a reputation of being a great choreographer and stepper. Most of the people at Cupperton University know about me.

I walk up to Tedran and begin my step with the last step I take to get in his face. I transition so smoothly that some of his brothers are in shock. I can hear the pledges and my sorority cheer for me too. I slap my hands on the opposite leg and hit the ground. I clap under my legs repeatedly in a circle. I clap my hands and have them hit opposite elbows. I do a butterfly motion in front of my chest three times. I put my hands in fists and pump forward in place while stomping. I also move backwards clapping above and under my legs from the left then from the right.

"Damn. She is real good," Patrick says. "I heard about her a few times. I didn't believe none of the stuff I was hearing. I needed to see it."

Tedran starts stepping while I am. I don't stop though. He makes a beat that goes with the one I'm doing. His arms go high and low. He squats and hits one thigh at a time before bringing his hands together one on top of the other a few times. He pretends like he's climbing a ladder silently, then stomps and claps a few times. He does a backbend and comes up and explodes into choreography. Sometimes we randomly stomp at the same time. It's real tight. I make sure I do the backbend and come up and do choreography just like him. I thought that was a nice move.

I'm a good choreographer, but I don't mind learning when someone does something that catches my interest.

When I turn in a circle, I see the astonishment on the pledges faces. My Sorors here are amazed beyond belief. They love watching me. I hope it's because I'm good, and not just because I'm a woman. I hope it's because I'm just as good as the boys.

This is real intense. This is real Greek life. It's a real competitive atmosphere. A lot of people don't get to witness nights like this. We're drinking, they are smoking and we are being real competitive. We have pledges here that are going through their process. This is what people envision when they think about Greek life.

I end my routine and go to my girl Casha. Tedran steps a few seconds more, then goes by his boys. He's hugging and hitting hands with them looking at me talk to my girl. I'm looking at him too. I wish Austin could have seen me, but oh well. I enjoyed myself.

"I love you girl," Casha says. "Don't let nobody tell you that you don't do this shit. You are the damn choreographer. You do this shit. You the best at it."

I love to hear people talk to me when they are drunk and high. I know the drugs relax them and make them feel easy so that they don't hold anything in.

Chaysa pulls me to the side and says, "Girl you need to teach them something." She's talking about the pledges. "Why you let them come over here with that routine?" Chaysa continues.

Chaysa is drunk and high. She's so pretty that I just can't stop looking at her.

"Teach them a routine," Chaysa continues. "Y'all staying the night anyways. They need some serious help. You know I could care less about some bitches that don't even go to my damn college, but this is about the sorority."

The frat boys go back to the front yard and chill in their cars with the sorority girls.

I teach the pledges a basic routine. They are tired as hell; I can tell. However, I am drunk as hell, and really don't want to waste how I good I feel on teaching them. Plus, I'm trying to get back to the party with everyone else.

I teach the girls to correctly stomp and clap above and under their legs. Then I have them stomp, clap, and hit the floor. Then I have them do their arms in a butterfly motion. I make them do that a couple times. It looks good just being repeated.

"That already looks way better than what they were doing," Chaysa says.

I tell the girls they can go back to sleep.

"Well, just so you know, our leaders told us to act like we were stupid as hell tonight while y'all were there," Jamia says. "They don't even like y'all asses."

"I guess this means that you have learned to like us more than the people you are forced to be with," Casha says.

"We just thought y'all should know," Trayna says.

"We get it," I say. "Y'all like us so much that you'll tell us the truth about your fucked up prophytes. Go to sleep."

Me, Casha, Chaysa, and one of her other line sisters named Nana watch the pledges fall asleep in the living room while everyone else has a good time outside. We don't want the girls to be whispering to each other while they're laying all close. They need to have everything they went through today heavy on their brains while they doze off. We don't want them getting up to get anything. We sure as hell don't want them on their phones texting each other, or anyone period.

"They better keep it down out there before the neighbors get mad," Nana says.

"The neighbors are cool," Chaysa says. "They knew this was a sorority house before they moved in."

The Greeks outside are playing basketball and making noise any time a shot is made. Whoever is on the losing team has consequences when they get back inside. The girls have to take their shirts off and expose their bras. The boys have to pull down their pants and expose their boxers.

"So tell me, Nana and Chaysa, when y'all were brought in, did y'all regret it?" Casha asks.

"Girl hell no," Nana says. "I just couldn't wait for the process to be over. Once I realized all the hell I heard about was real, I just wanted my letters to flaunt around."

"I mean seriously," Chaysa says. "It's a horror story pledging. It's not easy to make these lines."

"I know," I say. "It's supposed to just be a bunch of tests and community service. It's not supposed to be any hell."

"I felt like I was kidnapped when I was with my prophytes," Nana says.

Some of the pledges are moving around. My girls and I are too loud talking, but we don't care. We're trained to give them a hard time. I mean, pledging is just one hundred percent hell. The tests don't make it any easier. The pledges have everything they've went through in their heads while they're taking them.

"What was the worst thing y'all went through?" Casha asks.

I hear one of the pledges groan. I know whoever it is thinks that we will make them do whatever Chaysa and Nana say they did.

"Who the hell is making noise?" I rudely ask. "Don't make me make y'all get up."

"Please don't make us make y'all get up," Casha says. "Y'all have embarrassed us enough tonight."

"That show was weak as hell," Chaysa says. "But anyways, my line had to spend money on them niggas, and that wasn't cool."

"What did y'all physically have to do, I mean?" Casha asks.

"Them bitches that brought us in knew someone that worked at a place that had rock climbing. We had to do that shit because they knew we were scared of damn heights," Chaysa says.

"One time we had to go hiking," Nana says. "Do you know them bitches didn't want to give us no damn water. They liked watching our bodies break down. I never understood they trifling asses."

"I learn that a lot of prophytes be jealous of their pledges," Casha says.

"We weren't," I say. "It's that we didn't care what we did because we had to spend too much time on them niggas."

"True that," Casha says. "One time one of our prophytes cars broke down and we had to go get her. I was pissed the hell off. Anytime they were in trouble, they had hella pledges to choose from to go help them."

"Damn. I wish I would've thought to ask our pledges to help me when my car broke down," Nana says.

Somebody is outside throwing up. Tedran announced it real loud. Nana goes to see who it is. It's Mianala. Nana goes to get her and brings her to the bathroom. I hear her telling Mianala to get it all out. She's joking with her about throwing up all the good food we had tonight. She tells her to know her damn limit. I hate when people throw up because of their ignorant ass choices. Not knowing their damn tolerance level. I get mad when my food is thrown up, just like I get mad when I spend money.

Me, Chaysa, and Casha pull cards from the deck. Whatever number we get is to determine how many minutes the girls will be in the bathroom. Whoever is the highest card, has to take two shots. I pulled the King of Hearts. Chaysa and Casha are laughing at me. For sure I will be taking the shots. What are the odds they pull a higher card?

Casha lays her head on my shoulder. She loves me so much. She gives me a kiss on the cheek.

"We better always be girls," Casha says. "If something I do bothers you, you better let me know."

I kiss her on the forehead. "Girl you know I would be miserable if we ever stopped being friends."

We smile for a photo for Chaysa. "Y'all are so cute," Chaysa says. "I hope my line can develop the same love y'all have for each other. We are close, but I can tell we aren't as close as y'all are."

Tedran comes to see what we're doing.

"Aye look y'all," Tedran says. "They acting like lesbians." A few members of Phi Phi Alpha come to see what we're doing. My damn sister only has her head on my shoulder.

"Boy, take your ass back outside," Chaysa says. "Coming in here with all that noise."

Mianala and Nana are taking forever in the bathroom. I hear bath water running. Me, Casha, and Chaysa go to the bathroom.

"Girl, hurry up and clean yourself up," Chaysa says. "Why you drink more than you can handle?"

"Fuck you," Mianala says. "I don't want to hear that shit. Get me some clothes."

I go with Chaysa to get Mianala some clothes from a room in the sorority house. After, we go check on the girls in the living room.

I start looking sad. My thoughts took a sharp turn. Fuck. I hate when this happens.

"Girl, what's up?" Chaysa asks.

"I keep having this nightmare," I say. "Looking at them just reminded me. Maybe if I tell y'all, it won't be as bad."

After Mianala finishes taking a bath, me, her, Chaysa, Casha and Nana sit in the living room. I tell them how I keep having this nightmare that I'm in a big stadium on stage with a step crew I formed. People keep picking me a part, and my own mother acts like she's set on showing people that I'm a bad child. My mother is acting like she wants to be me. She's enjoying watching me make a fool of myself in public. All I'm doing is complaining. I can clearly see that something is wrong with me. It's so disturbing that I'm trying to figure out what it is.

I just hate Nadia so damn much. What the fuck could she have went through that made her so damn bitter? What could have made her so much of a nothing ass bitch? I'm really starting to get convinced that I'm adopted. It's to a point where I am just willing to accept any alternate thought to cleanse myself of Nadia. She's so evil, she's not worth even thinking about.

Some of the pledges are probably awake, but I don't care. I wish one of them would throw anything they heard me say in my face. I'll admit that sometimes I say things that get me emotional in front of pledges, and I start to feel sorry for them because of all the hell they have to go through. I just make it seem like I'm not paying the pledges any attention when I'm with my Sorors, so they can think I just slipped up. I don't like to seem like a weak Alpha Eta Nu member.

"Girl we all go through hell with our mothers and fathers," Casha says. She loves me too much. She always tries to comfort me. "That's why it's important to spend time with other people you love," Casha continues. "We didn't choose our parents. My mom is dangerous too. She would hit me for no reason sometimes. After she did, she would just stare in my eyes. She knew I wouldn't hit her back."

"I hate how parents know we are vulnerable as kids, naturally want their love, and take advantage of it," Mianala says. She looks me in my eyes and says, "There's some people that wish their parents would just hurry up and pass away."

Sometimes I feel like I am in a ghost land. Who could possibly know anyone like Nadia? "Y'all don't have to say y'all have bad parents because I have a bad mother," I say.

"Where is your dad?" Nana asks.

"I don't know him," I say. "My mother was the real deal when it came to being a bitch to her daughter."

"I don't know mine either," Mianala says.

"I'll admit that my mother and I have a good relationship," Nana says. "We have our arguments, but we still are real cool."

"I mean I watch the news, so I know things could be worse," I say. "But…"

"But that's no excuse," Casha says. "No one deserves fucked up parents. We didn't ask to be here." She gives me a hug. "If you want, I can be your mom," she continues.

"So you love me enough that I can call you Mom?" I joke.

"You know that I do," Casha says.

Chaysa gets up and starts strolling by herself. She is damn near about to fall every step she takes. She is drunk as hell. She looks so ridiculous that I'd be surprised if she even remembered any of her routine. It looks like she's just doing anything. Chaysa strolls between the pledges. She falls on Scalina and Jamia who are lying next to each other. The two pledges say they have to use the bathroom.

"Hurry up," Casha says.

Scalina and Jamia powerwalk to the bathroom.

"Girl why do I feel like this liquor is making me stupid? Like it's making me forget things?" Chaysa asks.

"Because it is," Mianala says. She rests her head in my lap. My Sorors love me. Even when they just meet me.

As Greeks, we are taught to trust each other with even our deepest, darkest secrets. We are taught to strengthen each other with the bad things that have happened to us, so we never feel alone. When I got older, I realized how stupid that was. The hazing is bullshit, and so is trusting each other just because we are in the same sorority.

Every organization has fucked up people in it; however, me and my line are real close, so it's not a problem to share personal information. We are Greeks, but we are still regular people. We sometimes get caught up telling people personal things who we haven't known long. Me and Casha didn't know Mianala and Nana until tonight.

"Damn. We just saying all of this not knowing if these niggas are really sleep," Casha says.

Scalina and Jamia return to the living room. Scalina puts her hands on my shoulders from behind. I look back and she whispers in my ear, "I hate my mother too. She wishes I would die every second she looks at me." She kisses me on the cheek.

"Girl lay your ass down," Casha says.

I say, "You gone get your ass in trouble if you repeat anything you heard."

"Girl go get the wood," Casha says.

"Relax," I say. "It's late. The last thing we want is for somebody else to throw up."

I don't want Scalina to get hit. I'll take any help I can get when it comes to Nadia. It helps to know someone has been through the same thing. It doesn't matter who it is. I hate that I need strength from anyone to get over Nadia's behavior. She's nothing, and it shouldn't require help from others to get over anything that she has done.

"She told me that," Scalina says getting in her sleeping bag. "I don't care if I get in trouble for telling you that."

Scalina gives Jamia a little push.

"Her mom chased her with a steaming hot flat-iron," Jamia says. "She didn't have her shoes on, and her mom dropped it on her feet."

"Okay ladies, go to bed," I say. I have to admit that what Scalina and Jamia said to me warmed my heart. I learned a lot about Scalina's character. She wants me to feel better. She wants to ensure that I am alright. She cares about me despite all the things she's been through tonight.

"So, to switch the subject, since the pledges clearly aren't sleep," Nana says. "Is it true that you and your homegirl Reeya went to Ann High School and destroyed the advisor's office?"

"We thought the cameras weren't on that day," I say.

"Then y'all went to her house and broke the windows," Chaysa says.

"We were young," I say. "She should have never implemented all those rules into the step organization that I started."

"Then you got kicked off the team you started," Nana says. "That shit is crazy. I would've killed that bitch kicking me off the team that I started."

"You think I don't have homicidal thoughts about that stupid bitch?" I ask. "Anytime I think of her, I wish she would just disappear."

"She needs to kill herself for being so damn ugly," Casha says.

"What happened with you at Musteegan College?" Chaysa asks.

"I was coaching there for a year," I say. "The man that gave me the job tried to end my term early. First off, I love stepping too much for someone to guarantee me a year, then take it away after three months. Second off, I am grown. I have bills. That shit isn't cool to just take away someone's income."

"Didn't he tell you it was your last day, on your last day?" Casha asks.

"Girl yes," I say. "I went to his house and put three lighters on his front porch. I put a glass candle next to them. Then I put birthday candles on the porch."

"How did you get off on all those charges?" Chaysa asks.

"It's simple," I say. "I was lucky."

"You know people say you're like the villain that haunts Ann High School right?" Chaysa asks. I can't believe that even she has heard about what I did at Ann. "They think one day you gone turn into some killer," Chaysa continues. "You scared the hell out of some people so much, that they think when you die, your ghost is always going to haunt Musteegan College."

"Look. I'm gone tell y'all the truth," I say. "I was young. Nadia, my mom, was a bitch. I was my mother's daughter. She had my mind, and I was lost. She is the reason I got kicked off Ann's step team, and she is the reason I didn't handle myself well at Musteegan College. She trained me since the day I was born on what to do when I faced all types of situations that I would go through in life. She was the devil. My mind, it was gone. I didn't have one. Everything, I blame it on Nadia."

I fall into another negative trance.

"There's a lot of blood going into you still being alive," my grandma says. I don't know what she's talking about. We're sitting at my dining room table. "There's this thing called private practice, and Nadia's been doing it on you since you've been born," my grandma continues. "I worked my ass off to keep you alive. I want these projects done, and I want them done right. I'll tell you exactly what to write."

My grandma always takes all the credit for everything I do. I'm not mad at all. Without her, I wouldn't be here. And she knows how we like to ride for each other. We know the message that we want people to take from us. She, my grandma, is the head of our duo.

I'm hysterical right now. I see myself with tape over my mouth sitting with my knees to my chest.

"Shh," my grandmother says. "Don't touch that damn phone." She opened my eyes to what Nadia wants to say to me in remembrance of her birthday coming up. "Just remember that I did everything already," my grandmother continues.

I can't believe this bitch Nadia is about to try me the rest of my life by saying bad things to me on and off because of some thoughts she's having of *me being just too pretty and no one should envy me the way they do.* She feels the envy others have for me is dangerous and that I should be dead. She feels that's how she is a grown woman by wishing her daughter would die so others good days wouldn't be interrupted with suicidal thoughts when they see me because they're so ugly. This bitch Nadia has me fucked up.

My grandma just saved me from this shit.

"She's not as sneaky as she thinks," my grandmother says.

Nadia has me so fucked up. She's not just gone be talking to me like I'm an old rag, the rest of my life.

First, Nadia can't remember telling me one of my cousin's was smoking cocaine in her backyard. Then she says her friend

202

Nikki was on a hike with her and that bitch Mrs. McGruder, but Nikki is the only close friend that didn't make the photos. Then she can't remember saying my sister asked my twin brothers for ninety dollars on their birthday.

"Who the hell does this bitch think she's talking too!?" I yell. "Who the hell does Nadia really think she is?" Fucking nothing ass bitch.

My grandmother pops me on my mouth.

"I'll tell you everything you need to know," my grandmother says. It's like we're on a secret mission. She has a plan.

I don't talk to my sister anymore. There's no reason to be calling each other sisters in the first place.

I'm getting tired of using these family terms with people I hate.

I hear my Sorors start laughing, and I'm back to my right state of mind.

I hate talking about Nadia. She just made me super angry. When the pledges get into a deep sleep, I get the idea for me and Casha to pour cold water on them. I wish we could record this, but we can't. The pledges quickly stand up. They are mad as hell. Chaysa, Mianala, and Nana are laughing. They are copying the girls' reactions to the cold water.

"That was a great idea Shona," Mianala says. "Perhaps next time you will think about the short supply of clothes we have left because it's so many pledges on this line."

I give Mianala the middle finger. I feel stupid. That's what Nadia's ass does for me. I should have thought twice about pouring the water on the girls. I feel a little better, and not so stupid, when I remember that Casha poured the water with me.

The pledges stay in the living room and complain while me and my girls go in the bedroom and look in the closet for more clothes. We don't have enough. We have some of the girls sleep in their bras and shorts, and the rest of them sleep in shirts and panties. We give them new sheets and blankets to share.

"We'll do hair in the morning," Casha says.

"Girl I am not doing no hair," I say.

"I meant they gone do they own hair in the morning," Casha says. "I'm not about to keep chaperoning them all night."

"Let's have them go in the bedrooms," Nana says. "We can sleep out here and watch TV since we don't know when everyone is leaving. Plus, they don't have on enough pajamas."

"Alright girls. Grab your things and go to the bedrooms," Casha says.

Me, Chaysa, Mianala, Nana, and Casha go in the laundry room and wash the pledges' clothes.

Tedran finds us downstairs and asks if he could use one of the pledges' cars. I know he's just trying to give the pledges worse memories of their experience. I hear one of the pledges yell *no*.

"We'll deal with them tomorrow," I say.

"For that, let him use one of they cars," Casha says.

"Patrick wants to use one too," Tedran says.

"Where the hell y'all going?" I ask. Tedran comes over to me and puts his arms around my waist. "You know I got a man," I say.

"Oh, that's right," Tedran says. He puts his arms around Mianala who is real friendly right now and gives him a kiss on the cheek. All I can do is shake my head and look away. "So where they stuff at so I can get the keys?" Tedran asks.

Patrick comes downstairs right on time to ask, "Yea, where they purses at so we can get the keys?"

Oh hell no. I can't take a chance on someone else's money coming up missing. I let the boys know when the girls fall asleep, I'll find where they put their keys.

We go in the living room and the rest of the Greeks are already in there. I guess everyone got tired of being outside. Some of the girls are sitting on the boys' laps.

Nana puts on some slow rhythm and blues and some people start dancing. I love watching people dance to slow music. Rhythm and Blues is my favorite type of music. I'm drinking and eating nachos again.

I'm gone need to go to the gym and work out after tonight.

Casha comes over to me and says, "The pledges should be knocked out by now." It's almost three in the damn morning. Them niggas better be knocked out.

I go in the bedrooms and search purses. I search Jamia and Scalina's purses first. They both have their keys in them. I toss them to Tedran and Patrick.

"We need to wake them up to find out where they parked," I say.

"Relax. Have some fun," Tedran says. "Let's go on a hunt in the neighborhood."

We have to walk all around to search for where the girls parked. It's all of the Greeks at the party out on the street searching for cars that could be anywhere. I'm walking close with Casha, Chaysa, Mianala, and Nana. We are following behind Tedran waiting to hear two beeps from a car.

Everyone is out in the street having conversations, doing Greek calls, drinking, smoking, and messing with people that drive by. When some of the frat boys start hitting peoples' cars that are driving by, I tell the girls we need to get back to the house.

"We can't just leave them with Scalina and Jamia's keys," Casha says.

"Yea. They need to get out the house tomorrow," Mianala says. "We don't want them stuck with us until they get their keys back. Hell, they may end up needing replacement keys considering how fucked up everyone is."

Thirty minutes passes and we still haven't found the cars.

Me and my girls of the night end up venturing off our own direction. We're drunk and just enjoying being close to each other like real friends do. We're saying how good we all look and giving each other advise. We're being real women and lifting our sister up whenever bad things are brought up. We never get mad when someone says something hurtful that has happened. We just respond accordingly to whatever our sister wants to say.

Tedran and Patrick finally find Scalina and Jamia's cars and drive by me and the girls. Me and Casha hop in the car with

Tedran. Chaysa, Mianala, and Nana hop in the car with Patrick. We all get in the backseat because we want to be close and play around. We are driving all over New Orleans.

I love when we're high on the interstate and I can look down at neighborhoods. I just love scenery. Just looking at apartment complexes where everyone has the porch lights on is beautiful.

I look over at Patrick and see Mianala, Nana, and Chaysa taking their tops off and riding in just their bras. They in the car jamming to the damn radio.

"Shona is The One!" Chaysa screams.

"We turned up!" Mianala says and winks at Casha.

Casha turns up the radio. It's on the same station our girls have theirs on. We start dancing hard just like them.

"Turned Up!" Chaysa screams.

"Sssskkkiiioooo!" me and Casha scream. We're flying all over the damn car. We don't have our seatbelts on and neither do the other girls.

"Y'all making me feel young again!" I yell out the window.

"Girl you are young," Mianala says. "You're only thirty-five."

"You sure as hell still move like you're young!" Chaysa screams out the window. She starts rocking her shoulders back and forth like me.

Casha leans over me and screams out the window, "We feel like we're in college again!"

The boys are driving side by side on the freeway. I'm in this car with Tedran, and I'm making sure he doesn't open the glove compartment or anything else that has something he can steal. We're in Scalina's car.

"I wonder where the hell everyone else went," Tedran says to Patrick on the phone. He has him on speaker.

"Derrick is calling me right now. I'll see where they went," Patrick says.

We're so drunk that me and Casha are trying to reach Chaysa, Mianala, and Nana's hands in the other car. Tedran starts making siren noises, and I hit him on his head. He takes his shirt off.

"Why y'all not down to y'all bras like the other girls?" Tedran asks. "I know y'all not thinking about no nigga on a night like this. Y'all need to fucking live."

Casha looks at me. "Girl this been one crazy ass night," she says. "I say we get crazy just this one time."

"Girl we been crazy all night," I say. "We just haven't stripped."

"Just do it with me. Please," Casha says.

I take my shirt off. Me and my girls are smart. We know better than to take out a phone.

Tedran pulls in a neighborhood, and me and Casha wonder where the hell we are. We put our shirts back on. We pull on the side of the street.

"We not there yet," Tedran says. "I need to get high some more before we get where we're going."

Patrick gets in the front seat with Tedran. Me and Casha sit on the car with Mianala, Nana, and Chaysa. I'm not even drinking. I'm just watching them smoke.

We hear Patrick and Tedran talking about going to see Phi Phi Alpha's pledges. He's getting angrier while he talks about them.

When we get to Arkin's house, a Phi Phi Alpha member from another university, I know why. There's two members of Omega Zeta Phi that are being held hostage here. I take a quick shot. They're in the basement chained to the floor.

One day the two boys from Omega Zeta Phi were at a party with Phi Phi Alpha members. They started clowning Phi Phi Alpha's performance at a step competition they got second place in. They started clowning the members parents and prophytes. To be honest, it didn't matter how the Omega Zeta Phi boys insulted Phi Phi Alpha. Greeks are looked at as people that don't tolerate any disrespect.

The hidden truth is that Arkin has relatives that are in Omega Zeta Phi. His cousin Edwin got the two boys to willingly come to his house. The thing with Greeks is because we are a sisterhood and brotherhood, it's easy to just hop in the car with people that are in the same organization. We are taught to trust all of our sisters and brothers, and some people are dumb enough to do that. I know Alpha Eta Nu has over three hundred thousand members worldwide. I would never trust that many damn people. It sounds stupid that someone even has to say that.

Edwin led the two members of Omega Zeta Phi that were talking shit to Arkin's house. The way I heard the story is that everything started out as one big party. The boys played pool and the two boys in Omega Zeta Phi willingly chained themselves to the ground. They thought they were just playing some crazy Greek games. However, they learned that they would be held hostage and not released.

I know for a fact that Arkin has many parties. Lots of people see the two members of Omega Zeta Phi in the Phi Phi Alpha member's house. Somehow the two boys never open their mouths about being held hostage.

"I can't believe this shit," Casha whispers to me.

"You know what the hell it is at this house?" I ask her.

"Girl hella people know them two boys is down there," Casha says.

"You think the girls know?" I ask.

"They might if they talk to the right niggas," Casha says. "You know they cool as fuck, and people like talking to them. They not snitches. I can't believe them two niggas Jordan and Brentin."

"That's they names?" I ask. "What the hell you know? You might know more than me. I didn't even know their names."

"Them niggas crazy. They sick in the head. They be giving girls date rape drugs and all," Casha says. "Word is, Arkin threatened they damn family. He threatened to snitch on them for illegal shit he knew they did. It's all types of ways they got those boys down there. You know Edwin is a little bitch. He don't give a damn about nobody in his frat. He'll snitch on they asses in a heartbeat."

"Edwin need his ass beat," I say.

Me and Casha are maliciously smiling. We know damn well we some bad girls. We done been through too much damn shit in life. So much that we don't give a damn about knowing where people are being held hostage at. Arkin is one bold ass nigga.

He's not worried at all about one day being snitched on and getting locked up.

"This nigga Arkin is a cocaine head," Casha says. "He not worried about a damn thing."

We get in the house and go straight to the basement. Jordan and Brentin are laying on the floor complaining and arguing with each other while three bricks are on Jordan's back and five bricks are on Brentin's back. That's that bullshit I swear. One brick is enough, so I know the Phi Phi Alpha members don't give a damn that one boy has more than the other.

Both Jordan and Brentin have blood dripping from their backs. The bricks are cutting them a little.

There's about thirteen Phi Phi Alpha members here surrounding Jordan and Brentin. They all are thirty or over. They don't give a damn about some college boys that came to an adult party and acted a fool.

"Aye, take one brick off y'all backs," Arkin says. Everyone starts laughing. It smells like that good weed down here. I hope no one asks me to smoke. I keep feeling embarrassed and like a loser saying no.

"Stand up," Derrick says. "Shake each other's hands and thank each other for being good men and coming to the Arkin Suite." Okay, this nigga is being a complete asshole. The Arkin Suite? He's being evil as hell.

Jordan and Brentin don't do as they're told. They've been here for almost three years and no one has said a word, despite all the gatherings that Arkin has had.

"Okay, since niggas don't want to listen," Arkin says holding his beer cup in his hand, "we'll beat that ass again."

Jordan and Brentin have basically been here so long that it doesn't matter if they do as they are told or not; they know no matter what they do, the punishment that is the worst can still happen.

Arkin grabs an extension cord and hits both boys on their stomachs. They start throwing up.

"Oh hell no," Mianala says. "I don't want to even end my night like this. Do something where these niggas won't be throwing up."

Me, Casha, Chaysa, and Nana look at Mianala like she's lost her mind. We sure as hell didn't forget about her just a few hours ago.

"Girl shut the hell up. You were just throwing up earlier," Nana says. She doesn't care to blast her. We are all on our own level now. It's been a long night.

"Why you telling my got damn business bitch?" Mianala asks. "I thought you was my girl?"

"Alright ladies," I say. "Calm down. Our damn pledges done got on y'all nerves." I'm saying anything to calm them down.

"Yea. Maybe we should have brought them another night," Casha says putting her arm around me. "We hate to have our pledges make our Sorors start bitching to one another."

"Yea. My bad girl," I say to Chaysa who's going in on Mianala too. "I didn't know the young bunch would take a toll on your mind."

"It wasn't them," Chaysa says looking at me sad. "This bitch is just crazy thinking we forgot we had to pause things to take care of her." Chaysa loves being around me. I knew she would quickly try to cover up why she's arguing with her line sister. I'll always be titled her sister, but she never wants to lose me as the good friend that I am towards her. She wants me to continue to act like a real sister to her. She doesn't want us to be like those Sorors that really hate each other and treat each other like shit although they are bound as sisters for life.

"I think it's about to be a cat fight," one of the Phi Phi Alpha members says.

"Nigga shut up," Chaysa says. "This shit y'all have going on with these two boys is weak as hell, and your sex probably is too."

"Bitch, shut the fuck up," the same Phi Phi Alpha member says. "You ain't all that bitch."

"Nigga sit your whack ass down," I say defending my girl. "Focus on your weak ass prey, and figure out why the hell you get mad when somebody talks about your sex."

"Fuck you and this whack ass shit you have going on," Casha adds.

"Bitch, you lucky you a woman," the same Phi Phi Alpha member says.

"Nigga, be lucky I stopped weight training a long time ago," Casha says. "If I didn't, I could whoop your ass."

"Yea. Don't be trying to clown me and my girls," Mianala says.

Arkin knees Jordan and Brentin in their growing. They both fall to the floor and groan.

Derrick has Patrick and Tedran go upstairs to talk to him for a bit. I have the girls follow me to go with them.

"Help y'all selves to whatever is in the kitchen," Derrick says.

Me and the girls been eating and drinking all night. We never stop getting hungry though because we won't stop drinking. It feels too good eating after drinking. My girls are smoking too. I know they keep getting the munchies.

Me and the girls sit on the counter in Arkin's kitchen. We're eating from a vegetable platter that has dip.

The girls keep talking about everything that's happened tonight. Chaysa and Mianala are acting like they never argued downstairs. I'm listening to Derrick, Patrick and Tedran. Derrick is telling them that Arkin is getting tired of having Jordan and Brentin down there. He's thinking about killing them. Chaysa and Mianala look at me when they hear that.

"Don't worry girls," Casha says. "They not really gone kill them niggas."

I look at Casha like what the fuck. Chaysa, Mianala, and Nana couldn't possibly think that Arkin would want to keep them niggas down there his whole life. Whatever. Me and my girl have to keep these young Sorors' minds in a good place.

"They just trying to sound all hard," I whisper to the girls. "They know we can hear them."

The three young Sorors don't want to buy me and Casha's story.

"We mean it. Don't listen to a thing them niggas say," Casha says. "They stay trying to make us think they some gangsters. Half the time, they just want to feel bigger than what they are by discussing crazy ass stuff."

"Y'all know they treat women like they are beneath them," I say. The three girls start to relax. They can believe that statement. All these damn frat boys think they are bigger than all women alive.

I'm tired as hell. I can't wait for this night to be over.

After hearing Derrick's statement about Arkin getting tired of Jordan and Brentin, I tune out of his conversation. It can't get much worse than that. I want to hear him say something good, but I don't want to keep listening to the hell he's talking about just to get to the good.

"I want some ice cream," Casha says.

"Ice cream and vegetables?" I say. I'm so fucking tired.

"I mean I want some more damn nachos," Casha says.

"I think we are all beat up by this night," I say. "It's time to call it a night."

I let Tedran and Patrick know it's time to get back to the sorority house. They need to get they own cars, and come back to Arkin's house.

Once we get back to the sorority house, we make sure all the pledges are still laying down, then my girls and I go in the bedroom. Now that we're comfortable being in the place we will sleep, we're not as tired as we were. We get close to each other on the bed and watch television until we fall asleep.

I wake up in the middle of the night and decide I want to go home. I wake Casha up and tell her.

"It's okay girl. Go," Casha says. "I'll take care of the pledges."

When I get home, I sit by my fireplace, pour myself some wine, and mix it with a blended mix of fruit. Afterwards, I sit in a warm tub of water and drink. Thoughts of my grandmother come to mind. I space off.

I felt like I experienced a mid-life crisis and at the same time I reached a state where I needed to have family love. I walked right in that girl saying good stuff about herself who was lacking love and didn't know.

"Without real love, you wouldn't be here," my grandma says. "Sit up straight. You're too pretty to be slouching." I sit up straight at the kitchen counter where my grandmother and I are sitting. "They knew one day you would need that love of a family. They're all grown," my grandmother continues. "They know how your momma acts. Some of them know how she was practicing on you since you were born. They can't believe you still here. You do what I say do, and get these projects done."

My grandmother knows I have lots of talents other than stepping and coaching. I like to write, dance, and sing. My grandma gets on my case a lot about finishing these books I'm writing. She's very strict.

"You make sure you let them know how I raised you," my grandmother continues. "Let them know how we love each other."

I rub my forehead and snap back into reality.

I'm not someone that can relax feeling good about her mother. I'm not someone that gets to enjoy knowing that my mother was a good woman, who felt good that she had a beautiful daughter. I'm someone whose mother gets uglier by the second. The thought of her makes her get more painful to look at. I hate seeing new pictures of her.

I can't wait for the day that I just look at Nadia as nothing. I'm going to convince myself that I am adopted. It will work. I know it will. Soon nothing Nadia says to me will matter.

It's terrible that my reality with family is so bad, that I can make up anything I want and be content with it, and not even care.

When I get out the shower, I put on my robe and go sit by the fireplace. I miss smoking my weed, having my drink, and sitting by my fireplace. I need some type of damn substitute for the marijuana.

213

I get up and bang my fists on my counter in my living room. I'm so frustrated that I can't start smoking again.

11

I'm rushing to get to my homegirl Dayla's house. Her sister Isyss goes to Ann High School. She is a student helper for that witch Jessie McGruder. Isyss said she had some information that is real deep to tell me. I'm trying to drive safely, but I keep getting honked at so I know I'm not.

Isyss said I would want to hear everything in person, so here I am on the road.

"Girl come in," Dayla eagerly says when I get to her house. "Isyss told me a little, and I made her stop. I was getting mad as hell. I don't think I can listen to that shit twice in one day."

Me, Dayla, and Isyss sit in the living room.

"Girl I was with Jessie McGruder all day," Isyss says. "She walked in our school theater angry about something while Jasmine coached the step team."

"How many people are on it?" I ask.

"Ann High has fifteen members," Isyss says. "Jasmine was telling the team to make their arms stiff and their claps crisp. She demanded her members, who were slowly going through their movements, to show her they weren't leaving anything out and could deliver the beat properly."

Isyss tells me how Jasmine's very impressed with her members because they catch on fast, they practice after hours, they aren't scared to ask questions about moves and positions they don't know, and most importantly, she loves that they respect her.

Isyss lets me know that Mrs. McGruder sternly observed the practice for a minute then said she needed to speak to Jasmine who had no clue what had her old advisor in a bad mood.

"Jasmine and Mrs. McGruder are close. Mrs. McGruder treats her like a daughter," Isyss says. "She takes her out to eat, she buys her clothes, and she even allows Jasmine to chill with her in her office during school hours, despite the fact that some of the other staff members are trying to reduce the amount of visitors' people have during school hours. I heard people say that Mrs. McGruder was more than happy to allow Jasmine to continue coaching Ann's step team when she graduated because she herself is not good at creating choreography, and neither were any of the returning members. So when Jasmine graduated, she had no problem paying her to continue being the coach."

"How often do you be with McGruder?" I ask.

"Girl, a lot. I need these hours to help me win some scholarships," Isyss says. "Jasmine has no clue that the only reason Mrs. McGruder treats her like she's her own is because she wants to make sure she continues to coach Ann High's step team as long as she lives in Louisiana. I heard Mrs. McGruder was planning on paying you to come back, but when y'all fell out, she had to go for Jasmine."

"Tell me more," I say.

"Jasmine told her team she would be right back and had them continue practicing," Isyss says.

"Girl please," Dayla says to Isyss. "Shona started that team. Don't say that team belongs to that bitch. I don't care if she coaching it now or not. Them bitches were wrong for what they did to my girl."

Isyss says she went with McGruder and Jasmine to her office. She says McGruder has one of the biggest offices in the school being that she is the vice principal.

"Mrs. McGruder always dresses professionally," Isyss says. "She works out a lot. Anyone can tell just by looking at her muscular arms."

"That bitch has more muscle than her husband," Dayla says.

Isyss says that Jasmine asked McGruder what was going on.

216

She said Jasmine was nervous as to what she would hear because it's not often she sees McGruder disturbed. McGruder had Jasmine pull a chair up next to her and sit down.

"Jasmine took a seat by her and asked what was up again," Isyss says. "I was anxious myself to hear what the issue was."

Isyss says McGruder turned the computer towards Jasmine and they looked at The Big Bang Step Off website.

"Jasmine said she checked out the website a couple days ago," Isyss says. "Mrs. McGruder pointed intensely to something on the screen, then moved her finger. She touched the screen so hard you could hear her finger when it made contact with it."

Isyss says that Jasmine read *Mission High School* in a low voice looking confused and wondering why McGruder was showing her the site.

"Mrs. McGruder pointed again to *Mission High School*, then slid her finger down," Isyss says. "You should've seen Jasmine's ugly face when she read *Shona Jackson*."

"They don't know my sister knows you," Dayla says. "She not gone never tell them. Any time them bitches discuss you, she will let you know."

I met Dayla at someone's party a while ago. We been cool ever since.

"She already knows that," Isyss says to her sister. "Anyways. Jasmine was angry. I know her heart was beating fast. Her mouth sure dropped. The girl was super upset that you are a part of the competition. She said she never thought she would have to see you again after high school, let alone compete with you."

"I don't know why," Dayla says. "She knows Shona loves to step."

"Jasmine started cracking her knuckles and her face kept

217

getting more serious while she kept staring at your name on the screen," Isyss says. "Jasmine looked at the photo of you, and then at the one hanging behind Mrs. McGruder on the wall. It was the same photo, except you cropped all the old members out of yours, and Mrs. McGruder just cropped you out of hers."

I look at Isyss crazy and so does Dayla.

"I need something to drink," Dayla says.

"You telling me she cropped me out of the photo in her office?" I ask.

"Girl, let's face it," Isyss says. "That woman hates you, but you know I got your back."

"Just listening to this shit has me wanting to beat the hell out of Jasmine," Dayla says. "If McGruder wasn't so old, I'd want to whoop her ass too."

"Jasmine started saying you must've just entered Mission High into the competition," Isyss says. "She said they weren't there when she checked. She started wondering how you even got hired there."

"Jasmine knows it would be hard for anyone to reject someone like Shona with her natural stepping ability," Dayla says. "Mission High is one of the top high schools in the nation. It's swarmed with so many different activities, that a lot of people, including Jasmine and Mrs. McGruder who are familiar with the school, didn't think another program could be implemented, let alone find a time slot for students to do another activity."

"I love how you go from using so many curse words to sounding educated," Isyss says.

"Finish telling my girl the story," Dayla says.

"Mrs. McGruder started talking about how you were a part of the Luminous LA program," Isyss says. "She sounded so disgusted. She told Jasmine you coach at a site for thirty days

218

for two hours in the afternoon, then they transfer your arrogant ass to another school."

"She's always been that bitch to detail every fucking thing going on with someone else," I say.

"Jasmine and Mrs. McGruder both looked like they wanted to punch the walls," Isyss says. "Jasmine said she couldn't believe you got in. She said that usually that proper, uptight, and prestigious staff over at Luminous LA only hires relatives or people they know. They don't just let anyone join their program. She said they're real picky about who they pay their high salaries too. She said she knew you couldn't have crossed paths with anyone that would give you one of the programs that require going to various schools. Those people never leave their desks. She kept wondering how and why they hired you. She called you psycho."

"And she got the face of a bitch that can break concrete," Dayla says. "Concrete face. I need to come up with a better name."

"Mrs. McGruder looked Jasmine square in her eyes," Isyss says. "She said Ann's step team needed to be on point. She said she didn't want you walking away with that trophy."

"I'm surprised she didn't bring up what you did to her," Dayla says to me.

"Let me finish my story," Isyss says. I didn't tell her about me losing my mind. "Mrs. McGruder poured herself a glass of water and asked Jasmine if she remembered what you did to her."

"What did she say?" I ask.

"Jasmine just nodded her head yes," Isyss says. "Mrs. McGruder said she couldn't sleep for days. She said she was terrified."

"She didn't say any details about what happened?" Dayla asks.

"Nope," Isyss says.

"Good, because your ass don't need to know," Dayla says. "And just what were you doing all this time they were having this conversation?"

"Being nosy," Isyss says. "I was writing in a notebook. They thought I wasn't paying attention to them. They don't even know I like step. But anyways, Mrs. McGruder started asking Jasmine how the team was coming along with the choreography and Jasmine said they were doing alright."

"From what you saw, how were they doing?" Dayla asks.

"To be honest, they were doing alright," Isyss says.

"Girl you know they not fucking with you," Dayla says.

Isyss says McGruder was not happy hearing the word alright. McGruder said alright was not good enough.

"Mrs. McGruder asked Jasmine if she needed to make practice more than four days a week and longer than two hours every morning," Isyss says. "She told Jasmine she knew she could and would do it if she had to."

"They need to," Dayla says. My girl is not happy that I have to listen to this bullshit.

"Jasmine kept talking about how she was not that familiar with Luminous LA's program, but she said she did know y'all are only allowed to practice no more than two days a week, unless a day is needed to make it within the thirty practice three month contracts," Isyss says. "She said Ann High already practices double what Luminous LA's students do. She said they would be fine."

I'm getting happy knowing that McGruder is worried about Ann High's performance level. "It's good to know she still acknowledges my talent in a bitter old lady way," I say deviously. "Tell me more."

"But get this," Isyss says. "Mrs. McGruder kept asking

220

Jasmine if she was sure the team was doing well enough. She was thinking hard about having more practices. She started to say your name and only said the beginning. She couldn't say the full name."

"I know that bitch hates saying her name after what she did to her," Dayla laughs. I playfully push her and lean my head on her shoulder.

"Mrs. McGruder told Jasmine that she better know that you are going to go twice as hard being that Ann High is in the competition," Isyss says. "Then she asked her if she had been looking at those frat videos she sent her for ideas."

"Why the hell are they using other peoples' steps?" Dayla asks.

Isyss says Jasmine rolled her eyes at McGruder. She says Jasmine asked McGruder if she was saying that she didn't think she could come up with good choreography. Jasmine said they copied the frat videos last year. She said she was done with that. She said she was coming up with the choreography this year.

"Jasmine said, and yes, she could do it better than you Shona," Isyss says. "She said the steps they were in there doing, she came up with them. She started getting madder and saying she's just as good as you, if not better than you. She told Mrs. McGruder she couldn't prove that if she kept making her use recycled steps from other teams. She said she was under your instruction for three years."

Me and Dayla look shocked again.

"What the hell is that supposed to mean?" I ask. After what Isyss just said, it sounded like Jasmine was trying to hint to McGruder that she was tired and hated being under me.

"She better had meant that she learned a damn lot being under you," Dayla says.

"Mrs. McGruder asked her to stop saying your name," Isyss says. "Jasmine said she'd been under your instruction for three years, so she knows what you are capable of. She said she knows how you like to do fast and complex steps."

Isyss says McGruder was wondering where Jasmine was going with her comments. Jasmine kept going on and on about how she knew what to expect from me, but said that I didn't know what to expect from her. She said I would probably think that she was going to come to the table with steps other people made up. She said she'll show me though. She said she would make me feel stupid. She said she could create everything, and could do it better than me. She said that Jasmine Pent is the choreographer. Not Shona Jackson.

"And Isyss you remember all of this?" Dayla asks. "You got that fire memory."

"Mrs. McGruder's forehead wrinkled as she took a step back and caressed her forehead at the sound of Shona's name," Isyss says. "She hates to hear it period."

"How she think I feel hearing hers?" I rhetorically ask.

"Don't worry," Isyss says. "I'm almost done."

"Girl, I'm not rushing you," I say. "I'm happy you're telling me this. You know I don't want to make you upset. I love Dayla too much to be getting smart with her little sister."

"Girl, say whatever you want to her," Dayla says. "She ain't nobody." I know better not to do that though.

"I'm almost done," Isyss says. "Jasmine had an attitude and asked Mrs. McGruder why she was shaking her head. She started to think Mrs. McGruder didn't have faith in her coaching ability."

"The damn team probably don't have faith in it either," Dayla says. She has me laughing.

"Mrs. McGruder said she was just shocked," Isyss says. "She

said she never thought she'd have to look at that evil thing again in her life."

"Who's that evil thing?" I ask.

Isyss nods her head and says, "She was talking about you. She said it hurt to say or hear your name, that's how much you got under her skin. She said she would never forget what you did to her and her husband. She said you should be in prison right now, not coaching step teams."

"Hell naw," Dayla says.

"Jasmine asked Mrs. McGruder if she had just found out today that you were coaching Mission," Isyss says. "Mrs. McGruder said yes."

Isyss says McGruder said her husband had just called and told her. She said he was just as upset as she was. Neither of them thought they'd be cursed and have to see me again. Mr. McGruder said he almost spilled his coffee when he looked at the website to see any new additions. Mrs. McGruder said Ann High needs to annihilate us. She said she didn't want that criminal walking out of the arena smiling with her team. That criminal would be me. She said she wanted me in tears. She wants me to hate her so much that I think about coming for her and her husband again.

"If only that bitch knew how much I hated her," I laugh. Dayla does too.

"Mrs. McGruder said she knew you hated watching them perform and throw it in your face with their smiles, so she knows you'd hate losing to them," Isyss says. "She said when y'all lose, and she said y'all better lose, she said you would come to their house again. But this time her husband and herself would anticipate it. Then they could do what they should've done the last time, which is beat your ass until you're unrecognizable, and make sure you're unable to get away

223

without leaving evidence and drive off without a prison sentence."

"That bitch needs to check herself," Dayla says. "She is talking too much shit."

Isyss says Jasmine had confidence that Ann High would beat my team.

"Mrs. McGruder said she didn't just want to beat your team; she said she wanted to make y'all regret joining the competition," Isyss says. "She said she wanted to make y'all not even want to perform if they go before y'all! She said she wanted to be able to smile and laugh in your face, and make you lose sleep at night because you're so furious that they beat y'all. She told Jasmine she knew it would eat you alive if you lose to the man and woman that took you off the team, and the girl who took your head captain spot."

Isyss says at first Mrs. McGruder's main focus was getting her students another performance and a shot at viewing some of the best step teams in Louisiana, and she didn't care about winning first place or placing at all, despite the team never coming in second to anyone.

Now that I'm in the competition, it's bigger than just getting to experience other teams. Now it's about making me, her worst enemy, want to pull up in front of her house again. It's about making me lose sleep at night thinking about the loss I suffered to the three people that made my senior year not worthwhile. It's about Mr. and Mrs. McGruder having another opportunity to smile bright in my face as I watch them enjoy holding a first-place trophy that she had no contribution in them getting.

"I'm not even trippin'," I say. "I just wish I could've picked up on her being a nothing ass bitch before I asked her to be our advisor."

224

"Mrs. McGruder said she wanted you to leave the arena angry," Isyss says. "She said she wanted your arrogant self to see you're not the best stepper, let alone the best choreographer. She said her and Jasmine both know you think you're the best stepper to walk the planet. Mrs. McGruder says she hates you, and wants Jasmine to make you hate them even more than you did when you were kicked off the team and she gave her your spot."

"What did Jasmine say?" I ask.

"She told Mrs. McGruder not to worry," Isyss says. "She said she'd make sure the team was ready. She said she'd been working hard putting together different moves, formations, and beats, and she'd been drilling in everyone how important facials are. She said they would be fine. She said they are going to show up and show out. She said if they go before *Shon* and corrected herself saying, if they go before the arrogant witches team, that y'all wouldn't want to perform and would probably leave."

"Don't worry about it Shona," Dayla says. "Your name is too pretty anyways."

"Jasmine looked at your face on the computer screen again," Isyss says. "She said *it's on*."

12

I remember a day back when I was in college and I was just sitting in my teddy bear pajamas watching step competitions from all over the world on my computer. Their energy, loudness and sounds were crisp as they stomped and clapped. Watching the crowd turn up was turning me up just watching through my screen. I knew I was capable of creating the same reaction; I did it three years at Ann High.

More inspired and anxious, I turned on some music and started making up steps. For a second, I forgot I was at my dorm. I temporarily forgot I had roommates and lived on the second floor because I stomped like I was on the concrete outside. My neighbors below were poking the ceiling with a broom. That was their way of telling me to stop. I didn't. After about ten minutes, Melinda was knocking on the door.

"Yes?" I answered.

"Some people are at the door for you," Melinda said.

"Yes," I said to the three girls at the front door.

"Can you stop all the stomping, we live downstairs and we're trying to study," one girl said.

"Some of us are trying to sleep," another girl said.

"Sure," I said with a fake smile.

I closed the door and turned around to Melinda who was being nosy with her hands across her chest. I pushed my room door and Melinda caught it before it shut.

"Can you turn down the music too?" Melinda rudely asked.

"Yes," I forcibly said.

Melinda left without saying anything. All she did was roll her eyes as she shut the door.

I put on some sweats and a hoody and went to the outdoor basketball court in the dorm area to continue practicing. The pole lights towered above the court, so I had plenty of light that late night.

The wind was blowing and I was doing what I loved as the breeze went through my hair. It was paradise. Some dorm residents were watching me from their windows and porches, but it didn't bother me. Stepping is as natural as breathing for me.

Exhausted from stepping all night, I slept past my alarm. Ciera knocked on my dorm room door.

"You ready for class?" Ciera asked.

I tried to roll back over, but fell off the bed.

"I been doing more research on the competition," Ciera said talking about a competition I had entered Cupperton's team in while I was back and forth between my room and the bathroom putting on clothes, brushing my teeth and washing my face. "They want people to showcase during the intermissions."

"We are competing. We don't need to showcase," I said.

Ciera looked at me dumbfounded.

"It wouldn't hurt to get more exposure. You never know who will be in attendance," Ciera said. "You've been trying to find other places to perform besides basketball games, so why not do it at the step competition? You'll already be there."

I couldn't believe she was suggesting I let Legit perform considering how they acted at rehearsal. And at this high level step competition at that.

"I don't think it's a good idea," I seriously said. "They can't even show up to practice on time, and none of them are willing to put in extra time to perfect our routines. They already got my nerves bad."

Legit didn't need to do more than what they already were. They were undeserving of extra. I bet they wouldn't even care if I told them and decided not to do it. They made it loud and clear that they didn't appreciate anything I'd done to get the

227

team going, and the things I did to keep it running.

The members in Legit changed, but the attitudes and ways they treated me didn't.

"Girl forget this team," I said. "I'm not even sure if I'm coaching here next year. I'm just going to finish this year off with the team, get us maybe three more performances, and not wreck my nerves next year and create a team with these ungrateful people on it."

"Just think about it," Ciera said.

I snap out of it and start making up choreography for Luminous LA. I can stomp as loud as I want in my own damn house.

I go chill with Professor Tobin again. He's walking back and forth as he looks through the graded papers in his hand. He looks mean and seems pretty upset, but no one takes him serious. Everyone is paying for their education, so as long as he passes them, that's all they care about.

Me on the other hand, I actually liked to make A's and B's whether or not I would apply the class in my future or not.

"It is important to take notes," Professor Tobin states. "I don't understand why I have to keep explaining this."

The students look at Professor Tobin, but no one is actually listening. The girl front and center is playing tic tac toe, and the girl next to her is texting under her desk.

Not wanting to listen to Professor Tobin nag, I drift off.

I visualize myself in Nadia's car during the early morning during my high school years.

"You're not that good of a stepper anyways," Nadia evilly said to me. "Get out my car little girl."

I exited Nadia's car and walked in Ann High School's theater looking angry and like I was ready to kill someone. Even though I knew I was a great stepper, it still hurt that Nadia didn't hesitate to tell me I wasn't a good one.

One of my teammates said, *"Hi Shona,"* when he saw me in the theater. Boiling mad, I didn't say anything. I just continued to walk to the audience seats where I put my things down and released my tears.

One of my male teammates came to comfort me. "Momma know, momma know child," he said as he put his arms around me.

Mrs. McGruder was standing to the side of the theater appearing to be upset.

I got myself together and walked on stage.

"Let's review where we left off. Five, six, seven, eight," I said.

Everyone did the step, and after only eight seconds a few people got off beat.

"That sounds terrible!" I loudly said. "This is how a real stepper does it!"

I did the step alone and at a faster pace than anyone else could. Some of my teammates looked at me like I was a showoff. Others acted like they didn't care.

"That's how a real stepper would do it!" I said loud.

Mrs. McGruder was so angry at what I was saying, my attitude, and my actions, that she picked up her things and left the auditorium.

I wake up at the sound of everyone getting their things and leaving class.

Professor Tobin stops me before I make it out the door.

"Shona how do you expect to learn more, and for free at that, in this class if you're asleep?" Professor Tobin asks.

"I do a lot of reading on my own," I say. "I will be okay."

"Stay awake in my class if you're going to be visiting," Professor Tobin sternly states.

"Sorry Professor Tobin," I say. "I have a lot on my mind."

"Is everything okay?" Professor Tobin asks.

"Yes, but I have to go," I say. "See ya."

I wonder if Mrs. McGruder was wanting and waiting for me to say the wrong thing. Everything about her posture, vibe and facials in the theater that day were that of a mean scrooge.

What kind of advisor doesn't even check on her student that is in tears?

I head straight to Cupperton's gym after class and only see Abbey and Charity who are playing cards. I hold myself together as I approach them while they sit on the bleachers.

"Hey, do you guys know where everyone is?" I ask.

Abbey shakes her head no.

Charity says, "No."

I know they can tell I'm fed up because I'm turning in circles with my hand on my forehead.

"Well let's get started," I say.

I rehearse a simple combination with the girls. I don't like to waste time. I have to reteach it when everyone else decides to arrive. I definitely don't want to give the other members the satisfaction of thinking that practice can't resume without them. Especially not Regina and Shanell.

As practice continues, all the members lollygag in sporadically.

Towards the end, everyone makes it and I am able to go through the entire routine once with everyone. It's not perfect, but it's decent.

"Okay great job everyone," I say. "Tomorrow is the game. Let's try to be here at seven when it starts."

"Is there any time I can come to your place because I need more help?" Shanell asks.

I can't believe this girl. This is the first time Shanell has ever asked for extra help, and it's the day before our performance. I want to say: *if you don't have it by now, chances are you won't tomorrow because you haven't been practicing it the right way,* but I know she will say I'm wrong and feel like I don't have any confidence in her.

If I thought Shanell was awful and would completely ruin the routine, I would suck it up and help her, but she has the moves and the beat, so I'm not. She wants to practice extra so she can go all in with her facials and attitudes which will throw her off because she hasn't been doing them thus far.

Shanell's lost her mind. It's sickening to me that a member that comes when she wants and at what time she wants would have the nerve to ask for extra help.

"No, I'm busy," I say. "Can anyone here spare time to help Shanell?"

"I will help her," Regina volunteers.

"Alright, I will see everyone tomorrow night," I say.

While everyone exits, I start to get weak. My grandma pops in my head. I need to sit down. I take a seat on the floor behind one of the basketball rims.

13

I'm at home about to read a magazine. I sit on my couch in my living room and space off.

I see my grandma sitting in front of me in the dining room.

"They saw me and said they love me," I say to my grandma. "They called out to me for help through all of their pain. They envisioned me just the way I am."

My grandma wants to tell me another story of people who loved me who got caught up in some of the worst bullshit this world has to offer.

"Help me. They're torturing me," one girl said to me. "I was good to you."

"Listen to me," my grandma says.

My grandma has me thinking about this crazy society. This society is so hurtful that it picks people a part in ways I can't imagine. But these peers of mine said they loved me and no one could break that love they had for me no matter how others broke me down. They wanted me to really feel the love they had for me.

"Focus. While Man Man was on drugs, it was sad to listen to his stories," my grandma continues. "But I didn't have a choice."

My grandma tells me that Olifus told her of a man named Canel. Olifus is Man Man.

"There was a man named Canel. Olifus always started his story about Canel that way," my grandma says. She says Olifus told her Canel was almost fifty years old. He was a brown man that knew he was ugly to anyone he ever took interest in. He settled for a woman he thought was ugly because he knew the woman of his dreams who was model type would never fall for him.

Canel liked to hang out at spots that young people did, just to see how they would look at him. After so many bad looks, Canel couldn't even take the good ones serious anymore. This is a world where people have to have tough skin. Someone would look at Canel in a nice way and then later regret it and come back and look at him ugly.

"They probably were always looking at him in an ugly way and he took it the wrong way," I say. "That's why they came back to make sure he knew they didn't take any interest in him."

"There's a lot of people that don't want any misinterpretation of how they view others," my grandma says. My grandma continues to say that Canel would visit places like amusement parks, skating rinks, and theaters just to be around young people. "Olifus told me he would bring his young relatives with him just to disguise more what his intentions were," my grandma continues.

She says Canel's favorite spot was a record store though. He took interest in the spot because he noticed a certain group of individuals would go to it often. He even started to learn specific days they would go. He would change his appearance so these specific individuals wouldn't recognize him.

Canel was desperate for a day that people would continuously look at him like he was a fine human being, but it never came. The rude stares would continue. The quick glances then looking away at anything that was next in sight continued. People falling at the sight of him continued.

"Wait. People would fall when they saw this man?" I ask. "He was that ugly?"

"See. There are things that you never had to deal with," my grandma says. "There are some real mad people out there baby."

Olifus would tell my grandma how Canel just wanted better thoughts, which were a solid group of nice-looking people in his head. Canel came upon a certain batch of them, and never made eye contact with them. He wanted to just enjoy how they looked physically and get to sleep at night. He wanted to please his natural desires in his thoughts. He didn't want them ruined.

"So was he just walking around the record store or socializing with someone he knew?" I ask.

"He would pretend to be interested in purchasing something," my grandma says. "He usually walked out with some headphones, speakers, movies, or CDs. He didn't want to cause any attention he didn't want. He's a black older male. If he's constantly seen at a place without purchasing something, especially a small record store, people will take notice. There were plenty of times he bought a few things."

My grandmother tells me Canel brought small kids with him to the store before too. He knew how to get the attention he needed the store employees to give him.

"Grandma, who were these people Canel liked so much?" I ask.

"They attended Freshtin High," my grandma says. "The record store was down the street from the school." My grandma tells me that Man Man told her a story about a group of high school kids that went to Freshtin High. "This was no ordinary group of kids," my grandma continues. "This was a real classroom full of kids with good looks and personalities. These kids were many different colors."

She says Man Man named all the students. My grandma only tells me of Tina, the main girl in Man Man's story. Leonard, the main boy in his story. Marissa, Tina's best friend. Devon, Leonard's best friend. Marla, Alana, Alisa, Kevin, Dennis and Alonzo. All of the kids were eighteen at the time.

"These kids knew how to have a good time," my grandma says. She says they were in class early all the time. They would have rap battles. They would clown each other and not take it personal.

My grandma says the high school students were all talented; however, they all specialized in singing, and some could sing and rap. They could all play instruments as well.

"Each student I tell you about is very important," my grandma says. "Olifus told me about this boy Leonard. Leonard was fine beyond reason. He was very light, tall, and was in shape. He wasn't muscular, but he had a nice build that would make any man that worked out wonder how Leonard kept his fit body. He was just someone that people would question where he came from because he looked so good."

My grandma says Leonard didn't have to say anything. He didn't have to smile. He didn't have to smirk. Even on his worst

234

day he looked good. He would have to factually get up and say okay, today I'm going to make myself look bad. He would have to create someone that was drastically different than him. A little bit to nothing of effort wouldn't work. Leonard would have to change his face completely.

My grandma continues to say that Leonard was smart in that aspect too. He knew the face was an important part of his body that made people attracted to him. He wasn't stupid at all in that department. Leonard knew he didn't really have to change his body type at all. He just needed to do something about his face if he wanted different attention. However, Leonard was a normal boy. He was who he was.

Leonard was like any other boy that was fine as hell. There were days he would look at people and see their reactions. He would see people go from complete shock looking at him because he looked so good, to barely able to move. He eventually laid in bed one day and understood that those people did not look good to him. They were people that he wouldn't even give the time of day. While they were looking shocked because he looked so good, he was looking at them with disgust and didn't even realize it.

"I recognized that I do that to people to grandma," I say. Recently I've been noticing that I unconsciously look at ugly people like *where the hell did they come from?* At work at the warehouse, one girl I noticed was super hideous. Warehouse work is my main job. Anyways, this girl was short, had blue eyes that could blind you because they were just so fucked up on her face, and she was fat. I recognized that she was the type to actually pay attention to how many times someone would look at her, and how they would look at her.

"I said to myself that this girl has killed some people before," I say to my grandma. "There's no way she could deal with the pain of how the people of this world would look at her frightened. Especially children who are the same height as her, and she is a grown woman." This girl was the first person I said off sight has killed someone. I was just so disgusted. I was wondering how she just couldn't kill herself. I mean, if someone knows she looks like that, she should just kill herself. The majority of people here have a unique way of looking, but here we are looking in this girl's eyes and she resembles that of a creature from a horror movie. I wanted to hurt this girl. She doesn't just get to kill people because she's an off looking person. She probably can't even look at herself in the mirror. I know she keeps track of how many times someone looks at her, and how quick they are to look away or not look at her at all once they recognize she can possibly ruin their thoughts, sight, and take their life just by looking at her, or the thought of her in a dream.

This girl was one that I knew thought *well I'm here, and no one has the right to tell me I shouldn't be. I'll get everyone back and if they can't fight me, oh well.* I know she has a killing facility where she gets all of her anger out. There's no way she likes anyone that looks good.

I had my moments where I wanted to look at this girl like *what the fuck are you doing here,* but thought she had a good strategy to get people in her killing facility. This girl makes me sick to my stomach. I can't believe a person could be so ugly in the eyes alone and her face and body type make it even worse.

There's no way people would flirt with this girl with their eyes. They would just want her to drop dead as if she was hit by electrocution.

"Grandma, I know there was a day when this girl realized the only thing she could do was kill people," I say. "She cracked. She knew there was more people out there just like her, and anyone with sense who was built like her would know that all the nice-looking people would have to go."

Even if I could look at this bitch for a long time, or wanted to be her friend, which would never happen, I know so many more nice-looking people have pissed her off that she would just plan to kill me one day and play along like she liked me. She so damn hideous in the eyes and appearance in general, that she makes me want to look at her mean like *why is she here.* She's used to it though. She's had so much prey or has so much still waiting

236

on her return from work, that she can now look everyone in the eyes again.

"Let me get back to Olifus' story," my grandma says. She continues telling me about Leonard. She says Leonard didn't have to do much to make friends. He was the cool cat in the classroom. He was the main one people didn't want to say anything bad about them. He was someone that had followers that weren't even a part of his clique.

"One day when Leonard was at the record store, he was really into himself. It was just one of them days," my grandma continues. "Leonard was at the store acting as cool as he wanted to be. Not one bad word could ruin his day. He was feeling fly and didn't care about anything going on around him."

She says Leonard spoke to a few of the workers about some of the artists he was looking for in the CD section of the store. He was making conversations with a lot of people that walked by him. He was very social this day. Nothing sneaky or conniving crossed his mind.

"Okay grandma. I get it. He was having a really good day," I say.

"Be patient with me baby," my grandma says. "Canel was in the store this day."

My heart drops. The way my grandma worded all of that saying nothing but good things about Leonard, then switched to saying Canel was in the store, makes him seem like a real villain.

She continues with her story. She says Canel was browsing many sections and talking to workers too. He pretended to read a lot of the information sections of the items he was picking up. He spent a lot of time making facials that made it seem like he couldn't make up his mind on whether he wanted to purchase certain things. Canel would ask for prices and even ask about returning some of the things he had purchased.

Canel was an older man, but he had more stabilization in his mind than he made himself out to have. He played the part that he felt society had given brown men like himself. He acted impatient at times, and angry about the items he was talking about. He thought that made him appear attractive in front of younger people when he showed he was an adult that didn't settle for anything less than what he wanted. These were twisted ways he acted, thinking younger people would see him as a cool person.

"Does that make sense?" my grandma asks.

"Canel was messed up in the head," I say. "It makes perfect sense."

My grandma says Canel noticed Leonard in the record store this particular day. He saw that Leonard was being very social and knew he felt real cool. This was a day that Canel didn't want to pass by. Once Canel recognized that Leonard was on his A game and thought he was in a one hundred percent good mood, Canel wanted to make eye contact with Leonard. Leonard was dressed to impress, had a fresh haircut, and his personality was very fun and cool.

Canel thought of how to go about getting Leonard to notice him. He went to the CD section and stood next to Leonard. The old man dropped his keys on purpose and Leonard picked them up for him because that's what people usually do.

"Leonard's eyes got real big when he looked in Canel's eyes," my grandma says. Canel was so used to bad looks though, that no matter what look Leonard did, he didn't feel handsome enough to get a genuine nice and friendly look from the young man. All of the thoughts Canel had about Leonard were crushed.

"The girl named Tina reminds me of you," my grandma says. My grandma says Tina was the most talented person in the class. She could play the flute, violin, and piano. What she was the best at was singing. "The entire class wanted to be around Tina," my grandma continues. "She was a rare individual. She had a fun and loving personality that could draw anyone in."

"Tina was a brown skinned girl. For eighteen years old, she looked like she could be in her twenties. She had a nice thin shape, and a good height to her too," my grandma says. "Tina could dress well and was always willing to say things to cheer people up."

238

My grandma smiles at me. She knows I know kind words can go a long way from someone that is beautiful to an individual. She knows any chance I get to cheer someone up, I'll do it. There's no hesitation. I've always been this type of person.

Now I'm thinking about telling Nadia about the assault again.

"Keep writing," my grandma says. "I've never let you down. I never will."

My grandma says in her day it was so racist, that it was unbelievable that Tina was even alive. Brown people with talent don't last long on this Earth. First, we have our own kind that don't want us to succeed. They make our lives harder by their evil spirits and conniving acts towards us. "Tina was like you," my grandma says. "She never thought it was her talent that made people hate her so much. She couldn't figure out why she was disliked. Tina was like you also because any time she could get revenge she would."

"Then those people messing with her get to hold their heads high knowing she might wind up in jail one day behind them," I say.

"This world is wicked baby," my grandma says. "There's a lot of evil behind closed doors you'll never know about. People are disappearing. Some of them are being cloned and replaced. You'll never know."

My grandma continues to tell me that the class Tina and Leonard were in was one that most blacks wanted to be a part of. These kids weren't scared to tell anyone off that wronged them. They all looked good. They had fun spirits. They were cocky and arrogant in all departments.

"So they had loved ones around them that genuinely loved them," I say.

"They had enough so that they could live their lives enjoying the essence of their being," my grandma says.

"Each and every last one of them?" I ask. "And how would you know?"

"Although Man Man was on drugs, sometimes I knew he was himself. The drugs couldn't break him entirely. He wasn't that weak of a man," my grandma says.

She says the class Tina was in was very diverse. There was many different ethnicities in the classroom; however, Tina's main crew was brown skinned just like she was. Leonard and a few of his boys that came around were the main light skinned people that she knew.

Tina knew she was special. She knew it was difficult to be accepted as a brown skinned woman. When she would be out and about, different races that didn't know her would give her a hard time because of her skin color. "Tina usually had a serious face on when she wasn't engaging in anything," my grandma says.

"Why did Tina have a serious face?" I ask my grandma. I usually have a serious face on and I know my grandma is working hard to change that. My face was serious because of my bitter mother. Nadia didn't care though. Nadia wanted to know her life wasn't completely wasted.

I put my pencil down.

"Pick your pencil back up," my grandma says. "I want all of that written. You don't have anything to worry about. When this Earth is tired of you, it will get rid of you. There's too much hell on Earth. You know you can die in your damn sleep anyways."

My grandma says Tina's face was usually serious because of all the racist she had to deal with. Racist don't see our kind as beautiful, but they know who we consider beautiful. They study us in various ways to lure us into traps. They're willing to do the work to get rid of our people. "Racist really see us as non-human, but we're still here," my grandma says.

"Everyone knew Tina would be a star one day. The only way someone like Tina survives with all that talent and the hate that comes along with it, is if there's a strong following keeping her safe," my grandma continues. "I'm talking safe in ways that you can't imagine. She probably doesn't even know some of the people looking out for her. Some of them are so old school that they would pick arguments with her and let her stay mad. They'll throw in a few words that will stay in her mind, but all

240

she'll know as a young adult is that it was an argument and it couldn't be used for good."

My grandma says people in high positions are responsible for people like Tina being alive.

"One late night when Tina was at the record store, she was just as loud as she wanted to be." my grandma says. "It was just one of those days you could just tell she had been out with her girls and had a good time." Tina was so beautiful, people told her often that she was so pretty to be brown.

"I've heard that a lot too," I say.

"I know you hear it," my grandma says. "You don't have to tell me that."

She says that this particular day, Tina was outspoken about many things in the store. No one could dampen her spirit. Some of her friends stopped by the store and they were very social speaking of cutting class, not getting caught, and still passing some kind of way. "All of the things I would beat your behind for," my grandma says.

Tina would see someone dancing and look at him and dance too where she was at. She wasn't a shy brown girl. She never acted inferior or scared to just be herself and enjoy a good time in fear that a racist would come around and ruin her day.

"I like Tina. She seems like an older sister I wish I could have," I say.

"There's so many things wrong with that older sister of yours," my grandma says. "My love was all for you. All I can do is be thankful for that."

"So what else can you tell me about Tina?" I ask.

"I have to tell you that Canel was in the store that day," my grandma says.

My heart falls again. Canel is starting to sound like a horror story.

Canel saw that Tina was feeling herself this day. My grandma is continuing with her story. There was no way Tina could get upset. She was well put together. Her hair and nails were done. She had on a cute outfit.

241

"Tina was one of those girls that knew she was beautiful," I say. "I can tell. No one could tell her otherwise. She had heard it too many times before."

"What stood out the most is that she didn't have on any makeup," my grandma says. "When Man Man told me that, she really reminded me of you."

I start smiling really hard. My grandma really thinks I'm beautiful and never hesitates to tell me. I can tell it warms her heart to say nice things to me. She's nothing like Nadia. I wish I never had to say Nadia's name again.

"So Olifus told you about Leonard and Tina being at this store when Canel was there," I say.

"Let me finish my story please," my grandma says.

"I apologize Grandma. I want to hear everything you have to say," I say.

My grandma kisses my forehead. "I know when you're desperate for affection because of Nadia never showing you any," my grandma says. "I don't want you to feel like that. I only want to do right by you."

"I love you grandma," I say.

"I love you too Shona," my grandma says.

My grandma continues her story. She says Canel always wanted to be one of those old cats that felt young. He thought acting like he didn't care about sneaky ways in children was one of those ways. He overheard Tina and her friends' conversations and acted like he didn't care. He hadn't made eye contact with any of them, but still had that hope that maybe one or two of the people in the crew took notice of him, so he played his part of a nonchalant old man when it came to youth being devious.

Tina would go around the store and put headphones on at different spots listening to music. She was a great singer, so she naturally got lots of attention. Canel did his usual routine of talking to the workers, figuring out what was new in stock, and talked about exchanging things.

"When Tina got in line, Canel got in line behind her," my grandma says. "Man Man started choking before he told me this next part. He said Canel tapped Tina on the shoulder so she had

242

to turn around and look at him. Tina's expression was very serious. It was a mean expression. Canel could tell she didn't like the sight of him."

"What did he ask her?" I ask.

"He asked her if she knew of any places nearby that sold good hamburgers," my grandma says. "All he wanted was to see how she would look at him at first sight."

"On a day that she was really into herself like Leonard was?" I ask shocked. "But you already said he was so programmed that all looks at him were of disgust, so her serious face shouldn't have even mattered."

"You're paying attention really well," my grandma says. "I need you to learn of a few more kids from Freshtin High before I go onto anything else."

There was Leonard and Tina's friends, Devon, Marissa, Marla, Alana, Alisa, Kevin, Dennis, and Alonzo.

My grandma says Leonard's best friend was Devon. Devon was just as cute as Leonard. He always had a nice haircut and his eyes were so cute. His fade was always nice. Devon was one of those cute boys that always had on a nice button up shirt with jeans, and didn't care what anyone would say about him. Devon was talented too. He was a saxophone player, and he could sing. He was a great dancer too.

"If he's as cute as you say he is, then he hears too many good things from people that really look good to care what a hater will think," I say.

Devon knew people liked to look at him. He never hesitated to look disgusted at a girl that he felt was ugly that would admire him. The slightest smile from someone he didn't like would piss him off because it was easy for girls to think he would date them. He didn't like how he could smile or speak to a girl at times, and the girl would not stop blushing or could barely speak sometimes.

One late night, Devon was at the record store.

I'm already thinking Canel will show up.

Devon was having a good old time singing. Some of the workers knew he went to Freshtin High and didn't mind letting him play his saxophone outside of the store. People would give Devon cash and let him know how talented he was all the time. Devon was a huge fan of jazz music, so he played it often.

One evening Canel was at the store. He saw Devon having a good old time.

I'm nodding my head. The story for these kids keeps being the same. "Let me guess. He was enjoying his nice looks and never having to worry about taking anyone serious that said anything negative about him," I say.

"Canel was in the store," my grandma says ignoring my statement.

My mouth drops.

"Remember, any story that Nadia told you that made your mouth drop, I can do a lot worse," my grandma says. "Only now, there's real love involved, and you know I don't want to do anything but right by you."

"Yes ma'am," I say. "What did Canel do to Devon? He wanted his attention too?"

"Canel walked up to Devon and asked him how long he'd been playing the saxophone," my grandma says. "He didn't really care. All he wanted was to see how the young man would look at him in his eyes the first time they made eye contact."

Devon's eyes got big and his mouth opened wide. It took him a few seconds to respond that he'd been playing the saxophone since he was ten years old.

"What did Canel say?" I ask.

My grandma laughs. "Canel was messed up in the head, but he wasn't that crazy to get angry enough to make a scene at the store," my grandma says. "He ignored Devon's reaction to him as if he was a mature adult, and told him he was a good player."

"He should have told him to get more lessons if he was hurt by the expression," I say. "He should have lied."

"Canel liked Devon so much that he still had hope that the next time he saw him, he could outdo his first expression," my grandma says. "Canel just didn't have it in his heart to say something negative to the good-looking youngster in fear that the youngster would look at him worse, or act like he didn't want him to speak to him again."

"Canel sounds like he needs a good ass beating," I say. My grandma hits me on my behind and tells me to watch my mouth.

I tell my grandma I've had dreams about male singers while I was on drugs too. I would be dating the lead and the other four boys and I would be really close. The drugs made me have real feelings for these boys. I'm learning while I'm recovering that the feelings were really enhanced.

"There was a girl named Marissa that would hang out at this record store too," my grandma says. "Marissa was one of those girls that had little to no hair. People that saw her from behind often mistook her for a boy."

Canel got in line behind Marissa and asked her if she liked his haircut. Marissa didn't understand why the old man wanted her opinion, and her face showed that. She looked disgusted at Canel, which upset him because he had been observing her in the store for over twenty minutes and she showed no signs of any frustration. He felt she looked at him in a displeasing way because he was ugly. Canel stood bitter in line staring at the ground behind Marissa. When he came to, he recognized people were staring at him. He was even more upset. Marissa didn't see how angry she made the old man.

There was a girl named Marla that Canel liked. She would go to this record store often. She went there the most Olifus told my grandma. She had more hair than Marla, but she wore baggy jeans and big shirts. People looking at her from behind as well, would mistake her for a boy. She wore hats often, and boots.

Canel saw that Marla was having a good day and wanted to make eye contact with her.

"What is wrong with this old man?" I ask. "Grandma, he's giving me the creeps."

I want her to change the subject now. Canel is too much.

"You're going to listen to each and everything I have to say," my grandma says. "This is to help you, not hurt you. You think something is wrong with Canel, just imagine what was going on with you when Nadia wanted to know how you would look at her while she was practicing on you and training you to be who she wanted."

My grandma starts tearing up.

"There's certain things a real mother doesn't want her child to hear," my grandma says. She's considering herself my mom instead of Nadia. That's how I like it anyways.

My grandma continues her story. Canel pretended to accidently bump into Marla and apologized to her. Marla, who was looking in a book she had, went from looking relaxed, to uneasy when she looked at the old man. She told him not to worry about bumping into her, then proceeded reading her material.

"Grandma, is he about to turn into some serial killer?" I ask.

"Just let me finish the story," my grandma says sternly.

The girl Alana had a bit more weight to her than Marla and Marissa, but she still was a cool kid. She was very popular. She had a great singing voice and was good at playing the drums.

Alana would sure enough be having a blast one day at the record store.

Canel told Alana she was beautiful and asked for her number. Alana's mouth dropped like most of the other kids. She didn't like to look at the old man. Her quick response *no*, and walk away made that quite obvious.

My grandma says Alisa was the only girl in Leonard and Tina's main crew that was light skinned. She had hair that went past her shoulders and she loved to wear skirts with button up shirts. She was a great singer and played the piano.

Alisa was playing in her hair and looking in her small portable mirror when Canel would approach her and say that the store had a bathroom if she wanted a bigger view. He laughed after his statement. He thought that was a good punch line. This naturally got Alisa to look the old man in his eyes. She started coughing and told him she actually did need to go to the restroom. Her disgusted face let Canel know the young lady didn't like him, and her response was to let the old man know she took no interest in him talking to her.

"Let me guess. She was having a great day until she looked the old man in his eyes," I say.

"That's right," my grandma says.

"Canel's name is starting to sound like one from a horror movie," I say.

My grandma tells me about Kevin. Kevin was a chubby brown skinned boy. He worked at a barbeque spot. Man Man couldn't figure out how the boy made it to his senior year, and rumor has it that he was always falling asleep in class. Kevin was a great singer and he played the saxophone as well.

I'm shaking my head. I already know my grandma's going to say he was having a great time at the record store, and Canel wanted to know what his first impression of him would be. That's exactly what she says in her own words.

I know when my grandma keeps repeating things to me, it's something serious. One thing she says a lot is, these kids are just like me: nice looking and talented.

"There's a lot of predators out there," my grandma says. "This world is full of mentally ill people."

Canel gave Kevin some money while he was outside playing his saxophone. Kevin's eyes told a story Canel didn't like. Kevin looked at the old man, then said thank you looking another way. Kevin called someone he knew down the street and quickly left the old man's sight.

The old man knew Kevin was a cool kid from Freshtin High School, so he got to witness how someone so popular and nice looking with extra weight would respond to an ugly old man like himself.

My grandma says the boy named Dennis was a great singer and rapper. He loved to wear hats and wear button up shirts. He was outside of the record store talking to a group of older men. He was having a good time listening to their jokes while they were drinking beer.

Canel came up and joined the circle. He began a conversation with the other older men. Dennis couldn't believe the sight of Canel and kept staring at him as if he was trying to figure out what he was. Canel continued talking to the other men and pretended like he didn't see Dennis staring at him. When Dennis finally looked away, Canel wrapped up his conversation and left.

"He wanted to see how long the boy would stare at him?" I ask.

"He sure did," my grandma says. "He wanted the truth in any form he could get it. He was also one of those people that wanted to know how worse things could get for him. If Dennis would have stood there for ten minutes staring at him, Canel would've kept talking for ten minutes."

Then there was Alonzo who could sing, dance and play the piano.

He was at the record store on a late night. He was looking and feeling good. He was browsing through CDs when Canel approached him. Canel offered to purchase whatever CD Alonzo wanted because he was feeling generous. Alonzo looked at the old man and his speech started to slur. He told him *no thanks* and left.

"So Canel approached all of these kids just to see how they would react to him?" I ask.

"Yes, and those weren't the only ones that he liked that looked at him crazy from Freshtin High," my grandma says. "But that should be enough for me to fully get you to grasp this story."

"But back to Canel," my grandmother says. She says Canel lived in an apartment with his wife. He hated himself. He was always suicidal because he didn't have money for a big house and had to look his woman in the face knowing this every day. He thought his woman was secretly making jokes about him not being able to provide for her like he should as a man. He couldn't give her the fancy house she wanted or car. He couldn't give her the bank card and let her splurge on things she wanted. He hated himself.

Canel knew having money could get him the girl of his dreams. This also made him suicidal. Canel was a typical ugly man angry all the time because he wished he had better looks. Because he didn't have looks, he wished he had money to get the people he wanted to come around him.

248

Almost every day Canel would be looked at as if he were a monster by people in society.

"Stay with me," my grandma says when I start looking around. "After Man Man told me about the students, he told me of this place called The Land Spot. He said someone would be crazy to willingly go in the place. It was easy to get lost in the area. It was a forbidden human life place. Once in there, life would change for the trespasser for the worst."

My grandma says Canel was out and about one day. He was at the record store that he goes to. This particular day, Tina, Leonard, their close friends, as well as other people from Freshtin High, were at the store. Some to purchase some CDs, movies, and other electronics, and others just to hang out. They were in and out of the store. The owners knew they went to a school nearby, so they let the kids enjoy a good time. There were lots of smiles and laughter. They talked about work, family, and many other things. They were really enjoying each other's company.

Canel kept a low profile. He knew the kids wouldn't recognize him anyway with his hat and glasses on. It was his spot to get to look at people he wished he could every day. He hated observing Tina. She was too confident. She was by far the prettiest brown girl he had ever seen, and he hated her for that. He wanted to know what it was like for a brown girl in a hateful world to be so conceited and cocky. He saw how the other kids admired her. They played in Tina's hair, invited her places, and a smile or some type of expression showing content in her entire being would be on her face. Canel was jealous.

Canel got to witness how the kids interacted together.

My grandma says Canel was having issues with his woman one day. He desperately needed to get out of the house. He left and started drifting off with his thoughts. He was walking and not really paying attention to where he was going.

Twenty minutes out of his mind and walking not really knowing where he's headed can get him to drift into a lot of trouble.

Canel ended up going into The Land Spot.

Canel came to his senses when he reached a mansion. When he saw it, he wanted to turn around and leave, but knew he couldn't. He saw someone that looked just like him. Then he saw the kids from the record store as well as a few other people. He knew they weren't the real kids because the real ones would not act how these replications were.

Canel was on the brink of a heart attack. He knew he was trapped when he recognized that the replications of himself and people he knew were acting how he would want them to. It was like they knew his inner most desires and how he wished he would act normally. The kids were doing things that he wanted them to for his sexual desires. Canel's replication was doing things he always wanted to do in public, but wouldn't because he would feel uncomfortable.

Canel tried to remember things he saw along the way on his walk. He needed help and he needed it quick. All he had was himself. Canel quickly had thoughts that his replication would try and kill him. He knew The Land Spot was the real deal. He had come across a place on Earth that human life was never supposed to reach. He had crossed a terrible path.

"Grandma, this Olifus man sounds like he's really out of his mind telling you this story," I say.

"Listen to it all," my grandma says. She says Canel realized he was supposed to have had a heart attack at the sight of a copy of himself, but he didn't. It was that moment he knew when he first saw his copy that the response it gave was important. He had to figure out how to control it.

Canel saw television screens that were depicting things he had seen when he entered The Land Spot. He started to feel very weak and knew he didn't have much time. He couldn't believe the way he wanted those kids to act towards him was happening in their replications, and the copy of him was joking about it. He had no time to cry. He knew he would die.

Canel quickly changed into a stern man that demanded the copy to change the way he acted. He knew this copy was Earthly. All he could do was try to save his life. The copy wanted

250

competition out of Canel. Canel knew they copy was greater than him, but it wasn't enough.

Canel had to try drugs and knew he would need to befriend one of his copies to take his place, otherwise he would die. He had to look his clone in the eyes and make sure his heart was stable. He learned what drugs he could use and which ones would kill him.

Canel had to eat things that he didn't know what they were. He had to have sex with beasts. He did all types of things to train these copies of people to act a different way. He had to learn how to be a producer, director, and many more things dealing with television. He had to live a working life in record timing.

Canel racked up on money. He asked himself several times where all of this equipment came from. It was then that he knew Earth was real in ways most of mankind would never know. It was then he recognized he had drifted off so much that he wound up in a place that rare individuals would make it out of. Canel did everything he could and ended up making it out of The Land Spot.

Canel went home and lived a regular life for a couple months. Then he would move him and his wife into a bigger house. His wife knew something was off about him. He would lose his mind several times and say things he never wanted to about The Land Spot. He knew he would, which is why he was always so uneasy and never seemed to be comfortable. He met people and told them about The Land Spot against his own will. He couldn't help himself.

When Canel finally came to his senses, he went out and sought out the kids from Freshtin High. He promised them money and that he could get them on television because now he knew where one of the studios was located. He knew the replications were getting around and they would have to return to their original state and place of their emergence to stay strong. They would need him there too.

Canel told the students that they would have to sleep with him whenever he wanted, eat things they didn't want to, do activities with beasts, and many more things to get their role on television. The kids went to a talented school, but they were all from low-income families. These were kids that knew people laughed at them for looking so nice but never being able to make a lot of money and live a luxurious life. Their good looks would be walking around the projects and never plastered onto a screen or poster.

These were kids that had real talent. Singers, dancers, and instrumentalists. They knew if they ever wound up on television that they would be successful. They just didn't know the real of how television came about.

"Those drugs Olifus took were something serious," I say.

"Keep listening," my grandma says. She says all the kids signed Canel's contracts over the course of two months on separate occasions. Canel took most of them to a restaurant and got them to sign the contracts. Some of them he went to their houses. The kids started to notice odd things going on in their neighborhoods and people acting different towards them. It was because of the replications going around town. The copies of them would disguise themselves at times. They were playing a real-life game that my grandma calls *Danger*.

"None of them, I mean not one of those kids remembered the time they saw Canel at the record store," my grandma says.

There was about twenty-five students that met at The Land Spot. They sat in a classroom together. They all were shocked when they realized they all knew each other from school. They knew what they did to even be given the role in the film, so that made them feel awkward around each other.

A man walked in the classroom. At first sight and based off of how their feelings shifted, the kids knew that they were going to die, but always held onto the fact that they may get lucky and live. They would still have to film the movie; real dialogue or not. It wasn't Canel that walked in the classroom. It was his replication. The kids could tell it wasn't him because his height was slightly off, and there were marks on his body that Canel didn't have. The copy moved awkwardly and his voice was different. Too much time had passed.

252

The kids were all chipped. Canel controlled their chip. He liked to mess with their private areas the most and get them to do what he wanted them to do. Every move they made was watched. When that chip was expired, so was their lives. Canel couldn't have the copies think he wanted the kids dead. At first, he didn't and the copy of himself would go around town and have people laugh at him. There would be a day when Canel didn't care about those kids lives. He had money now, so he could easily get attention from people. He was a well-known producer. The only thing those kids knew was that they had to finish the film.

My grandma gets teary eyed. The lies about these kids make her angry. I feel like she's telling me I could've been one of them.

She says there was enough students in the class for each of them to have hope that another one would have a connection to get them out of their situation.

The kids were given scripts. Canel did in fact write the movie. He titled it *Music from the Soul*. He only wrote uplifting songs. He didn't want the kids to sing anything that showed their naughty ways which was popular. Canel made the wardrobe for the students similar to how they dressed on the streets, but didn't allow Tina to wear anything that she would like. He always made her wear a plain shirt with a regular pair of jeans. Her hair was always the same in the film: some up and some down or all of it down. He didn't want people to know who she was at all. They could hear her sing and that was it.

Canel's copy said his name was Canel as well. The students were horrified. Some of them that had seen similar looking people of their friends around knew that something was wrong. They knew Canel had to have stumbled on the place and got them involved. Some even remembered seeing him at the record store. Canel got to feel those feelings. The Land Spot is a twisted place.

The classroom setting looked similar to Freshtin High School. What the students didn't know until the film was released was that there were cameras in their real school as well. The other students not involved with Canel noticed that the replications of the chosen students were now coming in and out of the school. The students started to think that their lives were in danger too. Tina and Leonard's crew who weren't involved with Canel, didn't care. They wanted that chip out of them.

The students were required to return to the place to film the movie. It was the only place they knew they all would be at the same time. They weren't all in the same class at Freshtin High, and some of them never even saw each other at school. They didn't want to talk about their situation at all. They already felt embarrassed around each other for sleeping with Canel and doing other lustful acts he wanted them to do to even get involved with the film.

"It was a big slap in the face," my grandma says. She says the real Canel would see the kids around and have them thinking the town had gone mad with clones. They were all scared. They would eventually learn that he was controlling their replications. He was the real producer for The Land Spot. He had all of their scents on him and his thoughts were heavy with them in his head. "Olifus told me it was like Earth swallowed Canel up and spit him out," my grandma says.

"Damn. I'm glad I quit smoking when I did," I say. "Man Man is out of his mind."

My grandma says the students had friends and families that learned about what happened and believed their crazy sounding stories. "Like I said, the kids were out of their minds a lot and desperate for help," my grandma says. "They said what was going on at The Land Spot several times. This helped them feel alive. Their friends and family would help them get time to be free."

She says Tina, like the rest of them, had friends that pretended to be her and let her pretend to be them so that she could get some free time. They basically gave her a part or their life and took on some of her dirty deeds so that she could live again before she died. Eating dog food was one of the small things their friends would have to do. Eating dog feces is just something I can't think about, but I know they had to do it. They

254

would use all of them to let Tina know they knew every breath, she couldn't wait for a good sigh of relief. They knew Tina wouldn't care if they died or not. Some of her friends let her know they could die together. "There were people that really loved these kids," my grandma says. "We all have to play ignorant to this Earth, but the real ones stick by their family and friends."

The kids had friends that knew movements they would recognize. They would learn more ways to speak to each other with their bodies and simple sound effects. Every twist and turn would count for something.

The student's friends would get in the facility and alter the script. They wrote in songs that their friends had already written. Most of them could sing and rap, but Canel only allowed them to sing. Their friends also changed around some of the dialogue. This was real love at its best. The captured friends crew had to do devilish things to get in seats that changed the final product. They had to work together to steal equipment that was not sold in stores. They even sent kids in that they didn't mind dying to try and steal things. They needed live cameras that would get footage of The Land Spot to educate people on what was going on and to try and find a way to free their friends.

"Olifus was on drugs bad," my grandma says. "When he started to learn the story of Canel and these kids, he had dreams that Leonard was a famous singer named Tim James, who was in a group with his six brothers: Deon, Mitchell, Ken, Kentel, Reginald and Brandon. Leonard was just that talented. There were rumors that Tim had been killed and replaced."

My grandma says that Tim's father, Angus, was approached by a brown man named Ronald who worked at The Po Boy Spot. Angus would always go to the Po Boy Spot with his sons and boast about how talented they were. Ronald knew Angus was a hot head that knew he had nice looking children. Angus would always have the biggest smile on his face talking to Ronald and Ronald was always jealous. He hated to hear Tim, Deon, Mitchell, Ken, Kentel, Reginald, and Brandon call Angus father.

255

One day Ronald was driving around and stumbled on Forsa Territory, a forbidden land. He would get in and see the replications of himself. He would have to kill a few. He would stumble on the main room where he would take the information of someone he would kill and steal their identity. He would live in the deceased man's mansion.

Ronald approached Angus and his wife Theresa with their five children. He offered them a record deal. Angus would sign over his whole family. They would go to Forsa Territory and be chipped. Angus could not believe he had ruined his perfect life with his family.

Angus would learn Forsa Territory and give his kids access to chipping the public. Ronald still had control over the family.

Angus in all of his misery would take his brother, Don, who had seven children of his own and get him to sell his family's life over to him. He had his brother's family chipped. Angus along with Tim would write a script about their families lives up until the day they gave their lives to Ronald and have Don's family act it out. Angus didn't want any of his brother's family to act as Tim, so he had his son choose someone else.

Tim knew a neighborhood boy that was very talented and idolized him named Garvy. He would get the young boy, Garvy, to give him his life.

Angus knew his family was well known. He lied about things in the script, but he knew people would figure it out because his family was always performing at events. Don's family was not as good looking as Angus', and Tim would love that the public didn't get to see the real James family. He didn't think they deserved too. He was bitter about how entertainment runs.

Tim hated his cousin Markel because he was talented and always got any girl he wanted. Tim would make Markel sing back up instead of giving him the lead. He would make Markel believe that he didn't think he was that good of an entertainer. He would make his ego go down singing back up for Garvy.

There was a young man named Tinson that begged Tim to be in his family movie. He was very good looking and Tim was now regular in wanting new friends. He made Tinson do rituals before giving him the part to play one of his brothers in the film.

When my grandma says give him his life, she means chip him.

Tim being a respected artist made it hard for Olifus to believe the rumors of his death.

Tim was in fact Leonard's cousin.

My grandma says that all of the students Canel had chosen were related to other entertainers. She says the chip allowed Canel to know exactly how the students felt about all types of people: fat, skinny, short and tall. Just name it. It even allowed Canel to know how arrogant the kids felt about themselves. The things he learned would get around town. He had money to sleep with young people so the rumors easily spread to Freshtin High. This made people that felt less than them in the looks department furious. They would befriend the clones and make life worse for Canel's chosen clan. They would make it harder for the students to meet up with their regular friends, boyfriends, and girlfriends. The bitter students would try to get Tina and her class killed faster.

"Just imagine the hell the girls wanted to cause Leonard who was only into petite and fine-looking women," my grandma says. "Canel had everything Leonard thought about ugly girls going around town. He even had recordings."

Leonard's cousins had to act like they hated him and orchestrate a way to see him. With the recordings, it was bad for anyone to show that they were fond of who Leonard really was internally. They had to steal from him, beat him up a few times, and set him up in order to lead him somewhere he could talk to them and be comfortable. "I know it sounds crazy," my grandma says.

The clones could feel the anger in Tina and Leonard's crew. It was getting worse and worse to a point where the priority to kill them kept going up in the clones. "There was something very real about these copies. No one knew what hit New Orleans," my grandma says.

The kids even pretended to be each other at times. They knew the rooms in The Land Spot to go to for transformation.

There wasn't a single evil room that didn't exist. If it could be thought of, it was there. The students slept with each other and played many roles in each other's lives whether it be relatives, associates or friends. They wanted to be anyone else.

The DVD would be released. It was at this moment that the students realized that television was real footage of the last days of some of the actors and singers. Television became horrifying to watch.

All of these kids got a following. People tried to give them many outlets to escape, but the real about cloning is just unbearable. Some people were shocked that the students lasted after the film had been completed and released. The kids played the game the best they could. They pretended to be their copies, pretended they were living normally, and even got bold enough and told people what they saw.

People couldn't stand watching the pain the kids at Freshtin High were going through.

Tina and Leonard's friends ended up blowing up the school on a day that all of the kids that were chipped were in it. They didn't care about anyone else in the school who wasn't involved.

Over time, the students started to see Canel age. Canel ended up dying by getting sick from the chip inside of him. The students that knew what Canel was into said he was murdered. They never really knew what happened to him.

Canel coming across The Land Spot hit the kids of Freshtin High really hard. They couldn't believe they had got chosen for those parts in the film. Canel was a monster. Of all the people in the world, here they were being recorded for ways that many more people had towards this man that made it through an awful experience at The Land Spot. Canel did reveal to them the truth about why he chose them. He said they were the IT kids he always wanted around to make him feel good as an older man. He told them they hurt his feelings with how they looked at him. He went into detail about Tina, Leonard, Marissa, Devon, Marla, Alana, Alisa, Kevin, Dennis and Alonzo to all of the students. He really wanted them to feel how he felt as a human being. All of his feelings were in those replications. He put DNA in a spot on Earth that it was forbidden. Now many of one person is walking around in various forms.

All the way from the time they arrived at The Land Spot and were chipped up, until the day they died, the chosen kids from Freshtin High who always hung out at the record store acted as sex slaves to Canel in hopes that he would free them from their chip and give them their lives back. They were forced to make people feel good that they didn't want to. They had to do sexual acts with their enemies and strangers as well. Canel controlled them completely. He knew how to operate the chip one hundred percent. He had to learn lots of things about computers while in The Land Spot. The kids did all types of bestiality, lies, gossip and drama, betrayals to each other, and gang related activities to please Canel.

Canel was a man who had enough though. He also did too much alone to make it out alive. He had to learn things that could give the average person a heart attack. He fought to keep his life in ways those kids would never understand. He would never care about them living. His whole agenda was to keep luring more people into The Land Spot so that he could live.

The Land Spot was later nicknamed Dead Man's Territory by people that knew about what happened to the Freshtin High School students.

"It's not until it happens to your city and someone you love that you really understand what's going on out there," my grandma says. "Saying certain things can get you killed. Keeping silent about them can get you killed even faster."

Canel wanted everyone to know why he hated those kids. He never wanted Tina to smile. He always had Leonard just show his face with his mouth opened as if he was shocked. He had the kids joke about Leonard and copy his facials a lot because he liked Leonard the most; however, Tina was the star of the classroom. Canel didn't like that due to all the racism in the world. He knew Tina's spirit was high and she was confident because of her surroundings. He didn't want people to see that in the film.

Marissa would be looking up for a few seconds then down a lot. Devon wouldn't get much camera time, but when he did, he would always be on his feet walking. Marla would quickly engage in another activity, looking bothered a lot in the film. Alana looked sad while in class in the film a lot when Canel was there. Alisa would start talking to someone else. Kevin would start drifting off a lot. Dennis fell asleep a lot in class. Alonzo would start arguing with people in frustration to Canel's appearance.

Canel let everyone know in the film how those kids looked at him when they saw him. The chip allowed him to know the kids' real feelings. He got them to change their minds due to pain. He got to feel them internally and see their outward expression. The film was twisted around with a different teacher who wasn't Canel, but people got the word around on who really was the villain, which was Canel.

Canel was so evil that he had some of the kids' parents killed and would dress as their moms and dads to be around them. He had the money and training to make everything possible and easy for him. He would meet more producers and they would sit around knowing they beat an unbelievable area to stay alive. They felt they deserved to torture people. It was a matter of time anyway before the population was sought out.

I'm crying. I can't believe that bastard got all those kids involved in that bullshit. That's way too many damn people to have been in his fucked-up ass head. His damn copy was laughing at his ass. He was a sorry ass ugly ass brown skinned old man that lusted after several high school students. The copy got to witness how Canel wanted those kids to act and know that the old man knew how a real man should act, but didn't want to. Canel wanted to be around a bunch of disobedient kids and sleep with them. Now the copy wants to be just like him, show him he can do it, and take his spot. The copy knows just how to act to piss Canel off. It can feel how he feels. Canel really crossed into a deadly territory.

"Grandma, what did you want me to take away the most from this story?" I ask.

"All you need to know right now is those kids remind me of you," my grandma says.

14

The crowd erupts as the buzzer goes off because Cupperton University is up at halftime of their home game. The roar is loud as hell. I cover my ears.

I lead six members of Legit on one side of the court to the free throw line, and Regina leads the other members to the other free throw line.

We take our beginning positions: hands in fists to the side and heads down. The rap instrumental begins, and Shanell is swaying her hands in the air out of position before anyone is supposed to move. I'm already upset because I made it clear to her and everyone else that it is vital to not break our positions or formations.

Shanell looks stupid to me, but the crowd thinks she was supposed to lift her arms and swing them side to side. Hopefully most of the people here don't know I'm the coach because they'll think I'm responsible for Shanell's stupid sudden movements.

A couple beats play to the song and everyone marches in on beat, and end in a pyramid where the team does a ripple step that I start off. Everyone goes one beat behind the person in front of them. Our feet are stomping, but the main thing that gives the ripple effect is our arms.

Although the crowd is going nuts, I can hear some members messing up. There's claps where stomps are supposed to be. Stomps where claps are supposed to be. Heads turning to the right when they're supposed to be to the left.

Despite all these mess ups, the audience keeps cheering so they obviously don't recognize them, but that's not what counts. It's the principle that has me upset. I taught this routine over and over, but because sometimes people didn't show up and came late, they didn't get all the practices they should've gotten.

I'm doing great, but no one can pick me out because so many people are doing different things when we're doing steps that we do everything the same.

The audience doesn't know who's doing right and who's doing wrong because they don't know our routine.

This is the worst crew I've ever performed with.

Every time we transition and I move behind a few members, I notice their mistakes. People's arms look weak because they're movements aren't stiff, some of their faces look boring while they just go through the motions, and some of the claps and stomps are weak, which is why we're not as loud as we should be.

Despite this horrible performance I'm a part of, the audience continues to cheer and I struggle to hide my emotions and stay in the routine.

Legit and I get in one line in the center of the court and start our stroll. Shanell's, *I can't keep my arms to my side like I'm supposed to,* self is jumping up and down before we even get out the gym doors. So, to start the routine, she's out of position swaying her arms back and forth, and to end it she's jumping up and down in the middle of the stroll instead of doing the proper movements like everyone else.

When we get completely out the gym everyone is congratulating one another. Everyone's excited about that terrible performance we just did. Everyone except me. I don't care how loud the crowd was, I know that everyone messed up on one part or another except me.

I know that if everyone would've respected me and allowed me to help them outside of practice, I could've gotten them to be good steppers and to do our routine properly. However, because they were too lazy and just wanted something to tell mommy and daddy about them being involved in on campus, they have me looking like I can't coach to anyone in that gym that knows what a step show should look like.

Legit also made my nice steps that I put lots of time into creating look like garbage. I'll be honest and say I put together most of my steps in less than two hours, and sometimes thirty minutes, but that's not the point. The point is my steps are legit and tonight *Legit* made them look like the average ones you see on the internet that don't *wow* anyone.

I can't get past the issues I am having with this team.

Overall, the performance was great to the audience but dreadful to me.

I have never been one to force an emotion I wasn't feeling, outside of work. I can only give off what is going on inside of me. However, when it comes to performing, I'm good at faking my emotions. Usually, I don't have to do that, but tonight I was upset ever since Shanell swayed her arms back and forth. That told me she doesn't even listen to anything I say at rehearsals, on top of coming late almost every day.

I grab my things from the bleachers where I get a lot of compliments from people in the audience and wait in line for nachos with Ciera at the concession stand right outside the gym area.

"I thought the performance was good," Ciera says.

"Girl, I'm glad everyone enjoyed it," I say. "Everything that sparkles isn't gold. I am dealing with a lot of foolishness with this team. I know one of these days I am going to lose it."

I pay for my nachos and when I turn around I see the last two people I expected to see and want to see right now: Teasha and Queela and three other Alpha Eta Nu Sorors.

I have the worst fucking luck. I haven't seen them in years. I'm trying not to show how fucking mad I am. Damn it. They

264

would be attending a game on a day I had a damn performance.

"That performance was uh, interesting," Queela says. The Sorors with her are smiling and laughing.

"Now tell me something," Queela says. "Why would you guys perform when you're not ready?"

I want to take my nachos and Ciera's, who just turned around from paying for hers, and throw the hot cheese in Queela's face.

I'm getting angry, so it's best that I walk out of this gym now. Ciera follows me out the doors and so does the sorority.

I can't believe these supposed professional and prestigious women are being childish and following us.

"Tell whoever started that team that they should terminate it," Queela says. "Stepping is for Greeks for a reason. I thought you knew that. That mess you guys displayed out there makes us look bad. That is not how stepping should be done."

Queela and the Alpha Eta Nu girls with her are still following us.

"Don't you guys have better things to do besides stalk us around this campus?" Ciera turns around and rudely asks.

"Don't worry about it," I say.

"And who are you?" Teasha asks.

Ciera tosses her nachos to the ground.

"Someone that's gone mess your face up so bad that all that make up you're wearing won't do it any justice anymore," Ciera says. "Leave us alone."

Me and Ciera start walking again and these particular members of Alpha Eta Nu are still behind us. I'm so disgusted at their childish behavior that I lost my appetite. I toss my nachos in the trash. I didn't even get to eat one chip.

"Don't think we didn't notice everyone messing up," Queela says. "That crew you have is something terrible."

Queela gets quiet waiting on my response, but I'm not saying anything. One thing I don't need is thousands of members getting on my case for not being the bigger person and not making more drama come from this fucked up situation. Hundreds in every state. Oh hell no.

The last thing I need is a bunch of my Sorors giving me a hard time on this campus and any other one I visit.

I'm furious that my team didn't do well tonight. I never want to give anyone a reason to speak bad about my performance.

Tonight could've been so special if my team had it together. I could've showed my Sorors how good I am at choreography and how great of a stepper I am; however, being that everyone was messing up on one thing or another, it made it hard to know who was doing the right movements.

Queela would have no reason to be in my face right now if the team showed out, because we would've been so good that her anger wouldn't have allowed her to get out of her seat. I didn't even see her or any Sorors in the gym, so they must've been all the way at the top of the stands, or watching from outside the doors.

"It actually seemed like she knew what she was doing out there," one of the sorority members I don't know says. "I could tell she was on beat and got skills. She had the attitude, good facial expressions, and solidarity that the other people didn't have. She has talent, but unfortunately she should be removed. That team is so not it."

My Sorors all laugh. These are some hating and jealous girls. I know now that they're intimidated by my ability.

I want to keep my mouth shut, but Ciera and I are going home. I don't want these sorority *kids* knowing where I stay, so I turn around and Ciera follows my lead.

"Look, I don't know what the problem is," I say. "I haven't done anything to any of you."

"The problem is, I got word that there would be some steppers performing at the game tonight," Queela rudely says. "Steppers that aren't Greeks. And to my surprise, I get in the gym and see that you're disrespectful behind is one of the performers."

"People that aren't Greeks that step are offensive to us," Teasha says. "They need to have letters. I thought you knew that." Teasha points to her Greek letters on her line jacket. "To put on a step show," Teasha continues. "I don't care if the school allows you to perform or not, you need to have respect for our Greek organizations."

I don't know why anyone would support a show that they are against.

"And you need to have that team shut down," Queela says.

I was actually going to call everyone when I got to my room and tell them I was terminating the team because I couldn't handle it without much respect, which is the truth. I was going to terminate it because I'm so angry about tonight's performance. But I can't do that now. I can't give these broads the satisfaction.

"I'm not shutting anything down," I rudely say. "I started this team and I'm going to continue it. Who lied and told you people that weren't Greeks are disrespecting them if they put on step shows?"

These particular members of Alpha Eta Nu are looking angrily at me.

"Stepping started in another place, so Greeks didn't even do the dance first," I say. "*Our* ancestors created it as slaves. It's how they communicated because they weren't able to speak. So I suggest you learn your history before you approach someone else who is a part of a Greek organization that knows more about stepping than you do, because you sound stupid."

267

"I do know my history," Queela says offensively walking towards me.

If she knew her history she would've spared me her last few sentences. I put her up on game and now she's angry, which is why our noses are an inch away from each other. The Sorors with her get close behind her and Ciera gets close behind me.

"Now you listen to me you non-stepping little girl," Queela says. "You're not that good of a stepper, and what your team displayed tonight is a disgrace to all steppers. It's disgusting to watch other races that are Greeks make stepping look like a joke, so imagine how much my stomach hurt when I saw a team full of black people that couldn't stay together. You need to let that team go."

Queela walks away and all the Sorors with her follow her except Teasha who is still staring me in my eyes.

I hear Queela laughing and saying that she never met someone who was more ridiculous than me. She says she can't believe that I would perform with this team. She keeps repeating herself. She's getting on my nerves.

"You are just too disrespectful," Queela says. Now that she's seen me step, I know she's bitter. Her own friend in the sorority said she could tell I was on point despite everyone around me, so I know Queela had to take note of that too.

Queela knows I can step, so considering her bad attitude and jealous vibe she gives me, I know she wouldn't allow me to perform with her and her besties in the sorority because I would take away all of the attention from everyone else, like I planned on doing when I performed with any of my Sorors.

I'm glad Queela didn't come to help bring me in when I was pledging. Queela would just put me through the pledging process so she could have an excuse to hit me, yell at me, and make me do whatever she said with no intentions of giving me

268

my letters. If she never saw me step until I joined Alpha Eta Nu, I'm sure she would've found a way to have me removed.

"Here," Teasha says and hands me a flyer. "Take this. If you're serious about community service, you can still come help us out, just know we would never let someone as pathetic as you in our organization. The other Sorors got you your letters. Everyone knows that it's not our fault that you have letters. Get your stepping game up."

Queela catches up to the Sorors with her.

Ciera takes the flyer Teasha just gave me and starts to put it in the trash.

"Wait, give it here," I say.

I look over it.

"Girl, what do you want that for?" Ciera confusedly asks. "Are you thinking about going?"

"Yea," I say with a smirk on my face. "And I think you should come with me."

15

I sit with Ms. Ross as I watch Mission practice a step they learned.

"I want to see that one again," I say.

Mya counts to start them off.

The boys are extremely energetic and show a lot of attitude. Some of the girls are struggling, but they are trying which is all I care about.

Everyone has improved tremendously. We're sounding in sync and looking like an actual step team. Some people still look like they don't want to be here, but that's fine. As long as they learn these moves so we can perfect them and work on putting their own personalities in them, I'm good.

Everyone's working hard except Sheela, who is half stepping by hitting her thighs instead of clapping under her legs. When she messes up, she stands still as the rest of the team continues.

I'm furious but remain calm.

"Sheela, if you mess up, you need to try and come back in please," I say.

"No, I'm just going to stand here," Sheela says non-chalantly. "It's too hard to come back in."

If I was back at Ann High I would take her off the team, but according to Luminous LA's guidelines, I'm not allowed to remove anyone.

"No you are not," I say. "Do your best and come back in on beat. You look ridiculous just standing there."

My attitude is in full effect now and everyone in the room can see and hear it.

"Again," I say.

Everyone does the moves again. Sheela does them with very little energy.

"Alright that's it for the day," I say. "See y'all next week."

As I head to the door, Ms. Ross stops me.

"Hey, I wanted to talk to you for a minute," Ms. Ross says.

I can hear the worry in her voice.

"A couple of the girls, members, think that you are a little too mean," Ms. Ross says.

I keep my mouth shut until she finishes.

"I asked them why they don't practice hard and they said it's because you are too strict and mean," Ms. Ross says.

"Look Ms. Ross," I say. "You sit in here with me every practice. No disrespect, but I am just being a coach. I can't be happy go lucky with this team every second. I have to be serious most of the time. This is new to all of them. I don't have the time to play games and talk about what they had for dinner last night."

I need to whip this team into shape so I can win The Big Bang Step Off. I refuse to walk out of the arena without a first-place trophy and a smile on my face when I see the McGruder's and Jasmine.

"Can you just lighten up a little bit?" Ms. Ross asks. "Maybe you can ask them how they are coming along or how they are doing sometimes?"

"Ms. Ross, I am not here to be anyone's friend," I say. "Let me take a wild guess. The girls, excuse me, members you are talking about are Sheela and Alexis?"

Ms. Ross says nothing. I know I'm right though.

"If anyone has problems, why don't they quit?" I ask.

"That's the part that I find interesting," Ms. Ross says. "They are complaining and have all these issues with you, but they don't want to quit."

I'm upset about the complaints, but my heart softens when she says they don't want to quit. There's obviously something

271

about the class that they like: step or me. Who knows?

One thing I know is I don't want to take anything away from her students that they enjoy, like the McGruder's did to me.

I always remember my bad experiences growing up and how I felt going through them, before making present decisions in similar situations. Besides, like I said, I couldn't remove any students if I wanted to because the Luminous LA program does not allow it.

The students would have to willingly quit.

"I'll try to make a few adjustments," I say.

Stressed and tired from coaching two teams, each with their own issues, I go to Ciera's house.

I put on my black and gold fitted dress. I look at my curves and play with my hair in the bathroom mirror as I make sexy faces.

Ciera comes out of her bedroom in a nice red and gold dress. She hits me on my butt.

"You look good girl," Ciera says.

"So do you," I say.

Ciera hugs me.

"You know you are beautiful right?" Ciera asks.

"Thanks, so are you," I say with a big smile as I look at my friend in the mirror.

I always appreciate a nice compliment, especially from my best friend. Some people just don't know what one compliment can do for someone's day.

Ciera tightens the bun in her head and says, "You should put a bun in yours too."

"With what?" I disgustedly ask. "A sock?"

Ciera says yes.

"No thanks," I say.

"You ready?" Ciera asks.

"Yea, after we take some pics," I say.

I am the type of person that likes to have memories of everything I do. It doesn't matter if it's my dinner I prepared, or the scenery at the park. I like to take photos and put them in my photobook.

Me and Ciera take a few pics with my phone, then look at them.

"I think you should do a bun with a sock," Ciera says again. "That way we can be twins."

"I'm not putting no sock in my head! That's ghetto," I say.

I'm quite content with my flat-ironed hair going down my back.

We take a picture on Ciera's phone in the bathroom before heading out.

The big Paper Chase Night Club sign almost blinds us as we walk in the building. We hand money to the cashier and squeeze our way to the center of the dance floor to dance.

Paper Chase is where we always go when we need a night out. The crowd is always live and everyone always enjoys each other's company.

If there was ever a day me and Ciera's cars were broke down, and we decided to walk to the club, heels and all, we didn't care as long as we could get away from our house. We love going to clubs anyways because we never have to worry about the neighbors complaining the music is too loud.

"It's so packed tonight!" Ciera shouts.

"I know! I need a drink," I say.

"Don't trip. If you don't want to buy any, you know I got you at my house," Ciera says.

We both crack up. Ciera stays stacked on liquor.

We dance and even join other people's dance circles. Ciera sees a man break dancing and cheers him on. It's funny watching her motivate this man to stay on the floor and do more tricks with his off-beat self. I'm so enthused watching Ciera cheer him on, I don't realize a tall and well put together man is staring at me.

"Hi, my name is Jared. Would you like to dance?" he asks.

"Sure," I say.

I'm not turning down this fine man.

"Aye girl, I got to use the bathroom. Be right back," Ciera says.

I knew she would come up with something. Neither of us likes to be the third wheel. She heads to the bathroom, but the DJ plays a song she likes and she begins to dance again only a few feet from where she left me.

I dance with Jared. I can't help but examine him. He is taller than me with my heels on which is a huge must. He has nice brown skin. His profile is perfect. I think he likes me. Or at least the way I look since he did approach me. Jared starts to do old school moves and I copy him.

After a few songs, I start to stumble a bit.

"My feet are starting to hurt," I say.

"I understand," Jared says taking notice of me looking all over the club. "Looking for your friend?"

"No," I lie.

"Well when you are, she's over there," Jared tells me.

Jared points behind me and Ciera is talking to an older man at the bar.

"Well, I don't want to stalk you all night," Jared says. "If it's not too much, is there another time I can see you if we don't bump into each other again? Is there another night you will be here?"

"If you want, you can just straight up ask me for my number," I cockily say.

"Can I have your number Beautiful?" Jared asks.

"Where's your phone?" I ask.

Jared pulls out his phone and I put my number in it.

"Have a good night," Jared says.

As he walks away, Ciera walks up to me.

"Girl you better control that smile. Don't let him see he got you all mushy on the inside," Ciera says. "We got a reputation to keep."

"I'm trying," I say. "But it's naturally flowing out of me. Let's go stand by the wall."

We use our hands to fan our faces and watch everyone enjoy drinks.

"We need some friends with some money," I say.

"Yea we do," Ciera agrees. "But you already know my homeboy hooks me up, so we can have a few drinks at the crib."

"How much longer you want to stay?" I ask.

"I'm actually ready to go," Ciera says. "All these people crowding me has me hot."

We head out and the parking lot is one big party as well. People are playing music and dancing like it's one big block party.

Ciera hops in the driver's seat of her car.

"Aye can I drive?" I ask.

Ciera hops out and tosses me the keys.

We swerve off into the night.

"So you had a good time?" I ask.

"Yes, I had a good time," Ciera says. "I know you had a good time. What was that boy's name again?"

"Jared," I blush.

"When the next time you gone see Jared?" Ciera asks.

"I don't know," I say. "He has my number. I don't have his."

Ciera looks at me like I'm crazy.

"Girl, next time have him give you his number," Ciera says.

"Why?" I ask.

"That's just what you supposed to do," Ciera says. "How old is he?"

"At least eighteen," I sarcastically say kind of annoyed at all the questions.

Paper Chase is an eighteen and over club.

Ciera laughs.

"Felt good to get away and not think about all the stress that comes with being an adult. Sometimes I wish we were still in college," Ciera says.

"Who you telling? We need to do this even more than we already do," I say. "I want to feel relaxed like this all the time."

"Girl hush," Ciera says. "We do this enough. You know you just feeling good because you met somebody."

She's right. Ciera is absolutely right. I miss having an additional male companion. Sometimes I get nervous and think something might happen and Austin might want to leave me even if I've done nothing. I've seen too many movies.

Ciera changes the conversation as she stares at me drift off into wonderland blushing and playing with my hair. I'm thinking about how fine Jared is.

"Is everything going alright with Mission High?" Ciera asks.

"Yep," I snap out of my daze and confidently say. "Mission is definitely a breeze compared to Cupperton."

We reach a stop light and Ciera is fascinated by the man crossing the street.

"OOOOOO WEEEEEE!" Ciera exclaims.

"Which one is that for?" I ask.

"That nice yellow fellow crossing," Ciera says.

Anytime someone pleasing to the eye crosses our path, we have to alert the other one with our signal *oooo weeee.*

276

"OOOOO, OOOOO, WEEEEEE!" I shout.

"Oh, so you like him too?" Ciera laughs.

"No. I like that nice chocolate one creeping up behind him," I say.

"The chocolate one does not look better than the yellow one," Ciera says.

I take a second look.

"He absolutely does," I say.

Ciera takes her hair down, takes her heels off, and tilts her seat back.

"I should have sat there; my feet are killing me too," I say as I continue driving.

The rest of the ride we just relax and enjoy nice jazz music.

Ciera and I go in her house and we sip on alcohol mixed with orange juice.

I try to control my facials. These damn drinks are still strong as hell. Ciera can throw shots back left and right and her face won't wrinkle.

"You still a light weight?" Ciera laughs.

"Shut up," I say.

I get silent and stare at a plant that's sitting on the corner table. I'm thinking about Jared again. Just dancing and talking to him for a short amount of time was enough for him to win me over. He's a smooth talker and he looked so good.

"You still thinking about that boy?" Ciera asks.

"No," I lie as I snap out of blushing.

"Don't worry girl," Ciera says. "Your little secret is safe with me. I know he will call you. Give me a hug because I'm ready to call it a night."

"Alright girl. Have a good night," I say, then stretch out on her couch.

277

16

I'm walking in Dayla's house right now. She has snacks on the table and I'm hungry as hell.

"So, what's up?" I ask Dayla.

"Girl, nothing," Dayla says. "My life is uneventful these days. Isyss! Shona's here. Bring your ass on so we can know what the hell is going on."

"I got y'all," Isyss says. "Jasmine was sitting on the front row in the auditorium at Ann High School watching her girls and boys rehearse some of their steps. She said they sounded sloppy and she kept yelling and making them start over."

Isyss says Mrs. McGruder came in and sat next to Jasmine. McGruder had found out that I had a team performing during the dance team competition at Cupperton. Jasmine couldn't believe it. She wanted to know how I got the performance. McGruder said she called the school pretending to be a parent trying to get her child on the team. McGruder asked them what events they would be performing at and when she could check them out. She wasn't expecting to hear the dance competition since there are no step teams that are a part of it.

"Them wierdos finally thought it made sense that you got your team in being that this particular competition is Luminous LA's main event," Isyss says. "Jasmine slouched in her seat and looked at her team." Isyss says that Jasmine kept screaming that the moves needed to be tighter." Isyss continues saying that Ann's team kept starting over and Jasmine would never be satisfied. Jasmine kept telling the team to get it together clapping her hands. Isyss says McGruder was getting upset because she felt the team was not where they needed to be.

"Jasmine ignored Mrs. McGruder because she didn't want to admit that her team is not as good as she would like them to be," Isyss says. "McGruder wanted to know how the choreography was coming along and Jasmine ignored her again because she didn't want to admit that she was struggling coming up with complex choreography. Jasmine's angry because creating steps isn't easy for her like it was for you."

Isyss says Jasmine had to spend days trying to think of different movements, which ticks her off because she remembers watching me come up with steps in less than an hour. She's a little discouraged, but she has faith she'll pull off a good show in time that will be good enough to win first place.

Jasmine's determined to show the world that she's the best choreographer, not for her own joy, but for my misery. Jasmine knows I will hate the world acknowledging her as the first choreographer to lead her team to victory during the first Big Bang Step Off.

Ann High's step team was just a check to Jasmine, but now it's something she's using to prove to Mr. and Mrs. McGruder that she is better than me, as well as prove to me that she is better than me.

"Jasmine asked Mrs. McGruder when your next performance was," Isyss says. "She told them it was Friday."

"It is Friday," I say.

"Jasmine had the team take a seat and she stood in front of them," Isyss says. "She asked them if they were free to check out some competition on Friday at Cupperton. Everyone said yes."

Isyss says Jasmine told the team that Mission High was performing and their coach is none other than one of her ex-teammates, who is a girl that never got over her taking her head coaching position, and a girl their advisor Mrs. McGruder had numerous issues with.

"Jasmine said you're definitely not someone she would recommend any of the team to associate with," Isyss says.

"Then she said that you are the coach of one of the teams they will be competing against, and Jasmine did say that she had to admit you are good at what you do. Jasmine's face got angry."

Isyss says that Jasmine said despite the issues me and her had, she had to admit that I was a decent coach during my reign at Ann High.

"She probably admitted that because she knows that some of her members probably seen you perform before, so they know how great you are," Dayla says. "They just didn't say nothing because her ass always acting like a bitch when she talk about you."

Isyss says Jasmine told her team it would be a good idea for all of them to go check the performance out.

"One of the girls named Mariah Mency, was eager to speak after hearing Mission High School," Isyss says. "She told Mariah that the basketball team plays Mission High School in a couple weeks." Isyss says everyone looked nonchalant about what Mariah had mentioned. She says Jasmine told the team that she would give them more details later and had them get back to perfecting the steps, and everyone went back on stage. She says McGruder pulled out a packet from her purse and asked Jasmine if she remembered it.

"What was it?" I ask.

"Jasmine was flipping through the pages of the packet and it was the document you sent to the principal of Ann High and the head of all New Orleans high schools after school activities advisors trying to get Ann's step team shut down your senior year," Isyss says. Isyss says the main points that triggered Mrs. McGruder were the ones concerning why I felt that she removed me from the team which were: Mrs. McGruder wanted to prove the team could continue on without me and she wanted someone else to take over what I had created. I knew this to be a fact when she read the program for Step Spectacular and Jasmine's name was written as a founder. Me and Jasmine both know that I am the one and only founder of Ann's current step team.

"I talked about Mrs. McGruder's unprofessional attitudes while removing me from the team, as well as her husband's boastful demeanor every time he saw me," I say. "I then asked the president and the head of New Orleans high school after school activities how they could hire anyone of the McGruder's who have poor professional skills, and do not have the best interest of their students."

"Jasmine continued to read over the packet that completely bashed the McGruders'," Isyss says. "Mrs. McGruder still isn't over the fact that you went above her head in an attempt to have her fired, get back on the team, or simply have it shut down. She said you were selfish. She said if you couldn't be on the team, that you didn't want it to continue on."

Isyss says McGruder told Jasmine to take all of her frustration out on me and put it in the moves she makes up. She said I don't deserve a victory, and definitely not over Jasmine and her, then she left the theater.

17

I show the front and back rows on Mission High's step team how to switch positions as they clap under their legs, while Ms. Ross sits in the audience and reads a book.

After the step is completed, I can't help but compliment them.

"That sounded great," I say. "All you guys have to do is put a little more attitude into the routine and your own personality and you'll be ready to compete."

Mission High has come a long way. They're catching onto the movements faster every practice, and they're putting lots of energy into the routine. After a few more practices, I know I can get them to be just as good as I got Ann High to be when I was there.

My boys and girls at Mission High started rough because they had no experience, but once they got a few practices under their belts, stepping got a lot easier for them.

"I want to implement one little factor in our overall performance," I say. "I want everyone to hold both hands up and opened."

Everyone does as they are told.

"Now do this," I say.

I tuck my thumbs in. It makes the claps more crisp and has an effect on how they sound.

"From now on, every move you make will be done with your thumbs tucked in," I say. "I need you guys to also remember that anytime your arms are in positions three or four, you must turn your heads. Yes, having good steps is nice, but being able to deliver them the proper way plays a great part in the judges' decisions."

I have everyone go through some of the steps with their thumbs in. They all do exactly what I thought they would, which is start with them in, then naturally let them loose.

"Ms. Ross can you get me a role of tape?" I ask her.

When I was at Ann High, I taped everyone's thumbs and index fingers together because it was frustrating after three days of them unsuccessfully keeping their thumbs in.

I'm not going to wait to see if Mission will get the hang of tucking their thumbs in; I'm just going to start early and tape them now.

"Let me see your hand," I say to Desiree.

I tape her thumbs and index fingers together, then give some of the members tape to help put it on everyone.

We do the steps again.

"This feels weird," Alexis says.

"Good," I say. "I need you to get used to having those thumbs in."

"How long do we have to keep this on?" Desiree asks.

"Until you can do the steps without sticking your thumbs out," I say. "Every practice we'll start with no tape, and if you can't keep your thumbs in, then I'll put tape on them again."

Desiree sucks her teeth.

"Don't complain," I say. "You guys look better already."

After practice, Jason puts his tapped hand on my shoulder and asks, "How am I doing coach?" He's tapping his taped fingers on my shoulder.

"You know you can take the tape off now, right?" I ask.

"Yes, but I'm going to practice a little more outside before I go home," Jason says.

That's music to my ears. I'm glad to hear he's practicing on his own. It seems like everyone is, being that they're almost to professional status with me. However, I still want to have at least one intense rehearsal outside of school hours with everyone. There can never be enough rehearsals.

"You're doing great," I say to Jason. "Everyone is. There's still some attitudes that need to go, but as far as the routine, everyone has improved a lot."

"Don't worry about Sheela," Jason says knowing I'm only having a hard time with her now.

Alexis has fixed her attitude. Maybe now that she's been stepping a while and is really good at it, she no longer needs to make it seem like she's going through a bad teenage phase.

"She's got a problem with everyone," Jason says. "Bye coach."

I grab my things and try not to make it obvious that I can see Sheela looking like she wants to kill someone while she grabs her backpack. When her back is to me, I stare at her until she's out of the theater.

Sheela's really angry inside about something. She's starting to look worse than I did when Nadia told me she played a part in getting me kicked off my step team senior year. Just like I was unapproachable for a while my senior year when Nadia revealed to me her secret, so is Sheela. She doesn't look like she wants to be bothered.

I'm not going to say anything to her. She's putting a lot more effort into the steps despite her anger. She's been working so hard and sometimes she gets mad at herself for not having the choreography. I commend her for being able to practice through her anger. She's already proven that she's stronger than I was my senior year.

Sheela has yet to come into practice broken. I'm so angry at myself for walking into Ann High's auditorium and breaking down in front of the team instead of holding my emotions in until I was alone. I felt so unprofessional and weak.

I walk out of the theater before Ms. Ross, who locks it. When I get outside, I see Jason, Jose, and Michael practicing a few

284

steps with a small audience.

"Don't show too much," I say.

Delia's walking to her mother Chelsea's car.

"Bye Delia," I say.

"Bye," Delia responds.

"Bye Ms. Chelsea," I say.

Ms. Chelsea gives a forced smirk. I can tell something is bothering her by how forced it is. I think she's about to release some bad news to Chelsea. I need to think optimistic though.

As I walk down the school sidewalk, a few Mission students approach me.

"Hi, Ms. Jackson. Is it too late to join step?" a sweet girl asks.

"It is," I say. "They've learned too much."

"Desiree and Keasha are my girls. They can catch me up," the girl says.

"I'm sorry," I say. "There's a lot of different formations and adding just one person would cause me to have to change everything around."

"Do you teach a class anywhere else?" one of the boys asks me. "I want to learn how to step."

"Unfortunately I don't," I say. "But if I ever do, I'll come by and let you guys know."

"Okay," the handsome boy says. "You're doing a great job with them. I see them practicing."

"Yea," another girl says. "Sheela's always in class practicing. Mr. Thompson stay telling her to *leave the stepping for step rehearsal.*"

Of all people, Sheela is the one that's practicing in class. The student that seems to hate being in my class every practice with her bad tone and attitude when she talks to me, is the same one perfecting the steps in class. So, her attitude is the opposite of what she feels on the inside. She acts like someone forced her to be in my class, but she loves it.

"Look," the first girl that spoke to me says. "I made up a step."

She does a cute routine. There's a lot of claps above and under her legs and a lot of hits to her thighs.

"That's good," I say.

"You inspire me," she says.

"Thank you so much," I say.

They have me feeling like a celebrity right now. I love when people tell me in person that I've inspired them.

"Have a good day Ms. Jackson," the girl says and her and her friends head back inside the school.

I feel special and loved walking to my car. Mission's students really just warmed my heart.

Sometimes I feel like I'm a low and filthy person for seeing Mission's team as essential mainly to make a statement to the McGruders' and Jasmine. I'm basically using them as a weapon instead of my main goal being to help them get better at stepping, and inspire them to keep going with the art even when I've moved on to another school.

I need to get rid of the selfishness and vengefulness inside of me. Being a coach of Luminous LA is about teaching, inspiring, and encouraging the students. It's not about using them for my own personal gain. I'm vowing to myself that I will have the right mindset about my job from now on.

When I leave Mission High, I want the students to feel uplifted, accomplished and happy to have been a part of my program. Now, don't get me wrong, I am aiming to get that first-place trophy, and have confidence my diverse team will hop on stage and deliver at the dance competition, as well as The Big Bang Step Off.

I'm just no longer caring about the McGruders' and Jasmine.

My focus is my members and making them the best they can be at stepping. It's no longer stuck on that first-place trophy just so I can prove that I am the best choreographer and smile and laugh with my team while Jasmine and the McGruders' watch with pure hatred and disgust.

My car engine is acting up. I pull on the side of the road. I'm not that far from the school yet.

Someone's honking their horn behind me. I turn around and it's Jose.

"You want a ride Coach?" Jose asks talking through the passenger window.

"It's alright," I say. "I can call someone."

"I don't mind," Jose says.

"I have someone who can come get me," I say. Jose insists that I sit with him in his car until Ciera comes.

I get in and Jose pulls on the side of the road.

"You can sit in here until she comes," Jose says.

I wanted to get out and enjoy the breeze, but my student seems to want me in his presence a little while longer, so I'll keep him company.

"So how's school going for you?" I ask to keep from an awkward silence.

"Good. I'm glad it's my last year," Jose says. "I'm tired of it."

"I feel you on that," I say.

"Do you really?" Jose sarcastically asks. "Don't you remember doing all this schoolwork?"

I nod my head.

"Then you're not too sick of it now at least. You're done," Jose says. "Once I get out of Mission High, I don't care if I work at a grocery store the rest of my life, I'm not doing another year in school. I can't stand it, so why would I take out loans? I'd have to pay the rest of my life for something I don't want to do?"

"It's not so bad," I say. "You just have to make sure you know what you want to major in beforehand, so you don't waste any loans on classes you won't need."

"I don't know what I want to do," Jose says. "I just know I'm tired of school. I wouldn't mind visiting a college campus though."

This is the perfect time to squeeze this in.

"If you and the team want, maybe one day I can ask the team that I coach at Cupperton to let y'all visit their dorms," I say.

"That would be dope," Jose says.

"Of course it would only be right to practice a little since you guys would be together," I say.

"I knew there was a catch," Jose laughs.

"Yep," I say. Ciera is here. "Alright Jose, I'll see you next time."

"I'll talk to the team about that practice," Jose says.

I get home, make some calls, and pay to have my car fixed.

Delia texts me and says she's going to put me on mute while her mom is talking to her. I'm at home lying on the couch eating popcorn.

Ms. Chelsea is driving and speaking disgustedly to Delia.

"Your teachers have said that your grades have been slipping the last month and a half," Ms. Chelsea says.

Delia texts me that her mom caught her completely off guard. This is the last thing she was expecting to hear.

"That means that right around the time you joined this stomp team, you lost focus of what's important," Ms. Chelsea fusses.

"Step team," Delia corrects her with an attitude.

"Oh whatever!" Ms. Chelsea shouts. "Right around the time you joined this team your grades started to fall."

I get up and start walking around my house.

Ms. Chelsea takes a deep breath. She says she's trying to come up with a solution. Ms. Chelsea finally says, "I'm removing you from the team until your grades get better."

"What!?" Delia says. I can imagine how bad she feels.

I know Delia is furious because she's now learned most of the routine and is really enjoying the class.

"I will call your coach tonight to let her know," Ms. Chelsea says.

Delia sounds like she's crying. "There are only a few more practices," Delia says.

Ms. Chelsea says nothing.

"I will do better!" Delia fusses. "I will make sure I put my school work before this team!"

Ms. Chelsea says nothing as Delia throws her head back on the head rest.

18

I practice outside with Legit in Cupperton's parking garage. I couldn't get the gym because the basketball team is rehearsing.

Everyone is in attendance except Regina and Shanell.

I start the choreography by myself as everyone else stands with their elbows out and fists touching across their chest. No one has any expression on their face except me. I intensely start off with a slow right stomp, followed by a hit on my chest to begin the choreography. The rest of the team comes in soft.

Listening to how weak they sound, I no longer hold my intense facials. I do the moves nonchalantly. I give up. It takes the entire team to be energetic for our shows to have a good impact. One person can't do it.

I have two more basketball games scheduled for us to conclude this year and be done with this team, and it looks like we're going to do just as bad as we did at the first one.

I hope my Sorors don't show up again.

Regina and Shanell arrive with thirty minutes left in our two-hour practice.

On sight, I walk over to them as they approach.

"I'm removing you two from the team," I say.

Regina and Shanell look appalled.

"You are the only two that consistently come late," I say. "I put too much time and effort into this team, and I can't deal with people taking it for granted."

The truth is, everyone comes late and shows up when they want, so they all should be getting removed; however, I don't want to terminate the team yet. I want to finish the year off because I know I'm not going to run this team again. So, I'm just going to make an example out of two people and see if their absence affects everyone else in a positive way.

"I have not been late more than three times," Regina pleads.

"I have been keeping track of how many times people come late and you have been late more than eight times," I say. "Not only do you keep coming late, you come late by a minimum of an hour sometimes."

Because everyone comes sporadically to rehearsals, no one knows who's been showing up faithfully on time and who hasn't, so it's easy to lie to them.

Regina has no idea that there's people here that have been late nine and ten times, and those people sure aren't going to admit it.

Everyone's looking at Shanell and Regina catch attitudes with me. They're all shocked that I'm removing members. I no longer care about having the maximum amount of people perform in fear of too many people dropping. If they were going to leave, they would have already.

The team will do fine with a couple of less people. I'm hoping removing these two will make everyone show up on time, if not early from now on. I don't care how anyone feels right now, I care about my sanity, and everyone here knowing that I am not to be taken advantage of.

"One time I was only late two minutes, so how could that even count?" Shanell asks.

"Late is late. You guys are finished," I say.

Realizing I'm serious, Regina begins to talk loud.

"You are hella wrong for this!" Regina yells. "I don't want to be on this stupid team no more anyways! It's not fun anymore!"

I hold my composure. This team isn't fun because of them, not me. They chose to make me miserable coming late or not coming at all.

I was so frustrated and had to spend so much time reteaching steps, that there was never any time to joke or play around. Let alone have a good conversation. I lost my patience for this team. Everyone has enough sense to know that no one wants to keep reteaching combinations over and over.

I'm angry that Regina and Shanell are acting like they really have been on time and they know they haven't. Not to mention, I feel embarrassed that this argument is happening in front of the entire team.

Shanell decides to gang up on me with Regina. She is the type to add fuel to the fire. When she sees that someone is on her side and she is on the side with more people, she takes advantage of it. It's only right to be judgmental about these girls.

"First off, you didn't have to wait for us to come here to say this," Regina says. "You should have called or something."

"Shanell you are finished!" I shout.

"Why do you even have everyone out here in the cold anyways?" Regina asks.

I look back at the team who is trying to not make it obvious they are listening.

"Good luck with this stupid coach. Regina let's go," Shanell says as she grabs Regina to leave.

I take a minute to catch my breath and analyze what just happened. I have actually removed people off of my team knowing how my removal caused me to act with the McGruders'.

I'm thinking: Should I have done this? Am I wrong? Was I fair? Am I now a reflection of the McGruders'? I did tell Regina and Shanell the rules on day one and the situation that just occurred was due to their own choices.

Although I'm not happy about kicking Regina and Shanell off the team, they needed to go. I let them do whatever they wanted long enough. Hopefully they are the only examples I need.

I didn't smile while I kicked them off the team, so I am not as evil as that Mrs. McGruder.

I slowly walk back to the rest of the team. My voice is shaky, but I manage to speak.

"I want everyone here to know that being a coach is not easy," I say.

One of the other members, Kim Reese, tries to console me.

"Don't worry about it," Kim says. "I've been a coach for a dance team before, and times like this are gone come."

"Thanks. Let's just pretend like none of that mess just happened," I say.

We continue practicing.

As I walk back to my car, I receive a phone call from Dion Bell, one of the members on the team that I just saw.

"Hello," I say having no clue why he's calling me.

Dion says, "Hey, I just wanted to call and let you know that I am removing myself from the team. It's not fun anymore."

I'm even angrier now. Why would he finish out the practice if he knew all along he was going to quit? I always knew Dion was a follower, but thought differently when it came to school and his activities. He likes to impress his rich mom and dad back in Florida, by letting them know how active he is on his campus, which ensures them that he's not involved in any gangs, drugs, or other stuff people think college students get influenced to do.

Dion's an ass to me now. He had to call me and say he quit, instead of saying it to my face like a man in front of the whole team.

I say, "Hello," again acting like I didn't hear him. Then hang up.

Angry and upset, I splash water on my face and stare at myself in my bathroom mirror. I call Ciera who is doing crunches in her bedroom.

"I think I'm about to call it quits with this team," I tell her.

"What?" Ciera asks in shock.

"They are wearing me down," I say. "I don't know why they feel they can act a certain way and take advantage of me, but I can't deal with this no more."

"I'm sorry to hear that girl, but do whatever is best for you," Ciera says.

"Hold on," I say.

I send out an email to all of the members of Legit: *The team is done*.

I tell Ciera.

"That's all you said?" Ciera laughs.

"Yea. What else is there to say?" I say lying in bed. "It's crazy how I already feel a huge weight lifted off of my shoulders. I got more time on my hands, I don't have to deal with their attitudes, I no longer have to stress about people showing up when they want to. This was a good move."

"That's what's important and I think it was a good move too

girl," Ciera agrees. "You don't need that extra stress. Especially not when you have another team. One that you are actually getting paid to coach."

She's definitely right about that. I coached Cupperton for free and they caused me way too much stress, and wasted a lot of my time. At least with Mission, when they give me a hard time, I have a check that keeps me encouraged.

"But at least you tried it," Ciera says. "If you wouldn't have, then you'd have always wondered what if you started this team and if it could've been successful."

I know from now on if I get involved with a team that I'm coaching for free, I'm removing people that don't follow the guidelines. The members of Legit knew the rules about tardiness because stepping is not something that can be learned over night. I made that rule because I knew I would hate reteaching; however, I did not stay true to it because if I did, the team would only be comprised of me. They were so unappreciative.

I'm getting more frustrated the longer I think and talk about Legit. I should have never called the team that name. They were far from *Legit*. I should've called it *Inaccurate*.

"Well, I'm about to take a small nap and just appreciate not having to deal with the shenanigans anymore," I say. "Have a good rest of the night girl. I love you."

"I love you too girl, and keep your head up," Ciera says. "Forget about that team. You know it's a matter of time before someone hits you up to coach another one."

"Bye," I say and fall asleep.

I dream about the time me and the senior dean for Ann High School sat across from Mrs. McGruder, who looked bitter and deceitful.

"Shona, the reason I called you in here and have Mr. Ruckus here is because when removing someone from a team, the staff member that is head over that particular grade has to be here," Mrs. McGruder said to begin the conversation that would lead to me being down and out the rest of my senior year.

"Jasmine is now head coach," Mrs. McGruder said.

That exact day, Jasmine went on a power trip and began acting uppity. I couldn't take it. Our friendship ended within hours of my removal.

Prior to the last meeting I had with Mrs. McGruder, Jasmine was my best friend. We always hung out together, had sleepovers, helped each other with homework, and she was the one that talked to me about going to college when I wasn't planning on going at first because I was just like Jose: sometimes I didn't want to continue on with school because I was tired of taking classes.

Jasmine sat down and questioned me about other things I liked to do besides step, and motivated me to enroll in Cupperton to learn scriptwriting. As soon as Jasmine was labeled head captain, she held her nose high and had a lot of pep in her step.

Jasmine didn't try to console me or talk Mrs. McGruder into giving me another chance at being on the team, despite the fact that she motivated a teacher to let me retake a test because she knew I was stressing because Nadia was so mean to me.

Jasmine just quickly told our circle of mutual friends that she took my spot, and went from holding conversations with me in the hallway, to saying *hi* sporadically, to not saying *hi* at all.

It was then that I recognized we weren't really friends. I feel like she kept me close until she could take my spot. She smiled in my face only because she wanted to take my place and wanted to disguise it. If she was mean to me, it would've been obvious there was jealousy, but she played her jealousy off by being my friend. She had me fooled for so long. She was good at acting like she cared about my future and my happiness.

I open my eyes furious.

That day in Mrs. McGruder's office ruined my senior year in high school. I lost my team and my best friend, and it was all because I couldn't keep my attitude from Nadia being evil to me at home outside of practice.

I see my grandma sitting in front of me in my dining room again. I keep losing my mind and thinking she's right in front of me.

"Nadia said my dad didn't want me," I say.

"She said your daddy didn't want you? What you think hers said about her?" my grandma asks. "How many times you think I told her she had book sense and no common sense?" my grandma asks.

The things my grandma told Nadia because she knew she would say them to me. My grandma knew I would be smart enough to figure it out. She said she knew every trick in the book. She had some tricks up her sleeve. I can see her playing poker right now.

"You have to tend to things to remember them in intricate detail. Especially when you're beautiful Shona. Ugly people with ugly ways have no limits, no bounds," my grandmother continues. "You have to release yourself from the problem."

My grandma warns me. She wants me to understand that I shouldn't have anyone's number that I have to worry about telling me some crazy stuff. "Tell her that's why I did it," my grandma says.

I remember visiting my grandma one day. I went in her trailer. When I got to the door to go in, I could feel her spirit and turned around and looked at Nadia and her sisters. My grandma motioned her head to the right and her youngest daughter moved to a different spot to stand.

"There's going to be some real crazy things people say to you. But a real love can cut through that Shona," my grandma says. "There's no reason someone should call you and say one negative statement that you can remember the rest of your life and you can't act nonchalant about it. Real love can do anything."

A pot on the stove is boiling with water. The lid is popping up.

"I know your mom didn't teach you how to cook," my grandma says. "She was no good."

I'm looking real sad now. Nadia just couldn't do a damn thing for me.

"I laid my life down, and so did a lot of other people because we were sick of the excuses. You will do right by me and finish what I started," my grandma says. "When I die, I will die in peace. Who the hell cares who goes first? If there's no love, there's no caring on my end. I loved all of my grandkids until I woke up to the truth."

"What's the truth?" I ask.

"If they ever try to exclude anyone that's mine, I will hate them until the death of me," my grandma says. "That's the woman they never knew."

Nadia needs to really learn how to hate. When someone is dead, they're dead. "How could I care how any of my damn kids are going to react when I'm dead?" my grandma says.

"Oh I see. They want to see how long I'm really going to make it without their love and support," I say.

"You always did think a little too quick for me," my grandma says. "You always had a smart mouth," my grandma says.

Whatever. I didn't think that was smart.

Now that I know Nadia's been practicing on me since birth, every past thought about her is dangerous, and yet I am still making it. Who the hell keeps hitting me in my grown woman like that?

I never recognized a time where I actually thought Nadia was a woman that felt sexual, but now I can look at the days I really endured pain and see how she respected herself as a woman.

"The thought of her having sexual tendencies towards herself is just a mess," I say.

My grandma laughs.

I remember screaming all the way to a rollercoaster and Nadia kept trying to stand right by me. She was looking down at her private area the whole time. I was maybe ten years old and she was out in public enjoying her sexual essence because I was screaming. I have tons of thoughts like this that could give me a heart attack. "Mainly because she's so ugly," I say. I don't get it though. She wasn't ugly when I didn't know the truth. My grandma tells me and now I completely dropped every good thought of her.

"It was quick as hell too," my grandma says. "You're a baby. I treated you like a child for thirty-five years. Now I need you to

297

trust me to continue to love you so you can make it through life."

"Okay Grandma," I say.

"I want you to hang onto the fact that I would lay my life down for you. I hated Nadia for how your older cousins would tell me she would treat you. Tell her I hated her when I was carrying her," my grandma says.

My grandma knows some of my older cousins were abusive towards me. All this writing I'm doing, and this bitch Nadia has our family with an attachment to them bitches.

"Damn. That's how bad being ugly can cut up?" I ask.

I get popped in my mouth again.

"There's blood behind this," my grandma says. "Believe me."

"I can't stand her and that Mrs. McGruder," I say.

"They the only two people thinking they sitting around with staff that can't see behind the hard work you do and their lives not amounting to anything," my grandma says.

I snap back into reality.

There were days when I was a show off, and days when I talked mean to my Ann High team members, I'll admit. But I don't think I should've been removed from the team. Definitely not since I created it.

19

The next week Mission High's step team meets me outside of the dorm area at Cupperton. Jose got everyone to come visit the campus.

Legit is finished, so I contacted the housing director at Cupperton and asked if there were any vacant dorms that I could allow my Luminous LA team to view. Luminous LA is well known and lots of people know the history of the organization.

I am being trusted with a key to a dorm room and having high school students with me on this campus, although I no longer attend it.

"Where's Delia?" I ask.

"Her mom wouldn't let her come," Desiree says.

I want to ask why, but I figure if she wants me to know why, she would tell me. They're not supposed to be here anyways, so it's not like I could call Ms. Chelsea and ask her to drop Delia off. I'm already taking a risk having the team here.

I might get away with saying two were just stopping by the campus, and we ran into each other if Mr. Stephen stopped by, but not the entire team.

"Now we all know we cannot talk to Ms. Ross or anyone else about this little gathering right?" I ask.

I'm not supposed to meet with my students outside of practice hours, and definitely not without Ms. Ross. It's standard policy, that way the students can't make up a story that I did something to them and for liability reasons too.

"We know," Jose says and looks at everybody to make sure they heard what I said, because he really didn't know.

"Dang where is everybody?" Casey asks looking at the vacant dorm area on the walk to the dorms.

"Either in their rooms sleep or off campus doing they own thing," I say. "It's just one of them days. We gone go to Greg Johnson University after this."

When everyone walks in the dorm I have access to, the first thing they notice is how spacious it is. They go in the kitchen, bathrooms, dining room, and the bedroom.

The entire apartment is clean because I came early and cleaned out the bathroom, wiped down the kitchen, and cleaned swept and vacuumed. I also took out the trash before my students arrived. I was pissed. I hate cleaning other peoples' places. In this case, this vacant apartment should've already been clean.

"Coach, they need some decorations," Jason jokes taking notice of my plain bedroom.

The most decorations this room has in here are bed sheets and pillows. I sit at the desk while a few of my members sit on the bed and others stand.

"I know this room is boring, but if you attend here, be thankful you don't have to walk far to get to class," I say. "Y'all ready to practice?"

"Can we chill for a second?" Alexis asks.

I say sure. Casey turns on the TV I brought with me and scrolls through the channels.

"Go back," I quickly say.

The words *Big Bang* caught my attention. A commercial promoting the competition is airing. We watch the promo for the show.

"You don't want to miss the hottest step show around," a reporter says. We can hear his voice, but can't see him because while he talks, photos of all the coaches pop up on the screen one at a time, very quickly.

My Luminous LA team cheers when they see my picture.

"Coach Jackson!" Kiara shouts.

Now a few teams are being shown from their step shows at their schools or other events. I'm happy none of the other teams knows anything about Mission High's step team. All they know is I coach them. Everyone will be completely amazed when they see me walk in my team that's comprised of non-blacks.

Everyone will be anxious to see what Mission High has to offer.

"I can't wait," Michael excitedly says when the commercial goes off.

I'm glad I caught the commercial because now the team is really pumped. I even saw Sheela do a little smile while she was watching the commercial.

"You think we gone do good coach?" Alina asks.

"I know everyone will do well," I say. "You guys have all improved so much since the first day we met."

I feel like my team is looking at me like I'm a mother giving them the encouragement they need. It feels great. I'm a lot older than them, and they're giving me the respect that I deserve.

I guess I'm shocked because of how Legit took advantage of the good thing I did, so they could have something to do on campus.

"I'm excited for this competition," I say. "I'm excited to see you guys on the stage in front of thousands of people showing off everything I've taught to you."

Some of the members look shocked when they hear me say *thousands of people*. Jason and Michael slap hands. Then Michael slaps Jose's hand.

"We will do good," Jason says.

"I'm so proud of all of you," I say. "I want you guys to go on that stage and show everyone that stepping is not just a black thing."

"I'm nervous," Keasha says.

"Girl you cheer in front of people all the time," Alexis says. "You'll be fine."

I remember back in college when I would have friends over and they would get loud. Melinda would slam her room door and shout, "It's too loud in here! I wish people would take their kindergarten friends to their elementary schools and not to our apartment!"

Melinda would then go slam the front door.

I can't stand when people indirectly talk about someone when they know the person they're talking about will know it's them. Melinda always called my friends kids, but she was always the one displaying the childish behavior. I hated witnessing this stupid type of irony from her.

301

Sometimes I would cuss Melinda out and other times I would have to remember I was a part of a sorority and the President of a team.

"And don't have them on our side of the apartment!" one of my other roommates that lived on the other side would shout after Melinda slammed the door of her choice.

"Aye, you need me to go check them?" Ciera would seriously ask.

I sometimes said no.

"I can make sure they don't use that tongue for nothing else but eating," Ciera would say. "We should pick the lock to her room and cut up her sheets. Break her window."

One time Ciera walked out of the room and I followed behind her. Melinda locked her room door and Ciera wanted a hanger to pick it. I told her to behave because I didn't want us to get into any serious trouble.

Ciera always told me to let her know if I needed her to pay Melinda a visit and regulate some stuff up in my dorm. I always told her I would be sure to do that.

I love hearing her treat me like I'm her relative or best friend. It makes me feel good and like we're a family.

My Luminous LA team and I have gotten really close. I've already developed a family with my students.

"Let's go ahead and get practice out of the way," I say to my Luminous LA team.

We practice outside in the quad in front of the housing office. I was skeptical about practicing outdoors in fear of Alpha Eta Nu coming out. Not because my team isn't ready to showcase, because they are, but because I don't want to deal with no drama. Definitely not in front of my team.

Shanell and Regina were enough.

I have Mission go through the routine, and I walk around making a mental note of the small mistakes I'm seeing, such as a thumbs poking out, facials not being intense enough, stomps being late or early, and arms not being stiff enough when they stretch out.

I have everyone break into groups and help each other while

302

I go around from group to group correcting their mistakes.

People are walking by and some are at a standstill watching us. It's not until I see someone pull out their phone and point it our direction that I shut the rehearsal down.

I don't like for people to record my routines before I perform them at least once.

The team cools off for a bit in the vacant dorm living room for a while. "You guys ready to head to Greg Johnson?" I ask.

"No," Alexis says and the rest of the girls look at me like I'm crazy. "We want to go home and get fresh."

"Meet us back here," Jason says.

"We can meet you at the school," Kiara says.

The girls head out, and Jason, Michael, and Jose stay and relax with me in the living room. The boys and I watch music videos and eat sandwiches, chips and dip, while we wait on one of the girls to call.

When we finish eating, Jose takes all of our plates to the kitchen. When he comes back out, he stops in the middle of the floor and starts stepping.

I'm about to shed a tear. Jose's doing a step I made up to the song that's playing on the TV. He starts smiling when he sees me recognizing my own choreography that I know he learned by watching one of my tutorials on *Video Video Vault*.

"Took me two days, but I got it," Jose says while he's still doing the choreography. "I know I'm not as good as you, but I think I do alright."

"You look good," I say.

"Thank you," Jose says and wipes sweat off of his face. "I try my best to look good for the ladies."

"I meant the step," I say.

"Coach you stepped in high school right?" Michael asks.

"I did," I say.

"Do you have any videos of your shows?" Jose asks.

I grab one of the three DVDs from my bag and play it.

There I am, front and center on the stage with Jasmine to my left.

"A! H! S!" I shout and everyone explodes into my

choreography.

I know despite how evil Nadia was to me, I still was able to put together a show, and teach it to my team so we could showcase for our peers.

I look so good. I set the next step and Jasmine comes in along with everyone else.

People are shouting my name more than anyone else on the stage. I had respect, honor, leadership, and admiration amongst everyone at Ann High.

Everyone knew I was the founder of the team, coached the team, and was the one responsible for everything and everyone that was on stage delivering.

Most of the members were nowhere near as talented as they were when they first began stepping with me just like Mission High wasn't, not even Jasmine. She wasn't a natural when she came under my wing freshman year in high school. I had to teach her how to hold all the different basic positions. She wasn't a natural or the star on the team, I was.

Luminous LA's boys are watching the videos with complete admiration. They're watching a video from my junior year.

At the end of each year, the McGruders' create a disk with all the performances from the year, and give one to each student.

"Did you make up you guys routines too?" Michael asks.

"Yes," I say.

"Those steps are nice, but I think you made ours better," Jose says.

"Of course," I say looking at him like he should know that.

I get better as the seconds go on. Every step I create needs to be better than the last one I created. I'm smiling as I watch Ann High stroll off stage, and I'm in the front, and Jasmine is behind me.

I'm killing my choreography and people are still shouting my name as I lead my team down the aisle.

The disk automatically goes to the next performance, so the boys and I continue to watch.

We're all so tired from practice that we fall asleep on the couch.

We don't wake up until Alexis calls Jason's phone asking where we're at. Jose drives the boys, and I drive myself to Greg Johnson where we're meeting the girls in the parking lot.

As soon as we pull in the lot, the boys are amazed by what they see. Frats holding their canes, a bunch of students socializing by their cars, couples holding hands, and a man blasting music out of his car with people dancing to it.

"Now Coach, which college is better: Cupperton or Greg Johnson?" Jason asks me over the phone.

Jason pulls up behind Alina's car where all the girls are talking and observing their active surroundings. I'm lucky I spotted someone pulling out. I hop out my car and join the girls while the boys find a parking spot.

Alexis is really feeling herself while she sits on the front of Alina's car with her shades on. She's looking at the frat boys. Her freshman behind is no more than fourteen or fifteen looking at those grown men that look a minimum of twenty-five.

I walk over to Alexis.

"I'm going to attend this school," Alexis says when she notices me out of her peripheral. "I'm the addition that this campus needs to make it even better than what it is. Beauty and talent," she says with one of her legs extended up.

"You just make sure you come here because what you want to be in life excels here and nothing else," I say.

"Coach why didn't you come here?" Casey confusedly asks approaching me from behind.

I start laughing because of how she asked. She's really puzzled that I go to Cupperton instead of Greg Johnson University. Luminous LA members must be mad we had to rehearse today.

I turn around and say, "I'm starting to question that myself," even though I know I chose Cupperton because it has a good film program.

Every time I walk on Greg Johnson's territory, I start to wish I would've just majored in dance, even though stepping is not an art form they offer. However; I wouldn't want to waste my major on stepping because it is something I already know how to do.

Greg Johnson looks like it is one big party today.

Luminous LA's boys walk up and everyone heads on the campus. There are more people than I've ever seen when I've came here before outside walking around. The campus has red, black, and white balloons all over the buildings with streamers.

I spot a bulletin board and watch the words scroll across: *Basketball Game Tonight.*

"Let's go," Casey says.

"We in there," Michaels says.

The team and I roam around the campus. We come across the football field and see people tossing a football back and forth. There's people running on the track too.

At Cupperton, the track stays packed even if it's not track season too, just like the basketball court stays packed even if it's not basketball season. Some people hated when I reserved the gym for Legit to practice. It cut into their free time in there.

Greg Johnson's concession stands are open behind the bleachers and there's not even an event going on yet. People are eating nachos and hot dogs watching the boys have fun on the field and the track stars sprint around it.

One girl is doing suicides on the field racing against one of the boys. She's not beating him, but it's the effort that counts. It's clear her drive and passion for her talent causes her to want to compete against the best.

"You guys see that girl running against that boy on the field?" I ask the team. They look at her. "I bet one of these days she'll be able to beat him, if not finish at the same time as him," I continue.

"She's passionate," Sheela says.

"I want you guys to be as competitive as her when you perform, whether it's for a competition or just to showcase," I say.

"She's almost catching him," Jason says.

It's clear the boy has slowed down a little to let the girl beat him, and she knows it, which is why she laughs and hops on his back. She gets down and kisses him on the lips.

"Well, shows over folks," Jason says.

We continue walking around the campus and come across some of the cheerleaders practicing outside. Alexis, Desiree, and Keasha are staring at them with disgust.

"We are better than them," Keasha says.

"You didn't need to say that," Desiree says. "We can come up with better cheers, look better than them doing the routines, and sound better saying the chants."

"Look at that," Alexis says. "They can't even hold the girl up that well."

Alexis is clearly hating and jealous. Greg Johnson University's cheerleaders are flawless, and they're doing great with their choreography. Some boys are passing the cheer team.

Alexis is shaking her head.

"The boys just walked past them like they were ghosts," Alexis says. "There's no way I would be cheering and showing off what I can do, and the boys wouldn't take at least two looks at me."

"That's right," Keasha says. "We usually get three looks, and it would be four, but people don't like to be rude so they mosey on about their business and wait to attend the games so they can stare all they want."

While Alexis and the twins continue to hate, the rest of the team and I observe the cheer team with admiration. Even though Alexis and the twins probably can outdo these cheerleaders with their style, personality, and ability, I still don't like to hear them bash the crew.

I'll be honest and say that listening to them is making me think about how I am when I talk about stepping.

Yes, I know I'm one of the best steppers alive, but do I really need to say it so much? No. I need to just continue to let my routines and work ethic speak for me.

My goal from now on will be to reduce saying that I'm the best stepper and choreographer. I've only heard Alexis and the twins boast about themselves consistently once, and that's today, and I'm annoyed. So, I can't imagine people that have to

307

listen to me repeatedly say how good I am at what I do, and the things my teams have accomplished.

I get everyone to continue walking since we're going to the game tonight. I don't want to see the entire cheer routine before everyone else.

We pass the food court and some of my students say they're hungry. While they all go in, I go to the bathroom in one of the buildings that hold classes. When I finish washing my hands, I wander around the building.

Once again, I am fascinated. The rooms holding classes are lively. The students are laughing and smiling with the instructors while they learn the subject material, some are eating lunch in their classes, and some are sitting on their desks. This is how me and my crew were when I was in school.

I walk up and down the hallways just to kill time because I'm still full from the sandwiches. A nice-looking man starts walking my direction. "You look beautiful," he says with the cutest smile and keeps walking.

A few minutes after he passes, another nice-looking man tells me I look nice.

The people here are so friendly and make me feel special.

Back in the day when I would visit Greg Johnson, people here did not want to compliment me. There must've been something in the water or some type of life taking poisonous pollen coming from the plants that everyone inhaled every day that caused them to be so rude.

Class lets out from one of the rooms, and I follow the students out of the building. As soon as they get outside, they head to their cliques and start socializing. They don't head straight to the housing area or to their cars; they hang around and enjoy the college atmosphere.

"Did you meet someone?" Alexis asks when I join them at the table at the food court.

"Nope," I say. "Just wandering around."

"You want some?" Casey asks offering me some of her chow mein and orange chicken.

Jose grabs me a plastic fork from one of the counters and I

take a bite of Casey's food.

"You guys want to hang around here until the game?" I ask.

My members all say yes, so we go to Alina's car, play music, and relax. Some of the team sits in the car with their legs hanging out like Kiara who is eating her leftover food, and the rest of us stand, dance and talk surrounding it.

Greg Johnson's students and alumni watch us act like we're at a block party.

This is how I wanted to bond with my team at Cupperton: Legit. I'm enjoying feeling like I'm in college again with my high school students, and not the people I actually coached at the school I attended. I feel so good right now enjoying a good time with my students. This is how life should always be.

Yes, I terminated Legit, but it was so worth it. I'd rather have them gone and enjoy this moment I'm sharing with Mission High steppers without having a negative thought in my brain about them, than still have them in my head and not enjoy this time because I can't get over how they didn't appreciate what I did starting that team.

Students and alumni of Greg Johnson University join us at the car and dance with us. One of the frat boys' of Phi Phi Alpha from Greg Johnson parks his car behind Alina's and gives us waters, sodas and chips he had in his trunk. Some of his brothers hop out the car and talk and dance with us.

Afterwards, me and the members of Luminous LA walk in Greg Johnson's packed gym to screaming and hollering. I'm feel so refreshed that this atmosphere is so lively just like the dance competition that was at Cupperton, and there's a lot of support for the players.

People are blowing horns when their team scores a basket, frustrated dads are yelling at the referees for calls they feel are bogus. Moms are up cheering on their sons. Little boys and girls are excited to watch older people play the game.

It's so packed in here that there's nowhere for me and my team to sit together. We split up and the twins and I sit together on the far side of the bleachers.

We were having such a good time outside that we forgot

about the game. There's only a minute left in the first quarter. Greg Johnson University is up by five.

The game stays close all the way to halftime and Greg Johnson is up by two.

The cheerleaders take the floor with their pom poms and do some bomb ass choreography. Better than all the teams in the movies. They're choreography is fast and complex the entire way through; they don't even slow down for their transitions. They toss people in the air and hold them firmly a lot while people are on the floor tearing up the other choreography.

They look better than the professionals that are on TV.

This reminds me of my junior year in high school when Ann High's cheerleaders and step team performed together in the gym. It was my idea. The cheer team looked so good in their black tights with silver and black tops.

I met up with the cheerleaders' head captain four or five times so she could get used to the beats I created, and she created choreography to match them. The beats I created went perfectly with the movements she created.

A step team collaborating with a cheerleading team is something that I've never seen done before by anyone else. Ann High's students were amazed, and so was I when I was creating the routine, coaching the routine, and definitely when I performed the routine and got to listen and watch the crowd go crazy as they watched.

The collaboration with the cheerleading team was my favorite performance at Ann High. I love to work with different dance styles. Stepping is so advantageous because using the body as an instrument allows music to be excluded. There's no second or third party involved.

That performance motivated me to work with the drumline at Ann High. The drumline collaboration was great as well. They would do a beat and my team would do the same one with our bodies. Then they would do a beat then stop. Then we would continue it. Then there were times when they did a specific beat and we did a separate beat I created to remix it. The parts the crowd loved the most were when we all did the beat to a

310

popular song.

Those were the good old days.

Ann High didn't do any collaborations my senior year. I wonder why?

After Greg Johnson's cheerleaders finish their routine, their dance team takes the floor. Considering how the gym is a lot louder now, I can tell the dance team is about to show out. The team gets to work with their intense choreography. The crowd never quiets down. The dance team does a small step in their choreography. I learned it just by watching; that's how simple it was.

I'm not really impressed when I see dancers adding step choreography in their routines because it's becoming more common.

"Coach you saw how they combined dance and step?" Casey asks me as we walk to the cars after the game.

Instead of saying anything, I just do the step the dance team did. I wish I would've noticed the dancers walking beside me and my team in the middle of this crowd because they're staring at me like I'm a cocky girl, and they don't like one bit that I just delivered their choreography better than they did.

Unfortunately, the dancers keep looking at me, like I would if I came across someone doing my choreography.

"What you think you better than us?" one of the girls on the dance team asks rudely.

The rude girl and her crew walk in front of me and Mission's team.

I'm at a loss for words.

"No, she doesn't *think*, she *knows*," Alexis says.

"Oh really," the same rude dancer says walking close to my face.

Alexis steps in front of me and crosses her arms.

"You need to back up," Alexis says. "Don't start nothing you can't finish."

Even though Alexis is a freshman in high school, she has a lot of heart stepping to these college girls.

Sheela walks closer to Alexis and the rest of the team follows

311

her lead.

Now all the dance members on Greg Johnson's team are close behind who's clearly their offended coach and teammate. There's only a few inches separating Mission High and I from Greg Johnson's dance team.

"Fight!" a little boy shouts.

We now have a big huddle of people surrounding us.

I move Alexis out the way and say, "Don't get offended that I learned your routine just by watching it once."

The same rude dancer mean mugs me.

"How long do I need to let you stare at me for you to realize that you're not intimidating?" I ask the rude dancer. "You're face doesn't scare me."

"But it is frightening to look at," Alexis smartly says.

There's a few seconds of nothing but silence and mean stares until we all hear, "Break it up," from the security guard. He's shining his flashlight in our circle.

No one moves, so the security guard pushes and squeezes his way to the center of the circle where me and the dance coach are staring at each other.

"I said break it up," the security guard repeats.

The dance coach and I are the last ones to start slowly moving. I wait until she turns her back to join my team that's waiting off to the side for me.

Jose decides to follow me home to make sure none of them bitches from Greg Johnson follow me. I shower and get in the bed.

Despite the last encounter at Greg Johnson University today, I had a great time and accomplishing day with my students. We started the day lounging in a dorm, we rehearsed, we walked on another college campus, ate together, and attended a basketball game. On top of that, my students showed to me once again, that they'll defend me if anyone disrespects me.

Although I'm an only child, I feel like I now have a bunch of little brothers and sisters with Luminous LA members. I should've felt that way with Legit, but I know if I ever got ganged up on, they would not defend me. They didn't care about me not one bit. They just cared about what I could do for them. I don't even look passed Legit siding with the opponent. They probably would've jumped behind that dance coach and defended her, or simply just walked off like they didn't see any argument about to start. But Shanell and Regina were definitely quick to get in my face because they didn't want to be removed. I'm still a little upset about them ganging up on me; I gave them an inch with the absences and tardies, and they took a mile.

I'll never understand why people disobey the rules and get shocked when they're removed. I'll take a small portion of the blame for not removing the first person to exceed the maximum amount of absences and tardies.

When I fall asleep, I dream about a story my grandma wants me to know.

"Olifus told me a story about a girl named Malana Devay," my grandma says. "She was a light skinned stud. Malana was eighteen years old and developed very nicely. She had the perfect shape. She was tall and her stomach was as flat as can be. She loved to wear belly shirts and jeans that were baggy. She wasn't afraid to wear boxers and have them showing. She was a confident stud, and she knew she looked really good. No one could tell her any different."

My grandma says Malana had a real cute face. Her eyes were very pretty and so were her nose and lips. She had hair just beneath her shoulders. She loved to wear bandanas and glasses also. She had a lot of style. Malana knew she attracted a lot of attention due to her swag and unique look. She was someone everyone expected to see on television just for modelling. A lot of people don't think of a sexy stud when they first hear modelling, but Malana was it.

Malana's voice was very cute. She didn't talk manly. She talked like a regular girl. She didn't try to speak in any way other than what was natural to her.

Malana's personality was very nice and friendly. She knew a lot of people wanted to be in her company just because she was so fly. She enjoyed feeling like a star just because she was flawless. Most of her life all she heard was how cute and cool

313

she was from both girls and boys. The good definitely outweighed the bad.

One thing that came with her good looks was any bad look she gave people that liked her was heartfelt. They couldn't get over it. People would walk by her and bump into her. They would talk shit about her. Malana wasn't scared to fight though. She had been suspended several times from school for beating the hell out of somebody. People would get on her nerves because they would lust after her and she didn't want them.

"So not only was Malana a cute looking stud, she also knew how to fight," I say.

"You sound like you like her," my grandma says.

"She seems interesting," I say. "Did she have a girlfriend?"

"Olifus said she was always in and out of relationships," my grandma says. "Sometimes she had a long relationship, but most of them were short. It was hard for her to remain loyal when so many people took interest in her."

Malana went to a school called Creshform High. It was in Slidell, Louisiana. It was in the projects. She was a well-known thug. She stole any chance she could whether it was stuff right off the shelf, or money. Girls like Malana that had looks and were thugs were in high demand amongst women in need of a relationship, and men that wanted a woman in their crew. She had looks, personality, and wasn't a snitch. She had connections to get drugs and liquor. She was a cool girl.

There were times Malana had to deal with mean people because she was a girl that was into girls, but she had a loving family that always told her to be herself. They always encouraged her and wanted her to be happy. She was a stud that was envied by other studs because it was obvious she had a strong support system.

Malana lived with her mom Kinaya, dad Reginald, and brother Marvin. The Devay family was a strict household, but also a fun one. Malana's parents taught her well. They didn't tolerate her being a bad ass out on the streets. They told her the dangers of doing wrong. They told her how kids her age were being killed repeatedly for hanging with the wrong people.

The Devay family didn't have much money. Kinaya worked at a fast-food restaurant and Reginald worked as a teacher. They saved a lot incase their kids ever needed money for anything.

The Devay family lived in a small one-bedroom apartment. Malana and her brother slept in the living room. They ate dinner together and had family nights where they would play games or watch movies. The parents never really liked to invite people over because they were embarrassed that they had two kids and one bedroom. They didn't allow their kids to invite people over either.

Marvin and Malana always wanted to make something of their lives to get their parents in a better living situation. They cared more for their parents than they did themselves.

"So what's about to happen with Malana and Marvin? Canel's not coming is he?" I ask.

"Man Man told me about this group of friends: Cambridge, Lamaya, Denaya, Chaylani, and Arlina. They all had a brown skinned or pure dark complexion. Cambridge and Lamaya were the only ones that attended Creshform High School. This group was very unique. Cambridge wanted to be a girl. Lamaya wanted to be a boy. Denaya was insecure because she had a long and flat ass, Chaylani and Arlina were bitter because they were overweight.

Cambridge and Lamaya would see Malana around at school sometimes. They couldn't help but notice her because they wanted to be popular just like she was. They saw the attention she would get and envied her. They felt like losers when people looked at them. Malana was a real *it* girl. Lamaya was jealous that she couldn't get attention from girls the same way Malana did. All the girls Lamaya wished she could date all took interest in Malana. Lamaya knew she was ugly compared to her in the eyes of the students at Creshform High. Cambridge was really upset that the girls took more interest in Malana than they did him.

Denaya, Chaylani, and Arlina would pick Lamaya and Cambridge up from school sometimes and they would notice Malana. They couldn't stop staring at her having a good time

315

with her friends. They wish they knew what it was like to be perfect. They wanted to know what having a nice body felt like. All they could do was stare and watch Malana enjoy the essence of her being.

Sometimes the crew would come across her at the store or see her around town at an event. The response they had was the same. They couldn't stop staring at Malana doing anything. She could just be getting something off the shelf and the crew would just stare at her. They wanted to know what such a cute looking stud like Malana felt like inside. They wanted to know what she thought of herself and what she did in her personal time.

Sometimes the girls would catch Cambridge laughing at them for staring at Malana. Cambridge was happy he wasn't a girl that had to compete with Malana. He was sometimes happy he was a boy because he felt it would hurt worse if he was a girl that couldn't try to look better than her. Denaya, Chaylani, Arlina, and Lamaya couldn't even use make up to try and look close to Malana. Their body was nowhere as neat as Malana's. Lamaya had height, but she was not cute in the face and she was dark. She could never look like Malana.

Cambridge and his crew would walk past Malana and say evil things sometimes; however, she never could confirm it was about her. His crew has five people. They just make general statements that could be mistaken for them talking to each other. They would call Malana a man, say she was slow, and say she was unattractive.

Cambridge and his crew thought Malana never paid it any attention, but they would still mumble things around her as if she had no feelings. Malana knew a lot of people didn't think she cared about a word they said, but she was just like everyone else who could do without hearing negative bullshit. She knew people thought she was nonchalant because she looked good, and she hated that.

One day the crew sought out Malana just to get on her nerves. They knew she would be at an outdoor basketball event. They wanted her to see them. They thought it hurt her to look at such ugly people, and it did, but they couldn't prove that. They wanted and were desperate to see what the hood rat was up to. They walked by her and mumbled things like: *That bitch needs to pull her pants up. She's an ugly stud. She is not it.* Malana would say something like *them bitches better shut the fuck up* even when she was unsure if they were talking about her. Cambridge and the girls didn't care how Malana reacted. They just wanted her to say something.

Cambridge, Denaya, Chaylani, Arlina, and Lamaya were wandering around town one day. They noticed they reached an unfamiliar area and stopped. Lamaya was the one that took initiative to inform her crew that they didn't have anything to do anyways. They might as well test the waters and see what was in the area they stumbled upon.

They read a sign that said *High Class Territory*. They went in the place and walked on a rocky road. They talked and laughed until they noticed that the people seemed very serious and focused. The people had lots of electronic equipment that they had never seen before.

Cambridge and his crew started to see things they'd never seen before like televisions showing what they were looking at in that very moment.

Lamaya saw someone she recognized from television that was a news anchor and rushed to her. She was shocked by the celebrity appearance, but really wanted to ask for help. She wasn't feeling like her normal self.

Cambridge noticed someone that looked like him and his scared facial expression got the rest of his crew to follow his eye path. They noticed the look-a-like and realized they were in danger. A little while after, the girls noticed some of the people looked like them.

Denaya tried to keep everyone calm. They recognized that the copies were making a mockery of them. They all started to feel weird and realized that it was the clones that were making them want to vomit. Denaya was the first one to recognize that they had to adjust how they were acting so the copies would too.

The crew was losing time because they had to fight the feelings of not wanting to be embarrassed in front of each other. It didn't take long for them to recognize that when the clones moved, they were making them feel weaker when they didn't have control of their emotions. The crew got it together and started to act civilized. They changed their way of thinking. Everything bad that they liked was thrown out. They had to become good people to adjust the replications, but the replications knew them inside and out.

The crew had to act like good people to change the replications somewhat, but the replications were them. They wanted to play the game of life just like Cambridge and his crew were. Too much of a change would cause the crew to be killed quicker.

Cambridge and his crew reached a forbidden zone like Canel did. They had to do things the replications did. They had to eat disgusting things, drink disgusting things, and make sure to enjoy them to make the replications feel good. They had to learn the camera operating system. They had to learn how to direct, produce, and write films.

They had found one of the real entertainment spots. They found where television was coming from.

They recognized that everything they had been taught was a lie. They learned that the land was in fact real. They knew it was something they could never talk about.

There was a room Cambridge stumbled on. Lamaya was right behind him. In the room was fifteen copies of him. He quickly shut the door and went on about his business.

Cambridge, Lamaya, Denaya, Chaylani, and Arlina's main focus was to get out of the place. They were so distracted by everything going on and the fast pace all the robotic people were moving in, that they couldn't remember how they got in the place.

Some of the robotic people would talk to them and befriend them. They had to play along until they were led to the exit. They ate with these robots. Had sex with these robots. Had sex with animals. Witnessed killings.

The crew got out of High Class Territory at separate times. Once they all were able to meet up again, they shed instant tears. They couldn't believe they made it out of the toughest part of life: the electronic world and cloned world.

"Olifus said they recognized that they had walked on land that would change their lives forever," my grandma says. "Real humans were not supposed to step foot in High Class Territory."

My grandma says Olifus told her while the crew was in High Class Territory, Lamaya was the first one to come across a copy of Malana. The copy acted like she liked Lamaya and flirted with her. Lamaya couldn't believe the girl wanted to have sex with her. It took her a few seconds to remember that her crew was all copied. They had robots walking around of them. This was the first Malana she had seen, but she noticed the height was slightly off. Still in fear for her life, Lamaya slept with the copy of Malana.

Lamaya would see Denaya and tell her she saw Malana in one of the recording studios singing, only to hear Denaya say she saw Malana on a movie set. Chaylani, Arlina, and Cambridge would all say they saw Malana in a different area around the same time. Cambridge being terrified, admitted to sleeping with her. Arlina said she saw him having a good time.

The crew became suspicious when Malana's replications started seeking after them. They started to notice too many of her. They all lusted after her tremendously. Malana's replications were doing anything good and bad because they knew Cambridge and his crew didn't think she could do any wrong. Malana's replications started to get too much energy. They got so much energy that they started to act rude all the time to Cambridge and his crew. They acted like his crew didn't exist. They would walk past his crew and act rude.

All of the replications of Malana became arrogant and acted as if they were above Cambridge and his crew. They started to make jokes about the crew. It was getting really bad. The crew believed that the replications were acting how the real Malana felt. Most importantly, they were all embarrassed that they lusted after Malana. This is the same girl they talked bad about.

Now they have to look each other in the eyes and know that they are twisted in the head. They do what is wrong knowingly and have to admit that to each other. They know that such an act causes trust issues. The next time something goes wrong with them, they know none of them can be trusted to narrow anything down. Their past situations are all questionable when something went wrong.

The crew would have to learn how to use cameras, record, write music, sing music, produce films, and direct them. They would have to keep performing tasks until they got involved with the right system of people from High Class Territory that would reach the exit.

The crew recognized the copies were acting off of their feelings and were taken aback. They couldn't believe what they were walking on their whole life. They knew Earth was a serious platform. Life was not to be taken for granted.

The crew had to try many drugs. They knew they had to find a way to fake taking them, otherwise they would die. They had to figure out ways to trick their replications into taking their spot. They had to look beings in the eyes that looked just like them and become friends. The group had many copies and they all functioned in different ways. Some were studious and others were crackheads.

Cambridge and his girls would get out and create new lives for themselves. They had learned the money structure and had plenty. They were hit with new lives. They got new homes and cars just like Canel. Their friends believed they had made it big in the entertainment world. All their friends were was more prey to keep them alive longer. They were sacrifices to the land so they could get more time to live.

Cambridge, Denaya, Chaylani, Arlina, and Lamaya knew they needed the original Malana to deal with all the clones that emerged because they were around them, her scent was on them, and they had strong feelings for her.

Cambridge was the one to approach Malana with the deal of becoming a famous singer. She knew he had money because she researched him online. He told her about Denaya, Chaylani,

Arlina, and Lamaya and how she would have to sleep with them before she signed the contract.

Malana wanted desperately to save her family from such a rough neighborhood. She also wanted to be on television because she knew she looked good. She wanted people to see her and be jealous of her. She knew people loved seeing her living in such poverty with her handsome brother and good-looking parents. She wanted to be all over everyone's televisions and always hear how great she was as an entertainer and how good she looked. She knew she would get more girlfriends.

Malana agreed to have sex with Cambridge and his girls. She met them at a hotel and slept with them all together. Then she met them all individually and had sex with them. She signed the contracts and was given the location to High Class Territory.

Once Malana walked in the studio in High Class Territory, she knew she was going to die. She saw someone that looked exactly like her walk by. There's so much money involved with television that there wasn't much room in Malana to see something unusual that wouldn't cause her to think she would die. She started to have second thoughts, but waited for Cambridge and his crew.

The first person Malana saw was a clone of Cambridge. Her heart dropped and she became very stiff. She was scared. Cambridge's clone gave her the songs to sing and checked out the ones she had written. Malana was chipped and Cambridge, Denaya, Chaylani, Arlina, and Lamaya all had access to control her.

Just like Canel, Cambridge and his crew had to fight feelings of not really caring whether Malana died. They had been through too much in High Class Territory and now had so much fame and money that people naturally wanted to sleep with them and be their friends.

Their minds were focused on survival. Malana couldn't believe her entire body was being controlled by who she would refer to as her handlers. She was a singer and had no idea how long her life was going to last. She hadn't heard any stories

321

about anybody successful being chipped and controlled throughout their careers. She couldn't believe what had happened to her life in a few days. She was heartbroken.

Malana couldn't believe the type of monsters Cambridge and the girls were. She started to remember all the things they said when they were around her. She almost had a heart attack when she remembered what she said about them. The crew got to feel all of these feelings. She was completely sold out to them. Once the chip is put in the human body, it cannot be removed.

Malana felt so stupid and realized how real ugly people are. She couldn't believe she was the one that got taken by this ugly crew. They were going to make all the decisions for her in life. They would know where she was going and who she was with. They got to know the life of a real-life girl that was a fine ass stud. They could hear her conversations. They could know things that they never would get to know in life. They could tell her what to say.

Malana had to remember that they had to do things to get those jobs, but she didn't know how deep it was. She was an artist. She didn't have to do all the work to survive in a spot that Cambridge and the girls stumbled upon with no knowledge of anything. Their crew was first and made it easy for Malana. She didn't have to do anything but perform, but she would also sell her life to evil people; the true meaning of being sold out. Malana was chipped and had to do any and everything the people that despised her told her to.

Malana would return home and look into her parents' eyes and start crying. They knew she was in a pain that they'd never seen before. She needed them to know something was wrong, but didn't want to tell them because she cared about them and knew if they went to High Class Territory that they would be chipped too.

When Malana was by her brother in the living room, he wondered what was wrong with her. Malana wouldn't say anything. No matter how much Marvin hugged her, played with her, told her he loved her, and that he would keep quiet on

322

whatever it was, Malana would not tell him. Marvin and his parents knew Malana loved them to a point where she wouldn't want to involve them in any trouble.

Malana was smart enough to know that she would lose her mind anyway and tell them one day, and she would feel more comfortable knowing she informed them that way. She also knew her parents and brothers would fight to find out what was troubling her.

Malana started singing and dancing around the house a lot more. She would leave to go to High Class Territory and meet up with Cambridge and the girls. They would rehearse and record songs. Malana had to tell them everything about her. She hated this and struggled to say things, but once she realized all the pain the group could cause her, she straightened up. It took her a while to get used to being such a cute thug that was forced to be surrounded by people she felt were ugly.

It was hard for Malana to look the group in their eyes almost every day. She learned the material and was happy that she got to take some of it home. She knew her parents would go through her things and find the song lyrics with professional labels on them.

One thing Malana couldn't believe was that she was being paid very little. She was making the same amount her mom did at the fast-food place.

Cambridge, Denaya, Chaylani, Arlina, and Lamaya made Malana tell them her entire schedule. They wanted to know where she usually went and who would be there. They ruined everything in her life. They didn't care because they made it out of High Class Territory, but they also didn't care because they got the truth out of her about how she viewed them.

All five of the individuals controlling Malana wanted to treat her like a baby. They wanted to date her.

They were so frustrated at how Malana treated them that they would drug her and get her to fight the natural person she was. They made her want to kill herself because she hated them.

When the group of five was out in public, they felt less shame when people looked at them in mean ways. They knew they had a high-class thug that looked one hundred percent flawless that they got to torture. They knew other people were doing the same. It didn't hurt them as much dealing with society.

Malana would go home and her parents and brother would find out what she was involved in. They would find a way to get her free time and do some of the acts she had to do. High Class Territory is real evil, vindictive, and twisted. Someone who was dark and fat could pose as Malana on a crazy day. The place had no limits. Questions would be asked, but depending on the handlers for the day, anything could happen.

Malana had relatives that looked similar to her that would help her as well.

All hell broke loose when Malana's music videos started to appear on television. Marvin made sure to appear in the videos. He was down for his sister. People wondered why Malana looked so similar to the artist on television that had a different name. All the work Malana did, and her real name wasn't even used on television. Cambridge and his crew didn't go by their original names either. Everyone was hidden.

Malana went by Vayla Shores on television.

Malana did lots of interviews. Her parents and her brother showed up in a few of them. The Devay family wanted to show themselves to let everyone know how sorry they were for what their daughter was involved in. They knew the love people had for celebrities was real. They knew their immediate family would know they were in trouble and would do all they could for their daughter who was in so much pain.

Malana got to witness how everyone loved Vayla Shores. She felt good emotions in that department. She still went to school and socialized with people. Only now she was willing to socialize with anyone. She needed help. She really felt that some of the students at Creshform High knew what was going on and would try to get the chip out of her. It was making her sick.

It was unbelievable the amount of success she was having and she didn't get to enjoy any of it. Malana's relatives that went to school with her were in shock. They would sit in class as her and take her place on many occasions. They wanted to learn who Cambridge and his crew were so they could try and have them killed.

"Olifus couldn't believe what he learned about television, and how those kids were even strong enough to make it seeing how people reacted to them," my grandma says. "Malana Devay, better known as Vayla Shores, was walking around like a regular person. People always told her how much she looked like Vayla. She couldn't believe they didn't know it was her. She couldn't believe how fooled everyone was."

My grandma says this made Malana think of other artists. She knew some that she got to work with were dead.

Malana's dad, Reginald, had a brother, Darrel, that would play his guitar outside on the street. Reginald lied and told his daughter a story about Darrel wanting to be an entertainer. Malana quickly hoped her dad would say that Reginald made it away from his handler.

Reginald told Malana that Darrel had gotten offered a deal by a record label. He read through his contract with a lawyer and decided to join. Malana knew that this meant that her Uncle Darrel had been chipped. She knew he was playing an instrument on the street, but wasn't around him enough to know if he was in any trouble. She also knew that the chip could control her emotions and at times she would want to show pain and she couldn't. Malana was unsure if her uncle had been released from being controlled.

Reginald continued to tell Malana about stories that Darrel had told him about being in pain and in and out of the hospital when he would work long hours. Darrel said he would get sick at times and not know why. Reginald said he knew something was going on with his brother and wanted to help him, but his brother was never straight forward with him. He said whatever the problem was, it was hard to put his hands on.

Darrel got really dizzy one day and was in and out of consciousness. Darrel told Reginald that he thought he was going to die soon. Darrel told his brother that he thought someone put something in his body that he couldn't get out. Days later Darrel passed out at one of his friend's house. He came back to himself and felt different. Days later her realized that he felt normal again.

Darrel didn't want to continue on with music. He wanted to focus on his health; he decided to just play an instrument on the street.

Reginald made this story up to help Malana believe that one day she would be free from her handlers. Malana trusted her parents and knew they wouldn't lie to her about anything concerning the unfortunate situation that she was in. Malana often spoke about her Uncle Darrel in interviews. This helped her feel important and a way to feel normal again with high rank she really was living in amongst her friends. She thought they would look her uncle up because she was so famous. Not many cared to look up anyone other than Malana though. She was the star.

Darrel was a well-known instrumentalist with a great voice amongst many crowds, and many people did articles on him. So when Malana went to look him up, it was as if he did have a career.

Darrel knew people that had gotten into trouble trying to be entertainers. He told Reginald and Kinaya the dirty truth about television. He was a better story teller than Reginald. Darrel knew he had to inform his brother who had two very nice-looking kids that there was real danger in the world.

Malana's uncle knew she liked to sing and caught her dancing a few times. He thought his niece and nephew might take interest in becoming famous. Darrel knew it wasn't easy to be chosen, but he didn't risk the chances of his family being the lucky ones' that got to be on television. He told his brother everything and made sure he told Kinaya.

Darrel told Reginald that the people behind entertainment were very angry. He told his brother that it was through anger, that entertainers were chosen. Signing the contract is signing someone's life over to another person. Darrel made sure to completely explain that. He told him every move he made

326

would be controlled if he wanted to be famous. The producers could always know what he was up to. He told his brothers the producers could cause him pain whenever they wanted. Darrel let Reginald know that the famous life was not what he would expect. Darrel let him know that he wouldn't get much more money than he was making on the street playing an instrument.

Darrel's confession to Reginald helped him talk to Malana. When Malana was sent to all kinds of facilities. There were places where she had to stay handcuffed with a bag on her head while people watched television. Her mouth was used as a fingernail filer. She was to make darker girls that wanted to be lighter feel good about themselves. She had to sit around for days bleeding in different spots. Malana had to sit in rooms that smelled horrifying. She had to put living things in her mouth.

Malana's parents would continuously drill in their daughter that she would get out.

Malana's mind was getting worse and faster. She was being shopped around to different crazy places. The videos were real footage of her. She was controlled. There was real robots and clones of her.

Malana had many surgeries over the course of her fame. She couldn't believe that most of the public really thought she looked the same. She couldn't believe no one would fight to have it aired that she kept having surgeries. What tripped her out the most is after surgery, she would go to school and people could see it for themselves that the famous Vayla Shores kept being operated on. She felt like people should've been putting up a fight so she didn't have to undergo so much surgery.

Malana's parents worked hard to get in offices so that they could get her surgery that made her still look appealing. The surgery was a must, so the most they could do is get in a seat of someone who knew the artist deciding how her face would look. There was a lot of killing going on. If Malana did not look good, she would lose her audience and that would give her handler a reason to kill her quicker.

Cambridge and his crew had too much money. They'd met more good-looking girls that were studs. They didn't care for

Malana anymore. They just didn't want anyone to say anything good about her. They tried to erase her original image from television completely. There was five of them, so it was hard to keep the way Malana originally looked in her videos. The Devay family, along with the help of Darrel, had to decide on a clip to continuously keep Malana's real face. Anytime it was taken out, they would find a way to put it back. They had other relatives willing to help. The process would keep happening to a point where the copies would even get used to the clip Malana was originally in and put her back when it was taken down.

Malana went from being in many videos, to being in a few seconds of one video. The editing seats were hard to get in.

One day Malana's parents just sat and stared at her. She was acting like a baby, but fully conscious as an adult. She was in pain. Trying to speak hurt abundantly. She was aware of how she sounded. It hurt Chaylani and the girls to hear how Malana would talk like a baby to girls that she liked. Especially when she was clowning ugly girls that would want to be around her. Malana admitting she knew how both girls and boys she didn't like wanted her attention and being arrogant about not caring because she looked so good, really got under the girls skin. They learned how Malana was such a confident light skinned woman. They made her act like a baby most of the time.

Cambridge made Malana walk around as a dark skinned woman. They had all the supplies at High Class Territory. The girls would make her act like a man because it turned them on.

Malana's friends at school that were clueless to her being on television despite watching some of her videos with her in their presence, wondered what was wrong with her. She lost many of her friends. Cambridge and his crew controlled how Malana acted in public. If she didn't do what they said, they would give her more pain. Her life was gone.

Malana would have nasty things injected in her private areas by the girls. She would be forced to sit in uncomfortable positions in pain for long periods of time. Cambridge and his crew would treat her as if she was a piece of furniture. They could stare into her eyes while she was in pain as long as they wanted to.

The girls would make her say things they wanted to hear in a baby voice like: *You look cute. I want some pussy. Oh my God! Shut the fuck up. Keep.* They made her say them in different tones too. It was real childish and messy. They made her say *keep* as a baby when it came to parts of their bodies that they didn't like. They had already got an honest confession out of Malana that she hated how they looked, so it was more for irritation purposes. She had to put her head in toilets. She had to hold things over her nose that smelled awful. There was no limit to the pain she could be caused.

The girls wanted to hear everything negative Malana had to say about them. Malana made them feel like shit with her real emotions towards them as the rough neck she was before being under their control.

Malana's mind was always thinking to try and get rid of the pain. She remembered she had a friend who sung a lot. Over time she noticed a change in his behavior and even his appearance. She noticed his height was messing with her mind sometimes, but thought she had just gone crazy. Now that she was aware of what was really going on in the world, she knew he had been replaced and she was friends with a clone for a long time. So there was a clone being the entertainer saying he was alive and a clone walking around as him. Her friend didn't have a funeral. She wondered what happened to his body.

Malana's friends would find ways to drastically change what people thought about her. One of her close friends, Darius, pretended to start liking her more and wanted to be her boyfriend. Malana didn't think anything suspicious. She wanted any and everything new because it gave her more hope that she would be free from being controlled. She always hoped that she would fall asleep and someone would perform surgery on her and take the chip out of her. Reginald and Kinaya had her thinking that they had to wait until a certain date to have someone take it out of her, but in reality, they knew they couldn't touch it. If it was removed, she would die.

Darius knew what was going on with Malana. He knew it was her on television, but acted like he didn't know. He didn't want her to think that he knew ways that could remove her chip. It hurt Darius to see his friend witnessing what fame and fortune was all about. The fortune only goes to the producers. The fame is a ghost. No one knows that the real entertainer walks amongst the crowd. "It hurt Darius to know Malana had made the worst decision of her life," my grandma says. "She said *yes*, and you have to remember that Shona. It hurt him too that she couldn't cry sometimes when she was in pain. She had to hold it in."

I look at my grandma very sad.

Malana thought that Darius didn't know it was her on television, so that made her angry at times. She would watch the television and wonder how he couldn't know it was her. She noticed her original face was starting to show up less in the videos. Darius would notice that too.

He noticed that the more time he spent with her, more often he would see people coming around that either had a similar personality to him, walked like him, talked like him, or even looked like him.

Darius really loved Malana. He knew he had to tap into every part of her emotions so whenever she wasn't around him, she could think of something he said to help her when she needed.

Although Malana was a stud, she began enjoying sleeping with Darius. It made her feel better that Cambridge and all the people she was forced to sleep with weren't the only boys she was with.

Malana would be waken up out of her sleep by the chip. Made drowsier and forced to go to sleep earlier. She would start to hear things that weren't there.

Cambridge was one to sleep with many copies of Malana and tell them Malana's thoughts that he would learn. The copies would use what they learned against Malana. They enjoyed knowing she was being controlled. It aroused them and added to the game called *life* that they were learning and adjusting to play. Cambridge would tell Malana the things he told the clones.

He would watch and feel her pain. There was nothing she could do.

Malana's parents cared about their daughter. They knew they had to do something. Malana could try all she wanted, but she couldn't force herself to talk normal. It even hurt for her to talk. Reginald and Kinaya found a way to kill her with drugs quickly and put wounds on her. They left her to be found. They knew she needed to be free from the pain.

Before putting her to sleep, Malana's parents made sure to do a few interviews with her. They wanted to show the public that they were strong and if they could make it, so could her fans. They made sure to stand and look in the camera in ways to let people know they understood the real feelings that come about from celebrities.

The Devay family wanted people who were aware of what was going on to know that they were sorry that their daughter signed the contract. They knew their family that was aware of what was going on would know they had no choice but to end Malana's life so she could be free. Reginald did more interviews with Malana than Kinaya.

Reginald and Kinaya did the interviews when Malana's face had been transformed tremendously. She still looked okay, but nowhere near as good as she originally was born. Reginald knew her face wouldn't be able to take well to many more surgeries. He reached a point where he would signal his family through the interviews in ways that only they would know, that Malana was reaching her end. He made gestures to let them know it wasn't much more he could have done to her face for her to remain marketable, let alone be able to look at herself.

Reginald and Kinaya wanted people who were aware of Malana's situation, which wasn't many, to know that if they could still make it with their daughter not living, than so could they.

"The clones had the ability to form off of scent and feelings," I say shocked. "Olifus must've been smoking some of the same stuff I was."

"Olifus was on very hard drugs," my grandma says.

"So what did people do when they learned Malana died?" I ask.

"Shona you have to remember that the majority of the public thought she was Vayla Shores," my grandma says. "Vayla Shores was not Malana Devay to almost everyone. Only a small amount of people knew that the real artist had died. The rest of the world thinks she is still alive."

Why do I want to just punch the wall right now? I'm mad as hell.

"I feel like I knew Malana," I say. "I wish I could've met her. Did she get to do any concerts?"

"She did a few small shows, but never got to do them with her regular face," my grandma says. "Cambridge and the girls fought hard to make sure that happened."

"When you say fought hard, what did they do?" I ask.

"They did sexual favors for people. Fulfilled people's most private desires like eating nasty things. They danced at strip clubs. They sold themselves basically," my grandma says.

"Malana was the real deal," I say. "She must've really looked good. Wait." I feel so stupid right now. My grandma is giving me a lot of information though. "Vayla Shores?" I say hesitantly. I'm getting teary eyed. I've seen many videos with Vayla in them. She is a good-looking stud and she really did have a nice shape.

"What's wrong baby?" my grandma asks.

"I'm... I mean... You've just been saying so much that I couldn't register the name. I'm a huge fan of Vayla. I liked how she dressed. Her flat-ironed hair was so pretty under her bandana. I've seen movies with her in them." I'm looking shocked. My mouth drops. "That's not her in those movies," I say.

Tears are going down my face. Remembering how my grandma said Malana was in school and people didn't know it was her, they just kept saying she looked similar to Vayla just made me real sad.

"How many videos have you seen with her in them?" my grandma asks.

I'm wiping my tears from the face. I'm thinking about all the different faces I've seen her with. Sometimes I've seen her with three different faces in one video.

"Are some of those people clones in the videos?" I ask.

"What did I ask you?" my grandma says.

"I've seen over twenty videos with her in them," I say. "But I'm unsure if she had surgery or if those are clones."

"They could be her friends or relatives that swapped places with her to give her a break and let the public that was aware know that they had her back in those videos," my grandma says. "They wanted the people who would wake up later to know too. They knew people would do research. This world is unfolding. Everything is going to be out in the open real soon. Life hit here."

We were never supposed to exist. We're in space. Forgive me. I'm still recovering from drugs.

"I'm trying to locate Malana's real face," I say. "How do I know?" I think about the girl that floated through my mind a lot while I was smoking. The one that I always treated like my daughter in my dreams. "I think I know which one she was," I continue. My head drops to the floor. I'm crying. My grandma is not though. She's sitting looking serious. "There's not much footage of her in the one video I know she's in," I say.

"And Cambridge and the girls never stopped trying to get rid of those clips," my grandma says. "You have to remember that they had a crew too, and they knew other producers who hated their clients as well. To this date, people who know that's Malana in that one video are trying to get rid of it."

My grandma pulls out a picture of Malana.

"Grandma, this picture looks like it was taken with one of our cameras," I say.

"That girl was your cousin Shona," my grandma says. "You have no idea how sick this society is. The real world is out there baby. Don't do those drugs again."

I slowly say, "Wait. Malana Devay is my cousin?"

"Yes," my grandma says.

"How come I never met her?" I calmly ask.

333

"My father had many kids by many different women," my grandma says. "He didn't even introduce me to all of them, but with a little help from other relatives, I got to know a few of them. I got to know my sister Kinaya. I never told my dad though. I sent Kinaya pictures of you. Malana knew who you were. She said lucky me that I get to kiss you on the left and right cheek. She said she wished you were her baby."

I'm smiling. I'm starting not to feel well because of what Malana went through.

"When did she die?" I ask.

"She died in 2001," my grandma says. "She was eighteen. Remember the public still thinks she's alive though."

I wake up out of my dream and go in the bathroom and splash water on my face. Malana's story touched my heart.

20

I'm sitting in Hollow's Cave. I have on a baby pink top and blue jean shorts. I'm looking all over. I'm just not myself tonight. I'm in deep thought about my grandmother.

"You don't get to just be talented here. You were under mind control," my grandma says. "Starting a step team is not small. Them crazy niggas are all over. I'm one of them. You can't just do that shit. You ran all of those kids. They don't know you or who knows you. People have fucked up mindsets. They think when you're talented you're intertwined with people in high places. You could be cloned for all they know. These robots out here have people's minds fucked up. You think in Louisiana they just gone let you start a step team? Hell no. You entered a dangerous territory and you will feel the wrath of it. Your mother was ugly. They knew what to do with that. They knew you could barely speak. Real racist exist. Sit up straight damn it."

" I am," I say. She's getting on my nerves. She's already hounding me about my weight. Now she's getting on my nerves about being talented. This is bullshit.

"You always find a way to make them remember you," my grandma says. "That's how you fight here. Fuck them racist niggas, and they life as it is. You know when someone dies, the real niggas here are over it and move on as if it never happened. They happy it wasn't them. That's why I need this done. Real mind control. They'll all fall victim to what we do."

"But grandma, why couldn't you snap me from writing bad things about some of my friends?" I ask.

"You're an image of me," my grandma says. "I needed it done. If they're your friends, they will always be that way, but you know pretty people have a lot of shit going on here. You do right by me. Get it done. This place is not for the weak. Friends don't matter. Making it another day around here matters."

"I hear ya," I say.

"You're fine. Pretty soon you'll be able to think of the scenario and it won't even matter," my grandma says. "You've made it through a lot of abuse," my grandma continues. "You don't have much to look back on. Just know those times that Nadia did help you were hard to come by. But the spirits moving around this Earth are real. She can only be so evil. All the hell she put you through, that's why I did it."

"It's hard to believe all of this," I say. "You really want me to write this? They gone cut up."

"Let them," my grandma says. "I'm pissed the hell off. Once Nadia told me a story about how she got assaulted before. Then I turned around and told her one of her aunts said she molested her son and step brother when she was coming up. I told her which aunt said it too."

21

Everyone walks in Mission's practice happy.

Sheela doesn't smile, but she's giving off a happy vibe.

"Hey Coach," Kiara says and winks at me when she walks in.

Jason, Jose, and Michael give me a hug, and everyone else waves. Practice goes smoothly. Everyone's attentive, asking questions, standing firm, doing the movements great, and saying the chants loud.

"Hold that position," I say.

Everyone keeps their right leg in the air with their right arm extended to the right. At the same time, they have their left arm in with their hand in front of their chest. Their bodies are also bent down a little.

"Don't drop it," I say.

A few people are shaking and struggling to hold their balance. After twenty seconds I let them drop the position.

"Shake your legs out because you're about to hold it again," I say.

I spend the entire practice getting everyone used to holding positions that are easy to lose their balance in if they're moving too fast, which they will be because my steps are fast paced. This way their bodies are so equipped to the stance that there's not a chance they will accidently fall during their shows.

"You guys are sweating hard, that's good," I say.

Mission High members are in pain. Their faces are so tight and frowned because they're so uncomfortable.

I let them take a water break, then they get back to holding the positions. At the end of practice, I make them go through the routine and they all break down. Some can barely lift their legs because they're muscles are so tight. Some stomp softly, and others pick their legs up, but hesitate to stomp them.

"Alright you guys. We gone call it a day," I say. Some of them walk out limping.

I'm so happy. Today was by far the best rehearsal we've ever had.

"You know you could get fired for meeting up with the students and practicing without me," Ms. Ross says to me when we get out of the building.

I freeze and can't make any facial expression. I should've known someone would tell her.

"Don't worry," Ms. Ross says. "I won't say a thing. And so you can sleep good at night, I was told about the meeting before you told them not to inform me at your old university. Just like you can trust me, I'll trust you and tell you that Kiara told me. She was very excited and anxious to go to a college campus when she told me. I know she didn't know she was supposed to keep her mouth closed because she casually told me with a smile on her face and good graces. I told her to make sure she never mentioned it again, and most importantly why she shouldn't. I like you, and think you're good at what you do. I honestly enjoy what you teach the students more than the cheerleading and dance team here. I don't want you to get fired, and neither do the students."

"Thanks," I tell her.

Despite knowing Ms. Ross and Mission's step team have my back, I do want to ask Mr. Stephen about the team doing a community service event.

I send Mr. Stephen an email asking to have a clothes drive outside of the community center in one of the parking lots right next to Alpha Eta Nu's Mentor and Encouragement Program Building.

Alpha Eta Nu's Mentor and Encouragement Program gives parents an opportunity to sign their kids up to have a personal mentor that will give them advice and encouragement when

338

they need it, as well as help with homework and take them out a few times.

It takes Mr. Stephen a week to respond to me with a *yes*. He says Luminous LA will provide the bus transportation.

I pick up the flyer Teasha gave me. I read the words *Alpha Eta Nu* and say, "See you there," with a smile on my face sitting on my bed.

22

The days leading up to the Mission High Clothes Drive, I make sure my students have the choreography down pact, as well as teach them some new moves because the ones I have them display at the clothes drive will not be used in their shows.

There's going to be our event and Alpha Eta Nu's event, on top of the people that will be just visiting the community center, so hundreds of people are bound to show up, and I know some will record.

I told my students that I am just focusing on them because technically I am at work. I'm not even wearing my letters. I can get in serious trouble if I put my organization before watching over my students. I'm laughing inside. If only people knew how stupid some Greeks can act putting the sorority before their actual job that pays them money.

I can't wait for my students to show off what I've taught them while I watch impressed and some of my Sorors of A. H. N. stare over at us with disgust. I hate Queela and Teasha.

Delia is still a no show.

"Do you know where she's been?" I ask Ms. Ross.

"No," Ms. Ross says. "But she has been at school."

I know I said I wouldn't use my students for my own personal revenge on anyone again, but I'm going to swear not to do it again after this clothes drive. I'm just so upset that some of these girls in sororities don't think anyone can step better than them, and I don't appreciate them bombarding and stalking me when I was at Cupperton.

I'm also upset that Legit didn't deliver my routine well. They did it no justice, and I need these particular Alpha Eta Nu members to see what my choreography looks like coming from dedicated members that have been working hard.

I'm noticing that I'm getting so excited for Mission High delivering at the dance competition, The Big Bang Step Off, and the clothes drive, that I can barely focus at times. All I can focus on is how well they are doing at practice. My mind is consumed with how far they've come as a team.

Ciera stops by my house a few times to spend time with me while I'm so excited for my upcoming shows. I'm having parties by myself a lot. It's tough working two jobs.

"Girl you better focus," Ciera says. "Remember, you have a job. Two jobs at that. You want to keep them both."

Ciera's absolutely right about that, but it's still so hard for me to think about anything other than Mission High. We're really like a family. A family that I won't be around forever.

My stomach just turned and I no longer want the breakfast tacos I just made.

I give Ciera her plate at the dining room table and sit down looking like my feelings are hurt.

"Don't trip," Ciera says. "You'll see them again. Your students love you, which is why they're quick to want to knock someone out for you. You have their numbers, and they have yours. I know they not gone forget about you after you move on to another school."

The bad thing about Luminous LA is that you have to leave the students that you develop a bond with. We, as instructors, get close with our kids, then have to turn around and leave them.

I'm thinking about Jose doing my step choreography, Alexis getting in front of me when the coach for Greg Johnson's dance team got in my face, the entire team showing me consistently that they are down for me, the rehearsal we had in the dorm at Cupperton that they were supposed to keep their mouth shut about, and our time on Greg Johnson's campus.

We had so much fun together, and best of all, they've become great steppers and are getting better than the people on TV. I'm really going to miss my students if they delete my number and plan on forgetting me the second we walk out of The Big Bang Step Off.

Who's to say I'll bond with the students at the next high school I get sent to?

"I'm going to miss them so much Ciera," I say with my head resting on my hands on the table.

"They not gone forget you," Ciera says.

The next week, Ciera and I follow behind the bus to the community center. Mission High gets off the bus with their suitcases full of clothes, shoes, and other things that they can't fit or don't want any more, such as toys, games, household appliances and more.

Ciera and I both have a suitcase full of clothes as well. I wanted to keep it completely anonymous that we came out here to step, so I let the team wear whatever they wanted.

I set up two tents and portable tables that Mr. Stephen dropped off at one of my rehearsals. It felt so good to listen to my students tell him how much they loved me and hoped I'd come back to their school again.

I had the students show Mr. Stephen a step before he left and he was amazed and said, "I'm very impressed. Keep up the good work Shona."

Delia is a no show again.

Mission High, Ciera and I put some of the folded clothes on the table and leave some of the suitcases open lying on the ground with clothes in them.

After we get set up and wait for people to arrive, a big truck pulls up in the parking lot followed by a bunch of cars. Queela and Teasha are in the car that's right behind the big truck. They get out the car and look at me and Mission's team. They don't look happy to see me at all.

Men hop out the huge truck and pull out some black boards. I'm so upset I didn't anticipate this. These A. H. N. members, my Sorors, are setting up a stage so they can perform for the people that stop by their booth. I thought they would step on the ground like I plan on having Mission do, but it turns out they have a better platform.

People start to show up sporadically for the clothes drive, and most of them flood my Sorors' mentor program tables. They must've done more promotion besides flyers, word of mouth, and posters and bulletins. They probably called Sorors from other schools and told them to promote their event. Having people that will do anything for you on pretty much every college campus is definitely a plus of joining a sorority, but I don't care. I don't want to participate with those snobby, stuck up, and uneducated about the history of step Sorors, Queela and Teasha.

Despite me wanting to join this event to make these particular Alpha Eta Nu girls' mad, I truly am happy watching everyone dig through the suitcases, take things off the table and put them against their bodies to see if they'll fit, play with the toys, and grab the things they want.

One little boy is having fun playing with the remote-control car that Jason brought.

Everyone's enjoying themselves.

My Sorors' Alpha Eta Nu stage is now put together. I see Queela huddling up with Sorors, so I have Mission High show the crowd around us two steps.

I purposely have Mission High's backs towards Queela and Teasha's crew and the crowd surrounding them.

Our crowd gets cheers, claps, and look astonished as they watch my students give a great performance. Some of the little kids try to do the steps while they watch. One little girl has her two fists together in front of her chest just like my members do when they finish most of their steps.

"Coach, do one with us," Jose suggests.

I stand front and center of Mission High and do one of the routines with them. The crowd gets even louder.

People in the crowd say: *You guys are good. I want to be on a step team. How do they move so fast?*

When Mission and I finish the step, I look over at my Alpha Eta Nu Sorors and they are not happy. Teasha has her hands on her hips frowning at me. Her as well as the rest of her crew know I had my students give that performance just to make them mad. Some of their crowd is walking over to us, so I have Mission do another step. Besides a little kid just asked them to do another one anyways.

Queela and Teasha don't care to announce that I'm their Soror, and I don't care to let people know I know them.

One of the Alpha Eta Nu girls that I'm not familiar with is whispering in Queela's ear. Now Queela is smiling at me and nodding her head. When she starts walking towards me, I already know what she's about to ask.

"You guys want to use the stage after us?" Queela asks my members.

Mission High looks at me for approval.

"Sure," I say.

If these particular A. H. N. members want some high school students to make them look like the sorority should be shut down, then I would love to help them out. The sorority could never be shut down for being upstaged.

"As soon as we're done, we'll make our way over there," I say.

Queela walks back to her crew.

When Mission High and I are out of everything we brought with us, we head over to where Queela, Teasha, and other Sorors are on their side of the parking lot and me and Luminous LA's entire crowd is following behind us.

Teasha is mean mugging me holding one of the flyers she knows she gave me a copy of in her hand with her arms crossed in front of her chest. She knows I held this event on purpose, and she knows I brought my team out here to make her, Queela, and the rest of our Sorors that are with them angry, and I don't care.

They think they are the best Greek steppers, and I want them to prove it. I want them to show that they are the best and that high school students can't outdo them.

Queela, Teasha, and their crew take the stage. Queela invites me to stand on it with one of my members so we can introduce ourselves. I have Alexis come up with me. We stand off to the side while Queela gets everyone's attention.

"Good evening everyone," Queela says. "I am Queela James, an alumni of Cupperton University, and a proud member of Alpha Eta Nu Sorority Incorporated."

Queela sounds bougie, proper, and educated. She doesn't sound ghetto, attitudish, hood, and loud like she did when her and her crew of friends stalked me and Ciera.

"We want to thank everyone for coming out and signing your

344

kids up for a positive program," Queela continues. "We are positive that our Mentor and Encouragement Program will inspire, encourage, motivate, and uplift your children. Since everyone took time out of their day to come here, some of my Sorors and I thought it would be a great idea to put on a step show."

The crowd cheers.

"We noticed these two lovely ladies and their team stepping on the other side of the parking lot," Queela says. "So I thought it would be a great idea to invite them to put on a small show on our stage." Queela still won't acknowledge that I'm a member of Alpha Eta Nu.

I'm going to have Mission do the same steps they did in front the area our clothes drive is in. We are not doing anything we're performing at the dance and step competition.

"I was going to give them time to introduce themselves, but I can see someone telling us to wrap it up," Queela continues.

I follow Queela's eyeline to a man that's standing in front of one of the buildings to the community center, and he's not paying us any attention. He doesn't even look like a staff member in his grey sweats and grey shirt. I don't know why Queela had to lie about that.

I tap Alexis' arm so she can follow me off the stage, but Queela says, "Oh you two are fine. Don't worry. We won't bite you."

Queela hands someone off of the stage the mic, winks at one of our sorority members that's the closest to me, and Queela and the member nod their heads, and take their position front and center.

Alexis and I look at each other wondering what that was about, but we don't worry about it. Something is seriously wrong with Queela. If I had someone recording my show, which I do have Ciera recording so I can make my students a DVD of our performances before I head to another school, I would not want anybody on the stage with us. If I wanted extras, I would've brought some. Maybe Queela wants to catch me and Alexis on camera looking jealous, but that's not going to happen.

Queela sets the first step for her crew. I'll give it to her. Her facials, movements, and body positions are nice; however, she looks sloppy without her thumbs tucked in. I'm shaking my head. I shake it harder when the sorority members join in and their thumbs are all over the place too. I can tell these alumni have gotten rusty over the years when it comes to stepping.

It's unfortunate I'm not performing with them. Queela and Teasha should've allowed me or some of my line to perform with them, but they choose to be bitches to us. This step line and any other line that's never been taught to keep their thumbs in, needs me desperately. No one taught me to keep my thumbs in when I'm stepping to look more professional. I just already knew.

I'm so used to keeping my thumbs in that sometimes I catch myself walking around with them tucked in. One time at practice, Michael asked me if I walked everywhere ready to break out into a step.

Alexis and I watch these particular Alpha Eta Nu members perform with serious faces.

These particular members of A. H. N. are not impressing me with their basic steps that I'll remember when I get home, even if I didn't practice or think about them until I got there. These girls haven't even changed positions on this long and wide stage.

Despite this pathetic performance, the crowd is cheering and clapping. The louder the crowd gets, the more Queela gets into the choreography.

It's sad that Queela thinks what she's doing is a masterpiece. It probably took her weeks to come up with this basic routine. I could teach this to elementary kids and have them deliver it better than this batch of Alpha Eta Nu.

I can tell this crowd has never seen a step show before, because if they did, they wouldn't be so into this weak choreography. It would give them pain to watch it.

I know Legit gave me a hard time and I hate to keep talking about them because they didn't deliver when them bitch made

346

Alpha Eta Nu members observed our show, but if I threw them on this stage despite some of their mess ups, they still would be more entertaining than this performance because their steps were better and not possible to learn by observation.

I clap along with the crowd, even though I don't want to, to make it more evident to Queela that I'm not jealous of her and this awful step line.

I look at my Mission High members in the audience and most of them are just watching. Kiara and Casey do a few claps. I look at Jason who's staring at me laughing. I hold my laugh in and mouth to him *clap*. He does and gets the rest of Mission High to.

As Alpha Eta Nu continues to perform, I can't help but let out a little laughter with my hands folded across my chest. All of these girls think they have a first-place routine, when really what they're displaying wouldn't even get them entered into any competition.

Four minutes into this Alpha Eta Nu routine, they decide to turn a different direction for their step. One of the members, the same one that Queela whispered to, is facing me and Alexis' direction. Poor girl doesn't realize how stupid she looks getting into the choreography. I smile at her and nod my head so she can think I respect her as a stepper; I don't think she sees me though because she's staring so hard at Alexis. My face gets serious because she's mean mugging her now.

I recognize the girls facing the other direction, have now turned back to the front for the rest of the routine. Only this girl staring at Alexis is not facing the audience. I drop my arms and look like I want to push this girl off the stage when she does her step approaching Alexis. I look at the rest of her crew and they're still facing the front.

I know Queela can't be that bad of a choreographer to have one member throw off the formation by approaching someone that's not even supposed to be on the stage.

This broad is now less than two inches from Alexis' face stepping. I'm hot. Alexis doesn't move, but I sure do approach the girl doing my own remixed beat to the simple one they are doing.

There's people here, camera's rolling, and my reputation is on the line, so I'm not about to let this disrespect take place. The girl is still stepping and facing Alexis, pretending like she doesn't see me, so I get closer to her doing my routine. My face is facing the side of hers while she stares into Alexis' eyes.

I'm so into my choreography and my remixed beat, which is so tight that the crowd's trying to figure out where the nice beat is coming from. Once they spot me, they are fixated on me and not my Sorors who are performing.

The girl in Alexis' face never looks me in my eyes before she decides to back off and step her way back to her position and face the front with her crew. However, I'm so angry that she got in one of my students' faces, that I keep doing my remixed step as I make my way through this group of Alpha Eta Nu's three lines.

I'm on the second row behind Queela, staring at her while I add the rhythm to their routine that it needs. She starts to frown, but holds her composure because she knows it's not good for Greeks to get caught acting ghetto in front of people. Especially at a community service event.

I'm still stepping. When Queela and her crew switch directions, so do I doing my solo freestyled choreography. When they turn back to the front, I do. When they stop, I do, and when they start back up, I do.

I am going to stay on this stage until the show is over. This Alpha Eta Nu batch will be lucky if I don't hop on their stroll line, *if* these terrible girls even have one. I'm hoping they don't, because if it's as bad as their steps, which shouldn't have been showcased, then it shouldn't be performed either.

The nerve of Queela to have a stage set up to put on this show, and the nerve of her to allow this show to happen. I can't believe she has confidence in this slow routine.

I can feel the anger on this stage. These girls will definitely want to beat me up when the show is over and everyone's gone, but I don't care. I'm passionate about stepping and my team. I'm not going to let anyone disrespect them, and definitely not with stepping when I'm around. These girls will learn to respect me and Mission High on the step scene one way or another. They might be able to beat me up, but they'll never outstep me.

I can tell some of the crowd knows I'm not supposed to be a part of this routine, despite Queela allowing me and Alexis to be on the stage, by their shocked looks. Some people literally look at me, then at Queela and her girls. We have yet to do any of the same choreography, and not to mention, I'm in casual clothes and they're in their step shirts with their letters on them and blue jeans. I'm in tights and a shirt.

Ciera is still recording and I can't wait to watch it when I get home.

Mission High is looking on like they know it's about to be a show down.

Sheela is cracking her knuckles getting closer to the stage and staring at one of Queela's girls who's trying to hide her frustration the best she can while she listens to my nice beat, and is upset that I would join in on their slow routine that probably took them months to learn.

Teasha starts another step and her crew comes in.

I want to fall to the floor. I join in the step doing the exact same movements that Queela and her girls are doing. I look at Queela in pure disgust.

The nerve of these girls to try and diss my student, then turn around and do my choreography from my website, *and* say the chants I put with it.

I'm furious as I watch Queela do my step no justice, and I'm even more furious when the girl next to her messes up on it.

I disgustedly wave my hand in the girl that didn't practice enough face, and I now use my step to transition to the front of the front row. I say the chants and do my moves better than everyone on the stage.

Mission High is looking on in disbelief. They don't know I'm doing my own choreography.

When the step ends, Queela and her crew stop, but I keep going.

They saw the first video to the step I entitled, "It's

349

Complicated," but they must've missed the part two I uploaded months later, which is why I'm still going on with the routine and they're not. If I did all of part two, I'd be stepping longer, but I decide to cut it short.

Queela's fist is coming at me with her deathly looking face. I duck and elbow her in her cheek. Teasha pushes me and Ciera jumps in. Me and Ciera are now fighting Queela and Teasha.

Now we have a fight between Queela's crew of Alpha Eta Nu and Mission High.

Everyone's pushing, punching, and throwing each other to the floor. Police officers rush over to us.

"Shows over folks," one male officer says.

"You think you tight, but you not!" Queela shouts with her hair messed up and shirt all wrinkled.

An officer is pulling Queela away because she's still trying to come at me.

"You'll never be better than me!" Queela continues. "You'll never be good enough to step with me and my crew of Alpha Eta Nu!"

The crowd is completely wowed by what they just witnessed. The people that are supposed to be their mentors and encourage them about life were fighting and couldn't hold their composure until a later date.

Mission High, Ciera, and I grab our suitcases and put the things Mr. Stephen bought in the trunk of Jose's car.

Alexis gives me a hug and says, "Thanks Coach," before getting in the car with Alina.

"No problem," I say. "No one is going to disrespect you. Not while I'm around."

Ciera and I pull off. She's shaking her head.

"I can't take it with some of them stuck up sorority girls," Ciera says.

"Why in the world would they use my step?" I ask.

Ciera can't believe her ears. I buck my eyes at her and nod my head to let her know I'm not playing around.

"Yes, them bitches got on stage and performed my step," I say a little louder.

350

I wouldn't be surprised if they thought I wouldn't recognize it because it's been uploaded to *Video Video Vault* for three years now.

"I wanted to break each and every last one of their necks," Ciera says.

"As soon as I saw that girl from that one night pull her arm back, I dropped my camera and ran," Ciera says. "I was trying to get to her, but by the time I got up there, it was like a jam-packed boxing ring. I know I punched one of them real good though."

"I don't even feel bad about the situation," I say. "That girl should have never got in Alexis' face. The crazy part is, I saw Queela wink at the girl, but didn't think it was code for *get in her face.*"

"That goes to show you how much of a bitch she is to have someone else do the dirty work," Ciera says about Queela. "If anyone's going to be blamed for what happened back there, it's gone be that stupid broad that got in Alexis' face."

Ciera is right. I can't believe this shit. Alpha Eta Nu is a family. We don't snitch on each other, and one will take the blame before we all go down for doing something.

"I wouldn't be surprised if my step was the last step they used because it was better than everything they did before it," I say.

Ciera's looking all over the car for something.

"What you looking for?" I ask.

"I left my phone in the community center," Ciera says. She was in a rush to get back outside and record, so she thinks she left it at the front desk when she was finding out if they were hiring. They weren't.

"You think it's still there?" I ask.

"Yes," Ciera says. "That's why we going back."

We drive back to the community center and Ciera runs in one of the buildings. While she's inside, I notice Queela, Teasha, and another A. H. N. member still in the parking lot. They still look angry.

Ciera happily gets back in the car with her phone and says,

"The man at the front desk held onto it for me. He said he knew I'd be back."

Ciera notices me looking out her window and does the same. She starts the car up.

"Let's go hear what they're saying," Ciera says.

Ciera turns the car lights off so it's not clear that it's us in the car. Queela and her girls won't see us unless we get real close to them, and I know they weren't expecting us to drive back to the community center.

Ciera gets on the road the closest to the parking lot and drives slowly. I roll my window all the way down.

"You so stupid for teaching us that mess!" Queela yells at her member named Whitney that taught the girls my choreography. It's also the same member that got in Alexis' face doing the step. "We are Alpha Eta Nu and we don't bite off of anybody's stuff unless they want us to!" Queela continues.

"Whitney did you recognize Shona when she walked over?" Teasha asks. Whitney has an attitude and doesn't say anything. "You did," Teasha continues. "That's why you're quiet."

"The second you recognized her, knowing you done took her choreography and taught it like it was your own, you should've told us to cut the routine early," Queela says. "I would've been angry still, but not as angry as I am now."

"Now you got that girl with a head bigger than what she already had before she got here, and thinking our line needs her to be the best," Teasha says. "People recorded the show Whitney!"

I can tell Whitney is angry at herself. Teasha and Queela don't care though. They look like they want to fight the girl.

"When you asked me to implement a step you created, I trusted you to do just that," Queela says.

Ciera and I are still creeping down the road. I'm hoping I get to hear everything before we get too far.

At first, I felt bad for this Whitney girl because I was thinking she honestly just wanted to add a good step to their routine, but now that I know she tried to pass my step off as her own. I want to hop out this car and drag her to a ditch.

352

"And the nerve of you to try and battle the girl knowing we would eventually do a step that her coach created!" Teasha screams. "Just stupid."

Teasha walks away, exhales, then walks back. She's shaking her head and walking in a circle around Whitney.

"I just wanted us to have a better step," Whitney says. "We are way better than what you are teaching us."

I can't believe this girl just indirectly told Queela that she's not a good choreographer.

Queela folds her arms across her chest.

"Excuse me," Queela angrily says.

"I just wanted..." Whitney says and starts to tear up.

"You just wanted what?!" Teasha screams. "To teach a step you stole, then pass it off as your own so you could seem like you're better than her? You not better than your Big Sister Queela and neither is Shona."

"Them girls are delusional," Ciera says to me.

"That's right," Queela says. "You messed up doing this. You had us looking like fools to everyone here, and pretty soon we'll look like them to the world. You didn't have enough sense and respect for the sorority to tell us not to do the stolen routine that was done by the very person I told to remain on the stage, but you do have enough sense to know that people will post what happened today online right?"

"I wouldn't be surprised if it wasn't already up there," Teasha says. "Whitney, you are just one low-life person. It's disgusting to look at you now. You don't even deserve to be in this sorority anymore. You're now as ugly as those ugly bitches who we call *bears* in other sororities."

Alpha Eta Nu members refer to other sororities that are known to have the ugliest members as *bears*.

"I'm sorry," Whitney says.

"Sorry?" Queela mocks. "Sorry is not going to take away the embarrassment you're responsible for."

Ciera turns the corner onto the main street and we can no longer hear what the girls are talking about.

"I'm sorry," Ciera says. "Some sorority girls are so fake. They

353

put on a front for people that aren't in the organization, or people they want to be a part of it, so they can have a line the following year, but once they think no one is around, they'll act how they really want to."

Queela, Teasha, and Whitney were just defending each other, and back there they were angry with each other.

"The world puts Greeks out there as these perfect people making it seem like they work everything out in a calm and collective manner when they have arguments, but that's really not the case," Ciera continues.

If one of my members pulled what Whitney pulled, I would honestly be angry, but I wouldn't call any of them out of their name. If only Whitney didn't try to pass my choreography off as her own, I would still like her all for the simple fact that she didn't have a problem getting help from someone that has more talent as a choreographer.

While Ciera's driving, I start thinking about my grandma. We're at the dining room table.

"Those drugs are messing with you," my grandma says.

"It's crazy how I can know that I have to keep reciting the evil story that ended with love, but I'm too run down to do it when I am recovering from drugs," I say.

"It hurts to think, doesn't it?" my grandma says. "That's how strong drugs are. They are inside of you. They know what you are trying to think of to get them out of your system, and they make it that much harder for you to think about what you need to in order to find the love."

"These drugs play with my memory the same way Nadia does," I say. "She acts like she doesn't know I will remember what she says. She acts like she's dumb and thinks I will forget what she said the same day. She has me feeling so stupid."

"She is nothing," my grandma says. "You don't play with no one's memory like that. You know damn well you can remember things forty years after they happen."

"So, it is people out there dying because they want to say devious things," I say.

354

"Yes. And just like your sorry momma, they getting off sexually on saying stuff like that too in they spare time. Ya momma not a woman at all. A real woman knows her body and mind and what is nourishing to fulfill it."

"Okay. So again, there is three hundred and sixty-five days in a year," I say.

"And I know you're not worried about not one of them she may pass on," my grandma says.

"What the hell did you have?" I ask.

There's a pot boiling on the stove again with water overflowing. I turn the heat down.

"I can teach you how to cook pigtails and red beans and rice like a real mother would," my grandmother says. "But right now there seems to be a few pounds that you need to shed."
She's getting on my nerves talking about this weight, but I know it's not going anywhere without a fight.

I went to the store and brought some oranges, apples, peanut butter, mushrooms, tofu, brown rice, red peppers, green peppers, onions, and water for my new diet. I already told her I was drinking wine and alcohol on my days off. This drug recovery is beating my ass.

My grandmother has me throw out the mustard, ketchup, popcorn, pasta, and anything else that she recognizes is not a part of my fast.

My grandmother used to always drink beer. She isn't in my visions for a few seconds while I take a few swallows of beer. Then she reappears.

"When you were in Baton Rouge, you coached a lot of step teams. Some you couldn't believe. You gone run into your relatives and not even know. That's how crazy some of them fools are out here to a point where we lie about who the hell we are. No one was taking my granddaughter away from me," my grandmother says. "I needed your senior year of high school for personal reasons. Just like I needed those five years of you going to college. Does it make sense for you to be worried about a team when you needed a scholarship?" My grandmother pops me on my mouth. "Act like I raised you right," she continues. "There's been people out to get me since I was young. They still around. They know you." She says she was involved with drugs that I will never even hear about in my lifetime.

My grandmother is starting to scare me. Sometimes I feel like she wanted to know that I loved her more than the activity of stepping. Of course I would give up anything for my grandmother.

"Only list the dates I tell you in the book you're writing," my grandmother says. "You're doing things three or four times that you used to only do once. You can't keep your memory. Do you think these drugs are something to play with?" my grandmother asks.

I come back to myself and am shedding tears. My grandmother is really counting on me to use my talents and make sure to input the things she says.

"Now how did this happen?" Mr. Stephen asks when I walk into his office for our mandatory meeting the next day. He has the fight scene from the clothes drive playing on his computer.

A tear rolls down my face because I feel like I'm about to get fired. I should have never held that event. That's what I get for using Mission for revenge after how good they've been to me lately. I don't deserve to coach them, but I'm hoping I still get to keep my job.

I take a deep breath.

"I was defending one of my students," I say. "One of the girls got in her face stepping, and that's looked at as disrespect in the step world. If I wouldn't have stepped in, then right now the whole world would think I'm a weak girl and wouldn't take me seriously. The video already has a hundred thousand views, and that's one hundred thousand people that wouldn't take me serious as a coach if I wouldn't have done what I did. They couldn't handle me outstepping them, so they started a fight."

Mr. Stephen takes his glasses off and wipes his forehead.

"There's nothing I can do about naturally being better than them," I continue.

"There wasn't a better way for you to keep your respect?"

Mr. Stephen asks.

"No," I say.

The only way to let Queela, the other Alpha Eta Nu girls, and the rest of the world know that it's not okay to step to me or anyone I'm coaching, was to step in on their routine.

"Actions speak louder than words," I continue.

Mr. Stephen can tell by my nonchalant attitude that I'm a lost cause and he should not try to convince me on how to handle the matter the next time, if there is one.

"Whatever," Mr. Stephen says. "I contacted The Big Bang Step Off and they still want Mission High to perform."

I'm smiling.

"They're defending your actions, but I know better," Mr. Stephen says. "They still want Mission to perform because now there's a demand for people to see them. A show that only had half of the seats filled is now sold out. I'm going to still let them perform because I want to show the world that you guys are capable of acting civilized at more than just the dance competition, but I never want anything like that to happen again."

When I get home, Ciera calls and tells me to stop by her house.

"Look," Ciera says.

Ciera has up the Alpha Eta Nu national website. The website is warning members that if any more fights break out, that they will be suspended from the organization for two months or possibly removed from the organization. President Deon left a comment. He did not like the footage he saw on the internet making his college look like it graduated a bunch of heathens. Fraternities and definitely sororities are thought to have some of the most well rounded and respected individuals in them, and Alpha Eta Nu has the world thinking differently.

It may have helped that Ciera and I sat down and talked with President Deon before, and he liked us. Maybe that played a part in members being warned. I'm sure President Deon knows about The Big Bang Step Off too and didn't want me to lose my teams' spot in it.

I hate that other members of Alpha Eta Nu saw the footage of the fight. I'm so embarrassed. When I meet more members of Alpha Eta Nu, I don't want them to think I'm violent.

Ciera and I look at each other and laugh. We're so happy I didn't get into any trouble. I'm grown as hell and don't want to be removed from Alpha Eta Nu.

"Damn, I dodged a huge bullet," I say completely surprised.

"It's only right," Ciera says. "Hell, I'm mad Whitney didn't get removed. She is the one that taught them *your* step."

23

Keasha calls me and tells me that her and Desiree are going to Delia's house to catch her up on the routine. She has me on video chat so I can watch. The girls practice outside in Delia's big backyard on her basketball court.

Delia's so far behind on the routines that she gets irritated trying to retain all of the movements and put her all into them.

"We can take a break," Keasha says.

The girls grab their water bottles and go to the front porch and sit down.

"Do you think your grades will be up before the competition?" Keasha asks.

"I'm not sure, I let them slip too low," Delia says. "I just want to learn what I don't know just in case a miracle happens."

Keasha turns her phone towards the window. Ms. Chelsea looks through the window at the girls sitting on the porch.

"Delia, did you finish your homework?" Ms. Chelsea asks.

"Yes," Delia lies.

Ms. Chelsea shakes her head and closes the blinds.

"Hurry and teach me the rest so I can go finish it," Delia whispers to the twins.

"What homework didn't you do?" Desiree frustratedly asks.

"Math," Delia says.

"Math? We are good at math," Desiree says. "You want us to help you?"

"Can you do all of it?" Delia asks.

The twins look at her like she's crazy.

"We really want you to perform with us, so you need to learn how to do the work so you can pass your exams," Keasha says.

"So make sure you put a lot of time into your homework," Desiree says.

"I know you guys," Delia sadly says. "I really want to perform with Ms. Jackson before she goes."

"I want you to perform too," I say. Delia gets startled. She forgot I was watching.

The girls all look sad now.

"You're so nice," Desiree says. "Even though we gave you a hard time at first, you still stuck with us."

Ms. Ross explained to Mission's members that if I got overwhelmed and couldn't handle the students, that I could remove myself from the site, and Mr. Stephen would happily employ me somewhere else.

Ms. Ross also told the students that Mr. Stephen has been bragging to everyone about his new step choreographer because she is running one of the best programs Luminous LA has ever had.

"I'm so mad you didn't get to see her on stage with those girls," Keasha says.

"What girls?" Delia asks.

Desiree and Keasha fill their friend in on what took place at the clothes drive with Queela and her girls.

Delia grabs her computer and the girls watch the footage from the fight on the front porch.

"No they didn't watch her tutorials, step to Alexis, then do her routine right in her face with her on the stage," Delia says.

"We were just as shocked when Coach told us it was her step," Keasha says.

"I need to get back out there," Delia says.

"And you will," Desiree says. "Just study more. We miss you out there, and so does Coach. She's always asking where you are."

"I sure do ask where you are a lot," I say. "I love my team."

Sometimes when I say *love*, I think of my grandma. She's the only real love from family that I have.

I'm laughing because I remember my grandma giving me a spanking when I was growing up. It didn't hurt.

I see my grandma in front of me again. I'm dazed off again.

My grandmother has a few cards laid out on the table. "I have a few tricks I want to show you," my grandma says. "I know your momma lied to you about who some of your relatives were. She had you thinking your aunts were your cousins and a lot more crazy stuff. I know every trick in the book. I lied to her too. It's people laughing at her too. You've

360

met people you don't even know are related to us, but they tried to show you so when you thought back you would wonder why they did certain things. Flip over two cards."

The first card I flip over is a gun. I'm looking confused. What kind of cards are these that my grandmother has? I flip over another card, and it's a gun as well. I look my grandmother in her eyes. She looks serious. I don't feel any bad vibe though. I can still feel that she has nothing but love for me. My heart isn't bothered either. I just wasn't expecting a matching game with my grandmother to be comprised of any guns.

"You got a match. Go again," my grandmother says.

I flip over two more guns. Now my mind is empty and the only thing engulfing me is the naturalness of feeling uneasy with what is in front of me. If I were to move, I would react in a way that was backwards. I would probably do the opposite of what I thought was right. I naturally don't want to be bothered with guns. I can't even believe someone that's supposed to love me has them in my face.

"Tell your momma I can teach you what she did to you. I can also do a lot worse than she can. Now if I know how to figure my granddaughter out, imagine what I did to her," my grandmother says. "It's your turn again."

I flip over two more guns. My mouth drops and I can recognize that I'm about to develop an illness. One that's so deadly I will react the wrong way. Just like I did outside of the store with those kids that assaulted me.

"You were young," my grandma says. "A baby. You had nowhere to run. You can't remember when you were five or six years old, but your momma has been playing games with you like this since you were small."

My grandma has me flip over two more cards, and sure enough it's a match of guns.

"Now I can do that to you all day. Sit here and watch your mouth drop to the floor until I'm satisfied enough to go to sleep and feel like a woman," my grandma continues. "I can do that all day until I believe your expression is strong enough for me to know I did my job right and am doing well in developing your mind to think stupid and become suicidal. Now just imagine the things your mom was doing when you were a child. You had no choice but to sit there. There were times she was suicidal because she recognized in this world that people viewed her kind as pure ugly. She would use you and your sister to get uglier images out of you two so she could walk around. Nadia hated your sister for not succeeding in killing you. She tried to train your sister's mind to want you dead, but my love is stronger than that. I made you a fighter, and you won the battle against your sister every time."

"I knew the day would come when she told you how much she hated you," my grandma says.

My grandma says she gave me time to know that I was a good person by thinking Nadia may have issues with old age. Then my grandma told me Nadia did evil on purpose. My grandma says she showed me what lacking love in areas could do. But reminded me I was supposed to have committed suicide a long time ago. The day I was born. My grandma's love is stronger than Nadia's. Even dead she said she would always be smarter than any of her kids. She said a lot of people with families like this don't make it.

"So just know in this life you would reach that point where the love wouldn't be in you," my grandmother says. "You would stray off and naturally think you shouldn't be here. And that's what your mother thought of you. That's how beautiful you are. You were supposed to hit that point a long time ago, but I showed you I was able to love you. I loved you all along."

I'm just out of my damn mind hearing all this shit.

"It's not easy for a mother to have a beautiful daughter that's talented and takes all of the attention from her when she's born," my grandmother says.

"Do you really think I'm that beautiful?" I ask.

"Tell her that's why I did it," my grandmother says. "Of course I do."

"Grandma, am I supposed to be dead right now?" I ask.

"My love is too strong," my grandmother says. "You recognized that I loved you. That means I did everything right.

362

You got to a point in your drug recovery where you needed real love. Without it, you would have died. Sometimes life will get a hold of you and you won't want to deal with anyone but family. That's where your love is supposed to always be. That will happen. I know what you were dealing with, and I knew you would search for me. And when you did, I wanted you to know just how much I loved you. I would die for you. Tell her that's why I did it."

So now I understand that my whole life my grandmother's love was strong within me. She wasn't around much because my mother moved away from her when I was young.

"Love is real strong. It can cut through any devil there is," my grandmother continues. "It's stronger than getting kicked off of that team. The reason you were kicked off is simple. I needed you to. This is blood we're talking about. None of your relatives know how serious this game called life is. The story of the assault and Jania, all the way up to you recognizing why I did what I did, is what type of hell you need to keep in you to cut through these drugs. It's too much. Drugs will play with how you think someone loves you. But I knew my grandbaby knew I loved her. I was just waiting for the right time to tell you. When Nadia told you about Jania, that was it. I knew that day would come. You would search for the love and I would be there."

My grandmother looks at the phone. I follow her eyes. Now she's looking at me again.

"I will teach you how to get back what they were trying to take from you. Something you already had," my grandmother says.

"What did I have?" I ask.

"Wipe your face," my grandmother says. I take a napkin and wipe my face even though I don't think anything is on it.

"You had a natural tendency to let people go quickly that did something wrong to you," my grandmother says. "It didn't matter how big or small it was." I look sad. "I know sometimes you wish you didn't let people go for small stuff now that you're older," my grandma continues. "I don't care though. Because I do get jealous. Nadia specialized in making you very intolerant of giving people second chances. Now you're older and you know better. Look at how much hell you have to recite to get to the love I have for you."

My grandmother gave me a way to forget about being nothing but a practice to Nadia. My grandmother says she'll use anything to show me the type of love that is out there fighting to keep people in situations like me alive.

I snap back into reality.

"I need you guys to help me every day," Delia says.

"Girl just come on," Keasha says grabbing Delia's hand to lift her up. "Let's study then practice some more."

The girls go to Delia's room and help her with her math homework.

Once Delia gets the hang of her math problems, the girls go back to the backyard and practice the steps.

Ms. Chelsea peaks out the screen door a few times.

The girls practice until the twins get picked up by their older sister.

The next week, I attend a luncheon hosted by Mr. Stephen for the 25th Anniversary of Luminous LA. All of the art instructors are here.

Everyone's sitting at a table chatting about how well their students are coming along and eating sandwiches with chips and sodas, while I sit quietly at a table with two older ladies. They ask my name and about what I do. I tell them and don't bother asking them because I don't feel like talking. I don't even want to be here, but decided to show my face for Mr. Stephen. I want him to know I appreciate him giving me the opportunity to work for Luminous LA.

Mr. Stephen grabs a microphone and stands at the front of the room to thank everyone for coming out.

"Good afternoon everyone," Mr. Stephen says. "Thanks for taking the time to come out to Luminous LA's 25th anniversary."

Mr. Stephen gives his speech on wanting to keep kids off the streets, and give them something positive to do like he did when I met with him for the first time.

"I'm so proud of this program and to have all of you as my

instructors," Mr. Stephen says. "Twenty-five years ago when we started, we only had fifty-two schools we were involved with, and now we've branched out to almost two hundred."

Mr. Stephen concludes his speech thanking everyone again, and letting them know to eat everything because he doesn't want to take a bunch of sandwiches home.

"My family won't be able to finish all of this," Mr. Stephen continues.

People laugh and smile; not because Mr. Stephen is funny, but because they know he's trying to be.

I grab my purse, put my jacket on, and walk over to Mr. Stephen when he finishes talking to almost everyone here. There's literally been someone approaching him every time someone walked away from him.

"Hi, Mr. Stephen," I say. "Thanks for having me."

"Shona, no problem," Mr. Stephen says. "Are you enjoying yourself?"

I say yes.

"Have you met Talia?" Mr. Stephen asks me.

The lady that was walking past us turns around, so I know she is Talia.

"She's one of our instructors," Mr. Stephen says. "Talia teaches students to tap dance."

"I also teach ballet, the drums, piano, flute, theater, dance, and a lot of other things," Talia says.

I can't stand her uppity tone. I can't stand people that have to make themselves feel bigger and more important by going through their entire resume.

"Excuse me girls," Mr. Stephen says when he notices a girl standing behind him.

"I'm about to head out in a minute Mr. Stephen. I'll see you," I say.

If he thinks I'm about to hold a conversation with this Talia girl, he's lost his mind. He's turned his back, so he can't see me when I do what I was planning to do.

Talia starts to say something and I turn my back and walk out the door.

When I get back to my house, I just flop on the couch. I'm bored as hell and don't have anything to do tonight. I was supposed to stick it out and stay at Mr. Stephen's event, but I couldn't last.

Sheela calls me and says she desperately needs some company. I'm not supposed to let my students come in my house, but I would hate to tell her *no* and she ends up doing something crazy to herself.

I give Sheela my address. She comes over with a backpack of clothes.

"Can I spend the night?" Sheela asks.

"Sure," I say. "Can I ask why you need to stay here, and if someone knows you're here?"

"The people responsible for me think I'm at Alexis' house," Sheela says. "She already knows to cover for me. I just wanted to come here and not be around any adults."

I look at her like she's crazy. I *am* an adult.

"Parents," Sheela says correcting herself.

Sheela brought a blanket and pillow with her so she's good. She sits quietly in the dining room and does her homework, then goes to sleep.

I used to go to bed early when I was frustrated because the pain goes away temporarily while I'm sleep, so I think Sheela has a lot on her mind.

I see my grandma and me sitting in the living room on the couch.

"While you're writing this for me, you can reread it after. It'll help you beat the drugs faster," my grandmother says. I didn't even think to say the drugs are responsible for some of my actions at the store while I was being assaulted. No, I blame Nadia only. Sounds like my grandma really is trying to make me finish this book. She says reread this to beat the drugs. I guess that's one way to put *get this done*.

My grandma's gritting her teeth like the drugs had me doing. I remember when the drugs had me practicing my smile as if I was a model.

"I made you write this with all of them in your head, while

dealing with drug recovery. Tell her that's how crazy I am," my grandma says.

"Your mom has said worse stuff to you," my grandma says. "You've just always been one to need to hear or go through something four or five times for it to register. Look at that crazy shit she said to you. You finally heard her. Imagine how long it took me to think of ways to get you to understand. Saying something negative after someone pours their heart out to you about a bad situation, that's one of the oldest tricks in the book."

"Enjoy yourself and your privacy," my grandma says. "I'm teaching you patience. Tell her I told you to mess up that text message. Who the hell did she think she was bringing up Jania to you after you told her not to? Let her go. She's going to bombard you with another crazy statement," my grandma says.

"With Nadia, you will go around people you've said bad things about and think they won't harm you," my grandma says. "She practiced that."

"But grandma, I don't feel like detailing everything in this book," I say.

"Do as I say damn it!" my grandma says.

"You mean I have to tell this story and write about the pain it is with little to no time to do it and the drug recovery being pain?" I ask.

"That's what I said," my grandma says.

Fuck it. Nadia told all those lies while I was recovering from drugs. She has me fucked up. Let me get all this shit typed up.

I snap back into reality and start thinking.

When I was removed from Ann High's step team, some nights I was able to force myself to sleep, but most of them I couldn't because the thought of that evil quad that consisted of the McGruders', Jasmine, and Nadia would haunt me at night.

When I finish doing my homework in the living room, I get in my bed. Sheela's in it. She's not sleep though, and she thinks I didn't notice her tears before she rolled over.

"Do you need a ride to school tomorrow?" I ask.

"I can take the bus," Sheela says. "It's not too far."

I can hear the pain in her voice.

I have Ciera drop her off at Mission the next day.

"What's wrong with your student?" Ciera calls and asks me on her way back to her house after dropping Sheela off. "She looked depressed and like if someone doesn't talk to her or she doesn't get the attention she needs, she's going to hurt herself."

"Girl, I don't know," I worriedly say. "She doesn't tell anyone what's bothering her."

"If you love your student, I suggest you start doing a little digging," Ciera says.

I wake up early to go to Mission High before the bell rings to talk to the principal. I need to get some information on what's wrong with Sheela. I don't want to lose my student, and at the same time know I didn't try to figure out what the issue with her was so I could try and get her help.

I was angry most of my senior year when I was removed from the team, but I wasn't suicidal. But me and Sheela are two different people.

"I'm not allowed to give any information on my students to anyone that does not work here at Mission High," the principal says. "I understand you work for Luminous LA, and I've heard nothing but good things about you; however, I have rules and guidelines like everyone else. I can't tell you anything I know about Ms. Gonzalez."

"Do you think she's okay?" I ask concerned.

"Sure," the principal says. "She's most likely going through a bad phase. Maybe it's a boyfriend, or she lost a relative, or her and her best friend are no longer talking. There are so many things that can cause these teenagers, or any kid at that, to seem angry all the time. What I can assure you is if I, or anyone else in this school, thought she was a threat to anyone including herself, we would sit her down, question her, or talk to her family. But Sheela's a straight A student, and she's never given anyone a problem since she's been here. I'm sure she's going through a rough storm and it will be over soon."

I like how Sheela making straight A's and never giving anyone a hard time *before* is supposed to mean that she will never do harm to herself or anyone else.

I hope the students at Mission High aren't as stupid as their principal.

I need to figure something else out to find out what's going on with Sheela without asking my students for help. People like to talk, and I'm almost certain that one of them will tell someone what I said, who will end up being friends with Sheela and tell her.

Sheela already looks unhappy most of the time. I don't want to take a chance on her being upset that I'm snooping around trying to figure out what's wrong with her, when she clearly doesn't want anyone to know.

I really care for my students. They have proven to be dedicated and loyal to me. They are like my little sisters and brothers.

I would be devastated if something bad happened to any of them.

I leave the principal's office.

I see my grandmother sitting at the table again. I'm in my feelings.

"You are to never do drugs again," my grandma says. My grandmother says we'll beat these drugs together. It's not going to be easy. It's been a while since I've smoked and I'm still not clear of my brain being a natural wreck. "Now you need to keep repeating things to fight the drugs," my grandma continues. "I know how it goes. With these drugs, you're going to have to repeat a lot of things. To get to the love, you will have to recite things that cut. The drugs are very much real. The effects are some that you will never read or hear about. That's how serious they are."

"I regret using them so much," I say.

"The point that I'm trying to make is that you have to repeat the bullshit your mother said in the first place. That's the only thing you say twice. You pour your heart out as a woman to her and she makes it worse? Late at night at that?" my grandmother says. "You do what you have to do to beat these drugs effects. I want these projects done."

"Nadia did me so wrong," I say.

"Just know I did the same thing to her," my grandmother says. "Your cousin told me she had you to a point where you could barely talk. Nadia can barely talk her damn self. *Day* and *they* are not the same word. *Mout* and *mouth* aren't the same word either," my grandmother says.

I'm sitting alone at the table for a minute. Then I'm back to reality sitting in my car.

24

Delia and I sit next to the announcer at the dance team competition at Cupperton. The rest of the team waits patiently under one of the basketball rims to hear the music begin.

I am filled with excitement as I sit in this loud atmosphere filled with a competitive and lively vibe.

I am back in the mix.

Even though Mission is not competing, I'm still excited just for them to showcase.

I look in the section where my students' parents are sitting and see Jose's mom holding up a big poster that says: *Jose is the Best*. A row down from her is Keasha and Desiree's mom and sister, who are holding up a poster that says: *Keasha and Desiree are here to stomp it out.*

The judges sit back and relax as Mission waits to begin in their red, black, and white designed pants, black beaters, with black hats on backwards.

All of which Luminous LA funded for.

I continue scanning the gym with a smile that slowly fades when I see Jasmine and Ann High's step team sit at the very top of the stands. Jasmine's entire team has attitudes on their faces.

I cue the audio man to start the music.

Mission High gets to their beginning formation.

Jose, Jason, and Michael make the first row. Alexis, Alina, and Desiree stand in between them on the second row. Keasha, Aisha, and Sheela stand in spaces on the third row between everyone on the second row, and Kiara, Casey, and Mya make the fourth row standing in the spaces the third row created.

The song cuts off and everyone stands with their hands in fists to the side and their heads bowed.

Jose shouts, "Mission!"

Everyone looks up, left, right, then straight before doing one stomp and shouting, "In the house!"

The crowd erupts.

Someone in the audience yells: *Okay! Let's Go Mission!*

Jose shouts, "Ladies and gentlemen, we are Mission's step

team! We come to step for you, and do! Our! Thing!"

The boys drop down to the floor and do the step sitting and the girls keep the same beat standing.

Upon completing step one, the boys stand up and stretch themselves out and the girls stand with their hands on their hips.

The crowd is still loud. Other teams come in the gym from the hallway and concessions and stand at the doors to watch.

Mission is really showing off.

I take note that Kiara and Casey are not tucking in their thumbs all the way, and Delia and Desiree drop their faces because they're getting tired.

We're definitely going to work on the minor mistakes at the next practice. I'm so critical about every step, every position, every look, and every move. What I see, no one else will, because they're not me. I've been stepping and coaching so long, that I can pick out the little things that most coaches can't. I want everything to be sharp. There's no room for mistakes. Errors are not an option.

I believe if people work hard enough with step or any type of dance, it'll be so drilled into them that even if they start to drift off in thoughts, the movements will still be accurate.

Mission High continues to give a stellar performance. They are loud, have good spacing when they move around, keep their heads up looking into the audience, and never lose the beat.

Jasmine and Ann High are watching with serious faces. They look jealous and envious, as they should.

Michael shouts, "Step it up!"

The boys do complex movements and the girls come in after the first eight count. The second line transitions in front of the first line, and the third and fourth rows switch positions. They freeze. The DJ plays another song and the team mixes step and dance choreography, then they stroll out of the gym.

We get a standing ovation while we do our stroll from everyone except Ann High's step team and Jasmine.

I don't care because I know the sound of the roaring crowd is enough to make Ann High's members blood boil, and at the same time let them know that Mission High can deliver. This is the loudest the crowd has been the entire competition.

Mr. Stephen even came out to support the teams today, and he's looking amazed as he stands off to the side of the gym.

I look over at Jasmine one last time. She's staring at me so hard, I feel like someone has a red target on my forehead. She looks at me, then at Delia at the announcer's table.

I smile and look around pretending like I can't still see Jasmine looking at me, but I observe her out of my peripheral vision. She's now staring at me with a smirk shaking her head.

Some of Ann High prepares to leave and of course Jasmine is one of them. Others stay to watch the end of the dance competition.

When Jasmine walks to the doors, she looks over at me again. I'm already looking at her. The world seems to be going in slow motion as we make eye contact. I look at her with a smirk until I can't see her anymore.

I grab the CD from the announcer and meet Mission High outside of the gym, where Ciera is giving them hugs. Nothing but excitement is in the atmosphere as the parents congratulate their kids.

Other teams and their coaches congratulate Mission as well, saying: *I've never seen anything like that. You guys were amazing. Can she come to our school?*

Some people request for me to coach their schools.

Mr. Stephen comes up to me and personally says, "You did an amazing job with them," then goes back inside the gym to support the other students.

"Great job!" I shout to Mission High.

Everyone says thanks.

"I will see you all in a few days," I say. "The Big Bang Step Off is next."

The team cheers.

Mission High's parents smile and tell me how impressed they are with the show.

Delia walks over to me and gives me a hug.

"I hope your grades are getting better," I whisper in her ear.

373

I overhead the twins telling Alexis what was going on with Delia. Ms. Chelsea smiles at me when I release from Delia. I'm glad she allowed her to attend the performance even though she didn't allow her to perform, so she can get a feel of the intense and loud environment.

Ciera's just as happy as I am that the show was a huge success.

I never had this much fun on any high school team I have ever been a part of. I enjoy coaching Mission more than most of the other teams' I've coached in the past.

Ciera and I slow down as we walk to our cars. "I saw Jaz," I tell her.

"Who?" Ciera asks.

"The head coach of Ann High," I remind her.

"You worried?" Ciera asks.

"About what?" I ask.

"Her potentially being as stupid as some of your sorority sisters you don't fuck with and using some of your steps?" Ciera asks.

"No," I say.

I know for a fact that Ann High recycled steps from fraternities my senior year because Jasmine was a rookie head coach, so she didn't know how to make up her own when I was removed. If she can even make a small step, it's because of all those days she watched me banging on walls and tables to make beats, then trying to copy the beat using my body and different movements.

I actually feel like the McGruders' want to beat me fair and square; it's the only way the win would be worth it. They know I'm aware of how they got down my senior year with their routines. I wonder if Ann High will hire a professional coach. Either way, I'm not worried about what they will do.

Mission High will be ready. They'll have great steps, formations, attitudes, put their personalities into the steps, as well as their good looks to go along with the performance.

Mission is the real deal.

"I'm sure she saw some footage of us with Queela and her

girls," I say. "She won't be stupid to do something that the whole world is clowning my sorority on. Besides, if she knows I'll show out with my high school students against members of my sorority, whether it's for a job or not, she won't be stupid and test me. We have a bad history, and we didn't end off on good terms. She let our friendship go the day she took my position. She knows I'll take any opportunity to let her know that *I'm The Choreographer* and *Thee Stepper*. She can't outdo me. She'll get embarrassed. Besides, I can't be worried. The competition is coming up. I'm going to teach them a few new steps, and merge some of them together with what they already know, because they still need to work on a few things like keeping them thumbs in and staying into the routine when they start getting tired."

"That's smart," Ciera says. "Are you going to extend the practices now that it's crunch time or add a few? Have it somewhere else if Mr. Stephen doesn't allow it."

"I'm way ahead of you on that," I say.

Ciera goes home.

I go to the park and watch children play on the monkey bars, swings, and slides in a neighborhood close to my house. I don't feel like being bored at home right now. I just want some fresh air.

I'm so proud of Mission's performance today. I feel so accomplished and reassured that I'm the best choreographer.

I'm so happy Jasmine and her team got to witness a great performance. She has a lot to be worried about. I know she's going to make a lot of changes to make her routine compete with mine. Her members that never worked with me, now know that I'm the real deal. They're probably worried, and they should be.

No matter what Jasmine and the McGruders' bring to the table, stolen, recycled, or created by themselves, it won't be better than what I bring. Mission High will be the step team that's known across the nation under my direction after The Big Bang Step Off.

I drift off when I see a little girl drinking out of the water fountain. She reminds me of the time I was walking down the hallway and passed Mrs. McGruders' office to get a drink of water. While I was drinking, I recognized Nadia's voice coming from Mrs. McGruders' office.

"You did the right thing by taking Shona off the team," Nadia said. "Don't feel bad about it."

I picked my head up from the fountain and listened a lot harder than I was. I toned out everything around me. All I could hear was Nadia and Mrs. McGruders' voices over all the random conversations by people sporadically walking around, print machines going, and doors shutting behind people going into their offices.

"She was very disrespectful," Nadia continued. "Not only to you guys, but to me at home also. She was always talking negatively about me, and I've done all I can for her my whole life."

I was full of rage listening to Nadia spread lies to Mrs. McGruder about me. I wanted to walk into the office to see if she would lie while I was in there, but I knew she would.

"She was bitter for no reason," Nadia continued. "I heard her on the phone making up all types of lies saying you were just messy, and didn't want her on the team because you were jealous you don't have talent like her. She was very arrogant, conceited, and she only cared about herself."

My blood was boiling so bad listening to Nadia lie, that a student walked by and asked me was I okay, and I looked at him so mean that he started walking fast to get away from me.

Nadia was good for making people think that I was a problem child instead of telling them the truth, which is she blamed me for my father leaving her, so she wanted to ruin my life. She was the one depriving me of a social life, and making me stay home just because she wanted me to be angry all the time. She was the one spreading lies about me like she did to Mrs. McGruder, saying I was the problem, when in fact, I was never a problem. I just got stuck with a bitter mom.

What Mrs. McGruder didn't and still doesn't know is, I managed to successfully run Ann High's step team for three years dealing with an insane mother.

I admit I talked nasty to the team when they asked for my help. I admit that some days practice couldn't carry on because I was unwilling to teach. I admit I was angry at a lot of the rehearsals, and I admit I said I would clean up my act time and time again, but I never did.

I caught an attitude a few times my senior year, and Ms. McGruder kicked me off.

My senior year I had enough and I did the best I could to hide my problems and control my attitude, but I exploded a lot. Nadia messed up my mind and attitude. Mrs. McGruder should have given me more than a few chances. She's an old lady so she should know that a person who snaps has a lot going on internally. She should've tried to figure out what the problem was instead of being so quick to throw me off the team.

Angry is an understatement to describe how I felt when I overheard that conversation between Nadia and Mrs. McGruder. Despite my rage increasing, I still wanted to hear more. Something told me to stick around because something would be revealed that I didn't want to know, but needed to know. I sipped more water as students walked by, so they wouldn't think I was about to kill someone.

"I've already seen a huge improvement in her attitude towards me and everyone in this school ever since you took her off the team," Nadia said. "I want to thank you for teaching her a lesson."

So not only was Nadia making up lies, she was also giving Mrs. McGruder a pat on the back for taking me off the team.

When I was a senior, I always questioned whether or not Mrs. McGruder ever questioned why a mother would get her daughter taken off the team she started.

I just recently came to the conclusion that no, Mrs. McGruder did not and would not question that. She wanted me gone and to no longer see me running my team so she could hand it over to Jasmine.

Nadia made her feel a lot better about her decision.

"Ms. Nadia, I want to thank you for supporting me

throughout the entire time I was contemplating removing your daughter," Mrs. McGruder said. When Mrs. McGruder said this, I'm not kidding, if both her and Nadia dropped dead that day or a few weeks later, I would not have cared. I had the upmost hate for the both of them.

Despite me not caring whether they lived or died, I continued to listen on knowing that my blood was on fire.

"A lot of mothers wouldn't let school staff know that their child was planning on putting little effort into the choreography and quitting the team when they needed her most," Mrs. McGruder continued.

Nadia was and is so low down for making up a lie like that. I would never half do any steps, and Mrs. McGruder knew that.

Why in the world would I put a little effort into my choreography, knowing I would have to perform it, and everyone would know I created it? I had and have a reputation to keep. I don't care how mad I get, I would never not put my all into my choreography whether I am performing it or not.

"I took those statements as a sign from God," Mrs. McGruder said. "What you told me was the confirmation I needed to remove her. I'm really happy with my decision to do so. The teams doing so much better without her."

They weren't doing too much better if all the steps they used were mine or from Greek videos.

The part that trips me out about Nadia, is when I think back, I did see her going into Mrs. McGruder's office a lot during the time that led up to my removal from the step team. It never crossed my mind that she could stoop so low to make me angry.

Nadia didn't care whether I liked or loved her or not. She just wanted me to be as miserable as she was when my dad left her. I hate my dad for leaving me with her. By now, he's probably married with children and taking care of them like he should've manned up and did me. But no, he didn't want that responsibility in his twenties.

All I had was Nadia, who worked in the kitchen at Ann High my senior year, so it was nothing for her to walk around the corner and pay Mrs. McGruder a visit whenever she wanted.

"Oh yea, don't tell her I spoke to you," Nadia's sneaky and conniving self said when she left Mrs. McGruder's office.

I quickly went into the nearest bathroom.

Nadia really used her lunch break as a time to talk to Mrs. McGruder. She went to her office just to influence her decision on removing me prior, and I just heard about it that day.

I knew Nadia was evil and bitter, but never thought she would play a part in getting me taken off the step team. I forced myself not to break down completely like Nadia would have wanted me to in the bathroom. I fought my tears.

How bitter could Nadia be to try and have her own daughter removed from the only thing she enjoyed being a part of?

Despite how mean she is, I don't even fault that evil witch Nadia. I fault the McGruders' for not seeing past her lies. Mrs. McGruder was fifty and her husband was fifty-two at the time. They should've seen straight through Nadia's lies. I just can't make my mind up on who to put at fault with this shit.

However, when someone wants someone gone, they'll play their part and get them gone. That's what I did with Regina and Shanell. If anyone tried, they would have failed at getting me to keep them on the team.

Nadia gave the McGruders' the benefit of explaining to the staff at Ann High that my own mother said it was good that I was taken off the team.

It's sad that I didn't overhear this conversation until a couple of months after I was removed.

The little happiness I gained from being happy that I was almost about to graduate and head to college, left the day I heard this conversation.

A car slams on the brakes and I snap out of my evening nightmare.

Now I see my grandma sitting next to me.

"All those years she was out there fighting you and pushing you in the middle of the street, and all because she was fighting her suicide. That pissed me off. There's blood behind this," my grandma says. "I treated you like a baby for thirty-five years. It took all this time for you to wake up and understand why I waited so long to tell you the truth. You are my baby because I said so. Not hers. I know how to love you."

"I love you Grandma," I say.

"You're a woman. You should be comfortable paying bills and getting up every morning with or without a man," my grandma says. "Really remember what the hell you went through when you were pledging. You remember how them ugly girls were to you. It was easy for them to make each other hate you more. List all the dates I tell you. You are not to fear anyone but me."

"I really wish I could smoke without any side effects," I say. "I know I'm not the only one."

"Think about the first users of drugs," my grandma says.

"I am," I say. "What do you mean they need a worse situation to snap them out of the thoughts that they are having?" I remember one day when I saw someone almost get hit by a car. The hell from the drugs went away because I had something severe that shifted my thoughts.

I'm thinking of Nadia now, and when I was telling her about the assault. I had to say that, then remind myself that she went into talking about Jania. Then two months passed, and I wound up in a girl saying all good things about herself that was supposed to walk off a bridge. Then she somehow was released and didn't know by who. She didn't register the love, so she was just moving. She didn't know it was real love moving her. She wound up remembering what she had said to Nadia about the assault. Then she remembered Nadia's response saying she harmed two boys. Then she got released from that and didn't know it was *love* releasing her. She made it to a hard thought. One that hit her. It gave her the answer and response. The answer was, "Tell her that's why I did it." She recognized it was her grandmother. Then she had to keep repeating the whole scenario to feel the love.

"Really think about how crazy the first users of drugs were," my grandmother says. "There are people looking around and suicidal off of who they see because they are so ugly. It's in and out of them. That's how nasty these streets really are."

This is all so crazy to hear. My grandma keeps switching subjects quickly. She has a lot she wants me to include in the book I'm writing.

"You remember how you walked up to that girl that was captain your senior year of the team?" my grandma asks. "The year you won the scholarship. You were at a distance from her and you couldn't believe how hideous she looked. Your eyes got big and her mother couldn't believe how you looked at her and her daughter. You knew when her mother saw you that she thought you were beautiful. Just like she did when she saw you at her church. Then you couldn't help but walk closer to them. You looked at her mother as if you couldn't believe she had such a hideous looking daughter. You stood right next to them. You could tell her mother remembered the story of the candle and the note hitting the door of your enemies. The mother didn't care about anything. She couldn't believe her daughter was so caught up in your response of how you looked at her as if she was ugly as opposed to how serious you were about being taken off of a team you had started. The girl's mother looked at her as if she would kill her for being so stupid to how that dumb woman was for taking you off of a team with the talent that you had. Shona, those women are real psychologist. They hate how people look at them. They're really bitter about how their kids look and changed their lives once they were born." My grandma says those women want to know how pretty people view them. "That lady's daughter looked like road kill to you," my grandma continues. "How were you going to make it two years with her? It was no way to do it."

My face is in complete shock. I can't believe I met one of them fucked up ass families. Some people I only expect to hear about in the movies.

I was out so long that it's now pitch-black outside, and the park is vacant. Once again, no one cared to wake me up when I fell asleep on a bench. People are so careless these days.

A woman is outside alone in the dark at the park, and they just keep walking like they don't see her, not caring if she could possibly be on the news the next day for being kidnapped.

I bet if I was their daughter they would care, and would also want someone to wake her up if she dozed off in a public area with nothing but space and opportunity for a kidnapper to cover her mouth and take her to his or her car.

The people of today are so messed up.

On my way home, I take my phone out and see that I have a missed call. I dial it back.

"Hello Shona," a manly voice answers.

"Hello, who's this?" I ask.

"Jared."

It sounds like he's watching a basketball game.

I cheer up from my nightmare and ask, "Hey, how are you?"

I definitely remember the nice-looking man I danced with at Paper Chase Night Club.

"I'm good," Jared says. "Where are you at?"

Jared hears cars honking their horns. Three people are trying to figure out who has the right of way at a four-way intersection where I'm at.

"On my way home from the park," I say.

"Alone?" Jared asks.

I don't say anything.

"You know you don't need to be out there by yourself," Jared says. "Now that you have my number, give me a call next time and I'll pick you up. But listen, I was wondering if I could take you out to dinner?"

"Why now?" I ask. "I haven't seen you in a while. I'm surprised you even still have my number. What? You got tired of some other girls or what?"

I really don't want to go. I don't want Austin to find out. If I do decide to go, we're going to have to go somewhere on another side of town.

"No," Jared says. "I've just been busy with a lot of things that I can tell you about if you let me take you out to dinner."

"Sure," I say. "When?"

"Tonight," Jared says.

"Let me check my schedule real quick and I will call you right back," I say knowing I don't have anything to do.

"Alright. Bye," Jared says.

I quickly call Ciera. She says she's flat-ironing her hair.

"Jared just invited me out to dinner tonight," I say. "I was wondering if you could come?"

"Girl you say *Jared* like I know who he is," Ciera says.

I remind her of the club.

"I still don't remember him, but whatever," Ciera says. "He got a friend, because I'm not trying to be no third wheel? Ah!"

I know the steam from the flat-iron burned her scalp because she always screams when she's straightening her hair.

"No. I want you to come and not make yourself known, just incase I need to do the signal so you can get me up out of there," I say. "I don't know him well yet."

I'm finally approaching my house.

"Well," Ciera says. "You don't know him at all."

No matter what situation I'm in, if it could potentially put me in a position where I would want to leave, I always make sure I have a way out.

"You're right," I say. "What if he is crazy, or lacks the intelligence that I need in a man?"

Jared seemed sweet the night I met him, but sometimes I learn the nice ones be the craziest ones after just talking to them for a few minutes. Plus, it's been a couple months since I've seen him, and not once did he call just to say *hi* and make sure I would remember him.

"Okay, so you want me to come observe, and if he is not what you want to keep around, get you out of there?" Ciera asks.

"Pretty much," I say. "So, you remember the code?"

"Yea, yea, yea," Ciera says. "If you put both hands behind your neck, I call and say there's an emergency."

If Ciera calls, I'll have the phone on speaker so Jared doesn't think I'm lying about the emergency.

"Alright. Thanks girl," I say. "I will send you some details later. Bye."

I call Jared back.

"So what time should I be ready tonight?" I ask.

"Ten," Jared says.

"Perfect," I say.

"Alright. See you then," Jared says.

As soon as I get inside, Alina calls me. Damn. I got too much going on to talk to her right now. Fuck it. Maybe it's important.

"I'm gone put you on video chat," Alina says. "I'm at the basketball game. We're playing Ann High."

Alina and Alexis walk in the basketball gym at Mission High School. It is crowded. Ann High's basketball team has always been Mission's number one rivalry.

"Good luck girl," Alina tells Alexis.

Alexis looks real cute in her warm-up suit.

Alina takes a seat on the bleachers. Alexis puts her things on the bench and shoots around with her teammates, not recognizing Mariah from Ann High eyeballing her evilly as she warms up on the opposite end of the court.

Alexis gives her teammates high fives and pumps them up while they do their lay-up drill. While running back to the halfcourt line after making her shot, she makes eye contact with Mariah and gives her a fake smile. Mariah mugs Alexis. However, Alexis has no idea who she is.

There's twenty seconds left on the clock before the game begins. The starting five for both teams take off their warm ups and head to center court.

This is Mission's home game, so they wear their white uniform with red outlining. Ann High wears their black *away jersey* with yellow outlining.

Mariah is jumping up and down and Alexis is slapping hands with her teammates.

Alexis is now jumping up and down at the center circle pumped to begin. She winks at Desiree and Keasha who cheer behind the baseline. They wink back.

Mariah makes it a priority to stand next to Alexis.

I keep my phone close by me while I get ready to go out. Alina goes to give Alexis a towel for her face on one of the breaks. Alexis tells her that Mariah said she didn't understand why they put freshmen on the varsity team that still play on a middle school level, while they were waiting for the referee to toss the ball up.

Then Alina tells me that Alexis responded that she didn't understand how immature idiots got a pass to make it to high school just because of sports, when they didn't even pass their middle school exams. Alexis told Mariah to keep looking at her because she knows she's a nice sight to see in anything she has on.

"That's my girl," I say.

"Them niggas are real rude," Alina laughs. She puts her phone at an angle so I can see more of the game.

Mariah gives Alexis a dangerous stare. Alexis can see her out of her peripheral vision.

Alexis' teammate throws the ball to her. Alexis gets it and goes in for the layup. Mariah chases behind her; she gets in front of her and looks like she's about to take a charge.

Alexis goes up for the layup, Mariah elbows her in the stomach, and Alexis falls hard on her back.

The referee gives Mariah a technical foul. Alexis' coach snaps at the ref because she feels Mariah should be ejected from the game.

"That's a bogus call ref!" Alexis' coach shouts.

Mission's parents chant *Throw her out.* Mariah stands with her hands on her hips without a care in the world for elbowing Alexis.

Alexis didn't know, but Mariah really does have issues keeping her grades up because she's not good at retaining a lot of information, and Mariah hates girls that boast about their good looks. Mariah is a girl that believes people shouldn't brag about their looks, especially when there's so many people struggling with insecurities. I know this because Dayla's sister Isyss told me.

Alexis' mom is worried while she watches her daughter struggle to get up with the help of her teammates. Once Alexis gains her strength and composure back, she goes over to Mariah, who is walking towards the bench with no remorse, and shoves her in the back.

Mariah turns around and tries to punch Alexis in the face, but Alexis ducks, then punches Mariah in her face. Mariah's nose starts bleeding.

The referees quickly break up the fight and escort both girls out of the gym.

Alina, Desiree, Keasha, and the rest of the crowd look on in disbelief.

After the game, Alexis and Alina lie in a tent in Alexis' backyard. Comfy in their pajamas, they sit in silence and think about what just happened at the game.

Neither of them even know why Mariah targeted Alexis.

"Did you know her?" Alina asks. "Because that was personal."

"Nope," Alexis says. "Never seen her a day in my life. I don't even know her name."

"Man, that had to be the earliest fight in all of basketball history," Alina says. "I mean y'all didn't even finish the first quarter. I didn't know the school rivalry was that bad."

"It's not. That was just some jealous girl that came over to me talking mess, then got upset when I called her an idiot," Alexis says. "I can't believe she would show out like that at what's supposed to be the most exciting game during the regular season for both teams."

Alexis phone rings. One of her basketball teammates checks to see if she's okay, and tells her they won by fifteen points. Alexis puts her on speaker phone so I can hear. Alexis tells her she's fine and glad they won without her.

"I definitely didn't want to lose to them after they had that girl attack me like that," Alexis says.

"You think that was planned?" her basketball teammate asks.

"Probably," Alexis says and tells her basketball teammate she has to go.

"You know I'm not even mad about being suspended five games," Alexis says to Alina. "I was defending myself."

"I agree," Alina says. "I'm so glad you ducked in time."

Alexis looks at Alina like she's crazy.

"Girl my reflexes are on point," Alexis says. "I can't have these jealous girls out here messing up my face because they're

386

jealous they don't have it. I don't care about being suspended. At least I still have the step team."

Alina sadly turns away from Alexis. Alexis looks at her a little worried.

"I'm pregnant," Alina says.

Alexis sits up and looks at her in disbelief. Eighteen and pregnant? Alexis instantly forgets about the brawl she was just in. Alina's mom will be a grandma at thirty-four.

"I can still do the competition," Alina says and sits up. "This is just one curve ball I wasn't expecting."

"You of all people?" Alexis laughs.

Alexis wasn't shocked to hear Alina's revelation, she was shocked because Alina is considered a *good girl* at Mission High.

Of everyone on the team, the twins would be the ones that everyone would vote for if the question was: *Who would get pregnant first?*

"It's always the people you least expect," Alexis laughs, then stops when she sees Alina is still in her serious state.

"Who?" Alexis asks.

"This boy named Terry," Alina says. "He's in college. I met him at the store on my way home from practice one day. We exchanged numbers. He had good conversation. I went to his dorm one day when my mom was away on business, and what can I say. The chemistry was there. I couldn't say no."

"How was it?" Alexis asks.

"It was good," Alina says.

"Your mom know?" Alexis asks.

"No. I'm not going to tell her until after the competition," Alina says. "I don't need that stress."

"Does he know?" Alexis asks.

Alina shakes her head no.

"Do you plan on telling him?" Alexis asks.

"Girl yes. Stop asking so many questions," Alina frustratedly says.

Alexis says *sorry.*

The two girls lie back down and listen to the ambient noise.

Alina asks, "Do you want to be the Godmother?"

387

Alexis smiles, says sure, and gives her friend a hug and kiss on the forehead.

"I can't wait to meet my Godchild," Alexis says. "Don't talk too loud because my mom is still awake. I don't know when she's going to give up on trying to make me think she's not listening in on my conversations. I know her ears are wide opened when I have company over. All the eavesdropping she does has yet to pay off."

Alexis says she hopes it's a girl so she can do her hair, paint her nails, and put her in nice skirt outfits. Alina says she hopes it's a boy, that way she doesn't have to worry about her child getting pregnant.

The girls laugh and talk all night until they fall asleep.

I don't say anything about Mariah being on Ann High's step team because I don't want to raise Alexis' adrenaline anymore tonight. I want her to go to sleep. I want her to rest. Alina is right. That fight happened too damn quick.

I don't say anything about the pregnancy because I'm just too damn shocked. My ears feel like they have been raped. No this high school Luminous LA girl did not just open my eyes even wider tonight with this revelation.

Grown ass kids.

25

Jared calls and says he's outside. While I walk to his car, I see Ciera on the phone in hers. She looks me up and down and mouths: *You look good.*

Jared opens the door for me to get in the car, then we head to dinner.

"You look beautiful," Jared says as he looks me up and down in my two-piece red and gold skirt set.

Jared licks his lips as he looks at my legs and goes down to my four inch heels.

"Thanks. You look nice too," I say. "So where are we going?"

"To one of my favorite restaurants," Jared says. "Just sit back and relax."

Jared's car is super clean. There's literally nothing in the car except me and him. Seems like the car just got pulled off the lot before he picked me up.

I see Ciera trailing us a few cars back dancing and nodding her head to whatever's playing on the radio.

Poor Jared has no idea how I will flip the switch on him if he says anything that is an indication that I don't need to be around him like: *I like to paint my toe nails* or *my baby momma is getting on my nerves.* But so far so good with Jared. He's been the perfect gentlemen opening my door and complimenting me.

Jared pulls the sunroof back.

Jared pulls up in front of Papa's Fancy Seafood Restaurant. How did he know I love seafood?

I can't believe this menu. I would never come here on my own. The food is too high for the portion offered. The buffet down the street from my house costs twenty-eight dollars, and it has unlimited crab as well as a fruit bar, salad bar, sushi bar, and all types of different Chinese foods.

This place is a rip off. Seafood is seafood no matter where it's being served or the size of the restaurant.

Jared watches me and laughs at my disgusted facials looking at the menu.

"You have a nice smile," I say.

"Thank you. Have you found anything you want to eat?" Jared asks.

"I haven't looked at the foods yet. I've just been looking at the prices," I say.

Jared laughs.

I glance at Ciera who is sitting a few tables behind Jared with her wig she put on before she came in. She's on the phone talking to someone about the ridiculous prices on the menu. The waitress asks Ciera if she wants to take off her coat, but she says no.

I'm glad Ciera came, but I hope she quiets down a little. I know she's frustrated about this expensive food. She asks the waiter for water and says she needs more time to think.

"You know I got you right?" Jared flirtatiously says to me.

I snap out of my gaze at Ciera. Shoot. Jared's turning around and trying to find who I was looking at. Ciera turns her head towards the back when she sees Jared turning around.

"Yes," I say. "I'm going to get the crab leg platter."

"I'll have the same as you," Jared says.

The waitress comes over in her short black skirt and dressy white shirt with her black bra showing and asks, "Hi, are you two ready to order?"

I go from looking my regular self, to looking disgusted, to putting a fake smile on my face. I thought Papa's Fancy Seafood Restaurant was supposed to be a classy and upscale place. Why are all the waitresses walking around looking like cheap hookers?

"Ladies first," Jared says.

"I will have the crab leg platter," I say.

"And you sir?" the waitress asks.

I observe Jared closely. I want to see how he converses and reacts to this woman who appears to be someone who thinks she should be on the menu.

"I will have the same," Jared answers as he stares at the menu, and doesn't even look up at the waitress.

I'm staring at him so hard, he can probably feel my eyes on him.

"Okay. I will be right back," the waitress says and she takes the menus.

The waitress looks a little hurt Jared won't look at her. Oh well. I'm content that he didn't want to take a chance on making me feel like he took interest in another woman. Or maybe he wanted to show me women that walk around showing all their assets, whether it's at work or not, don't capture his attention, and he doesn't take any interest in them.

"So what type of things do you like to do besides go to Paper Chase Night Club?" Jared asks.

"I like to step, play basketball, and listen to music," I respond.

"Oh so you're a stripper?" Jared asks surprised.

"No. I said stepper," I say. "I am a high school coach."

"Oh, stepper," Jared says. "I'm sorry. My hearing trips at times."

"Now I know why someone I was walking by around my house looked at me like I was crazy when I told him I was a stepper that coached high school kids," I say.

"That's wasup," Jared says. "How do you like it?"

"I love it," I say. "Every now and then I have one student that will give me a hard time, but for the most part it's cool."

"Why don't you just take that one person off the team?" Jared asks.

I drift off into a late night at Nadia's house. I was sitting at the dining room table with my friend Reeya. I didn't say a word while I was creating my weapon. I just did what I had to do as fast as I could. I was sitting in a house with all the lights off, except for the one in the dining room. My face was serious, and I didn't have a care in the world. I was on an assignment that I assigned myself, and I was ready to make the biggest statement in my life.

The McGruders' had me angry for removing me from my team, but all the smiles at the performances and watching me walk around the school with some of the people that were on the step team that had their shirts on while I didn't, kept adding fuel to the fire.

I was tired of the McGruders' hateful acts, and I was tired of letting them enjoy my misery, so I needed to take action to make sure I had something to laugh at whenever they smiled at me again.

I was on a mission to make sure the McGruders' knew not to ever mess with me again. They had Jasmine cocky and conceited for taking my spot, and they also had Nadia walking around the school happy as she watched me mope around.

The McGruders' needed to pay.

I grabbed a lighter, turned the dining room light off, and hopped in Nadia's car with my weapon and Reeya. I was focused. I couldn't wait to reach my destination.

The McGruders' were too old to be so evil towards a teenager. I hoped they never smiled again after my mission.

I pulled up in front of the bushes in front of the McGruders' house.

Reeya got out of the car. Like a killer, she walked slowly and angrily down the McGruders' driveway. She stood staring a few feet away from their screen door. It was pitch black outside, and their porch light wasn't on as Reeya stared angrily at the home of the people that ruined my senior year and her junior year.

I was breathing heavily, but my heart was still calm. After a few seconds, Reeya took the lighter out of her pocket and lit the candle. Reeya stared at the candle, then at the glass screen door. She threw the candle at the McGruders' door. The door quickly shattered and the porch quickly caught on fire.

I watched the fire spread for a few seconds while Reeya walked backwards up the hill.

I started smiling.

It wasn't until I saw the neighbor's lights turn on, that Reeya turned around and ran to the car. I bet she never ran so fast in her life. I guess when people do criminal things that could get them locked away for years, their body will naturally do things they didn't think it could, to avoid dealing with the police.

I still didn't have an expression on my face or a care in the world when I drove off in the car. I was still nonchalant. I put the pedal to the metal and sped off.

The porch fire must have expanded faster than it did when I was watching it, because by the time I reached the first light to the main street, a fire truck was headed in the direction I just came from. I drove past it like I didn't see it. I didn't even pull over to the side of the street like I was supposed to.

The only thing I thought was *mission accomplished*.

"Shona? Shona?" Jared says.

I snap out of my flashback.

It took me one day to plan the day I would get the McGruders' back, and that was the day prior to me executing my plan.

To this date I don't regret it.

I set their house on fire a few months before I graduated high school.

When word spread around Ann High about the fire, I couldn't help but laugh when people looked at me like I was crazy when they passed me.

Jasmine no longer laughed with her new friends when she saw me. Instead, she looked down at the ground, and like she was afraid of what I would do to her. And I was happy her fake-friend-self would fear me at least until I left Ann High, or didn't know where she lived.

"Huh!?" I shout uncontrollably.

"Are you okay?" Jared asks.

"Yes," I say.

I drink some water.

That whole fire scene is one of the most memorable moments of my life. If people knew it was me and thought like me, they'd feel like I haven't shaken the arsonist gene in me. They would fear that I'm still capable of doing the same thing, especially since I didn't get arrested for it.

I'm so happy I went through with my plan, otherwise I would be very bitter towards myself because I would know the McGruders' didn't have any consequences for their actions. After I got them back, I no longer cared if they smiled at me, which they didn't. They would see me and look away after the date their house caught flames. Even Nadia was scared to leave me in her house after that date, so she started *asking* me to go to my friends' houses while she wasn't home.

If I'd have known being a suspect in the McGruders' case would get me the respect I deserved from them and Jasmine, as well as get Nadia to give me a little bit more of a social life outside of school, then I would've burned their house down days after they removed me.

All the people I couldn't stand feared me after being a suspect, and I loved each and every moment of it.

The McGruders' had to stay in a hotel for a few weeks until they found another house to move into. Putting their house on fire was the second-best thing I ever did. The first is becoming a choreographer my ninth-grade year of high school.

Every day I saw Mrs. McGruder after the fire, she sounded bitter and angry, and like she wanted to transfer jobs, but I knew she would never give me that satisfaction, nor want the students to think that I am capable of making her switch jobs.

"I don't think I will kick her off the team," I say to Jared. "Maybe I will have a talk with her."

I know what getting kicked off of Ann High's team caused me to do to the McGruders', and not have an ounce of remorse for it to this date, so I'm not going to quickly kick Sheela off the team. Besides, she's proven time and time again that she has my back no matter how mad she is about whatever's bothering her. I'm not going to make her think I don't care about her like the McGruders' did me. I want to be like a big sister to Sheela, and try to figure out the problem.

I know at first I didn't want to get in Sheela's business, but I need to do something before she catches an attitude with me on the wrong day, and I do decide to let her go.

I didn't have a problem removing Shanell and Regina because they didn't have a problem taking advantage of me. Coming late or not coming at all is not something I take lightly. If people like them put flames to my house, I would come for them, and in a worse way than they did me.

Shanell and Regina's situation was different than mine and Sheela's. And definitely different than my relationship with the McGruders'.

I was always on time, and *I* was the coach and founder of Ann High's step team, so I should've been granted some leeway whenever I had an attitude, or the McGruders' should have tried to talk to me. Sheela is always on time as well, so I'm going to sit her down one day and have a talk with her.

"Aw okay. To each his own," Jared says. "I personally love to play basketball. Do you follow college sports or the NBA?"

"No. Not really, but I still enjoy playing," I say.

Jared pulls out his wallet and shows me a picture of him in his basketball uniform when he was younger. Braces and thin as a toothpick. He was so adorable.

"Do you still play basketball?" I ask.

"Yes. I play a lot actually," Jared responds.

I try to think of something else to say. I'm not the best when it comes to thinking of topics.

To avoid seeming boring, I quickly ask, "Are you an only child?"

I wish I could have thought of a better question.

"I have two younger brothers," Jared says. "One is fifteen and the other is eighteen."

"How old are you?" I ask.

"Thirty-six," Jared says.

Thank God. He is perfect. Taller, handsome, and only a year older than me.

"And yourself?" Jared asks.

"Thirty-five," I say.

"You still a baby," Jared says.

I hate how people won't be that much older and still refer to me as *a baby*.

"How long have you been out here?" Jared asks.

"My whole life," I say. "I was born in New Orleans. Are you from here?"

"No. I'm from Kansas," Jared says. "I came out here for…"

Jared is interrupted when the waitress comes back. This time I don't look at Jared. Aware my keen eyes may have caused him to play it safe the first time, I look at the waitress as she speaks.

"Here you are," the waitress says and sets the food on the table.

Jared begins to eat. He grabs his plate and still doesn't look at the waitress. She doesn't look too happy he's not paying her any attention.

"You're not that cute anyways bra," the waitress says.

"Yea whatever," Jared says so she can hear him.

Jared pays her no mind. He struggles to pull the meat out of the crab leg.

Behind him, Ciera's waiter is asking her if she's going to buy something to eat. She's still getting refills of water.

"You know what? Let me see the menu again," Ciera says knowing good and well she's not going to buy anything, and also that she's taking up space and will be put out if she doesn't purchase something.

The waiter brings Ciera a menu and stands over her.

"I'll come to you when I'm ready to order," Ciera says.

The waiter looks like he doesn't believe her as he turns away and goes to another table.

"You came out here for...," I say to get Jared to finish his statement.

Jared rushes to swallow his crab.

"Oh, you don't have to rush," I say. "Sorry about that. You can finish telling me when you are done."

Jared swallows his food.

"My cousin is an NBA player and I'm just here to support him," Jared says.

NBA player? Now I know this is just a casual encounter that may only be for a hook up, so I'm confident I'm not giving Jared any sex. I sip my water a bit more.

"So the last time you were here you were just visiting your

cousin?" I ask.

"Yes. Then I went back to Kansas," Jared says. "I come out here a lot to see him. He's my closest relative. He flew me out here to support him. I probably was here another two days that night after we met at the club, then went back home. I'll only be out here a few more days before I go back. Part of the reason I didn't call you was because I wasn't out here."

Jared changes the subject. "So how long before you go visit somewhere else?" Jared asks.

Jared probably thinks that I, like so many other women, get more excited about a man that has money, rather than a good heart and mind. I'm not like that. Besides, I know I need to focus more on the good heart and mind because that's what's going to help me keep my peace of mind. I don't want to get into a relationship with a man that will make me want to set his house on fire because he's mentally unstable when it comes to being with one woman.

"I've visited a few other places," I mumble.

Upset at myself for not realizing this acquaintance and his timing were too good to be true, I try to keep a semi-happy look on my face.

Jared's only here temporarily, so he obviously only wants a fun night. I wonder if he hooks up with a different woman in every place he visits, takes her out to eat, then tries to get in her pants. Even though he wasn't in Louisiana, he still could've called and said *hi* occasionally.

I try to detour my thoughts from being negative.

Ciera can see me kind of looking sad, so she puts her hands behind her head and looks at me inquisitively. I look down and shake my head no, then text her and tell her she can leave. Even though Jared clearly only wants some fun, he's still cool and I'm not bored with him. I can make it through this date.

"I don't want anything," Ciera says and hands the waiter her menu.

Jared seems to not have a worry in the world while he devours his crab meat.

"You should probably start eating your food before it gets cold," Jared suggests.

I crack one of my crab legs and the meat comes out perfectly. I softly broke it down the middle, then pulled the two ends apart, and it came out as one long and whole piece of meat.

"You are a pro," Jared says about me cracking the crab leg.

"Yep. Haven't had crab in a while, but the technique has always stuck with me," I say.

Nadia used to take us to visit my grandma and I always paid attention to how my grandma would crack her crab legs, crawfish, and peel her shrimp. I pull out another piece of crab meat and try to hand it to Jared, but his hands are wet and buttery, so I put it in his mouth. I make the most out of this time with him because I don't care to see him again. Plus, I still have Austin.

I enjoy Jared's company and play along with his flirtatious ways the rest of the dinner. Might as well enjoy the small amount of time I have with him.

We finish our food, and Jared pays for the bill that is given to us by someone other than the waitress that was helping us before.

"I can't believe you are leaving her a tip," I say to Jared while he puts cash on top of his card.

"I'm not. Here you go," Jared says giving our new waiter the tip.

I see our old waitress looking angry when she sees the tip she didn't deserve go to the nice man that brought us our bill.

"She better hope the people she's waiting on now give her a

tip," Jared says.

When Jared and I step outside, I decide to be humorous.

"You know I have a team entering the *stripper* competition that's coming up right?" I ask.

Jared looks at me crazy then laughs, recognizing I used the term *strip* instead of *step* because of him mishearing me earlier.

"Very funny," Jared says. "So, are you inviting me to this *step* show?"

"Yea. It's The Big Bang Step Off," I say.

"I heard about that," Jared says. "I'm in town for another month, so I guess I don't have a choice but to stop by and support you."

Jared pulls up to my house.

"I had a good time with you tonight," Jared says.

"I enjoyed myself too," I say and give him a hug. "Thanks for a good night."

Unsure of whether this is the last time I will see him, being that he is the finest brother I have ever had the pleasure of enjoying scompany with, I give him a kiss on the lips and slowly release from him.

"What was that for?" Jared asks.

"Just for being a nice man," I say and get out the car.

I head inside. I turn around and Jared's watching me walk. I turn around one last time before I know he can no longer see me, and he still is watching me. I wave. I don't hear him pull off until a few seconds after he can no longer see me.

Soon as I walk in my house, I regret the kiss. This was our first date. I wish I would've gotten over my hormones and physical attraction to that man. However, the optimistic side of me says I would have been even more upset if I never saw him again, and I didn't take the opportunity.

I go in my bedroom, slam the door, and slam my back against

400

it.

I put my hands on my forehead and shake my head back and forth as I mess up my hair up.

My heart is in pain. Not because of kissing Jared, but because I'm thinking about the McGruders' again.

I space off.

I'm remembering the day I walked in Mrs. McGruder's office.

"Shut the door," Mrs. McGruder demanded angrily.

I shut it and smirked while I took a seat because I knew what the topic at hand would be. I was just found innocent of the arsonist crime I committed. There were no fingerprints found anywhere.

The McGruders' put me down as a suspect, stating everything that went on with me and the step team, but there was no evidence to convict me.

I'm not going to lie, I sat in the court room scared as I've ever been listening to the judge talk about the case. My heart was racing.

When the judge told Mr. and Mrs. McGruder that she didn't have any evidence to convict me, even with Nadia's testimony against me, her disobedient child, I felt like I couldn't be touched. I was free to go.

I smiled and shed a happy tear. Nadia was there in support of the McGruders'. All she did was shake her head when the judge said she had no choice but to let me go.

The McGruders' just cried. I watched them walk out the courtroom with Nadia following behind them.

That was one of the saddest days of my life watching Nadia sit behind the McGruders' bench and looking angry our entire ride home.

That day I wanted to poison every drink in the fridge knowing Nadia would drink at least one of them, and hope she would have to spend a few days in the hospital.

"You know we know you did it," Nadia said on our ride home, not knowing I saw her put the phone on voice record when I was getting in the car.

I looked Nadia straight in her eyes and said, "I don't know what you're talking about."

"Play stupid if you want Shona," Nadia said. "God is watching and He knows everything you do."

I can't stand hearing evil people talk about God. That should be illegal, and there should be a jail sentence behind it. It's not right for people that do evil intentionally to talk about God like He's only good for correcting others and not themselves.

Nadia's never been diagnosed with a mental illness by a doctor. She just chooses to be evil. She obviously never had a day in court because that day in the courtroom was so intense, it's what really gave me the confirmation to swipe the thought of doing more damage.

I don't like my future residing in a stranger's hands. That judge didn't have any reason to care whether or not I spent some years in prison.

Anyways. I kicked my feet up on Mrs. McGruder's desk when she walked to her seat. When she sat down, she threw them off.

"I don't care that the case is closed and there's no way to prove that you tried to kill me and my husband," Mrs. McGruder said. "I know you did it."

I continued to smirk.

I wanted Mrs. McGruder to feel the same pain I felt when she removed me from the team. I actually wanted her to feel worse.

"Why did you do it?" Mrs. McGruder continues. "And it better not have anything to do with you getting removed off of this team."

"Look here Mrs. McGruder," I said. I sat up from my slouched position. "The plan was not to kill you. It was to scare you. You smile as you kick me off the team that I started. I STARTED THIS TEAM! After I tell you I have personal things going on at home, write you notes apologizing, I even apologized to the team like you asked me to. But did you have a heart and give me another chance? Huh? Did you? No. You were just a woman that utilized the power she had to the fullest."

"Shona I gave you plenty of chances," Mrs. McGruder said. "Your attitude was out of control. Your apology was rehearsed."

"Jasmine should have minded her business," I said. "I had a hard time putting together everything I wanted to say to the team, so I got help. That does not mean it wasn't genuine."

I talked to one of my friends about everything I should include in my apology, because I wanted to make sure it was perfect, so I only had to say it once. I saw Jasmine eavesdropping off to the side, but didn't think anything of it because we were best friends.

It wasn't until I got kicked off that someone on the team told me Jasmine told Mrs. McGruder that my apology was rehearsed.

I wish I would've known Jasmine was such a fake friend. Then I would've known she was trying to find something to guarantee me getting kicked off Ann High's step team.

Prior to my termination, Mrs. McGruder gave me a week to figure out a way to show her I knew I was wrong for having an attitude towards people that did nothing to me, all along knowing good and well it didn't matter what I did. She wanted me off of my team, and for Jasmine, who she knew was my best friend, to take my spot.

So not only did Mrs. McGruder want to hurt me by taking away my baby which was the step team, she also wanted the

403

joy of knowing the person I spent most of my time with at school, my best friend Jasmine, would remind me of what I lost every day just by her presence.

Anyways. I sat in Mrs. McGruder's office looking nonchalant and like I didn't care about anything I did.

The only thing I cared about was not having to do time for setting the McGruders' house on fire. I think God looked out for me because He knew they deserved it.

Mrs. McGruder sat looking at me as devilish as she could.

"You took away the only thing I had to look forward to," I said. "The only thing I had to try and get my mind off of the pain my mother was causing me. I know I had a bad attitude! You should have helped me! You should have been a caring adult and tried to help me get through what I was going through! You don't know what I go through at home! You didn't even care! You or your boyfriend..."

Mrs. McGruder cut me off.

"Husband!" Mrs. McGruder said.

"Whatever!" I yelled. "You two think you're funny, smiling and laughing every time I walk past the team perform? Using the steps I made up? Seeing Jasmine get those papers in my face gave you an orgasm, huh?"

Some people are so stupid they really don't put all the pieces together, so I took that particular day as the opportunity I always needed to get off my mind everything I wanted the McGruders' to know.

I knew Mrs. McGruder would tell her husband everything, so I let it all out.

Mrs. McGruder's stupid-self thought that being kicked off my team was the only reason I ambushed her house. That alone made me want to set her office on fire. The thought that her and her stupid husband really thought being terminated alone was the reason they had to move to another house, made me want to choke Mrs. McGruder then hang her from the ceiling.

The McGruders' minds thought on a small scale, except when it came to throwing me off the team. Despite me breaking down everything that led up to my criminal activity, Mrs. McGruder still acted like the dummy I knew she was.

"What are you talking about?" Mrs. McGruder asked.

I didn't want to go into detail, but I definitely wanted to make sure she knew every little thing that led up to her house catching flames for three reasons. One is so she can look back over all the things I say and know her actions were not okay. Two, so I can have a peace of mind. And three, so her and her husband will never make the mistake of throwing someone off the step team again just for an attitude, without trying to figure out what's causing the attitude first, and if they could help the student feel better.

"The day of prom, I went to support one of my friends on the step team at the competition," I said. "Jasmine came over and started talking to my friend, which I know she did on purpose. I kept a smile on my face so your little precious new head coach wouldn't see me sweat. My smile turned into a frown when your boyfriend, excuse me, husband, put his hand right in front of my face and handed Jasmine the judges' critics; and of course he looked me in my eyes and smiled while he did it."

I was angry as hell that day.

"He could have easily went on the other side of Jasmine and handed her the papers, but he just had to come up right beside me to reach in front of me, because he knew it would make me mad because the judges critiques should have been going in my hands," I continued.

I know the judges didn't have much to say, because most of the members on Ann High's step team my senior year were under my wing. There were only three people that were freshmen, and they are probably the only people that the judges had something to say about.

"You're petty Shona. Just petty," Mrs. McGruder angrily said.

I didn't care. I continued to clear my mind. I wanted her to know everything that bothered me, and I wasn't leaving that office until I did.

It didn't cross my mind that she could possibly have a tape recorder going. That's my only regret. If it was ever played for anyone, I would make something up saying it wasn't me, or I was acting.

"And why was Jasmine named a founder of the team in the Step Spectacular program?" I ask. "Huh? What was that about? I am the ONLY one responsible for opening up an opportunity for each and every person that will EVER be a part of Ann High's step team. Jasmine was around, but that's it. She didn't put in any work. I know you knew that."

Mrs. McGruder knew I was the only person that asked Ann High's first advisor, Mrs. Right, to be the advisor for Ann High my freshman year, and the one demonstrating my ability to her. Mrs. Right walked by when I was teaching Jasmine a step and said *we did good.* I asked Mrs. Right to be the advisor and we went to her office and talked about basically just needing a supervisor in the school to watch over us.

"Did you even know if we were home?" Mrs. McGruder asked.

I said no.

"You're insane," Mrs. McGruder said not admitting that she was wrong for giving Jasmine credit where credit was not due.

I was hurt even more that never during the time I was coaching was there a Step Spectacular, but the year I was kicked off they had one. I took it personal because I knew they only created it so they could list Jasmine as a founder to make me angrier, because they knew I would attend, just like I did other performances to support some of my other friends.

I saw the program and ripped it up in my seat, then threw it on the floor before the show even started.

Not only did they list Jasmine as founder, but they listed her name before mine.

"No, you're insane if you think you can play around with somebodies heart and they won't come for you," I said. "You want to know if I had something to do with your house catching flames? You want to hear me *say* it? Yea I had something to do with it, but the case is closed now. So, what can you do?"

I began to walk out of Mrs. McGruder's office, but remembered I forgot to say something.

"Oh, and Mrs. McGruder," I said.

Mrs. McGruder stared devilishly and bitterly at me.

"Be glad you found my little letter when you did," I continued. "Because I was going to go back."

I was lying just to make her angrier and lose more sleep. I caught word from some of the people I knew on the step team that Mrs. McGruder told them she lost sleep many nights after her house caught on fire. But like I said earlier, after that courtroom situation with that mean looking and intense judge, I knew I wasn't going to do anything mischievous again to anyone else.

Now I might think some evil things, I may even hire someone to execute them, but I, Shona Jackson, will never do the dirty work again. However, just like my steps always get better, so do my evil plans. I would've came up with something that was worse than putting flames to a house that I wasn't sure if anyone was in. But thankfully for the McGruders', walking in that courtroom was enough for me. Nadia supporting them was bullshit, but not more than being cut from the team.

I was embarrassed that the judge witnessed my own mother being against me and hoping and praying that I would get thrown in prison. And when I say praying, I mean Nadia was sitting in her seat with her hands together pointing up. I caught her a few times closing her eyes and tilting her head up to the ceiling.

Nadia was quite the actress that day.

It shouldn't be possible for the founder of a team to be removed from it. Ann High and every other place that has organizations needs to add a rule in the guidelines book stating founders are exempt from termination.

I can't believe the McGruders'.

If the McGruders' would've looked like they hated the fact that I was kicked off the team at least once, maybe things would've been different. If they acted like they really hated that I wasn't performing when I watched the step team, instead of smile with evil happiness at my clear anger, then just maybe their house wouldn't have caught flames.

Even though I hated the courtroom process and never wanted to visit a judge, I'm actually happy I did despite how scared and on pins and needles I was all the way up until I was declared innocent. The fire would have been pointless if Mrs. McGruder and her husband didn't know it was me.

A scorned teenager is no one to play with.

I had to let Mrs. McGruder hear it clear as day from my lips that myself and Reeya burned her house down. I honestly didn't expect the house to get ruined to a point where they would have to move.

I wanted to look the McGruders' straight in their eyes in the courtroom under oath and say, "*Yes. I did it.*"

This thought about the courtroom process fucks my mind up

so much that I remember having this thought back in college. Melinda snapped me out of it. I can't even get rid of this memory.

"There's a party upstairs," Melinda opened my door and said. "Thought I'd ask everyone before I throw this flyer out."

Melinda was all of a sudden trying to be nice to me.

"Please don't just take a step in my room," I said. "I don't care if the door is unlocked." I'm never in too good of a mood after thinking of the past with the McGruders'. "Thanks, but I'll pass," I continued.

I didn't trust Melinda so much that I wouldn't be surprised if she had someone create the flyer to lead me down a dark alley.

"Since when did you start caring whether I knew about a party or not?" I asked.

"Since today," Melinda said. "Now do you want the flyer or not?"

"Shut my door," I said. I was happy she snapped me out of my negative thoughts though.

Melinda tossed the flyer in my trash by the door as she left and rolled her eyes.

"Stupid," I silently said as I slammed my head on my pillow.

Melinda always did the little things that she knew would irk someone and not cause a physical altercation, because if the residential assistant stopped by it would be stupid to say, *I fought her because she threw something in my trash.*

I was trying to force myself to sleep that night in my dorm, but couldn't because I couldn't stop thinking about the McGruders'. That thought alone would not let me rest. And on top of that, someone was in the living room playing music really loud, and I heard a bunch of people laughing.

I got up to see what was going on and Melinda, the other two roommates, and about fifteen other people were dancing, taking shots, eating, and smoking, when no one was allowed to smoke in the dorm area.

I couldn't stand my housemates. Melinda wanted me gone because she didn't want me attending her little party and knew the loud music would annoy me.

It was late and I knew someone was going to call campus police. I put on a hoodie, grabbed some clothes for class the next day, and went by Ciera.

I still couldn't fall asleep on her couch.

"I can't sleep," I said to Ciera who was in bed.

"I can sleep on the couch and you can sleep in here," Ciera said.

"It doesn't matter where I'm at," I said. "I'm not going to be able to sleep. You got something to drink?"

"You got class in the morning right?" Ciera asked.

"Yea, but I'll make it," I said. "I'm not gone drink that much."

Ciera poured us both a small amount of liquor and mixed it with juice.

"You alright?" Ciera asked as she handed me my drink and sat close to me.

"Yes," I said.

I felt like it was the perfect time to reveal to my best friend one of my deepest darkest secrets. I took a sip of my drink and told her about Nadia, the McGruders', Jasmine, my step termination from Ann High, and my visit to the McGruders' house.

"Dang girl," Ciera said. "I had no idea."

"It's not something I like to talk about," I said.

"Well, it's over now," Ciera said. "I'm happy you got off, and I'm happy you taught them McGruders' a lesson. Now it's time for you to remind them of the mistake they made and win The Big Bang Step Off. Show them and Jasmine that they could take

410

away your team and your spot in high school, but they can never take away your passion. You are the best, and there's nothing they can do about it."

Ciera gave me a hug. I dried my face.

I was so glad I told Ciera and she knew everything about me. She's always trusted me, and it kind of hurt that I didn't trust her with certain information about me. I just hate telling people things because I fear that if we fall out, they will throw it in my face. I shouldn't have put Ciera in a box just because of raggedy *Ann* Jasmine. Ciera's cool, loyal, trustworthy, and a good friend. She's always had my back if anything bad popped off between me and someone else without knowing if it was my fault or not. I love her so much.

Ciera's calling me now.

"Are they ready?" Ciera asks talking about my Luminous LA team.

I smile.

"It's about to go down for real," I say.

26

I smile as I walk up to Professor Tobin to give him a script that I've been working on for almost a year. He's going to edit it for me.

"Told you I would do it," I say with a smirk and leave the classroom.

I wrote my script on a teenager that was removed from her high school step team and sought vengeance on the people that did it. I ended it with being proven innocent by the judge and watching the McGruders', who are the Jefferson's in the story, walk out the courtroom frowning while I am smiling at them.

After leaving my old professor, I head to Mission High early.

Sheela sits with me on the bleachers on the football field. The football team is practicing and the cheerleaders are rehearsing on the track. A few students are sprinting and jogging on the track as well. There's people sitting with their cliques eating and having a good time too.

Observing these kids reminds me of my high school days and how much I miss attending Cupperton. I miss how much fun I used to have in high school prior to my removal, but I would never want to return to it just because of the bad memories floating through it.

I still don't like the sight of the McGruders' to this date. They're evil old people that get happiness from making teenagers they don't like bitter.

"So why did you call me out here before practice?" Sheela asks.

"I just wanted to talk to you in private," I say. "Is everything okay with you?"

Sheela looks away.

"Look, I know it's not my business whatever is making you look so mean and have attitudes at times, but I did want to at least try to get you to open up to me. Believe me when I say you can trust me."

Sheela knows I know something is up with her because of the sporadic attitudes she's been having since day one at practice.

"No," Sheela says.

Desperate, I still try to get it out of her.

"Sheela please tell me what's bothering you?" I ask. "Maybe I can help."

"No. I like to try and fix things myself," Sheela says.

Even though she doesn't tell me, I already know what the problem is. I had Ms. Ross do a little snooping on her own because I wasn't sure if Sheela was suicidal, and I didn't want to take a chance on losing my student.

Sheela is smart and beautiful, and I would hate to lose her, and on top of that find out it was because of something I could've helped her with.

Ms. Ross went into the principal's office at Mission High and expressed her concern for Sheela, and said she wanted to figure out a way to help her, but she needed to know what's going on with her.

The principal told her Sheela is tired of being tossed around from foster home to foster home.

I know that's not the easiest thing to talk about. Sheela was taken away from her parents at five years old due to them being caught giving her marijuana. They had already been arrested multiple times for possession.

Sheela never tells anyone about it because it is a soft spot, and she doesn't want anyone to use this delicate information to try and hurt her. Her attitude is the reason she keeps being bounced around. She's only been attending Mission High for six months thus far.

The principal told Ms. Ross everything. Especially when she

told him she would call Mr. Stephen and have Sheela removed, which wouldn't happen because Luminous LA wouldn't allow it. Ms. Ross lied to get Mission High's principal to spill the beans on everything we needed to know. He knows Sheela is a stellar student and didn't want her to be taken out of the program, which he clearly wasn't that familiar with since he believed Ms. Ross could have Sheela removed for just an attitude alone.

Even though Sheela won't open her mouth and tell me what's going on so I can let her know she's not the only person being moved all the time and there's people going through a lot worse than her, I still try to soften her up a little.

"You know I used to be just like you," I say.

"How?" Sheela asks like she doesn't believe me.

"I needed help, but didn't want to ask anyone for it," I say. "My attitude got me kicked off my high school step team, got the cops called on me, caused me to do crazy stuff, and have a miserable senior year in high school."

Even though I got on Mrs. McGruder for her and her husband not trying to figure out what was wrong with me, I will admit that I never asked them for help. I just expected them to give it to me being that they were older, and that could be what Sheela thinks about me and Ms. Ross.

Sheela looks shocked when I admit I was removed from my team.

"I don't want you to have to go through anything I went through," I say. "I wish my high school advisor would have sat me down and tried to figure out what was wrong with me, but she didn't. She just kept giving me a lot of chances to try and fix my attitude without knowing what the problem was. So, when she got fed up with my attitude, she kicked me off the team. The team *I* created."

I quiet down for a bit watching the students on the field

414

enjoy their extracurricular activities. I remember the days I used to mope around high school when I looked at the members that remained on the team every day because most of them were my friends. My friends knew I was hurt so bad that they wouldn't even talk about the team in front of me unless they were saying something bad like: *step team sucks now,* or *it's boring,* because they could tell by my demeanor that I was still bitter about being detached.

"Do you want to be on this team still?" I ask Sheela.

"Yes," Sheela says.

"So act like it," I say. "I love having you on it. You got a lot of talent. But I need you to fix your attitude because it can be contagious. If you don't want to tell me what's going on, that's fine, but talk to someone you feel comfortable with releasing your inner emotions to."

Sheela laughs when I say *inner emotions.*

"There goes a smile," I say. "I will be honest with you, I hate that I got kicked off my step team, and I was angry when I found out my mother influenced my advisors decisions to take me off, but I am glad at the same time the McGruders' called the cops on me."

"Why?" Sheela confusedly asks.

"A, I learned that I should never allow someone to get me to act in a way that can put me in prison," I say.

I let Sheela know that not only would the McGruders', Nadia, and Jasmine have had the joy of playing a part in getting me removed, but they would've been granted more happiness if I would've gotten thrown in prison. They would've loved calling all over the city telling everyone that I was locked up. Nadia would have definitely loved it. I already know she called everyone when I was *accused* of burning down the McGruders' house, and told them *I told you so* when it came to her lies about me being a disobedient child. I know she enjoyed that I gave her a reason to make everyone believe everything she's ever lied to them about me.

"B, I know to keep my issues from my private life outside of school, and now that would be work for me," I say. "Plus, I would rather learn things the hard way, especially ones involving the cops, as a minor as opposed to an adult. I don't want you to have to deal with anything like I have; I just want to share my story so that maybe it can help you. Try to leave the attitude from your personal life out of practice, alright? You're still here and working hard at practice, so that tells me you're one strong individual and better than any negative situation that comes your way. When I was kicked off my team I could barely function, so you're definitely better than me. I learned that I need to practice self-control, because at the end of the day, no one cares where your life ends up, or what you're going through. You got to look out for yourself. I know it's hard, but do the best you can. I am willing to work with you if you work with me."

"Alright Coach," Sheela says. I give her a hug and we head to the theater.

"Aye Coach," Sheela says on the way. "Why did the cops get called on you?"

"Sheela, if I give you that hardcore information, you gone have to detail for me everything that's bothering you," I say at the theater doors.

"Coach do you and your advisor still talk anymore?" Sheela asks. I close the theater door and talk to her in the hallway. "Because I don't think I could do it," Sheela continues.

"No. But if I saw her today, I would never thank her for calling the cops even though I really needed that life experience badly," I say. "Look at me." Sheela looks me in my eyes. "If you ever need to talk, I am here," I say. "Believe me, I am very wise for my age. I been through a lot growing up. If you need someone to talk to, I'm here to listen. I don't like to gossip, and I'm not one to spread peoples' business because I don't want no one to do that to me. Alright?"

"Alright," Sheela says.

Sheela and I walk in the theater while everyone is stretching. I see Kiara catch Jose staring at her. He quickly turns away and snaps out of it once she smiles at him. He tries to play off his embarrassment by practicing some of the step movements. Kiara blushes as she turns back to the front.

I'm smiling and shaking my head. My students are so cute.

I walk on stage and get straight to business.

"Alright you guys," I say. "The show is coming up. Let's go. We're going to be learning some new steps. Let's get down to business."

While Sheela comes on stage to join everyone, I notice Alexis is looking uneasy for some reason.

"Get loose. Do a few stretches," I tell everyone. "Alexis, let me talk to you for a minute." We take a seat. "Ms. Ross talked to me about the fight." Ms. Ross gave me a call the day after it happened. "You remember the fight within the first quarter of the game? That has got to be a record," I continue. "But are you okay?"

"Yea I'm fine," Alexis says. "I got suspended for a few games. Please let me still do the performance."

"You can still do the performance," I say. "Stay out of trouble."

"I try to, but people make it hard for me," Alexis says. "It's not easy when you're talented and beautiful. You know that Coach."

"Thanks for the compliment," I say. "You're right. It's not

easy when you have beauty and talent, and definitely not in this jealous world we live in. I know you were defending yourself and hey, if it means anything to you, I don't think you should've gotten suspended for any games being that you were standing your ground."

"I don't even know who that girl was," Alexis says.

"And you don't need to," I say. "Forget about her. You got more important things to worry about, and at the end of the day, Mission High still beat my alma mater, so you're still on that girl's mind."

"Wait, you graduated from Ann High?" Alexis asks.

"Let's go," I say getting up. We go back on stage. "Focus is key as always," I continue. "The show is around the corner. There's no time for playing around. Follow my lead and pay attention."

I'm teaching new moves because it's better safe, than sorry. If the McGruders' and Jasmine do decide to use, add to, or remix anything Ann High saw at the competition, then so be it. I always make up a step that is better than my last.

The advantage I'll always have is I'm a natural stepper. I can make up a step in my sleep or lying on my back. I don't even have to get up or move. All I have to do is get up to make sure I can actually do what I visualized in my head, and at the pace I did it with the movements.

Everyone learns the new step pretty quick. Everyone has all the basics step movements down, so they catch on fast, and have been for a while.

After I finish the choreography, I place my students in different formations.

After they practice moving side to side with the beat and not looking down or at anyone else, I tell them, "Break off into groups and help each other with whatever you're struggling with."

Jose, Michael, and Jason stay with me. I make sure their arms extend all the way out and their heads turn sharply with the movements. The boys are on point. They don't miss a single beat.

I move around from group to group and the girls are doing a great job helping each other as well.

Sheela is helping Casey and Kiara.

"Make sure you remember not to let your thumbs out when you're clapping under your legs," Sheela says.

I make my way to Alexis' group and she's going through the step in slow motion with the twins and Delia.

"Great job girls," I say.

I go to Alina's group and she's watching Mya and Aisha go through a step. Once Mya and Aisha finish, I have all three of them do the routine.

I tell the girls they did great and they slap hands and give each other hugs.

"We're almost as good as you Coach," Aisha says.

"Almost as good?" I rhetorically ask. "You all are almost better than me."

And I'm not lying, trying to make them arrogant, or buck their heads up so they can become conceited.

"Stop playing," Mya says. "We will never be as good as you."

"Mya honey, I would not lie to you," I say. "I give credit where credit is due, and you all have gotten so much better."

I almost shed a tear.

"Aw," Alina says. "Coach is about to cry."

"No I'm not," I say and hold in my tears. "But I am really proud to get the opportunity to work with each and every one here."

Alina, Mya, and Aisha give me a hug.

419

"We're happy to have gotten to work with one of the best steppers in the world," Aisha says.

"Best stepper and choreographer," Mya says. When the girls release from me, I go back over to the boys and watch them do one of the steps. They are doing great with their necks snapping each and every direction, voices loud, thumbs never getting out of place, crisp claps, energy, and facials on point.

"Everyone come here please," I say when the boys finish.

Everyone huddles around the boys.

I have the boys do the same step again for the girls.

The girls applaud them for their deliverance.

I want my girls to be sassy and cute with their steps, but be able to switch it up and step like men with hardcore faces and intensity.

"Coach, do a step for us," Mya says.

"At full speed," Jose says.

Of course everyone cheers, motivates, encourages, and insists that I do one of the steps by myself. Without hesitation, I hop in the center of everyone.

I erupt into one of the steps that I taught Legit. Everyone looks on amazed. I freestyle some moves at the end of the routine and end slowly moving my arms down in fists to my side.

"You could do a whole show by yourself," Casey says with an impressed tone.

"Alright, you guys can go back to your groups," I say.

I just wanted the girls to watch the boys so they could match their intensity level.

At the end of practice, everyone comes together and we put our hands in and say our chant.

I shout, "Mission!"

Everyone says, "Step Team!"

I chant again, "Mission!"

Everyone says, "Step Team!"

I energetically say, "Let's do this! A few more practices left baby! We need to go hard! Forget about Ann High coming to scout us! They don't got nothing on this team! We gone hit them with some moves they never knew existed!"

"Let's go!" Sheela says.

"I have faith in this team!" I yell. *"On a Mission* on three! One, two, three!"

Everyone says, "On a Mission!"

27

I'm at Dayla and Isyss' house. Isyss has more information to give me about Jasmine and Mrs. McGruder.

"Jasmine was walking back and forth in Ann High School's auditorium and waiting for the bell to ring so her team would show up," Isyss says. "I heard her say the competition is heavily on her mind. She would hate for the worst to happen, which is Mission placing higher than her team."

Isyss says that Jasmine doesn't care about getting first place; she just cares about beating my team. She knows I hate her for letting go of our friendship the day she took my spot. She also knows she needs to prove to the McGruders' that she is a better coach than me, and always has been, despite not being head captain until I was terminated.

"That girl is full of shit," Dayla says.

"She has something to prove to the McGruders', and to herself," I say. "I didn't know she was someone that could make herself believe a lie she made up. She will never be better than me."

Isyss says Jasmine first entered The Big Bang Step Off to allow her students to compete on a bigger scale against step teams from all over the U.S., but once Mrs. McGruder told her I had a team in the competition, it was no longer about a nice outing and experience for Ann High.

"Jasmine's entire being is now focused on proving to the McGruders', you, and herself that she's better than you at choreography and turning rookie steppers into pros in a short period of time," Isyss says. She says Jasmine's been working day and night to come up with step routines, chants, and formations that she feels will be better than anything I can come up with.

"Beating Mission High at The Big Bang Step Off means more to Jasmine than anything in the world right now," Isyss continues. "She wants to keep the last laugh, like she did when her and you graduated from Ann High. She definitely wasn't expecting you to have an opportunity at getting the last one." Isyss says Jasmine wants and needs to beat Mission High so she can forever have the victory over me. She doesn't care if she never wins another competition in her life. If she wins the first Big Bang Step Off, she will be content. She won't even care if she ever comes across me and the team she's coaching again, or if she herself even coaches a day after the competition.

Isyss says that Jasmine just wants to beat me with the choreography she made up herself, and prove that she's the better stepper, and she's the choreographer.

Not me.

"Ann High's students came in the auditorium and Jasmine had them sit down in the audience seats so she could give them a pep speech," Isyss says. "She wanted to get them as excited as she could to win the competition. They don't have the slightest clue her focus is not on them enjoying themselves, but on making her statements to their advisors and you. Jasmine no longer cares about her members. She just cares to beat you Shona."

Isyss says Jasmine told her team it was crunch time. She said they have seen one team, but there will be better ones. She said they needed to practice hard. She didn't want any complaining, laziness, or breaks. Then she rudely asked the team if they understood her. They all said yes.

"Jasmine had everyone come together in a huddle," Isyss says. "They connected their fists."

Isyss says Jasmine had everyone count to three and everyone said *Ann*. They stomped twice and said *You know*. They went to their positions. Jasmine was smiling a lot while Ann's steppers practiced their routine. She is very confident that what she put together will outdo anything I put together. While she watched her team do everything she's taught them perfectly, it seemed like she lost any worry she once had. She gave the choreography everything she had. She studied fraternities and sororities and even regular step teams from across the country. She saw the things that made the crowd go wild and the things that made them yawn.

"Jasmine's expecting you to look high and low in an attempt to find a step that was copied, but you won't find anything because everything Jasmine's taught for The Big Bang Step Off is original," Isyss says. "Jasmine has two freshmen and everyone else has stepped before, been in numerous competitions. She's confident you will have a bunch of first timers because Mission High has never had a step team before. She thinks for sure the team of rookies will shrivel up at The Big Bang Step Off, which is more intense than the dance competition."

"Jasmine has trained her mind to believe that she alone is responsible for her own success as a stepper," I say. "She no longer had respect for anything I did to help her after she took my head captain spot."

"She kept making her team do steps over again because she liked how they sounded," Isyss says. "When they got tired from doing the steps, she would get mad. Ann High just continued on with their routine."

Isyss says Jasmine is ecstatic that she finally came up with a routine on her own. She wishes she would've always came up with her own moves, especially when I was still at Ann High. Isyss says Jasmine feels like she didn't know her own strength or capability.

"I mean, just watching and listening to Jasmine, she seems completely self-centered, self-absorbed, conceited, and selfish," Isyss says. "She's convinced herself that she would've been just as great at stepping and coaching whether or not she ever would've met a girl named Shona Jackson in her life."

Isyss says Jasmine walked through her students' routine while they continued practicing. Isyss says that Jasmine is overly confident that what she's done will send me home after the competition just as angry as the day I was kicked off of Ann High's step team.

28

I go through some old photos before bed of my journey with Ann High's step team. I flip through pages of me, my friends, and step mates at parties, football games, volleyball games, and concerts.

I get to the section I labeled *Freshman Year Step Team* and look at how happy I was with my team in our Barbie doll uniforms.

I get to the sophomore year section and we're in our school girl uniforms backstage before the performance.

I get to the junior year section and smile at the jailbird uniforms we wore. The smile goes away when I see a photo of just me and Jasmine in our Ann High long sleeve purple step shirts together. I look at myself, then at Jasmine and smirk.

This was one of the many days since I began Ann High's step team that Jasmine had me fooled thinking she really was my friend, but really was just pretending until she was granted the opportunity to take my position as head captain.

If I was still on the team senior year, no one would respect Jasmine because they would know that someone that is better and more educated about stepping was in their presence.

When I get to my senior year pictures, I look angry because I am in a picture with the step team in their long sleeve Ann High black shirts, but I don't have one on.

Jasmine's not in the photo because I hated her, but I did snap one with my friends that were still on the team, and still respected me as head coach even though I was no longer a part of them.

I took the picture just so the McGruders' would think that I didn't care about being kicked off of the team. This photo was prior to me and Reeya setting their house on fire, which automatically told them that I did care and was truly hurt that I was denied coaching and performing with the team I created, during what I hoped would be my best year in school.

Senior year, the last required year of school for everyone, is supposed to be the most fun, memorable, and craziest in a good way, of all the years of required school, and yet mine was just so miserable because I got kicked off of the team I created.

Jasmine got the last laugh in high school, but I'll get the last laugh at The Big Bang Step Off. No matter what routine she steals, or if she comes up with her own choreography, she'll never be better than me. Most importantly, she'll never be me, or get the respect I have at Ann High as a choreographer.

Jasmine is nowhere near my level.

The next couple of weeks, Mission perfects our routine. I am ecstatic about their progress. They have come a long way. They went from not being able to do one simple stomp and clap, to being able to pick up eight counts very quickly.

I make sure everyone is in their exact spots and hits every move properly. Anytime someone stomps off beat, which is very rare being that I now have a team of professionals, I make them start over. Anytime someone says a phrase in the wrong part of the routine, I make them start over. If I feel that not enough energy is being given, I make them start over. Especially the last couple of weeks before the show which I entitle: *Go Hard or Get Out*. The team titled it *Hell Week* because every little thing, whether it was a facial being dropped or someone not saying a word, they started over.

During these weeks, I made my Luminous LA team stop at random parts of the routine just so they could hold their positions. I made them hold the squat position so their legs could gain more strength. I even made them run around the track a few times.

By the end of every practice, everyone was drenched with

427

sweat and tired beyond reason. They didn't even talk to each other when they got their things and struggled to leave out.

Mr. Stephen pops in a few practices and observes. He is very happy with what he sees.

Our relationships are becoming stronger as a team. Everyone has a lot more patience when they don't understand one of their teammates' actions or what they say.

Sheela no longer comes in with an attitude. I can tell she is still a bit uneasy, but I can appreciate that she is fighting to control her attitude.

During Mission's last few weeks of rehearsals, Jared comes by a few nights to keep me company. We play cards, I make dinner, and we watch movies. I always wondered if I was wrong about him. Could he actually want a relationship with me? We did meet at a club. I always tell myself to stop playing; he's just doing and saying what's right until he gets what he wants. But what if I'm wrong? Just play it safe I tell myself. Don't develop any feelings. I have a man anyways and our relationship is strong. I love Austin. It's just something came over me, and I want to have a little more fun these days.

My mind doesn't know what to think of Jared though. The kisses get longer every time I see him. I have to pull it together. He's only in town for a few weeks.

I go to a friend's house to have him put together a CD for Mission's show. I've been using my iPod thus far for rehearsals so Mission could practice their entrance, exit, and a few transitions, but The Big Bang Step Off requires a CD to be handed into the DJ before the show, so he can download the songs from each team onto his computer ahead of time.

29

I watch Mission High run through their performance for the last time.

"Keep it up!" I shout to them so they know I'm proud and that they are doing great.

"Everyone bring it in," I say when they finish.

I do slow claps as they walk to me. Jason decides to join in as he walks to the huddle and everyone else follows his lead. The claps get faster as everyone gets closer. We begin shouting.

We are pumped for the performance. Sheela is so pumped she is jumping up and down.

"Go ahead and clap it up for yourselves," I say. Everyone claps faster. "We have come a long way," I say. "I know everyone's ready. Don't be nervous."

"I'm never nervous," Mya says.

"Ready is my middle name," Kiara says.

They make me smile.

"Make sure you all get a lot of rest these next two days," I say. "One, two, three!"

"On a Mission!" everyone shouts.

Keasha and Desiree have a team dinner at their house. Desiree has me on video chat so I can observe their gathering.

Keasha and Desiree's mom, Ms. Armstrong, brings out a strawberry cake while Mission's team sits at the dining room table in her house and finishes their lasagna and salad at their team dinner.

I suggested the team have a bonding night together before their show. I had Ms. Ross convince Delia's mom to let her attend the dinner.

"Tastes good Ms. Armstrong," Jason says.

"Has anyone ever told you it's rude to talk with your mouth full?" Casey asks.

Jason acts like he didn't hear her and continues to eat.

Ms. Armstrong places a slice of cake on everyone's plates.

"Does everything taste alright?" Ms. Armstrong asks.

Everyone says *yes*.

"Does anyone want any more of anything?" Ms. Armstrong asks.

A few people say *yes*.

Alexis grabs Desiree's phone, laughs, and whispers to Alina, "Do you want a little more, since you are eating for two now?"

Alina looks at Alexis seriously and shakes her head no. She doesn't want the entire team knowing.

"Alright enjoy yourselves," Ms. Armstrong says and heads back to her room. She is just as beautiful as her two daughters.

"So, I was thinking," Alexis says placing Desiree's phone back in a place where I can see everyone. "Let's come up with some line names."

"Some what?" Kiara asks.

"Line names," Alexis says. "You know, nicknames for each one of us."

"We're not in college," Casey says.

"So," Alexis says.

"So, we're not in college and I heard they take offense to that stuff," Casey says.

"Who's they?" Alexis asks.

"Sororities and fraternities," Casey says.

"Who cares," Alexis says. "Besides, half of them are hazing and getting suspended, if not banned permanently. Hell, some of them are accidently killing their pledges."

"Watch your mouth in my mother's house," Keasha sternly says.

I'm just listening not giving a damn what the girls decide to do.

430

"Well I personally agree with her," Jason says. "My sister's sorority was banned for hazing their pledges in the ocean. One of them drowned."

Everyone looks at Jason in pure shock.

"This happened three years after my sister graduated," Jason continues. "She had nothing to do with it. She said they change their initiation every year."

"You see," Alexis says. "We don't need to take their advice, nor care about what they have to say. I personally do not care about anything concerning the college frats and sororities; that includes their thoughts and opinions. Did you guys already forget those ugly witches that tried to jump Coach at the clothes drive?"

Everyone looks angry remembering the fight between Queela and her girls. I don't think I ever told Mission High officially that I'm a member of Alpha Eta Nu as well. I don't care though. I'm just listening to them not caring what they decide to do as far as the names go. They need to enjoy this night in its entirety.

"Exactly," Alexis continues.

"I think you should be called *Her Cockiness,*" Jose says.

"I think that works for you too," Jason says. "I like it."

"Why does that suit me?" Alexis asks.

"You are always bragging about all your talents," Jose says. "When I first met you, the first thing you said when you introduced yourself was: *My name is Alexis Thomas. I am a freshman. I am on the Culinary Arts team, head captain of the cheerleading team during football season, I also play basketball, and am the future valedictorian.* You said the same thing when you introduced yourself to Coach."

"Yea, you introduced yourself to me that way too," Alina says. "Did you rehearse that?"

"No," Alexis smiles. "But I do like the title *Her Cockiness*. I'm conceited, with a reason. Okay next, Alina. I think you should be called *Quiet Time.* You talk really low sometimes. We struggle to hear you at times."

"I think *Question* fits her better," Aisha says.

"No, I think I like *Quiet Time* better," Alina says. "I think it's pretty funny too."

"I want to be called *Diamond,* and I think my sister should be called *Jewel,*" Desiree says. "We are what every girl wants to be, and we shine always."

"Oh, I like that. I agree," Keasha excitedly says. "All in favor, say *I.*"

All the girls look at Desiree and Keasha and look away without saying a word.

"I want my name to be *Strictly Business,*" Michael says. "I like to get things done. There's no playing around when it comes to business."

"I want my name to be *Unbreakable,*" Sheela says. "No explanation needed."

"You guys can call me *The Baddest,*" Kiara says.

"*Zero Tolerance,*" Mya says.

"*Poison Ivy,*" Casey says. "I look and seem like I won't mess you up, but if you touch the right spot, whether it's physically or mentally in my nerves the wrong way, I will beat you into next week."

"*Anaconda,*" Jose says. Everyone looks at him. "I would be happy to prove I deserve that name, but that would be inappropriate," Jose continues.

"*Pretty Girl,*" Delia says.

"*Money Machine,*" Jason says.

"Why *Money Machine*?" Alexis asks. "You got money?"

"No, I'm predicting the future," Jason says.

"Well I want to be called *Baby Blue* because it's my favorite color," Aisha says.

"Wow Aisha," Alexis says. "You officially have the most boring name out of the crew."

"Whatever Alexis," Aisha says.

"Okay, now we need a crew name in general," Alexis says.

"I think Mission is cool and I like when we say: *On a mission*," Kiara says.

"Yea, that's cool, but let's think of something better," Alexis says. "Just for us. Not school affiliated."

"New Step Movement," Mya suggests.

No one says anything.

"Divine Stomp," Jose says.

No one says anything.

"Louisiana Steppers," Michael says.

"S.I.P." Sheela says.

"What?" everyone says inquisitively.

"S.I.P." Sheela says again. "Step Into Perfection. That's what we do."

Everyone is quiet for a minute.

"I like it. It's different," Casey says.

"So let's propose a toast to S.I.P., and make sure we *step into perfection* at The Big Bang Step Off," Alexis says.

Everyone raises their glasses of soda and share a toast.

After eating, everyone plays Dance Phase, a video game.

Ms. Armstrong and her oldest daughter check in on everyone.

"Your coach really has done a great job with you guys," Ms. Armstrong says. Her and her oldest daughter go back in her room and shut the door.

After the team finishes dancing, they go outside and run through their routine in the driveway. They use the light in the garage.

Neighbors and people walking by watch and smile.

Jason pumps up a water balloon with the hose and throws it at Mya, who picks up the hose and starts squirting it at him with her finger making the water squirt out all over.

Jason runs down the sidewalk until the water can no longer reach him.

The night turns into one big water balloon fight.

Mission High enjoys an evening of laughter and fun.

I call Sheela the next day.

"Hey Sheela how are you?" I ask her over the phone.

"I'm doing good. Did you enjoy watching us at our team dinner?" Sheela asks.

"I sure did. Is everyone excited for the performance?" I ask.

"Of course," Sheela says.

"What did I miss at the dinner when I stepped away from the phone?" I ask.

"The lasagna, salad, and strawberry cake were bomb as hell," Sheela says.

I'm jealous. I love me some strawberry cake.

"Was the cake from scratch?" I ask.

"Yep, so was the lasagna," Sheela says. "And the salad had everything from banana chips, to tomatoes, to raisins, to eggs..."

I cut her off.

"Okay okay. You're making me hungry, and I'm too lazy to prepare all that," I say.

Sheela laughs.

"Did you like our line names?" Sheela asks.

"I heard some of them. They are cool. What's yours again?" I ask.

"Unbreakable," Sheela says.

"I love that. It fits you perfectly," I say.

"Hey Coach, can I ask you something?" Sheela asks.

"Yes, wasup?" I ask.

"Did you have a line name on your college step team?" Sheela asks.

"I sure did," I say. I assume she's talking about the most recent team I had and not from fifteen years ago. *"The One,"* I say.

"That's the coldest name I ever heard," Sheela says.

I smile.

Ironically that's the name my no good team, Legit, came up with for me. If I remember correctly, Regina came up with it for me, and everyone cosigned immediately.

Sheela is right. It is the coldest name anyone could have. I love it. I don't care that it came from those fools. That's going to be my name on any team that I join or coach.

Sheela and I hang up and I go in my room and look up at the ceiling. I think back on how I even made it to this point. Watching the dance competition. Getting the business card. Emailing Mr. Stephen. Meeting Mission's step team. Mission's first day of practice and their very low skillset. The improvements. The huddles at the end of practices. The attitudes. The trip to Greg Johnson University. The clothes drive. The fight with some of my sorority at the clothes drive. The team defending me against Greg Johnson University's dance team. Talking to Sheela on the football field. Mr. Stephen coming to observe the team. And the final practice.

It's amazing how one day changed my entire life.

I sit on my bed and say aloud, "Show time."

30

Me, Ms. Ross, and Mission High stare out the windows on the bus as we wait for the traffic guards to direct the driver to the drop-off spot at Louisiana's Dance College (L. D. C.).

The campus is flooded with people. Huge banners welcome all the participating parties.

L. D. C.'s sororities and fraternities stroll on the sidewalks and do their calls while huge crowds surround them. Vendors sell bacon hot dogs with the onions, pico de gallo, and avocado. Kids swarm the fruit vendors for the mangos, pineapples, strawberries, kiwi, and oranges' bags. There's even a taco truck selling everything from tacos to chili cheese fries to double cheeseburgers. L. D. C. even has their band out on both sides of the sidewalk as the teams walk onto the campus.

It looks like one big festival on the entire campus. Everyone's dancing, having great conversations, and meeting other people from other teams and areas.

It's one big party.

The bus pulls off and stops close to the gym area where competitors sign in and the staff makes sure everyone is present, and gives wristbands to family and friends of the participants.

"Alright, grab your things and follow me," I say to my team.

While waiting in line behind other teams, we continue to take notice of our surroundings. It's obvious that this is one of the most active places any of us has ever seen.

Jason hangs up his phone.

"My mom says her and the other parents are looking for parking," Jason says.

I notice Ann High walk in the building next to the gym.

"Don't worry Coach," Kiara says putting her arm around me. "We gone do this. And we gone do it right."

"That's right," Mya says. "We ready."

We finally make it to the front of the line.

"Mission High," one of the staff members says.

"Yes," I say.

"This is Thomas," the staff member says pointing to a male in a Big Bang Step Off shirt. "He will be your escort for today. If you have any questions, feel free to ask him. If he doesn't know the answer, he will be sure to find it, right?"

Thomas nods his head.

"Right this way please," Thomas says.

He leads us into the building next to the gym.

The hallways of L. D. C. are lit with white and red bulbs. Disco balls flash from the corners. Adults, teenagers, and toddlers dance around inside and outside as the loud music plays.

Thomas leads us up the stairs to our classroom which is decorated just like the hallways minus the flashing lights. As soon as we walk in, there's a huge banner that says *Welcome Mission.* Everyone is astounded. We get settled.

"Put your things down," I say. "Let's take some before and after pictures. Let's take one now, and another after you put on the uniforms."

I had everyone wear grey sweatpants with black t-shirts to the show.

Before me and Sheela hung up the other night, I had her text me the line names everyone came up with, and put them on the back of their shirts. She told me about their group name, *Step Into Perfection,* as well.

I had the designer put a logo on the front of the shirts with two steppers in different positions with their group name.

It was a hassle trying to find someone to do the shirts for me, and in such a short time, but it's true what they say: money talks.

I had to use money from my savings to pay for the shirts.

I want the first experience at The Big Bang Step Off to be as perfect as I can make it. This is my last performance and day with Mission, and I want it to be perfect.

No one's make-up and hair is done. This way no one has a clue of what our theme is.

Mission High members form two rows in front of the banner. I pull out my phone.

"Would you like me to take it?" Thomas asks.

I hand my camera to him and say, "Thanks."

"Can you take one with mine too?" Casey asks.

Sure enough everyone hands Thomas their phones and cameras and he takes photos for us all before he exits the room.

"I'll be right back," Thomas says.

Alina sits down at one of the desks and Casey sits on top of it.

"I'm getting nervous now," Alina says.

"You'll be alright," Jose says. "We all got a little jitters just like we did when we were at the dance competition."

"Believe me," I intervene, "Once you begin, the nerves will go away. You will be fine. Just have fun out there."

I pull out bags of wigs.

"Alright girls, you should start putting on your uniforms, or at least the tops so we can start doing hair," I say.

"Boys can you step in the hallway for a minute?" Casey asks.

"Actually, go to the restroom and put your uniforms on so we don't have to do this twice," I say.

Jason, Jose, and Michael grab their uniforms and go to the bathroom.

The girls put on their black and white corset with a black flared skirt that has white flares underneath it. They put on sashes that say *prom queen* over their shoulder. They wear black stalking's that have horizontal cuts all over them with

438

black boots.

They're Zombie Queens!

Delia puts hers on as well for team spirit.

I go in the hallway after a few minutes and my boys are waiting. They look so nice. Jason, Michael and Jose are in their battered suits. They have a black jacket with a white boutonniere, with a white dress shirt and black bow tie, skull cufflinks and jagged hems on their shirts and jackets. The pants are distraught also to complete the fresh-from-the-grave look.

"Y'all ready?" Jason asks.

"Hell yea," Jose says. "I invited everyone I know at school."

"So two people from Mission are coming," Michael laughs.

"Very funny," Jose says. "All the cheerleaders, all the volleyball team. Just know when you see them, it's because of me. Maybe a few of our female members are responsible too. And while you laughing, keep them thumbs in," Jose says to Michael.

"Yea, I got some tape in my bag if you need me to tape it to your index finger," Jason laughs.

"Yea whatever. I got this," Michael says.

I let the boys in. The girls pair up and put their curly wigs on. They puff out the wigs everywhere except the bangs so the hair can look a little rough.

I'm so happy sitting at the front desk observing my students. I feel like we're all family. It's unfortunate that we've gotten so close and today is most likely the last day we will see each other.

Keasha does her sister's hair and says, "I can't wait to go on stage."

"I can't wait to hear all those people cheering for us," Desiree says. "I love how they decorated."

"Me too," I agree.

"Coach you got a man?" Sheela asks.

"Don't worry about what I got," I say. "I got confidence in each and every one of you, and that's all y'all need to know."

"Aye Coach, will we see you again after the show?" Alina asks.

"Of course," I say. "You guys have my number, just call me whenever."

I'm so happy to hear that they want to keep in contact with me. Today may not be the last time I see them after all.

"We can kick it sometime," I say.

"How old are you?" Jose asks.

"Thirty-five," I say. "I'm old."

Sheela is just like me when I was a senior. Had a lot going on and a bad attitude. I'm glad I took the time out to talk to her before she got so bad that I would have had to talk to Mr. Stephen about her. I would hate to do that to any of my students, and definitely my seniors. Plus, Sheela seems just as passionate about step as me these days. There's no telling if she would have developed the same insanity I did if she got kicked off the team.

The girls finish touching up their wigs as I go around and put white zombie make-up all over everyone's faces.

Everyone takes pictures in groups, then go through certain parts of the steps. Some people practice alone, and others practice in groups.

"It's hot in this room," Kiara says.

"Who you telling?" Aisha says.

"Try to open those windows," I suggest.

Michael and Jose open the windows.

"Look at all these people waiting outside?" Michael says. We all go to the windows to see.

The line is moving slowly because the staff are trying to find seats to accommodate everyone.

"I will be right back," I say.

I head toward the bathroom and as I'm walking down the hallway, Jasmine approaches and slows down when she sees me.

A boy walks up behind Jasmine and asks her, "Aye Coach, is this our room?"

"To the right, yea," Jasmine tells him.

The young man proceeds to the room.

"It's not nice to see you, but at the same time, I *love* that we are competing against each other so you can know that I was better than you all along," Jasmine conceitedly says. "And let's not forget, a way better coach for Ann High than you ever were."

I keep a straight face.

I proceed to the restroom without saying a word. After all, I see myself as a mentor to my students now. What would it look like if they caught me arguing in the hallway?

Jasmine stomps and claps as she watches me the entire way down the hallway.

I stop without turning around.

"So what, you want to battle?" Jasmine asks. "Huh, *Shona Mama*?"

I take a deep breath and continue walking.

Today's not about me. It's about my students. I don't want to be the highlight of tonight because someone recorded me outstepping the heck out of Jasmine.

"I didn't think so," Jasmine says.

31

The host begins the show.

There's speakers blasting all over the school, so I can hear everything.

"Ladies and gentlemen, welcome to The Big Bang Step Off. I am your host Wilson, and this is my cohost Rachel," Wilson says as Rachel waves. "We are delighted to have such a big crowd tonight. We have a very special show for you guys. We still have lots of people outside we are trying to squeeze in, so please scoot as close to your neighbor as possible. Please, and thank you. Now let's get this party started!"

The crowd erupts.

I look at myself in the mirror in the bathroom. It's finally time. The moment I've been waiting for.

"Ladies and gentlemen, put your hands together for Marina High School!" Rachel shouts.

Someone in the hall is on the phone with someone watching the show. There's also screens projecting the show in the halls and bathrooms. Louisiana's Dance College is about the business. The energetic Marina High's students are dressed as orphans with pink and white dresses on with white stalkings.

I call Desiree and she tells me what's going on in the room. Mission High listens in amazement in their room at the sound of the crowd that has not settled down once. Marina High School's routine lasts about eight minutes before they stroll off stage to an upbeat instrumental and the announcer calls Gates High School to the stage.

Looking in the mirror I say, "This is it."

I remember sitting in Ann High's theater and watching Jasmine smirk at me at Step Spectacular. I remember Mrs. McGruder kicking me off the team. I remember overhearing Nadia's conversation with Mrs. McGruder. I remember my conversation with Mrs. McGruder in her office. I remember the sound of the door shattering. This is my chance to show that none of that negative stuff defines me. That I am better than my past mistakes. That I would not kill my dream because of one situation. That my talent never left. That I still have it. That I will never stop. That I, Shona Jackson, am The Choreographer.

These speaker systems are off the hook. I'm so glad I can hear everything that is going on.

Gates High School finishes off their routine in the gymnasium. They stroll off the stage with their cheerleading and football uniforms on.

Rachel and Wilson come back on.

Wilson says, "Awesome job Gates. Everyone give it up one more time for Gates High School."

The crowd erupts.

"Up next, we have Ann High School," Wilson says.

The music begins and Ann High dances to their positions to the smooth sounds of a New Orleans jazz beat in their green, yellow and purple Mardi Gras costumes.

The beads around their necks and beaded bracelets on the girls give their costumes more significance.

They begin in a triangle with their heads down. Instantly the female stepper who is the tip of the triangle begins the step and everyone comes in one beat after the person in front of them. They do a full cross with their arms going in all four directions.

They sound great and as one.

Their routine begins slowly, then speeds up.

They move into every basic shape from ovals, to triangles, to diamonds, and stars very smoothly.

"Ann! High! Steppers!" Mariah, the girl that started the fight against Alexis at the basketball game, shouts as she breaks into her solo and everyone joins in.

The DJ plays bounce music from New Orleans and Ann switches it up to dance movements. Wobbling, shuffling, and moving side to side.

The audience is amazed.

I stand next to the door to watch Ann High's performance.

I look out at the crowd, and almost everyone is standing, dancing, and shouting.

Jasmine is standing next to the DJ and nodding her head as her team keeps the beats.

As Ann High strolls off stage to New Orleans bounce music, Jasmine waits for me to make eye contact with her. When I do, she winks and smiles harder, then walks backstage to meet her team.

I have to give it to her. That New Orleans theme was something spectacular and her members definitely delivered.

I stay to watch a little of the next team. After only thirty seconds into their show, I want to rush the stage. The nerve of them to use my choreography knowing I would be here.

Know what though, I don't even care. If they want to use the steps I made months and years ago, they can be my guest.

Mission High will definitely beat them with the new steps I made up.

I head back to my team's room.

Delia's mom is now here. She walks over to me.

"Hi Shona, Delia's grades have been improving and I am willing to let her perform if you are," Ms. Chelsea says.

The sad part is Ms. Chelsea is actually serious. How dare her come in the day of the show and pretty much suggest that her daughter should perform?

"Delia doesn't know some of the routine," I say trying to hint that she should not perform.

Delia whispers in my ear, "I have everything down. Trust

444

me."

I hesitate to speak.

I look over at Desiree and Keasha who are staring at me with hope.

"Okay," I say.

Delia's mom smiles and leaves the room.

I turn to Delia.

"I am going to trust you," I say. "I want you to fall into the back. There is one part where the formation is too complicated for you to squeeze in. I want you to freestyle dance to it as they step, and come back into the routine afterward."

Thomas informs us that we are next. We head downstairs.

"Coach did Ann High do a good job?" Casey asks.

"Honestly, they did good," I say. "But you guys are better."

The curtains close as Albion High School walks off the stage in their Joker costumes. Many people are shaking their keys.

"Coach why are people rattling their keys?" Alina asks.

"Basically saying the team should drive home because they're no good," I inform her.

Alina gets nervous and starts biting her nails. I pull them out of her mouth.

"You will be fine," I say.

Ann High walks past us.

Alexis sees Mariah and looks very serious at her.

I recognize Jasmine look at me cockily out of my peripheral vision, but don't give her the satisfaction of looking at her again.

"Good luck. You will need it," Jasmine laughs.

I say nothing. One of us has to be an adult.

The rest of Mission High looks on as Jasmine continues to walk by and stands at the doors to watch us.

"You guys got this," I say. "Just do the routine like we rehearsed and we are good. Hands in."

Everyone puts their hands in.

"On a Mission on three. One, two, three!" I shout.

"On a Mission!" everyone shouts.

I head to the DJ booth on the side of the stage.

The team goes to the waiting area.

I see Jared waving to me from the stands and smile at him. He mouths *Good luck*. I mouth *Thanks*. My line sisters are here too. I see Austin as well. Thank goodness him and Jared are nowhere near each other.

I keep looking around and spot the McGruders' laughing and smiling.

Surprisingly, I naturally don't roll my eyes.

Mission High does one last huddle before hitting the stage.

Wilson announces, "Up next we have Mission High School!"

The crowd gets loud.

"Let's do this," Jose says.

"Let's give it our all," Alexis says.

"Yes. This is the last performance," Mya says.

"Alright. Mission on three! One, two, three!" Jose shouts.

"Mission!" everyone shouts.

32

I cue the DJ to start the scary sounding music.

Fog covers the stage, white lights flicker, and Jose, Jason, and Michael march on as the girls slowly crawl into their rows and take their positions.

Jason is in the middle and the twins are on his sides on the front row. The beat cuts off and they freeze with their hands in fists to their sides with serious faces on.

The crowd is loving it.

Jason shouts, "M! H! S!"

Mission High jumps up in the air and hits their thighs. They come down on both feet, stomp twice with their hands in fists together in front of their chests. The crowd gets louder.

"Break it down!" Jason shouts.

The two outer lines do the same complex movements and the middle row does a different combination and keeps the same beat. Everyone's thumbs are in as they clap and hit their chests, clap and hit the floor, and clap and hit their thighs with both hands. Their elbows are stiff when they have a hand in front of their chest and the other hitting their thigh.

Mission High claps and keeps their hands together and move their elbows to the right, then to the left. They do one arm in a semi-circle in the air and hit the sides of their thighs repeatedly.

Jason does a step, everyone joins in and transitions. All the boys end on the first row. Alina, Mya, and Alexis squat over them and clap above and under their legs while the boys stomp their feet. Everyone else keeps the same beat standing.

Mission High points their arms in many directions and holds their position in a couple parts of the routine. Their heads are turned the way that their arms are pointing. Sometimes they hold one leg in the air. All those days of squatting, holding positions, and jogging really paid off.

Mission High claps above and under their legs in a circle. They also hit their thighs with one hand and have the other hand go in the air and hit the side of their thigh. Their heads are being thrown forward and thrown back up intensely.

My members of Mission High transition to two lines from shortest to tallest. Jason and Jose end the lines. They do a ripple step that starts slow and ends fast.

Their movements are very sharp. Everyone's thumbs are tucked in. The crowd is loud. Everything's going great.

I cue the DJ to play the music again and Mission steps to the beat. The song cuts off and they continue to do the beat.

The audience goes crazy when they recognize how well Mission does the beat with their bodies.

Now everyone is facing outward in a circle with Michael in the middle.

Casey, who stands front and center of the circle, starts the step off, and everyone does complex moves while Michael krumps.

Mission High says a few words during most of their steps: *We the best. Louisiana's Finest.* No one misses a single move or forgets a single word.

I cue the DJ again. Mission High steps to the beginning of the song and dances to the second half.

Delia notices this is where I was saying she needs to freestyle dance. Not only does she dance, but she does a flip where she notices extra space.

Mission transitions back into the original four rows that they began in and do another step.

"Rewind!" Alina shouts.

They do the step backwards and repeat it twice.

Everyone gives a standing ovation, including the judges.

The DJ starts the music again and Mission strolls out.

448

The crowd goes insane.

Mission's students and parents hold up signs and cheer.

The crowd continues to roar.

I cue the DJ to lower the music when my team is off the stage.

Rachel and Wilson go back on.

"Great job Mission High!" Rachel says. "What a performance. Up next we have Grant High School."

33

Mission High members are jumping up and down and hugging each other in our room.

"Win or lose, I am so happy to have been a part of this program," Alexis says.

I spin around in a circle with Alexis in my arms. When I put her down, Jose puts me on top of his shoulders.

"I am very proud of each and every one of you," I say. "This is by far the best team I have ever coached."

Everyone quiets down while Wilson begins to speak.

"We would like all the teams to come on stage so that we can announce the winners," Wilson says.

All the teams come out on stage.

"We want to thank everyone for coming out today and supporting these teams," Rachel says. "We would like to thank all the schools for coming out and competing this year. We would also like to thank all the coaches that put time into their programs to give our future another activity to be involved in."

The crowd claps.

Delia gives me a hug.

"And with that being said, let's get straight to it," Wilson says. "In third place, we have Ann High School!"

Jasmine's smile quickly turns to a frown. Two members from Ann High get the trophy. Ann High does not even try to hide that they are not content with the results. The McGruders' look angry.

"Great job," Wilson says not caring that Ann High is very angry at the judges' decision.

"This is a mistake," Jasmine angrily says to Wilson.

"In second place, we have Sheridan High School!" Rachel says.

The crowd erupts.

Two members from Sheridan's team get the trophy. I love their blue, black, and white sexy maid costumes.

Everyone's anxious to hear who won first place. Some teams have their fingers crossed and eyes closed. It's obvious they are praying.

"And in first place we have Mission High School!" Wilson shouts.

The crowd roars.

Mission High members and students in the audience jump up and down.

Desiree and Keasha grab the trophy. Jasmine and Ann High head off of the stage while the remaining teams clap for Mission High.

I'm in tears.

"You all are winners in my book," Rachel says. "We want to thank everyone for coming out again. Have a nice night and God bless."

34

Mission High and I are on our way back to the school. We sit on the bus still excited. Everyone either talks on the phone to their family and friends or converses to one another about their favorite parts of their show, the other teams, and what costumes they liked the best.

Jose comes and sits next to me.

"Aye Coach, I mean Shona, since we are finished and I'm no longer your student, we can go on a date some time, right?" Jose asks.

"Boy we can be friends and nothing more," I say. "And I'll always be your coach."

"Can't blame a brother for trying," Jose says.

Alina's sitting across from me talking to the twins behind her. She notices me looking at her rub her stomach with one hand, then stops.

I smile at her.

I feel so good right now.

I did start off only wanting to get the last laugh and beat the McGruders' and Jasmine, but I'm happy to say I'm more content that my students hard work paid off, and they have something to look back on from their high school years.

Mission High under the direction of me, Shona Jackson, won the first ever Big Bang Step Off.

Even though I have the right mindset now, as far as, why I'm happy Mission High won the competition, it still didn't hurt to see Jasmine and the McGruders' upset that they did not beat Mission.

I got the last laugh.

Drained from all their excitement earlier, everyone falls asleep on the bus except me.

I hold the trophy tight and look out the window.

When I get home, I walk in my bedroom and my grandmother pops up.

"We have a year to complete this," my grandmother says.

Today is May 24, 2024.

"I need this done," my grandma says.

I'm headed to my favorite restaurant. It's my last meal for real before I do the fast. The only thing against the fast is the liquor I will be drinking. The weight should still go away in three months. I mean it. Weight loss is a bitch. My grandmother is gritting her teeth because she says I'm being disobedient still drinking. She has me messed up. All this damn stress and me not doing drugs anymore? Please. I'm drinking.

"You starting to sound ridiculous," my grandmother says. She means that stopping the drugs was a good thing. They were only messing with my mind and body, but the drinking is bad too. Right now, I don't care though.

"Look at what you have to go through for you to get your mind back," my grandma says.

I'm regretting telling Nadia about the assault. It's probably because of the drugs that I told her.

"I trained you on how to not care how Nadia acted when you told her personal information," my grandma says. "I didn't want you to tell Nadia anything personal because if she had something going on, she could use what you were saying to try and get over it," my grandma says. "You know what I mean."

What is it about this ninety's music while I'm recovering from these drugs? It just hits me and makes me feel good. "I finally feel like listening to music from the nineteen forties since that's when you were born," I say to my grandma.

I remember the day I ate only fries with cheese on them. I couldn't believe I had several days like that and the weight really didn't go anywhere.

"You know it's not worth it to be around anyone willing to storm your head with negative thoughts. Your mom is sick. She's waiting for you to say something crazy to her to help her. She can't stop being suicidal because she's so damn ugly. You already have the notes for everything I needed you to say. The next time you come to my house, I need more. Repeat it again for me," my grandma says.

I'm just not about to repeat point A to point infinity again. Point A being I told Nadia about the assault. Point infinity being my grandma saying she loved me all along and that's the only way I'm still here. Then there's the fact that the only parts mentioned more than once is me talking about the assault to Nadia's response.

"I remember when I turned sixty," my grandma says. "Tell her I want her to think about it the whole time."

"Think about what?" I ask.

"She'll know," my grandma says.

I wish I could know. I'll just remember I was about to die and she said she would die for me. That's where the love was. She couldn't help how much she loved me. It was natural.

"How the hell am I supposed to write this story, recover from drugs, and do this diet at the same time?" I ask. "You do know I have to think about them niggas to complete this right?"

"Watch your mouth young lady!" my grandma says. "There's blood behind this."

So the drugs took me to a place of solitaire. Told me bold facts about the creation of the world. Told me the truth about fat and ugly bitches. Told me animals got more sense than some of these humans and there's no way we're sitting here house sitting them. They had spots to kill us too. Drugs had it easy for me to believe my relatives don't exist. They told me I'm here alone, and just to label them as animals in general. I'm supposed to snap back into my original way of thinking with these bullshit thoughts in me?

"Grandma, how did y'all come up with those nicknames?" I ask.

"That's how twisted the place is," my grandma says. "You think I'm crazy? You have no idea."

I remember all the times I spent with my grandmother.

"It's gone feel so good when you really recognize all the love I have for you," my grandmother says. "I needed you and your brothers and sister to see how stupid your mother was."

"Grandma, how am I going to really not go to this restaurant every off day? I need these drinks," I say.

My grandma's smiling real hard at me. Sometimes I have flashes of her talking to me while I'm sitting on the table as a toddler. "I'm enjoying you having a good time," my grandma says.

"So you like to watch your granddaughter enjoy a good time?" I ask.

"Do me this one favor," my grandmother says.

"You've been making me make videos," I say. "I've been writing. I'm doing all I can while I'm working at the warehouse."

"There's ways to make it through the weekend without thinking about work or stress," my grandmother says. "Make sure you're enjoying the process."

"Once your name is on these projects, I'll feel like I have lived," I say.

"I'm glad to hear that," my grandmother says.

"What the hell?" I say. These niggas keep getting my order wrong. The wings are not as hot as they usually are. And I asked for extra onions because I know they don't give but two circular onions in the regular order. "Are these wings fresh off the grill?" I ask the waiter.

"Yes they are," the waiter says.

I ate two and they are not as hot as they usually are, and now I have eight left when I ordered twelve. When I see him again, I let him know I need some new wings. I can't believe when he comes back I have six habanero wings and six barbeque wings. I asked for twelve habanero wings. I definitely know I will have eaten fourteen wings instead of twelve when I get my new order.

My grandma pops up.

"So, you know the workout you need to do is serious?" my grandma asks. She keeps up with everything I eat.

"Can I get extra onions?" I ask the waiter that brings me my drink.

During the course of my time at this restaurant, my wings are wrong. My salad did not come with the extra onions which I asked for. They bring my salad before the rest of the order when I wanted it all together. I don't care if I didn't ask for it all together, they should have asked me if I wanted everything to arrive together or separate. So, it's not wrong for me to want them to be able to read my mind. If they didn't ask, they should already know what I was expecting.

I woke up after noon today because I only got an hour of sleep today after getting my computer. I got up and washed clothes and made my fast meals for three days. Then I came to my favorite restaurant for them to continuously get my order wrong.

I have two strawberry margaritas and a lime margarita. I need this liquor. I keep getting bombed with facts under this drug recovery.

My grandmother pops up again.

"You enjoy yourself doing what you love to do. If anything happens in this process, I already got everything taken care of," my grandmother says.

"This month of May has been crazy as hell," I say.

"I'm telling you, don't pick up that phone," my grandma says.

"So you're telling me she's sitting by the phone to blast me with a thought I will remember forever and nut off of that?" I ask.

"She believes you can do that for her," my grandma says.

"I know. You already told me what she is," I say. "That's nothing. She's just a reaction. She has to see something to have an emotion. Nothing's there."

"They merge Shona. Just know that this world is crazy. Your name creation and all. There's real spirits. There's real wickedness," my grandma says. "You'll learn what a real OG is. A real OG knows how you can be swiped of internet materials as well as motherly skills to a daughter. A real OG knows that the internet is nothing to play with," my grandmother says. "Any mistake you make, I can use it. Don't forget how much younger you are than me."

"You're going to tell and show people how I can take my thirty-five-year-old granddaughter and tell her a year in advance that I need a project done and she still does it for me," my grandma says. "I need this book written. For my street credit and school knowledge nobody thought I had. I can take a school girl and make her write like a thug would. I need this done. I'll show people what patience really is. You have to be patient with me. They already know how impatient you are. Now you will show them I can get an impatient girl to take a year and do what I say. This is blood money. Your memory is gone to the drugs and you're still recovering. I know I can get you to do what I want. They will remember me forever as I, a drug addict, put my knowledge in a recovering smart girl who didn't want nothing to do with individuals like me."

"Grandma you are starting to sound a bit crazy. You mean to tell me you are one of the *original gangsters* that knew about the real behind these drugs and could teach a young girl like me how to write from a real young thug perspective?" I ask.

"I mean I got the knowledge to make you a real thug. If you don't know the truth about these drugs and making it, you won't know anything. When you know someone on drugs, you'll know naturally that it's not a game to stay alive in this world," my grandma says. "Only a thug could know how it is to know how to create anything and that the world could still strip you of it. Only that thug could know what real survival is. You wanna mess with the old school? How do you feel reciting this same spiel about what you told your mother, to waking up and realizing you need me to feel complete?" my grandma asks. "If you don't know what we did, then there's nothing for you to figure out. We know all about what it's like to survive here first."

"Grandma I can still remember myself going into the gym for Cardinals' tryouts when I was I think maybe ten years old," I say. "I had jeans on for my first basketball practice. How the hell am I still here? I can now see this woman was really not caring about me. She was trying to get rid of me since then?"

"If a child says the wrong things, a woman can get in real trouble," my grandma says. "I used that. That was the one thing you had on your side. That's one of the ways I studied in depth about you. I knew I could beat your mom in training you to have good thoughts over her negative ones. It wasn't a doubt in my mind if I did the right thing and studied a real psychopath with a beautiful daughter she carried for nine months, that I could beat her."

"You're amazing Grandma," I say.

"Its real out here," my grandma says. "These women are real bitter. They see kids doing things they never got the chance to."

The part that trips me out is negative things have always been so easy to remember, and the drugs can take those memories from me as well. I have to keep talking about the assault and Nadia's response to make it to the part about the love. My grandmother keeps saying there's more she has to tell me.

I had to recite the monstrous story and even cried about it because the love my grandmother has for me is so strong that I made it. There was no love anywhere else.

It's like I was empty without reciting the story. I had to build myself back up while recovering from the drugs. Now the question I kept having was how the hell could anyone remember anything if they didn't write it down? I spent months writing down what the drug effects were doing to me because I knew there was no possible way for me to remember what they did to me once the effects were gone.

The drugs even bothered me to a point where if I didn't do what I wanted to do, I would feel sick.

"You'll never understand who the people who tried those drugs first really were," my grandmother says.

My grandmother tells me I have to understand life with love and drug effects being that I did them. If no one really loved me, with the type of good person I am that doesn't go out and do malicious things, I would have died.

"Just look at your momma as a drug. You won't care about anything else she has to say," my grandmother says. My mouth just dropped. "You know one statement can put somebody in they place," my grandma says. "I need you to get these projects done."

My grandma keeps saying she'll make it up to me. I keep saying I hate her. If I don't do what I want to do right when I

458

think it, I know I will forget and the drug messes with me. It makes me sick.

This story to feel the love is like a six-step process. The love was supposed to be inserted after telling her the story, but it wasn't. It was cut out. It was replaced with hate. Some time passed and I was without the love of Nadia and I hopped into a shell where I said nothing but good things about myself. I was supposed to keep walking with those thoughts to a place where I could fall and kill myself.

I can still see myself walking into the shell as if someone was leading me into it.

Somehow, I got out of those thoughts in that shell and I still looked confused. That's when I remembered the part where the love was snapped out. I thought of telling Nadia about the assault and her supposed to have inserted love there. Or even cut me off while telling the story and say something that showed love through the phone.

"She don't know how to do that," my grandmother says.

Instead, Nadia brought up Jania saying I harmed those boys. Then I got let out of that shell. Then I heard my grandmother's voice say, "Tell her that's why I did it." I believe I was about to question whether anyone loved me. I was supposed to somehow kill myself there.

I kept making excuses for why Nadia didn't say anything to console me.

"She's the walking dead," my grandmother says.

At home, I cooked some brown rice, red bell peppers, green peppers, onions, mushrooms, and tofu. That's going to be my lunch at work for the next three days. I'm only going to drink water. If I need to, I'm going to drink an energy drink to stay awake at work. So, I will be cheating in that aspect on my diet. But I already told my grandmother that I was going to drink liquor on my off day. I'm going through too much hell right now.

I'm tired as hell, but my grandma tells me this is the last realization I need. The love she has for me. "My spirit and you. I know you're a woman. You will make it," my grandma says.

"Everything in here, you let them know I told you to write it," my grandma says. "I'll take the credit for everything you've done thus far. Books. Choreography. Dancing. Writing. All of it. You let them know this is blood money. I needed you to do all of this for me. You don't know what the original gangsters were like. They'll sell you stuff and let you die using it without a care that you ever existed."

My grandma has a lot to say again.

"You did ask her if she remembered saying your cousin was using cocaine and she said she didn't remember," my grandma says. "You did ask her if she remembered saying your sister called the twins on their birthday and asked them for ninety dollars. And what did she say? She said no. Then she said *okay, I remember.* She told you her best friend Nika went on that hiking trip and when you looked at those pictures, her best friend out of them all, in over forty pictures, was not in them. So, to hell with her being mad you said you didn't want to look at the McGruders' again."

I was crying because my grandmother had a real love for me. I can't believe how she returned in my life. She believes I will be okay once I am done recovering from smoking marijuana and cigarettes.

"You know you would have had sense to not use those drugs if your momma was a momma," my grandmother says. "But she was nothing. She was what people couldn't look at. She didn't like that she couldn't flirt with her eyes. She didn't like not getting stared at for a long time like the pretty girls do."

"I just don't get how you can carry someone for nine months, then say fuck it," I say. "Nadia acts like such a baby. I can hear her say: *she's prettier than me and I never got attention, so I'm gone treat her bad.*"

"It's crazy how you can carry someone for nine months too, and they turn out ugly and you don't want them," my grandmother says. "Tell her that's why I did it."

I just couldn't see myself carrying anyone for nine months, then not wanting them. It would be one thing if I was mentally ill like Nadia. Okay so that explains it.

460

"She's getting older too Shona. That's gone make her ugliness act out. That ugliness is cutting up. It hurts when people keep cutting their eyes at her. That's something you don't know what it feels like," my grandmother says.

These drugs keep fucking with me. It really is hard to think. I'm tired of being banged with hard facts too.

Drugs can make me say anything. Drugs can make me do anything. Drugs can make me feel any type of way. Drugs can make me think things happened that didn't. Drugs can put hard images in my sight that aren't even there. Drugs can make me have real feelings for people I've never seen or met. Drugs can do anything. The drugs become me and take over my entire conscious. Yet somehow, magically I can still walk around.

"You're lucky you didn't get into any trouble while using those drugs," my grandma says. "You'll recognize how tough real love can cut one day."

The drugs have me reading the screen on my device wrong at work. Thinking in general has my vision messed up. I can't wait to be fully recovered. How the hell I'm going to remember what these damn drugs did to me is a damn mystery.

"No it's not," my grandmother says. "You're going to write it down. I need this done. Don't use the drugs anymore. This is the last straw. I'm here with you now getting you through this. I know you are a woman. I'm gone. My spirit lives inside of you," my grandmother says. "You've already made it this far. You've been practiced on your whole life. That's how sharp my love is. Tell her that's why I did it. Real love can fight through words. I've already shown you that. You made it this far. You weren't supposed to. I'm teaching you what it's like for goddesses like you. No one's seen anyone around that resembles you. You are unique. An automatic weapon. It takes a lot to get people like you to make it another year. I need this done."

My grandma is getting emotional.

"Shona," my grandma says and smiles. "You made it through a lot of crisis'. I'm proud of you. You're scared of being alone, but understand some girls like you have walked off bridges. Stabbed themselves to death. Overdosed. Many things they've

461

been practiced on to do because people couldn't deal with the things they could naturally do just by walking in a room," my grandmother says. "I worked my ass off to keep you here, and you will do right by me and finish these projects."

"Yes ma'am," I say.

"Sit up straight," my grandmother says. "I'll teach you everything your momma didn't."

I remember I text Nadia on the 20th of March. I told her that she was the only one telling me outrageous stories. It wasn't the first time either. I had already told her she was the only person I knew that kept talking to people she said she didn't like.

"Pour some more orange juice in the glass," my grandmother says. Now that I have my grandmother, I'm aware of more ways Nadia was playing with my head. "All Nadia is, is confusion," my grandmother continues. "Walking suicide. Scaring people with the sight of her."

I told Nadia I didn't want her mentioning the twins' dad side of the family to me again. Then I text her and asked if she said anything to Jania when she said that bullshit about her daughter and she said yes she did. She didn't elaborate at all. "Place the forks on the table," my grandmother continues. I was trying to get some type of humanistic motherly response and all Nadia said was that Jania's side of the family has problems. It was something for the record books. "It was nothing," my grandmother says. "I'm going to raise you right. I've treated you like a baby for thirty-five years. You'll always be my baby. You have more relatives here. Some of the family you do know, doesn't even know they exist."

"I'm proud of you," my grandma says. "You've made it this far with pure hate. You're not stupid. You defeated all the odds against you. I made good with some people. That's how you got away from your mom."

"Tell them I told you to write all of that. You were under severe mind control," my grandma says. "I needed your school years bad. Especially when you made it to college. You didn't have no choice, let alone control over yourself with anything you've written. Mind control ain't shit to fuck with. I knew your mom would lose her mind one day. I was waiting on that moment. Don't forget that," my grandma says. "I knew she would break. That ugliness on and inside of her is severe alone. Just remember you've heard worse, it's just at that moment I woke you up. You're not stupid Shona. Be a woman and accept how things worked out for you."

So first I have to accept that my grandma says she died when she did with many intentions. Then she says to hold onto that. Then with love floating around me, I made it to thirty-five years old. She knew I wasn't stupid.

35

My line sisters and the pledges from Cupperton are at my house. The pledges are in my pool lined up horizontally in the water. They have been in the same position waiting for over thirty minutes.

It's a nice sunny day and my Sorors and I have our bathing suits on. Some of us are walking around the pool eating fruit and drinking wine, and the rest are in the kitchen cooking and drinking.

"So what's the time needed for a pledge to get out of the water?" Telana asks.

"They not gone last," I say. "They sorry as hell." The pledges have to hold their breath under water. "I guess whoever holds their breath the longest, can help cook," I continue.

On my cue, the girls dip their heads in the water. Most of them pop back up after less than five seconds.

"Oh, hell no," Casha says. "These damn girls are not good at anything. Who the hell can't hold their breath for at least five seconds?"

"I know none of they asses plays sports," Caya says. "Who plays sports?" she asks the girls.

A few of them raise their hands. Caya feels like being a jackass so she tells them she didn't say raise their hands; she wants them to speak.

"Girl just because they play sports doesn't mean they can hold their breath under water that long," Shemina says.

Canila holds her breath the longest. She goes inside with my other Sorors and helps prepare dinner.

I have the rest of the pledges race in the pool two at a time. Me and Casha always cheer on the pledge who is winning. We make the winner feel good and the loser feel as low as possible. We don't raise losers in this sorority.

The losers have to do push-ups and recite their line sisters' names. They have to clean the dishes and any other part of my house that gets out of order while they are here.

My line and I let the girls swim for a while. They can't get out the pool though.

Caya gets in the pool and swims with the girls. Me and Casha are dancing, so we don't get in yet. We're enjoying another day together.

Deliana and Asayla start making barbeque chicken on the grill outside. They made the potato salad, pork and beans with hot dogs, salad, and greens while they were inside.

Deliana tells me and Casha to follow her inside. She spoon feeds us some potato salad.

It tastes so good that I say, "I love you so much girl. You know you can throw down in the kitchen."

"Thank you. I love leaving my positive spirit in your house," Deliana says. "Whenever you come in this kitchen, I want you to think of me."

"It sounds like she's trying to be your girlfriend," Casha says throwing her arms around my waist from behind.

Deliana spoon feeds Casha some potato salad.

Scalina comes in and says, "Big Sister Shona I'm going to the bathroom."

"Girl just go to the bathroom," I say.

"Yea. You don't have to let us know you're going," Casha says.

"At least not today," Deliana says and slaps Casha's hand laughing.

"We love you," I say.

"I love all my big sisters too," Scalina says.

"Hurry up and go to the bathroom girl," I say. "Then get your ass back in that pool."

Today me and my Sorors on my line are just going to haze the girls a bit in the pool. That's it. We're going to enjoy a good day with these girls for the most part. We want to have a great dinner.

I have the pledges do circles with their bodies in the pool. I make them doggy paddle from one end to the next. Casha has some of the pledges pretend like they are drowning. She has the remaining ones save them.

After that, I have the girls dip their partner in the pool and hold her head down until she tries to come back up for air. I know it's dangerous, but I know they can do it.

Caya has the girls jump in the pool and touch the bottom of the five feet end.

My line and I run out of ideas and start making up dumb stuff for the girls to do.

I have the girls and their partners get on opposite sides of the pool. At the sound of my whistle, they have to swim to the center of the pool and touch hands. After they touch hands, they have to swim back to their starting points.

"Are you keeping up with the score?" I ask Casha.

"Girl how the hell am I supposed to keep up with who keeps winning when they keep switching partners?" Casha asks.

"Damn. Well, they all can crawl up and down the stairs," Caya says. She changes her mind real quick. She makes the girls pretend like they are drowning again and has their partner save them. They wet as hell.

Caya better had changed her damn mind.

Shemina and Telana run inside the house because they can't stop laughing so hard. They are acting real ignorant pretending like they are dialing nine one one.

The last thing I have the pledges do is jump off of the diving board and swim to the end of the pool. Once they touch the end of the pool, they have to submerse themselves in the water and hold their breath as long as they can.

Casha and I go back inside and Deliana spoon feeds us some greens and salad.

"Girl, I wish you were my personal chef," I say.

"Anytime you want me over, I'll be here," Deliana says. "There's no one like you."

"People have been telling me that ever since high school," I say.

My Sorors and I go outside and enjoy swimming with the pledges.

It's hot as hell and the cold water feels so damn good to me. I swim from one end of the pool to the other. My favorite thing to do is just be submersed in the water. Sometimes I do circles, and sometimes I touch the bottom. Sometimes I stay under and count how long I can hold my breath.

The girls and I are throwing each other in the pool for fun now. They are jumping off of the diving board. Some of them try holding their breaths underwater so much that I think they actually like doing it. They stop when they realize Caya is paying close attention to them. They think she is going to compare how they hold their breath on their own, versus how when we told them to.

I'm not talking to anyone. I'm just enjoying my body. I love my shape and how I look in a two-piece bikini. It's not easy staying in shape.

I daze off and think about my grandma.

"That weight is not going anywhere easy is it?" my grandma asks. "I want it gone within the next three months. You're not that big. It shouldn't take long. You have a photoshoot and a video shoot you need to do. I want it done correctly."

I was supposed to had started my diet already, but completely failed. I had cravings like a mutha fucka.

I'm always on my feet at the warehouse, but I still can't lose any weight.

"I can show you how to enjoy an eight-hour shift," my grandma says.

"I'm looking forward to it," I say. I get popped in my mouth. "I wasn't getting smart Grandma," I say.

"Make sure you do some typing today?" my grandma says.

"I can't," I say.

"You just typed sixteen pages in one day," my grandma says. "So, what do you mean you can't do it again?"

I've been writing and stepping a lot because I keep hearing my grandma tell me to do it. She wants me to utilize my talents to show off who I am, and at the same time tell people the truth about what went down with our family.

It's the end of the month of May.

I got one hour of sleep. I work the night shift at the warehouse. I came home and slept for an hour, then went to buy groceries. I knew I had a lot of errands to run. I had to go buy this computer and Microsoft Office which ran me $463.68. I had to go to the phone store and the library. I mean my first check from my new job at the clothing store just vanished.

"This is blood money Shona. I need this done," my grandma says. "You were dying. You didn't have a choice but to spend that money. I'm giving you time. You have plenty. I'm giving you plenty of time in between. Another year before the next eighteen of your life passes to get this work done. What's happened to you in your life is not small. They still sitting around waiting for you to die, but you're going to use your talent and keep showing them who I am. Something was taken from me."

My grandma is getting on my nerves.

I'm so done with this woman. I ate one meal today. Egg fu yung, three chicken wings, and three cheese won tons from the Chinese place. I'm officially about to start this diet on Sunday. Tomorrow's my last day eating good. Then I'm doing the fast.

I'm about to drink before bed.

"Make sure you type up some of the pages tomorrow too," my grandma says. "You're behind." I just got this new computer, so prior, I was writing on notebook paper. My grandma is saying transfer the pages to the computer as soon as I can. "I need this done," my grandma says. "Work on your choreography tonight while you're drinking too. You have to understand that something was taken from me."

There's no way I can do this diet with this work schedule. I'm definitely drinking on my day off. A beer, a Lima Rita, and a shot of E and J.

"I have food to clear out of the fridge. I'm not throwing anything away," I say to my grandma. "I already haven't been eating fried foods, fast foods, drinking soda, and eating junk food, and I still haven't gotten to the size I want."

"So if that's not working, you need to make some better choices," my grandma says. "I don't want my grandchild out of shape. You are to represent me well. I have a lot riding on this."

"Grandma, my shoulders and my behind have been hurting,"
I say.

"Make the adjustments," my grandmother says. "There's
blood involved in this."

I'm trying to figure out what she means when she says blood
is involved in this. The drugs are really messing with me. I
haven't smoked marijuana since April 5th, 2024. It's now May,
2024, and the withdrawal is pissing me off.

"Really think back to your junior year when you met that
woman," my grandma says. "She's the one that came with all
the paperwork. She said freshmen shouldn't be captain. Let
alone on the varsity team and you started it as a freshman. The
captain process. There was some things you didn't understand
there. Think about the girl who kept telling you not to try out
for captain. There's blood involved in this."

I snap back into reality.

I open my eyes underwater. I just enjoy swimming. I love
pools.

"Big Sister Shona, am I doing good?" Scalina asks.

"Doing good what? Swimming?" I ask.

"No. Pledging," Scalina says.

"Girl of course you are," I say. "That don't mean things are
going to get any easier for you."

"I need all my Sorors to get they asses out of the pool and
grab a shot," Caya says holding shots on a tray. My line sisters
surround Caya and we raise our shot glasses. "This is to us still
being the divas we are and loving each other," Caya says. "We
never let any argument or fight cause us to lose our
relationship."

"That's right," I say. "We always work it out. I love y'all so
much."

We all raise our glasses and cheers, then we grab a glass of
wine and get in the pool on floats. We're eating and drinking in
my pool.

"I feel fancy," Telana says.

"Whenever you at my house, you should feel good and
fancy," I say. "You should feel like you living the life. Come by

again on one of my grown and sexy nights. I can make you feel even better than the last time."

On my grown and sexy nights, I'm usually alone. I cater to myself. I usually wear panties and a bra around my house. I have candles lit all over. I have either rhythm and blues playing or jazz music. If the television is on, it has Christmas lights shows playing or jazz musicians on it. I have my fireplace going. I celebrate me loving myself. I celebrate me not breaking because of any of the negative things that have happened in my life. I celebrate knowing Nadia is at home knowing I could be enjoying a good time by myself. I know she could be jealous.

On my grown and sexy nights, I dance all around the house. Most of the dances are real sexy. I stare at myself in the mirror for long periods of times.

Sometimes I put a bathing suit on and get in my pool with candles lit outside. I'll hang Christmas lights around my backyard and walk around and think about my successful life. A life with loving people in it.

Sometimes I'll drive around and listen to jazz music. I'll pour my drink in a container and park somewhere that I can look out at the city. I'll have on short shorts and a belly top.

"Sounds like you want to be my girlfriend," Telana says.

"Girl I can show you a real good time," I say. "I think you will really enjoy yourself and love me even more of course."

"I want to spend the night at your house," Trayna says swimming over to me.

"If you make the sorority, I'll be sure to have y'all over," I say. "I like to feel young with young girls."

"I'm not a snitch," Trayna whispers to me. "Just invite me only. I'll keep my mouth shut."

"I'll think about it," I whisper back sarcastically.

Trayna gets out of the pool and jumps off the diving board. When Trayna comes up from the water she says, "I wish we could drink. The big sisters are having such a good time. They are turned up."

"Sssskkkiiioooo!" me and my Sorors shout because of Casha.

"Wait. Did I hear the pledges say it too?" Caya asks.

"No girl. You are drunk and high," Shemina says.

The sun is going down. I go in my bedroom and sit on the balcony. I sip my wine and watch my sorority and the pledges have a good time.

Shemina and Telana grab buckets and pour water on people.

The pledges are running around the pool and acting like they weren't just hazed a while ago.

Caya is squirting some of the girls with water guns. Casha is taking it too far grabbing the damn hose. It's really a water day at my house.

"Big Sister Shona, can I get in the jacuzzi?" Scalina comes in my room and asks. Clearly she's having so much fun that she didn't think twice about asking to come in.

"Hell no," I say. "I mean not now." I'm trying to be a little nicer today. "Come sit next to me," I continue. "So what's it like knowing the fun side of Alpha Eta Nu members?" I ask.

"It's real cool," Scalina says. "I want to come back to your house and chill with you one day."

"Why does everyone want to come back to my house and chill with me?" I ask knowing that I just have a good spirit and am a loving person.

"Because you're so pretty and we want to be like you," Scalina says.

I look at Scalina in her eyes. She looks like she adores me. I give her some of my wine. I pour some liquor and let her take a shot. I can tell this isn't her first time drinking.

"Can I have another shot?" Scalina asks.

"Sure," I say. "It's the least I can do for someone that may be my sorority sister one day."

Scalina's smile is contagious.

"I wish I looked like you," Scalina says. "You have the perfect profile. It doesn't matter what angle someone approaches you from, you look good."

"What if they approach me from behind?" I ask.

"You have a nice figure," Scalina says. "It doesn't even matter."

"Thanks girl," I say. "But don't be taking no chance on thinking someone looks good in the face when you approach them from behind. Make sure you turn they ass around. A cute shape is not enough."

"I love your house," Scalina says. "I know you enjoy it even when you're alone. You're too pretty to not love staring at yourself."

"What you think I'm conceited or something?" I ask. "Cause I am," I say before she can answer.

"Can I ask you something Big Sister Shona?" Scalina asks.

"Of course you can," I say. "I can do whatever I want to you if I don't like the question, right?" I'm smiling. I let her know I'm just messing with her.

"When I cross, can I come by you?" Scalina asks.

"You mean *if* you cross," I say.

"I want to be like you. You speak conceitedly. I mean confidently," Scalina says.

"Look. To tell you the truth, you should be fine," I say. I'm drunk and just not giving a fuck right now. The truth with pledging is we always need a new line. The more people we get, the more money the sorority will make each year. Me and my line aren't stupid. We know damn well the president, vice president, secretary, and treasurer of the entire sorority are using some of the money we spend each year to stay active, on their mansions and cars.

Each year, members of the sorority have to spend four hundred dollars. We pay it to the treasurer of the entire sorority, and she spends it on people in need is what we are told. My line and I are not idiots. Them people in them offices are living the life off of our money. We don't believe a word they say.

Sometimes if we only have around ten members come out for the group, we won't even cut anyone. If they fail their tests, we let them retake them.

This line has twenty-three people, but we like to meet the cap for Alpha Eta Nu which is thirty-three. Anything beneath that means we may not cut anyone.

Sometimes a lot of people don't want to come out for the sorority because they know we are some crazy ass Alpha Eta Nu members. They know we will give them a run for their money. They've heard stories. We always deny them though.

"So we gone be buddies when I cross?" Scalina asks.

"We might," I say. "I just don't be chilling with people because they are in this sorority. If I like them, they can come by."

"A lot of sorority members like you, huh?" Scalina asks.

"Girl no. Some don't like me right when they look at me," I say.

"Because they jealous you're so pretty," Scalina says.

"They judge me just by looking at me," I say. "I don't give second chances when it comes to people looking at me crazy. I know too many people. I have too many friends to give a fuck."

"You have the prettiest shaped face," Scalina says. "You look great looking from the side. Your earrings are real pretty."

I look at Scalina. I'm in a good mood doing all this drinking. "You're a pretty girl too," I say. "You have a nice-looking shape too. Make sure you keep yourself together. When you get my age, it gets harder." I remember that Scalina likes to smoke. I wrap a blunt for her. I feel good just doing that. I love the smell too. I'm mad as hell I can't hit it.

I watch Scalina smoke. She's feels real good. I'm loving watching her smoke. She can tell I love to inhale the second-hand smoke, so she blows out a lot in my direction. I'm nodding my head to the music playing. I'm in my feelings as usual watching someone else smoke. Sometimes I just want to cheat and hit the blunt again. One time shouldn't do much. It took a long time for me to even realize that I needed to stop.

All this second-hand smoke takes my mind to another place. I rock side to side and see my grandma sitting next to me instead of Scalina.

"Olifus told me of four girls that were cousins that formed a singing group. Their names were Stalaya, Anna, Abigail, and Valory," my grandma says. She says these girls were all twenty-two or twenty-three. They all still lived at home with their parents. They were very close and never let anyone ruin their relationship. Stalaya, Anna, and Abigail were all light skinned and Valory was brown skinned. They were singers and rappers. They performed at talent shows and at parties.

Stalaya was the one that had the idea for the girls to form a group and the girls were forever grateful that she did. They all wanted to make it big on television one day.

The four girls were very popular. Stalaya, Anna, and Abigail were studs. Valory was the only girly girl. They worked regular eight-hour jobs and performed in their free time. Sometimes they would get paid and other times they'd just get exposure. They kept trying to figure out who they could talk to so they could become famous, but never had any luck. They went into many offices and studios, but never got called back. The girls weren't having any luck, but they would never give up on their dream coming true.

Stalaya was a cool kid. She was always calm and settle. She was the one that would come up with new catchy phrases for the girls to use and others to catch onto. She had short curly hair and wore big shirts with baggy clothes. She was a fly girl. People loved her style. Despite her good looks, she was really nice. She was arrogant internally. She never said or showed anyone that she was. She just naturally knew she looked good and that was enough for her.

Anna was more outspoken. She had a hard time biting her tongue because people couldn't stop staring at her. She knew it was because they liked how she looked, and she was the type to let them know she knew why they were staring. People liked that about her and thought it was comical at times. Anna's personality can naturally make people laugh. Anna was serious though. People had been staring at her most of her life. She needed a break.

Anna had short hair and wore big shirts and baggy pants just like Stalaya. Anna was very confident. She wasn't scared of anyone either.

Abigail had a little more weight to her than the other girls. She was light skinned but not as light as Stalaya and Anna.

Abigail hated her weight, but couldn't get rid of it. She wasn't overweight, but she wasn't as thin as the other girls. She liked to wear big clothes too.

Abigail was the comedian of the group. She told jokes a lot and loved to make people laugh. She was also the one that used to sneak out the most when they were kids and skip school. Now that she's grown, she has a hard time coming home at a time that doesn't wake her parents up.

Valory was a girly girl. She loved to wear dresses and skirts. She loved to wear her long hair flat-ironed down her back. She was the one always trying to decide where the girls should go hang out and who they should bring with them. She always had her nails and hair done. She loved to dance provocatively while the other girls were more of hip hop dancers.

Valory was into boys while the other girls liked girls. Whenever they had a function, Abigail, Anna, and Stalaya had fun with Valory's male companions. None of the girls had a hard time making any friends despite some of them only wanting to date girls.

The girls are grown so Valory would get on tables and act as a private dancer for the night. She was a very confident brown skinned girl. She had confidence just like Tina. So many people have said good things to her, that negative ones were hard for her to believe. On top of that, she has real love in her family that comes from her cousins. Her mind is conditioned to flow to the love whenever something bad comes her way. She never is stuck in a bad place despite her parents being passive aggressive. She had cousins that were going through the same things she was. Her life just happened to work out in a way that she always had a strong defense to help her get out of a bad time.

"I know you don't have the same relationship with your cousins," my grandma says. "But look at me damn it. I'm all you need. This world is real. You have no idea how easy people in higher positions can walk in your house."

My grandma says the girls lived in neighborhoods that were really close. They could walk to each other's houses. They were well known thugs. They were popular in their neighborhoods. Their families had lived in their current locations since they were kids. The girls had many sleepovers where they told each other secrets and wanted to know more of each other's business.

Anna, Stalaya, Valory, and Abigail had real love in their lives. On top of that, they all looked good. They could look into each others eyes and fall asleep off of the love they shared. Many people wish they had what these girls had.

The four girls were close growing up since elementary school. They would lie for each other. Defend each other whenever someone bothered them. They would ask their parents to hang out together and throw their birthday parties together. They snuck out the house together. Abigail, Valory, Anna, and Stalaya were so close that other families were jealous. The girls didn't care who got jealous of them. They gave them a reason to hate even more. They would whisper to each other, put their arms around one another, and make jokes and laugh at people who they knew were jealous of them.

A terrible thing all of the girls shared in common was that their home lives weren't that great. They didn't have family support. Their families knew they had talent and constantly told them they didn't. They ridiculed their singing and dancing abilities. Their families didn't care how late they stayed out. What their parents did care about was getting calls because the girls were in trouble. That's when the girls would be disciplined. Sometimes the girls did bad things on purpose just to make sure their parents still cared about them. Misbehaving to feel love from discipline is what they did.

The girls were thugs that weren't scared to do anything for the attention that they wanted.

The girls talked about the problems they dealt with at home and trusted one another to never tell anyone else. They cried together and consoled one another.

"Olifus told me of a couple. Gerica and James," my grandma says. She says they were two people that pretended to date just for family. They didn't live together and they didn't do anything a couple would unless they were with their relatives. They didn't like how it felt to be single in their forties.

Gerica was a heavy-set light skinned woman and James was a slimmer dark-skinned man. They both hated their lives and their families. They wanted money quick like everyone else.

"Everyone sees entertainment as the way to make quick money, right Grandma?" I ask.

"They see it as a way to make millions," my grandma says. "And yes, it comes quick."

Olifus told my grandma that Gerica and James both worked at the same food store. They conversated one day and realized they had similar interest in keeping their families out of their business. All they had to do is say they were seeing someone and a lot of nosy questions would stop. They seemed very weird and awkward to both of their families but they did not care. They wanted less attention on them for being single in their forties.

Gerica and James were the type of people that had a lot of sexual partners. They didn't want to settle down anytime soon. However, they did want kids.

"Okay, what is wrong with these people?" I ask. "Gerica and James are messing with my mental stability."

Gerica was very bitter because she didn't like her weight. She was rude most of the time and picked fights with people for stupid reasons. She was bothered very easily because of her shape.

"That's probably why no one would settle for her. You kept saying how Malana looked good from head to toe," I say. "What about Gerica? Did the weight at least look nice on her?"

"She looked good to have some weight to her, but if people don't like their weight, they will be unhappy," my grandmother says. "James and her had an agreement. That's the only reason he was with her when he has sex with better looking women. She was just a front for his family. James wasn't the best-looking man, but he didn't have trouble picking up women. He couldn't get the girls of his dreams just like Canel, but he could get his sexual needs met at times."

One day Gerica and James were driving around. They were arguing about how their families were acting at an event they threw at their house. Their families didn't seem happy about the relationship and had harsh words to say to both individuals. Gerica had lots of relatives that she didn't like at her house, but she cared what they thought so she didn't hesitate to give them an invitation just so they could know she had a man.

Gerica's family would criticize her house and how it was decorated. They would let her know she had picked up a few pounds and also judge her cooking. They said more judgmental things than anything else. They didn't care that she was in a relationship.

"That's why I don't want to be around no relatives that I don't like," I say. "That doesn't make any sense. Just because we are blood doesn't mean we have to keep each other company."

"You've always been smart like that," my grandma says. "Don't let nobody tell you different. You're not around the bullshit that's going on with our kin folk. Remember why I did what I did. Any time you go through anything, know that I took care of business to get anyone that messed with you back. I know you're innocent. I loved you and always have. Don't let no one brainwash you."

"There's all types of people that wish they could take back a time they visited a relative they didn't like," I say. "I don't want to be one of those people that gets in trouble because I lost my mind."

"They already crazy," my grandma says. "They're trying to make you crazy. I knew you would reach a point where you could be alone and really understand who I was. Once you know me completely, none of the things they say to you will matter. You're a beautiful girl. Enjoy your life. It can be taken from you at any moment."

These drugs are messing with me. My thoughts are turning negative again. My grandma is all I have. When the thought of my other relatives comes to mind, the drug recovery gets real bad. I start feeling like something is pulling at my brain again.

When I think, my mind gets frustrated and it hurts. I think I'm in the last phase of the recovery. I can't believe it's been over two months still that I haven't smoked and the effects just won't go away. I do understand that I smoked in the drugs real easy. It will be a fight to get rid of the effects. They did make me feel really good. Now they are showing me the opposite.

I mean, I still have points where I just get so mad that I can't believe the drugs would take so long to go away. I started to think someone put something in my food or drink and that's why these symptoms are so severe.

"The drugs can give you those thoughts too," my grandma says. "They can do anything. That's why I can't stress to you enough not to use them again."

James' family was just as bad as Gerica. The men would make jokes about how his girlfriend looked. They would also ask him when he was going to get someone else. "They had dysfunctional families," my grandma says.

While they were driving, James kept getting them lost. James didn't care though. Gerica would take the wheel a few times out of frustration. The thing was that they kept arguing and it was distracting their minds. They both knew that but wouldn't shut up. They were the type to want the other person to act mature at times and this was one of those times.

Gerica and James would ask people how to get home. They would pull over and smoke a cigarette. They didn't want to go home. They even argued in public.

"Did they remember anything good their relatives said to them?" I ask.

"Some of Gerica's relatives let her know that they were happy she had a job and was able to take care of herself," my grandma says.

"She's over forty," I say. "Believe me I know it can be hard to maintain a steady lifestyle these days no matter what age you are."

"This world is real hard to make it in," my grandma says. "Any day and at any moment what you've worked for can be taken from you. People are real messed up out there. A lot of people with money are screwed up in the head. You have to remember the words I tell you to live a healthy life. You have to stay strong and when something goes wrong, remember that love can fight through it. Something else good will happen for you, but you have to do the work. Keep taking chances. Don't let constant no's being given to you, overpower the fact that you are alive. Life is tough. People can be cruel. Hold yourself together and find the resources you need. There's plenty of help out there. You aren't the only one that is struggling."

"I will remember everything you told me grandma," I say. "Thank you for loving me so much."

"James' family made jokes the entire time they were there," my grandma says. "Both James and Gerica expected a genuine love from some of their relatives, but they both belonged to people that didn't even think they cared about a single word they said. Their families were odd. They should just tell people that they are associates."

James and Gerica got back on the road and came across Castle Whitmaker. It was a land that had very gory things going and very extravagant things going on. They came upon the place on accident. When they first saw the entrance, Gerica was hesitant to go in. She knew they were in an area that they weren't familiar with. James convinced her they should go in and get help. They had no idea how far they were from home. Not one of them wanted to use their phones to get home. It was just one of those days where they were being childish.

They parked on the side of the road for a while before entering into Castle Whitmaker. They saw people walking by and noticed that they would make them feel weird. Gerica opened the car door and threw up. She didn't know why she was getting sick all of a sudden.

James didn't know why all of the people seemed odd. He couldn't put his hands on what was going on around him that made him feel weaker and unsure about himself.

Some of the people walking by were telling horror stories. Some were fighting. There was no security around to break up the fights. The fights were so bad that people were being injured. Gerica and James didn't care though. Their spirits were vexed because they didn't have any real love with family.

When Gerica cleaned herself up, she got out the car and asked someone for directions. This person lied about the directions. Gerica talked to him for five minutes and listened to how he was trying to have her go in circles and wind right back up in the same spot. She wanted to see how long the old man would go on with his story. She got back in the car and could barely move. She told James she wanted to hurt the old man. She said he was trying to have them drive twenty minutes around the area and knew they would end up in the spot they were in now.

James wanted to try his luck with talking to someone. He talked to a woman. Gerica noticed James was flirting with the woman, but she didn't care. She didn't even know where they were at and she knew no one she knew was around. James talked to the woman for a few minutes. He seemed to be enjoying the conversation. Gerica couldn't hear him, but he was complimenting the woman and asked her to look up directions on her phone. He lied and said his was dead.

The woman said her phone was not working. Gerica was getting impatient so she rolled down James' window and told him to hurry up. James ignored Gerica and the woman did not like that. The woman pointed at a kid on his bicycle coming from Castle Whitmaker and James looked. The woman took off running.

Some people knocked on the car and startled Gerica. They wanted to know if she knew them. Gerica would tell them no.

When James got back in the car, he was embarrassed that the woman had ran away from him. He lied and said she knew the kid and didn't want him to see her. James and Gerica looked around and felt out of place.

Despite all the unwanted occurrences, James and Gerica did not want to leave. They wanted to go inside the area and ask for help on how to get home. They were still stingy and didn't want to show maturity by using their phone. They really wanted the other one to act like an adult.

Once cars started pulling up behind them, they really couldn't leave. James drove into Castle Whitmaker. Him and Gerica could not believe all the buildings they were seeing. They parked in front of a large building and went to the front desk where they were told to have a seat and someone would help them. When they turned to have a seat, they both saw people that looked like them. The couple stared at each other and didn't want to look anywhere else. They knew they had to leave immediately.

Gerica noticed that some of the people walking by had her mannerisms, some had her body type, some of them talked like her, and some of them walked similar to her. She didn't think her and James were going to make it. James tried to remain calm when he saw a man placing cups on a table and arguing with a woman. Him and Gerica were arguing earlier that day while he was putting cups on a table.

The couple started to notice people were doing things that they do a lot. They noticed that some of the people were developing skills similar to them right in their faces. They couldn't believe they were in such a fancy building with people using computers and remotes to operate things. There were lots of flat screen televisions with shows playing on them. They saw live views of streets in many areas. Some of which they were familiar with. They saw live views of people in stores. They even saw an area where the weatherman was being recorded.

There was an area where someone was moping the floor. James noticed that this man looked like one of his friends. James grabbed Gerica's hand. They both thought they would die. They were too scared to leave. They could barely move. They sat down close to each other still holding hands. They needed to gain their strength and calm down before making any moves.

Gerica and James' mouths dropped to the floor when they heard their names being called.

"Grandma, I remember when I visited Alhambra in California and I went to a clinic. The doctor came out and called someone with my last name," I say. "It only struck me because I started to notice some strange things happening and being said when I would enter places. Some of the people..." I pause for a second. My mouth drops. "I started to notice that some people would look like you years after that day I remembered being at the clinic. I was on drugs though."

"You'll become wise about this world," my grandma says. "It's the only way you will survive. You have to know the truth."

My grandma says someone told Gerica and James how to exit the area and get home. The couple managed to get up and go to their car. Once they got in, James quickly started the car, but cones were directing him where to go. He drove deep into the area before being able to make any turns to go back the direction he came.

James and Gerica noticed that Castle Whitmaker was starting to look like the slums. It was looking rougher and dirtier. They'd only driven five minutes from the fancy building they asked for directions in, and the place was starting to look horrendous.

They drove through a housing neighborhood where they saw people standing on the side and beating animals. They saw people cutting themselves. They heard people screaming threats that had their voices. They saw people drinking blood and urinating outside. The couple witnessed people being beaten to death. They even saw people being held at gunpoint. They just knew they were about to die.

James kept trying to drive to an area where his sight wasn't effected so bad, but it seemed like the more he drove around to flee from violent and gory scenes, he would see things that were worse.

James ended up running over a piece of glass and the couple was stuck. They were both scared to get out of the car, but they had no choice. James put a knife he had in his pocket and Gerica held onto her pepper spray.

Both James and Gerica's hearts were racing. They were out of place and felt like they had no control of what was going to happen to them. James remembered seeing the man that looked like him in the first building they went in. He remembered that because he was so scared, the man was slow

483

to respond to people and slow to move. He knew Gerica was smart enough to know that these people were operating off of their feelings. They tried to remember everything they saw when they first came in. They needed to remember how everyone was more controllable when they were naturally fearful to a maximum, before they calmed down. They would need those feelings again.

The couple knew they would have to kill individuals that looked like them and blend in, otherwise they would be killed by one of their copies or other individuals that didn't know why there was two of them. Luckily, they found a couple that was kissing that looked just like them sitting on the side of a house. Gerica and James knew that couple wanted their attention.

Gerica and James looked at each other. They knew if they made it out of Castle Whitmaker that they would be changed forever. They knew they would need to take lives to beat the memories they were already getting. Their feelings were being adjusted by the beings and objects.

James and Gerica approached the couple that looked like them. Gerica pepper sprayed the woman and got into a fist fight with her. She banged her head on the wooden house and she became unconscious. James stabbed his copy to death and stabbed Gerica's copy to ensure she was dead. They drug the dead bodies to the back of the house.

The backdoor to the house was opened. It was a one-story house, so James and Gerica scoped it out really quick. No one was home. The pictures lying around didn't look like the couple they had just killed, but the two knew nothing they saw mattered. They were in a freaky town and had no idea how to get out.

They were only in the house for a few minutes before they heard people knocking on the door. James found a gun. He gave Gerica the knife and put the gun in his pocket. They heard people going around to the back of the house. With nothing but fear in him, James opened the front door and let the new couple in. Him and Gerica quickly left out the front and went to a nearby shed where they looked around for a solution to their problem.

James saw a car that was running and him and Gerica quickly got in it and drove away from the crime scene they were involved in. They had no idea where they were in Castle Whitmaker. They came across places that were filming shows they had seen on television. They came across an area where lots of people were headed somewhere. James learned they were going to a late-night screening of a film. He parked the car and him and Gerica joined in with the large audience.

They arrived to an area where everyone was standing watching a film outside. The couple witnessed people putting paint on themselves, chanting gory things, wearing ripped clothing with blood stains on them, and holding weapons. They had no idea what was about to happen at this film screening. Gerica noticed another couple that looked like them. They watched the couple to see who their friends were, then followed the couple to an isolated area where James shot them dead. They switched into their clothes.

James and Gerica befriended the people that were with the couple they had killed. The film they were viewing had people shooting and killing animals, then eating them. The crowd would do the same thing. Gunshots were all over. The film had people drinking blood in it. The crowd would do the same thing. James pulled out his gun and pointed it at Gerica's head because he had become hysterical. The couple they befriended offered to take them home. They left the event early and James and Gerica arrived at a house. They just hugged each other and looked at each other in shock. They didn't want to die. They knew they had no help.

They learned what Earth really was. They learned how serious television was. They had mistaken how serious those high-priced electronics were.

They were trapped at Castle Whitmaker for weeks. During those weeks they would get separated. They would have to continuously kill replications of themselves to survive and have a spot in a place where the people were strange. They needed to naturally feel a great amount of fear to control the beings around them. They had to do unimaginable things with animals. They had to eat gruesome things. They had to fit in with the strangeness around them. The longer they stayed, the more people that they knew from their regular lives were popping up.

Both James and Gerica saw replications of Stalaya, Anna, Abigail, and Valory. They noticed how the girls were making jokes about them. These were the people they had the most sexual desires about. They wanted them to be their kids as well. The clones of the four girls would laugh at the fear James and Gerica had. This is what they needed to make it out of Castle Whitmaker, but that didn't mean they weren't hurt that the replications knew exactly how to act to make them feel shame and regret wanting kids that weren't even theirs. The replications knew how they fronted for one another as a couple and acted like they didn't want stud girl kids, but really did. James and Gerica were separated but still held onto their phones. They called and let each other know they had come across the quad. They knew they were dealing with the same hell from the replications.

Gerica and James would come across each other again. She would have to pretend to be him and he would have to pretend to be her. They would have to eat road kill, sleep with animals, act physically impaired, ridicule all types of people, be bums, then turn around and clean up and be computer geniuses. They had many tasks to complete before they learned which replication to kill and how to make it out of Castle Whitmaker.

They knew they would have to figure out how to get in the computer buildings that were near the entrance. They had to get jobs and learn the technical world. They would learn how to produce films, direct films, write scripts, and many more things that were mind blowing to them because they never took any interest in them. On top of that, these jobs were things they had no knowledge in.

James and Gerica even stumbled on rooms that had over fifteen clones of them. There were too many replications of them and too much technical things going on. They knew they needed to keep in contact with these flawless robots as well as get into an office to keep up with what was going on at Castle Whitmaker.

Gerica and James would make it out of Castle Whitmaker with stolen identities. They would find the office of the new person and their home and take over. They had plenty of money and would have to return to Castle Whitmaker to survive. They would need people to go with them so that these people could be prey to be killed and little to no attention would be on them.

Gerica and James would get married and start their lives again. Only now they were not scared to kill people or have them killed. They had skills they never had before. They knew how to cover things up.

Gerica and James would get in contact with Stalaya, Anna, Abigail, and Valory and tell them about a singing career. The girls were very interested and the couple gave them a time to meet them at a dinner to sign the contracts. James told the girls not to inform anyone of their decision until the contracts were signed.

All of the girls were excited that they had finally gotten their big break. They spent a lot of their savings because they knew they would make it back.

Stalaya was a real bad ass though. She went to her friend Kima's house. Kima was a cute looking white girl that was best friends with all of the girls. Stalaya had to tell her girl that she was offered a singing contract and would be signing soon. She couldn't help but notice that Kima was no longer excited about her visit. Kima became very serious and looked like something was wrong with her.

"We need to go somewhere and talk," Kima told Stalaya. "We need to go now. Do you have somewhere we can go?"

Stalaya knew Kima well and trusted her. They had been friends for seventeen years. They knew each other since they were little.

"Take it easy," Stalaya said. She started to look serious too. "All I did was tell you," Stalaya continued.

"Say no more," Kima said. "Take us somewhere no one can hear us."

"Nobody's at my house," Stalaya said.

The two girls went to Stalaya's house and Kima scoped out the entire place to make sure no one was there. She even went in Stalaya's parents' room to make sure it was vacant.

Kima told Stalaya not to sign those contracts. Stalaya's mouth dropped to the floor. Kima told Stalaya about the chip that would be inserted in her body. "You'll be controlled and in pain by someone day and night," Kima said.

"You think Gerica and James are trying to put something in my body to control me?" Stalaya asked confused.

"Listen, my cousin signed a singing contract," Kima said. "He told us who the producers were. My family learned that the producers had came across a place they were never supposed to step foot in. They had to do all types of evil and malicious acts to get out of the place. They even had to kill a few people for the first time in their lives. They learned where clones were being created. They had to kill some to get out of the place. The producers are twisted and sick. They learned how to produce in the place they were never supposed to step foot on. They learned many jobs there. Stalaya, they learned how to chip people with a device and control them. Make them do whatever they wanted at any time of the day. If the chip is turned off, you will die. Sure you'll get the career, but you won't get any money. My cousin made less than my mom did when she was working at a restaurant. You'll be on television, but you won't be happy. You'll get a new name. You'll still go to school because you won't be able to pay for tutors and that high class life you thought you would be living. You won't be able to afford a mansion for your family, let alone yourself. You'll be on television Stalaya, and you won't care. The pain those people endured on whatever land they came across was infinite. Most people die when they step on the soil of the places that produce films. Some people are fortunate to make it out."

Kima told Stalaya that she knew she'd seen people floating around town that looked like other people. She let her know that strange things start happening in towns where people start making it on television. Only people that know someone who made it and are smart enough to know it's them under new names, know the truth about what's going on with celebrities. Kima told Stalaya that the people who want her, have seen doubles of her.

"Trust me I know," Kima said. "It's only a matter of time before you see them if you sign that contract. Don't go to the location to record in the studio. They are setting you up. They most likely don't really like you. Hell, they probably don't care about anyone after all they've been through on those forbidden grounds. There's not many on this Earth, but they exist. In this area, Castle Whitmaker is not far. It also goes by Deadly Sorrow. No one really talks about it. Not many know the truth about entertainment artists."

Stalaya looked in Kima's eyes and told her, "I believe you."

"I could be killed for telling you this," Kima said. "My family told me they would slit my throat if I was ever caught telling anyone the things my cousin revealed when he was in so much pain. My family put him to sleep. However, Julian Court still has a spot on television. His clone took his place. You'll be in school and no one will know it's you on television. They'll say you look like the individual, but surely with all the money people think celebrities have, you wouldn't be sitting in their school. Definitely not with a lot of fame."

"We have to tell Anna, Abigail, and Valory," Stalaya said.

"We can't," Kima said. "I took a risk telling you. I can't have all my best friends sold out. It would devastate me. Especially knowing the truth about what happened to my cousin and the truth about celebrities and their handlers. You came to me and I know all of my girls. If it was one of them that came to me, I wouldn't have said anything. I seen you girls performing at parties. I seen how into performing y'all get. But I noticed that you would let them shine more. You were more into them and getting them recognized. You even told me that. You said if they wanted you out, you would do it. I spent time with them alone too. I know them. They won't believe what I'm saying and even if they did, they would think they could handle a little bit of pain. However, it's not a little pain. It's your enemies controlling you. They will learn you inside and out. You will pay for wanting to be famous. Your life will be over. You'll drink blood and sleep with animals. These are your enemies we're talking about."

"So you're saying let them sign the contract and ruin their lives?" Stalaya asked.

"You can't help them if you're chipped too," Kima said. "Believe me, you'll notice instantly the change in them when you see they have become entertainers. They'll say things they never said before. They'll be comfortable doing things they know are disgusting for other people to look at. They will be crying out for help in ways that most people won't know. A lot of people will shun them. They will have no clue that the girls are in trouble. They can't talk about the chip. They are under oath. If they break that oath, they can be killed. The clones won't care, so the producers can call it quits on their lives the second they run their mouth. You will know the girls need help and I will help you. You won't be naïve to their irregular behavior. Neither will I. When they are on television, more people will wake up. Our school isn't the best. We don't have many people that have sense to know that real entertainers sit with us, but some of us do know the deep secrets of Height Daze."

Height Daze is the name of the entertainment industry. There's only a few areas where artists are given their careers and appear on television. Castle Whitmaker, High Class Territory, and The Land Spot are only a few.

"We fight to turn down the chip in the people we love," Kima said. "We fight to fuck with the people fucking with them. We don't care if it's a car accident sometimes. No one deserves to have all that power over someone. Anna, Abigail, and Valory will need us to take their place a few times for strength. They'll need to know that we've always been real and loyal friends to them. When they know we are willing to get down and dirty with them and are trying to get them their lives back, it will give them better thoughts. Believe me Stalaya. Just believe me. Don't sign that contract and take the oath."

Stalaya let Kima know how their families didn't really care about them. She knew if her girls were in trouble that they wouldn't get the family help.

"There's rumors that sometimes people have to sacrifice a blood relative to be famous," Kima told Stalaya. "Have that relative killed. Not everyone has to do it. People hear these rumors and panic sometimes. They'll kill the artist faster if they think they're trying to have them killed. Do you think they are under this type of contract?"

"I have no idea," Stalaya said.

"Whatever the case may be, they will need us now more than ever," Kima said. "We can't take a chance on their families wanting them dead for putting their lives in danger. It's said that most artists only live for three years after being chipped, but that's just a rumor."

"If they have to do all those nasty things you said with the chip in them, then I'm sure it malfunctions. It's probably true," Stalaya said.

"I need you," Kima said with tears falling down her face.

"Can I ask you something?" Stalaya asked.

"Anything," Kima cried.

"Why would you take a chance on telling me something that could get you killed?" Stalaya asked.

"If I lost all of my friends to the music industry, I would want to kill myself," Kima said. "Those people are really wicked. It would hurt them if someone made it and didn't have to suffer under their control. That's what that *no* means. That's how serious turning down a deal for popularity and money is. That's how big that decision is."

Stalaya never showed to sign the contracts. When Anna called her, she said that she changed her mind. Stalaya wished her girls the best.

Anna, Abigail, and Valory signed the contracts. They would meet Gerica and James at Castle Whitmaker where they would be chipped and see replications of themselves. They would have to kill people. Eat gruesome things. They had to do many rituals. The three girls really felt like they had made a terrible mistake when they recognized they were being controlled.

They began to wonder if they were really talented or if Gerica and James chose them for another reason. Without confirmation, they thought their talent was the worst thing they could've ever exposed in their lifetime. Gerica and James told the girls how they wished they were their kids. How they saw them around and loved to watch them interact, but the girls never paid them any attention. They told them how they loved how they dressed, and talked about how pretty they were. The couple held nothing back. They knew how old they were bothered the girls and how ugly they were bothered them too. They knew they weren't people that Anna, Abigail, and Valory could stand to look at unless they had something to offer them.

Gerica and James had fun making the girls hold guns at each other's heads. They shot them for fun and had all the healing medicine. Gerica and James met people that could help them have all the fun they wanted torturing the girls.

Gerica and James had the girls go to their family events and make them look good by telling good stories about them. All the while, the trio was hoping someone would help them.

When Stalaya saw the girls around, she noticed they couldn't stand the sight of her. She could tell something was wrong with her girls. Stalaya spent so much time with them that they would eventually slip up and tell her what they were going through and wouldn't remember saying it. Stalaya realized Kima was right.

Anna, Abigail, and Valory hated Stalaya. They wondered if she knew all along that signing those contracts meant that they would be living in hell on Earth. Stalaya never said anything.

Stalaya would meet up with Kima and tell her who Gerica and James were. They would have to follow them around secretively to see their whereabouts. "We have to turn down their chips," Kima would constantly say to Stalaya to let her know those things were no joke.

The girls' music videos began airing on television. One day Kima was around the girls when their videos came on. She could not believe she was witnessing her girls watch themselves on television under different names, and it was like they didn't exist in the television world. Kima would look completely shocked and stare at them in disbelief. Their own families wondered why they looked so similar to the famous group *Real Gold*. Anna's name was Kelina. Abigail's name was Helena. Valory's name was Delilah.

Anna, Abigail, and Valory never told their families they got record deals. They knew their families didn't really care about them anyways, so it didn't matter how much pain they were going through, their families wouldn't care.

Stalaya knew the girls couldn't stand her. She knew they hated that she wasn't dealing with the same amount of pain. She found a way to swap spots with Anna and Abigail who looked the most similar to her. She did the rituals and even went in Gerica and James' house pretending to be them, while they were out and about being able to deal with their stress. Stalaya stayed away from her girls unless she was letting them know that she was working to give them a part of her normal life.

Kima would use sneaky ways to tell people who knew Anna, Abigail, and Valory and weren't naïve to the fact that it was them on television, who Gerica and James were. These people who saw the videos and knew the three girls were furious. Kima would constantly let Stalaya know how ignorant the majority of the world was when it came to entertainment, but she told her that the small amount of people who are aware do real evil things to these producers to ruin days of their lives whether it be at a store, a parking lot, the library, or a mutual friend's house.

Stalaya would know where the girls were headed and find somewhere she could just see them. She noticed that they walked different and talked different at times. Kima told her they could control her second by second with that chip in her.

One day the girls were at a friend's party while people that wanted to help them took their place in Gerica and James' lives. Anna, Abigail, and Valory were shot to death. People knew they couldn't endure anymore pain.

"Gerica and James are still alive. Unfortunately, some people will still die of old age even with the chip," my grandma says.

No one but Kima knew that Stalaya was supposed to be a part of *Real Gold*. Stalaya noticed that the videos were being altered and what her girls really looked like was disappearing.

Stalaya fought to get in seats in front of computers that would let people know who she was. She was able to let people know she started the group. She knew with what she would call, *the realness of the wind*, that people would figure out that she had made it. That she was alive. That someone that knew the girls and was supposed to be in the group was still out there.

It was a battle to get rid of the real image of celebrities from television. They were really hated. They were for an agenda that was ran by racists. They didn't care. They wanted the money. People that looked good were really despised by people like Gerica and James who got to learn the real thoughts of real narcissists.

"There's lots of killings still to this date for these entertainers," my grandma says. She says their families and people who knew them or know what's going on, won't let their image or voices die. People like Gerica and James have their crews too. It's a real battle to not let those entertainers be forgotten. Stalaya telling the world that she was still around scared the hell out of Gerica and James. They had no idea how some of their relatives were winding up dead so quickly. Stalaya knowing exactly who they were helped her to get rid of people trying to take Anna, Abigail, and Valory off of television all together.

Stalaya couldn't believe real people could go to Castle Whitmaker and kill off a clone and pass as the trio. There's real wickedness and evil in this world. Their own family would try to make it in Castle Whitmaker so they could be the girls because they didn't like them.

The trio had many surgeries, so it was becoming harder and harder to keep up with them. People that knew them and had pictures of them knew which clips were real. They could tell the difference between clones and their friends.

The very few people that know about Height Daze got wind of Stalaya's story and tried to keep her strong. Stalaya knew most of the world was believing a lie when it came to her friends. It hurt her to know that her friend's had died and people were replacing them on television. Most of the world thought they were watching the girls get older when they had already passed away. Fortunately, she got to meet other people who knew entertainers and the truth about Height Daze.

Gerica and James didn't want the real stories out there. They would die one day and didn't want people to experience *Real Gold*. They didn't want people to get the real hype, let alone see them.

"These people were real entertainers. They were really good-looking people that most people don't get to see. They had real talent. The producers were one of a kind too. People really wanted them dead. They made it through hell stumbling upon a place they never were supposed to enter. They had real bitterness for their own mistakes and took it out on people they envied," my grandma says. "They learned the hard way what this land was about. Smart people were able to pick up on things and learned from their mistakes. They didn't like that. They wanted everyone to know the truth about life and this place we walk on. They wanted them to go through it too. A lot of the producers wanted people to stumble upon the place like they did. They can hire people and have them chipped, but that wasn't good enough sometimes to those that had to fight to survive with all of their feelings in the hands of strange creatures that resembled them."

"How did Olifus know all of this Grandma?" I ask.

"It's drugs Shona," my grandma says.

"Grandma, I've been up all day listening to your stories," I say.

"And you're going to listen to more," my grandma says.

I hear a boom effect from the radio and snap out of my thoughts.

"So what you like to watch on TV?" Scalina asks.

"I like to watch *Trust in These Ladies,*" I say.

"Oh, that's that show with them women who are married to rich men," Scalina says. "I know what you talking about. When them women start arguing, I can't even pick a side. I like too many of those girls."

"I know right," I say. "They all look beautiful, have good personalities, and seem cool as fuck."

"You know they go through all that bullshit too just to be on television," Scalina says. "They the realist."

I can't believe Scalina just got real with me on that level. I know them bitches on *Trust in These Ladies* go through hell behind closed doors just to be on television.

"What's that damn shit called that they are involved in?" I ask.

"The Baplisan," Scalina says. "They done sold out and they got to deal with the consequences."

This scary ass shit makes me drift off. I hear my grandma's voice. I see me and my grandma sitting in my living room on the couch. She's lighting a candle.

"She used you and showed you how you could really manipulate a child's mind and get things out of her. She got those stories out of you and said don't touch them," my grandma says. "She knew all about the one statement rule and how it can change everything." My grandma said she got everything out of me so if anything did happen to me before I finished this book, basically all of her projects to date, she wanted me to know that she already got my enemies back.

"You make sure you experience me when you're not on drugs," my grandma says. "No matter what choices you made with money, she drug it all out of you."

My grandmother says she treated me like a baby for thirty-five years and now she's going to teach me how to be a woman. She wants me to write that. What do I look like? I've always been a woman.

496

I shake my head and snap out of my thoughts and start talking to Scalina again.

"They didn't know what the hell they was getting into," I say.

"They did, it's just they didn't know how bad it was. They didn't know it would keep getting worse," Scalina says.

"Them niggas want out and can't get out," I say.

"People just say they ain't shit for selling out, but don't know they didn't know all the shit that came with it," Scalina says. "Them niggas want out like a mutha fucka."

"The fact that they can even live through that mess is what makes them still attractive to me," I say. "People clown them and make they lives a living hell when they get lucky and see them out in public, but know damn well the shit they have to do is bad as all hell to a point where they shouldn't even be thinking about them selling out in the first place."

"Them niggas sold out to the damn devil," Scalina says. "That shit is bullshit."

"Hell yea," I say. "I look at the women on *Trust in These Ladies* and can't believe they sold out. I can't believe they doing all types of hellish shit to be on television."

"If they don't do it, they'll be killed," Scalina says. "The Baplisan is nothing to play with."

I'm so damn drunk, I'm talking about this crazy shit the Baplisan. I hate talking about it. When I talk to my friends about it, they get scared. They hate to say the name. They think the government will come after them.

Scalina keeps smoking, and I drink looking down at our lines having fun by the pool.

"See. It looks like they becoming cool. Hopefully we can too," Scalina says.

"Finish smoking so we can go back downstairs," I say.

Scalina's eyes give away that she has been smoking. They're dim and turning red. When she gets outside with me, her line sisters know she was having a good time upstairs. It doesn't matter though because my line and I were always planning on letting the pledges let loose tonight and get drunk and high. The thing with them is, if they don't smoke or drink, we will force them to.

When Scalina and I get downstairs, I catch Trayna's eyes. I sit on the side of the pool and have her swim over to me.

"I been thinking," I say. "I think I will invite you over one night to experience how I like to get down when I need a night to acknowledge all the things about me."

Trayna gets happy. "I look forward to it," Trayna says. She's being flirtatious naturally.

Caya passes Jamia the blunt. The pledges are shocked. They are getting happy knowing that my Sorors and I are relaxing and letting them feel the buzz and high. Caya gives Jamia a shot to take. Jamia is looking at her line sisters that are in the pool and dancing. She's feeling good instantly. Her line sisters are cheering her on and smiling.

I can tell this line is a cool batch of college kids.

"Girls get out and drink and smoke with us," Shemina says. She shares her blunt with Delisha.

My Sorors and I let the pledges drink and smoke while we play in the pool. I grab a beach ball and me and the girls play catch. We call each other's line names when we throw the ball. We have our drinks near us on the concrete while we're in the pool. We're smiling and throwing water on each other. We're jumping off the diving board and pushing each other in the pool.

The pledges are enjoying smoking more than drinking. They are happy they can do something that relaxes their nerves from dealing with all our bullshit.

Some of my line sisters get out the pool and start strolling. I stay in the pool and throw the beach ball. I keep drinking. Stressing because I can't smoke makes me drink more.

My mind wanders off.

"Some people need new real life situations to beat the drugs faster," my grandma says. "Why you think some of them start killing people?"

I'm mad because the drugs really do take my thoughts. They are running away with everything I think.

There was three times I realized the drugs were pulling anything in my brain that I had ever witnessed. The drugs showed me chairs in a puzzle that I did. I remembered them and wished I could relax there. I knew that puzzle was nowhere in my mind, but I had seen it before is the point the drugs were trying to make. I left it alone. Then the drugs showed me a picture of a brown hole in one of my books. I did not have that on my mind at all or anything that would lead me to it. Then when the drug showed me the word *care* that's in red, white, and blue in one of my books, I woke up and believed them. They could make me remember anything.

The point is I've seen the images before. The drugs can find them. The word *careless* I wrote and remembering *care* in the book. Things started to make me feel real weird.

Writing a book and wanting to feel my grandmother's love at the same time. This is real love. At work I have to stay focused. I shouldn't even be out of the house while recovering from drugs, but I do need new thoughts and they can mess with me anywhere.

The drugs have me not wanting to do more than one thing in a day. Wash, cook, clean, go to ride some rollercoasters. The drugs are taking everything I see and making it negative. I had to keep repeating the negative stories over and over. I must've said the story about fighting those boys over fifty times over the course of twenty days. I could become suicidal reciting shit like this, but the realness in these drugs is nothing to play with. Imagine people that can't cut through the drugs quick like this.

I hear a lot of movement and snap back into reality.

Some of my line sisters are grabbing floats.

Scalina says, "So who's going to hold their breath underwater?" Her line sisters laugh with her. They are really feeling their blunts and drinks.

My line and I are laughing as well. The pledges already know why. "Of course, if we don't forget what you said we can always get you back later," Telana says. We can't say that enough. I slap hands with Casha.

"So, my Big Sisters," Trayna says. "How long do we get to smoke and drink?"

"Until we say you can't," Caya says. "Enjoy yourselves."

It's dark outside now.

I get in my jacuzzi with my sorority sisters, while the pledges keep smoking and drinking.

My line sisters and I talk bad about the people that brought us in. We are out of our minds with all the shit we had to deal with to be Alpha Eta Nu members.

I switch the conversation to all the good nights we've had. No matter what we went through, we always get to say we're members of Alpha Eta Nu. So many people are jealous of us for being in a sorority. They know we get hazed. They just don't know how. They know we get our asses beat to wear these letters. They think we are capable of dealing with any bullshit that comes our way from bitches mad we are wearing the letters. People fuck with us on purpose because they know we are supposed to act civilized in public. They want to make us lose our letters.

My girls and I drink to that.

We have the pledges bring us drinks. My Sorors have them bring the blunts. They pass them back and forth.

"Are we not supposed to talk about this night with our prophytes?" Delisha asks.

"Y'all can tell them whatever y'all want," Shemina says. My Sorors and I laugh again. We let the pledges get in the jacuzzi with us. We talk bad about their prophytes.

"Tashina ain't shit," I say.

"Neither is that slutty Amy," Caya says. "Them niggas are weak ass fuck. That's why we needed to get in with this new line."

The pledges are learning that me and my girls don't even like their prophytes. By now they know that they can say whatever they want to their prophytes about what my line and I say about them; we can always deny it. The pledges have to make it through their process anyways. The pledges can tell that me and my girls are close. We could give a damn about anything they go back and tell their prophytes. We don't care to hang around them.

When the girls and I get out the jacuzzi, we chill around the house in our towels. I have a few showers. Me and the girls take turns in them. Some of the damn pledges forgot to wash their hair in the shower. I don't get real mad because I know we played with their minds in the pool. Whenever they are hazed, they are bound to forget some things.

My Sorors and I put on our pink tops and blue jean shorts. We compliment our outfits with sparkly silver flats. We have on silver jewelry. We all have on silver earrings. Some of us have on silver bracelets, and some of us have on silver necklaces. A few of us even have on silver anklets.

When my Sorors and I finish getting ready, we help wash some of the pledges' hair. I wash Trayna's hair. We're in the bathroom in my room using the sink. My bathroom is decorated with gold rugs, a toilet cover, and towels. It's very spacious. Getting all this chlorine out of this girl's head is nothing to play with. I hate the damage that shit can do.

"Don't you love to swim without a swim cap, and then have to wash your damn hair?" I rhetorically ask.

"Girl I hate wearing a swim cap," Trayna says.

"I do too," I say. I mainly hate it because when I'm showing my damn body off, that damn cap does me no justice. When I have a two-piece bikini on, I like to feel completely sexy. That means my hair is showing. Wearing that cap makes my damn head hurt anyways.

"So who are you the closest with on your line?" I ask shampooing Trayna's hair.

"I like them all the same," Trayna says. "It's like it's hard to even develop a strong relationship with them while I'm being... I mean while I'm going through this process."

"While you're being hazed you wanted to say?" I ask.

"No. I said it right. When I'm going through this process," Trayna says.

"Good answer," I say. "So what you like most about my crib?"

"I like how it's so big for just one person," Trayna says. "I think I may want to stay single. I know you enjoy just coming home knowing you can afford your own living."

"I sure do like feeling good because I can provide for myself," I say. "I don't need help from no damn body."

"It's good you don't have to rely on your mom or dad," Trayna says.

"Girl who you telling," I say. "I'm in debt to my mom right now, but I'll pay her back when I can. She's put me through too much shit. She shouldn't be telling me to pay her back a fucking thing. That's how I know she's not remorseful for a fucking thing she's done to me."

I start looking real bitter and drift off.

I need a break from writing. I was at the amusement park the other day, and I was writing in line for a total of six hours.

"With love, you know to be patient with speech," my grandma says. "You also know to do what the hell I say. You gone get it. I need it all there."

I always thought people knew my thoughts under the influence of drugs. I thought they knew what I was thinking and how I was feeling, and my body would give them feelings. I know people get killed a fucking lot behind these damn drugs.

"You have to play tricks to live here. I needed you to write those books exactly like that," my grandma says.

"But Grandma, why did you have me talk about my friends in them? Why would you let me write dark secrets in there?" I ask loudly and frustrated.

"You have the same birthdate as two of your relatives that mistreated you and you never think of any of them on your birthdate. Real love can do that," my grandmother says. "Don't worry about what you already wrote."

I look down and sad.

"What's wrong?" my grandma asks.

"I'm still having a hard time shaking telling Nadia about the assault," I say. "I wish I wouldn't have told her."

"Nadia did this before when the cops came and addressed you vandalizing those people's property with that girl," my

502

grandmother says. "She told the cop she never was pushing you repeatedly down the street. She thought you were going to jail and still put her bullshit in so you could think about it when you left. When she walked in with the cop, you knew she was mad them advisors didn't get to sit comfortable in what they did to you. She didn't give a damn about you possibly going to prison. Just you giving them damn people a way to interrupt their nights of comfort when they removed you. Then she realized that's all she had and decided to wait on the cop to arrest you with her sick ass and he didn't."

My heart feels like it has an irregular beat. I get myself together and focus on the conversation with Trayna.

"Can I tell you something?" Trayna asks.

"You sure can," I say. "If you need to snitch on your line sisters for something they've done, go ahead," I joke. I'm rinsing her hair now.

"One time while my mom was washing my hair, she told me she didn't care if I drowned in the water," Trayna says. I stop massaging her head for a minute. "I couldn't believe it," Trayna continues. "I don't know why she decided to say it, but she did. I never forgot it. Every time I get my hair washed, I think about what she told me."

"I know exactly what you mean," I say. "It's like we're lucky if we get parents that are bigger than any abuse they've been through. Verbal abuse hurts like hell."

"It's like she wanted me to remember her telling me that for the rest of my life," Trayna says.

"My mom, excuse me, Nadia, is the same way," I say. "Only thing with her is I know she wants to keep being a verbal abuse bitch for the rest of my life. If I pick up the phone, I have to worry about her saying something outrageous to me. I just hate her."

I start looking real angry and space off.

I see my grandmother at my dining room table eating.

"Don't worry about not one smile she has on her face," my grandma says shaking her head and eating a piece of chicken. "Tell her that's why I did it."

503

Me and Nadia hung up and she didn't say a single thing to uplift me.

Days before Mother's Day, I was stripped of life completely, but something kept me moving. There was something that made me think my sanity was there too. I would walk into a shell confused, then look both ways as if someone might be there. It was my grandmother's love that kept me going. She hopped me into a girl that kept saying she was pretty and beautiful. I was released from this girl and brought into another one. I looked forward for a few seconds, then both ways again. My grandmother wanted me to know I wasn't completely lost. The next shell had the thought of me telling Nadia about the assault that came over me and how she told me Jania said I bloodied her nephew and son. Then I was released from this shell and started walking. I walked forward and started looking both ways again.

The next thing I heard was, "Tell her that's why I did it." Then I remembered I went two entire months without thinking about what Nadia had said. I talked to her for an hour for days in April and for days in May. I didn't think about anything negative.

I had to keep repeating the story to understand how my grandmother's love came about. She told me she always loved me.

I remember Nadia forgetting three things I asked her. I did text her to release my feelings because she obviously needed a reminder I didn't want or need to hear from that side of the family. I was friends with some people Nadia said were distant cousins on social media, then somehow, we weren't friends anymore. My first thought was Nadia made up some lies. That happens all the time.

"So what does that tell you?" my grandma asks. "You need to make some decisions."

I also remember I needed to clear the unwanted feelings I had and text Nadia if she said anything in response to Jania. She said *yes I did* and she said they side of the family has problems.

I have to remember my grandma say she was waiting on this situation to step into my life real heavy when I lose strength.

All of these suicide feelings from all of these people while I'm recovering from drugs. "You're a gangster," my grandma says. "This is good for you."

I shake my head and get frustrated with myself for spacing off. I come back to reality and apologize for losing my head for a few minutes.

"That's why you not supposed to answer the phone no more," Trayna says. She picks her head up and starts dripping water on the floor when she says, "I mean you're supposed to make a big decision on how to deal with your mom." She's breathing hard now. She thinks I will get mad at her for giving me harsh advice.

"You're alright," I say. "I know I'm not supposed to talk to this crazy woman again. Sometimes I just wish the doctor would call me and say they had it wrong. I could live with that my whole life." I want to drink to that. "Asayla can you bring me two shots?!" I shout so she can hear me downstairs.

I'm almost done washing and conditioning Trayna's hair.

"But look, I don't want to spend this night like this," I say. "We in here doing your hair. It's about to be a cool night. Let's talk about some good things, like what you got for Christmas last year. I love to talk about Christmas."

"I got four hundred dollars," Trayna says.

"What else?" I ask.

"As long as I get money, I don't care what else," Trayna says. She quickly remembers I asked her a question and says, "I got clothes, CDs, movies, board games, shoes, and a new phone from relatives. Even my mom gave me some things."

"I didn't get anything from family," I say. "I mean, girl let's just switch conversations."

Asayla comes in my bathroom with three shots and margaritas on platters. "What we drinking too?" Asayla asks.

"Me being adopted," I say.

"Girl, I'm with it," Asayla says.

505

Me, Trayna, and Asayla take our shots. I feel so good. One day the doctor might actually call me and tell me a deep secret. We drink some of our margaritas. Asayla sits on my bathroom counter while I dry Trayna's hair.

"What y'all doing downstairs?" I ask. "Those of y'all not tending to someone's hair?"

"Drinking and smoking of course," Asayla says. "And dancing."

"I hear people stepping," I say. "Who down there getting down?"

"That's Caya and Casha," Asayla says. "I told the pledges they better take visual notes." Asayla knows what step they are doing downstairs because of the beat and joins in and does it. I do it with her.

Me and Asayla are doing the butterfly motion with our hands in front and hitting the floor. Our stomps in between are together, and we don't miss a beat with the girls' downstairs. We do movements hitting each-other's hands and clapping between the other person's legs when she jumps in the air. We bend down and clap between our leg with it remaining on the ground, clap behind our back, then clap between the other leg while it's on the ground. We stomp, clap, then hit our chest and move in a circle. We are really showing out.

Trayna is loving watching us. She has a big smile on her face.

"I wish I was on y'all line," Trayna says.

"Don't say that," I say. "Do what you have to do. Make the sorority," I sternly say. "Damn. You should have brought more liquor up here," I say to Asayla.

"Let me go get some sister," Asayla says flirting with her eyes.

I finish drying Trayna's hair. "Do you know how to flat-iron your own hair?" I ask.

"Of course Big Sister," Trayna says. "I can't wait to be a part of Alpha Eta Nu. I love this sisterhood. I wish y'all were bringing us in."

"I knew you would say that eventually," I say.

Asayla comes back up with more shots. She has wine, just incase we want to chase it. She's also smoking her blunt.

"You want to hit the blunt?" I ask Trayna. It's not mine, but this is how me and my girls do. I can offer someone some of their blunt with no problem.

Trayna is scared to say *yes* or *no*. I take the blunt from Asayla and give it to her. The smoke smells so amazing. I miss it so much. I'm ready to break my recovery, but I can't. I hate myself right now. I know it's the weed that gave me these terrible side effects in my head. I want to get rid of them, and if I smoke again, it will take longer. I want to cheat so bad.

The smoke makes me drift off.

"There was a man named Baron Din," my grandma says. "He was a dark brown skinned man."

"Grandma, I don't think I can take another story. These stories are getting too messy," I say. "I feel like I'm becoming mentally ill when these stories come to mind throughout my day."

I get up to leave.

"Sit back down got damn it!" my grandma demands. She's looking at me sternly.

She says Baron worked at a seafood restaurant. It sold burgers, fries, nachos, and other fatty foods too. It was one of the hot spots in New Orleans. He was very popular amongst residents, people from other cities, states, and visitors from other countries. He had a big smile that was welcoming and he always made sure his customers were happy.

When people walked in his place of business, he made sure to greet as many as he could. He learned some of their names and even told jokes to them. He asked them if they were having a good day and if they weren't, he would try to cheer them up. He would give them extra food sometimes and slide in some samples of other things. No one would snitch on him. Every now and then some crazy person would say something, like your cousin Halaya, but Baron was the manager, so he wasn't worried about getting in any trouble.

Baron was well known for giving food to people in need on the streets. When people that slept on the streets came in and purchased something, he made sure to give them an abundant amount and tell them to keep holding on.

"Baron knew that his kind acts would get people to keep coming back," I say. I'm just not in the mood for any of Man Man's characters. If they do anything good, I think it's because they have something to lose. In Baron's case, he needs people to keep saying good things about him, so if one day something goes wrong, he'll have a lot of folks vouching that he always did his job correctly.

"He didn't want to lose his job," I continue looking restless. I know this is going to end bad. I can't believe how much mess the other stories Man Man told had in them. I'm just going to let my grandma finish.

"Cajun Lovin'," I say. "Is that where he worked?"

"That was the name of it baby," my grandma says.

My grandma continues to say that Baron was an obese man. At work he was consistent with pleasing everyone that came through the door. The only times he ever lost his temper is when his employees weren't doing their job correctly. Olifus said Baron took out any issues with customers, his weight, or his life in general on his employees.

Sometimes the employees would catch Baron spaced off talking to himself when arriving to work or while cleaning up when no customers were around. Baron would be snapping as if he was talking to someone. Every occasion was different. Sometimes he would be going on and on about how much he hated his mother. His employees knew it was because of his weight because he wouldn't stop looking at his stomach. Other times he would be saying racist things about other races. He would be out of his mind. He was able to snap out of it to perform well for work.

"He was gaining his needed energy for the day because he was so fat," I say. "I bet on his days off he goes off about something for a long time and has a hard time stopping because he can't get rid of his gut."

508

My grandma pops me on the mouth. Sometimes I feel like she does it for no reason. I didn't think what I said was smart at all.

"I'm having issues too Grandma," I say. "This weight is not going anywhere. I can't believe I haven't eatin' at Cajun Lovin' or any other fried food places, and I haven't cooked any fried food and I still can't get back to how skinny I was before."

"When you were living out on the streets all those days, it's easy to get caught up in the pain of life that you don't even realize you're losing the weight," my grandma says.

I was on drugs hard and it was days I couldn't even be inside. I needed to be out for long periods of time. I never told anyone but my grandma. There were days I stayed with strangers. Some drug addicts let me stay at their home, and other days some store owners let me stay in their home.

I would lie and tell my family that I was living with roommates and things just went bad so I had to leave, otherwise I would be locked up for fighting.

"Grandma, you know I haven't been in a real fight before. I mean, there was the time Nadia was pushing me repeatedly in Halaya's neighborhood asking me where I was going," I say. "She had called me a bitch and I started walking away from her. She came after me like a monster. Something was wrong with her."

"If she would've spoke the truth, she would've kept saying *I'm stupid and diagnosed as mentally ill.* She would've said she was ugly repeatedly and said it was true because of how people looked at her every day. She was suicidal Shona," my grandma says.

My grandma is starting to look sad again. She tells these stories so serious and firm though.

She says Olifus told her Baron had two daughters and a wife. His wife was a drug addict when he met her. She wasn't fat at all. It bothered Baron that his wife had two kids and never got as big as him.

"I hate when men can't stand looking at their woman who is in shape knowing good and well they don't want to walk around with another fat person," I say. "Baron is the type. I know it's not all of them." I say it's not all of them, but I don't mean it. I've met too many men that can barely stand looking at themselves because they are so fat and ugly.

My grandma says Baron's daughters were eighteen and nineteen at the time that these next events happened. He often told the mother to hit their girls for the smallest things like not doing their chores on time. He never cared to hear the excuse. His weight was getting the best of him. He hated to eat at the table with his family. His girls Halesta and Mania were very thin and very pretty light skinned girls. Halesta was the oldest. His wife Toraya was brown skinned just like him.

Toraya wanted to leave Baron, but was too afraid. During some of Baron's rants when he was mad about his weight, he would threaten to hurt his family. Toraya was too scared to lose her children. She was staying. Baron would say real evil things about how his daughters looked. He needed to see them cry. He would damage their brains with thoughts he knew they would never forget from their father. The mother tried to help her girls with kind words, but they wouldn't work. The girls would go out, drink, and smoke just like their mother.

There were days when Toraya, Halesta, and Mania were scared to go home. They would get a hotel or stay at a friend's house to avoid being around Baron. Toraya knew every day Halesta and Mania were away from him could keep their hearts with a good feeling for a long time knowing what it was like to be away from their father.

Halesta and Mania told their mother that they began smoking and drinking because they couldn't take Baron's behavior. Toraya did what any mother would do and told her girls not to engage in those activities. She knew it would be hard to get her children to not partake in such events with a dad she knew was suicidal almost every second of every day. Toraya always wondered how Baron was making it, and it was because he had her and their daughters to take his frustration out on.

Toraya was strong enough to not smoke with her children. She wanted them to know she was strong enough to handle their father.

"So the only time the girls felt any type of freedom in their teen years was when they were away from their dad?" I ask.

"That's what Olifus said," my grandma says. "Man Man told me about a boy named Junior." She says Junior played many instruments and was a great singer. He attended Juliendard University. That school was the best of the best. It was a school for musicians. Many celebrities' kids would attend this school.

I know who celebrities' kids are. The kids that knew their families were on television under different names. Only the educated really knew who these kids were.

The kids at Juliendard University were most known for their Rhythm and Blues and Jazz music. Those kids got down. They could change people's bad moods into good ones. They were unbelievable and Juliendard was definitely a one-of-a-kind school.

My grandma has a big smile on her face. She can't believe how talented the kids at that school were. The part she loves is that they were mainly black kids. Light, brown, dark, red bones, I mean just all the pretty shades that black is considered. I still separate myself and say brown is not the same as black. I'm not the only one. Somewhere along the way of this world, things got twisted. We all know brown and black are two different colors. I don't care what the job applications say, I'm a brown woman. They can have me write whatever the hell they want.

My grandma says Junior was a popular student at Juliendard. He was a handsome young brown fellow. He knew he had a smile that was enjoyed by a lot of his colleagues. As a freshman, he was well known for his voice and his skills on the piano. He knew he was talented and had a look that could make it on television.

I turn my head quickly to my grandma. I can't stand the sound of television right now. I'm learning how evil it really is.

Junior spent a lot of time in the coffee lounge. It was called The Brown Sugar Spot. It was a beautifully lit three-story circular area with round wooden tables. It was the perfect spot to listen to relaxing music and talk with friends. People could even study in the soothing area.

Junior could make friends easily, but he was selective. Whenever he was at a social event, people really enjoyed his personality. He was friendly to everyone and he knew that made more people want to be around him. He knew he had a look that made people want to look at him, so he knew being kind would make people want to be around him more. He always knew he would be on television one day and wanted to build an audience early. He was also arrogant in knowing when he left a setting, people would wish they could see him again.

"At least he was kind," I say. "No matter what his cocky ways were."

Junior spent a lot of time on campus because he wanted to really enjoy college. He knew it would be over quickly. He loved the campus vibe and energy of the students.

"What was his home life like?" I ask.

"He was a regular kid from the projects in New Orleans," my grandma says. "There was something about the young folks in Olifus' stories. These kids were loved as project kids by many that knew they were just like them. Junior went out and hung on corners drinking early and missing his curfew too."

"It was like there was pressure on them to make it out the projects," I say. "People didn't know they were doing that to them I guess."

"There was a girl named Eliza," my grandma says. She was a bright skinned girl with curly hair. She had a short haircut like a boy would have. This Eliza was one of a kind. When people saw her, they couldn't believe their eyes. She had the perfect eyes. It's like they naturally made people think she was flirting with them. Her lips and nose were perfect. She had a cool and pretty voice. She knew how to dress and was into herself. She knew she looked really good.

Eliza sometimes got tired of catching people just staring at her, but a lot of people like her do. She didn't mind showing she was irritated sometimes. Her circle of friends was just as nice to look at as her. They hung out in spots that a lot of people hung out in and got to know others. They liked to have fun and just enjoy a good time.

Eliza and her crew loved the spots on campus that played jazz music. They liked to dance and watch others enjoy a good time too.

Eliza attended Juliendard University too. She spent a lot of time in The Brown Sugar Spot too. It was really relaxing. She loved to talk to people. She got lots of compliments. She loved to make people feel good just by looking at her and hearing her voice. You have to know the people she dated told her the truth about how they felt about her before they dated her. They would tell her things their friends would say about her. Eliza knew just how to get all the information out of them.

Eliza wasn't one to stay in relationships long. Too many people liked her.

"She was a player," I say.

"That's a good way to put it," my grandma says.

"What was her personality like?" I ask.

"She was friendly," my grandma says. "If someone said something stupid, she was the one to try and fix it so whoever it was didn't feel embarrassed. She was very calm. She seemed like the type to take on a job as a lawyer but could still maintain herself and have fun in life."

"You know a lot of them lie about being about that type of life," I say. "I wish I would've known Eliza."

Eliza was very popular although she wasn't a musician or singer. She studied Science while attending Juliendard University.

Junior went to Cajun Lovin's on numerous occasions. Baron knew Junior by name. The two would always have conversations. Baron loved to see the youngster having a good time with his friends. Junior knew Baron was bothered by his weight. A lot of people looked at Baron and assumed that.

Baron knew Junior could sing and play instruments. He overheard a lot of his conversations. He would sometimes give Junior and his friends their food for a cheaper price. He always listened to hear if Junior would say anything bad about him, but he never did. He was too smart to say anything about Baron in his place of business. He knew someone could be sitting close that would tell the old man.

Baron had Halesta and Mania come in on a day he heard Junior saying he would come back. Baron wanted to know how the youngster would look at his daughters. Junior took a lot of interest in them. He spoke to them and got them to eat with him and his crew. Baron observed the whole thing. Junior couldn't get the smile off of his face. He would blush at times and touch the girls on the cheek. He couldn't stop telling the girls how beautiful they were.

Halesta and Mania's father would continue to serve people and talk to his coworkers. He would act like he wasn't paying the girls any attention. The girls liked Junior so much that they didn't pay their father any mind. At times they forgot they were in his place of business. The girls flirted with Junior and even exchanged numbers with him.

Once Baron noticed that the youngsters exchanged numbers, he went over to their table. "How are my beautiful girls?" Baron asked.

Halesta and Mania looked startled. They quickly stopped blushing over Junior. Their smiles dropped. They looked completely shocked. It's like they forgot they had such an unattractive father. Baron did not take their reactions lightly, but hid his inner feelings because he was at work. The girls did not want to say *dad* at all, but they knew that's what Baron was waiting on. They knew their dad wanted to know if they would acknowledge him in front of the person they'd been enjoying themselves with.

"Hi Daddy," Mania said. She knew if she didn't, their home lives would be even worse. They knew they had already lost the joyful expressions they had, but felt like they could make it seem like they were startled their dad saw them smiling so hard with a boy.

Baron said he just wanted to make sure his girls were alright and that they had enough to eat.

514

"His fat self probably hated to say the word eat," I say. "I can't believe how bitter these people are that got so big and realized the weight was not easy to lose. Hell, I'm getting bitter myself and I'm not even that big." My grandma hits my mouth. Dang it. I can't curse talking to her. "I don't even want to say I'm not that big because if I brainwash myself into thinking that, then I might get bigger," I continue.

Junior had no idea that Baron was the beautiful Halesta and Mania's father. He thought the girls looked too good to be his, just like they knew he would. "Shona, sometimes people will decline your offer if they don't like what your surroundings look like," my grandma says.

"I know that grandma," I say.

"Alright baby," my grandma says. She tries to be careful with what she says to me because she knows Nadia always wanted me to feel stupid.

"Did Junior hang out with the girls after learning who their dad was?" I ask.

"No. He always had an excuse to why he wouldn't go around them," my grandma says.

My grandma says Junior did however take interest in Eliza. He would see her around in The Brown Sugar Spot. He loved her look. It wasn't often that he saw a girl with really short hair that looked good. Junior wanted to talk to Eliza really bad and meet her. He wondered if she would even like him because he wasn't tall like girls like her liked. All of Eliza's male friends had height to them. Junior wasn't short but he wasn't as tall as them.

He made eye contact with Eliza a few times. She would just glimpse at him and get back to her conversation. She knew her beauty was compelling. Junior loved to watch Eliza engage with whoever she was around. He wished he looked good enough to be in her circle. The sad part was he thought it was his height that caused her to not take interest in him.

"Did he even try to talk to her?" I ask.

"He never did," my grandma says. "Whenever he made eye contact with her, he tried to figure out what her facials meant towards him."

"Okay. He can't just wait for her to look at him and try to read her mind," I say. "One look could mean anything. He doesn't even know what she's talking about. This boy just made me want to puke. He sounds like one of them stupid people that need to just get lost and don't think."

"Then what?" my grandma laughs.

"Maybe he won't come back," I say.

My grandma laughs and says, "I can't believe you really understand the eye contact thing when someone is not even talking to you. If you have no idea what is being talked about or just happened to get looked at while someone is browsing around the room, there is no reason to be trying to figure out what someone is thinking."

"That's bizarre," I say. "I can't take it with people like that."

Olifus says that Junior took a lot of interest in Eliza and always hoped to come across her just to observe who girls like her hanged around and just to see her.

Baron was driving around one day. He was cutting up bitter behind his weight. He was going off about how racist against blacks were no good people that should be put to sleep. He said they were the dumbest beings to cross the planet and had no logical explanation to call another color non-human. He talked about hurting these evil people. He had a confidence in it. Sometimes he would remember how outnumbered blacks are after his rants and that would make his mind go blank. He would become glad that no one heard him because he knew racist would take him out if they heard what he was saying. He would go a while without caring about his weight when he thought of the consequences of being heard by the wrong people.

Baron was saying things he only said when he was trying to get his mind off of his weight.

"Well his stomach is attached to him. There is no way for him to forget it," I say. "He had no way of not being bitter. I can't imagine all the things Man Man doesn't know about this bitter man and what he would do to other people to take his mind off of his situation."

Baron's mind froze after going off on racist. Then he began going off on his mother. He would say she was wrong for not keeping him informed that he was getting bigger. He blamed her for not teaching him to eat healthy at home.

"Is he still driving?" I ask.

"Yes he is," my grandma says. "He was heading straight to Fashon Grove. Another portion of land that is forbidden to humans."

"So he's out of his mind thinking about his weight," I say. "Now he's headed in the wrong direction?"

"He drove straight into Fashon Grove," my grandma says.

Olifus said as soon as Baron entered into Fashon Grove, he wanted to turn around but couldn't. He knew he had gone the wrong way when he saw people walking by that moved like he did as a heavy-set man. His sight became real keen. He understood that something was very off about the place. He saw a boy that looked like Junior peeing on the side of a building. He knew this boy was a character because he had saw so many prior. The boy's height wasn't the same and neither was his voice.

Baron learned quickly that it was his fear that caused the boy to act in a way that would spare his life. If he was fearful, the boy would go away and live his life. Baron knew it was natural fear that was keeping him alive. Him being naturally uncomfortable would make him less fearful of the people around him. The second he relaxed, these beings would act in a way that scared him. He recognized the clones were reacting off of his feelings.

Baron's mouth dropped to the floor. He couldn't believe what was walking on Earth. He couldn't believe what was happening. He had nothing to relate his experience to.

"His weight finally left his mind," I say.

"He was in fear for his life," my grandma says. "He knew he had no help. There was other people there that had stumbled on the area, but he had no way of knowing how to separate them from replications. He saw another person that looked like

517

him and knew he would have to kill him and blend in with the crowd."

"So the people that make it out of these forbidden spots are smart enough to know they have to kill one of their look a likes and follow whatever lifestyle it has," I say.

They have to not only do that, they have to learn how to get in the right spots to get out. They see all the electronics and fancy buildings that are close to the slum areas and learn that they have to learn the highest positions to figure out why so many people resembling them are being made. They have enough sense to know that if they don't figure out how to operate the clones and slow down the making of them, that they will have a hard time in their regular ways outside of the forbidden land and will eventually die.

"Right. People would not take kindly to seeing too many of one person. Bullets will start flying from all over," I say.

Baron had to have eating contests with his replications as well as regular people. He would have to use the restroom in public so people could know he had a small penis and was embarrassed by it. He would have to find ways to make himself very uncomfortable and fearful naturally to make it into the offices where the chips were being made.

Baron would learn that the clones were trying to implant something inside of him. They were trying to become him. He couldn't believe they were trying to become him completely. He felt like Earth had been invaded. He didn't know how to describe these creatures that resembled humans. He would look one direction, then look the other and see someone that wasn't there before. He didn't know what had landed on Earth.

"Did he wake up?" I ask.

"When you ask *did he wake up*, what are you asking if he woke up to?" my grandma asks.

"Did he wake up to this Earth being alive?" I ask. "Believe me I know it's a lot to take in Grandma, but the land is real. Air and space is nothing to play with. Well the drug recovery could be speaking for me."

"Baron knew that something strange was going on, on the land we live on," my grandma says. "He knew anything on Earth, whether it be trash or human wastes, was not just being disposed of. He knew he was seeing things he could never tell of. He would be killed telling people about the scary things he was seeing and how they were being created."

Baron had to tackle everything that was bothering him as an obese man. He had to admit to things he knew he was doing that were wrong. He had to admit it was because he was upset that he was obese. He had to say he treated his children wrong because he hated how he looked, then he had to admit that no punishment was great enough for his actions. He had to admit he knew it made his girls suicidal to hear his father say such negative things. His punishment would be created off of how he was feeling.

"When you know and feel that you should be killed for your actions or what you have said, how do you stay alive with these creatures?" my grandma rhetorically asks. "You have to find that room of chips. You have to hope more beings of you are created and kill another one. You have to keep trading places with your clones. You keep learning how much of a low life you are."

"But naturally Baron didn't want to die?" I ask.

"He reached that point like the others did where he knew if he found the right spot, he could get out," my grandma says. "He could get society to pay for him making it out of the place. He knew he had something on his hands. If he kept being created, he knew there wasn't many other people that could endure the pain that he was going through. He learned that he would have to do disgusting things, but if he found the right place, he could get out. He couldn't believe how low he felt. He couldn't believe that all of his inner secrets were revealed and he had to deal with them."

"So the bastard was forced to accept that he wasn't shit to begin with. He was nothing but a fat bastard getting on everyone's nerves and making people suicidal," I say. "He couldn't get out of his low state."

"He got the pain that he knew even his worst enemy couldn't think of," my grandma smiles.

I'm smiling too. "I'm starting to like the place," I say.

"It's crazy what those producers have to go through, but if they make it out, it's dangerous. It's deadly for people," my grandma says.

Baron had to go through many rituals. He had to sleep with animals. He had to eat large consumptions of food and show how much fun he was having. The clones would look at him stupid to show him that they knew he was really enjoying eating a lot. Junior was amongst these clones.

Baron learned that these clones were squeezing all of the feelings out of him and somehow figuring out the people he thought about the most. Clones of Halesta and Mania started to show up. They would act like the girls wanted to in order to show their father how disgusted they were with his weight.

Baron had to kill children. Most importantly, he had to kill clones of himself. He would have to implant a chip in him to register where his clones were going. He would make it to the offices where he learned how to produce and direct films. He would learn how to write scripts and how to cast for films. Baron would learn the real about the first shows to air on television.

"The first shows had the smartest people in the world on them, right?" I ask.

"They did," my grandma says. "Life was never supposed to exist. Remember Halaya used to always call you a nerd?"

"Yes, I remember," I say.

"Well, it doesn't hurt to be smart when it could save your life," my grandma says.

"I've had it," I say. "The place is alive."

Baron knew there was other people in Fashon Grove trying to make it out. He would befriend a few of them and would remain close to them when he got out. They would know each other's new identities. Most people that go in, don't make it out. You do have to a have a certain level of smarts and intelligence to make it out of the portion of land that no one was supposed to walk on.

Baron would learn the entertainment world and try to attach to a group that was leaving Fashon Grove. He found a group that was looking for him to be conceited and arrogant in the fact that he was served. He found a group that wanted him to being conceited in the fact that he was taught a lesson and he was wrong for being alive. This group let him know they wanted him dead. Baron still walked with his head held high that he had made it out of Fashon Grove. He remembered everything he needed to, to find the building where he would work under a new identity.

Baron had his credit and debit cards with him.

"I know he was pissed that he had to learn how the money system came about," I say.

"He was even more pissed when he had to get into the main office and look up people that looked similar to him," my grandma says. "He found a rich man that lived in a mansion that was in an area far from where he lived and wrote down his identity. He went to the mansion and killed the man. Baron had learned what was going on in the world."

Baron would live in his new mansion and go home to his wife and kids occasionally. He filed for divorce eventually.

"He was happy he had that money," I say.

"He was miserable. He had been made to feel so low that it was no coming back to having a regular mind. He was a pure killer," my grandma says. "He needed to see dead bodies to snap his terrible mindset from being in Fashon Grove."

He quit working at his Cajun Lovin' spot.

After a few months, Baron sought out Junior. He met him around the corner from Cajun Lovin'. He had on a suit and his limousine driver was waiting on him. Baron told Junior that he became a producer, writer, and director. Junior had no idea that Baron had moved on to such a great job. No one that knew Baron did.

"Wait, how come we hear of producers all the time on television, but no one knows that Baron became one?" I ask.

"He was under a different name," my grandma says. It's crazy how we as the viewers will sit at home and look at someone famous that we've known, and say it's not him because he goes under a different government name.

Baron offered Junior a contract and told him what day and time to meet him for the signing. Junior ended up signing at Cajun Lovin'. In his contract he was required to perform sexual favors for Baron and sacrifice a relative. Junior had no problem giving over his uncle that raped him as a sacrifice. He always knew one day he would kill him when he got educated on how to not leave any evidence that it was him. His uncle didn't know Junior overheard him speaking of mistreating him.

Junior's uncle went to Fashon Grove first thinking he would be getting a contract to be on television. Instead, Baron stabbed him to death.

Once Junior entered Fashon Grove, he knew his life was over because he had started to see replications of him, Baron, and other people he had in his mind or was just around. Junior met Baron in a room where he was chipped.

"Is that chip basically selling your soul?" I ask.

"It's basically giving your life over to someone else," my grandma says. "It's not the devil. It's a regular human being."

"Fashon Grove must've looked nice when people first entered since they wouldn't turn around," I say.

"It's not that all the forbidden spots looked good upon entrance that people wouldn't turn around and leave. It's that they were too scared to leave once they saw the clones. The clones operated off of feelings. They know how to make people second guess leaving," my grandma says.

Baron would give Junior a schedule with when he was to shoot his music videos and rehearse in the studio. Baron had experimented with the chip in Junior, so the young man knew he was doomed. There was no turning back. His life was over.

Baron would take Junior through Fashon Grove and have him meet copies of himself. Baron had gotten used to the clones. He would turn Junior's chip up so he didn't have a heart attack when looking at the replications. Baron made Junior sleep with animals, sleep with his replications, and eat disgusting things. Junior threw up at the sight of some of Baron's clones. He knew the old man was trying to have the clones want to kill him. Baron asked Junior if he remembered how shocked he looked at him at Cajun Lovin' when he told him who his daughters were. Junior lied and said no, but he really did. The old man having the chip allowed him to feel how Junior really felt. He knew Junior remembered. The clones were snitches too.

Junior was a smart kid though. He knew there had to be a spot that Baron learned to chip him in. He would kill off several of his clones and take their spots. He would date animals, walk around like animals, dress as women, talk like women, find people others wanted dead and kill them, and he would drink blood for breakfast. Junior spent days in Fashon Grove trying to find the office where Baron learned to chip people.

"Did he find it?" I ask.

My grandma says Junior found it and had to find someone that looked like him that was living well somewhere. It was like once people got in the main office where the chipping was learned, they instantly had access to someone that was living as them in another place. The clones merged. It's like they were mechanical, but they weren't. These clones in Fashon Grove were Earthly.

Junior found his match, went to his house and killed him. He had a new life. Baron was still in control of Junior though. He was very upset that Junior learned how to chip people. The other clones would know Junior was even smarter than he was bargained for and it would be tough to have Junior killed with all the robots operating off of Baron's real feelings of him being an asshole that would know what was right and still want to do wrong. The robot looks would be worse when Baron thought about doing something they already taught him was the reasoning behind their personalities.

Baron got so mad one day he showed Junior the place in Fashon Grove where the animals had human characteristics and voices.

"Damn. This place was really freaky," I say.

"That's a good way to put it," my grandma says. "The animals being able to take on human features and characteristics to teach them a lesson was really insane."

Junior's videos would start to air on television, but because he had gotten into the main office, he was able to live like a real celebrity away from the general public. He wasn't like Malana, Anna, Abigail, and Valory who had to keep going to school and watch their videos with people that didn't know they were sitting right next to them.

The first person Junior sought out was Eliza. He would go to Juliendard and ask her to be in his video. She had seen a few on television and wanted to escape the projects. She would sign the contract and go to Fashon Grove where Junior would chip her and be her controller.

"She knew her life was over too when she saw people that looked like her, huh grandma?" I ask. She says yes. "I can't believe Junior learned how to be a handler," I continue. "He was a real genius college student."

"None of that matters," my grandma says. "Some people when they are in danger become smart in ways they never thought they would."

Eliza had to attend school still. Once the video aired, people had no idea it was her because of the name change, but she knew there wasn't anyone that looked like her except the clones. She noticed weird things happening at Juliendard because of her. People started to sound and act strange.

"Once your DNA is in Fashon Grove, it's over," my grandma says. "The slightest scent of someone can be registered."

Eliza started to notice people acting like her and laughing like her even though they looked nothing like her. She knew Juliendard had clones prior to her going to Fashon Grove. She was furious she had Junior controlling her life.

Junior would make Eliza teach him how to act like her. He made her tell him the things she would talk about with her friends. He made her tell him why she chose the friends she had. He wanted to know the most arrogant things she would say to herself because she looked so good.

524

Once Junior and Eliza's video aired, some people did recognize that it was her. They helped her get time away from Junior. She had relatives that helped her too.

"Everyone is not as fortunate as these kids I'm telling you about were Shona," my grandma says. "Everyone didn't have a following that would take their spots and mess with their handlers."

My grandma says Junior and Tim James are cousins. Junior knew he was on television but had no idea what television was about until Baron got him to go to Fashon Grove. Tim and his brothers sought out everyone in their families to go to Fashon Grove, but Junior wasn't around them. Junior knew his cousins were full of shit. He knew he was lucky he wasn't around them. He knew how they played games and acted like they didn't mean any harm to anyone. They were cool cats. Junior thinks he would've been smart enough to decline an offer from the James' family.

I hear stepping and it gets me back to reality. I hear loud stomps and claps. We hear the girls downstairs do another step and me and Asayla join in. This step has a lot of movements. The girls downstairs are probably in the living room, so they are switching formations easily. Me and Asayla do the same transitions, we just use smaller steps. This step called *Thunder* has the girls on the front row switch spots with the girls on the back row. The people in front will hop in the air and hit their thighs, then the girls on the back row with do the same thing. It's a ripple motion. Then there's the actual ripple that we do with arm movements. When me and Asayla only hear stomps, we know the girls have to be doing the ripple step.

The girls downstairs hear me and Asayla stomping and do our call. Me and Asayla do it back.

This whole time Asayla and Trayna are passing the blunt back and forth. The music is playing too. Me and Asayla wait to hear what step they are doing downstairs to the beat of the music, then we join in. Me and my Sorors are doing the step to the beat of the music. We are playing no games doing our thing.

A smooth Rhythm and Blues song comes on and I start combining dance in the step. Asayla steps the whole time. Trayna is shocked at what she sees. She loves how I can freestyle by including dance in the step routine.

"You are really good Shona," Trayna says.

"Girl I just love me some R and B music," I say. "I'm feeling too good right now."

"What about me?" Asayla asks.

"You both are really good," Trayna says looking at me. I know she thinks I'm better.

Trayna is flat-ironing her hair sitting on my bathroom counter. Asayla sits next to her so they can continue passing the blunt back and forth. I'm still dancing, stepping, and enjoying my drink.

"You still thinking about letting me come over and chill one day?" Trayna asks. She is really high if she's asking me that in front of Asayla.

"I'll be honest and say I thought about it a little," I say. "I'm focused on tonight. After tonight I'll think about it more."

"What y'all got planned?" Asayla asks. "You better invite me."

"If I decide to let this girl come over, I will let you know," I say. "Don't say shit to nobody though Asayla."

"You know I'm not gone say shit," Asayla says with a little attitude. "If you about to have a girls' night with some of the new pledges, I want to come. You know I love how you chill."

"Hurry up and finish your hair," I tell Trayna. "We need to head downstairs. Tonight is going to be a good night. It's going to be fun."

Asayla goes downstairs. Me and Trayna can hear that the girls have started some card games. We hear the cards being called out. We've heard Ace of Spades and Ace of Hearts. My line sisters are playing Spades. Asayla says she wants to join in on the fun they are having.

"Girl you should not have said anything about coming over when Asayla was up here," I say. I'm drunk. Usually I don't tell no damn pledges that something they did is something I didn't want my Sorors to know.

"I'm sorry," Trayna says. "I want her to come too. She seems cool."

"She's my line sister," I say. "Of course she is cool." We are both drunk and she is high. We gone be saying all types of stuff that we wouldn't usually say.

Trayna finishes her hair and we head downstairs.

Trayna goes to talk to some of her line sisters. I start strolling with my line sisters and doing steps. It's safe to say that none of us are in our right minds. We can't even keep our balance doing our strolls and steps. Casha falls on the ground and all me and the rest of my line can do is laugh. It's only a matter of seconds before someone else falls. I just hope no one throws up.

I go in the dining room. The dining room table is fixed nicely. I have pink table clothes on them. I have blue napkins on top of pink napkins. The food: barbeque chicken, potato salad, pork and beans with hot dogs, salad, and greens are on platters on the table.

My Sorors, me, and the pledges all take our seats at the table. We are all drunk and they are high as well. We all know this food is about to taste spectacular.

We quickly grab the platter that is in front of us and place a portion on our plates. Then we pass the platter to the next person. Caya is so drunk and high that she places the potato salad on her plate and begins to eat. I notice a few of my Sorors place one food on their plates and start eating like there isn't another type of food on the table.

I at least put barbeque chicken and pork and beans with hot dogs on my plate before I start eating and not caring about people passing food around. I mean, some of us are so out of it, that some of the people that have platters that need to be passed are right next to us. They have to reach over us to get the platter to another person.

Me and my Sorors want the pledges to enjoy some time with us, so we are eating and engaging in conversations. We've talked about pledging and they've seen enough of Greek life.

We want to have a good conversation about other things. We want them to feel as if they are one of us and talk to us freely without any worry.

"I want to know more about the pledges," Telana inquisitively says.

"Me too," Asayla says. "I like them actually."

"Me too," Shemina says. "They are fun."

"We gone have to do more with them," I say. I make sure to look at Trayna and Scalina. I shake my head no so they don't say anything about talking to me about coming over.

I can look at the pledges and tell they are unsure about if they should say anything.

"What's them college parties like these days?" Deliana asks.

"They are real fun," Delisha says. "But they are not as fun as being here."

"I had hella fun when I was in college," Caya says. "When I was a freshman, I loved being around the seniors. I loved being a part of the grown life for real."

"I know right," Shemina says. "Experiencing partying away from the parents. I couldn't wait to feel life away from my parents."

"How do y'all like our cooking?" Deliana asks.

"Yea. How is the loving *touch of soul* from Asayla and Deliana?" Asayla asks.

"I love it," Jamia says. "I wish we could eat like this all the time."

"Girl don't' we all wish we could eat meals like this all the time," I say. "I know I would gain the weight, but I would just buy me some workout equipment to stay in shape."

"I hear that," Shemina says. "I recognize just being five pounds bigger than what I want to be has me miserable. I don't know how women who are fat even make it day to day."

"They are miserable almost all of the time," Telana says. "It's no joke to stay in shape."

All this talk about weight makes me think of my grandma. I drift off. She's sitting in front of me at the dining room table in my house.

528

"There was a day where a girl named Arina, that Tim had chipped went home to her mother, Vanaya," my grandma starts. She says Vanaya knew something was wrong with her daughter but couldn't put her hands on it. Out of nowhere Arina would start acting like she was in pain and have odors. Arina would do things she never did before. Just like everyone else, she would break down and reveal what she was going through. Arina would ask her mom to come with her to see Fashon Grove.

"Why would I go there with you and you just said you saw clones of yourself and that's where you got chipped?" Vanaya asked her daughter. Arina was happy to hear her mother was smart. Vanaya knew what to say to her daughter to try and calm her down some. "Who put that chip in you?" Vanaya asked.

"Tim James," Arina said. His real name was Xavier Cray.

Vanaya and her sisters couldn't believe what they were hearing. The famous artist that everyone loved was chipping people. She knew it would be easy for such a good-looking man to persuade girls to sign the contracts.

"Why would you sign with Xavier and you knew he didn't like you?" Vanaya asked. "You knew all he ever wanted to do was work you up because you liked him and he knew he would never date you. Then you turn around and give him your life."

Arina would start scratching herself and barking like a dog.

"Is that him messing with that chip?" Vanaya asked.

Arina would keep barking.

Two of Vanaya's sisters, Wilma and Berenda, were at her house this day Arina was revealing her new lifestyle.

"I knew it," Wilma said. "That's not Brittany back at the house." Brittany's Wilma's daughter. "She started acted strange and she still makes me feel uncomfortable at times just by her being in the room. A lot of people noticed something was off about her. They had to kill and replace her. I didn't even get to bury my own damn daughter."

"You think it was Tim's family?" Vanaya asked Arina.

Arina was drinking milk out of the carton. She couldn't snap out of how she was acting.

"That's not Kela at my house either," Berenda says about her daughter. "I took her to the hospital one day and her blood and everything was still the same. They said she was mine, but I know somethings not right. They got her too."

Once Arina could speak again, she started crying. She said she wasn't sure, but Tim and his family didn't like her and her cousins. They liked to make the girls frustrated and argue with them.

"How we supposed to find Tim?" Vanaya asked.

"He's a handler. I don't know," Arina says. "He knows how to chip people."

"Is he chipped?" Vanaya asked.

Arina said she wasn't sure.

"That girl in Junior's video, that was her at the store that day huh?" Berenda asked.

"That was her," Vanaya said. The three sisters can't believe that these famous artists didn't really have fame. They saw them multiple times in one week sometimes.

"I always thought he was related to Tim," Wilma said. "It's something about him. I don't know if it's his presence, his level of talent, or his face structure, but he always reminded me of Tim. He might know him."

My grandma says Vanaya saw Eliza wandering around outside and approached her. She straight up said that she had people that could help operate her chip. Eliza was desperate like everyone else chipped to regain control of her life. She went with Vanaya to her house.

Vanaya had two of her kids that were four and five playing in a pile of shit in her kitchen.

"That's my two youngest kids," Vanaya told Eliza. "You can have them. You can do whatever you want to them. I don't want them. I'm tired. I'm sick. They daddy not around and I could use the time I spend taking care of them doing other things. I want my life back. If you don't want to kill them, I'll find a way to or get a dog and say it did it."

Eliza noticed how the kids were reacting to her. Eliza sat up straight with her neck poked out and sounded like a dog to let

Vanaya know that she would fuck her good for her to help her. Vanaya saw from how Arina was acting that she needed to prove to Eliza that she was aware of the painful state she was in. When Eliza did a sound like an animal, Vanaya's two kids would start having more fun playing in the shit and eating it. The two kids looked Eliza in her eyes often and showed sympathy.

"I need to know where to find Junior," Vanaya said.

Eliza's excitement would cause her to make animal sounds. She even would position her body to show Vanaya she would please her sexually to get her freedom back. Vanaya had her kids respond to those gestures.

"I can get in those offices," Vanaya said. "Help me so I can help you. I got people that will switch spots with you and do some of your dirty work."

When Eliza came back to her senses, she would tell Vanaya where she could find Junior. She would also let her know how Fashon Grove was always changing and having construction done. Vanaya would find out where Junior lived. She would also find out where Tim and his family lived.

Berenda and Wilma would meet at Vanaya's place. They knew they would have to get their youngest sister to go to Fashon Grove. "We know if one of us wasn't here, and she was, the odd man out would've been chosen. We can't have our families being chipped," Vanaya said. "Them low-life's are the scum of the Earth knowing they can prey on anybody. They need to be stopped."

The girls set their youngest sister, Tesalaya up. They get her to go to Fashon Grove with Eliza. They don't tell her about the chip and who Eliza really is. They knew Tesalaya would call on them for help and that's when they would guide her to find that room with the main office.

Tesalaya was so bitter and knew it was a possibility her sisters set her up, but one thing she had was control. After all the rituals, she had the power to pick and choose people to chip for herself. Berenda and Wilma would tell her about their children.

531

Tesalaya along with her sisters' would start getting other members of the James' family to sign contracts and go to Fashon Grove. They would let the families know their relatives were the cause of them being targeted. This would cause chaos amongst them. Leonard, Tim, and Junior would have to create rumors about how they got into arguments and fights over the way they would treat overweight black girls. They would lie about stealing from black men. They would say racist things to people. They would make up infinite lies and have to remember them so that Vanaya and her family would get out of their business and stop torturing the James' family's extended family.

Vanaya knew the only way to get even with the boys' was to get in the main office too and chip their families.

Vanaya and her sisters met up a lot at her apartment. They started to discuss other people they had seen around who they thought were on television.

"Olesa Malin," Berenda would say.

"That was her," Vanaya says. "We see her at that store almost every week. Now how the hell is one of the most famous female singers prowling around a store with no one running her over?"

"The industry is wicked," Berenda said. "She's not a handler. The James' family is on television and in movies a lot because they have access to the main office, but Vanaya, I'm a huge fan. I know that's clones of Olesa on television. It's hard not to like that music."

Vanaya saw Olesa at the mall with a famous rapper named Cameron.

"I know who you are," Vanaya said at the counter to Olesa. She works at the mall. "That's my sister's kids over there acting mentally ill. If you want them, you can have them. You can do whatever you want with them. She don't want them. I can't stand looking at them. If you don't want to kill them, we'll take them dogs barking outside home, and let them eat them alive. The cameras are off right now. Tell me who put the chip in you?"

Olesa quickly told Vanaya everything she wanted to know when she realized the kids were responding differently when she had a different reaction.

Cameron made his way to the counter and Vanaya had another set of kids that acted mentally ill and also off of his emotions.

Cameron told Vanaya everything she wanted to know.

Vanaya followed Olesa and Cameron's handlers around. She was able to find people that helped her distract them.

"That chip is instant," my grandma says. "They can make it trigger at any second."

Vanaya and her sister's met at her apartment again.

"That was those kids at the gym wasn't it?" Wilma asked.

"They are starting to sound like a horror story themselves at these house meetings saying they saw famous people that are walking amongst them and living in areas close to them," I say.

My grandma starts laughing.

"That was them," Vanaya said. "That one young girl Valeesha is a video girl. Jasmine plays all those serious roles in movies, and Carlah stars in her own show on that kids' network. They all get a lot of air time on all types of networks."

"Even they chipped," Berenda said.

"That was Faysha and Fayla from that family show too," Vanaya said. "Faysha is the younger one that always wears those barrettes. If we get them, we should know enough handlers to get our hands on anyone that tries to mess with our family."

"Think of a few more people," Vanaya said. She was greedy about saving her family. She wanted some type of control and she wanted it bad. She was willing to be as messy as she had to.

"That one girl," Berenda began.

"Come on," Vanaya said. "This not the time to be in your feelings. I'm probably gone remember more myself."

"That one girl in that video with that boy that looks like Junior," Berenda continued. "She's from Georgia. Shalima. She has that strong voice. She's light skinned. Sometimes she has a short haircut and other times she has shoulder length hair.

She's known for her song *Too Fly For You*. I know where she hangs out."

"There's that caramel girl Tila in that famous R and B group. I see her walking around sometimes. I know it's her because I hear her voice. There's that girl Shalima performed with at the video awards. Her name was Kendra," Wilma said. "I saw her at the record store." Wilma started crying. "She's a little older than Shalima, but they perform together a lot. She dies her hair blonde and has brown in it at times. She sings *It is Me*. I talked to her before. I even told her she looked like Kendra. We should talk to her."

"That's what we will do," Vanaya said.

"That famous R and B boy, Dashawn," Berenda said. "He can do all that damn dancing."

"There's that young girl that has short hair. She's a singer and does a little acting. Jayma." Wilma said. "Then there's that girl that was in that group with Olesa. Sesia. She was light skinned just like her. She works at a restaurant. I see them around a lot. They want the public to notice them. They want help."

"That brown girl that we always see at the park. Miracle." Berenda said. "She's desperate for help. I always see her leave different apartments in one neighborhood. She's never happy when she leaves. Sometimes she has a bad odor to her. I want to help her."

"We'll do what we have to do to get a yes out of them," Vanaya said. "We'll trade blood for blood with them people messing with us."

"Olifus told me the story of a racist Caucasian woman," my grandma says. "Her name was Carli. She lived with her husband and two children. She was arrogant about being white. She was uppity. She thought she was better than everyone that wasn't white. She really felt that all the other races were jealous of white people."

By now I know that most people sold out lived in apartments. Only a few were fortunate to live in a house.

"I definitely understand that this is a cloned world. The money, the houses, the fancy cars, it's all television sucking

534

people in," I say. "Only the people that have been to the forbidden lands can afford those houses. We landed here and some people got lucky and found houses that were cheap or abandoned. They found loop holes to get those houses. They saved to get those fancy cars. I know Grandma."

My grandma says there was a woman named Simpty. She was a brown skinned overweight woman who hated her appearance, but most of all she hated her eyes. She hated herself. She didn't care about anyone. If anyone she knew passed away, she would not care. She hated her existence. She never wanted to say a kind word to anyone, but did occasionally. It hurt her to leave someone with kind words. She didn't think they would take them serious because she was so ugly. She never thought she would get the chance to be pretty. She knew it was hopeless. She was too ashamed of her face to want to work out to stay in shape. She didn't have any motivation.

Simpty would steal from people and they would never suspect her. She didn't understand why people trusted her so much. They would never accuse her. Simpty would believe that the people she was around couldn't picture a brown woman like her stealing from them. It was something about her that would detour their minds of suspicion.

Simpty didn't have any friends. People would come around her for a season, then leave. They would get tired of seeing her space off and look bitter. Simpty's associates would catch her looking really angry and not be able to snap out of it. They would start off having a good time, then Simpty would lose herself. Some people wouldn't shun her after one instance, but some would. Simpty would sometimes say things and recognize she did later. She would say things like *that mean old bitch didn't have to look at me like that.* She would say *I'm so ugly* and *no one will ever care for me.* She would say it so evilly. She would regret it of course because she didn't want to lose her company. She recognized she had a problem that she couldn't control. She would become angrier. She had no idea how long her murmurs were going on. She knew if she asked, her acquaintances could lie to her. She only trusted herself when it came to the truth about how people viewed her.

Simpty didn't have children. She lived alone. She would sit on the couch and just stare at the wall most of the time she was at home.

"Why do so many of these women hate their eyes?" I ask.

"They just don't like them because they are not like the majority," my grandma says. "These are the women Man Man told me about. This is how he described them. He said it was important for me to understand his stories and to keep paying attention no matter how many times he had to repeat something."

My grandma says that Simpty was the type to see someone standing on the steps and think they were joking about her not being tall enough. She would see someone stand by a tree and think they were joking about her being too tall.

"Simpty is really mentally ill," I say.

Simpty would see Carli at a grocery store often. She thought Carli was so beautiful and had a lovely voice. She never heard Carli say anything bad to anyone. However, Carli always looked at Simpty like she was disgusting to see. She would turn away quickly and walk the other direction. Simpty couldn't get herself to think anything ill of Carli. It was mainly because she was used to people looking at her disgusting.

"She had a real problem," I say. "If that many people look at you like you're ugly to a point where you become naïve about obvious ugly looks, you are in a bad state in your life."

Simpty would speak to Carli and Carli would breathe hard and look mad. She was obvious about the fact that she didn't like Simpty.

"You said she was racist," I say.

"Simpty didn't think Carli was racist," my grandma says. "She just wanted to try and make the pretty white woman like her. Maybe get her to say something nice about her. She knew a compliment from such a beautiful white woman would uplift her. She knew she would be able to fall asleep easily and stay sleep longer."

536

"Where was Simpty's family?" I ask. "They raised her, so they were used to her."

"Some parents will let you go the second they get the opportunity," my grandma says. "Man Man said Simpty was raised by her mother. The father left. Simpty's mother had a hard time looking at her daughter. She got used to treating her daughter like she didn't want her. She wanted Simpty to leave as soon as she was old enough to."

Simpty would approach Carli on a day she had her children with her. Simpty would smile at her and her family. She didn't think Carli would be rude to her in front of her family. Simpty said *hi* to Carli and the lady would grab her children by the hands and walk away.

It's like Simpty was obsessed with this woman. She would enjoy watching Carli talk to the black cashiers at the store. It was always about her purchases, but that alone made Simpty stray away from thinking the woman was racist.

Carli would be upset at her husband and children one day from throwing a party without her knowing. One day she would be driving and fussing to release her anger. She would come across Placement Avenue. The Caucasian woman drove straight in. She was out of her mind. She hated when her husband did things he knew he could ask her and she would say yes. She was completely submissive to him.

When Carli entered Placement Avenue, she recognized a replication of her walking into a building. She couldn't bring herself to turn around. She wasn't feeling like herself. Her mind was telling her to leave, but the way her body was feeling would cause her to keep driving in the restricted area.

"Did Placement Avenue have a restricted sign?" I ask.

"No, it didn't. Some of the forbidden places do have signs up, but you have to remember these replications operate off of feelings. It doesn't matter what anyone reads. These clones are not to be played with. The property itself is fucked up too," my grandma says.

She's cursing more often around me. Telling me these stories is really getting under her skin.

Carli saw a fancy building and thought to go ask for help. She would go in and see all the computers, holograms, televisions, live recordings, news anchors, street views, famous people on television, and much more. What shocked Carli is that she saw two of some people standing right next to each other. She saw two people that looked like Tim James talking to each other. She saw two people of Tila from that R and B group drinking and having a good time with executives and producers she recognized from television. She knew something crazy was going on. She looked weird and felt weird.

Carli didn't act stupid to recognizing that most of the people in the building were white people. She really got to feel how other races thought highly of how smart white people were. She would have to meet the expectations of the world and she was not happy at all about that.

"Did she think she was going to die?" I ask.

"She did," my grandma says.

One replication of Carli was a news reporter talking about a collision on the freeway and a house that was burglarized. The collision and the burglarized house happened just hours before she arrived. Carli noticed how some of the people that didn't look like her would move like her and talk about things that really happened in her life.

When she saw people that looked like her husband and children, she had a heart attack. She was rushed to Placement Avenue's hospital where she was put to sleep. When she awoke, she almost had another heart attack because one of the women had her voice. It was a clone of Simpty. Carli wanted to get out of the place desperately and really wanted to kill that clone of Simpty. Carli knew she would have to kill a clone of herself and take her place.

Carli would leave the hospital and not know where her car was. She would ask the front desk worker in the hospital. The worker would make a few calls and learn that Carli's car had been stolen.

"What am I supposed to do?" Carli asked.

"Walk," the front desk worker said.

Carli was too scared to put on a scene, but she did recognize that these beings were not to be played with, yet they could feel pain. That is all she cared about. They could die. She wanted to kill them bad.

"Right. Like who the hell do they think they are?" I ask.

Carli didn't care if the clones were created off the shit from her ass or the piss from her pussy. She didn't care if they were electronic or made from natural components of the Earth. She wanted to kill them. She knew they were operating off of her emotions.

Carli witnessed the white women acting arrogant and like they were better than other races. She heard the conversations whites were having and how they would degrade other races. These were beings that were feeding off of who she was. Although their conversations were degrading to other races, they were still making a mockery of Carli. They knew how to talk in code. They knew how to make one sentence mean many things. They were her.

Carli wasn't going to let the clones think that they knew how to act as a real white woman.

Once Carli realized that doing the right thing was getting her to experience her real emotions alone, she really had it. The clones let these people know that all their childish ways could be dealt with. The clones let these people know that all the hell in them would have to be defeated for them to feel regular again.

Carli would find a clone that was with clones of her husband and children. The clone's name was Devela. Once Devela left, Carli would go to the house and make up a story of the clone's car being stolen like hers really was. The husband knew it was not his real cloned wife, but still played as if he didn't. The children would hug Carli and front like they really thought she was their cloned momma.

Carli had been scared to death too many times already. She could handle the family life for a day. She would learn where the mother worked and go to the job on a day she wasn't there.

Devela was a movie editor. She worked on the twentieth floor in a fifty-floor building. Carli had no idea what she was doing. She would sit in a room full of clones that knew she was an original human and act as if her personal life was interfering with her performance. She would go to the bathroom and throw up a few times. These clones felt electronic at times and it's too much for the human body to handle.

Carli would end up meeting Devela in the parking lot. She would use a gun that she obtained and kill her. Carli took the car and went to Devela's house. She killed the husband and the kids. She felt real good about it. She went in the fridge and prepared herself some shrimp and lobster with butter. She poured herself a glass of wine and sat over the three dead bodies.

Carli would drink her wine and say, "You could never be my husband and kids. My family is way too good for this shit. We never had to pretend to be someone else. We are originals. You dumb bitches tried to steal our lives. You're paying for it. The rest of these amateurs will pay for it too." Carli would walk around the house sipping her wine and smiling. She was out of her mind although her expressions didn't show it.

"She became a killer," I say. "She wasn't going to be able to shake that."

All it took was for Carli to see her entire family had been cloned, for her mind to snap. After that, she was an official killer. She didn't care about anyone. She was someone that took the time she carried her children very seriously. She did everything right. Sure she was racist and didn't care, but she felt she was right for being a racist. She didn't think she was paying for being evil towards other races. She heard it was wrong to be racist and didn't care. She was a woman that was raised to be racist and thought it was right.

Carli knew her misfortune was because she was angry at her family and wandered into a forbidden area. This area had people mimicking her in all types of ways. Her life was over and she knew it.

Carli found some liquor and drank it heavily. She wanted to enjoy the new person she had become. Just one bad day with her family turned into the worst day of her life.

Carli was trying to figure out how she would leave the place. She had no idea where she was and didn't want to ask anyone else. She knew they knew she was a regular human.

Carli would eat and drink over the dead bodies all night.

She turned on the news and saw footage of her killing Devela. Her heart didn't drop. She was drunk.

Carli knew people would start looking for her cloned family really soon, especially since a woman that looked exactly like Devela had killed her.

Carli couldn't believe that the news anchor reporting the incident was one who was in the large building when she first arrived. She couldn't believe what she was hearing either. The news anchor named both Devela and Carli. He knew they weren't related although they looked alike. He referenced people that said one of the girls might've been a clone. Carli couldn't believe how deceitful the news anchor was. She knew he was a clone himself. Once Carli saw how these clones went about broadcasting the robots as if everyone should know they are real, she threw up. She had enough sanity to know that she had to leave the house.

The next few days Carli would find more clones of her and kill them. She would take their places in hopes of getting out of Placement Avenue.

Carli would eventually come across the main office in Placement Avenue where she would be taught how to chip the population. She was in complete shock that the chip would allow her to have control of a person entirely. Carli had become a legit killer. She would learn how to put the chip in people and get even more anxious to leave the avenue.

Carli kept being in fancy buildings and living a high-profile life in Placement Avenue. She would start attending events for high school kids and college kids. She would see people that looked like her when she was younger. She saw that these kids were attending concerts and other popular events drinking blood and daring themselves to eat disgusting stuff. Some of the kids would cut themselves and lick the blood off of each other. Carli would have to partake in the events.

Carli noticed clones of Simpty wandering around Placement Avenue. Some would go into slave houses and return to their masters. One clone of Simpty would be at a table eating without any silverware. She would be eating feces, throw up, and other bodily wastes. She wanted Carli to see exactly who she wanted Simpty to be.

"Carli would have to beat all of that," I say. "I can't believe folks made it out of these forbidden places. It's no wonder they are messed up in the head."

Some people that didn't look like Simpty, but acted and moved like her, would make sure Carli saw them. They would follow Carli into stores and act uppity just like she would. The clones of Simpty would make Carli hurt just like she made the real Simpty hurt. They would make her feel so uncomfortable that she would apologize for how she treated Simpty. Carli realized the clones viewed themselves as the original person. They felt they were Simpty. They had real anger and bitterness towards Carli and wanted a genuine apology.

Carli would get out of Placement Avenue and find the home of a woman that looked like her. She would kill her and learn her hectic life.

Carli would get Simpty to sign a contract for acting. In the contract, Simpty would have to kill her parents, and abide by how racist white people wanted her to act to her own kind. Simpty would do so with no hesitation. She would get chipped and realize that she had given her life to a racist woman.

Simpty was treated like a slave. She was hung. Sometimes upside down. Ate out of dog bowls. Forced to perform yard work. She was forced to eat feces and drink urine.

"Nothing was there with that woman," I say. "Catch her and do whatever to it. It's simple. Only the realest would understand shit will be created. We have to catch it and dispose of it. Or in Simpty's case, torture it."

Carli wanted to make sure Simpty never left her possession, so she would get some of her friends into the main office in Placement Avenue. She would teach them how to use the chip and control Simpty. If Carli were to die and for some reason Simpty lived, Carli wanted to know that she had taken care of everything so that Simpty would endure pain for the rest of her life.

Carli was a rare individual that sought out a slave instead of one of her close enemies from past friendships or relatives she hated. Simpty hated herself as a brown woman so much that she would become a well-recognized clone. Carli didn't take lightly that Simpty would catch her with her family and test her behavior.

The place is registered. It can feel how everyone feels when it comes to individuals. It knows who the most popular people walking are. It knows who is considered the best-looking people.

"I'm telling you this because this could have been you," my grandma says. "You never were going to make it in the entertainment industry. Evil is real. Suicide is real."

My grandma's last statement shocks me and my heart starts racing. The talk of suicide is nerve wrecking.

I snap back to reality.

"How y'all like our steps and strolls?" Caya asks.

"I loved it," Delisha says. Some of her line sisters agree with her. The rest of them keep eating.

The pledges, me and my Sorors continue to engage in friendly conversations. My Sorors and I know the pledges wish they could hear us talk about their sets, but we don't. There's no apologies. They need to experience all the hell they go through.

My Sorors and I start talking about other sorority and fraternity performances that we didn't like.

I tell everyone about Queela, Teasha, and their crew at the clothes drive with Luminous LA.

My line and I start getting hype about battles and competitions we have won. All the while we are still proper and staying tidy while eating. The only thing we didn't do was wait to fill our plates with all the food we wanted before eating. We were too drunk for that.

The pledges tell us about the battles they have been in with other pledges. They tell us they have won a few and lost a few. Usually the battles are step battles, but sometimes they are information battles. When it's pledges of the same sorority, the pledges can tell what they are fucking up on. It's nothing like watching and listening to another line of Alpha Eta Nu recite information better than another line of pledges.

My Sorors and I are so out of our minds that we laugh while the pledges tell us about the battles they lost. We get so out of control that Scalina urgently starts talking about a battle that they won.

"Remember the battle we won?" Scalina asks her line. "Them other girls went away crying."

"We tore they asses up," Jamia says. "You know I wanted them to see me acting like I was the best and smiling and hugging my girls."

"We all were turned up," Delisha says. "I was so happy we won, that I don't even remember what we did afterwards."

"You don't remember because we won and had to report to our prophytes," Jamia says.

This line of pledges keeps sounding like they want me and my line to bash their prophytes. They sound like they want us to say *fuck their prophytes* and like they want us to consider ourselves their real prophytes that brought them in. They want us to talk bad about their prophytes because they are having a way better time with us than them.

"I remember skipping class and having people do my homework," Caya says.

"Girl you not the only one," I say. "I couldn't keep up with my damn homework doing that pledging shit."

"Girl, I would've had straight A's if I studied for my much-needed classes like I did for Alpha Eta Nu," Caya says. "I know any member that made it through college with a degree had to have had someone doing their homework."

"I think some people made it through college doing their own school work," Shemina says.

"Not me," Caya says. "Did you make it?"

"Hell no," Shemina says. "I needed help with my homework."

"Don't try to make it pretty," Telana says. "You needed someone to do your school work. We were missing all types of sleep because we were pledging."

"Y'all just make sure y'all do y'all work," Caya says to the pledges. "Get the most out of your college education."

This food is bomb as hell. The girls have blunts going around the table. I'm bitter as hell not smoking. We are chowing down and drinking.

"This is living the life," Delisha says. She loves how she is eating, drinking, and smoking with her line sisters and some cool ass Alpha Eta Nu members.

I have to have my crab and lobster to feel like I'm living the life most of the time.

"I'm glad you are enjoying our company," Telana says.

We start playing Spades while we are eating. Some of the girls on the other end of the table start playing Dominoes. The table if full of food and cards because we're playing card games.

The girls and I continue to engage in conversations. We are smiling and laughing at each other. My Sorors and I know the pledges are feeling at ease and at the same time are wondering if the fun will end soon. My Sorors and I don't want them to get in their feelings and think we will ruin this good time.

I place bubbles next to some of my Sorors' legs. When I sit down, I nod at them and tell them to blow them. Some of us get up and blow bubbles in the pledges' faces. The pledges are scared to get up.

"Don't let them burn your eyes," Telana says. "Get up." Telana ran in the living room as soon as me and some of our Sorors started blowing bubbles.

After blowing bubbles, me and the rest of the girls go in my backyard. They are smoking and not caring about drinking. Meanwhile, I have my drink.

My backyard is lit with white Christmas lights. I don't care if it's Christmas time or the end of July, my lights are staying up. I like for it to feel like Christmas all year because I just love lights. I love the decorations. I can't say that enough. I have chairs outside and stools, yet some of the girls are still sitting on my fence. It's a nice and cool night. It's not too windy.

The radio is on. It's playing some good stuff. The pledges dance way better than they step. The girls and I do line dances and have soul train lines. We form a circle and people get in the center and dance.

"Some of these damn girls dance better than us," Asayla says.

"It's always like that," Telana says. "Most people I know dance a lot better than they step."

Caya is blowing bubbles.

"You're such a big kid," I say going over to her and giving her a hug.

"We all are," Caya says. "Ain't nothing wrong with enjoying things we did as kids."

Telana comes over and tries to get me to hit the blunt.

"I can't," I say. "I wish I could."

"Why don't you smoke again?" Telana asks.

"I don't want to talk about it," I say. "I still love to smell the smoke though."

"Girl you need to get back on board," Telana says. "Ain't nothing like getting high."

"I feel you on that," Caya says. "Getting drunk is not enough."

"It's enough for me," I lie. I hate how much I miss smoking. Weed did used to make me feel good, then things went downhill. "Tell me something, did my behavior change at all since I stopped smoking?" I ask.

"I think you were more relaxed and free flowing when you were high and drunk," Telana says. When she says *free flowing*, she means I was willing to do more things that I wouldn't sober. I would say and reveal things that I wouldn't if I was just drunk.

546

"Well I'm glad I got a grip on my mind," I say. "I hate regretting things that I say."

I sit on one of my speakers and enjoy watching everyone have a good time. After a few minutes, Jamia comes and chats with me.

"What you thinking about?" Jamia asks.

"How I want to travel more," I say. "I love to be on the road. I just want to be the passenger."

"Of course. The passenger gets to do all the site seeing," Jamia says. "I hate traveling. I wish I could just close my eyes, make a wish, and be at my destination."

"Girl you are boring," I say. "How's the weed?"

Jamia hugs me. "It's the best as usual," Jamia says. "I love y'all so much for letting us get high. Can we tell our prophytes or no?"

"Girl y'all can tell them anything my line let's y'all do," I say. "We forced y'all to do it. They not gone get mad at anything we let y'all do. If anything, they gone assume we got y'all back for doing some shit y'all had no business doing."

"I like y'all more," Jamia says.

"You not the first one of y'all to say that," I say. "I'm glad you came over. My mind almost shifted to a place I didn't want it to go."

"Do you mind me asking where it was going?" Jamia asks. "We keep getting taught that we should reveal secret things that hurt us to each other so we can become closer. I want to give you advice, if I can. I like you. I want us to be cool if I make Alpha Eta Nu."

I'm drunk and about to have a moment just like Telana was talking about. "First off, let me tell you Jamia, this is real fucking life," I say. "You not supposed to be telling people all your business. People fall out all the time. You know folks are fucked up and throw things in peoples' faces."

"Sometimes I do get nervous telling my line things that happened to me," Jamia says. "I sometimes do fear they will throw it in my face, but that's just because it's happened to me before."

"You're a smart girl," I say. "You know people only know what you tell them. You can make up a dumb ass sad story and tell your line."

"That's true," Jamia says.

"Just don't forget that damn story," I laugh. "That's the last thing you want is to make up something and someone wants to talk about it again and you don't remember."

"Yea. Then I have all my line sisters that heard it," Jamia says.

"It's some fucked up things with this Greek life," I say. "I keep my mouth shut about certain things. Y'all can't tell nobody the stuff we tell y'all. These Greek organizations are real private. It's real serious."

"Why is it like it's mandatory for us to get in each other's business?" Jamia asks. "I feel like the big sisters keep wanting to hear more and more of the things we went through in life."

"We all went through the process," I say. "Somebody wanted to get all in they business too. I'll tell you the truth. Some of the things me and my girls told our big sisters, we regretted. Some of my girls even changed some of their stories around. They got hit with wood a few times for it. It's not wise to make the prophytes think you're a liar."

"They could have let them go, huh?" Jamia asks.

"They could have," I say. "But it's fucked up because we're not supposed to be forcing people to reveal deep things that have happened in their lives."

"What were you about to space off and think about?" Jamia asks.

"Huh?" I say choking on my drink. Jamia pats my back.

"Shona had too much to drink," I hear Asayla say.

"No, I haven't," I struggle to say. I can barely stand up right now. "This nightmare I have often keeps coming to mind. It didn't start happening until I stopped smoking marijuana. It's strange to me because when I first began smoking, I never had these thoughts."

"Tell me," Jamia says. "Maybe I have had a similar nightmare before."

"Well, I hate my mother," I say.

548

I really just want to get up and fight the damn air. No one should have to say they hate their mother. Nadia is just one fucking stupid ass bitch. There is no word or phrase to describe what she was. I should call her *The Beauty Killer*. She is so fucking ugly that she goes around harming people that are beautiful. I'm pissed the fuck off that I have this bitch as my mother. I can't go insane though. I need to keep it together. My grandmother has gotten me too far for me to even think about displaying any crazy behavior.

Jamia rubs my back. "It's okay. You can trust me," Jamia says.

"She's the lead horror character in my nightmare," I say. "I can't believe how she treated me. I did nothing to her."

"What's she doing in your nightmare?" Jamia asks.

"She's laughing at me get embarrassed," I say. "She's also staring deeply in my eyes because she knows I'm about to die. She wants to witness all the terrifying looks I'm making before I go. Me being angry is fuel to her. My anger arouses her."

"So your mother likes to watch you miserable and hopes you die in this nightmare, is what you're trying to say?" Jamia asks.

"I'm at an event with one of my Sorors," I say. "One of them that I don't like. Some kind of way this dream is in a big venue. Lots of people are there."

"Damn, and your mom wanted to see you like that?" Jamia asks.

"Call her Nadia," I say. Her name just translated to *No Idea*.

"Got it," Jamia says.

Delisha comes and sits next to us and I fill her in on everything I have been telling Jamia.

"In this dream I put my all into helping people, just to have it thrown in my face by a bunch of hating ass bitches that are there," I say. "The events in the dream change all the time. It's like everyone hates me. It just keeps getting worse every time I have it."

"Damn. If I ever stop smoking, I hope I don't have a bunch of nightmares about my relatives," Delisha says.

"Gee, that's thoughtful and helpful," Jamia sarcastically says.

"I think it's just tough in general when someone's mother is just a bitch," I say. "I told myself to get strong enough to live without her love. I hate that I even know this woman."

"I hear all the time that people that quit smoking go through all types of things," Jamia says. "Hang in there. The nightmare will go away."

"You are a brave woman Shona," Delisha says. "You are strong. You are very positive."

"And you know you're real pretty," Jamia says. "You know what it's like in today's world. Them ugly bitches wish real beauties would drop dead. They can't stand looking at us."

"They know they asses are ugly too," Delisha says. "I've known people that stopped hanging around pretty girls because they said the pretty girls made them feel less than human."

"Ugly is ugly," Jamia says. "It's like your mom, I mean Nadia, is in the dream heavy because she really does act real mean to you. It's not hard to shake a fucked-up parent, but stay strong Shona. I'm telling you, just being alive makes people mad."

"Look how beautiful you are Shona," Delisha says. "I know your mom..."

"Nadia," I say.

"Sorry. My bad," Delisha says. "I know Nadia feels inferior to you. You are a rare beauty."

"If only looks could really kill," I say.

"That's a good one," Jamia says.

"I just never knew why this bitch didn't like me," I say. "I'm just starting to get answers. I can really believe she's mentally ill. Ugh. I fucking can't." I'm getting frustrated.

"What?" Delisha asks.

"I hate acknowledging that this woman exists," I say. "I wish..." I don't even say what I want. I wish Nadia would just pass away. I don't care how or on what day. All the fucked-up memories she gave me. She should be giving me kudos and off herself just for knowing I made it through her hell. I hate referencing her as a she, her, girl, or woman.

Jamia rubs my back. "It's going to be okay," Jamia says.

"You know mutha fuckas are trying to get us locked up," Delisha says. "We can't let them win."

"This bitch has always been a walking stone," I say. "She wanted me to have no good memories from childhood. That, or she was too dumb to know that any good she did was heavily outweighed by how much of a nothing-ass-mother she was."

"When my dad gets on my nerves, sometimes I steal from his ass," Delisha says. "I can't let him keep making my heart feel bad. I can't keep having my mind fucked up too. The only way I can keep my sanity is by getting his ass back."

"My sister used to steal money from Nadia," I say. "I never stole a damn thing from her. I always wanted to be a good person, but I had a fucking tall and gigantic gorilla as a mom. Nadia is just pure fucking hideous these days. I never had a chance to think she was pretty."

"She probably never was," Jamia says. "My mom is ugly as fuck. There's some people who have good parents and can barely look at them because they so ugly."

"It's fucked up how jealous parents can be," Delisha says. "Is that the main reason you think your mom…"

"Nadia," me and Jamia say.

"Sorry. I'm high as hell," Delisha says. "Is that the main reason you think Nadia hates you?"

"I don't have anything else to think," I say. "My grandma's spirit touched me and told me to recognize the truth. I felt real love from my grandma. A love I never knew from Nadia. Nadia's not even human to me anymore. Nothing was wrong with me. It's just that she is a fucking bitch. I got to know what an ugly bitch is like. I got to see the eyes of a bitch that I could say and do anything to because she wanted to learn how a true beauty would react when it came to anything. Especially the hell she put me through."

"Don't let her see you stumble," Jamia says.

"I don't let her see me period," I say. "I haven't seen her in so damn long. I haven't had to hear about any of my fucked-up relatives because I didn't answer her damn call. She's fucking sixty, I think, and seems like she wants to start being messy."

"She probably always was, and you just didn't know," Jamia says.

"I need these damn effects to go away so this nightmare can," I say. I start getting teary eyed. "And look at me," I continue. "Here we are at my place supposed to be having a good night, and I can't stop complaining about Nadia. This is exactly what she wanted to happen to me. How the hell am I going to cheer up? I need to get out of my feelings."

"Girl it's okay," Delisha says. "You talking about Nadia is not worse than the things y'all put together for us to do in the pool."

I look at Delisha and smile. "You know you are quite the character," I say. Now I'm laughing.

"What do you mean?" Delisha asks smiling. "You look like you've cheered up."

"You have to know that people will get what they deserve," Jamia says. "You may not get to see it, but Nadia will pay for everything that she's done to you."

"I don't believe in karma," I say. "Life is life to me. My thing is, I know Nadia goes through hell even today like we all do, whether it's work or whatever dumb ass people would befriend her. She's still a bitch to me. She doesn't care. Ugh. I think she doesn't even think that bad things happen to her because she is just so fucked up in the head."

"Maybe your grandma already paid Nadia back for everything that she's done, and would do to you," Jamia says.

"I'll be right back girls," I say.

I go in my room and fall on the floor. I'm laid out on my carpet. I wish I never smoked. I can't reduce the pain of these thoughts. The effects are storming hellish things in my head. It's hard to place good things over them.

When I join all of the girls again, a song comes on that Jamia likes and she grabs my hand and pulls me up to dance with her. I can't even think of anything else to talk to her about.

After everyone is tired of being outside, everyone goes in the kitchen and sits on the counters, chairs, and table.

552

I place air mattresses in my living room, unfold the couches, bring out some sleeping bags and blankets for the pledges to sleep on. Everyone changes into their pajamas. Many of them go in the restroom at the same time. No one cares to change in front of anyone here.

Everyone could have changed anywhere in the house if that was the case.

My Sorors sit on the couch close while the pledges sit on the air mattresses.

I'm so glad I have company tonight. When my drug recovery is fucking with me, I hate to be alone. The symptoms are severe when the parent is basically absent and an asshole. In my case, Nadia was never there mentally as a mother to me. I have Nadia's hard stare in my head.

I serve everyone vanilla and sherbert ice cream. I have the lights dim and jazz music playing. The pledges get to witness me and my line tell each other how much we love one another, and how we will always be there for each other. Sometimes I feel like they can sense when Nadia is heavy on my brain.

My head is leaning on Caya's shoulder. I need my grandmother so much. I can't believe how messed up this family I have is.

My Sorors sleep in my room.

I cry myself to sleep.

In my dream, I hear my grandma.

"I made good with her momma," my grandma says to me. "That's how you got away from your momma. Jacqueline owed me. She owed me real bad. You have no idea what that cocaine did to me. She owed me. That's how you got away. I need this done."

"I believe you Grandma," I say.

The next week, Trayna, Scalina, Asayla, and Telana come to my house for a grown and sexy night.

I bought different gold lingerie sets and gold silky pajamas for me and the girls. I also got us some gold slippers. My hair is flat-ironed, and I just feel real sexy.

I have champagne on the tables as well as liquor and wine. I brought weed and blunt wraps for the girls. Dinner tonight is fajitas and shrimp with mashed potatoes and asparagus. I have canned sodas in the fridge. My house is decorated with white lights going all around the house, up and down the stairs. It just looks amazing. The fireplace is going. I have candles lit. My house is a place of peace and fulfillment.

The girls and I take a shot first, then I have them grab their blunts and whatever drink they want and walk around the house for a few minutes.

When I wander into my room, Telana is in there. She's sitting on my bed thinking. I walk over to my mirror and just keep looking at myself. I'm dancing sexily moving my hips side to side and belly dancing. I'm playing in my hair and caressing my body. I see Telana look at me in the mirror and I wink at her and smile. I look and feel stunning. My silky gold gown is just beautiful.

Trayna and Scalina make it to my room while me and Telana are still in it. They get close on my bed. Me and Telana give them a massage while they look in the mirror. Then they do the same for us. I give the girls numerous compliments on their beauty and let them know that their company is to be appreciated by anyone that they are around.

The girls and I kiss on the lips. We are drunk as hell. They are smoking too. They acting like my nigga.

"You look so sexy in that gown," Telana says.

"Thank you. You look lovely as usual," I say.

We start to play house. I'm the woman who's married to a beautiful husband named Telana, and Trayna and Scalina are our kids. I play in the girls' hair and keep telling them things that make them feel sexy. I'm boosting their egos.

"I love how my daughter is such a lovely and confident woman," I say about Trayna. "She knows how to move her hips and cross her legs to attract attention."

"Thank you, Momma," Trayna says.

"I love how my daughter Scalina shows how her mother makes her so happy," I say. "I love when she shows that lovely smile of hers."

"Thank you, Momma," Scalina says.

I'm not even thinking about Austin. I'm living tonight. Telana's ass is making me disobey the rules. I know damn well I can't risk Trayna and Scalina snitching.

Telana pulls me to the side and says, "If they snitch, you know we will just deny it." We both start laughing and slow dance. She pulls me close then stretches out our arms and twirls me in circles.

Trayna and Scalina sit on the couch. Me and Telana stand behind them and drink wine. Afterwards, we walk around my backyard.

Telana is being such a good friend to me. She continuously uplifts me and keeps a smile on my face.

I'm having too much fun with these girls. I feel full of love. Nadia is not even a damn thought. I never got to be one of those girls that walked around the park with a loving mother. Nadia is so damn ugly that I don't even care.

I love my girls' company so much that I suggest we go to a hotel the next day. I already miss them and they haven't left yet.

When we get to the hotel and after we place our suitcases down, the first thing I do is prepare our drinks. The girls start wrapping their blunts.

Sometimes I wonder if I smoke just once or twice a month, if it would fuck me up. It took over ten years for me to want to quit. My grandmother is in my head now. As long as I think of her, I should be fine. I won't go back to smoking.

Me, Telana, Trayna, and Scalina are walking around the hotel and speaking to people we pass. Some people are having parties in their rooms and we get invited into one. We go in and socialize. We meet new people and I see Trayna and Scalina exchanging numbers with folks.

There's a DJ and bartender making margaritas and other drinks. We spend most of the night at the party, and just watch movies and chill all hugged up on each other the rest of the night.

36

I'm sitting at my dining room table. I see my grandma sitting in front of me. I smile at the sight of her. Sometimes I am conscious enough for a short while, that she's not really there, and I just can't wait to lose that feeling and believe she's still with me.

I look at my grandma sit across the table on the other side from me. We're close to the edges.

"I'll tell you the truth about sororities and fraternities. Sit down and pay attention closely," my grandma says.

My grandma says there was this couple: The Harris family. The husband's name was Earnest and the wife's name was Helta. "They had a daughter named Cherra, who was sixteen at the time of what I'm about to tell you," my grandma continues.

Earnest and Helta were a very bitter couple, but the wife played her part of trying to always cheer her husband up. The couple hated their weights. Earnest was more bitter than Helta, and he wished she was thin even though he was not. They stayed in a nice apartment.

When Helta first met Earnest, he was very lazy and not ready to live as an adult, even though he was of age, but Helta wanted and needed a man. She also wanted a lot of kids, but only had one because she started being skeptical about staying in the relationship. Earnest was always overweight. Helta didn't get big until after she had the child. She couldn't believe how hard it was to lose the baby weight. She would stare real mean and hard at Cherra because she knew having her caused her to gain all the weight.

Sometimes Helta would lose focus, daze off and say things to Cherra to make her feel guilty about her gaining so much weight. She would say: *I wish I never had you. I wish you would just go away.* Cherra knew her mom wasn't in her right mind. She could tell when Helta was shameful because of her appearance. She never said anything to disrespect her parents though.

Earnest was a man that liked to dress like a woman. Helta never wanted Cherra to find out due to embarrassment. Earnest would come home in women's clothing pretending to be someone else, so that Helta would think he was trying to fool his daughter, but in all actuality, he didn't care. He wanted Cherra to know it was him.

"Did Cherra know her dad wanted to be a woman?" I ask.

"She did," my grandma says. "She played stupid though."

My grandma tells me that Earnest was a bastard. He would talk like himself in the women's clothes and scare Cherra sometimes. He would even say things he normally would as her father to get Cherra to know he wanted her to know he wanted to be a woman.

"Did Cherra ever admit she knew it was him?" I ask.

"No, she did not," my grandma says. "She thought she would get in trouble if she did. Her father was a real bastard. He was bitter she never told him she knew it was him because he never had a confirmation. Had Cherra told him though, the bastard would've just denied it anyways."

"I hate men like him," I say. "It doesn't matter what someone acts like, he'll just respond however he wants to in the moment. If he wanted to be a woman, all he had to do was say so."

"The mother was so bitter about her weight, she didn't care that Cherra began to get scared of her dad being bitter that he wasn't a woman," my grandma says.

My grandma says that Cherra couldn't believe her mom was sitting around with her father in women's clothing having girl conversations about trips to the nail salon and getting relaxers for their hair. She saw her dad was comfortable more as a woman.

"Let me guess. Cherra tried to fool her dad into thinking that she was okay with him not wanting to be a man, so that he would be comfortable in his life?" I say.

My grandma says Cherra definitely tried to fool her dad because she knew he was always getting on her case for the smallest things, and she knew it was because he was unsure if she knew he was Fala, Taya, Mia, and all these other names she had to learn. Cherra hated when her father would fight her mother in women's clothing.

"Helta should've left his ass," I say.

My grandma slaps me. I got to watch my mouth.

"Baby, I used to do hard drugs," my grandma says. "But I still want you to hear me out with this story."

My grandma tells me Earnest worked as a cashier. One day when he left work, he drove by Lithium's Stadium. He noticed that someone pushing a cart on the third floor outside looked very similar to him. The strange man had on a *Lithium* shirt as well, so Earnest knew he worked at the stadium. Earnest couldn't stop staring at him. He listened to the stranger talk and he sounded nothing like him; however, the man talking to the look-a-like did sound like Earnest.

Earnest began to feel uneasy. His body was falling asleep in certain areas. His feelings kept changing. His emotions were all over the place.

Earnest noticed the look-a-like moved similar to him. He saw that the strange man was energetic and making moves to do his job, until he stopped his car. When Earnest stopped driving, the strange man started taking a break. He was laughing with his coworker.

"Grandma, how is this Earnest man going to lead into how sororities and fraternities were created?" I ask.

"Just listen. Everything I say is important," my grandma says.

I'm just going to keep in mind that she said she used to do drugs.

My grandma says Earnest had pulled over to watch his look-a-like in action. He started to wonder if his father had another child with another woman and didn't say anything. He took a picture of the man.

The look-a-like would turn around and face the street Earnest was on. Earnest would start to feel uncomfortable even more. When the look-a-like had Earnest in his presence, he would feel good knowing Earnest was unsure of who he was.

Earnest's emotions were all over the place. He knew something wasn't natural about them, but couldn't figure out what. He kept paying attention to the look-a-like.

My grandma says Earnest finally heard someone call the strange look-a-like man Gavon. The staff wanted him to do some work on the other side of the building. Gavon was feeling too good knowing Earnest was close. He didn't want to leave where he was. A woman that was thin and had really long hair approached Gavon and told him to continue working instead of conversing with his coworkers. Earnest could not believe that the woman moved like his wife and stood like her.

"They were clones right?" I ask. "They operate off of feelings. Earth, right? It has secrets no one will discuss. Those clones are nothing to play with."

"The lady knew just how to stand to register certain emotions in Earnest," my grandma says. "She knew how to make him feel shocked. This was his first time seeing Gavon. The lady knew she didn't look like Helta, but she knew she could get Earnest to think of her when he looked at her."

My grandma says Gavon would hold onto the bar in front of him and make eye contact with Earnest. Gavon was conceited and feared nothing. He knew he had more strength than Earnest.

"He could rob him of his strength. That's why," I say. "Grandma, did you used to smoke weed?"

"I smoked way more than that," my grandma says. "But that doesn't mean this story has no value."

My grandma says Gavon could feel all of Earnest's inner being. Gavon licked his lips, made his look sincere in letting Earnest know he knew how to look sexy as a bigger man, and looked at Earnest like he wanted his life. He looked at him like he knew he would see him again. Earnest's heart dropped and he was in complete shock and disbelief. Earnest couldn't believe this man had looked right at him knowing they had the same face and build. While Earnest felt low, unsure and scared, the clone looked at him like an arrogant bastard.

Something wasn't right, and Earnest knew it. Earnest was lost though. He noticed that his feelings changed and his body could move easier when the man he thought was a look-a-like moved away. He was so shocked because he'd never seen someone that looked just like him. He felt like he was looking in a mirror.

Gavon had muscles and a fat face just like Earnest.

Earnest went home and sat with Helta in the living room. He looked her straight in the eyes. The first thing Gavon did was say, "Helta, I apologize for everything wrong that I've ever done to you. I need you." Earnest was getting teary eyed. "I know you're a smart woman," Earnest continued. "That's why I'm apologizing to you first, so you can know that I mean it. If you never want me to dress like a woman again, I won't. I'm sorry for everything. I need you. Our family is in trouble. I need to know that you are down for me like you say you've always been."

Helta couldn't believe the person in front of her. She didn't remember who Fala, Taya, and Mia were.

"What is it Earnest?' Helta asked.

Earnest showed Helta the picture of Gavon. He looked her in the eyes while she looked at the photo. She took the phone. Her mouth had dropped and she began to cry. Earnest even captured footage of Gavon and the woman that reminded him of Helta and showed her.

"These people," I say. "They had a humanistic sense that the majority of folks don't have. That's why they survive so long, huh grandma?"

"You're right when you say *these people*," my grandma says. "Keep listening and stop interrupting me."

"Sorry Grandma," I say.

My grandma continues to say that Helta knew something was wrong. The times she felt genuine natural emotions from Earnest were becoming less and less as he wanted more and more to be a woman. When he had the picture and footage of Gavon, he didn't care about being a woman at all. Helta knew it was a fact. She saw the fear in him, and cared deeply. She was smart and knew that Gavon was someone to fear. She knew it wasn't just her and her family that was in trouble. It was everyone in the world. Something was going on that her and Earnest needed to find out.

"It's like he knew that the two of you could not live on this Earth together," Helta said.

I tune in harder to my grandma's story. I do know drugs can take the mind to places of wonder.

My grandma continues to tell me the story of Earnest and Helta.

"Remember the time we were at the mall on our vacation in Georgia? Cherra was with us." Earnest said to his wife. "I'm sorry." Earnest had tears going down his face. "Remember when we walked in? I was so embarrassed at my weight, my skin color, my fat face. Just my existence in general. I felt like a little kid. The first people I saw when I walked through the door made me turn left and walk towards the wall with my bags."

Earnest was waking up to the fact that Gavon was reacting off of his emotions.

Helta remembered the situation. Her eyes got big because she knew her husband was showing her how much of a man he could really be.

"I quickly turned away from the wall and went to the bathroom," Gavon said. "I was in there out of my mind. I was looking in small openings. There was one white brick missing from the wall. I kept looking in it. I needed to make myself feel small, so I tried any and everything. I looked through the space for a long time. Something was wrong with me."

"Baby you came out and we got our movie tickets," Helta said.

"The ticket man," Earnest said. "Remember what he looked like?"

"Yes," Helta said with tears coming down her face.

"He looked like me when I was in my twenties. Before you even knew me," Earnest said.

"How come you didn't say anything then?" Helta asked.

"He was fucking with me," Earnest said nodding his head. "He knew how to fuck with my emotions, so I didn't think about him looking like me."

Helta was looking in complete shock. She believed everything her husband was saying.

"I seen him in a few music videos on television," Earnest said. "I can show them to you." Earnest had more tears coming down his face.

"I know what videos you're talking about," Helta said. Earnest adjusted his body.

Helta wanted to prove to her husband that she was going to be in on whatever endeavor he was thinking about. She knew she would be able to figure something out once she got her head together from all this heart felt information. Helta turned on the video called *Touch* for the artist Trace; the man that worked at the theater. Helta chose *Touch* because she knew Trace's two coworkers who were women, that were at the theater that day, they were in it.

Earnest held his fist tight and shook it.

"That day at the theater, there were three men there that we saw before we approached Trace's counter," Earnest said. "They were acting real cocky and conceited. They were slim, tall, and nice looking."

Helta looked real serious at her husband who had never wanted to come across as sincere about saying another man looked good to him.

"They looked at me like I was disgusting. Like they couldn't believe I existed. When I got to the counter I paid for our tickets. I noticed that the two girls were loving Trace and making him feel like a man. I've snuck up on Cherra a few times and saw how she acted with her friends. They..."

"I remember. They were acting like her," Helta said referring to the two girls.

Earnest really needed Helta to understand that those clones were the real deal. They couldn't hide anything from them.

Earnest was realizing more and more that the bastard Gavon really knew him inside and out. He knew he could feel him at that very moment.

"Helta. I want this man bad," Earnest said nodding his head with the tears falling from it. He wanted to kill Gavon.

I interrupt my grandma telling me Helta and Gavon's conversation.

"Wait. If these are Earthly beings, then why would he want to fuck, I mean mess with them? He'll lose," I say.

"No Shona. You don't understand. There's something really real about these clones that come from those forbidden areas. It's like they're real monsters. Earth's way of saying get lost. There's a real price to pay to live here," my grandma says.

My grandma says, with tears in her eyes, Helta said, "We're not going to separate. We're going to do what we have to do."

"During the movie, I left and went to the bathroom," Earnest said. "I saw two men dressed as women. I went in the bathroom and they followed behind me. While I was using the restroom I heard someone scream, and I heard bones break and shatter. All I know is that Trace came in and I heard him say someone must've pulled the string to disfigure their body. I couldn't believe what I heard. Trace said he was just kidding and told everyone to leave the restroom while he helped the screaming man."

"These were men dressed as women in the men's bathroom," I say. "Right Grandma?"

"Keep listening, and yes you are right," my grandma says. She says Earnest didn't think anything of what he heard. Trace and his coworkers were laughing. Hearing screams and not seeing why, didn't equal someone really being seriously injured at the time a staff member came in and told everyone to leave and that he had it covered.

Earnest heard someone hit the ground before making it out of the bathroom. He knew it was on the level beneath him. He heard more voices. He waited on an ambulance to show up and one never did. Earnest stood in line at the concessions so he could make sure the two men dressed as women were alright. They never came out.

"You got to understand Helta, that I was a regular man," Earnest said. "I didn't know my feelings were being taken out of me and acted out."

Helta understood that her husband was trying to tell her that him wanting to be a woman in the past was backfiring bad. She knew he was telling her that him putting on a front of not wanting people to know he would pose as a woman, and the anger he had wishing they did know, basically him being a real jerk, would get him killed.

Earnest recognized just how empowered Trace and Gavon were. It was hard to process that he had a clone that was a young version of himself, and a clone that looked like him presently.

"Lithium's Stadium. That's where they work," Earnest said.

My grandma says Earnest and Helta went to the stadium a few times and parked. They would eat and pretend like they were waiting on someone. They had went four times, and on the fifth time, Gavon finally came out with one of his coworkers. He looked Earnest in his eyes with arrogance. He knew Earnest wanted him dead. Gavon couldn't believe how bold Earnest was, but he knew he still had the upper hand.

Helta and Gavon would go park nearby. They knew everything they did was being registered by natural emotions to Gavon. They would trail Gavon a few times, and once they got used to his path, they would try and find his car. The point wasn't to hide from Gavon because he knew when they were close, it was to change his emotions naturally and find out where he lived, and who he was involved with.

My grandma says the couple followed Gavon and one of his friends around the store. Gavon knew they were around. He would talk about some of the women and men that Earnest had been with. He would talk about an anonymous couple that had a daughter who was upset her dad dressed like a girl. He would bring up all the problems he knew Earnest and Helta had. Gavon would keep proving to Earnest that he was the true man. He

564

wasn't going to go by any low life creation that came about when Earnest's DNA hit the planet. He was going to prove to Earnest that he was a real gangster that would use everything against a natural human who he felt was cocky and conceited off of that notion alone.

Gavon wanted to prove that he should have arrived first. He didn't want to live knowing that he only existed because Earnest's natural DNA hit the planet. He wanted Earnest to have to fight him like a real arrogant bastard granted life could. Gavon, like the other clones, knew feeling humans off of emotions was an extreme advantage, but overlooked it. They knew humans were arrogant that they were natural creations. They also knew all the sins that humans did. Clones wanted to be greater than their master. They wanted to kill them and be them.

I think my grandma was on cocaine or meth. This story is getting to me.

My grandma says Earnest and Helta overheard Gavon talking about sabotaging a few things at work. He was going to hook up some cords incorrectly and hope some of his coworkers tried to fix them. He wanted them to get caught in a fire. He was going to do it in a couple weeks. He said a specific date.

Gavon would talk about how cocky and arrogant Earnest was. He always wanted Earnest to hear him talk about him dressing like a woman and treating his daughter like she was stupid. He also talked about killing Earnest. Gavon said his name. He knew it would trigger Earnest's heart.

Earnest and Helta would travel by Lithium's Stadium on numerous occasions to see if Gavon would show his face. Earnest wanted to see him. Helta loved seeing her man want to face another one. It was important for the couple to remember what brought about their natural emotions while they were going through a tough time with clones.

Once a woman came out that looked like Helta. Gavon was nowhere in sight, but this lady was. Helta's heart started beating really fast. This lady even sounded like Helta. She didn't want to make eye contact with her though. When Helta's heart sped up, she noticed the lady stand as if she was more superior to her. The lady would let Helta know that she had no mercy on her. She stared at her as if she was more than her. As if she was mighty and majestic. Her chin was held high and she smelled the air as if she was more deserving to live than Helta. She would close her eyes and twist her head as if she were a queen.

Earnest heard Gavon talk of there being a crushed spot in the ground at Lithium's Stadium. Gavon covered it up so no one would see it.

"There's no telling what else he's done. I can't have him frame me for something I didn't do," Earnest said.

Earnest and Helta knew they had to think of something and think of it quick. When they went home and brainstormed, they looked up events that were going on at the stadium. They decided to tell people that they would hold a food tasting event and have a party for Cherra at Lithium's Stadium.

The guest list was comprised of hundreds of people. They put everyone they knew on it. Even people they hadn't talked to since grade school. They wanted everyone to see that they had been made. They wanted people to know that they were in trouble. They also wanted to know if anyone they knew was responsible for people walking around that looked exactly like them.

The day before the food tasting and party at Lithium's Stadium, Cherra and two of her cousins would make meatballs, macaroni, meatloaf, and greens in the kitchen. Cherra told her relatives how some of the kids at school would bully her.

"They probably saw her dad trying to front like he wasn't the one in a woman's clothes," I say.

My grandma says Cherra would detail everything.

Earnest and Helta would invite three relatives over the day before the food tasting event and party: Cami, Marla, and Jane. These were people they knew were smart like them. If they saw something or felt something strange, they wouldn't think twice to figure out what was going on. They would do some serious investigating.

Marla was the only person that felt uneasy about being invited to Earnest's apartment. She thought he was up to something, but had no confirmation, so she let it go and didn't waste time thinking about it. She was still excited to see what the event would be like in Lithium's Stadium.

When Marla heard Cherra discussing the negative times she had in school, she would add more negative things to the conversation instead of consoling her. Marla was someone that never had anyone to give her good words after she confessed negative things others said and did to her. She never got the chance to have those special feelings. She knew Cherra wanted guidance, but was not going to give it to her.

Marla would say things to Cherra like: everyone has to deal with negative words from other people. If her mother and father have said negative things to her, why wouldn't people that aren't even related to her. Marla told Cherra she could stand to get her eyebrows done and her lips injected. She would tell the girl that her face could stand to be pretty. She needed make up. Sometimes Marla would try to make her statements seem like jokes, but even she knew they weren't funny. She couldn't bring herself to say not one good thing to comfort Cherra.

"Cherra was like you," my grandma says. "She wondered who this witch was that was in her kitchen that couldn't garner enough strength to uplift her before her party the next day. Cherra stared at Marla with her face in shock and her mouth dropped to the floor. She couldn't believe this woman was in the kitchen in her house. She didn't like Marla's spirit. She didn't know who this demon was that couldn't say anything positive. She thought of death quickly. It was the first time a woman had caused Cherra to wish death on someone else."

My grandma says Marla didn't care though. Marla liked to see the troubled facial on the young girl.

"What was wrong with the bitch?" I ask.

I get popped in the mouth.

"She was an ugly bitch, if you really want to know. Her eyes were way to far apart, and she had some weight to her. She hated how she looked. She was a bitch that didn't want to be brown," my grandma says.

"All that negative shit," I say. "She must've been suicidal since she was born. How dare that bitch walk up in anyone's house. It doesn't surprise me that she wanted to pound down negative things on that child."

My grandma tells me that Earnest and Helta would get tickets to a football game and have everyone meet them in the parking lot.

Gavon would approach everyone and let them in the stadium. Some of Earnest and Helta's guest almost had heart attacks seeing that Gavon looked just like Earnest. Everyone knew Earnest well enough to know he didn't have any siblings. Some would leave in fear, and the others would want to go inside Lithium's Stadium because they never got the opportunity.

The guest that left didn't like how Gavon made them feel internally. They saw that he would do things with mannerisms they had, but didn't think anything of it.

Everyone would take a seat on a chair in the grassy area after the football game.

Earnest had left the prepared food in the car. He did that on purpose. His guests knew him well enough to know he would never make such a mistake without a good reason being behind it.

Earnest and his family would get the food and return with only enough to feed him, his wife, Cherra, and the three guest that came with them: Marla, Cami and Jane.

"I definitely thought you had more food already here," Marla said.

Earnest looked at his guests like he meant to make them wonder and mad. He wanted to witness their anger. He wanted them to know he did it on purpose. He used his body language and his voice to piss his guests off. He never let go of his expression that he was being malicious. He had already invited couples he knew didn't like each other from prior events, so the tension was already thick.

"There's not enough food for everyone to taste," Earnest said. "You want to eat, go home and make something." Earnest was getting sick and knew he would have to kill Gavon to be released from his illness. Him acting like a child made his guests really think about Gavon. Some of them realized that it was the look-a-like that was bothering Earnest.

Gavon was upstairs in the concessions area with a few of his coworkers' eating nachos. He overheard Earnest's guests say they were going to leave. "Where the hell are they going?" Gavon asked. He found a microphone and got everyone's attention in the arena. Everyone was startled because Gavon sounded just like Earnest. His voice had switched. "Cherra, take the floor," Gavon said. "Everyone wants to see the party girl." He told her exactly where to stand. He told her to wait a few moments while he had a stage set up.

Once the stage was set up, Cherra would make her way to center field. She would wave at everyone knowing she was a gorgeous girl. On her way, she would fall in a hole and become seriously injured. Her face would scrape on something in the hole and become bloody, disfigured, and unrecognizable.

My grandma says one of the men got excited Cherra got messed up and nutted through his jeans.

At the time, Helta was in a hallway with her friend Galie. Helta screamed at the sight of her daughter and quickly put a gun to Galie's head and duct taped her to a chair.

Helta was the type to cover up her daughter messing her face up, but here she was faced with a situation where she couldn't deny something had happened to her daughter. They were in public. She knew her friends and family would love to witness her anger with a daughter that was disfigured in the face. She was not about to let them sit comfortable the rest of their lives. Helta knew there was no way for Cherra to heal.

Two of the workers in the stadium rushed to help Cherra. They took her to a room in the building. Earnest and Helta didn't have time to care. They thought she would be killed. They knew their lives were in danger. They pretended to care about their daughter by screaming her name, but knew whatever was going on in the world was bigger than her.

A woman that looked like Helta on the third floor would start flashing her titties moving her shirt up and down. Everyone would notice her and be scared to leave their seats. Someone that sounded like Galie took the microphone and told everyone that it was time to depart. The event was over.

My grandma says there was seven girls sitting in a room with the door opened in the stadium. They were all no good. They all had something they hated about themselves to a point where they became nothing but liars and deceivers. Some didn't like their height. Some didn't like their big asses. Some had diseases. Some had relatives that they had to deal with, but couldn't stand looking at. They were damned.

Once the seven girls realized that the clones were operating off of who they really were and getting a kick out of making them feel sorry for who they were, they knew they were in trouble. The clones enjoyed feeling that human kind knew they shouldn't live how they were living and did it anyways. They knew they had reason to want to replace them, and at the same time they wanted to be them. They wanted to be the assholes that were responsible for their being in all of their bullshit ways. They found a way to believe they were not just some second hand being.

"But they were," I say.

"And that made them madder," my grandma says. "They had to live with knowing they were second. Just imagine how easy it was for them in all their bitterness to use knowing how real humans felt not wanting them around."

My grandma says the seven girls were replicated. They started noticing that the clones were taking on their shapes. It hurt them when they saw Gavon was imitating them. He knew things that they couldn't believe. These clones were touching human kind that knew what they were in the wrong way. The seven girls wanted to get out of Lithium's Stadium by any means necessary to show the clones that they could beat them.

It was tough because how does someone who is being completely bullied off of their feelings and stripped of anything that they've done with the help of other creations, even move with that type of fear?

My grandma says these girls were willing to do anything. They started to converse bad about one another. They would get caught staring at each other in ways they never had before. They would tell secrets that they've told one another.

They would see that these clones were squeezing and pulling at all of their emotions. They could barely walk at times. They were throwing up. They were fighting and making each other bleed.

The girls couldn't believe these creations could take from each of them individually. The clones had control over them. It was like they could do anything.

"I'm still trying to find the right words to tell you how bad these people wanted to kill these clones," my grandma says.

"It's like they had stolen something from them. They were very arrogant," I say. "I'm trying to think of how to say it too. I can't believe this struck the Earth."

The seven girls would end up sleeping with each other and drinking each other's blood.

One of the girls was named Tiela. She was a short brown girl that hated being short. She was also a girl that wished she was a boy. She stopped caring about people the day she stopped growing.

Tiela started an argument with a beautiful brown girl named Crishonda. This girl Crishonda had lost her mind looking at the craziness going on in the arena. She started performing for the audience. Crishonda had a beautiful smile and she could dance really well. Out of nowhere, Tiela would send three other brown girls that were in the arena to get on stage and talk bad about Crishonda.

Tiela was dishing dirt on the three brown girls to the entire arena. She would say they slept with her knowing they would be embarrassed by it because she was so short. They didn't want anyone to know. Tiela made up countless lies she told the girls boyfriends. She would go on and on until the girls did what she said. She was a smart girl that paid attention to detail. When she saw some of the people running around the arena were starting to move like the girls she was messing with, she would start going in and out of consciousness. She did recognize that her clones were not making her feel as ill as they were before she started messing with the three brown girls. Tiela ended up shitting on herself.

My grandma says to get the clones emotions to change for freedom, everyone had to tell the truth about themselves and act how they really wanted to act.

The three brown girls would tell Crishonda she was a terrible performer. They would walk in circles around her and look her up and down. Crishonda was already out of her mind. She started to panic when she realized the girls that got on the stage with her were hating.

After a few minutes of the girls turning down Crishonda's offer to learn choreography with her, Tiela would talk bad about three light-skinned girls she wanted to sleep with, but turned her down. She knew it was because she was short. Tiela was always bitter because she knew she had a cute face, but she was short so none of the taller girls wanted her. Tiela would send three light-skinned girls on the stage to bother the brown girls.

The clones running around started to act like the light girls. They were operating off of feelings. Tiela and her crew as well as others that were in attendance began to realize that it took a group effort for the clones to switch gears. Tiela's eyes got real big. Her heart would drop. She had no idea what she was seeing. One thing she knew is that no man alive could create such beings. She had it clamped in her that these clones would kill her if they wanted to or needed to. She knew they didn't care if she died at all.

Tiela would make her way to the stage and sit on the side. She had her hands behind her head while she sat in a chair. She didn't care what was going on. Tiela's clones had relaxed while she was in this state. They were acting as if they were regular citizens in the arena. Tiela had found a way to be comfortable for a while. Tiela's relaxation mechanism made the girls she sent on stage furious, but the girls really treated Tiela bad. The girls knew they were being punished. They recognized it was all types of people in Lithium's Stadium. Everyone is different, but the girls all had it mainly in their heads that there was fat people, skinny people, people in bad relationships, people that were short, and people that were tall. The clones would register the maximum thoughts from everyone.

My grandma says the brown girls would not perform with Crishonda and the light girls kept saying all the brown girls weren't shit. All the while, Tiela was sitting in a chair like a man. She made it clear to everyone that they needed to do whatever they had to do so that everyone could get out of Lithium's Stadium.

Tiela noticed that the clones were acting even more suspect. She noticed it was because no one was making a scene towards Cherra and it was her event.

Tiela made up lies about Cherra. Cherra wouldn't stop crying about her face and kept asking certain people to console her. They had to do it. It made the clones heads turn. Doing things that were good that really made them uncomfortable was a strategy they needed.

Clones that were white, and mixed with white and black would end up doing the routine with Crishonda. The mixed clones appeared white. Clones like Earnest couldn't believe what was going on.

There was a black, and I mean dark ass woman in the arena named Rola, that had a brown-skinned daughter named Rolaya. Rola started making conversation with another woman who was hideous and dark brown. Rola was so fucked up in the head that it was like she didn't change anything about her. She would look at her daughter who was clear across the arena and tell her to come to her.

Rola knew she was ugly and faced ugly stares most of her life when she left the house. Rola knew Rolaya was so beautiful that ugly girls would become suicidal looking at her. Rola wanted attention and popularity and one way that she got it was by giving people awareness that she would kill her daughter if she could so that their kids wouldn't feel in one of the worst ways possible when they saw someone so beautiful that they didn't want to look in the mirror.

Rolaya was hesitant about walking to her mother because she had been abused by her. She knew her mother was ill in the head and sometimes did things hurtful to her so that the people around her would think she was a good person for doing it because she felt they knew Rolaya was a real beauty that should leave the world due to others feelings.

Rolaya went to Rola. Her mother took her head and banged it on one of the brick walls. Rolaya couldn't bring herself to hit her mother.

Tiela and her crew from the room would notice Rola and Rolaya. Earnest and Helta as well as others would see them too. They noticed that a copy of Rola had came out of the restroom. Shortly after, a copy of Rolaya had came out of the restroom. The clones knew it was common for black folks that were all about color to clown dark parents who were ugly.

"Those black folks need to get the electric chair," I say. "They didn't amount to shit but color. Hell no."

"You going to get it," my grandma says.

"I'm sorry grandma. I just can't believe what I'm hearing," I say. "And you're leading up to how the sororities and fraternities were started right?"

"Let me finish," my grandma says. "I did hard drugs, but I was no dummy."

My grandma says Rola would start acting like she was all that. She would snap her neck to the side like she was an *it* girl. Rola was sixty years old thinking she was the bomb because she felt people sympathized with her because she had a daughter that many ill minded people would want dead because many don't get to look like her every day. Many don't get to go home and enjoy their privacy knowing they are sex symbols. Knowing they are vixens.

"Rola sounds like Nadia," I say. "She seems like she doesn't realize she's only getting attention because of her daughter. She seems to forget or not realize that the very person she hates, is the only reason she gets the sympathetic love she craves. She gets to feel babied because of her daughter. There's really no love for me in Nadia because she is so ugly. And..."

"Go ahead. It's okay to say you're beautiful," my grandma says. "Just understand baby, I am here for you. I love you, and I told that bitch that."

I hate when I feel like I make my grandma curse. Sometimes she wants to act young herself though. Other times I think she is real pissed at the child she had. The truth is, I have moments at work where I'll drift into thinking that Nadia threw my head on something. She would smile and pick at strands in her hair. She would be in deep thought that she brainwashed me to never touch her the wrong way or say anything bad about her. She would feel like she won something. Like she overcame something. Like she beat a thought that was bothering her. She would think she was all that. I feel like Rolaya.

My grandma continues her story. She says Earnest was still sitting with his guests near the stage area. Helta was trying to find more people to hold hostage. They recognized that after Rola's act, and registering the color difference and how fucked up blacks can be, everyone in the arena was in trouble.

One of the men sitting with his wife was getting really hot and uncomfortable. He started to bleed in between his legs. The guests knew it was because he had lost his penis. The wife was so embarrassed. Her and her husband would sit on their kids and suffocate them. They weren't the only ones that killed their kids to pay for the wicked people they turned out to be.

The clones were going around the arena doing ridiculous things. The arena was turning into a revenge arena; a freak show.

The clones would hear all the things they already felt and knew. They knew all the way from light-skinned blacks to the darkest blacks that these people in Lithium's Stadium this day had thought processes that centered on the lightest blacks being the prettiest ones. This batch of people were very fond of light-skinned men. They said many things to praise them. The bright men would sit around and listen to people praise their looks. The bright women were like most of the women in the arena that would do anything to keep their man while he treated them however he wanted.

The bright women knew the darker women were getting upset. They fought each other. Some of the light girl's brown homegirls would help them get out of trouble. They knew the darker girls were getting mad and the clones were picking up on it.

The dark black girls were making it harder for everyone to escape the building. They wanted to be treated the same way browns and light people were treated. Everyone had to make the dark women feel the same way as the bright woman got to feel.

Everyone was messing with whoever they saw. They had to make their clones switch gears.

People started having animal features and smells. Daniya was one of the dark black girls that wanted to have her way. She was the first one that recognized that a lady that looked like her was reminding her of a gorilla. With the browns and lights in the stadium talking so disgusting of dark women, Daniya did not care that her clone could turn into a beast at any moment.

The people that recognized Daniya's behavior seeing and knowing what she knew, their faces began to look sadder and sadder. They kept having knew realizations.

Things were getting personal. One of the girls in Tiela's crew was a big light girl named Erika. She wouldn't move. Her clone, like most of the other ones, wanted her to do everything sitting still. Erika knew it was impossible. She was such a lazy girl that gossiped and made lies up about people because she had an incurable disease. Her clone would tell everyone.

People in the arena would make jokes about Erika. They wanted to get out. They also remembered that Tiela's entire crew had slept with her during this time at the arena. Some saw it. Tiela's crew had to do things they didn't want to so the clones would relax a bit.

My grandma says two big brown women named Angelisa and Vinika would understand that they needed to come up with a way to show they were remorseful for being such terrible people. They got the idea to have everyone start a community service project.

Angelisa and Vinika said women should be with women and men should be with men. The men were giving the women a hard time because the clones were giving them the idea of going in the restroom with the women. They didn't want to think about blood and what they would have to do in the restroom as punishment that they shouldn't mind doing to themselves.

Everyone separated into groups. Twelve sororities and ten fraternities were founded.

"Angelisa would come up with group names for the sororities and fraternities. They were all to specialize in community service projects," my grandma says. Everyone got to sit in their groups and discuss what projects they wanted to take on. The clones were amongst them. They knew some they wouldn't recognize.

Everyone needed the clones to think a different way. Doing the right thing got the robots to act differently. It gave the people some control over how they wanted to act. Earnest and Helta's guests knew they were in trouble.

Angelisa recognized that the clones were responding unsurely to the community service idea, so she would have her group line up and lean back in a line. She would make them do things like get naked. She would make them talk about each other horribly. She would talk bad about them as well. She would talk about their families and make them eat and drink things they didn't want to as pain for the way they turned out to be. Angelisa and Vinika would make their crew crawl around like animals and make animal sounds.

The clones couldn't believe their eyes and that's what everyone needed. The clones were wondering how could someone starting a community service event and groups that could be so successful, start hazing their members. They started to question what these humans were. They needed things to get worse and that's what the Harris' family and their guest needed. They would get to control themselves more.

"So to get these clones emotions to calm down, these people who were no good, came up with something good, and that threw them off?" I ask.

"Keep listening," my grandma says. She says the darker colors still were bitter. Earnest, Helta, and their guests started to realize that animals would start to show up. The animals had more intelligence than they did. Some wondered if that was true and some believed it was. They knew they needed to act fast in the midst of their community service project talk, and of course they talked in code. The clones loved that.

Earnest's clones would toss everything they saw out the window. Anything bad, they didn't question if Earnest would do it. Earnest was someone that would wait for someone to tell him something and decide how he wanted to get on their nerves. This was before he realized his match was made. This was when he was comfortable dressing as a woman.

Women Earnest dressed like began to show up in the arena. He wanted to kill those beings real bad.

There was a skinny woman with her fat husband that smelled like blood. Her husband knew she would do this on purpose at their house to get on his nerves, and he hoped it would help them get out of the arena. The woman was naturally ugly and her husband was too. Kids hated to be around them and that made them bitter. So, they found children and made them look at them to get the clones to understand they knew they weren't shit.

There were maybe two guests that were white that Earnest invited. It took a long time for white clones to enter the building. One white woman, named Michelle, would take an obese brown woman named Tifia that didn't like herself, mainly her eyes, and show everyone how the woman hated beautiful brown children. She did an experiment to show the attendees that no matter what, it hurt Tifia to treat an innocent brown child with love.

Michelle got Tifia to her right state of mind with all the hell going on in the stadium. She told her that everyone was in danger and terrorists were in the building. She said there was bombs underground and that children of all colors were trapped with a teenage brown girl. Tifia said the brown girl had already saved a few children and just needed a boost to save more. She said the brown girl would stay because she couldn't fit in the hole that the kids could get out in. She told her there was only one chance to get out of the place. Tifia let Michelle know she had to say something to the brown child, but didn't tell her what to say. Tifia told Michelle that she had a few seconds before the cameras would cut off.

The teenage brown girl appeared on a big screen in the building. Michelle chose to ask the teenage brown girl why she came to the arena that day. The teenage brown girl was in shock. She would complain from that moment on and not be capable of helping those children escape. She would become easily irritated. Unable to answer questions without being rude. The audience would begin to really hate her. Michelle showed no mercy. She wanted the girl to crumble to death. The teenage brown girl would pick and choose the kids she liked and let them go.

Michelle put Tifia in an electric chair and tortured her. She said she would hang her and blow her up later. Michelle was to tell the black race that they weren't anything.

Two clones of Tifia appeared in the stands. They were in separate sections. They would talk bitterly and nonchalant. They were really frustrated that this lady Michelle existed. They couldn't believe how she would treat people wrong on purpose and never expect anything bad to happen to her. She got her match and thought she wasn't going to deal with it whole heartedly.

The thing about the clones of Tifia is that they had already been sitting in those seats for a while. It's like they just changed voices and slightly changed their appearance. People couldn't believe how long they knew those two clones were sitting where they were.

The clones of Tifia would talk bad about Cherra. They would even confess that they hated their eyes, and that's why they treated their own color like shit. They were saying what Tifia should have been admitting. The clones would say it wasn't their mothers' faults that they were ugly; it was society's. The clones were pretending to be mentally ill. One would be ignorant and say: I wish you would die Tifia. Some of the men would laugh.

The teenage brown girl would make jokes while she thought she was about to die.

"I can't believe they can survive with pure hell of themselves walking. That don't mean anything. Them niggas need to be put to sleep," I say.

I tell my grandma that I need to know how Michelle lived everyday life knowing Tifia was breathing. Even dead she could and will be a problem.

"Michelle knew that even dead, Tifia's existence would still bother her," my grandma says. "She had to figure out a way to torture Tifia for every thought that was really bothering her. Just learning about her will fuck with you."

Hell no. If I could, I would have to make glass break the second I thought of Tifia. I would put Tifia in a room and make her hear loud shattering sounds at the thought of her. I would make her walk on glass. I would take her out of her right mind until she came to herself as the person she should have always been.

"Those white women did a lot to Tifia," my grandma says. "Tifia wouldn't die. She was suicidal a lot, but she kept surviving. She didn't want to die."

"All the hell she would cause, she had plenty of reasons to understand why she knew she deserved to be tortured," I say. "That's why she didn't' die." When I hear someone is so bitter that they don't care who dies and treats her own color or darker like hell, it's like they don't exist. Now I've been told in detail things that Tifia would do, and the pain of her only goes away with coming up with an antidote. Some way to torture her that will match.

My grandma says Earnest and Helta's guests began to see people that were from different countries show up. Some were terrorists. The newcomers would question the guests that had very little people that weren't considered black.

The clones would instantly register that the other countries people would relax Earnest and Helta and their guests just by their presence of being another color; a lighter color at that. The clones felt like they were all about to die. The other countries accents bothered everyone, even the clones, and yet the clones still got to feel and witness that these people would bow down to others because of their color. The Harris family and those that weren't already crying would begin to. They were being made a mockery of.

It's like there was a panel in the building. These clones were there to blow up the world and the fucked up and messy people the Harris' invited weren't shit but bitter beings. It was to a point where the clones were trying to get out of the building. This was when everyone got a sigh of relief when they got another confirmation that these clones really existed and could be tortured. The clones would register the emotions. Gavon would spot Earnest sitting in his group from the third floor and look at him conceited. He didn't care that Earnest had tears in his eyes. He knew Earnest was a bullshitter. He always thought Earnest was on top of his game trying to manipulate people and make himself feel more than what he was. Gavon wanted to be that person. He wanted to control that person. He wanted to show and prove to himself that he was more of a bullshitter than Earnest. He wanted Earnest bad.

Gavon loved that he got to feel Earnest's pain for wanting to kill him. He loved that Earnest knew he could do that and didn't care. He never thought Earnest felt genuinely weak about having a clone. He thought Earnest was going through emotions that he would get over. Gavon didn't waste time thinking Earnest sincerely regretted anything, even though those were real feelings the Harris man was giving.

The clones would die if they weren't given enough time to develop into someone else. They would need new feelings. They would need their match to continue to fear them and do things that were out of the ordinary to them. When the terroristic clones began to show up and people with animal features, the clones of the guests would have to help them escape. Gavon loved that he got to feel like Earnest's Dad. He got to feel like Earnest needed him.

The clones had to adjust to how the Harris' guests were feeling to help get everyone out of the building that weren't terrorists. They didn't take a chance on anyone getting upset that someone was left behind. They didn't have time for those feelings. The clones would say ignorant things to bother the humans for their stupid ways of thinking.

Erika finally was able to move when she got everyone in her group to do something they didn't want and told herself that she was a fat bitch that was bitter for not being cured. She had to really believe, which was easy, that she was wrong for how she lied on people. She had to admit that she knew a lie could get someone arrested or even killed. She had to admit that she could not be upset that people wanted her dead. The clones would start taking on odd features when they heard these things, but it had to be done. The clones would do hideous faces when hearing these things.

"That's what we see," my grandma says. "People's faces get disgusted when they see certain things. These clones could do the most with their existence."

Once everyone was free from the building, they would go to each other's houses and steal. They would break into cars. They would do stupid things like eat in stores. They would take bicycles and tricycles from children. Some would get arrested. They needed new emotions so that the clones would change feelings. They needed to feel a different way for one another. All of the searching and anger was needed to take their minds off of the unbelievable things they had seen.

There was a man named Charlie that was in Lithium's Stadium for the Harris' event. He had been to The Land Spot before. He was able to find the chip room and become a handler. Charlie would approach people he met at the stadium and tell them he could give them careers that made them money. He knew they wanted to leave town. He made sure to approach someone from each sorority and fraternity. They would all have someone that said yes. Now Charlie was running both sororities and fraternities alone.

"What happens if Charlie dies?" I ask.

"He would have done too much damage," my grandma says. "The pattern of how the sororities and fraternities get down would be instilled in everyone. It would have gone on for too long," my grandma says. "That's why you guys are still hazed today. Charlie took all the credit for starting all the organizations. Only special people had the truth revealed to them about the creation of sororities and fraternities. Most of the world doesn't even believe in clones. Then some people that do, don't know what they really are. They aren't just machines that are manmade. They're not manmade at all."

Charlie would have Cherra sent to foster care. He didn't want to look at her. He knew Helta didn't want her anyway with a disfigured face and no voice. Helta was the lead of her sorority. She was real bitter. She was over Tiela and Erika's crew. Many lines of Sorors would come after them.

Earnest ended up divorcing Helta and dating someone he hated so they could have hell in their house every day to throw off the clones. They needed what they deserved for being dumb ass humans that amounted to nothing but what their selfish pain caused them to be. They needed what they deserved for the clones to calm down.

Cops, cloned and not cloned, would arrive. They would act racist and question Earnest and Helta's guests to make them feel low and aggravated. They would ask them where they lived and their phone numbers so that everyone could hear. Many arrests would be made.

Lithium's Stadium would get back to normal. More events would be held. Over the years, that arena would be burned down.

Tiela and Erika's crew absolutely despised these clones. The clones didn't think real humans could fuck with them.

These were creations that were capable of feeling pain. They were technically the worst version of the person they were cloned after. Them robots were created off of who them people wished they were, and used their emotions to be their enemy.

"I'm making things narrow so you can have a path to follow Shona, but them clones could do anything," my grandma says. "Their main passion, their main focus was for them themselves as clones, to develop an emotion that would make their reason for existence, humans, just drop dead."

"Those fucked up people got they asses hand to them," I say. "I always wanted them to sit in all their ways and have to deal with themselves." My mouth drops. "I wanted them to meet their clones," I hesitantly continue. "I just didn't want everyone to have to deal with it."

My grandma nods her head. "We all wish for our enemies to deal with the pain triple fold of what they give us," my grandma says. "These clones are the real deal. They give their reason for existence one hundred percent more of the hell they need to feel, but we all have to deal with them." She says the lighter colors had to work hard to get the darker blacks to snap out of feeling not wanted. The brown girls couldn't believe what they were witnessing. They would lie and say they were dealing with the same thing. Everyone had to fool the dark black girls.

"The pitch-black girls, right?" I ask.

"You know it," my grandma says.

"Brown girls and them are completely different," I say. "We don't act nothing alike. How the hell do other colors think we are similar?"

"It's bad enough they labeled us all the same color," my grandma says looking me in the eyes. My mouth drops again. Light-skinned people, red boned people, and brown people are not the same color.

"So this really happened?" I ask. "All of these fucked up people landed in one place?"

"Listen. I was sick," my grandma says. "A lot of thoughts came over me. But I knew people who knew the truth. Everyone has a twin. You hear people say it all the time. Talking about the secret will get you killed."

37

I'm at home making spaghetti and meatballs with corn and salad. Deliana and Telana are coming over because they have to tell me something important. I'm adding spices to the spaghetti sauce.

I'm straightening up my house and getting ready while the food is cooking. I get in the shower and wash my hair. I feel so good. I'm thinking about my first successful school job with Luminous LA. Working two jobs at once is not easy. Especially while I'm recovering from using drugs.

I'm really an extravagant woman. I am exactly who I want to be. I've struggled at times, but I'm fine. I will beat these drugs and I will remember all they put me through so I don't ever use them again.

Austin is honking for me to come outside. Damn. My hair is soak and wet. I put a towel around it.

I miss Austin a lot. I didn't get to spend a lot of time with him while I was working at my first school with Luminous LA.

Austin comes in the living room, gives me a kiss and hug. He gives me some red roses as well. I place them in a vase and he picks me up. We kiss for a while.

"I just wanted to stop by before I went out of town to visit some family," Austin says. "What are you cooking?"

"Some spaghetti and other things," I say. "A couple of my girls are coming over from the sorority. It's not ready yet though. I got some leftover quiche if you want some."

"No. That's alright," Austin says. "I got to get on the road."

"Thanks for stopping by," I say. Austin gives me a hug and heads out.

I blow dry my hair in the living room and watch Mission High's last performance.

Deliana and Telana arrive. I open the door and give them a hug.

"Come right in," I say.

"It smells good in here girl," Deliana says.

"You know I had to cook for my girls," I say and tell them

what I'm making.

Deliana and Telana come in the kitchen with me.

"So what's up? What's this news you have to tell me?" I ask while I'm putting pasta on our plates.

"Girl, my cousin Vincent is in trouble," Deliana says out of breath.

"I don't know your cousin Vincent," I say. "But you know whatever I can do to help one of my girls family members, I will do it."

I place our plates on the dining room table and me and my girls sit down and converse.

"Girl, Beta Beta Gamma dropped out of his competition," Telana says.

"What?" I almost choke on my spaghetti. "Which competition is this? Why weren't we invited?"

"Girl this some underground shit Vincent and his fraternity do every once in a while. I need to tell you how much of a hoe Vincent is," Deliana says. "He invites two sororities every time him and his boys have this competition."

"Yea girl," Telana says. "And he invites the sororities that have the most hoes on them. The ones with them bitches he be fucking."

"And don't think for a second that them bitches don't know they all fucking the same nigga," Deliana says.

"So Beta Beta Gamma dropped out and they need us to fill in," Telana says.

"What the hell happened?" I ask.

"Someone got sick and it spread," Deliana says.

"Sick with what?" I ask shocked.

"We don't have those details," Deliana says.

"They all fucking the same niggas," Telana says. "That's all I need to know."

My girls let me know that the competition is in two weeks. It's held in Vincent's backyard and his basement. Only select people get to come.

"He wants us to fill in for Beta Beta Gamma," Deliana says. "All we need is a five minute routine."

587

"You know I'm down for whatever y'all want," I say. "I'm just not down to be using a bunch of old steps when I feel like the other team is going to come with new ones."

"Theta Kappa Beta is coming with new steps," Telana says. "But Vincent doesn't care what we come with. He just doesn't want to cancel a part of his regular show. There will be four fraternities there and the sororities are just showcasing. The crowd will decide who won."

This competition sounds ghetto.

"What?" I say. "We're doing all new steps. I can't believe y'all want to perform all old stuff."

"Desperate times cause for desperate things to be done," Deliana says.

"So Vincent doesn't care whether we win or lose?" I ask. "He sure as hell doesn't care who thinks our line has slept with him and his crew."

"Come on," Deliana says. "I need you to be down for this."

"Besides, all of your steps are bomb as fuck," Telana says. "We can do steps we haven't done in a year. Just refresh us. If them niggas ever seen us step somewhere, they not gone remember."

"The competition is in two weeks. That's plenty of time for y'all to learn new stuff," I say. "But we need to meet up at Hollow's Cave tomorrow. I'll come up with something tonight. It will be the easiest step y'all learn of them all of course. Y'all can record me and practice it at home. I will have all the steps we need lined up before the last week."

Deliana calls Vincent and lets him know that Alpha Eta Nu will fill in for Beta Beta Gamma. I can't believe she told me this right now.

Deliana and Telana finish eating and I let them know I need to get to work on our new routine. I have them help me move all of my furniture against the wall in my living room so I can practice in it before they go.

I'm full as hell and can't lay my fat ass down. I put on some hip-hop instrumentals and start thinking about the moves I want my crew to do. I use my table to practice coming up with

588

some beats, then I find ways to make those beats with my body.

I'm walking all over my house. I damn near stop in all of the rooms and start stepping when something comes to mind. Since there's only so many ways to move the body when it comes to stepping, it gets difficult sometimes to come up with new movements. The beats aren't hard to make different. It's the actual body movements. Especially when I've been stepping for so long. I like my routines to be very different. I don't settle just because I know that this is a body that can only do so many different things.

I'm moving backward clapping above and under my legs in my hallway. I'm beating on my walls trying to come up with new beats. I'm holding one leg in the air and moving my arms around trying to think of new positions. I'm standing with my legs apart at different angles thinking of new positions.

I start playing around and dancing to the music when I get in my feelings a bit trying to think of something new.

When I start to get into a rhythm and liking the beats I'm hearing and making with my body, I start smiling and nodding my head getting into what I put together. I'm visualizing me and my girls doing the moves in my head.

I do the moves more intense. I turn my head to the side sharply and move my arm at three different angles while stomping. I bend down and clap over and under my leg that's planted on the ground and do the same on the other side.

I go through the step very slow to pay attention to what leg I'm using. That's super important so I'm not teaching and causing the girls to make mistakes that are my fault.

I record myself and watch what I've done. I'm happy as hell. I did that shit. This first step is nice as fuck. I go through it a few more times, then I write a rough draft of what I want the last minutes of the routine to be like. I note where I want transitions, what I want the formations to look like, who will start some of the steps, and I also jot down some movements I want to make sure I incorporate like someone jumping in the air and the two people on her side clapping in between her legs.

I spend four hours trying to come up with our first step. This step is going to be at least a damn minute of the routine.

When I finish stepping, I set my alarm for the next day. I eat some more spaghetti, salad, and corn, then go to bed. My plans of watching soap operas, gossiping on the phone, and eating all day definitely did not succeed.

My Alpha Eta Nu line and I meet up at Hollow's Cave the next night. We sit together first and I discuss with them everything that I have planned for the routine. I read my notes to them.

"Girl I knew you were special," Asayla says.

"Hell yea," Shemina says. "I knew she wouldn't want us to do no old steps."

"So y'all ready to do this?" I ask.

"Let's do it," Deliana says.

Me, Casha, Caya, Shemina, Asayla, Telana, and Deliana spread out in the cave. For right now, it doesn't matter where they stand because we're all learning the same thing. Once we start getting to a part where we need to move around or do different things at the same time, I will have them stand in their designated spots.

I stand in front of everyone and do the first four count. Sometimes I go off of a three count. It just depends on the beat of the step I'm teaching.

I make sure the girls have the entire step in their heads during our first hour of practice. We're only rehearsing two hours, so that means the last hour, we should just be reviewing what we've done.

"How long did it take you to make this up?" Asayla asks.

"Hours," I say. "Lots of last-minute dedicated hours."

Shemina and Caya start laughing. I see Deliana looking at her liquor bottle and juice she has off to the side. When practice is over, I know she's going to guzzle it down.

Deliana catches me staring at her and says, "Hell yea I can't wait to drink it."

I have the girls run through what they've learned alone and it needs work. I'm not down for no frat boys clowning us; I don't care if we only have a short amount of time to learn an entire routine.

I have to practice one on one with some of the girls. Shemina caught on the fastest tonight.

"So you wasn't taking a chance on anyone recognizing some old stuff?" Shemina jokes.

"Listen girl. You know I wasn't," I say. "Girl, if I thought y'all couldn't do it, then we would've done some old stuff. I was gone be down to help Deliana regardless. I know y'all can learn some new stuff though. Y'all catch on fast enough. Besides, I've stepped with y'all long enough to know y'all ability, so I can work around it so everything can be new anyways."

"I already knew you had some type of creative mindset to teach us all new stuff," Shemina says.

I have Shemina do a section of the routine where she has to move forward hitting her thighs then move her arms left to right sharply. I have her do the moves where we clap and extend one arm to the sky while the other one is in front of our chest, then I have her clap and extend one arm to the side while the other is in front of her chest. I have Caya join us and do the same moves with her.

At the end of practice, the girls and I do the routine together. Deliana records me and sends the video to all of the girls. Then I set up a camera to record us all together so they can know where they are supposed to stand and move.

After rehearsal, the girls and I sit and drink a little.

"That step is nice as hell," Caya says drinking some beer.

"You know I got y'all," I say.

"I don't care what they have going on after we compete against Theta Kappa Beta," Deliana says. "We are partying in Vincent's house. He stays in a three story house too."

"Who are the four other teams?" I ask. "Or which frat is Vincent in?"

"Vincent is in Omicron Rho Rho," Deliana says. "The other three frats are: Rho Psi Phi, Rho Omega Rho, and Omicron Phi Phi."

"Everyone's only going once," Telana says. "Then the crowd will decide who was better."

"This sounds crazy," I say. "The crowd has to make a

591

decision?"

"Majority wins," Deliana says. "Until there's a majority, there's no winner. That means if there seems to be a tie, people will have to convince other people to change their minds."

Telana bumps my shoulder and says, "This is going to be fun."

"Make sure y'all come to all the practices," I say. When an event is going to have a lot of fuckery going on, the routine really needs to exceed everyone's expectations. These events are comprised of people that clown too fucking much. The ones that don't quit until people are in tears. I can't stand them ignorant niggas, but Alpha Eta Nu is still performing, so we gone have to come with it.

My girls and I all have different schedules and it's hard as hell for us all to find time to meet up all together. I still don't care. I make sure to keep track of how much time we have left at practice so we move on when we need to so they can go home with as much as they need to with the step they've learned.

My line and I drink. They start passing blunts around. We talk about things we want to buy online and things we want to buy from the mall. Most of us want to buy some jewelry. We're saying how nice certain things will look on each other.

38

I'm in Hell Kin's Cave. I love this spot. I love to be alone in it. I love how the chairs are all close and there's a small standing area in the center. It's a real intense area. Greeks only come out here for meetings or just to sit down and relax to get away from everyone.

I have on my sorority colors. I have on a pink shirt with blue jean pants. My hair is a little rough, but I have it going down my back.

I'm staring at a barrel that's on fire. I needed to get out the house. I'm in my feelings again and I don't want to be around anyone.

I'm thinking about the assault again. I can't get over it.

I told Nadia about the assault that happened in February for over thirty minutes. She said *mmm* and breathed heavy as if aggravated a few times. Then she finally said Jania said I harmed her son and nephew. I disgustedly said Jania's name and said she was mad because every time someone looked at her, they forgot what they were going to say and went completely black because she looked like a beast. Then Nadia said Jania said they told her that. Then I kept going on talking bad about Jania for a long time.

I started to think about my assault again. I told Nadia at least I called the cops so that it would be on the kids minds even if they were never caught. I told her those kids harm people for fun. There's nothing there.

It never even crossed my mind to ask Nadia for comfort or to say something that was positive to help me. That's how trained she had me not to ask her for anything that was good. We hung up and Nadia sent me to bed with two horrible memories.

Days before Mother's Day, which was May 12th, I was stripped of my entire being. As if Earth had caught me. A mid-life crisis came over me. I felt like I was without love.

At least I thought I was without love. My grandmother's love was walking me into new realizations.

I was supposed to had died. I hopped inside of a girl that kept saying she was cute, lovely, pretty, and beautiful as well as many other good things.

Then my grandmother's love released me from this girl, and I hopped inside of another girl that remembered telling Nadia about the assault and her telling me about Jania saying I harmed her nephew and son, and that they told her that.

Then my grandmother's love released me from that shell and walked me into another shell with nothing but her love and said, "Tell her that's why I did it." I was looking for love and questioning whether there was someone that loved me. My grandmother's love gave me the question and answer at the same time.

I then had to repeat the entire situation to reach my grandmother's love and understand it. That's the situation that happened and that's what I have to repeat and go through to understand my grandmother's love.

Then I remembered I talked to Nadia on the phone the 13th, 14th, 15th, and 16th for an hour each day in April, and it never crossed my mind what she said about Jania. I was working with Luminous LA at the time and Nadia was just giving me pure hell.

Then I remembered I talked to Nadia the 1st, 2nd, 3rd, and 4th of May and it never crossed my mind what Jania said about me. My grandmother said true love can cut like that. She said we would use this story to cut through the drugs.

I told Nadia about the assault on March 7th. I got into my feelings and wanted to address her about continuously reminding me of relatives that I don't like, and I sent her a text message asking her to stop telling me outrageous things and let her know things like that were hard to erase from the memory. I had told her many times before, to stop bringing up people she knows I don't care for.

I asked Nadia if she cussed Jania out for saying those things about her daughter, and she said she did, but nothing else. Then she later said that the twins' dad's side of the family has problems. But she didn't say anything else.

594

My grandmother says she was waiting on that day I hopped into all those shells, to tell me that's why she died. She knew Nadia would pound down on me with a negative situation after I had already told her one, without giving me any comfort. She knew Nadia wanted me to know she wished I was dead.

Nadia's ways were one of the ways I was stripped and hopped into that shell. My grandmother held onto me.

I can't wait for Nadia's birthday to pass. She's called me four days in a row. I haven't answered.

Around the 20th of May, Nadia kept calling. "Don't touch that phone," my grandmother said. "You know she needs more memories to storm you with. Let her think about all the things she couldn't remember that she told you. Let her wonder how all you have to do is ask someone when I was born and they will know for a fact that she wouldn't tell you. Let her think no one thinks nothing is wrong with her with all the bullshit she spreads and her not wanting to tell you anything about me. That's how ugly she is," my grandmother continued.

"I'll let her think I died by a heart attack from her telling me that Jania accused me of that bullshit," I said. I'm just now finding out that Nadia gets off on that. Her body is fucked.

My grandma is getting real mad. I pick my pin up.

"So, what you're saying is with distance she's just going to feed me bullshit her entire life and hope I remember it every day?" I ask my grandma. "She's been practicing on me dying out of nowhere looking for damn near anything in my mind, and still with thirty-five years under her belt of abuse, she still isn't satisfied and she's still functioning. I can't do anything about her being retarded or mentally ill."

I can't believe Nadia. I asked her if she remembered saying that boy did cocaine and she said no. I asked her if she remembered the ninety dollars she said my sister asked my brothers for on their birthday and she said no. I told her I didn't want to look at them two scrooges and she said she went on the hiking trip to see her best friend who was not in the picture. Then I even asked her why Jania would say such a thing and she said she didn't know. She said Jania told her that a while ago.

She said it in a way to where it was similar to someone being out and about trying to handle some business and it was nothing for me to hear. Like she really needed me to not have any good thoughts when thinking about the assault.

"Those devils know the second round of eighteen is almost complete," my grandmother says. "I need this done."

I show my grandma a step that I taught Luminous LA. She's looking real serious. She has a glass of coffee now. I know she means business. She wants those step videos uploaded.

"Most of your relatives know about you losing your speech when you were in school at times, and your head being down a lot," my grandmother says. "Tell them you was always a baby to me, and that's why you couldn't talk. I wanted you to live again like you were a baby. You've always been one to me."

"Wow. You're good at making me forget bad things I remember," I say.

"You think your mom is crazy. I'm the one that's crazy," my grandmother says.

"Why is there so much mess in this family? And they think I'm going to stay in the messed-up circle," I say.

"Tell her your head was always down because I was showing her I didn't want to look at her," my grandma says. "You can count how many times you looked your mother in her eyes in your lifetime. You can count how many times you looked in those advisors and those girls that stepped in, in their eyes on two hands."

"That bitch you let take your spot, tell her you was living with a mom that wanted you to commit suicide and you still alive," my grandma continues. "You still ran it three years. Tell her you could barely look her or that damn gremlin short friend she carried with her in the eyes. Let alone that damn advisor. How could you have survived doing it again?"

"We look at them, they get a beauty queen, we get nothing. It's psychological. This is real life," I say.

"We get our vision fucked up. Tell them I died and came back. When they saw you, they saw me," my grandma says. "You don't realize you naturally look at them like the ugly looking people they are," my grandma says. I don't care though. Them niggas are fucking ugly.

"Remember you went to them people's house?" my grandma asks referring to the McGruders'. "With those books on the shelf, you still didn't think anything of the visit to their house. Them people hated that shit and you didn't even know. That's how mind controlled your mother had you. She had you brainwashed. Do you know how fucked up I am because Nadia practiced things on you, for you to not have realized that? I'm real fucked up being able to teach you things at three and you can still react to them when you are over thirty?"

"You smart enough now to know that you shouldn't have went back to them people's house," my grandma says. "Your momma practiced on you to do stupid things. She was stupid. You smart enough to know Nadia only wanted to remind you of people who did you wrong. Why do you want to go back to see if she will do it again?" my grandma asks. My grandma had me write all those books so she could confirm to me that she got everything she wanted out of me, incase, it was my time to leave this Earth soon. Incase, I was called home first. "I'm just about to sit around here and die, huh?" my grandma rhetorically asks.

One day I was in the car with the McGruders' and one of my brothers. That day Mr. McGruder looked at my brother in the car when I couldn't stand the sight of his wife. I was looking at her real disgusting. My brother looked at Mr. McGruder and I guess he was showing the old man that he didn't care if he killed his sister. "Tell her that's why I did it," my grandma says.

"If I was alive, I would've snapped you out of those drugs. That's how much I loved you to get you off those drugs now. April 5th, right?" my grandma says. "That's when you stopped?"

"Yes ma'am," I say.

"Don't do that shit again," my grandma says.

"My spirit got you to have that attitude in high school," my grandma says. "That's how bad I wanted to know how much you loved me. She don't know the old school. Old school don't care that some bitch they hate passed. Sixty years old. We will

597

still let her know we want her dead and tell her it hurts that she doesn't get it that we are nonchalant, and make the ones we love the same way. Tell that Scrooge your head was down because your mother was so evil knowing her life was gone. She would never be thought of as pretty. Just a wall. A dresser." My grandma takes a deep breath. "You know that woman and her husband were mentally ill," my grandma says. "People were in and out of her office. You not the only person that couldn't stand looking at them."

Damn. These drugs keep making me think the same damn thing. My grandma was waiting on that moment Nadia started trippin' hard. She put it in me. She didn't let me tell Nadia any sentimental stuff. I didn't think of anything intense and personal to tell her. "I had you say what someone else said and did to you, and kids at that, and let her get off in her bedroom off of that," my grandma says. "You told her about your assault in March, and you didn't think about it again until days before Mother's Day," my grandmother says. "I did what I had to do."

First, my grandma showed me what Nadia was trying to do to me. Make me die when I was thinking all good thoughts about myself. She waited two months to tell me. She knew I would be smart enough.

My grandma was waiting on that moment, so I could really understand that thoughts like that play over and over in my head. With nowhere to run, I could've went crazy. Committed suicide. She knew how to trick Nadia into being a bitch around the time she talked about Jania. My grandma played mind games with her. Things that she said, she knew she would repeat. I went my whole birthday without Nadia or Jania's negative shit in my head. My grandma's love can snap through it while I am recovering from drugs.

These drugs have me repeating things over and over. My repetitiveness is getting worse and worse. I have to do it though. A lot of my thoughts have vanished. I have to search for them while I'm trying to get these drugs out of my system completely.

598

My grandma wanted to show me her love could get the drugs out of me faster and show me she could teach me what the drugs really are capable of doing if I don't stop. My grandma wanted to get me to a point where I couldn't deny the times she saved me. Real love.

I do have to ask myself, as long as I've been smoking, why haven't I been experiencing these symptoms? I guess things have to build up.

When I was looking lost in that girl that kept saying she was pretty and beautiful, that girl looked like she was fifteen years old. The image kept looking younger and younger. At first, she kept looking eighteen. She still couldn't find what she was looking for, which was love. She didn't know. Her mind was naturally talking. Private Practice.

"Remember you've always been one to want to know what something was like," my grandma says. "Now you know what it's like to feel love like this. Love that kills drug effects."

"Ninety dollars she said your sister asked the twins for on their birthday. Then she said she didn't say that. Then she said *yes she did*. You not crazy. You know something is wrong there. You not supposed to spend your youth confused like that," my grandma says. "Your sister always said she would put her in a home since she was a teenager. Let her know you don't care what place she ends up in. You did what I said. That's all that matters."

"She didn't even remember saying my cousin did cocaine," I say. "She kept saying she didn't say stuff with the quickness."

"Love can snap you out of anything," my grandma says.

My grandma's telling me I'm looking for love and it's there, but the drugs are powerful and can make me feel like the love is not there. She wanted to show me that she could snap the drug effects out of me through my mom. She's a jealous grandma. She wants me to view her as my mom.

I went two whole months, including my birthday, and didn't think about Nadia.

"I wanted to wait 'til around Mother's Day to tell you," my grandma says. "That's how much I hated your mother. Tell her I

599

hated her when I was carrying her. I knew you were coming. You even talked to your mom around your birthday and you still didn't think about what she said about Jania." Around Mother's Day my grandma showed me what my mother was trying to do. Then she reminded me of what she said to me.

Dealing with Nadia, on top of these drugs is a fucking monster.

My grandmother wants her voice to be the last thing I heard, and not some crazy shit these crazy mutha fuckas made. Them crazy mutha fuckas are the people who created drugs. These damn drugs have me hearing shit. My grandma says the drugs have serious chemicals in them.

"Me and my friend Olifus, we call him Man Man, we were in an isolated area," my grandma says. "An area where crack addicts were heavy. We had our guns with us. We came across some drugs. We used them. Man Man started mixing the drugs. He started going crazy. There was buckets, bowls, flasks, and all types of convenient stuff for Man Man to use. I started to think the place was an old site that people started creating drugs in."

I can't believe Man Man mixed them damn drugs. I can't even imagine what my damn headache would be like if I mixed drugs. These damn drugs ain't shit. If I have the right thought that's bad for me, the weed will push me and tell my mind it's right. I can't question that thought. Drugs. Just fuck them.

"I knew you were an untouchable gangster," my grandma says. "You didn't need to be a physical fighter while going through this drug recovery."

"Grandma," I say. "I've been clean from drugs for two months now. These symptoms are still a hot ass mess."

I get popped in the mouth.

"What irritates you the most about using the drugs?" my grandma asks.

"The fact that they control all of me," I say. "They are really taking all of my thoughts and making them real heavy. They're giving me responses that I know I don't naturally have. They're changing my facials. I'll have a thought and the drug will cause me to have both *yes* and *no* responses as if I can't make up my mind. I'm seeing people. They're blinding me at times when I think."

"Now without your mother's statements and knowing how clear minded you are because I never would allow you to think certain things, how long do you think it would've taken you to get over these drugs? Now that you know the truth about them?" my grandma asks.

"The drug learns me. It's the drug recovery right now taking all of my thoughts and throwing them to the ground," I say. My grandmother laughs. "I have to stay strong throughout life and never touch them again."

"The drugs are alive as if they walk through the neighborhood," I continue. Drugs cause face mergence. People I've seen as a child and people I've seen recently will look alike, and I'll say they're the same person. Clones or robots that merge into anything. Really, I'm believing they either came back or just have came back around. A crazy existence at that.

The drugs cause major suicide. Really, the instant I sucked in the smoke the first time, it was turning all my thoughts into suicidal ones, but it didn't kill me instantly. It's smoke. It's not supposed to enter the body at all.

Through my drug withdrawal, it has the last person I thought of entering my thoughts to cause me hell.

"Don't do them again," my grandma says. "You didn't even know it was the drugs giving you all of those bad thoughts. You started to think more than one of some people existed. Don't touch that shit again."

"I got it my loving grandmother," I say playfully. I love her so much.

"Tell her I had your head down because I didn't want her looking into your beautiful eyes," my grandma says.

39

I'm walking back and forth in my room and I see my grandmother in a kitchen sitting at the counter.

"If you know you can remember and understand it, it is worth it. The pain," my grandmother says. "I need all of this writing done. The poetry included."

The power of my grandmother is so strong. She tells me instead of consoling me in March, she waited until May around Mother's Day to teach me a hard lesson. She was waiting for that day to show me her strength. She says she knew when she wanted to tell me that the family I knew wasn't shit.

Before Mother's Day 2024, there was a couple selling light up flowers in cones. I had so much love in me for my grandmother that I just had to get one. I couldn't decide which one to get. There was a pretty red flower with different color lights surrounding it that I loved. Then there were blue flowers. Some cylinders had a tornado effect, but no flower. However, they were still pretty. Then I saw the pink flowers. I always think of pink when it comes to my grandmother. I knew I would choose one of them.

The couple kept inserting triple A batteries into the flower cylinders, so that I could see each one light up. It was fifteen dollars. I never got the chance to get anything for my grandmother when she was alive. I felt like she was with me ever since she told me, "Tell her that's why I did it." That love cut so thick through that hate that Nadia had for me.

"This world is real Shona. You can naturally feel when someone doesn't love you. The drugs can take anything away from you though," my grandma says.

I remember me in that shell saying: *Well, I'm pretty, and no one says anything bad about how I look.*

"If someone told you something bad about how you look, you know they eyes was crooked anyways," my grandma says.

My grandma waited until days before Mother's Day to have me walk in a shell where I visualized myself being dressed in a white dress. I was naturally searching for something. I didn't know what it was. It wasn't in me. Then my grandma reminded me of my mother telling me about Jania after I told her about the assault. Then my grandma said that's why she did what she did. That's why she let go when she did. She said she always loved me.

I bought my grandma a gift on the day before Mother's Day this year. It was a pink flower in a cylinder vase that lit up with different colors. Even though she's gone, I spent Mother's Day with her this year. I got a beer, margarita, and a shot of E and J. I played old school music and really felt her presence. I had my pink flower with lights lighting up my room as well as some lights outlining my wall.

My grandma is just amazing.

How could Nadia stare at me my whole life like she wished I was dead and not be successful? How could she have all these demons surrounding her child since she was born all the way to eighteen and not be successful in her not committing suicide?

These drugs pull out memories I would be a fool to think I would remember alone. The drug is all of me. It attacks all of my consciences. With my beer in my hand, she's showing me what my mom did to me. My head was always down because Nadia trained me to be that way. My grandma is teaching me the hard truth and consoling me at the same time.

Dates, nothing mattered to Grandma. Just me. The person. Sometimes it feels like she's still alive.

"Not one picture with me and you is she willing to give you," Grandma says. "Tell her that's why I did it. For someone that never had any real love in that house, now you can tell your mom what real love is."

"Tell her even if you die before her, she'll never know how I enjoyed being with you, and how she, Nadia is resting in hell alive because of me. Tell her I didn't want you to have no kids. You're going through the hell of a real beauty queen," my grandmother says.

"Tell her I had you thinking of her as a friend and not a mother all of 2024 and 2025, and see if she can figure out the rest," my grandmother says. "Tell her all she is, is a thought. An idea."

"Tell her I taught you how food taste alone was more than she ever would be when you were thirty-five," my grandmother says.

"Tell her when she brought up Jania after the assault, that should've been the last time she heard your voice," my grandma continues. "Tell her that's why I did it. Tell her beauty comes from pain. That's why it was her who had you."

Nadia was a bitch and I have to accept that. All the hell she can look back on and get off on that she's caused me and it's still not enough. I hate to think of her in her personal time. She didn't show any motherly affection and I really didn't want it from her ugly ass anyways. She is a statistic. She never got over anything that happened to her. My father, he wasn't around. That's his fucking loss.

"Tell her you could never be her," my grandma says. "You know how to make people like you and you never gave a damn if someone liked you. Tell her I will teach you the real meaning of independent. She can't teach you."

My grandma has a lot she wants Nadia to know.

"Mine so fucked up, that they think I'm just gone sit around and die," my grandma says. "They didn't know me at all. That day she brought up Jania, make that the last time she hears your voice."

"Tell her I let you hear her scream how I made her scream. She doesn't know what real love is," my grandma says. "Real love will tell you at thirty-five you can feel eighteen years old and it's normal. No mixed feelings in between. Nadia wasted all of that personal time to herself thinking you were thinking about her response about Jania and you weren't. You were thinking about me. That's how much of nothing she always was."

"She thought she was doing something by training you to keep your head down," my grandma continues. "She wasn't doing shit. Even when she reads what I'm telling you to write, she still won't believe I told you to write it. Sisters and brothers.

You don't even know all of them niggas hate her. They still gone think you don't know what you talking about after reading everything I'm telling you to write. Sometimes your brothers want to know who you are. Tell them y'all never had a chance to be close with that Nadia, no matter what type of men they turned out to be. Let them know that's the reality of life. It doesn't work well for us all."

"You working hard on books, she's working hard on one statement for her daughter that's over twenty years younger than her. She could never beat you even when she could throw you. She don't even know what was wrong with her," my grandmother says.

I'm staring at my grandmother and admiring how beautiful she is. She doesn't look old to me. She looks like a woman that's on a mission. She does look pissed that some people tried to take something from her. She looks like she wants all of her revenge.

My grandma is beyond gorgeous. People would consider her a red bone. She's light-skinned and real pretty. Her face shape is so nice. She knew Nadia wouldn't give me anything. With no picture, I could forget how good my grandma looked. I remember her being able to fit in a door and have room to move. That's good enough for me.

"I had my kids thinking I was so stupid; they didn't know I was a grandparent that wanted to brag and boast with arrogance about my grandchild to my friends," my grandma says. "We compete too when it comes to our grandkids. We're old, but we still have fun. I need to look good. You are to complete everything just as I say."

"Yes ma'am," I say.

40

My girls of Alpha Eta Nu and I meet up to practice a lot during the two weeks we are given. Everyone is working hard and I can tell they are watching the recorded footage they have of us at Hollow's Cave. I'm confident that our show will be great as usual.

The early A.M. on May 31st rolls around. I'm at work and realize my grandma gave me instructions not to call Nadia at all. She said to just let the hours at work go by first and take it step by step. I've never not told Nadia happy birthday. Believe it or not, I didn't even think about her most of my shift.

I write during my two hours I stay at the job site. Then go home. I needed the discipline. I knew if I stayed at work, I could get it done. When I get home, I spend five hours typing up my written pages that I'm behind on getting in my computer on Word. I can't believe I was that behind. My grandma is very strict. It feels like she's alive at times. But it's just Earth. I can't wait to be over my recovery from drugs. This is not a game.

I'm eating out with my grandmother at one of my favorite restaurants, Ronnie's. She's sitting in front of me watching me eat.

I got the habanero wings, a house salad and fries. I also had three margaritas. The drinks make me feel my grandma's presence even more. I feel good.

"You know it's unladylike for you to be so pretty and not maintain your weight," my grandmother says.

I'm drinking. She can't ruin my mood. It's Nadia's birthday and I'm so happy because she just doesn't matter.

My grandmother said anything she said to Nadia and how she said it was all to help me.

I hear my grandma's voice say, "What type of love would have you questioning the way you look? I want these projects done."

"Just tell me what to do and I'll do it," I say.

"You don't got nothing good to tell they kids," my grandma says. "You know when people see you, they view you in another light. You are making it with all the hate mutha fuckas naturally give. You know all that. You not about to say shit good to they kids. They don't deserve it. You're not wasting anything. Because I said so."

I drunk that first margarita fast as hell. Fast as anytime I've ever drank any drink before. I was desperate. I'm not doing good. It's the 31st of May and I just downed all that food and drinks at Ronnie's. I got the twelve-piece habanero wings and a house salad with fries. It always feels good to get this food. I'm too scared to let that go and order something else. The steak and shrimp have been on my mind.

I got four hours of sleep today. I needed those pages typed up. I wanted that shit out of the way.

My grandma pops up.

"I need you to do a few more. I need this done. There's blood behind this," my grandma says.

"You got sense to know you moved away," my grandma says. "They never told you who your family really was. Your momma wasn't shit. Let her know I said it. I will tell you how to talk to people. Her telling you about the Jania situation. She had you thinking of being in court faced with embarrassment. You tried to find good in it. That's the love you supposed to have for a mother. The hate and pain from a mother can kill you," my grandmother says. "We provide for you. Ensure you know the basics of life like how to look both ways before crossing the street. You did have common sense. You know Nadia would never teach you that. You were walking blindly that day. You were supposed to drop dead or kill yourself. My love would never let you do that."

I'm loving this music that's playing at Ronnie's. This food is bomb. I hear my grandmother, but at the same time, I just can't register the negative things she's saying. It's like she's putting a spell on me, and I don't care. I need this spell. This liquor has me feeling so good.

"You've told her bad things that have happened to you before," my grandmother says. "Jania wasn't the first time Nadia responded with another bad situation. I loved you so you never paid attention to it. But this is real life Shona. Those drugs are strong as hell. I know my daughter better than you. Now you know how smart you are to take this information and utilize it properly. What makes you think she's sane?" my grandmother asks.

"I knew something was wrong with her," I say.

This margarita is on point. These wings are so damn good. The liquor is making my grandma's presence even stronger. I'm loving it. I'm celebrating Nadia's birthday with my grandma. I went out to eat alone on my birthday and never thought about what Nadia said about Jania. My grandma's love is fire.

"You went two months not thinking about it. Your birthday included," my grandma says. "You even talked to your mom on your birthday and a few days straight after, and those negative thoughts about her not consoling you or you searching for something good she said and never finding it, never came to your mind." One of the boys Nadia said Jania brought up, his birthday is the day before mine, and it still never crossed my mind what Nadia said.

My birthday came around in April. I spoke to Nadia on the phone for an entire hour. She kept telling me she was calling my old phone, and that's why she didn't get through to tell me happy birthday until noon. I didn't care though. I was happy she called. The drugs had me needing my mom to call.

I also spoke to Nadia the fourteenth, fifteenth, and sixteenth of April for at least an hour each day, and her comments about Jania never crossed my mind. My grandma kept telling me in May around Mother's Day, that real love can cut like that. Then my brother's birthdays' rolled around in May. I talked to them on the phone and Nadia as well. Nothing Nadia said crossed my mind about Jania, and her not having anything to say about the assault sure as hell didn't cross my mind.

I talked to Nadia on the first, second, third, and fourth of May for at least an hour and the assault and Jania never crossed my mind.

"That's what real love can do Shona," my grandmother says.

I'm buying another drink. I've never been one to wish I was

someone else. I remember when I had burgundy curtains in my house. I remembered a pretty brown girl in her room with the burgundy curtains in her feelings, always dancing and thinking about what she wants. She's always wishing for more: a man, kids, fancy house, car, jazz instrumental nights, just anything that makes her feel complete. The drugs gave me feelings for this woman and let me know everything about her and how she felt. I wanted to be her.

That woman was me.

The televisions in Ronnie's are playing music videos. I'm dancing in my seat and enjoying my salad. These fries are bomb as hell with these wings.

"There's a popular TV show called *Play Cards: It's Talent,* and the panelist don't even talk like Americans," my grandma says. She says she knows they are terrorists. She says some people are so stupid that they don't know we look evil in the eyes every day on shows we watch every day.

I'm so drunk, that I'm not even scared to put that in my story. I recognize that who I normally am, would not want to write about that damn television show my grandma just told me about.

"I'm almost done telling you everything I need you to know. There's many ways to say one thing," my grandma says.

Drugs causing me to be able to flip my thoughts and believe new things instantly is ridiculous. I believed I was alone and people were here decades ago, and when they realized their stupid ways would cause them to be extinct alone, they found ways to take the love out of the world. Then I believed everyone was separated from their families.

"Remember *The Touch Me Story* you wrote about and threw away?" my grandma asks. "Remember that man that really thought he looked like a gorilla? He thought he resembled a gorilla just like the woman in that prison."

The drugs caused me to have real feelings on objects and internal feelings. If I thought of a cat, I could feel it and smell it. I could feel bricks. I remember I was in bed with no feelings when I woke up. I couldn't move. I had to recite telling Nadia about the assault and her telling me about Jania. That was the only thing I remembered cutting through the drug.

I hate how the drugs can flip my thoughts to believe major things back-to-back. The drugs show me all of my thoughts, then has extra thoughts to use to try and kill me.

The drugs were telling me what was smoked. That person who was alive and tortured has flesh in these drugs. Smell. It's all in the drugs. These thoughts alone were making me crazy internally. My sense of smell increased and enhanced my thoughts. I felt mental. My negative thoughts started making me feel better. Drugs gave me reversed feelings.

I have to keep reciting the same shit.

I can't believe I text this woman about the assault. The children at the store in New Orleans were a fucking mess. Then the nerve of her to tell me about Jania. "Uh unh. She been told me that," Nadia said. What a fucking bitch. Just fucked up to a max. Uglied out. She may really be mentally ill. Maybe she did something similar and was mad. Maybe she was developing an old people's sickness. Maybe she was telling me to never come back around because she knew she was no good.

"Nadia always could fool you," my grandma says. "She could make you believe she had good intentions like saying something bad for you to stay away because she knew she was getting sick. Tell her that's why I did it."

It's to a point where I don't know if Nadia has Alzheimer's, or she's just cuttin' up to get rid of me.

Since before Mother's Day when Grandma came back, and still
in June, I have to keep reciting the memory from the assault to
my grandma saying *that's why I did it*, to going all that time
without remembering the conversation about Jania for months.

My grandma pops up in my room.

"Man Man lost his speech," my grandma says. Man Man
started getting smarter. Then he tried to make sense of what
the drugs were doing to him. Every day I go to work the filtering
of the drugs gets realer and realer. I can fight as long as I want,
but the drug won't leave or lose its strength until it is
completely gone.

Without the drugs, I wonder what would have happened to
me. I think I wouldn't have had anywhere to run to have an
excuse for these beliefs. I think I would've exploded and had a
heart attack ironically because without the drug my normal
mind would have kept being blasted with new big thoughts.

"This world will storm down on you," my grandma says.

"Grandma, can I ask you something?" I ask.

"Yes. Anything," my grandma says.

"Is there a good way to remember the love?" I ask.

"Complete these projects," my grandma says. My grandma
knows I am smart. She knows I can do it.

It's June 6th, 2024. It's the day of Vincent's competition at his house. His three-story house is nice as hell. I need to figure out how to make some more money so I can live in one of these someday.

All of the fraternities and sororities are in bedrooms getting ready. The guests are scattered in the backyard and basement waiting for us. This gathering seems like a party that Vincent wants people to showcase at. He must've figured since there's enough teams, he may as well turn it into a competition for his guests to enjoy.

My girls and I are in one of the bedrooms. It's big enough for us to have a rehearsal.

"Everyone straight?" Deliana asks.

All the girls have on their nice pink shirts that say Alpha Eta Nu and some cute white jeans. We have on pink and white shoes. Our hair is flat-ironed. We have on earrings. We look nice from head to toe, as always.

"We're good," Asayla says.

"We're first and it's almost time for us to go out there," Deliana says.

I'm proud of the girls. They've learned a lot in such a short time.

"You sure this not some early success party he is having for himself?" I ask.

"I know right," Shemina says. "It's turnt' the hell up in this house. Them people probably won't even remember we're competing until they see us."

"It's just a regular party he has that he added a competition too," Deliana says.

My girls and I get to the door for the backyard. One of Vincent's boys, Heldor, holds the door open for us, and we march to our places on the stage with our arms together across our chest. Theta Kappa Beta is marching to their spots as well.

The crowd is loud as hell.

Rondy, one of Vincent's friends, is the host for the night. He's waiting for the crowd to quiet down. Three minutes have passed and they still haven't quieted down. It's no problem though. My girls and I are used to holding positions for long periods of times.

Once the crowd quiets down, Rondy says, "Give it up again for our two sororities coming out tonight."

The crowd claps. Some people are inside not paying us any attention. We're really here just as extra entertainment.

"I want to welcome everyone to my boy Vincent's party," Rondy says. "We have some step performances lined up for y'all. I want to thank everyone for coming out tonight. Me and my boys, Ralin and Heldor flipped a coin, and Theta Kappa Beta is up first. Sit back and relax folks. Enjoy the show."

Theta Kappa Beta starts out with one person setting their step, then they all join in. They begin with a fast-paced step that is comprised of a bunch of claps above and under their legs as well as circular motions with sharp movements with their arms.

Theta Kappa Beta makes some real hideous faces at times during their routine. My girls and I used to make those hard-core ugly faces when we were in college and a couple years after, but we changed to just making serious ones.

The members of Theta Kappa Beta transition to new spots and do their call *TeeeeKiiiiBiii* a few times. They position their legs at different distances and do the butterfly motion with their arms. They squat and hit their thighs a few times. The girls of Theta Kappa Beta even jump in the air and hit their thighs, and do circular motions with their arms, and clap and hit their thighs as well.

There's people in the crowd shouting compliments, and people being ignorant. I personally don't care what anyone in this drunk and high as crowd has to say. The fact that the audience has to come to a decision on who wins, has me not caring about anything about this crowd. Some people are inside talking and eating, acting like stepping is something that can be learned the morning of the show.

I'm not in the mood for this crowd. I'm just here to make sure they know that my girls and I are the bomb, and that they have no reason to try and clown us whenever they talk about us.

Theta Kappa Beta does a few motions, then pause. They show that they are capable of holding many positions for a long time.

"Y'all can't compete with us!" Theta Kappa Beta shouts. "When we step, we turn y'all asses to dust!"

I motion for my girls and I to move our arms to our sides in fists.

The members of Theta Kappa Beta stroll around their section of the stage, then come back to their positions and end their routine.

The crowd is loud for them.

"Give it up for Theta Kappa Beta," Rondy says. "Alright Alpha Eta Nu. Let's see what y'all are about."

"My Sorors!" I shout. "Let's put it down!"

My girls and I explode into an intense combination. Our arms extend to all four directions with a stomp and our heads follow our arms. We stomp and bend down to hit our thighs, then place one arm in front of our chests horizontally moving in and out while the other one hits the side of our thighs.

My girls and I squat down and hit our thighs, then hit our hands one on top of the other going in opposite directions. This is one of my favorite moves. I have us do the butterfly motion with our arms crossing and flapping up and down while we stomp alternating feet.

"No one can resist the way we step and twist!" my girls and I shout. "When we battle, it's like the other team doesn't even exist!"

My girls and I transition to different spots and do a ripple effect with our legs and our arms. Sometimes our legs and arms do the ripple motions together with our arms extending in different directions and other times we do the ripple effect with our legs moving outward then inward, and with our legs moving up and down.

There's a step when I stomp first, then one person will join in so the sound gets louder during our ripple.

The audience is saying things like: *Who the hell are these girls that just went before them? What the hell did we watch before this? Theta Kappa Beta, y'all need to step the hell up, for real.* Of course there's people telling the ignorant ones to shut the hell up.

My girls and I do our thing. We stroll around the stage pumping our arms forward and backward, using our hands as mirrors, and taking a few steps forward and using our arms to push ourselves backwards. We go to a new position to end with our arms to our side and smiles on our faces.

Rondy comes back to center stage and looks shocked.

"Give it up for everyone," Rondy tells the crowd. Some people are clapping, some are fooling around trying to step, some are shouting foolish things, and some are shouting good things. "I'm going to give everyone a chance to decide who they think the winner should be," Rondy says. "Get with your group. I'll look around, see who has the majority, and that will be who the sorority of the night is."

My girls and I and Theta Kappa Beta stay in our positions waiting on the crowd to come to a decision.

Rondy takes the stage after a few minutes. "If Theta Kappa Beta is your favorite sorority of the night, make some noise, raise your hand, do a little step, do a little dance. Let me know."

There's many groups standing together and Rondy is looking around to see how many are for Theta Kappa Beta and how many people are in the group.

"Alright. If Alpha Eta Nu is your sorority of the night, make some noise, raise your hand, do a little step, do a little dance," Rondy says.

There's so much noise, this damn man Rondy shouldn't have to look around at different groups or try to add how many people are in them.

"Y'all know damn well what that means," Rondy says looking around at all the audience members. "That was loud as hell. Alpha Eta Nu is the winner."

Some of the crowd is mad as hell. Some fights start to break out.

"Y'all can go back to y'all rooms now," Rondy says to my girls and I and Theta Kappa Beta.

My girls and I march back to the door that Heldor let us out. He holds it open for us again and once we're inside, we go to our designated room. We sit on the bed, lean on the walls, sit in chairs, and gather our things so they're ready when it's time to go.

"Wow. That was fun," Asayla says.

"You not joking are you?" Deliana says. "We tore them bitches up. I thought they was at least gone have something worth watching."

"Shona, we definitely could have won using old steps," Shemina says.

"We had fun," I say playfully. "That's all that matters. We going to watch the frats or what?"

"Yea. Let's go check them out," Telana says.

Caya leads the way down the hall to the backyard. My girls and I join the crowd to watch the frats perform.

Omicron Rho Rho is battling Rho Psi Phi, and Rho Omega Rho is battling Omicron Phi Phi.

There's a lot more men in the crowd than there was before. Everyone, including my girls and I, are drinking. My girls are smoking. It's just too lit in this backyard.

All of the fraternities have complex routines. They do a lot of moving around as well as shout a lot of their sayings. Every move they do is intense and their facials are real intense as well. These frats have mainly fast paced steps. They hit their thighs in the air a lot. They extend both arms at the same time to their sides. They say disrespectful things about the other frats and bash their entire foundation.

I'm looking around expecting more fights to break out. I know there's people here who are not wearing their letters, but are involved in Greek life.

Once both groups are done performing, Rondy takes the stage. He asks the audience who had the best routine of the night? Rondy can't figure out who the audience wants the winner to be, so he has Heldor and Ralin help him decide. Rondy asks the audience again who they think the winner should be. Him and his boys decide that Vincent's crew, Omicron Rho Rho won. Of course the crowd is not having that. They think Vincent's crew only won because it's Vincent's party. Lots of fights break out.

After all the fights are broken up, the party continues on. I tell my girls I'm leaving. There's no way I'm sticking around to see how this party ends.

When I get home, I pull out my diary. I sit on my couch in the living room in my pink silky pajamas. I start writing in my diary talking about the love I have for myself and how no one could ever take my joy away.

I end my night with a glass of wine sitting at my dining room table.